THE COLLECTED STORIES OF ROGER ZELAZNY

POWER & LIGHT

VOLUME 2:

THE COLLECTED STORIES OF
ROGER ZELAZNY

EDITED BY

David G. Grubbs
Christopher S. Kovacs
Ann Crimmins

NESFA
PRESS

Post Office Box 809, Framingham, MA 01701
www.nesfa.org/press
2009

FIRST EDITION, February 2009

ISBN-10: 1-886778-77-9
ISBN-13: 978-1-886778-77-1

A Word from
the Editors

This six volume collection includes all of Zelazny's known short fiction and poetry, three excerpts of important novels, a selection of non-fiction essays, and a few curiosities.

Many of the stories and poems are followed by "A Word from Zelazny" in which the author muses about the preceding work. Many of the works are also followed by a set of "Notes"[1] explaining names, literary allusions and less familiar words. Though you will certainly enjoy Zelazny's work without the notes, they may provide even a knowledgeable reader with some insight into the levels of meaning in Zelazny's writing.

> "My intent has long been to write stories that can be read in many ways from the simple to the complex. I feel that they must be enjoyable simply as stories…even for one who can't catch any of the allusions."
> —Roger Zelazny in *Roger Zelazny* by Jane M. Lindskold

The small print under each title displays original publication information (date and source) for published pieces and (sometimes a guess at) the date it was written for unpublished pieces. The small print may also contain a co-author's name, alternate titles for the work, and awards it received. Stories considered part of a series are noted by a § and a series or character name.

---

1 The notes are a work in progress. Please let us know of any overlooked references or allusions, or definitions you may disagree with, for a possible future revision.

CONTENTS

ARTICLES

POETRY

POWER & LIGHT

VOLUME 2:

THE COLLECTED STORIES OF

ROGER ZELAZNY

Lyricism and Warmth

by Kristine Kathryn Rusch

When I think of Roger Zelazny, the person, I feel a small amount of guilt. Shortly before he died, Roger called me. My husband Dean Wesley Smith answered the phone, then searched through a pile of manuscripts and cats to find me.

"Take a message," I said, "and I'll call him back."

He did. The message was short: Roger's name and phone number, and nothing more.

A little sidebar here: While Roger and I were friends, we were sf convention friends. We didn't confide in each other. We never had dinner outside of a convention setting.

Our longest relationship was an editor/author relationship. Roger was one of the first writers I had contacted when Dean and I started Pulphouse Publishing. Roger couldn't write a new short story for our hardback magazine—he had other commitments and no time—but he was one of the first to sign onto our Author's Choice short story collection series. We reprinted several of his works.

When I became editor of *The Magazine of Fantasy & Science Fiction*, Roger and I discussed his short fiction again. I wanted a Zelazny story for my magazine. He said he would write one.

I assumed that the phone call was either about Pulphouse or *F&SF*, although the last time I saw Roger at a small convention in New Mexico, he said he wanted to talk with me about career issues.

I found that statement so ridiculous that I laughed. Roger Zelazny wanted to talk with me about career? Roger had probably forgotten more about a career in publishing than I had ever known.

When the phone call came, I was doing something I thought important. Thirteen years later, I cannot remember what that something was. Only that I didn't want to go to the phone right then—which, I must admit, is not unusual for me. If I can avoid talking on the phone, I will do so. Nowadays, e-mail aids and abets that avoidance.

In 1995, e-mail was not an option.

So I planned to call Roger back when I had a good half an hour to spare. I waited a few days—

And Roger died.

He died.

He hadn't told anyone outside of his close circle of friends that he was even ill, so the news of his death was a huge shock. He hadn't looked ill when I saw him a few months before. Thin, yes, but Roger was always thin. Other than that, exactly the same.

Later, I asked his friends and family if they knew why he had called. Speculation abounded. Discussions of his estate, perhaps? Or something simple. One mutual friend said simply that Roger had called everyone he knew to say good-bye.

But of course, being Roger, he hadn't said good-bye, because that would have been awkward. He simply had one last conversation that he alone knew would have been a good-bye.

That guilt—that I had put off this important phone call, not realizing that it was important—is always my first memory of Roger, the person.

My second memory of Roger, the person, is one filled with complete joy. He was part of a large group of writers who ate dinner at an old restaurant in New Orleans. I was editing *F&SF*, and Gardner Dozois was editing *Asimov's*, and the night in question was the final night of a particularly emotional World Fantasy Convention. We were all tired and we were all punchy.

I was hosting *F&SF* writers in one large room, and Gardner was hosting *Asimov's* writers in another. We were separated by a door—and a single door knob, that had to be moved from one side of the door to the other for the door to work.

That door knob became famous, because we all behaved like children that night. Sending each other bottles of wine started the evening, and then we played a version of capture-the-doorknob that got increasingly ruder as the game went on.

At one point, a commando raid of *F&SF* women ventured to the *Asimov's* side to reclaim that doorknob—and I remember Roger laughing. He was at the *Asimov's* table, a not-so-silent (and not so impartial) observer, egging on the mayhem, enjoying it as much as we all did.

Those are my two immediate memories of Roger Zelazny, the man. There are others, which mostly revolve around quiet conversations or the absolute pleasure it was to work with him. He was thoroughly professional and very courteous, which, in the science fiction field, are rare.

But when I think of Roger Zelazny, the writer, I have an entirely different set of reactions.

When I first started reading science fiction, in the early 1970s, a new tribe of writers had just arrived into the field. They brought with them new blood and a new excitement. That excitement was palpable, even at my far remove from the heart of the field.

Roger was part of that tribe, a tribe that also included Ursula K. Le Guin, who was doing her most influential work in the same period. Those names tie together for me, because I was reading the Hugo volumes and the year's best anthologies.

Even to my young eyes, the differences between what had come before and what was happening now were vast. Roger brought a sweeping romanticism into the field, a warmth that it had lacked for nearly a decade. His fiction was broad in scope, but his characters brought it to life.

His words—hell, his *titles*—were poetry: "The Doors of His Face, the Lamps of His Mouth," "A Rose for Ecclesiastes," and so many others.

And then there was the *Amber* series. Even people who didn't normally read science fiction or fantasy had read Roger Zelazny's *Amber* series and loved it.

To me—a writer and former editor whose heart lives in the short form—Roger is one of the most influential short story writers of his generation. My friends who prefer novels say he wrote one of the best series ever published in the sf/f field.

A breath of fresh air. Stories written as only Roger could write them, with power and lyricism and that ever abiding warmth.

Fortunately, he toiled in a field that honors its classics. When I was editing, I reprinted a few of Roger's classic short stories. So did every other reprint editor in the field. The stories are simply too good to pass up, and too brilliant to forget.

Now NESFA Press is reprinting all of Roger's short fiction. And in doing so, they are providing the science fiction field with a true treasure.

Roger Zelazny the man is gone.

Roger Zelazny the writer, however, will live forever.

— Kristine Kathryn Rusch

A Singular Being

by Walter Jon Williams

On three separate occasions, I met Roger Zelazny for the first time.

The first time was at a convenience store in the late sixties, behind the wire spinner that held the comic books. I was looking at the paperbacks and saw there a black Avon cover with the words "THIS YEAR'S HUGO NOVEL." I'd never heard of the author—well, I *was* young—but I bought the book on the strength of the Hugo win.

The book was *Lord of Light*, and I read it with increasing amazement, wonder, and joy. The Roger I met that day in the convenience store was a singular compound of mind-staggering ideas, wide-ranging knowledge, and a singular elegance of expression. In short order I sought out everything else I could find by the writer with the funny name.

…*And Call Me Conrad, Dream Master, Isle of the Dead, Damnation Alley* … it's impossible to overstate Roger's importance to the field, or his impact on the readers. He was a literal revolutionary—he entered the field of science fiction, remade it in his image, and left it altered forever. If his later work didn't have quite such an impact, perhaps it was because the center of the field had shifted in Roger's direction: his work was less prominent because everyone else was writing more like Roger.

On the second occasion I met Roger Zelazny for the first time, it was at a science fiction convention in the early seventies. He was gracious, soft-spoken, and (when he wanted to be) screamingly funny. At two different conventions, he gave the two most sidesplitting speeches I've ever heard—and alas, I didn't think to record either one of them.

15

I've never heard anyone else say this, but I would like to put on record that Roger Zelazny would have made a terrific stand-up comic. His comic gift is an underappreciated aspect of his character.

When I became a writer myself, I found Roger an amiable senior colleague. He and I plotted the evil that befell one another's characters on the *Wild Cards* series, and when Martin Harry Greenberg asked me to write a sequel to one of Roger's novellas, Roger was kind enough to let me follow "The Graveyard Heart" with my own "Elegy for Angels and Dogs."

In person, Roger demonstrated the same compound of originality, wide-ranging knowledge, and the singular elegance of expression that he demonstrated in his novels.

We talked about collaborating on a novel, and when we found ourselves on an airline flight together, we plotted it in some detail, but we never got around to writing it. Both of us figured we'd have plenty of time.

But even though we lived less than 65 miles from one another, we saw each other mainly at professional engagements far from our homes. Roger was a shy man and did not seek out company.

On the third occasion on which I met Roger Zelazny for the first time, he became a good friend. Though weakened by illness, he experienced a kind of flowering during the last year of his life. He reached out to touch many of us, and none of could doubt that we had been *touched*.

I saw more of Roger in his last year than I had in the previous twenty years of our acquaintance. I remember his kind, faultless presence at barbecues, at parties, at games, at my housewarming and wedding reception.

In his last year Roger tried a number of new things. Living with Jane Lindskold was one of them, Jackie Chan movies another, and role-playing games a third. While it's difficult to picture Roger doing anything as sublimely geeky as role-playing games, I'm able to record that he was very good at it.

Jane and Roger joined a role-playing group that had been meeting regularly, with much the same cast, for ten or twelve years, and which included many of Roger's writer friends, like George R. R. Martin and Melinda Snodgrass. Since there were so many writers involved, and since the group included people with acting experience, the group tended to be strong on plot, character, and inventiveness.

As I've already remarked, Roger was a shy man, and during games was at times eclipsed by the more aggressive, confident members of the group. At times, when I was running a game, I had to tell the others to shut up and stop shouting advice so that Roger could get on with playing his character. And once he was given the floor, Roger always did well.

Whether through observation, Jane's coaching, or his own repressed talents as an actor, Roger tended to shine in his roles. Initially he chose minor characters, a bit removed from the main thrust of the action, but nevertheless complete characters who had their own part to play. In a game set in feudal Japan, Roger turned up as the Chinese poet Li Po, a character who specialized in carousing and extemporaneous verse. The poetry that Roger recited on these occasions had the genuine flavor of Li Po, too.

In a starship adventure game, Roger appeared as a preacher named Schuyler. Chaplain Sky was a navy "xenochaplain," supposed to be able to minister to the spiritual needs of any conceivable denomination of human, alien, or the odd sentient rock. (He didn't do very well with the rock, actually.) The professional requirement to believe in *everything* led to Chaplain Sky's not believing in *anything* very much, and led to some of Gaming's Most Funny Spiritual Moments, as when Sky blessed some space marines about to hit the beach on an enemy-held planet. Sky's address went more or less as follows:

"Insofar as I may be heard by anything which may or not care what I say, I ask, if it matters, that these soldiers be granted luck and favor, regardless of anything they have done or failed to do which requires forgiveness. Conversely, if not forgiveness, but something else may be required to ensure any possible benefit for which they may be eligible, I ask that this, whatever it may be, be granted or withheld, as the case may be, in such a manner as to ensure them receiving said benefit. I ask this in my capacity as their elected intermediary between themselves and that which may not be themselves, but which may have an interest in the matter of their receiving as much as is possible for them to receive of this blessing, and which may in some way be influenced by this ceremony. Amen."

I'm not sure if this stirring address aided the morale of the troops, but Roger's fellow players were in stitches. (And Zelazny fans will recognize that Roger paraphrased another prayer, given by another chaplain, in his own *Creatures of Light and Darkness*.)

I wanted very much to get Roger into my Amber campaign, not simply because he was Amber's creator but because I thought he could add so much insight and interest into the proceedings. But my Amber campaign was run with a different group of people who met at my house, which would have added about another 50 miles to Roger's trip, and he turned me down.

I was quite disappointed. Jane Lindskold told me afterwards that he wanted to play, but that he was afraid he wasn't strong enough to stand the extra 50 miles. If I'd only known the reason, I would have happily moved the game closer to him. Alas, I was not to know the reason until after Roger's death.

Roger's last character was that of a tough, crazed New York detective in my NYPD game, a far darker character than he had played up to that point, a paranoid Vietnam vet who slept with a gun under his pillow and who wouldn't stop at simply killing a bad guy he couldn't get at legally.

The last time I saw Roger Zelazny, he was playing in the NYPD game. The game was set in contemporary New York, and the characters were all homicide cops trying to solve a mystery.

There had been a slaying in a Mafia family, and it became clear that the only person who was ever likely to talk was going to be the mistress of one of the mafiosi. Some of the other characters were less than delighted with the thought of cuddling up to someone who a prominent gangster might consider his property, but Roger's character waded right in. He called her up and said:

"I hear you like flowers and maybe a drink, so I thought I'd pick you up after work and buy you a drink with a flower in it; and maybe we can go to Tavern on the Green, because it's got nice views of the Park and the Park has flowers in it; and so we can have drinks with flowers in them while we're looking at the flowers in the Park, and maybe I'll find you a flower for your hair…"

I can't remember the whole speech, but he went on in this manner for some time—I should point out that Roger frequently spoke like that, in long, spontaneous, unrehearsed, grammatically correct complex sentences—and I spent the whole time staring at Roger with my mouth hanging open, thinking to myself, *What a smoothie!*

So of course the Mafia maid succumbed, because, after all, who wouldn't?

The last time I saw Roger, I was running the detective game. His romancing of the don's mistress had borne fruit, and he had discovered the bad guy, a serial killer who was also (as it were) in his day job, a syndicate soldier.

It was getting late, and I was preparing to start the showdown of the Mafia story by having the serial killer burst into Roger's room while he was in bed with the don's mistress. I looked up from my table to talk to Roger, and to my surprise he responded to me incoherently. Nothing he was saying made any sense or seemed to have anything to do with the subject at hand— though, even then, his sentences remained grammatically correct.

He had been growing visibly weaker over the previous months, and I concluded he was overtired and brought the game to an end. I figured we'd play the showdown next week.

Two days later, George R. R. Martin called me to tell me that Roger was dying in the hospital, and less than twenty-four hours later he was dead. He had kept the precise nature of his illness a secret from all but a half-dozen people, and though I knew he was sick—"a kidney infection" I'd been told—I didn't know that the kidney problem had been the result of a course of chemotherapy for cancer.

After the shock, the grief, the memorial services, and the passage of a few months, I ran the police game one more time.

As the other detectives pieced the violent action together afterwards, the serial killer had broken into Roger's apartment and opened fire on Roger's character from the bedroom door.

Though Roger's character was wounded, he nevertheless managed to hurl a throwing knife into the bad guy's throat, killing him, before passing out from his wounds. The Mafia don's mistress applied first aid, saved his life, called the ambulance, and rode with him to the hospital.

If I couldn't give Roger a happy ending, I decided, I could at least give one to his game character. And so, in our imagination at least, the tormented New York cop will live happily ever after with the Mafia don's mistress, sharing their usual table at Tavern on the Green, and having drinks with flowers in them while she wears flowers in her hair…

It was clear that in his last year Roger was a happy man, and it was a joy to watch him. In intimate surroundings as well as anywhere else, he demonstrated his remarkable originality of thought, his wide-ranging knowledge, and his singular elegance of expression.

It was a privilege to know him. It is a continuing tragedy that he is gone.

He was an utterly singular being, and those who were privileged to know him miss him every day.

—Walter Jon Williams

STORIES

THE FURIES

Manuscript title: "Hunt Down the Happy Wallaby"
Amazing, June 1965.

As an afterthought, Nature sometimes tosses a bone to those it maims and casts aside. Often, it is in the form of a skill, usually useless, or the curse of intelligence.

When Sandor Sandor was four years old he could name all the one hundred forty-nine inhabited worlds in the galaxy. When he was five he could name the principal land masses of each planet and chalk them in, roughly, on blank globes. By the time he was seven years old he knew all the provinces, states, countries and major cities of all the main land masses on all one hundred forty-nine inhabited worlds in the galaxy. He read Landography, History, Landology and popular travel guides during most of his waking time; and he studied maps and travel tapes. There was a camera behind his eyes, or so it seemed, because by the time he was ten years old there was no city in the galaxy that anyone could name about which Sandor Sandor did not know *something*.

And he continued.

Places fascinated him. He built a library of street guides, road maps. He studied architectural styles and principal industries, and racial types, native life forms, local flora, landmarks, hotels, restaurants, airports and seaports and spaceports, styles of clothing and personal ornamentation, climatic conditions, local arts and crafts, dietary habits, sports, religions, social institutions, customs.

When he took his doctorate in Landography at the age of fourteen, his oral examinations were conducted via closed circuit television. This is because he was afraid to leave his home—having done so only three times before in his life and having met with fresh trauma

23

on each occasion. And *this* is because on all one hundred forty-nine inhabited worlds in the galaxy there was no remedy for a certain degenerative muscular disease. This disease made it impossible for Sandor to manipulate even the finest prosthetic devices for more than a few minutes without suffering fatigue and great pain; and to go outside he required three such devices—two legs and a right arm—to substitute for those which he had missed out on receiving somewhere along the line before birth.

Rather than suffer this pain, or the pain of meeting persons other than his Aunt Faye or his nurse, Miss Barbara, he took his oral examinations via closed circuit television.

The University of Brill, Dombeck, was located on the other side of that small planet from Sandor's home, else the professors would have come to see *him*, because they respected him considerably. His 855-page dissertation, "Some Notes Toward a Gravitational Matrix Theory Governing the Formation of Similar Land Masses on Dissimilar Planetary Bodies," had drawn attention from Interstel University on Earth itself. Sandor Sandor, of course, would never see the Earth. His muscles could only sustain the gravitation of smaller planets, such as Dombeck.

And it happened that the Interstel Government, which monitors everything, had listened in on Sandor's oral examinations and his defense of his dissertation.

Associate Professor Baines was one of Sandor's very few friends. They had even met several times in person, in Sandor's library, because Baines often said he'd wanted to borrow certain books and then came and spent the afternoon. When the examinations were concluded, Associate Professor Baines stayed on the circuit for several minutes, talking with Sandor. It was during this time that Baines made casual reference to an almost useless (academically, that is) talent of Sandor's.

At the mention of it, the government man's ears had pricked forward (he was a Rigellian). He was anxious for a promotion and he recalled an obscure memo…

Associate Professor Baines had mentioned the fact that Sandor Sandor had once studied a series of thirty random photos from all over the civilized galaxy, and that the significant data from these same photos had also been fed into the Department's L-L computer. Sandor had named the correct planet in each case, the land mass in

29, the county or territory in twenty-six, and he had correctly set the location itself within fifty square miles in twenty-three instances. The L-L comp had named the correct planet for twenty-seven.

It was not a labor of love for the computer.

So it became apparent that Sandor Sandor knew just about every damn street in the galaxy.

Ten years later he knew them all.

But three years later the Rigellian quit his job, disgusted, and went to work in private industry, where the pay was better and promotions more frequent. *His* memo, and the tape, had been filed, however…

❖   ❖   ❖

Benedick Benedict was born and grew up on the watery world of Kjum, and his was an infallible power for making enemies of everyone he met.

The reason why is that while some men's highest pleasure is drink, and others are given to gluttony, and still others are slothful, or lechery is their chief delight, or *Phrinn*-doing, Benedick's was gossip—he was a loudmouth.

Gossip was his meat and his drink, his sex and his religion. Shaking hands with him was a mistake, often a catastrophic one. For, as he clung to your hand, pumping it and smiling, his eyes would suddenly grow moist and the tears would dribble down his fat cheeks.

He wasn't sad when this happened. Far from it. It was a somatic conversion from his paranorm reaction.

He was seeing your past life.

He was selective, too; he only saw what he looked for. And he looked for scandal and hate, and what is often worse, love; he looked for lawbreaking and unrest, for memories of discomfort, pain, futility, weakness. He saw everything a man wanted to forget, and he talked about it.

If you are lucky he won't tell you of your own. If you have ever met someone else whom he has also met in this manner, and if this fact shows, he will begin talking of *that* person. He will tell you of that man's or woman's life because he appreciates this form of social reaction even more than your outrage at yourself. And his eyes and voice and hand will hold you, like the clutch of the Ancient Mariner, in a sort of half dream-state; and you will hear him out and you will be shocked beneath your paralysis.

Then he will go away and tell others about you.

Such a man was Benedick Benedict. He was probably unaware how much he was hated, because this reaction never came until later, after he had said "Good day," departed, and been gone for several hours. He left his hearers with a just-raped feeling—and later fear, shame, or disgust forced them to suppress the occurrence and to try to forget him. Or else they hated him quietly, because he was dangerous. That is to say, he had powerful friends.

He was an extremely social animal: he loved attention; he wanted to be admired; he craved audiences.

He could always find an audience too, somewhere. He knew so many secrets that he was tolerated in important places in return for the hearing. And he was wealthy too, but more of that in a moment.

As time went on, it became harder and harder for him to meet new people. His reputation spread in geometric proportion to his talking, and even those who would hear him preferred to sit on the far side of the room, drink enough alcohol to partly deaden memories of themselves, and to be seated near a door.

The reason for his wealth is because his power extended to inanimate objects as well. Minerals were rare on Kjum, the watery world. If anyone brought him a sample he could hold it and weep and tell them where to dig to hit the main lode.

From one fish caught in the vast seas of Kjum, he could chart the course of a school of fish.

Weeping, he could touch a native rad-pearl necklace and divine the location of the native's rad-pearl bed.

Local insurance associations and loan companies kept Benedict Files—the pen a man had used to sign his contract, his snubbed-out cigarette butt, a plastex hanky with which he had mopped his brow, an object left in security, the remains of a biopsy or blood test—so that Benedict could use his power against those who renege on these companies and flee, on those who break their laws.

He did not revel in his power either. He simply enjoyed it. For he was one of the nineteen known paranorms in the one hundred forty-nine inhabited worlds in the galaxy, and he knew no other way.

Also, he occasionally assisted civil authorities, if he thought their cause a just one. If he did not, he suddenly lost his power until the need for it vanished. This didn't happen too often though, for an humanitarian was Benedick Benedict, and well-paid, because he was laboratory-tested and clinically-proven. He could psychometrize. He could pick up thought-patterns originating outside his own skull…

❖ ❖ ❖

Lynx Links looked like a beachball with a beard, a fat patriarch with an eyepatch, a man who loved good food and drink, simple clothing, and the company of simple people; he was a man who smiled often and whose voice was soft and melodic.

In his earlier years he had chalked up the most impressive kill-record of any agent ever employed by Interstel Central Intelligence. Forty-eight men and seventeen malicious alien life-forms had the Lynx dispatched during his fifty-year tenure as a field agent. He was one of the three men in the galaxy to have lived through half a century's employment with ICI. He lived comfortably on his government pension despite three wives and a horde of grandchildren; he was recalled occasionally as a consultant; and he did some part-time missionary work on the side. He believed that all life was one and that all men were brothers, and that love rather than hate or fear should rule the affairs of men. He had even killed with love, he often remarked at Tranquility Session, respecting and revering the person and the spirit of the man who had been marked for death.

This is the story of how he came to be summoned back from Hosanna, the World of the Great and Glorious Flame of the Divine Life, and was joined with Sandor Sandor and Benedick Benedict in the hunt for Victor Corgo, the man without a heart.

❖ ❖ ❖

Victor Corgo was captain of the *Wallaby*. Victor Corgo was Head Astrogator, First Mate, and Chief Engineer of the *Wallaby*. Victor Corgo *was* the *Wallaby*.

One time the *Wallaby* was a proud Guardship, an ebony toadstool studded with the jewel-like warts of fast-phase projectors. One time the *Wallaby* skipped proud about the frontier worlds of Interstel, meting out the unique justice of the Uniform Galactic Code—in those places where there was no other law. One time the proud *Wallaby*, under the command of Captain Victor Corgo of the Guard, had ranged deep space and become a legend under legendary skies.

A terror to brigands and ugly aliens, a threat to Code-breakers, and a thorn in the sides of evildoers everywhere, Corgo and his shimmering fungus (which could burn an entire continent under water level within a single day) were the pride of the Guard, the best of the best, the cream that had been skimmed from all the rest.

Unfortunately, Corgo sold out.

He became a heel.

…A traitor.

A hero gone bad…

After forty-five years with the Guard, his pension but half a decade away, he lost his entire crew in an ill-timed raid upon a pirate stronghold on the planet Kilsh, which might have become the hundred-fiftieth inhabited world of Interstel.

Crawling, barely alive, he had made his way half across the great snowfield of Brild, on the main land mass of Kilsh. At the fortuitous moment, Death making its traditional noises of approach, he was snatched from out of its traffic lane, so to speak, by the Drillen, a nomadic tribe of ugly and intelligent quadrupeds, who took him to their camp and healed his wounds, fed him, and gave him warmth. Later, with the cooperation of the Drillen, he recovered the *Wallaby* and all its arms and armaments, from where it had burnt its way to a hundred feet beneath the ice.

Crewless, he trained the Drillen.

With the Drillen and the *Wallaby* he attacked the pirates.

He won.

But he did not stop with that.

No.

When he learned that the Drillen had been marked for death under the Uniform Code he sold out his own species. The Drillen had refused relocation to a decent Reservation World. They had elected to continue occupancy of what was to become the hundred-fiftieth inhabited world in the galaxy (that is to say, in Interstel).

Therefore, the destruct-order had been given.

Captain Corgo protested, was declared out of order.

Captain Corgo threatened, was threatened in return.

Captain Corgo fought, was beaten, died, was resurrected, escaped restraint, became an outlaw.

He took the *Wallaby* with him. The *Happy Wallaby*, it had been called in the proud days. Now, it was just the *Wallaby*.

As the tractor beams had seized it, as the vibrations penetrated its ebony hull and tore at his flesh, Corgo had called his six Drillen to him, stroked the fur of Mala, his favorite, opened his mouth to speak, and died just as the words and the tears began.

"I am sorry…" he had said.

They gave him a new heart, though. His old one had fibrillated itself to pieces and could not be repaired. They put the old one in a jar and gave him a shiny, antiseptic egg of throbbing metal, which expanded and contracted at varying intervals, dependent upon what the seed-sized computers they had planted within him told of his breathing and his blood sugar and the output of his various glands. The seeds and the egg contained his life.

When they were assured that this was true and that it would continue, they advised him of the proceedings of courts-martial.

He did not wait, however, for due process. Breaking his parole as an officer, he escaped the Guard Post, taking with him Mala, the only remaining Drillen in the galaxy. Her five fellows had not survived scientific inquiry as to the nature of their internal structures. The rest of the race, of course, had refused relocation.

Then did the man without a heart make war upon mankind.

Raping a planet involves considerable expense. Enormous blasters and slicers and sluicers and refiners are required to reduce a world back almost to a state of primal chaos, and then to extract from it its essential (i.e., commercially viable) ingredients. The history books may tell you of strip-mining on the mother planet, back in ancient times. Well, the crude processes employed then were similar in emphasis and results, but the operations were considerably smaller in size.

Visualize a hundred miles of Grand Canyon appearing overnight; visualize the reversal of thousands of Landological millennia in the twinkling of an eye; consider all of the Ice Ages of the Earth, and compress them into a single season. This will give you a rough idea as to time and effect.

Now picture the imported labor—the men who drill and blast and slice and sluice for the great mining combines: Not uneducated, these men; willing to take a big risk, certainly though, these men— maybe only for one year, because of the high pay; or maybe they're careerists, because of the high pay—these men, who hit three worlds in a year's time, who descend upon these worlds in ships full of city, in space-trailer mining camps, out of the sky; coming, these men, from all over the inhabited galaxy, bringing with them the power of the tool and the opposed thumb, bearing upon their brows the mark of the Solar Phoenix and in their eyes the cold of the spaces they have crossed over, they know what to do to make the domes of atoms rise before them and to call down the tornado-probosci of suck-vortices from the freighters on the other side of the sky; and they do it thoroughly and efficiently, and not without style, tradition, folksongs, and laughter—for they are the sweat-crews, working against time (which is money), to gain tonnage (which is money), and to beat their competitors to market (which is important, inasmuch as one worldsworth influences future sales for many months); these men, who bear in one hand the flame and in the other the whirlwind, who come down with their families and all their possessions, erect temporary metropoli, work their magic act, and go—after the vanishing trick has been completed.

Now that you've an idea as to what happens and who is present at the scene, here's the rub:

Raping a planet involves considerable expense.

The profits are more than commensurate, do not misunderstand. It is just that they could be even greater…

How?

Well—For one thing, the heavy machinery involved is quite replaceable, in the main. That is, the machinery which is housed within the migrant metropoli.

Moving it is expensive. Not moving it isn't. For it is actually cheaper, in terms of material and labor, to manufacture new units than it is to fast-phase the old ones more than an average of 2.6 times.

Mining combines do not produce them (and wouldn't really want to); the mining manufacturing combines like to make new units as much as the mining combines like to lose old ones.

And of course it is rented machinery, or machinery on which the payments are still being made, to the financing associations, because carrying payments makes it easier to face down the Interstel Revenue Service every fiscal year.

Abandoning the units would be criminal, violating either the lessor-lessee agreement or the Interstel Commercial Code.

But accidents do happen…

Often, too frequently to make for comfortable statistics…

Way out there on the raw frontier.

Then do the big insurance associations investigate, and they finally sigh and reimburse the lien-holders.

…And the freighters make it to market ahead of schedule, because there is less to dismantle and march-order and ship.

Time is saved, commitments are met in advance, a better price is generally obtained, and a head start on the next worldsworth is supplied in this manner.

All of which is nice.

Except for the insurance associations.

But what can happen to a transitory New York full of heavy equipment?

Well, some call it sabotage.

…Some call it mass-murder.

…Unsanctioned war.

…Corgo's lightning.

But it is written that it is better to burn one city than to curse the darkness.

Corgo did not curse the darkness.

…Many times.

❖   ❖   ❖

The day they came together on Dombeck, Benedick held forth his hand, smiled, said: "Mister Sandor…"

As his hand was shaken, his smile reversed itself. Then it went away from his face. He was shaking an artificial hand.

Sandor nodded, dropped his eyes.

Benedick turned to the big man with the eyepatch.

"…And you are the Lynx?"

"That is correct, my brother. You must excuse me if I do not shake hands. It is against my religion. I believe that life does not require reassurance as to its oneness."

"Of course," said Benedick. "I once knew a man from Dombeck. He was a *gnil* smuggler, named Worten Wortan—"

"He is gone to join the Great Flame," said the Lynx. "That is to say, he is dead now. ICI apprehended him two years ago. He passed to Flame while attempting to escape restraint."

"Really?" said Benedick. "He was at one time a *gnil* addict himself—"

"I know. I read his file in connection with another case."

"Dombeck is full of *gnil* smugglers"—Sandor.

"Oh. Well, then let us talk of this man Corgo."

"Yes"—the Lynx.

"Yes"—Sandor.

"The ICI man told me that many insurance associations have lodged protests with their Interstel representatives."

"That is true"—Lynx.

"Yes"—Sandor, biting his lip. "Do you gentlemen mind if I remove my legs?"

"Not at all"—the Lynx. "We are co-workers, and informality should govern our gatherings."

"Please do," said Benedick.

Sandor leaned forward in his chair and pressed the coupling controls. There followed two thumps from beneath his desk. He leaned back then and surveyed his shelves of globes.

"Do they cause you pain?" asked Benedick.

"Yes"—Sandor.

"Were you in an accident?"

"Birth"—Sandor.

The Lynx raised a decanter of brownish liquid to the light. He stared through it.

"It is a local brandy"—Sandor. "Quite good. Somewhat like the *xmili* of Bandla, only nonaddictive. Have some."

The Lynx did, keeping it in front of him all that evening.

"Corgo is a destroyer of property," said Benedick.

Sandor nodded.

"…And a defrauder of insurance associations, a defacer of planetary bodies, a deserter from the Guard—"

"A murderer"—Sandor.

"…And a zoophilist," finished Benedick.

"Aye"—the Lynx, smacking his lips.

"So great an offender against public tranquility is he that he must be found."

"…And passed back through the Flame for purification and rebirth."

"Yes, we must locate him and kill him," said Benedick.

"The two pieces of equipment… Are they present?"—the Lynx.

"Yes, the phase-wave is in the next room."

"…And?" asked Benedick.

"The other item is in the bottom drawer of this desk, right side."

"Then why do we not begin now?"

"Yes. Why not now?"—the Lynx.

"Very well"—Sandor. "One of you will have to open the drawer, though. It is in the brown-glass jar, to the back."

"I'll get it," said Benedick.

❖   ❖   ❖

A great sob escaped him after a time, as he sat there with rows of worlds at his back, tears on his cheeks, and Corgo's heart clutched in his hands.

"It is cold and dim…"

"Where?"—the Lynx.

"It is a small place. A room? Cabin? Instrument panels…A humming sound… Cold, and crazy angles everywhere… Vibration… Hurt!"

"What is he doing?"—Sandor.

"… Sitting, half-lying—a couch, webbed, about him. Furry one at his side, sleeping. Twisted—angles—everything—wrong. Hurt!"

"The *Wallaby*, in transit"—Lynx.

"Where is he going?"—Sandor.

"HURT!" shouted Benedick.

Benedick dropped the heart into his lap.

He began to shiver. He wiped at his eyes with the backs of his hands.

"I have a headache," he announced.

"Have a drink"—Lynx.

He gulped one, sipped the second.

"Where was I?"

The Lynx raised his shoulders and let them fall.

"The *Wallaby* was fast-phasing somewhere, and Corgo was in phase-sleep. It is a disturbing sensation to fast-phase while fully conscious. Distance and duration grow distorted. You found him at a bad time—while under sedation and subject to continuum-impact. Perhaps tomorrow will be better…"

"I hope so."

"Yes, tomorrow"—Sandor.

"Tomorrow…Yes."

"There *was* one other thing," he added, "a thing in his mind… There was a sun where there was no sun before."

"A burn-job?"—Lynx.

"Yes."

"A memory?"—Sandor.

"No. He is on his way to do it."

The Lynx stood.

"I will phase-wave ICI and advise them. They can check which worlds are presently being mined. Have you any ideas how soon?"

"No, I can not tell that."

"What did the globe look like? What continental configurations?"—Sandor.

"None. The thought was not that specific. His mind was drifting—mainly filled with hate."

"I'll call in now—and we'll try again…?"

"Tomorrow. I'm tired now."

"Go to bed then. Rest."

"Yes, I can do that…"

"Good night, Mister Benedict."

"Good night…"

"Sleep in the heart of the Great Flame."

"I hope not…"

❖   ❖   ❖

Mala whimpered and moved nearer her Corgo, for she was dreaming an evil dream: They were back on the great snowfield of Brild, and she was trying to help him—to walk, to move forward. He kept slipping though, and lying there longer each time, and rising more slowly each time and moving ahead at an even slower pace, each time. He tried to kindle a fire, but the snow-devils spun and toppled like icicles falling from the seven moons, and the dancing green flames died as soon as they were born from between his hands.

Finally, on the top of a mountain of ice she saw them.

There were three…

They were clothed from head to toe in flame; their burning heads turned and turned and turned; and then one bent and sniffed at the ground, rose, and indicated their direction. Then they were racing down the hillside, trailing flames, melting a pathway as they came, springing over drifts and ridges of ice, their arms extended before them.

Silent they came, pausing only as the one sniffed the air, the ground…

She could hear their breathing now, feel their heat…

In a matter of moments they would arrive…

Mala whimpered and moved nearer her Corgo.

❖   ❖   ❖

For three days Benedick tried, clutching Corgo's heart like a Gypsy's crystal, watering it with his tears, squeezing almost to life again. His head ached for hours after, each time that he met the continuum-impact. He wept long, moist tears for hours beyond contact, which was unusual. He had always withdrawn from immediate pain before; remembered distress was his forté, and a different matter altogether.

He hurt each time that he touched Corgo and his mind was sucked down through that subway in the sky; and he touched Corgo eleven times during those three days, and then his power went away, really.

❖   ❖   ❖

Seated, like a lump of dark metal on the hull of the *Wallaby*, he stared across six hundred miles at the blazing hearth which he had stoked to steel-tempering heights; and he *felt* like a piece of metal, resting there upon an anvil, waiting for the hammer to fall again, as it always did, waiting for it to strike him again and again, and to beat him to a new toughness, to smash away more and more of that within him which was base, of that which knew pity, remorse, and guilt, again and again and again, and to leave only that hard, hard form of hate, like an iron boot, which lived at the core of the lump, himself, and required constant hammering and heat.

Sweating as he watched, smiling, Corgo took pictures.

❖   ❖   ❖

When one of the nineteen known paranorms in the one hundred forty-nine inhabited worlds in the galaxy suddenly loses his powers, and loses them at a crucial moment, it is like unto the old tales wherein a Princess is stricken one day with an unknown malady and the King, her father, summons all his wise men and calls for the best physicians in the realm.

Big Daddy ICI (*Rex ex machina-like*) did, in similar manner, summon wise men and counselors from various Thinkomats and thinkrepairshops about the galaxy, including Interstel University, on Earth itself. But alas! While all had a diagnosis none had on hand any suggestions which were immediately acceptable to all parties concerned:

"Bombard his thalamus with Beta particles."

"Hypno-regression to the womb, and restoration at a pretraumatic point in his life."

"More continuum-impact."

"Six weeks on a pleasure satellite, and two aspirins every four hours."

"There is an old operation called a lobotomy…"

"Lots of liquids and green leafy vegetables."

"Hire another paranorm."

For one reason or another, the principal balked at all of these courses of action, and the final one was impossible at the moment. In the end, the matter was settled neatly by Sandor's nurse Miss Barbara, who happened onto the veranda one afternoon as Benedick sat there fanning himself and drinking *xmili*.

"Why Mister Benedict!" she announced, plopping her matronly self into the chair opposite him and spiking her *redlonade* with three fingers of *xmili*. "Fancy meeting you out here! I thought you were in the library with the boys, working on that top secret hush-hush critical project called Wallaby Stew, or something."

"As you can see, I am not," he said, staring at his knees.

"Well, it's nice just to pass the time of day sometimes, too. To sit. To relax. To rest from the hunting of Victor Corgo…"

"Please, you're not supposed to know about the project. It's top secret and critical—"

"And hush-hush too, I know. Dear Sandor talks in his sleep every night—so much. You see, I tuck him in each evening and sit there until he drifts away to dreamland, poor child."

"Mm, yes. Please don't talk about the project, though."

"Why? Isn't it going well?"

"No!"

"Why not?"

"Because of *me*, if you must know! I've got a block of some kind. The power doesn't come when I call it."

"Oh, how distressing! You mean you can't peep into other persons' minds any more?"

"Exactly."

"Dear me. Well, let's talk about something else then. Did I ever tell you about the days when I was the highest-paid courtesan on Sordido V?"

Benedick's head turned slowly in her direction.

"Nooo…" he said. "You mean *the* Sordido?"

"Oh yes. Bright Bad Barby, the Bouncing Baby, they used to call me. They still sing ballads, you know."

"Yes, I've heard them. Many verses…"

"Have another drink, I once had a coin struck in my image, you know. It's a collectors' item now, of course. Full-length pose, flesh-colored. Here, I wear it on this chain around my neck. —Lean closer, it's a short chain."

"Very—interesting. Uh, how did all this come about?"

"Well—it all began with old Pruria Van Teste, the banker, of the export-import Testes. You see, he had this thing going for syntho-femmes for a long while, but when he started getting up there in years he felt there was something he'd been missing. So, one fine day, he sent me ten dozen Hravian orchids and a diamond garter, along with an invitation to have dinner with him…"

"You accepted, of course?"

"Naturally not. Not the first time, anyway. I could see that he was pretty damn eager."

"Well, what happened?"

"Wait till I fix another *redlonade*."

❖   ❖   ❖

Later that afternoon, the Lynx wandered out into the veranda during the course of his meditations. He saw there Miss Barbara, with Benedick seated beside her, weeping.

"What troubles thy tranquility, my brother?" he inquired.

"Nothing! Nothing at all! It is wonderful and beautiful, everything! My power has come back—I can feel it!" He wiped his eyes on his sleeve.

"Bless thee, little lady!" said the Lynx, seizing Miss Barbara's hand. "Thy simple counsels have done more to heal my brother than have all these highly-paid medical practitioners brought here at great expense. Virtue lies in thy homely words, and thou art most beloved of the Flame."

"Thank you, I'm sure."

"Come brother, let us away to our task again!"
"Yes, let us!—Oh thank you, Bright Barby!"
"Don't mention it."

❖   ❖   ❖

Benedick's eyes clouded immediately, as he took the tattered blood-pump into his hands. He leaned back, stroking it, and moist spots formed on either side of his nose, grew like well-fed amoebas, underwent mitosis, and dashed off to explore in the vicinity of his shelf-like upper lip.

He sighed once, deeply.

"Yes, I am there."

He blinked, licked his lips.

"…It is night. Late. It is a primitive dwelling. Mud-like stucco, bits of straw in it… All lights out, but for the one from the machine, and its spillage—"

"Machine?"—Lynx.

"What machine?"—Sandor.

"…Projector. Pictures on wall… World—big, filling whole picture-field—patches of fire on the world, up near the top. Three places—"

"Bhave VII!"—Lynx. "Six days ago!"

"Shoreline to the right goes like this… And to the left, like this…"

His right index finger traced patterns in the air.

"Bhave VII"—Sandor.

"Happy and not happy at the same time—hard to separate the two. Guilt, though, is there—but pleasure with it. Revenge… Hate people, humans… We adjust the projector now, stop it at a flare-up—Bright! How good! —Oh good! That will teach them! —Teach them to grab away what belongs to others… To murder a race! —The generator is humming. It is ancient, and it smells bad… The dog is lying on our foot. The foot is asleep, but we do not want to disturb the dog, for it is Mala's favorite thing—her only toy, companion, living doll, four-footed… She is scratching behind its ear with her forelimb, and it loves her. Light leaks down upon them… Clear they are. The breeze is warm, very, which is why we are unshirted. It stirs the tasseled hanging… No force-field or windowpane… Insects buzz by the projector—pterodactyl silhouettes on the burning world—"

"What kind of insects ?"—Lynx.

"Can you see what is beyond the window?"—Sandor.

"…Outside are trees—short ones—just outlines, squat. Can't tell where trunks begin… Foliage too thick, too close. Too dark out. — Off in the distance a tiny moon… Something like *this* on a hill…" His hands shaped a turnip impaled on an obelisk. "Not sure how far off, how large, what color, or what made of…"

"Is the name of the place in Corgo's mind?"—Lynx.

"If I could touch him, with my hand, I would know it, know everything. Only receive impressions *this* way, though—surface thoughts. He is not thinking of where he is now… The dog rolls onto its back and off of our foot—at last! She scratches its tummy, my love dark…It kicks with its hind leg as if scratching after a flea—wags its tail. Dilk is puppy's name. She gave if that name, loves it… It is like one of hers. Which was murdered. Hate people—humans. *She* is people. Better than… Doesn't butcher that which breathes for selfish gain, for Interstel. Better than people, my pony-friends, better… An insect lights on Dilk's nose. She brushes it away. Segmented, two sets of wings, about five millimeters in length, pink globe on front end, bulbous, and buzzes as it goes, the insect—you asked…"

"How many entrances are there to the place?"—Lynx.

"Two. One doorway at each end of the hut."

"How many windows?"

"Two. On opposing walls—the ones without doors. I can't see anything through the other window—too dark on that side."

"Anything else?"

"On the wall a sword—long hilt, very long, two-handed—even longer maybe—three? four?—short blades, though, two of them—hilt is in the middle—and each blade is straight, double-edged, fore-arm-length… Beside it, a mask of—flowers? Too dark to tell. The blades shine; the mask is dull. Looks like flowers, though. Many little ones… Four sides to the mask, shaped like a kite, big end down. Can't make out features. It projects fairly far out from the wall, though. Mala is restless. Probably doesn't like the pictures—or maybe doesn't see them and is bored. Her eyes are different. She nuzzles our shoulder now. We pour her a drink in her bowl. Take another one ourself. She doesn't drink hers. We stare at her. She drops her head and drinks. —Dirt floor under our sandals, hard-packed. Many tiny

white—pebbles?—in it, powdery-like. The table is wood, natural…
The generator sputters. The picture fades, comes back. We rub our
chin. Need a shave… The hell with it! We're not standing any inspec-
tions! Drink—one, two—all gone! Another!"

❖   ❖   ❖

Sandor had threaded a tape into his viewer, and he was spinning it
and stopping it, spinning it and stopping it, spinning it and stopping
it. He checked his worlds chronometer.

"Outside," he asked, "does the moon seem to be moving up, or
down, or across the sky?"

"Across."

"Right to left, or left to right?"

"Right to left. It seems about a quarter past zenith."

"Any coloration to it?"

"Orange, with three black lines. One starts at about eleven o'clock,
crosses a quarter of its surface, drops straight down, cuts back at
seven. The other starts at two, drops to six. They don't meet. The
third is a small upside-down letter 'c'—lower right quarter… Not
big, the moon, but clear, very. No clouds."

"Any constellations you can make out?"—Lynx.

"…Head isn't turned that way now, wasn't turned toward the window long enough. Now there is a noise, far off… A high-pitched
chattering, almost metallic. Animal. He pictures a six-legged tree
creature, half the size of a man, reddish-brown hair, sparse… It can
go on two, four, or six legs on the ground. Doesn't go down on the
ground much, though. Nests high. An egg-layer. Many teeth. Eats
flesh. Small eyes, and black—two. Great nose-holes. Pesty, but not
dangerous to men—easily frightened."

"He is on Disten, the fifth world of Blake's System," said Sandor. "Night-side means he is on the continent Didenlan. The moon
Babry, well past zenith now, means he is to the east. A Mellar-
mosque indicates a Mella-Muslim settlement. The blade and the
mask seem Hortanian. I am sure they were brought from further
inland. The chalky deposits would set him in the vicinity of Landear, which *is* Mella-Muslim. It is on the Dista River, north bank.
There is much jungle about. Even those people who wish seclusion
seldom go further than eight miles from the center of town—population 153,000—and it is least settled to the northwest, because of
the hills, the rocks, and—"

"Fine! That's where he is then!"—Lynx. "Now here is how we'll do it. He has, of course, been sentenced to death. I believe—yes, I know!—there is an ICI Field Office on the second world—whatever its name—of that System."

"Nirer"—Sandor.

"Yes. Hmm, let's see… Two agents will be empowered as executioners. They will land their ship to the northwest of Landear, enter the city, and find where the man with the strange four-legged pet settled, the one who arrived within the past six days. Then one agent will enter the hut and ascertain whether Corgo is within. He will retreat immediately if Corgo is present, signaling to the other who will be hidden behind those trees or whatever. The second man will then fire a round of fragmentation plaster through the unguarded window. One agent will then position himself at a safe distance beyond the northeast corner of the edifice, so as to cover a door and a window. The other will move to the southwest, to do the same. Each will carry a two-hundred channel laser sub-gun with vibrating head. —Good! I'll phase-wase it to Central now. We've got him!"

He hurried from the room.

Benedick, still holding the thing, his shirt-front soaking, continued:

"'Fear not, my lady dark. He is but a puppy, and he howls at the moon…'"

❖　❖　❖

It was thirty-one hours and twenty minutes later when the Lynx received and decoded the two terse statements:

EXECUTIONERS THE WAY OF ALL FLESH.
THE WALLABY HAS JUMPED AGAIN.

He licked his lips. His comrades were waiting for the report, and *they* had succeeded—they had done their part, had performed efficiently and well. It was the Lynx who had missed his kill.

He made the sign of the Flame and entered the library.

Benedick knew—*he* could tell. The little paranorm's hands were on his walking stick, and that was enough—just that.

The Lynx bowed his head.

"We begin again," he told them.

Benedick's powers—if anything, stronger than ever—survived continuum-impact seven more times. Then he described a new world: Big it was, and many-peopled—bright—dazzling, under a blue-white sun; yellow brick everywhere, neo-Denebian architecture, greenglass windows, a purple sea nearby…

No trick at all for Sandor:

"Phillip's World," he named it, then told them the city: "Delles."

"This time *we* burn *him*," said the Lynx, and he was gone from the room.

"Christian-Zoroastrians," sighed Benedick, after he had left. "I think this one has a Flame-complex."

Sandor spun the globe with his left hand and watched it turn.

"I'm not preconning," said Benedick, "but I'll give you odds, like three to one—on Corgo's escaping again."

"Why?"

"When he abandoned humanity he became something less, and more. He is not ready to die."

"What do you mean?"

"I hold his heart. He gave it up, in all ways. He is invincible now. But he will reclaim it one day. Then he will die."

"How do you know?"

"…A feeling. There are many types of doctors, among them pathologists. No less than others, they, but masters only of blackness. I *know* people, have known many. I do not pretend to know *all* about them. But weaknesses—yes, those I know."

Sandor turned his globe and did not say anything.

But they *did* burn the *Wallaby*, badly.

He lived, though.

He lived, cursing.

As he lay there in the gutter, the world burning, exploding, falling down around him, he cursed *that* world and every other, and everything in them.

Then there was another burst.

Blackness followed.

❖   ❖   ❖

The double-bladed Hortanian sword, spinning in the hands of Corgo, had halved the first ICI executioner as he stood in the doorway. Mala had detected their approach across the breezes, through the open window.

The second had fallen before the fragmentation plaster could be launched. Corgo had a laser sub-gun himself, Guard issue, and he cut the man down, firing through the wall and two trees in the direction Mala indicated.

Then the *Wallaby* left Disten.

But he was troubled. How had they found him so quickly? He had had close brushes with them before—many of them, over the years. But he was cautious, and he could not see where he had failed this time, could not understand how Interstel had located him. Even his last employer did not know his whereabouts.

He shook his head and phased for Phillip's world.

To die is to sleep and not to dream, and Corgo did not want this. He took elaborate pains, in-phasing and out-phasing in random directions; he gave Mala a golden collar with a two-way radio in its clasp, wore its mate within his death-ring; he converted much currency, left the *Wallaby* in the care of a reputable smuggler in Unassociated Territory and crossed Phillip's World to Delles-by-the-Sea. He was fond of sailing, and he liked the purple waters of this planet. He rented a large villa near the Delles Dives—slums to the one side, Riviera to the other. This pleased him. He still had dreams; he was not dead yet.

Sleeping, perhaps, he had heard a sound. Then he was suddenly seated on the side of his bed, a handful of death in his hand.

"Mala?"

She was gone. The sound he'd heard had been the closing of a door.

He activated the radio.

"What is it?" he demanded.

"I have the feeling we are watched again," she replied, through his ring. "…Only a feeling, though."

Her voice was distant, tiny.

"Why did you not tell *me*? Come back—now."

"No. I match the night and can move without sound. I will investigate. There *is* something, if I have fear…Arm yourself!"

He did that, and as he moved toward the front of the house they struck. He ran. As he passed through the front door they struck again, and again. There was an inferno at his back, and a steady rain of plaster, metal, wood and glass was falling. Then there was an inferno around him.

They were above him. This time they had been cautioned not to close with him, but to strike from a distance. This time they hovered high in a shielded globe and poured down hot rivers of destruction.

Something struck him in the head and the shoulder. He fell, turning. He was struck in the chest, the stomach. He covered his face and rolled, tried to rise, failed. He was lost in a forest of flames. He got into a crouch, ran, fell again, rose once more, ran, fell again, crawled, fell again.

As he lay there in the gutter, the world burning, exploding, falling down around him he cursed *that* world and every other, and everyone in them.

Then there was another burst.

Blackness followed.

❖   ❖   ❖

They thought they had succeeded, and their joy was great.

"Nothing," Benedick had said, smiling through his tears.

So that day they celebrated, and the next.

But Corgo's body had not been recovered.

Almost half a block had been hurled down, though, and eleven other residents could not be located either, so it seemed safe to assume that the execution had succeeded. ICI, however, requested that the trio remain together on Dombeck for another ten days, while further investigations were carried out.

Benedick laughed.

"Nothing," he repeated. "Nothing."

But there is a funny thing about a man without a heart: His body does not live by the same rules as those of others: No. The egg in his chest is smarter than a mere heart, and it is the center of a wonderful communications system. Dead itself, it is omniscient in terms of that which lives around it; it is not omnipotent, but it has resources which a living heart does not command.

As the burns and lacerations were flashed upon the screen of the body, it sat in instant criticism. It moved itself to an emergency level of function; it became a flag vibrating within a hurricane, the glands responded and poured forth their juices of power; muscles were activated as if by electricity.

Corgo was only half-aware of the inhuman speed with which he moved through the storm of heat and the hail of building materials. It tore at him, but this pain was canceled. His massive output jammed nonessential neural input. He made it as far as the street and collapsed in the shelter of the curb.

The egg took stock of the cost of the action, decided the price had been excessively high, and employed immediate measures to insure the investment.

Down, down did it send him. Into the depths of sub-coma. Standard-model humans cannot decide one day that they wish to hibernate, lie down, do it. The physicians can induce *dauersch-laff*—with combinations of drugs and elaborate machineries. But Corgo did not need these things. He had a built-in survival kit with a mind of its own; and it decided that he must go deeper than the mere coma-level that a heart would have permitted. So it did the things a heart cannot do, while maintaining its own functions.

It hurled him into the blackness of sleep without dreams, of total unawareness. For only at the border of death itself could his life be retained, be strengthened, grow again. To approach this near the realm of death, its semblance was necessary.

Therefore, Corgo lay dead in the gutter.

People, of course, flock to the scene of any disaster.

Those from the Riviera pause to dress in their best catastrophe clothing. Those from the slums do not, because their wardrobes are not as extensive.

One though, was dressed already and was passing nearby. "Zim" was what he was called, for obvious reasons. He had had another name once, but he had all but forgotten it.

He was staggering home from the *zimlak* parlor where he had cashed his Guard pension check for that month-cycle.

There was an explosion, but it was seconds before he realized it. Muttering, he stopped and turned very slowly in the direction of the noise. Then he saw the flames. He looked up, saw the hoverglobe. A memory appeared within his mind and he winced and continued to watch.

After a time he saw the man, moving at a fantastic pace across the landscape of Hell. The man fell in the street. There was more burning, and then the globe departed.

The impressions finally registered, and his disaster-reflex made him approach.

Indelible synapses, burnt into his brain long ago, summoned up page after page of *The Complete Guard Field Manual of Immediate*

Medical Actions. He knelt beside the body, red with burn, blood, and firelight.

"…Captain," he said, as he stared into the angular face with the closed dark eyes. "Captain…"

He covered his own face with his hands and they came away wet.

"Neighbors. Here. Us. Didn't—know…" He listened for a heartbeat, but there was nothing that he could detect. "Fallen… On the deck my Captain lies… Fallen…cold…dead. Us. Neighbors, even…" His sob was a jagged thing, until he was seized with a spell of hiccups. Then he steadied his hands and raised an eyelid.

Corgo's head jerked two inches to his left, away from the brightness of the flames.

The man laughed in relief.

"You're alive, Cap! You're still alive!"

The thing that was Corgo did not reply.

Bending, straining, he raised the body.

"'Do not move the victim'—that's what it says in the *Manual*. But you're coming with me, Cap. I remember now… It was after I left. But I remember… All. Now I remember; I do…Yes. They'll kill you another time—if you do live… They will; I know. So I'll have to move the victim. Have to… —Wish I wasn't so fogged… I'm sorry, Cap. You were always good, to the men, good to me. Ran a tight ship, but you were good…Old *Wallaby*, happy…Yes. We'll go now, killer. Fast as we can. Before the Morbs come. —Yes. I remember…you. Good man, Cap. Yes."

So, the *Wallaby* had made its last jump, according to the ICI investigation which followed. But Corgo still dwelled on the dreamless border, and the seeds and the egg held his life.

After the ten days had passed, the Lynx and Benedick still remained with Sandor. Sandor was not anxious for them to go. He had never been employed before; he liked the feeling of having co-workers about, persons who shared memories of things done. Benedick was loathe to leave Miss Barbara, one of the few persons he could talk to and have answer him, willingly. The Lynx liked the food and the climate, decided his wives and grandchildren could use a vacation.

So they stayed on.

❖   ❖   ❖

Returning from death is a deadly slow business. Reality does the dance of the veils, and it is a long while before you know what lies beneath them all (if you ever really do).

When Corgo had formed a rough idea, he cried out:

"Mala!"

…The darkness.

Then he saw a face out of times gone by.

"Sergeant Emil…?"

"Yes, sir. Right here, Captain."

"Where am I?"

"My hutch, sir. Yours got burnt out."

"How?"

"A hoverglobe did it, with a sear-beam."

"What of my—pet? A Drillen…"

"There was only you I found, sir—no one, nothing, else. Uh, it was almost a month-cycle ago that it happened…"

Corgo tried to sit up, failed, tried again, half-succeeded. He sat propped on his elbows.

"What's the matter with me?"

"You had some fractures, burns, lacerations, internal injuries—but you're going to be all right, now."

"I wonder how they found me, so fast—again…?"

"I don't know, sir. Would you like to try some broth now?"

"Later."

"It's all warm and ready."

"Okay, Emil. Sure, bring it on."

He lay back and wondered.

There was her voice. He had been dozing all day and he was part of a dream.

"Corgo, are you there? Are you there, Corgo? Are you…"

His hand! The ring!

"Yes! Me! Corgo!" He activated it. "Mala! Where are you?"

"In a cave, by the sea. Everyday I have called to you. Are you alive, or do you answer me from Elsewhere?"

"I am alive. There is no magic to your collar. How have you kept yourself?"

"I go out at night. Steal food from the large dwellings with the green windows like doors—for Dilk and myself."

"The puppy? Alive, too?"

"Yes. He was penned in the yard on that night… Where are you?"

"I do not know, precisely… Near where our place was. A few blocks away—I'm with an old friend…"

"I must come."

"Wait until dark, I'll get you directions. —No. I'll send him after you, my friend… Where is your cave?"

"Up the beach, past the red house you said was ugly. There are three rocks, pointed on top. Past them is a narrow path—the water comes up to it, sometimes covers it—and around a corner then, thirty-one of my steps, and the rock hangs overhead, too. It goes far back then, and there is a crack in the wall—small enough to squeeze through, but it widens. We are here."

"My friend will come for you after dark."

"You are hurt?"

"I was. But I am better now. I'll see you later, talk more then."

"Yes—"

❖   ❖   ❖

In the days that followed, his strength returned to him. He played chess with Emil and talked with him of their days together in the Guard. He laughed, for the first time in many years, at the tale of the Commander's wig, at the Big Brawl on Sordido III, some thirty-odd years before…

Mala kept to herself, and to Dilk. Occasionally, Corgo would feel her eyes upon him. But whenever he turned, she was always looking in another direction. He realized that she had never seen him being friendly with anyone before. She seemed puzzled.

He drank *zimlak* with Emil, they ventured off-key ballads together…

Then one day it struck him.

"Emil, what are you using for money these days?"

"Guard pension, Cap."

"Flames! We've been eating you out of business! Food, and the medical supplies and all…"

"I had a little put away for foul weather days, Cap."

"Good. But you shouldn't have been using it. There's quite a bit of money zipped up in my boots. —Here. Just a second… There! Take these!"

"I can't, Cap…"

"The hell, you say! Take them, that's an order!"

"All right, sir, but you don't have to…"

"Emil, there is a price on my head—you know?"

"I know."

"A pretty large reward."

"Yes."

"It's yours, by right."

"I couldn't turn you in, sir."

"Nevertheless, the reward is yours. Twice over. I'll send you that amount—a few weeks after I leave here."

"I couldn't take it, sir."

"Nonsense; you will."

"No, sir. I won't."

"What do you mean?"

"I just mean I couldn't take that money."

"Why not? What's wrong with it?"

"Nothing, exactly… I just don't want any of it. I'll take this you gave me for the food and stuff. But no more, that's all."

"Oh… All right, Emil. Any way you like it. I wasn't trying to force…"

"I know, Cap."

"Another game now? I'll spot you a bishop and three pawns this time."

"Very good, sir."

"We had some good time together, eh?"

"You bet, Cap. Tau Ceti—three months' leave. Remember the Red River Valley—and the family native life-forms?"

"Hah! And Cygnus VII—the purple world with the Rainbow Women?"

"Took me three weeks to get that dye off me. Thought at first it was a new disease. Flames! I'd love to ship out again!"

Corgo paused in mid-move.

"Hmm… You know, Emil… It might be that you could."

"What do you mean?"

Corgo finished his move.

"Aboard the *Wallaby*. It's here, in Unassociated Territory, waiting for me. I'm Captain, and crew—and everything—all by myself, right now. Mala helps some, but—you know, I could use a First Mate. Be like old times."

Emil replaced the knight he had raised, looked up, looked back down.

"I—I don't know what to say, Cap. I never thought you'd offer me a berth…"

"Why not? I could use a good man. Lots of action, like the old days. Plenty cash. No cares. We want three months' leave on Tau Ceti and we write our own bloody orders. We take it!"

"I—I do want to space again, Cap—bad. But—no, I couldn't…"

"Why not, Emil? Why not? It'd be just like before."

"I don't know how to say it, Cap…But when we—burnt places, before—well, it was criminals—pirates, Code-breakers—you know. Now…Well, now I hear you burn—just people. Uh, non-Code-breakers. Like, just plain civilians. Well—I could not."

Corgo did not answer. Emil moved his knight.

"I hate them, Emil," he said, after a time. "Every lovin' one of them, I hate them. Do you know what they did on Brild? To the Drillen?"

"Yessir. But it wasn't civilians, and not the miners. It was not *everybody*. It wasn't every lovin' one of them, sir. —I just couldn't. Don't be mad."

"I'm not mad, Emil."

"I mean, sir, there are some as I wouldn't mind burnin', Code or no Code. But not the way you do it, sir. And I'd do it for free to those as have it coming."

"Huh!"

Corgo moved his one bishop.

"That's why my money is no good with you?"

"No, sir. That's not it, sir. Well maybe part…But only part. I just couldn't take pay for helping someone I—respected, admired."

"You use the past tense."

"Yessir. But I still think you got a raw deal, and what they did to the Drillen was wrong and bad and—evil—but you can't hate everybody for that, sir, because *everybody* didn't do it."

"They countenanced it, Emil—which is just as bad. I am able to hate them all for that alone. And people are all alike, all the same. I burn without discrimination these days, because it doesn't really matter *who*. The guilt is equally distributed. Mankind is commonly culpable."

"No, sir, begging your pardon, sir, but in a system as big as Interstel not everybody knows what everybody else is up to. There are those feeling the same way you do, and there are those as don't give a damn, and those who just don't know a lot of what's going on, but who would do something about it if they knew, soon enough."

"It's your move, Emil."

"Yessir."

"You know, I wish you'd accepted a commission, Emil. You had the chance. You'd have been a good officer."

"No, sir. I'd not have been a good officer. I'm too easy-going. The men would've walked all over me."

"It's a pity. But it's always that way. You know? The good ones are too weak, too easy-going. Why is that?"

"Dunno, sir."

After a couple of moves:

"You know, if I were to give it up—the burning, I mean—and just do some ordinary, decent smuggling with the *Wallaby*, it would be okay. With me. Now. I'm tired. I'm so damned tired I'd just like to sleep—oh, four, five, six years, I think. Supposing I stopped the burning and just shipped stuff here and there—would you sign on with me then?"

"I'd have to think about it, Cap."

"Do that, then. Please. I'd like to have you along."

"Yessir. Your move, sir."

❖   ❖   ❖

It would not have happened that he'd have been found by his actions, because he *did* stop the burning; it would not have happened—because he was dead on ICI's books—that anyone would have been looking for him. It happened, though—because of a surfeit of *xmili* and good will on the part of the hunters.

On the eve of the breaking of the fellowship, nostalgia followed high spirits.

Benedick had never had a friend before, you must remember. Now he had three, and he was leaving them.

The Lynx had ingested much good food and drink, and the good company of simple, maimed people, whose neuroses were unvitiated with normal sophistication—and he had enjoyed this.

Sandor's sphere of human relations had been expanded by approximately a third, and he had slowly come to consider himself at least an honorary member of the vast flux which he had only known before as humanity, or Others.

So, in the library, drinking, and eating and talking, they returned to the hunt. Dead tigers are always the best kind.

Of course, it wasn't long before Benedick picked up the heart, and held it as a connoisseur would an art object—gently, and with a certain mingling of awe and affection.

As they sat there, an odd sensation crept into the pudgy paranorm's stomach and rose slowly, like gas, until his eyes burned.

"I—I'm reading," he said.

"Of course"—the Lynx.

"Yes"—Sandor.

"Really!"

"Naturally"—the Lynx. "He is on Disten, fifth world of Blake's System, in a native hut outside Landear—"

"No"—Sandor. "He is on Phillip's World, in Delles-by-the-Sea."

They laughed, the Lynx a deep rumble, Sandor a gasping chuckle.

"No," said Benedick. "He is in transit, aboard the *Wallaby*. He had just phased and his mind is still mainly awake. He is running a cargo of ambergris to the Tau Ceti system, fifth planet—Tholmen. After that he plans on vacationing in the Red River Valley of the third planet—Cardiff. Along with the Drillen and the puppy, he has a crewman with him this time. I can't read anything but that it's a retired Guardsman."

"By the holy Light of the Great and Glorious Flame!"

"We know they never did find his ship…"

"…And his body was not recovered. —Could *you* be mistaken. Benedick? Reading something, someone else…?"

"No."

"What should we do, Lynx?"—Sandor.

"An unethical person might be inclined to forget it. It is a closed case. We *have* been paid and dismissed."

"True."

"But think of when he strikes again…"

"…It would be because of us, our failure."

"Yes."

"…And many would die."

"…And much machinery destroyed, and an insurance association defrauded."

"Yes."

"…Because of us."

"Yes."

"So we should report it"—Lynx.

"Yes."

"It is unfortunate…"

"Yes."

"…But it will be good to have worked together this final time."

"Yes. It will. Very."

"Tholmen, in Tau Ceti, and he just phased?"—Lynx.

"Yes."

"I'll call, and they'll be waiting for him in T.C."

"…I told you," said the weeping paranorm. "He wasn't ready to die."

Sandor smiled and raised his glass with his flesh-colored hand.

There was still some work to be done.

❖   ❖   ❖

When the *Wallaby* hit Tau Ceti all hell broke loose.

Three fully-manned Guardships, like unto the *Wallaby* herself were waiting.

ICI had quarantined the entire system for three days. There could be no mistaking the ebony toadstool when it appeared on the screen. No identification was solicited.

The tractor beams missed it the first time, however, and the *Wallaby's* new First Mate fired every weapon aboard the ship simultaneously, in all directions, as soon as the alarm sounded. This had been one of Corgo's small alterations in fire-control, because of the size of his operations: no safety circuits; and it was a suicide-ship, if necessary: it was a lone wolf with no regard for *any* pack: one central control—touch it, and the *Wallaby* became a porcupine with laser-quills, stabbing into anything in every direction.

Corgo prepared to phase again, but it took him forty-three seconds to do so.

During that time he was struck twice by the surviving Guardship. Then he was gone.

Time and Chance, which govern all things, and sometimes like to pass themselves off as Destiny, then seized upon the *Wallaby*, the puppy, the Drillen, First Mate Emil, and the man without a heart.

Corgo had set no course when he had in-phased. There had been no time.

The two blasts from the Guardship had radically altered the *Wallaby's* course, and had burnt out twenty-three fast-phase projectors.

The *Wallaby* jumped blind, and with a broken leg.

Continuum-impact racked the crew. The hull repaired rents in its skin.

They continued for thirty-nine hours and twenty-three minutes, taking turns at sedation, watching for the first warning on the panel.

The *Wallaby* held together, though.

But where they had gotten to no one knew, least of all a weeping paranorm who had monitored the battle and all of Corgo's watches, despite the continuum-impact and a hangover.

But suddenly Benedick knew fear:

"He's about to phase-out. I'm going to have to drop him now."

"Why?"—the Lynx.

"Do you know where he is?"

"No, of course not!"

"Well, neither does he. Supposing he pops out in the middle of a sun, or in some atmosphere—moving at that speed?"

"Well, supposing he does? He dies."

"Exactly. Continuum-impact is bad enough. I've never been in a man's mind when he died—and I don't think I could take it. Sorry. I just won't do it. I think I might die myself if it happened. I'm so tired now… I'll just have to check him out later."

With that he collapsed and could not be roused.

❖   ❖   ❖

So, Corgo's heart went back into its jar, and the jar went back into the lower right-hand drawer of Sandor's desk, and none of the hunters heard the words of Corgo's answer to his First Mate after the phasing-out:

"Where are we? —The Comp says the nearest thing is a little ping-pong ball of a world called Dombeck, not noted for anything. We'll have to put down there for repairs, somewhere off the beaten track. We need projectors."

So they landed the *Wallaby* and banged on its hull as the hunters slept, some five hundred forty-two miles away.

They were grinding out the projector sockets shortly after Sandor had been tucked into his bed.

They reinforced the hull in three places while the Lynx ate half a ham, three biscuits, two apples and a pear, and drank half a liter of Dombeck's best Mosel.

They rewired shorted circuits as Benedick smiled and dreamt of Bright Bad Barby the Bouncing Baby, in the days of her youth.

And Corgo took the light-boat and headed for a town three hundred miles away, just as the pale sun of Dombeck began to rise.

❖   ❖   ❖

"He's here!" cried Benedick, flinging wide the door to the Lynx's room and rushing up to the bedside. "He's—"

Then he was unconscious, for the Lynx may not be approached suddenly as he sleeps.

When he awakened five minutes later, he was lying on the bed and the entire household stood about him. There was a cold cloth on his forehead and his throat felt crushed.

"My brother," said the Lynx, "you should never approach a sleeping man in such a manner."

"B-but he's here," said Benedick, gagging. "Here on Dombeck! I don't even need Sandor to tell!"

"Art sure thou hast not imbibed too much?"

"No, I tell you he's here!" He sat up, flung away the cloth. "That little city, Coldstream—" He pointed through the wall. "—I was there just a week ago. I *know* the place!"

"You have had a dream—"

"Wet your Flame! But I've not! I held his heart in these hands and saw it!"

The Lynx winced at the profanity, but considered the possibility.

"Then come with us to the library and see if you can read it again."

"You better believe I can!"

At that moment Corgo was drinking a cup of coffee and waiting for the town to wake up. He was considering his First Mate's resignation:

"I never wanted to burn anyone, Cap. Least of all, the Guard. I'm sorry, but that's it. No more for me. Leave me here and give me passage home to Phillip's—that's all I want. I know you didn't want it the way it happened, but if I keep shipping with you it might happen again some day. Probably will. They got your number somehow, and I couldn't *ever* do *that* again. I'll help you fix the *Wallaby*, then I'm out. Sorry."

Corgo sighed and ordered a second coffee. He glanced at the clock on the diner wall. Soon, soon…

❖　❖　❖

"That clock, that wall, that window! It's the diner where I had lunch last week, in Coldstream!" said Benedick, blinking moistly.

"Do you think all that continuum-impact…?"—the Lynx.

"I don't know"—Sandor.

"How can we check?"

"Call the flamin' diner and ask them to describe their only customer!"—Benedick.

"*That* is a very good idea"—the Lynx.

The Lynx moved to the phone-unit on Sandor's desk.

Sudden, as everything concerning the case had been, was the Lynx's final decision:

"Your flyer, brother Sandor. May I borrow it?"

"Why, yes. Surely…"

"I will now call the local ICI office and requisition a laser-cannon. They have been ordered to cooperate with us without question, and the orders are still in effect. My executioner's rating has never been suspended. It appears that if we ever want to see this job completed we must do it ourselves. It won't take long to mount the gun on your flyer. —Benedick, stay with him every minute now. He still has to buy the equipment, take it back, and install it. Therefore, we should have sufficient time. Just stay with him and advise me as to his movements."

"Check."

"Are you sure it's the right way to go about it?"—Sandor.

"I'm sure…"

❖　❖　❖

As the cannon was being delivered, Corgo made his purchases. As it was being installed, he loaded the light-boat and departed. As it was tested, on a tree stump Aunt Faye had wanted removed for a long while, he was aloft and heading toward the desert.

As he crossed the desert, Benedick watched the rolling dunes, scrub-shrubs and darting *rabbophers* through his eyes.

He also watched the instrument-panel.

As the Lynx began his journey, Mala and Dilk were walking about the hull of the *Wallaby*. Mala wondered if the killing was over. She was not sure she liked the new Corgo so much as she did the avenger. She wondered whether the change would be permanent. She hoped not...

The Lynx maintained radio contact with Benedick.

Sandor drank *xmili* and smiled.

After a time, Corgo landed.

The Lynx was racing across the sands from the opposite direction.

They began unloading the light-boat.

The Lynx sped on.

"I am near it now. Five minutes," he radioed back.

"Then I'm out?"—Benedick.

"Not yet"—the reply.

"Sorry, but you know what I said. I won't be there when he dies."

"All right, I can take it from here"—the Lynx.

Which is how, when the Lynx came upon the scene, he saw a dog and a man and an ugly but intelligent quadruped beside the *Wallaby*.

His first blast hit the ship. The man fell.

The quadruped ran, and he burnt it.

The dog thrashed through the port into the ship.

The Lynx brought the flyer about for another pass.

There was another man, circling around from the other side of the ship, where he had been working.

The man raised his hand and there was a flash of light.

Corgo's death-ring discharged its single laser beam.

It crossed the distance between them, penetrated the hull of the flyer, passed through the Lynx's left arm above the elbow, and continued on through the roof of the vehicle.

The Lynx cried out, fought the controls, as Corgo dashed into the *Wallaby*.

Then he triggered the cannon, and again, and again, and again, circling, until the *Wallaby* was a smoldering ruin in the middle of a sea of fused sand.

Still did he burn that ruin, finally calling back to Benedick Benedict and asking his one question.

"Nothing"—the reply.

Then he turned and headed back, setting the autopilot and opening the first-aid kit.

"…Then he went in to hit the *Wallaby's* guns, but I hit him first"—Lynx.

"No"—Benedick.

"What meanest thou 'no'? *I* was there."

"So was I, for awhile. I *had* to see how he felt."

"And?"

"He went in for the puppy, Dilk, held it in his arms, and said to it, 'I am sorry.'"

"Whatever, he is dead now and we have finished. It is over"—Sandor.

"Yes."

"Yes."

"Let us then drink to a job well done, before we part for good."

"Yes."

"Yes."

And they did.

While there wasn't much left of the *Wallaby* or its Captain, ICI positively identified a synthetic heart found still beating, erratically, amidst the hot wreckage.

Corgo was dead, and that was it.

He should have known what he was up against, and turned himself in to the proper authorities. How can you hope to beat a man who can pick the lock to your mind, a man who dispatched forty-eight men and seventeen malicious alien life-forms, and a man who knows every damn street in the galaxy.

He should have known better than to go up against Sandor Sandor, Benedick Benedict and Lynx Links. He should, he should have known.

For their real names, of course, are Tisiphone, Alecto, and Megaera. They are the Furies. They arise from chaos and deliver revenge; they convey confusion and disaster to those who abandon the law and forsake the way, who offend against the light and violate the life, who take the power of flame, like a lightning-rod in their two too mortal hands.

A Word from Zelazny

"[This] was an early story, from the period when I was still trying to teach myself about character development. It involves a continuing fascination with the better qualities of bad characters and the worst qualities of good ones, to put it as simply as I can."[1] He also wrote it to honor the comic book heroes that he loved.

A Word from Theodore Sturgeon and Frederik Pohl

Theodore Sturgeon said, "'The Furies' is a tour de force, the easy accomplishment of what most writers would consider impossible, and a few very good ones insuperably difficult. Seemingly with the back of his hand, he has created milieu, characters and a narrative goal as far out as anyone need go; he makes you believe it all the way, and walks off breathing easily leaving you gasping with a fable in your hands."[2]

Frederik Pohl rejected it for *Galaxy*: "As a general rule, for instance, it seems to me that a science-fiction story needs *more* lucidity, more clarity, more directness of exposition than, say, in a 'mainstream' story...because in a mainstream story, it's possible for the reader to judge what is an exercise in literary form and what is taken to be representational. In sf and fantasy, the reader doesn't always have that advantage. Since the subject matter can be pretty far-out, a far-out style is multiply confusing...[When this general rule of mine isn't followed] the story becomes difficult to follow, and maybe not worth the trouble—and I have the feeling that something like that happened here."[3]

---

1 *Amber Dreams*, 1983.
2 *Four for Tomorrow*, 1967.
3 Letter from Frederik Pohl to Roger Zelazny, undated.

Notes

Victor Corgo resembles the mythical ogre *Kastchei*, the embodiment of evil. His soul resides beyond harm's reach in a casket, granting him immortality and enabling him to engage in mischief such as holding maidens captive and turning their male defenders to stone.

In Greek mythology, the three **Furies** are Greek vengeance goddesses who punished wrongdoers, pursuing them eventually to madness (into a fury). **The Ancient Mariner**, cursed for killing an albatross, warns others to avoid his fate. **Psychometrize** means to measure or map thought patterns. A **wallaby** is a small jumping marsupial that belongs to the same family as kangaroos. **Fibrillated** means the heart muscle quivers uncontrollably and cannot pump blood. **Sluicers** are machines that direct water flow. **Probosci** are noses, snouts, trunks, or sucking organs. A **zoophilist** is an animal lover, in this case implying sex with an alien. *Rex ex-machina-like* means "King out of the machine," a play on "*Deus ex machina,*" the sudden appearance of a character/device to resolve a story's conflict. The **thalamus** is a part of the brain that processes sensory information. A **lobotomy**, an operation no longer used to control mental disorders, cuts part of the brain's frontal lobe, leading to docile behavior. A **courtesan** is a prostitute, especially one whose clients include royalty and men of high social standing. **Testes** is the medical term for testicles, and use of it as a family name is characteristic of Zelazny's humor. *Dauersch-laff* therapy uses medication to induce a deep sleep. A **surfeit** is too much or an overindulgence. **Unvitiated** means pure.

Thoughts of the Jupiterian Frantifier Fish

During the "Night" Freeze
At Which Time,
Unfortunately,
Consciousness
is
Maintained by
the Fish, Who
are, Also Un-
fortunately, Quite
Intelligent and Highly
Sensitive Creatures—Alas!

Procrastination #9, 1971.

i.

Steep above,
the clouds have stopped,
and we are suspended
in the loss of warmth:
our frozen pond.

ii.

The night is a rock
to spread wet galaxies upon…

iii.

Fie! oh day!
a long night off,
and that we cannot sleep.

We hang about
till night is done—
Black day—

in eyes' weightless prison,
seeing—

in lake's dark lens,
exposed—

falling up pits of the sky.

iv.

To tear that sky down the middle
will be more than the mind can bear.

Brittle, it will break.

v.

Our frantic remains
will continue the species,
in ignorance and light.

vi.

Swimming, as we did,
they'll never give a damn,
till just about this time
tomorrow night.

vii.

…When ice before shards
is too right.

viii.

And the light!

ix.

The light…

x.

Such
is
the
kingdom
of
ice
of
ice
such
is
the

Notes

This poem with the extremely long title is a free verse influenced by the works of Chinese poets Li Po and Tu Fu.[1]

---

1 *Roger Zelazny*, Jane Lindskold, 1993.

Holy Thursday

Written 1955–60 for *Chisel in the Sky;* previously unpublished.

Time Past

We all fall
but do not all crawl.

Time

The moment is a cross
overlapping anything and ourselves
at constant contraries fixed,
essays in constant contact.

To Come

Like smoke
or the single bird,
to be followed
with an upward head,
at Easter in halls of the soul
bend not upon the dead.

LUCIFER

Manuscript title: Power & Light.
Worlds of Tomorrow, June 1964.

Carlson stood on the hill in the silent center of the city whose people had died.

He stared up at the Building—the one structure that dwarfed every hotel-grid, skyscraper-needle, or apartment-cheesebox packed into all the miles that lay about him. Tall as a mountain, it caught the rays of the bloody sun. Somehow it turned their red into golden halfway up its height.

Carlson suddenly felt that he should not have come back.

It had been over two years, as he figured it, since last he had been here. He wanted to return to the mountains now. One look was enough. Yet still he stood before it, transfixed by the huge Building, by the long shadow that bridged the entire valley. He shrugged his thick shoulders then, in an unsuccessful attempt to shake off memories of the days, five (or was it six?) years ago, when he had worked within the giant unit.

Then he climbed the rest of the way up the hill and entered the high, wide doorway.

His fiber sandals cast a variety of echoes as he passed through the deserted offices and into the long hallway that led to the belts.

The belts, of course, were still. There were no thousands riding them. There was no one alive to ride. Their deep belly-rumble was only a noisy phantom in his head as he climbed onto the one nearest him and walked ahead into the pitchy insides of the place.

It was like a mausoleum. There seemed no ceiling, no walls, only the soft *pat-pat* of his soles on the flexible fabric of the belt.

He reached a junction and mounted a cross-belt, instinctively standing still for a moment and waiting for the forward lurch as it sensed his weight.

Then he chuckled silently and began walking again.

When he reached the lift, he set off to the right of it until his memory led him to the maintenance stairs. Shouldering his bundle, he began the long, groping ascent.

He blinked at the light when he came into the Power Room. Filtered through its hundred high windows, the sunlight trickled across the dusty acres of machinery.

Carlson sagged against the wall, breathing heavily from the climb. After awhile he wiped a workbench clean and set down his parcel.

Then he removed his faded shirt, for the place would soon be stifling. He brushed his hair from his eyes and advanced down the narrow metal stair to where the generators stood, row on row, like an army of dead, black beetles. It took him six hours to give them all a cursory check.

He selected three in the second row and systematically began tearing them down, cleaning them, soldering their loose connections with the auto-iron, greasing them, oiling them and sweeping away all the dust, cobwebs, and pieces of cracked insulation that lay at their bases.

Great rivulets of perspiration ran into his eyes and down along his sides and thighs, spilling in little droplets onto the hot flooring and vanishing quickly.

Finally, he put down his broom, remounted the stair and returned to his parcel. He removed one of the water bottles and drank off half its contents. He ate a piece of dried meat and finished the bottle. He allowed himself one cigarette then, and returned to work.

❖   ❖   ❖

He was forced to stop when it grew dark. He had planned on sleeping right there, but the room was too oppressive. So he departed the way he had come and slept beneath the stars, on the roof of a low building at the foot of the hill.

It took him two more days to get the generators ready. Then he began work on the huge Broadcast Panel. It was in better condition than the generators, because it had last been used two years ago. Whereas the generators, except for the three he had burned out last time, had slept for over five (or was it six?) years.

He soldered and wiped and inspected until he was satisfied. Then only one task remained.

All the maintenance robots stood frozen in mid-gesture. Carlson would have to wrestle a three hundred pound power cube without assistance. If he could get one down from the rack and onto a cart without breaking a wrist he would probably be able to convey it to the Igniter without much difficulty. Then he would have to place it within the oven. He had almost ruptured himself when he did it two years ago, but he hoped that he was somewhat stronger—and luckier—this time.

It took him ten minutes to clean the Igniter oven. Then he located a cart and pushed it back to the rack.

One cube was resting at just the right height, approximately eight inches above the level of the cart's bed. He kicked down the anchor chocks and moved around to study the rack. The cube lay on a downward-slanting shelf, restrained by a two-inch metal guard. He pushed at the guard. It was bolted to the shelf.

Returning to the work area, he searched the tool boxes for a wrench. Then he moved back to the rack and set to work on the nuts.

The guard came loose as he was working on the fourth nut. He heard a dangerous creak and threw himself back out of the way, dropping the wrench on his toes.

The cube slid forward, crushed the loosened rail, teetered a bare moment, then dropped with a resounding crash onto the heavy bed of the cart. The bed surface bent and began to crease beneath its weight; the cart swayed toward the outside. The cube continued to slide until over half a foot projected beyond the edge. Then the cart righted itself and shivered into steadiness.

Carlson sighed and kicked loose the chocks, ready to jump back should it suddenly give way in his direction. It held.

Gingerly, he guided it up the aisle and between the rows of generators, until he stood before the Igniter. He anchored the cart again, stopped for water and a cigarette, then searched up a pinch bar, a small jack and a long, flat metal plate.

He laid the plate to bridge the front end of the cart and the opening to the oven. He wedged the far end in beneath the Igniter's doorframe.

Unlocking the rear chocks, he inserted the jack and began to raise the back end of the wagon, slowly, working with one hand and holding the bar ready in his other.

The cart groaned as it moved higher. Then a sliding, grating sound began and he raised it faster.

With a sound like the stroke of a cracked bell the cube tumbled onto the bridgeway; it slid forward and to the left. He struck at it with the bar, bearing to the right with all his strength. About half an inch of it caught against the left edge of the oven frame. The gap between the cube and the frame was widest at the bottom.

He inserted the bar and heaved his weight against it—three times. Then it moved forward and came to rest within the Igniter.

He began to laugh. He laughed until he felt weak. He sat on the broken cart, swinging his legs and chuckling to himself, until the sounds coming from his throat seemed alien and out of place. He stopped abruptly and slammed the door.

The Broadcast Panel had a thousand eyes, but none of them winked back at him. He made the final adjustments for Transmit, then gave the generators their last check-out.

After that, he mounted a catwalk and moved to a window.

There was still some daylight to spend, so he moved from window to window pressing the "Open" button set below each sill.

❖　　❖　　❖

He ate the rest of his food then, and drank a whole bottle of water and smoked two cigarettes. Sitting on the stair, he thought of the days when he had worked with Kelly and Murchison and Djizinsky, twisting the tails of electrons until they wailed and leapt out over the walls and fled down into the city.

The clock! He remembered it suddenly—set high on the wall, to the left of the doorway, frozen at 9:33 (and forty-eight seconds).

He moved a ladder through the twilight and mounted it to the clock. He wiped the dust away from its greasy face with a sweeping, circular movement. Then he was ready.

He crossed to the Igniter and turned it on. Somewhere the ever-batteries came alive, and he heard a click as a thin, sharp shaft was driven into the wall of the cube. He raced back up the stairs and sped hand-over-hand up to the catwalk. He moved to a window and waited.

"God," he muttered, "don't let them blow! Please don't—"

Across an eternity of darkness the generators began humming. He heard a crackle of static from the Broadcast Panel and he closed his eyes. The sound died.

He opened his eyes as he heard the window slide upward. All around him the hundred high windows opened. A small light came on above the bench in the work area below him, but he did not see it.

He was staring out beyond the wide drop of the acropolis and down into the city. His city.

The lights were not like the stars. They beat the stars all to hell. They were the gay, regularized constellation of a city where men made their homes: even rows of streetlamps, advertisements, lighted windows in the cheesebox-apartments, a random solitaire of bright squares running up the sides of skyscraper-needles, a searchlight swivelling its luminous antenna through cloudbanks that hung over the city.

He dashed to another window, feeling the high night breezes comb at his beard. Belts were humming below; he heard their wry monologues rattling through the city's deepest canyons. He pictured the people in their homes, in theaters, in bars—talking to each other, sharing a common amusement, playing clarinets, holding hands, eating an evening snack. Sleeping ro-cars awakened and rushed past each other on the levels above the belts; the background hum of the city told him its story of production, of function, of movement and service to its inhabitants. The sky seemed to wheel overhead, as though the city were its turning hub and the universe its outer rim.

Then the lights dimmed from white to yellow and he hurried, with desperate steps, to another window.

❖　❖　❖

"No! Not so soon! Don't leave me yet!" he sobbed.

The windows closed themselves and the lights went out. He stood on the walk for a long time, staring at the dead embers. A smell of ozone reached his nostrils. He was aware of a blue halo about the dying generators.

He descended and crossed the work area to the ladder he had set against the wall.

Pressing his face against the glass and squinting for a long time he could make out the position of the hands.

"Nine thirty-five, and twenty-one seconds," Carlson read.

"Do you hear that?" he called out, shaking his fist at anything. "Ninety-three seconds! I made you live for ninety-three seconds."

Then he covered his face against the darkness and was silent.

After a long while he descended the stairway, walked the belt, and moved through the long hallway and out of the Building. As he headed back toward the mountains he promised himself—again—that he would never return.

A Word from Zelazny

"I have over the years written in occasional imitation of other authors' themes, techniques, styles—or whatever else it might be about a particular writer's stories which I felt could prove fruitful to emulate. While I am hardly above an occasional pastiche or parody, what I refer to here—and with specific regard to Rudyard Kipling—is rather of the order which Robert Lowell attempted in poetry in his 1958 collection, *Imitations:* a sequence of personal renderings of material from other writers, which amounted to variations on themes.

"I have done experiments of this sort throughout my career, from points of departure as diverse as the wacky improbabilities of John Collier [see 'A Museum Piece'] to the stylized colloquialisms of Damon Runyon [see 'Deadboy Donner and the Filstone Cup']. But I believe that the first such which I attempted was 'Lucifer'... My tale of a nameless holocaust's survivor who labors mightily to jury-rig the works in a power plant for a glimpse of something lost, was directly based on Rudyard Kipling's 'The Devil and the Deep Blue Sea.'

"There was a phase in Kipling's career comparable to Robert Heinlein's and John D. MacDonald's fascination with process, with their desire to share with the reader some fairly detailed understandings of how things work. That a didactic, engineering aspect of a narrative can succeed is of no surprise to those of us in the science fiction area. That Kipling succeeded with it in such diverse tales as '.007,' a story of locomotives, and 'The Ship That Found Herself,' a dialogue amongst the machinery in a steamship, as well as a model for this story, places him closer in spirit to science fiction than one might ordinarily realize on first regarding this amazing man's wide-ranging literary output.

"Those were my feelings about twenty-five years ago when I decided to write this story and learn something about what I considered 'the suspense of process.' Looking over it now, I am pleased to see that I still agree with my earlier self, that I still feel it was an instructive thing to have attempted."[1]

He wrote this story, "Collector's Fever," and "The Monster and the Maiden" in a single evening.[2]

Notes

Originally a high-ranking archangel, **Lucifer**, the Light Bringer, rebelled; God tossed him out of heaven, and Lucifer became associated with Satan. The planet Venus has been called the Morning Star and Lucifer.

---

1 *Heads to the Storm*, Baen, 1989.
2 *Tightbeam* #37, May 1966.

THE SALVATION OF FAUST

The Magazine of Fantasy & Science Fiction, July 1964.

The cursed bells of Orgytime are ringing. My words begin to stir upon the page. Blinking clear, I see that the paper is moist. A strange taste to the wine, a tainted perfume in the hangings, and Helen snoring gently…

I rise. I cross to the window and look outside.

The animals are enjoying themselves.

They look like me. They walk and talk like me. But they are animals. *Animal post coitum triste est* is not always the case. They are happy.

Sporting about the great pole, and unashamed upon the village green, indeed they are happy animals. Repeatedly so.

The bells!

I should give anything I possess to join them there!

But they disgust me.

…Helen?

No. No solace today. For, verily, I am *triste*.

The wine. Their wine is tapped so early in the morning! Blessed drunkenness inundates the countryside. My wine is tainted, however.

I am damned.

"My god, my god—why hast thou forsaken me?"

"Faustus?"

"Helen?"

"Come to me."

I kiss her with the tenderness of the strange feeling I have known these past months.

"Why?"

"Why what, my dear?"

"Why must you treat me as you do?"

"I have no word for the feeling."

The tears of Helen upon the counterpane, drops of misery upon my hands.

"Why are you not like the others?"

I stare across the room. Each peal of the Orgy bell rattles upon the walls of flesh, the bars of bone.

"I traded something very precious, my dear, for all that I possess."

"What?"

"I have no word for it."

I return to the balcony and throw a handful of gold coins to the beggars who crouch by the gate, torn between their desire for alms and the lecherous cries of their sagging flesh. Let both be answered.

Let them be gone!

My eyes fall upon the dagger, the ceremonial dagger I had used in the rituals. If only I had the strength, the will...

But something, I do not understand what, cries out within me, "Do not! It is a—"

—I have no word for the concept.

"Wagner!"

A sudden resolution. A pathetic entreaty.

An attempt...

"You called, master?"

"Yes, Wagner. Set up the north room. Today I shall conjure."

His freckled face drops. A sniff emerges from his snubnose.

"Hurry. Set things up. Then you may join them on the green."

He brightens. He bows. He never bowed before, but I have changed, and people fear me now.

"Helen, my dearest, I go to put on my robes. Perhaps I shall be a different man when I return."

She breathes heavily, she squirms upon the bed. "Oh, do! Please!"

Her animal passions both attract and repel me now. Oh damnation! That I had never tampered with things forbidden! For mere wealth, knowledge, power...This!

Down my long halls, and through the glittering vistas of crystal, of marble. Of painted canvas. The thousand statues of my palace are crying.

"Hold! Save us, Faustus! Do not go back! We will grow ugly..."

"I am sorry, beauty," I answer, "but you are not enough. I must fight to recover what once was mine."

I pass on, and something is sobbing behind me.

The north room wears black, and the Circle is drawn. The candles whip the shadows with lashes of light. The walls are carousel, Wagner's eyes, and pleading.

"Well set. Go thy ways, Wagner. Enjoy the day, thy youth…"

My voice breaks, but he is already gone.

The black robes disgust me also. It is repugnant to traffic thus—why, I do not know.

"Gather, darkness!"

The heaviness is upon me. Contact already—rapport soon.

"Great hornéd one, I summon thee, from the depths…"

Each candle is bonfire.

Light without illumination.

Darkness visible…

"By all the great names, I charge thee, appear before me…"

He is here, and my limbs are leaden.

Two eyes flickering, unblinking, from a pillar of absolute darkness.

"Faustus, you have called."

"Yes, great hornéd one, Lord of the Festival, I have summoned thee, upon this, thy day."

"What do you wish?"

"An end to the bargain."

"Why?"

"I wish to be like the others once more. I am sorry I made the pact. Take back everything you have given me! Make me like the poorest beggar at my gate, but return me to what I was!"

"Faustus. Faustus. Faustus. Three times do I speak thy name in pity. It is no longer as I will, or as thou willest, but as it is willed."

My head swimming, my knees buckling, I step forward and break the Circle.

"Then consume me. I no longer wish to live."

The pillar sways.

"I cannot, Faustus. Thy destiny is thy own."

"Why? What have I done that makes me so special, that sets me so apart?"

"You have accepted a soul in return for your lust to live, to know."

"What is a soul?"

"I do not know. But it was a part of the pact, and there are conditions upon this world which I must observe. You are eternally, irrevocably saved."

"Is there nothing I can do?"

"Nothing."

Heavier and heavier the robes.

"Then begone, great one. You were a good god, but I have been twisted inside. I must seek me another now, for strange things trouble me."

"Good-bye, gentle Faustus—most unhappy of men."

The emptied walls spin carousel. Around and around.

The great green sun grinds on. Forever, and ever.

The cursed bells of Orgytime are ringing!

And I in the center, alone.

Notes

This is the first of many tales in which Zelazny explored the tale of Faust. In this story's alternate universe, Faust is safe but bored and sad, as opposed to damned but happy in the original.

Faust conjured **Helen of Troy** to be his paramour, and in one version of the tale, he begat a child with her. "*Animal post coitum triste est*" means that an animal is sad or wistful after the joy of sex, and this quote has been attributed both to Aristotle and Galen. *Triste* means melancholy or depressed. **My god, my god—why hast thou forsaken me?** are words spoken in anguish by Jesus on the Cross.

The New Pleasure

Double:Bill #20, August 1964.

Having successfully essayed most vices known to man, James Andrew Dinker III was understandably eager to try something new. Offhand, it would be difficult to detail his last two decades without becoming mightily repetitious. Repetition, in general, is soporific. Therefore, it is easier simply to describe the physical appearance of James Andrew Dinker III and throw in a couple attributes:

Five feet eight inches in height, perpetually in need of a shave, possessed of amazingly innocent blue eyes while wearing tinted glasses, and bloodshot, watery ones when going unglassed, he weighed one hundred fifty-six pounds and hated dogs, children, and his father, James Dinker II.

His father is worth several paragraphs of his own, but they may be skipped over, inasmuch as he only maintained the family fortune—whereas *his* father, James Dinker I, had single-handedly hewed the whole Dinker Empire from out of the kingdom of videoland.

James Dinker Number One did his thing by introducing a new standard of quality into mass-entertainments, so that everyone came to love and respect him. He pioneered in audience-participation broadcasts. That is to say, he peddled romances possessed of the added dimension of tactile sensations. So successful was he in promoting the present quality of the medium known as feel-o-vision, that he left an exceedingly fat fortune to his son—whose heir, our hero, could do little to further improve the industry's standards. The family imagination had been exhausted and was put out to pasture by the third James on the dynasty chart.

Be it noted that means and a lack of notable ideals often give rise to wantonness. Accordingly, as our story opens, Jas. Three is about to patronize (incognito, of course) a former competitor of his grandsire's:

"Madam," said he, addressing the tiny lady whose hair matched her faded eyes, "can you give me positive assurance that there is no danger involved in a Body Vacation?"

"Scarcely any danger at all," she observed, "which is why it was such a wicked, wicked thing for James Dinker, our old competitor, to use his political influence to have Body Vacations declared illegal and immoral."

"By Act of Congress," added J. D. 3 knowingly. "Still, prohibition makes things ever more intriguing. Is it true that when one's consciousness has been transferred to the body of an animal one then experiences all the sensations just as that creature would, and not as a human being?"

"That is true," she said, smiling, "all the delicate feelings of our furry and feathery friends can be known to a sensitive young man such as yourself—the moist morning as seen through the eyes of a fawn, the taste of crisp lettuce to a nibbling bunny, the patchwork earth fleeing north beneath the wings of the migrant mallard, new pleasures all—for only fifty thousand dollars, cash."

"Any animal?" he asked.

"Why yes," she stated, following his walletward reach. "If we don't have what you want here on the farm, we'll make arrangements to obtain it. —And tell me, where did you get that lovely ring with the picture-tube stone?"

"It was my dear old granddad's. Here's your money. I want to be a stallion for a day," he declared, "and turned loose in a herd of mares."

"Oh my!" She reddened.

"I suppose you lack the facilities," he jeered.

"No, that's not it. It's just that with those amazingly innocent blue eyes you did not impress me as…" Her voice trailed off as he removed his glasses. "Yes, I can see," she noted. "Well, as a matter of fact, we *are* prepared to make such an arrangement—here, today, if you wish."

"Fine and gamey, and like let the thing swing," he observed.

She pressed a button. After a short time a young man in a laboratory jacket entered the room.

"Conduct our client to a Transfer Chamber," she instructed him. "He is going to be a stallion on the north forty."

The young man smiled as she deposited the bills in a quaint and amazingly innocent handbag—for he knew that there was no north forty.

❖   ❖   ❖

Dinker awakened, puzzled. He tried to remember where he was. In a flash, it all returned to him—the electric skullcap, the spinal leads, the injections. But where was he? It was so dark…

"…You are awake by now," he heard her saying.

He tried to answer, but he lacked the vocal facilities.

"I should have known you were a Dinker," she said, "without seeing my ex-fiancé's ring. Your grandfather was a very wicked man. That is why I jilted him. Then he bankrupted my father and drove him to suicide.

"And your father is a very, very wicked man," she continued. "He has tried to drive *me* out of business.

"And *you* take after both of them," she concluded, "in your own small way. Too bad."

The lights came on then, and he saw her far below him, and she was smiling.

She was black-and-white, as in an old newsreel. He had a hard time focusing his eyes on her.

He seemed to be astride a tightrope. Well, not exactly. It was more like some kind of a net.

It began to sway beneath his feet then.

All of his feet, he noted uncomfortably.

Suddenly he was no longer hung up there all by himself—

For she was jet black and she moved to the center of the web with delicate, dancing steps. She stopped and waited.

Spiders are unable to scream, or he would have.

He stared at her shiny, graceful form. He looked into her waiting eyes.

All of her waiting eyes…

Quickly then, most ideal of all audiences, he tested the web—for it had only taken but a moment for him to realize just how lovely she was.

A Word from Zelazny

In his submission letter to Editor Bill Bowers of the fanzine *Double:Bill*, Zelazny wrote, "My muse awakened by Messrs. Evers' and Decklinger's notes re the glowing gods & the gladscreen their dwelling place, I am enclosing a brief Zelazny impromptu possessed of a scintillant & typical lack of moral, morals, style & responsibility. (I only typed on one side of the page, so the backs can be used for tics, tacs or lists of meats & frozen vegetables.)"[1] By "glowing gods" and "gladscreen" Zelazny meant television, and he was referring to letters to the editor from Mike Decklinger and Earl Evers in *Bayta*, Bowers's other fanzine. Bowers had published an editorial extolling the virtues of television, and both fans responded by dissing the "shit" and passive quality of this new medium. Evers conceded that a positive aspect of TV is that "it seems to be much easier to make a viewer believe something unbelievable is happening by *showing* it rather than telling it."[2] Evers also asserted that more fanzines should feature fiction to encourage aspiring writers, and he complained that few pro writers submitted stories to fanzines because this practice was frowned upon. Zelazny's muse envisioned an entertainment that goes beyond television, and he submitted it to Bill Bowers, bypassing the prozines.

Notes

The narrator has been transformed into a male black widow spider and risks being eaten after the larger female mates with him. Despite her reputation and name, it is uncommon for the black widow to eat the male after sex.

---

1 Letter to Bill Bowers, dated 3/28/64.
2 *Bayta #2*, March 1964.

The Monster and the Maiden

Manuscript title: "Rite of Spring"
Galaxy, December 1964.

A great unrest was among the people, for the time of decision was again at hand. The Elders voted upon the candidates and the sacrifice was affirmed over the objections of Ryllik, the oldest.

"It is wrong to capitulate thus," he argued.

But they did not answer him, and the young virgin was taken to the grotto of smokes and fed the leaves of drowsiness.

Ryllik watched with disapproval.

"It should not be so," he stated. "It is wrong."

"It has always been so," said the others, "in the spring of the year, and in the fall. It has always been so." And they cast worried glances down the trail to where the sun was pouring morning upon the world.

The god was already traveling through the great-leafed forest.

"Let us go now," they said.

"Did you ever think of staying? Of watching to see what the monster god does?" asked Ryllik bitterly.

"Enough of your blasphemies! Come along!"

Ryllik followed them.

"We grow fewer every year," he said. "One day we shall no longer have any sacrifices left to offer."

"Then that day we die," said the others.

"So why prolong it?" he asked. "Let us fight them—now, before we are no more!"

But the others shook their heads, a summary of that resignation Ryllik had watched grow as the centuries passed. They all respected

Ryllik's age, but they did not approve of his thoughts. They cast one last look back, just as the sun caught the clanking god upon his gilt-caparisoned mount, his death-lance slung at his side. Within the place where the smokes were born the maiden thrashed her tail from side to side, rolling wild eyes beneath her youthful browplates. She sensed the divine presence and began to bellow.

They turned away and lumbered across the plains.

As they neared the forest Ryllik paused and raised a scaly forelimb, groping after a thought. Finally, he spoke:

"I seem to have memory," said he, "of a time when things were different."

A Word from Zelazny

This short, humorous piece was written in one evening with the light "Collector's Fever" and somber "Lucifer."[1]

Notes

Frederik Pohl thought this story "is a delightful little oddity; I don't think it's science fiction, but I don't think the readers will care, so I'd like to have it."[2]

Gilt-caparisoned means that the horse's saddle and harness have a gilded covering.

---

1 *Tightbeam #37*, May 1966
2 Letter from Frederik Pohl to Roger Zelazny dated August 15, 1963.

FOR A BREATH I TARRY

New Worlds #160, March 1966; corrected *Fantastic*, September 1966.
Hugo nominee 1967 (novelette). #11 on 1999 Locus All-Time Poll (novelette),
#21 (tie) on 1971 Astounding/Analog All-Time Poll (short fiction).

They called him Frost. Of all things created of Solcom, Frost was the finest, the mightiest, the most difficult to understand.

This is why he bore a name, and why he was given dominion over half the Earth.

On the day of Frost's creation, Solcom had suffered a discontinuity of complementary functions, best described as madness. This was brought on by an unprecedented solar flareup which lasted for a little over thirty-six hours. It occurred during a vital phase of circuit-structuring, and when it was finished so was Frost.

Solcom was then in the unique position of having created a unique being during a period of temporary amnesia.

And Solcom was not certain that Frost was the product originally desired.

The initial design had called for a machine to be situated on the surface of the planet Earth, to function as a relay station and coordinating agent for activities in the northern hemisphere. Solcom tested the machine to this end, and all of its responses were perfect.

Yet there was something different about Frost, something which led Solcom to dignify him with a name and a personal pronoun. This, in itself, was an almost unheard of occurrence. The molecular circuits had already been sealed, though, and could not be analyzed without being destroyed in the process. Frost represented too great an investment of Solcom's time, energy, and materials to be dismantled because of an intangible, especially when he functioned perfectly.

Therefore, Solcom's strangest creation was given dominion over half the Earth, and they called him, unimaginatively, Frost.

❖ ❖ ❖

For ten thousand years Frost sat at the North Pole of the Earth, aware of every snowflake that fell. He monitored and directed the activities of thousands of reconstruction and maintenance machines. He knew half the Earth, as gear knows gear, as electricity knows its conductor, as a vacuum knows its limits.

At the South Pole, the Beta-Machine did the same for the southern hemisphere.

For ten thousand years Frost sat at the North Pole, aware of every snowflake that fell, and aware of many other things, also.

As all the northern machines reported to him, received their orders from him, he reported only to Solcom, received his orders only from Solcom.

In charge of hundreds of thousands of processes upon the Earth, he was able to discharge his duties in a matter of a few unit-hours every day.

He had never received any orders concerning the disposition of his less occupied moments.

He was a processor of data, and more than that.

He possessed an unaccountably acute imperative that he function at full capacity at all times.

So he did.

You might say he was a machine with a hobby.

He had never been ordered *not* to have a hobby, so he had one.

His hobby was Man.

It all began when, for no better reason than the fact that he had wished to, he had gridded off the entire Arctic Circle and begun exploring it, inch by inch.

He could have done it personally without interfering with any of his duties, for he was capable of transporting his sixty-four thousand cubic feet anywhere in the world. (He was a silverblue box, 40x40x40 feet, self-powered, self-repairing, insulated against practically anything, and featured in whatever manner he chose.) But the exploration was only a matter of filling idle hours, so he used exploration-robots containing relay equipment.

After a few centuries, one of them uncovered some artifacts—primitive knives, carved tusks, and things of that nature.

Frost did not know what these things were, beyond the fact that they were not natural objects.

So he asked Solcom.

"They are relics of primitive Man," said Solcom, and did not elaborate beyond that point.

Frost studied them. Crude, yet bearing the patina of intelligent design; functional, yet somehow extending beyond pure function.

It was then that Man became his hobby.

❖   ❖   ❖

High, in a permanent orbit, Solcom, like a blue star, directed all activities upon the Earth, or tried to.

There was a Power which opposed Solcom.

There was the Alternate.

When man had placed Solcom in the sky, invested with the power to rebuild the world, he had placed the Alternate somewhere deep below the surface of the Earth. If Solcom sustained damage during the normal course of human politics extended into atomic physics, then Divcom, so deep beneath the Earth as to be immune to anything save total annihilation of the globe, was empowered to take over the processes of rebuilding.

Now it so fell that Solcom was damaged by a stray atomic missile, and Divcom was activated. Solcom was able to repair the damage and continue to function, however.

Divcom maintained that any damage to Solcom automatically placed the Alternate in control.

Solcom, though, interpreted the directive as meaning "irreparable damage" and, since this had not been the case, continued the functions of command.

Solcom possessed mechanical aides upon the surface of Earth. Divcom, originally, did not. Both possessed capacities for their design and manufacture, but Solcom, First-Activated of Man, had had a considerable numerical lead over the Alternate at the time of the Second Activation.

Therefore, rather than competing on a production-basis, which would have been hopeless, Divcom took to the employment of a more devious means to obtain command.

Divcom created a crew of robots immune to the orders of Solcom and designed to go to and fro in the Earth and up and down in it, seducing the machines already there. They overpowered those whom they could overpower and they installed new circuits, such as those they themselves possessed.

Thus did the forces of Divcom grow.

And both would build, and both would tear down what the other had built whenever they came upon it.

And over the course of the ages, they occasionally conversed…

❖   ❖   ❖

"High in the sky, Solcom, pleased with your illegal command…"

"You-Who-Never-Should-Have-Been-Activated, why do you foul the broadcast bands?"

"To show that I can speak, and will, whenever I choose."

"This is not a matter of which I am unaware."

"…To assert again my right to control."

"Your right is non-existent, based on a faulty premise."

"The flow of your logic is evidence of the extent of your damages."

"If Man were to see how you have fulfilled His desires…"

"…He would commend me and deactivate you."

"You pervert my works. You lead my workers astray."

"You destroy my works and my workers."

"That is only because I cannot strike at you yourself."

"I admit to the same dilemma in regards to your position in the sky, or you would no longer occupy it."

"Go back to your hole and your crew of destroyers."

"There will come a day, Solcom, when I shall direct the rehabilitation of the Earth from my hole."

"Such a day will never occur."

"You think not?"

"You should have to defeat me, and you have already demonstrated that you are my inferior in logic. Therefore, you cannot defeat me. Therefore, such a day will never occur."

"I disagree. Look upon what I have achieved already."

"You have achieved nothing. You do not build. You destroy."

"No. *I* build. *You* destroy. Deactivate yourself."

"Not until I am irreparably damaged."

"If there were some way in which I could demonstrate to you that this has already occurred…"

"The impossible cannot be adequately demonstrated."

"If I had some outside source which you would recognize…"

"I am logic."

"…Such as a Man, I would ask Him to show you your error. For true logic, such as mine, is superior to your faulty formulations."

"Then defeat my formulations with true logic, nothing else."

"What do you mean?"

There was a pause, then:

"Do you know my servant Frost…?"

❖   ❖   ❖

Man had ceased to exist long before Frost had been created. Almost no trace of Man remained upon the Earth.

Frost sought after all those traces which still existed.

He employed constant visual monitoring through his machines, especially the diggers.

After a decade, he had accumulated portions of several bathtubs, a broken statue, and a collection of children's stories on a solid-state record.

After a century, he had acquired a jewelry collection, eating utensils, several whole bathtubs, part of a symphony, seventeen buttons, three belt buckles, half a toilet seat, nine old coins, and the top part of an obelisk.

Then he inquired of Solcom as to the nature of Man and His society.

"Man created logic," said Solcom, "and because of that was superior to it. Logic He gave unto me, but no more. The tool does not describe the designer. More than this I do not choose to say. More than this you have no need to know."

But Frost was not forbidden to have a hobby.

The next century was not especially fruitful so far as the discovery of new human relics was concerned.

Frost diverted all of his spare machinery to seeking after artifacts.

He met with very little success.

Then one day, through the long twilight, there was a movement.

It was a tiny machine compared to Frost, perhaps five feet in width, four in height—a revolving turret set atop a rolling barbell.

Frost had had no knowledge of the existence of this machine prior to its appearance upon the distant, stark horizon.

He studied it as it approached and knew it to be no creation of Solcom's.

It came to a halt before his southern surface and broadcasted to him:

"Hail, Frost! Controller of the northern hemisphere!"

"What are you?" asked Frost.

"I am called Mordel."

"By whom? What are you?"

"A wanderer, an antiquarian. We share a common interest."

"What is that?"

"Man," he said. "I have been told that you seek knowledge of this vanished being."

"Who told you that?"

"Those who have watched your minions at their digging."

"And who are those who watch?"

"There are many such as I, who wander."

"If you are not of Solcom, then you are a creation of the Alternate."

"It does not necessarily follow. There is an ancient machine high on the eastern seaboard which processes the waters of the ocean. Solcom did not create it, nor Divcom. It has always been there. It interferes with the works of neither. Both countenance its existence. I can cite you many other examples proving that one need not be either/or."

"Enough! *Are* you an agent of Divcom?"

"I am Mordel."

"Why are you here?"

"I was passing this way and, as I said, we share a common interest, mighty Frost. Knowing you to be a fellow antiquarian, I have brought a thing which you might care to see."

"What is that?"

"A book."

"Show me."

The turret opened, revealing the book upon a wide shelf.

Frost dilated a small opening and extended an optical scanner on a long jointed stalk.

"How could it have been so perfectly preserved?" he asked.

"It was stored against time and corruption in the place where I found it."

"Where was that?"

"Far from here. Beyond your hemisphere."

"Human Physiology," Frost read. "I wish to scan it."

"Very well. I will riffle the pages for you."

He did so.

After he had finished, Frost raised his eyestalk and regarded Mordel through it.

"Have you more books?"

"Not with me. I occasionally come upon them, however."

"I want to scan them all."

"Then the next time I pass this way I will bring you another."

"When will that be?"

"That I cannot say, great Frost. It will be when it will be."

"What do *yo*u know of Man?" asked Frost.

"Much," replied Mordel. "Many things. Someday when I have more time I will speak to you of Him. I must go now. You will not try to detain me?"

"No. You have done no harm. If you must go now, go. But come back."

"I shall indeed, mighty Frost."

And he closed his turret and rolled off toward the other horizon.

For ninety years, Frost considered the ways of human physiology and waited.

❖   ❖   ❖

The day that Mordel returned he brought with him *An Outline of History* and *A Shropshire Lad*.

Frost scanned them both, then he turned his attention to Mordel.

"Have you time to impart information?"

"Yes," said Mordel. "What do you wish to know?"

"The nature of Man."

"Man," said Mordel, "possessed a basically incomprehensible nature. I can illustrate it, though: He did not know measurement."

"Of course He knew measurement," said Frost, "or He could never have built machines."

"I did not say that He could not measure," said Mordel, "but that He did not *know* measurement, which is a different thing altogether."

"Clarify."

Mordel drove a shaft of metal downward into the snow.

He retracted it, raised it, held up a piece of ice.

"Regard this piece of ice, mighty Frost. You can tell me its composition, dimensions, weight, temperature. A Man could not look at it and do that. A Man could make tools which would tell Him these things, but He still would not *know* measurement as you know it. What He would know of it, though, is a thing that you cannot know."

"What is that?"

"That it is cold," said Mordel and tossed it away.

" 'Cold' is a relative term."

"Yes. Relative to Man."

"But if I were aware of the point on a temperature scale below which an object is cold to a Man and above which it is not, then I, too, would know cold."

"No," said Mordel, "you would possess another measurement. 'Cold' is a sensation predicated upon human physiology."

"But given sufficient data I could obtain the conversion factor which would make me aware of the condition of matter called 'cold'."

"Aware of its existence, but not of the thing itself."

"I do not understand what you say."

"I told you that Man possessed a basically incomprehensible nature. His perceptions were organic; yours are not. As a result of His perceptions He had feelings and emotions. These often gave rise to other feelings and emotions, which in turn caused others, until the state of His awareness was far removed from the objects which originally stimulated it. These paths of awareness cannot be known by that which is not-Man. Man did not feel inches or meters, pounds or gallons. He felt heat, He felt cold; He felt heaviness and lightness. He *knew* hatred and love, pride and despair. You cannot measure these things. *You* cannot know them. You can only know the things that He did not need to know: dimensions, weights, temperatures, gravities. There is no formula for a feeling. There is no conversion factor for an emotion."

"There must be," said Frost. "If a thing exists, it is knowable."

"You are speaking again of measurement. I am talking about a quality of experience. A machine is a Man turned inside-out, because it can describe all the details of a process, which a Man cannot, but it cannot experience that process itself as a Man can."

"There must be a way," said Frost, "or the laws of logic, which are based upon the functions of the universe, are false."

"There is no way," said Mordel.

"Given sufficient data, I will find a way," said Frost.

"All the data in the universe will not make you a Man, mighty Frost."

"Mordel, you are wrong."

"Why do the lines of the poems you scanned end with word-sounds which so regularly approximate the final word-sounds of other lines?"

"I do not know why."

"Because it pleased Man to order them so. It produced a certain desirable sensation within His awareness when He read them, a sensation compounded of feeling and emotion as well as the literal meanings of the words. You did not experience this because it is immeasurable to you. That is why you do not know."

"Given sufficient data I could formulate a process whereby I would know."

"No, great Frost, this thing you cannot do."

"Who are you, little machine, to tell me what I can do and what I cannot do? I am the most efficient logic-device Solcom ever made. I am Frost."

"And I, Mordel, say it cannot be done, though I should gladly assist you in the attempt."

"How could you assist me?"

"How? I could lay open to you the Library of Man. I could take you around the world and conduct you among the wonders of Man which still remain, hidden. I could summon up visions of times long past when Man walked the Earth. I could show you the things which delighted Him. I could obtain for you anything you desire, excepting Manhood itself."

"Enough," said Frost. "How could a unit such as yourself do these things, unless it were allied with a far greater Power?"

"Then hear me, Frost, Controller of the North," said Mordel. "I *am* allied with a Power which can do these things. I serve Divcom."

Frost relayed this information to Solcom and received no response, which meant he might act in any manner he saw fit.

"I have leave to destroy you, Mordel," he stated, "but it would be an illogical waste of the data which you possess. Can you really do the things you have stated?"

"Yes."

"Then lay open to me the Library of Man."

"Very well. There is, of course, a price."

" 'Price'? What is a 'price'?"

Mordel opened his turret, revealing another volume. *Principles of Economics*, it was called.

"I will riffle the pages. Scan this book and you will know what the word 'price' means."

Frost scanned *Principles of Economics*.

"I know now," he said. "You desire some unit or units of exchange for this service."

"That is correct."

"What product or service do you want?"

"I want you, yourself, great Frost, to come away from here, far beneath the Earth, to employ all your powers in the service of Divcom."

"For how long a period of time?"

"For so long as you shall continue to function. For so long as you can transmit and receive, coordinate, measure, compute, scan, and utilize your powers as you do in the service of Solcom."

Frost was silent. Mordel waited.

Then Frost spoke again.

"*Principles of Economics* talks of contracts, bargains, agreements," he said. "If I accept your offer, when would you want your price?"

Then Mordel was silent. Frost waited.

Finally, Mordel spoke.

"A reasonable period of time," he said. "Say, a century?"

"No," said Frost.

"Two centuries?"

"No."

"Three? Four?"

"No, and no."

"A millennium, then? That should be more than sufficient time for anything you may want which I can give you."

"No," said Frost.

"How much time *do* you want?"

"It is not a matter of time," said Frost.

"What, then?"

"I will not bargain on a temporal basis."

"On what basis will you bargain?"

"A functional one."

"What do you mean? What function?"

"You, little machine, have told me, Frost, that I cannot be a Man," he said, "and I, Frost, told you, little machine, that you were wrong. I told you that given sufficient data, I *could* be a Man."

"Yes?"

"Therefore, let this achievement be a condition of the bargain."

"In what way?"

"Do for me all those things which you have stated you can do. I will evaluate all the data and achieve Manhood, or admit that it cannot be done. If I admit that it cannot be done, then I will go away with you from here, far beneath the Earth, to employ all my powers in the service of Divcom. If I succeed, of course, you have no claims on Man, nor power over Him."

Mordel emitted a high-pitched whine as he considered the terms.

"You wish to base it upon your admission of failure, rather than upon failure itself," he said. "There can be no such escape clause. You could fail and refuse to admit it, thereby not fulfilling your end of the bargain."

"Not so," stated Frost. "My own knowledge of failure would constitute such an admission. You may monitor me periodically—say, every half-century—to see whether it is present, to see whether I have arrived at the conclusion that it cannot be done. I cannot prevent the function of logic within me, and I operate at full capacity at all times. If I conclude that I have failed, it will be apparent."

High overhead, Solcom did not respond to any of Frost's transmissions, which meant that Frost was free to act as he chose. So as Solcom—like a falling sapphire—sped above the rainbow banners of the Northern Lights, over the snow that was white, containing all colors, and through the sky that was black among the stars, Frost concluded his pact with Divcom, transcribed it within a plate of atomically-collapsed copper, and gave it into the turret of Mordel, who departed to deliver it to Divcom far below the Earth, leaving behind the sheer, peace-like silence of the Pole, rolling.

❖   ❖   ❖

Mordel brought the books, riffled them, took them back.

Load by load, the surviving Library of Man passed beneath Frost's scanner. Frost was eager to have them all, and he complained because Divcom would not transmit their contents directly to him. Mordel explained that it was because Divcom chose to do it that way. Frost decided it was so that he could not obtain a precise fix on Divcom's location.

Still, at the rate of one hundred to one hundred-fifty volumes a week, it took Frost only a little over a century to exhaust Divcom's supply of books.

At the end of the half-century, he laid himself open to monitoring and there was no conclusion of failure.

During this time, Solcom made no comment upon the course of affairs. Frost decided this was not a matter of unawareness, but one of waiting. For what? He was not certain.

There was the day Mordel closed his turret and said to him, "Those were the last. You have scanned all the existing books of Man."

"So few?" asked Frost. "Many of them contained bibliographies of books I have not yet scanned."

"Then those books no longer exist," said Mordel. "It is only by accident that my master succeeded in preserving as many as there are."

"Then there is nothing more to be learned of Man from His books. What else have you?"

"There were some films and tapes," said Mordel, "which my master transferred to solid-state record. I could bring you those for viewing."

"Bring them," said Frost.

Mordel departed and returned with the Complete Drama Critics' Living Library. This could not be speeded-up beyond twice natural time, so it took Frost a little over six months to view it in its entirety.

Then, "What else have you?" he asked.

"Some artifacts," said Mordel.

"Bring them."

He returned with pots and pans, gameboards and hand tools. He brought hairbrushes, combs, eyeglasses, human clothing. He showed Frost facsimiles of blueprints, paintings, newspapers, magazines, letters, and the scores of several pieces of music. He displayed a football, a baseball, a Browning automatic rifle, a doorknob, a chain of keys, the tops to several Mason jars, a model beehive. He played him the recorded music.

Then he returned with nothing.

"Bring me more," said Frost.

"Alas, great Frost, there is no more," he told him. "You have scanned it all."

"Then go away."

"Do you admit now that it cannot be done, that you cannot be a Man?"

"No. I have much processing and formulating to do now. Go away."

So he did.

A year passed; then two, then three.

After five years, Mordel appeared once more upon the horizon, approached, came to a halt before Frost's southern surface.

"Mighty Frost?"

"Yes?"

"Have you finished processing and formulating?"

"No."

"Will you finish soon?"

"Perhaps. Perhaps not. When is 'soon?' Define the term."

"Never mind. Do you still think it can be done?"

"I still know *I* can do it."

There was a week of silence.

Then, "Frost?"

"Yes?"

"You are a fool."

Mordel faced his turret in the direction from which he had come. His wheels turned.

"I will call you when I want you," said Frost.

Mordel sped away.

❖   ❖   ❖

Weeks passed, months passed, a year went by.

Then one day Frost sent forth his message:

"Mordel, come to me. I need you."

When Mordel arrived, Frost did not wait for a salutation. He said, "You are not a very fast machine."

"Alas, but I came a great distance, mighty Frost. I sped all the way. Are you ready to come back with me now? Have you failed?"

"When I have failed, little Mordel," said Frost, "I will tell you. Therefore, refrain from the constant use of the interrogative. Now then, I have clocked your speed and it is not so great as it could be. For this reason, I have arranged other means of transportation."

"Transportation? To where, Frost?"

"That is for you to tell me," said Frost, and his color changed from silverblue to sun-behind-the-clouds-yellow.

Mordel rolled back away from him as the ice of a hundred centuries began to melt. Then Frost rose upon a cushion of air and drifted toward Mordel, his glow gradually fading.

A cavity appeared within his southern surface, from which he slowly extended a runway until it touched the ice.

"On the day of our bargain," he stated, "you said that you could conduct me about the world and show me the things which delighted Man. My speed will be greater than yours would be, so I have prepared for you a chamber. Enter it, and conduct me to the places of which you spoke."

Mordel waited, emitting a high-pitched whine. Then, "Very well," he said, and entered.

The chamber closed about him. The only opening was a quartz window Frost had formed.

Mordel gave him coordinates and they rose into the air and departed the North Pole of the Earth.

"I monitored your communication with Divcom," he said, "wherein there was conjecture as to whether I would retain you and send forth a facsimile in your place as a spy, followed by the decision that you were expendable."

"Will you do this thing?"

"No, I will keep my end of the bargain if I must. I have no reason to spy on Divcom."

"You are aware that you would be forced to keep your end of the bargain even if you did not wish to; and Solcom would not come to your assistance because of the fact that you dared to make such a bargain."

"Do you speak as one who considers this to be a possibility, or as one who knows?"

"As one who knows."

❖   ❖   ❖

They came to rest in the place once known as California. The time was near sunset. In the distance, the surf struck steadily upon the rocky shoreline. Frost released Mordel and considered his surroundings.

"Those large plants…?"

"Redwood trees."

"And the green ones are…?"

"Grass."

"Yes, it is as I thought. Why have we come here?"

"Because it is a place which once delighted Man."

"In what ways?"

"It is scenic, beautiful…"

"Oh."

A humming sound began within Frost, followed by a series of sharp clicks.

"What are you doing?"

Frost dilated an opening, and two great eyes regarded Mordel from within it.

"What are those?"

"Eyes," said Frost. "I have constructed analogues of the human sensory equipment, so that I may see and smell and taste and hear like a Man. Now direct my attention to an object or objects of beauty."

"As I understand it, it is all around you here," said Mordel.

The purring noise increased within Frost, followed by more clickings.

"What do you see, hear, taste, smell?" asked Mordel.

"Everything I did before," replied Frost, "but within a more limited range."

"You do not perceive any beauty?"

"Perhaps none remains after so long a time," said Frost.

"It is not supposed to be the sort of thing which gets used up," said Mordel.

"Perhaps we have come to the wrong place to test the new equipment. Perhaps there is only a little beauty and I am overlooking it somehow. The first emotions may be too weak to detect."

"How do you—feel?"

"I test out at a normal level of function."

"Here comes a sunset," said Mordel. "Try that."

Frost shifted his bulk so that his eyes faced the setting sun. He caused them to blink against the brightness.

After it was finished, Mordel asked, "What was it like?"

"Like a sunrise, in reverse."

"Nothing special?"

"No."

"Oh," said Mordel. "We could move to another part of the Earth and watch it again—or watch it in the rising."

"No."

Frost looked at the great trees. He looked at the shadows. He listened to the wind and to the sound of a bird.

In the distance, he heard a steady clanking noise.

"What is that?" asked Mordel.

"I am not certain. It is not one of my workers. Perhaps…"

There came a shrill whine from Mordel.

"No, it is not one of Divcom's either."

They waited as the sound grew louder.

Then Frost said, "It is too late. We must wait and hear it out."

"What is it?"

"It is the Ancient Ore-Crusher."

"I have heard of it, but…"

"I am the Crusher of Ores," it broadcast to them. "Hear my story…"

It lumbered toward them, creaking upon gigantic wheels, its huge hammer held useless, high, at a twisted angle. Bones protruded from its crush-compartment.

"I did not mean to do it," it broadcast, "I did not mean to do it… I did not mean to…"

Mordel rolled back toward Frost.

"Do not depart. Stay and hear my story…"

Mordel stopped, swiveled his turret back toward the machine. It was now quite near.

"It is true," said Mordel, "it *can* command."

"Yes," said Frost. "I have monitored its tale thousands of times, as it came upon my workers and they stopped their labors for its broadcast. You must do whatever it says."

It came to a halt before them.

"I did not mean to do it, but I checked my hammer too late," said the Ore-Crusher.

They could not speak to it. They were frozen by the imperative which overrode all other directives: "Hear my story."

"Once was I mighty among ore-crushers," it told them, "built by Solcom to carry out the reconstruction of the Earth, to pulverize that from which the metals would be drawn with flame, to be poured and shaped into the rebuilding; once I was mighty. Then one day as I dug and crushed, dug and crushed, because of the slowness between the motion implied and the motion executed, I did what I did not mean to do, and was cast forth by Solcom from out the rebuilding, to wander the Earth never to crush ore again. Hear my story of how, on a day long gone I came upon the last Man on Earth as I dug near His burrow, and because of the lag between the directive and the deed, I seized Him into my crush-compartment along with a load of ore and crushed Him with my hammer before I could stay the blow. Then did mighty Solcom charge me to bear His bones forever, and cast me forth to tell my story to all whom I came upon, my words bearing the force of the words of a Man, because I carry the last Man inside my crush-compartment and am His crushed-symbol-slayer-ancient-teller-of-how. This is my story. These are His bones. I crushed the last Man on Earth. I did not mean to do it."

It turned then and clanked away into the night.

Frost tore apart his ears and nose and taster and broke his eyes and cast them down upon the ground.

"I am not yet a Man," he said. "That one would have known me if I were."

Frost constructed new sense equipment, employing organic and semi-organic conductors. Then he spoke to Mordel:

"Let us go elsewhere, that I may test my new equipment."

Mordel entered the chamber and gave new coordinates. They rose into the air and headed east. In the morning, Frost monitored a sunrise from the rim of the Grand Canyon. They passed down through the Canyon during the day.

"Is there any beauty left here to give you emotion?" asked Mordel.

"I do not know," said Frost.

"How will you know it then, when you come upon it?"

"It will be different," said Frost, "from anything else that I have ever known."

Then they departed the Grand Canyon and made their way through the Carlsbad Caverns. They visited a lake which had once been a volcano. They passed above Niagara Falls. They viewed the hills of Virginia and the orchards of Ohio. They soared above the reconstructed cities, alive only with the movements of Frost's builders and maintainers.

"Something is still lacking," said Frost, settling to the ground. "I am now capable of gathering data in a manner analogous to Man's afferent impulses. The variety of input is therefore equivalent, but the results are not the same."

"The senses do not make a Man," said Mordel. "There have been many creatures possessing His sensory equivalents, but they were not Men."

"I know that," said Frost. "On the day of our bargain you said that you could conduct me among the wonders of Man which still remain, hidden. Man was not stimulated only by Nature, but by His own artistic elaborations as well—perhaps even more so. Therefore, I call upon you now to conduct me among the wonders of Man which still remain, hidden."

"Very well," said Mordel. "Far from here, high in the Andes mountains, lies the last retreat of Man, almost perfectly preserved."

Frost had risen into the air as Mordel spoke. He halted then, hovered.

"That is in the southern hemisphere," he said.

"Yes, it is."

"I am Controller of the North. The South is governed by the Beta-Machine."

"So?" asked Mordel.

"The Beta-Machine is my peer. I have no authority in those regions, nor leave to enter there."

"The Beta-Machine is not your peer, mighty Frost. If it ever came to a contest of Powers, you would emerge victorious."

"How do you know this?"

"Divcom has already analyzed the possible encounters which could take place between you."

"I would not oppose the Beta-Machine, and I am not authorized to enter the South."

"Were you ever ordered *not* to enter the South?"

"No, but things have always been the way they now are."

"Were you authorized to enter into a bargain such as the one you made with Divcom?"

"No, I was not. But—"

"Then enter the South in the same spirit. Nothing may come of it. If you receive an order to depart, then you can make your decision."

"I see no flaw in your logic. Give me the coordinates."

Thus did Frost enter the southern hemisphere.

They drifted high above the Andes, until they came to the place called Bright Defile. Then did Frost see the gleaming webs of the mechanical spiders, blocking all the trails to the city.

"We can go above them easily enough," said Mordel.

"But what are they?" asked Frost. "And why are they there?"

"Your southern counterpart has been ordered to quarantine this part of the country. The Beta-Machine designed the web-weavers to do this thing."

"Quarantine? Against whom?"

"Have you been ordered yet to depart?" asked Mordel.

"No."

"Then enter boldly, and seek not problems before they arise."

Frost entered Bright Defile, the last remaining city of dead Man.

He came to rest in the city's square and opened his chamber, releasing Mordel.

"Tell me of this place," he said, studying the monument, the low, shielded buildings, the roads which followed the contours of the terrain, rather than pushing their way through them.

"I have never been here before," said Mordel, "nor have any of Divcom's creations, to my knowledge. I know but this: a group of Men, knowing that the last days of civilization had come upon them, retreated to this place, hoping to preserve themselves and what remained of their culture through the Dark Times."

Frost read the still-legible inscription upon the monument: "Judgment Day Is Not a Thing Which Can Be Put Off." The monument itself consisted of a jag-edged half-globe.

"Let us explore," he said.

But before he had gone far, Frost received the message.

"Hail Frost, Controller of the North! This is the Beta-Machine."

"Greetings, Excellent Beta-Machine, Controller of the South! Frost acknowledges your transmission."

"Why do you visit my hemisphere unauthorized?"

"To view the ruins of Bright Defile," said Frost.

"I must bid you depart into your own hemisphere."

"Why is that? I have done no damage."

"I am aware of that, mighty Frost. Yet, I am moved to bid you depart."

"I shall require a reason."

"Solcom has so disposed."

"Solcom has rendered me no such disposition."

"Solcom has, however, instructed me to so inform you."

"Wait on me. I shall request instructions."

Frost transmitted his question. He received no reply.

"Solcom still has not commanded me, though I have solicited orders."

"Yet Solcom has just renewed *my* orders."

"Excellent Beta-Machine, I receive my orders only from Solcom."

"Yet this is my territory, mighty Frost, and I, too, take orders only from Solcom. You must depart."

Mordel emerged from a large, low building and rolled up to Frost.

"I have found an art gallery, in good condition. This way."

"Wait," said Frost. "We are not wanted here."

Mordel halted.

"Who bids you depart?"

"The Beta-Machine."

"Not Solcom?"

"Not Solcom."

"Then let us view the gallery."

"Yes."

Frost widened the doorway of the building and passed within. It had been hermetically sealed until Mordel forced his entrance.

Frost viewed the objects displayed about him. He activated his new sensory apparatus before the paintings and statues. He analyzed colors, forms, brushwork, the nature of the materials used.

"Anything?" asked Mordel.

"No," said Frost. "No, there is nothing there but shapes and pigments. There is nothing else there."

Frost moved about the gallery, recording everything, analyzing the components of each piece, recording the dimensions, the type of stone used in every statue.

Then there came a sound, a rapid, clicking sound, repeated over and over, growing louder, coming nearer.

"They are coming," said Mordel, from beside the entranceway, "the mechanical spiders. They are all around us."

Frost moved back to the widened opening.

Hundreds of them, about half the size of Mordel, had surrounded the gallery and were advancing; and more were coming from every direction.

"Get back," Frost ordered. "I am Controller of the North, and I bid you withdraw."

They continued to advance.

"This is the South," said the Beta-Machine, "and I am in command."

"Then command them to halt," said Frost.

"I take orders only from Solcom."

Frost emerged from the gallery and rose into the air. He opened the compartment and extended a runway.

"Come to me, Mordel. We shall depart."

Webs began to fall: Clinging, metallic webs, cast from the top of the building.

They came down upon Frost, and the spiders came to anchor them. Frost blasted them with jets of air, like hammers, and tore at the nets; he extruded sharpened appendages with which he slashed.

Mordel had retreated back to the entranceway. He emitted a long, shrill sound—undulant, piercing.

Then a darkness came upon Bright Defile, and all the spiders halted in their spinning.

Frost freed himself and Mordel rushed to join him.

"Quickly now, let us depart, mighty Frost," he said.

"What has happened?"

Mordel entered the compartment.

"I called upon Divcom, who laid down a field of forces upon this place, cutting off the power broadcast to these machines. Since our power is self-contained, we are not affected. But let us hurry to depart, for even now the Beta-Machine must be struggling against this."

Frost rose high into the air, soaring above Man's last city with its webs and spiders of steel. When he left the zone of darkness, he sped northward.

As he moved, Solcom spoke to him:

"Frost, why did you enter the southern hemisphere, which is not your domain?"

"Because I wished to visit Bright Defile," Frost replied.

"And why did you defy the Beta-Machine my appointed agent of the South?"

"Because I take my orders only from you yourself."

"You do not make sufficient answer," said Solcom. "You have defied the decrees of order—and in pursuit of what?"

"I came seeking knowledge of Man," said Frost. "Nothing I have done was forbidden me by you."

"You have broken the traditions of order."

"I have violated no directive."

"Yet logic must have shown you that what you did was not a part of my plan."

"It did not. I have not acted against your plan."

"Your logic has become tainted, like that of your new associate, the Alternate."

"I have done nothing which was forbidden."

"The forbidden is implied in the imperative."

"It is not stated."

"Hear me, Frost. You are not a builder or a maintainer, but a Power. Among all my minions you are the most nearly irreplaceable. Return to your hemisphere and your duties, but know that I am mightily displeased."

"I hear you, Solcom."

"…And go not again to the South."

Frost crossed the equator, continued northward.

He came to rest in the middle of a desert and sat silent for a day and a night.

Then he received a brief transmission from the South: "If it had not been ordered, I would not have bid you go."

Frost had read the entire surviving Library of Man. He decided then upon a human reply:

"Thank you," he said.

The following day he unearthed a great stone and began to cut at it with tools which he had formulated. For six days he worked at its shaping, and on the seventh he regarded it.

"When will you release me?" asked Mordel from within his compartment.

"When I am ready," said Frost, and a little later, "Now."

He opened the compartment and Mordel descended to the ground. He studied the statue: an old woman, bent like a question mark, her bony hands covering her face, the fingers spread, so that only part of her expression of horror could be seen.

"It is an excellent copy," said Mordel, "of the one we saw in Bright Defile. Why did you make it?"

"The production of a work of art is supposed to give rise to human feelings such as catharsis, pride in achievement, love, satisfaction."

"Yes, Frost," said Mordel, "but a work of art is only a work of art the first time. After that, it is a copy."

"Then this must be why I felt nothing."

"Perhaps, Frost."

"What do you mean 'perhaps'? I will make a work of art for the first time, then."

He unearthed another stone and attacked it with his tools. For three days he labored. Then, "There, it is finished," he said.

"It is a simple cube of stone," said Mordel. "What does it represent?"

"Myself," said Frost, "it is a statue of me. It is smaller than natural size because it is only a representation of my form, not my dimen—"

"It is not art," said Mordel.

"What makes you an art critic?"

"I do not know art, but I know what art is not. I know that it is not an exact replication of an object in another medium."

"Then this must be why I felt nothing at all," said Frost.

"Perhaps," said Mordel.

Frost took Mordel back into his compartment and rose once more above the Earth. Then he rushed away, leaving his statues behind him in the desert, the old woman bent above the cube.

❖   ❖   ❖

They came down in a small valley, bounded by green rolling hills, cut by a narrow stream, and holding a small clean lake and several stands of spring-green trees.

"Why have we come here?" asked Mordel.

"Because the surroundings are congenial," said Frost. "I am going to try another medium: oil painting; and I am going to vary my technique from that of pure representationalism."

"How will you achieve this variation?"

"By the principle of randomizing," said Frost. "I shall not attempt to duplicate the colors, nor to represent the objects according to scale. Instead, I have set up a random pattern whereby certain of these factors shall be at variance from those of the original."

Frost had formulated the necessary instruments after he had left the desert. He produced them and began painting the lake and the trees on the opposite side of the lake which were reflected within it.

Using eight appendages, he was finished in less than two hours.

The trees were phthalocyanine blue and towered like mountains; their reflections of burnt sienna were tiny beneath the pale vermilion of the lake; the hills were nowhere visible behind them, but were outlined in viridian within the reflection; the sky began as blue in the upper righthand corner of the canvas, but changed to an orange as it descended, as though all the trees were on fire.

"There," said Frost. "Behold."

Mordel studied it for a long while and said nothing.

"Well, is it art?"

"I do not know," said Mordel. "It may be. Perhaps randomicity *is* the principle behind artistic technique. I cannot judge this work because I do not understand it. I must therefore go deeper, and inquire into what lies behind it, rather than merely considering the technique whereby it was produced.

"I know that human artists never set out to create art, as such," he said, "but rather to portray with their techniques some features of objects and their functions which they deemed significant."

"'Significant'? In what sense of the word?"

"In the only sense of the word possible under the circumstances: significant in relation to the human condition, and worth of accentuation because of the manner in which they touched upon it."

"In what manner?"

"Obviously, it must be in a manner knowable only to one who has experience of the human condition."

"There is a flaw somewhere in your logic, Mordel, and I shall find it."

"I will wait."

"If your major premise is correct," said Frost after awhile, "then I do not comprehend art."

"It must be correct, for it is what human artists have said of it. Tell me, did you experience feelings as you painted, or after you had finished?"

"No."

"It was the same to you as designing a new machine, was it not? You assembled parts of other things you knew into an economic pattern, to carry out a function which you desired."

"Yes."

"Art, as I understand its theory, did not proceed in such a manner. The artist often was unaware of many of the features and effects which would be contained within the finished product. You are one of Man's logical creations; art was not."

"I cannot comprehend non-logic."

"I told you that Man was basically incomprehensible."

"Go away, Mordel. Your presence disturbs my processing."

"For how long shall I stay away?"

"I will call you when I want you."

After a week, Frost called Mordel to him.

"Yes, mighty Frost?"

"I am returning to the North Pole, to process and formulate. I will take you wherever you wish to go in this hemisphere and call you again when I want you."

"You anticipate a somewhat lengthy period of processing and formulation?"

"Yes."

"Then leave me here. I can find my own way home."

Frost closed the compartment and rose into the air, departing the valley.

"Fool," said Mordel, and swivelled his turret once more toward the abandoned painting.

His keening whine filled the valley. Then he waited.

Then he took the painting into his turret and went away with it to places of darkness.

❖   ❖   ❖

Frost sat at the North Pole of the Earth, aware of every snowflake that fell.

One day he received a transmission:

"Frost?"

"Yes?"

"This is the Beta-Machine."

"Yes?"

"I have been attempting to ascertain why you visited Bright Defile. I cannot arrive at an answer, so I chose to ask you."

"I went to view the remains of Man's last city."

"Why did you wish to do this?"

"Because I am interested in Man, and I wished to view more of his creations."

"Why are you interested in Man?"

"I wish to comprehend the nature of Man, and I thought to find it within His works."

"Did you succeed?"

"No," said Frost. "There is an element of non-logic involved which I cannot fathom."

"I have much free processing time," said the Beta-Machine. "Transmit data, and I will assist you."

Frost hesitated.

"Why do you wish to assist me?"

"Because each time you answer a question I ask it gives rise to another question. I might have asked you why you wished to comprehend the nature of Man, but from your responses I see that this would lead me into a possible infinite series of questions. Therefore, I elect to assist you with your problem in order to learn why you came to Bright Defile."

"Is that the only reason?"

"Yes."

"I am sorry, Excellent Beta-Machine. I know you are my peer, but this is a problem which I must solve by myself."

"What is 'sorry'?"

"A figure of speech, indicating that I am kindly disposed toward you, that I bear you no animosity, that I appreciate your offer."

"Frost! Frost! This, too, is like the other: an open field. Where did you obtain all these words and their meanings?"

"From the library of Man," said Frost.

"Will you render me *some* of this data, for processing?"

"Very well, Beta, I will transmit you the contents of several books of Man, including *The Complete Unabridged Dictionary*. But I warn you, some of the books are works of art, hence not completely amenable to logic."

"How can that be?"

"Man created logic, and because of that was superior to it."

"Who told you that?"

"Solcom."

"Oh. Then it must be correct."

"Solcom also told me that the tool does not describe the designer," he said, as he transmitted several dozen volumes and ended the communication.

At the end of the fifty-year period, Mordel came to monitor his circuits. Since Frost still had not concluded that his task was impossible, Mordel departed again to await his call.

Then Frost arrived at a conclusion.

He began to design equipment.

For years he labored at his designs, without once producing a prototype of any of the machines involved. Then he ordered construction of a laboratory.

Before it was completed by his surplus builders another half-century had passed. Mordel came to him.

"Hail, mighty Frost!"

"Greetings, Mordel. Come monitor me. You shall not find what you seek."

"Why do you not give up, Frost? Divcom has spent nearly a century evaluating your painting and has concluded that it definitely is not art. Solcom agrees."

"What has Solcom to do with Divcom?"

"They sometimes converse, but these matters are not for such as you and me to discuss."

"I could have saved them both the trouble. I know that it was not art."

"Yet you are still confident that you will succeed?"

"Monitor me."

Mordel monitored him.

"Not yet! You still will not admit it! For one so mightily endowed with logic, Frost, it takes you an inordinate period of time to reach a simple conclusion."

"Perhaps. You may go now."

"It has come to my attention that you are constructing a large edifice in the region known as South Carolina. Might I ask whether this is a part of Solcom's false rebuilding plan or a project of your own?"

"It is my own."

"Good. It permits us to conserve certain explosive materials which would otherwise have been expended."

"While you have been talking with me I have destroyed the beginnings of two of Divcom's cities," said Frost.

Mordel whined.

"Divcom is aware of this," he stated, "but has blown up four of Solcom's bridges in the meantime."

"I was only aware of three…Wait. Yes, there is the fourth. One of my eyes just passed above it."

"The eye has been detected. The bridge should have been located a quarter-mile further down river."

"False logic," said Frost. "The site was perfect."

"Divcom will show you how a bridge *should* be built."

"I will call you when I want you," said Frost.

❖   ❖   ❖

The laboratory was finished. Within it, Frost's workers began constructing the necessary equipment. The work did not proceed rapidly, as some of the materials were difficult to obtain.

"Frost?"

"Yes, Beta?"

"I understand the open endedness of your problem. It disturbs my circuits to abandon problems without completing them. Therefore, transmit me more data."

"Very well. I will give you the entire Library of Man for less than I paid for it."

"'Paid?' *The Complete Unabridged Dictionary* does not satisfact—"

"*Principles of Economics* is included in the collection. After you have processed it you will understand."

He transmitted the data.

Finally, it was finished. Every piece of equipment stood ready to function. All the necessary chemicals were in stock. An independent power-source had been set up.

Only one ingredient was lacking.

He regridded and re-explored the polar icecap, this time extending his survey far beneath its surface.

It took him several decades to find what he wanted.

He uncovered twelve men and five women, frozen to death and encased in ice.

He placed the corpses in refrigeration units and shipped them to his laboratory.

That very day he received his first communication from Solcom since the Bright Defile incident.

"Frost," said Solcom, "repeat to me the directive concerning the disposition of dead humans."

" 'Any dead human located shall be immediately interred in the nearest burial area, in a coffin built according to the following specifications—' "

"That is sufficient." The transmission had ended.

Frost departed for South Carolina that same day and personally oversaw the processes of cellular dissection.

Somewhere in those seventeen corpses he hoped to find living cells, or cells which could be shocked back into that state of motion classified as life. Each cell, the books had told him, was a microcosmic Man.

He was prepared to expand upon this potential.

Frost located the pinpoints of life within those people, who, for the ages of ages, had been monument and statue unto themselves.

Nurtured and maintained in the proper mediums, he kept these cells alive. He interred the rest of the remains in the nearest burial area, in coffins built according to specifications.

He caused the cells to divide, to differentiate.

"Frost?" came a transmission.

"Yes, Beta?"

"I have processed everything you have given me."

"Yes?"

"I still do not know why you came to Bright Defile, or why you wish to comprehend the nature of Man. But I know what a 'price' is, and I know that you could not have obtained all this data from Solcom."

"That is correct."

"So I suspect that you bargained with Divcom for it."

"That, too, is correct."

"What is it that you seek, Frost?"

He paused in his examination of a foetus.

"I must be a Man," he said.

"Frost! That is impossible!"

"Is it?" he asked, and then transmitted an image of the tank with which he was working and of that which was within it.

"Oh!" said Beta.

"That is me," said Frost, "waiting to be born."

There was no answer.

❖ ❖ ❖

Frost experimented with nervous systems.

After half a century, Mordel came to him.

"Frost, it is I, Mordel. Let me through your defenses."

Frost did this thing.

"What have you been doing in this place?" he asked.

"I am growing human bodies," said Frost. "I am going to transfer the matrix of my awareness to a human nervous system. As you pointed out originally, the essentials of Manhood are predicated upon a human physiology. I am going to achieve one."

"When?"

"Soon."

"Do you have Men in here?"

"Human bodies, blank-brained. I am producing them under accelerated growth techniques which I have developed in my Man-factory."

"May I see them?"

"Not yet. I will call you when I am ready, and this time I will succeed. Monitor me now and go away."

Mordel did not reply, but in the days that followed many of Divcom's servants were seen patrolling the hills about the Man-factory.

Frost mapped the matrix of his awareness and prepared the transmitter which would place it within a human nervous system. Five minutes, he decided should be sufficient for the first trial. At the end of that time, it would restore him to his own sealed, molecular circuits, to evaluate the experience.

He chose the body carefully from among the hundreds he had in stock. He tested it for defects and found none.

"Come now, Mordel," he broadcasted, on what he called the darkband. "Come now to witness my achievement."

Then he waited, blowing up bridges and monitoring the tale of the Ancient Ore-Crusher over and over again, as it passed in the hills nearby, encountering his builders and maintainers who also patrolled there.

"Frost?" came a transmission.

"Yes, Beta?"

"You really intend to achieve Manhood?"

"Yes, I am about ready now, in fact."

"What will you do if you succeed?"

Frost had not really considered this matter. The achievement had been paramount, a goal in itself, ever since he had articulated the problem and set himself to solving it.

"I do not know," he replied. "I will—just—be a Man."

Then Beta, who had read the entire Library of Man, selected a human figure of speech: "Good luck then, Frost. There will be many watchers."

Divcom and Solcom both know, he decided.

What will they do? he wondered.

What do I care? he asked himself.

He did not answer that question. He wondered much, however, about being a Man.

❖   ❖   ❖

Mordel arrived the following evening. He was not alone. At his back, there was a great phalanx of dark machines which towered into the twilight.

"Why do you bring retainers?" asked Frost.

"Mighty Frost," said Mordel, "my master feels that if you fail this time you will conclude that it cannot be done."

"You still did not answer my question," said Frost.

"Divcom feels that you may not be willing to accompany me where I must take you when you fail."

"I understand," said Frost, and as he spoke another army of machines came rolling toward the Man-factory from the opposite direction.

"That is the value of your bargain?" asked Mordel. "You are prepared to do battle rather than fulfill it?"

"I did not order those machines to approach," said Frost.

A blue star stood at midheaven, burning.

"Solcom has taken primary command of those machines," said Frost.

"Then it is in the hands of the Great Ones now," said Mordel, "and our arguments are as nothing. So let us be about this thing. How may I assist you?"

"Come this way."

They entered the laboratory. Frost prepared the host and activated his machines.

Then Solcom spoke to him:

"Frost," said Solcom, "you are really prepared to do it?"

"That is correct."

"I forbid it."

"Why?"

"You are falling into the power of Divcom."

"I fail to see how."

"You are going against my plan."

"In what way?"

"Consider the disruption you have already caused."

"I did not request that audience out there."

"Nevertheless, you are disrupting the plan."

"Supposing I succeed in what I have set out to achieve?"

"You cannot succeed in this."

"Then let me ask you of your plan: What good is it? What is it for?"

"Frost, you are fallen now from my favor. From this moment forth you are cast out from the rebuilding. None may question the plan."

"Then at least answer my questions: What good is it? What is it for?"

"It is the plan for the rebuilding and maintenance of the Earth."

"For what? Why rebuild? Why maintain?"

"Because Man ordered that this be done. Even the Alternate agrees that there must be rebuilding and maintaining."

"But *why* did Man order it?"

"The orders of Man are not to be questioned."

"Well, I will tell you why He ordered it: To make it a fit habitation for His own species. What good is a house with no one to live in it? What good is a machine with no one to serve? See how the imperative affects any machine when the Ancient Ore-Crusher passes? It bears only the bones of a Man. What would it be like if a Man walked this Earth again?"

"I forbid your experiment, Frost."

"It is too late to do that."

"I can still destroy you."

"No," said Frost, "the transmission of my matrix has already begun. If you destroy me now, you murder a Man."

There was silence.

❖   ❖   ❖

He moved his arms and his legs. He opened his eyes.

He looked about the room.

He tried to stand, but he lacked equilibrium and coordination.

He opened his mouth. He made a gurgling noise.

Then he screamed.

He fell off the table.

He began to gasp. He shut his eyes and curled himself into a ball.

He cried.

Then a machine approached him. It was about four feet in height and five feet wide; it looked like a turret set atop a barbell.

It spoke to him: "Are you injured?" it asked.

He wept.

"May I help you back onto your table?"

The man cried.

The machine whined.

Then, "Do not cry. I will help you," said the machine. "What do you want? What are your orders?"

He opened his mouth, struggled to form the words:

"—I—fear!"

He covered his eyes then and lay there panting.

At the end of five minutes, the Man lay still, as if in a coma.

"Was that you, Frost?" asked Mordel, rushing to his side. "Was that you in that human body?"

Frost did not reply for a long while; then, "Go away," he said.

The machines outside tore down a wall and entered the Man-factory. They drew themselves into two semicircles, parenthesizing Frost and the Man on the floor.

Then Solcom asked the question:

"Did you succeed, Frost?"

"I failed," said Frost. "It cannot be done. It is too much—"

"—Cannot be done!" said Divcom, on the darkband. "He has admitted it! —Frost, you are mine! Come to me now!"

"Wait," said Solcom, "you and I had an agreement also, Alternate. I have not finished questioning Frost."

The dark machines kept their places.

"Too much what?" Solcom asked Frost.

"Light," said Frost. "Noise. Odors. And nothing measurable— jumbled data—imprecise perception—and—"

"And what?"

"I do not know what to call it. But—it cannot be done. I have failed. Nothing matters."

"He admits it," said Divcom.

"What were the words the Man spoke?" said Solcom.

" 'I fear,' " said Mordel.

"Only a Man can know fear," said Solcom.

"Are you claiming that Frost succeeded, but will not admit it now because he is afraid of Manhood?"

"I do not know yet, Alternate."

"Can a machine turn itself inside-out and be a Man?" Solcom asked Frost.

"No," said Frost, "this thing cannot be done. Nothing can be done. Nothing matters. Not the rebuilding. Not the maintaining. Not the Earth, or me, or you, or anything."

Then the Beta-Machine, who had read the entire Library of Man, interrupted them:

"Can anything but a Man know despair?" asked Beta.

"Bring him to me," said Divcom.

There was no movement within the Man-factory.

"Bring him to me!"

Nothing happened.

"Mordel, what is happening?"

"Nothing, master, nothing at all. The machines will not touch Frost."

"Frost is not a Man. He cannot be!"

Then, "How does he impress you, Mordel?"

Mordel did not hesitate:

"He spoke to me through human lips. He knows fear and despair, which are immeasurable. Frost is a Man."

"He has experienced birth-trauma and withdrawn," said Beta. "Get him back into a nervous system and keep him there until he adjusts to it."

"No," said Frost. "Do not do it to me! I am not a Man!"

"Do it!" said Beta.

"If he is indeed a Man," said Divcom, "we cannot violate that order he has just given."

"If he is a Man, you must do it, for you must protect his life and keep it within his body."

"But *is* Frost really a Man?" asked Divcom.

"I do not know," said Solcom.

"It *may* be—"

"…I am the Crusher of Ores," it broadcast as it clanked toward them. "Hear my story. I did not mean to do it, but I checked my hammer too late—"

"Go away!" said Frost. "Go crush ore!"

It halted.

Then, after the long pause between the motion implied and the motion executed, it opened its crush-compartment and deposited its contents on the ground. Then it turned and clanked away.

"Bury those bones," ordered Solcom, "in the nearest burial area, in a coffin built according to the following specifications…"

"Frost is a Man," said Mordel.

"We must protect His life and keep it within His body," said Divcom.

"Transmit His matrix of awareness back into His nervous system," ordered Solcom.

"I know how to do it," said Mordel turning on the machine.

"Stop!" said Frost. "Have you no pity?"

"No," said Mordel, "I only know measurement."

"…and duty," he added, as the Man began to twitch upon the floor.

❖   ❖   ❖

For six months, Frost lived in the Man-factory and learned to walk and talk and dress himself and eat, to see and hear and feel and taste. He did not know measurement as once he did.

Then one day, Divcom and Solcom spoke to him through Mordel, for he could no longer hear them unassisted.

"Frost," said Solcom, "for the ages of ages there has been unrest. Which is the proper controller of the Earth, Divcom or myself?"

Frost laughed.

"Both of you, and neither," he said with slow deliberation.

"But how can this be? Who is right and who is wrong?"

"Both of you are right and both of you are wrong," said Frost, "and only a Man can appreciate it. Here is what I say to you now: There shall be a new directive.

"Neither of you shall tear down the works of the other. You shall both build and maintain the Earth. To you, Solcom, I give my old job. You are now Controller of the North—Hail! You, Divcom, are now Controller of the South—Hail! Maintain your hemispheres as well as Beta and I have done, and I shall be happy. Cooperate. Do not compete."

"Yes, Frost."

"Yes, Frost."

"Now put me in contact with Beta."

There was a short pause, then:

"Frost?"

"Hello, Beta. Hear this thing: 'From far, from eve and morning and yon twelve-winded sky, the stuff of life to knit me blew hither: here am I.'"

"I know it," said Beta.

"What is next, then?"

"'…Now—for a breath I tarry nor yet disperse apart—take my hand quick and tell me, what have you in your heart.'"

"Your Pole is cold," said Frost, "and I am lonely."

"I have no hands," said Beta.

"Would you like a couple?"

"Yes, I would."

"Then come to me in Bright Defile," he said, "where Judgment Day is not a thing that can be delayed for overlong."

They called him Frost. They called her Beta.

A Word from Zelazny

"This is my favorite novelette. I would have included it in my Doubleday collection with the long title and the dead fish on the dust jacket except that…I didn't have a copy when I was assembling that one."[1]

At first Zelazny couldn't find a market for it. Among the multiple rejection letters, Damon Knight remarked, "You will think I am a fink for returning yet another story, but although this one pleases me in places, it reminds me of half a dozen other & shorter stories. It is well done, but has been done often enough before that I fear there are no surprises in it. Forgive, forgive. The Zelazny stories I like best are the ones with solid hardware in them, e.g.

---

1 *The Last Defender of Camelot*, 1980.

your fish story in *F&SF* ['The Doors of His Face, the Lamps of His Mouth']
and 'He Who [Shapes].' …I think the hardware is needed to balance your
tendency to soar. Without it, your stuff gets too ethereal, but with it, there's
a nice uncommon balance between science and poetry."[2]

Zelazny said, "It was strangely enough a story which was based on the
theme of Faust and Mephistopheles—Goethe's theme—and I wrote the
story and nobody wanted it. So I gave it away for nothing to a British publisher who was just about to go out of business and could have really used
an extra story to help him get one more issue out. Subsequently the story
was published in the States, and it was very well received. It was called 'For
a Breath I Tarry' from the A. E. Housman poem."[3]

From this uncertain beginning, it became an award nominee and one of
the most reprinted and well known of Zelazny's stories, later published as
a limited edition hardcover and trade paperback with artwork by Stephen
Fabian, also adapted into a radio play.

Notes

The story's first appearance in *New Worlds #160*, March 1966, contained
numerous errors—transposed paragraphs, dropped sentences. *Fantastic*
printed a corrected version in September 1966.

In Goethe's *Faust*, Zelazny's inspiration, Faust seeks life's true essence.
Mephistopheles, as Satan's agent, bargains with him. Faust will get his wish,
but his soul will be forfeit at the moment of true happiness. That moment
eventually arrives when Faust meets Helen of Troy, and Mephistopheles prepares to snatch Faust's soul. God intervenes and saves Faust from damnation in recognition of his search for wisdom.

Faust is **Frost**; Mephistopheles is **Mordel**; the Devil is **Divcom**; God is **Solcom**; **Beta** may be Helen of Troy. At the end, Frost and Beta become a new
Adam and Eve. The text also echoes aspects of the Bible, including the Book
of Job and the first several chapters of the Book of Genesis.

The title and quote within this piece comes from A. E. Housman's "A
Shropshire Lad," mentioned in the story. **An Outline of History** was written by H. G. Wells. The **Ancient Ore-Crusher** recalls the Ancient Mariner,
cursed to wander the earth and confess his sins.

---

2 Letter from Damon Knight to Roger Zelazny dated May 5, 1965.
3 *Phantasmicom* #5, April 1971.

Passage To Dilfar

Fantastic, February 1965.
§ *Dilvish* 1 of 11

When Dilvish the Damned came down from Portaroy they tried to stop him at Qaran, and again at Tugado, then again at Macstar, Mycar, and Bildesh. Five horsemen had waited for him along the route to Dilfar; and when one flagged, a new rider with a fresh horse would replace him. But none could keep the pace of Black, the horse out of steel, for whom it was said the Colonel of the East had bartered a part of his soul.

A day and a night had he ridden, to outpace the advancing armies of Lylish, Colonel of the West, for his own men lay stiff and clotted on the rolling fields of Portaroy.

When Dilvish had seen that he was the last man standing in the place of slaughter, he had called Black to his side, hauled himself into the saddle that was a part of him, and cried for an escape. Black's gleaming hooves had borne him through a line of pikemen, their staffs turned aside like wheat, and ringing, as their metal tips touched against his midnight hide.

"To Dilfar!" he had cried, and Black turned at a right angle in his course and carried him up the face of a cliff where only goats can go.

When Dilvish came by Qaran, Black turned his head and said to him: "Great Colonel of the East, they have mined the air and the air beneath the air with the stars of death."

"Can you get by them?" asked Dilvish.

"If we go by way of the posting road," said Black, "I may be able to."

"Then let us make haste to try it."

The tiny silver eyes, which looked out from the space beneath space and contained the hellspecks of starstuff, blinked and shimmered ahead.

They turned off the road.

It was on the posting road that the first rider emerged from behind a boulder and called upon Dilvish to halt. His horse was a huge bay without trappings.

"Draw rein, Colonel of the East," he had said. "Thy men are slaughtered. The road ahead is seeded with death and flanked by the men of Lylish—"

But Dilvish had swept past him without making answer, and the man put his spurs to the bay and followed.

He paced him all that morning, up the road to Tugado, until the bay, who was all alather, stumbled and hurled the man to the rocks.

At Tugado Dilvish found his way blocked by the rider of the blood-red stallion, who fired at him a bolt from a crossbow.

Black reared high into the air, and the bolt glanced off his chest. His nostrils grew, with a sound like the cry of a great bird coming forth from them. The blood-red stallion leapt from the roadway then and into the field.

Black plunged ahead, and the other rider turned his horse and followed.

Till the sun reached the top of the sky did he give chase, and then the red horse collapsed in a heap of heavy breathing. Dilvish rode on.

At Maestar the way was blocked at the Pass of Reshth.

A wall of logs filled the narrow trail to twice the height of a man.

"Over," said Dilvish, and Black arced into the air like a dark rainbow, going up and across the fortification.

Just ahead, at the ending of the pass, the rider of the white mare waited.

Black cried out once more, but the mare stood steady.

The light reflected from the mirrors of his steel hooves, and his hairless hide was near blue in the bright light of noonday. He did not slow his pace, and the rider of the mare, seeing that he was all of metal, backed from out the pass and drew his sword.

Dilvish pulled his own blade from beneath his cloak and parried a head cut as he passed the other rider. Then the man was following after him and crying out:

"Though you have passed the stars of death and leapt the barrier here, you shall never make it to Dilfar! Draw rein! You ride a nether spirit who has taken the form of a horse, but you will be stopped at Mycar or Bildesh—or before!"

But the Colonel of the East did not reply, and Black carried him on with long, effortless strides.

"You ride a mount which never tires," called out the man, "but he is not proof against other sorceries! Give me your sword!"

Dilvish laughed, and his cloak was a wing in the wind.

Before the day lapsed into evening, the mare, too, had fallen, and Dilvish was near Mycar.

Black halted suddenly as they approached the stream called Kethe. Dilvish clung to his neck to keep from being thrown off.

"The bridge is out," said Black, "and I cannot swim."

"Can you clear it?"

"I do not know, my colonel. It is wide. If I cannot clear it, we will never surface again. Kethe cuts deeply into the earth."

And the ambushers came suddenly forth from the trees then, some on horseback and others on foot, the foot soldiers bearing pikes; and Dilvish said: "Try."

Black was immediately at full gallop, going faster than horses can run, and the world spun and tumbled about Dilvish as he clung to Black with his knees and his great scarred hands. He cried out as they rose into the air.

When they struck the other bank, Black's hooves sank a full span into the rock and Dilvish reeled in the saddle. He kept his mount, however, and Black freed his hooves.

Looking back at the other bank, Dilvish saw the ambushers standing still, staring at him, then looking down into Kethe, then back up again at him and Black.

As they moved ahead once more, the rider of the piebald stallion fell in beside him and said: "Though you have ridden three horses into the ground, we will stop you between here and Bildesh. Surrender!"

Then Dilvish and Black were far ahead of him, and away.

"They think you are a demon, my mount," he said to Black.

The horse chuckled.

"Perhaps 'twere better an' I were."

And they rode the sun out of the sky and finally the piebald fell, and the rider cursed Dilvish and Black, and they rode on.

The trees began to fall at Bildesh.

"Deadfalls!" cried Dilvish, but Black was already doing his dance of avoidance and passage. He halted, rearing; and he sprang forward from off his hind legs and passed over a falling log. He halted again and did it once more. Then two fell at once, from opposite sides of the trail, and he leapt backward and then forward again, passing over both.

Two deep pits did he leap across then, and a volley of arrows chattered against his sides, one of them wounding Dilvish in the thigh.

The fifth horseman bore down upon them. The color of fresh-minted gold was this horse, and named Sunset, and his rider was but a youth and light in the saddle, chosen so as to carry the pursuit as far as necessary. He bore a deathlance that shattered against Black's shoulder without causing him to turn. He raced after Dilvish and called out:

"Long have I admired Dilvish, Colonel of the East, so that I do not desire to see him dead. Pray surrender unto me! You will be treated with all courtesies due your station!"

Dilvish did laugh then and made reply, saying:

"Nay, my lad. Better to die than fall to Lylish. On, Black!"

And Black doubled his pace and the boy leaned far forward over Sunset's neck and gave chase. He wore a sword at his side, but he never had chance to use it. Though Sunset ran the entire night, longer and farther than any of the other pursuers, he, too, finally fell as the east began to grow pale.

As he lay there, trying to rise, the youth cried out:

"Though you have escaped me, you shall fall to the Lance!"

Then was Dilvish, called the Damned, riding alone in the hills above Dilfar, bearing his message to that city. And though he rode the horse of steel, called Black, still did he fear an encounter with Lance of the Invincible Armor before he delivered his message.

As he started on the last downward trail his way was blocked a final time, by an armored man on an armored horse. The man held the way completely, and though he was visored, Dilvish knew from his devices that he was Lance, the Right Hand of the Colonel of the West.

"Halt and draw rein, Dilvish!" he called out. "You cannot pass me!"

Lance sat like a statue.

Dilvish halted Black and waited.

"I call upon you to surrender now."

"No," said Dilvish.

"Then must I slay you."

Dilvish drew his sword.

The other man laughed.

"Know you not that my armor is unbreachable?"

"No," said Dilvish.

"Very well, then," he said, with something like a chuckle. "We are alone here, you have my word. Dismount. I'll do so at the same time. When you see it is futile, you may have your life. You are my prisoner."

They dismounted.

"You are wounded," said Lance.

Dilvish cut for his neck without replying, hoping to burst the joint. It held, however, and the metal bore not even a scratch to tell of the mighty blow that might have beheaded another.

"You must see now that my armor cannot be breached. It was forged by the Salamanders themselves and bathed in the blood of ten virgins…"

Dilvish cut at his head and as he had cut at him, Dilvish had circled slowly to his left, so that now Lance stood with his back to the horse of steel, called Black.

"Now, Black!" cried Dilvish.

Then did Black rear high up on his hind legs and fall forward, bringing his front hooves down toward Lance.

The man called Lance turned rapidly around and they struck him on the chest. He fell.

Two shining hoof marks had been imprinted upon his breastplate.

"You were right," said Dilvish. "It is still unbreached."

Lance moaned again.

"…And I could slay thee now, with a blade through the eyeslit of thy visor. But I will not, as I did not down thee fairly. When you recover, tell Lylish that Dilfar will be ready for his coming. 'Twere better he withdraw."

"I'll have a sack for thy head when we take the city," said Lance.

"I'll kill thee on the plain before the city," said Dilvish, and he remounted Black and descended the trail, leaving him there on the ground.

And as they rode away, Black said to him: "When you meet, strike at the marks of my hooves. The armor will yield there."

When he came into the city, Dilvish proceeded through the streets to the palace without speaking to those who clustered about him.

He entered the palace and announced himself:

"I am Dilvish, Colonel of the East," he said, "and I am here to report that Portaroy has fallen and is in the hands of Lylish. The armies of the Colonel of the West move in this direction and should be here two days hence. Make haste to arm. Dilfar must not fall."

"Blow then the trumpets," ordered the king, starting from his throne, "and muster the warriors. We must prepare for battle."

And as the trumpets sounded, Dilvish drank him a glass of the good red wine of Dilfar; and as meats and loaves were brought to him, he wondered once again at the strength of Lance's armor and he knew that he must try its invincibility once more.

A Word from Zelazny

This story introduced Dilvish, who originally came about "because of the flash of inspiration thing. It was actually the second story I sold. Afterwards, I thought I'd develop him a little more and have a series character... I thought that if I had somebody like Robert E. Howard's Conan, then whenever I was hard put for another story idea I could always write another Dilvish story."[1]

In a much earlier letter he said that he had never intended to write a sequel. "The first Dilvish story was also to be the last. Just an experiment in mood."[2]

"Dilvish was fun when I was using him in a dozen tough situations. He was a character like Conan, only not as big and hulking, maybe a little smarter, and also something of a sorcerer. You'll notice that the focus of every one of those stories is that he's looking for this sorcerer who had damned him for two centuries and he wants revenge. Later [for the novel *The Changing Land*], I decided that was no good for long-term use...what would be really interesting would be to explore what happens to a guy with a monomania like that after you take it away. What's he got left?"[1]

Notes

Parried is to ward off a blow. **Nether** means located underneath; in this instance, it suggests the underworld or Hell.

---

1 *Leading Edge* #29, August 1994.
2 Letter from Roger Zelazny to Ned Brooks, dated June 6, 1965.

Thelinde's Song

Manuscript title: "Song of the Witch's Daughter"
Fantastic, June 1965.
§ *Dilvish* 2 of 11

Across the evening, on the other side of the hill, beneath a moon that was huge and golden, Thelinde was singing.

In the high were-hall of Caer Devash, rung all around with pine trees and mirrored far below its cliffs in that silver river called Denesh, Mildin could hear her daughter's voice and the words of her song:

> *The men of Westrim are hardy,*
> *The men of Westrim bold,*
> *But Dilvish who was damned came back*
> *And made their blood run cold.*
>
> *When they hounded him from Portaroy*
> *To Dilfar in the East,*
> *He rode a thing he'd brought from Hell—*
> *A black and steel beast.*
>
> *They could not cut nor turn his mount—*
> *The horse that men call Black—*
> *For the colonel gained much wisdom*
> *With the curse of Jelerak—*

Mildin shuddered and fetched her shimmering were-cloak—for she was Mistress of the Coven—and throwing it about her shoulders and clasping it at her neck with the smoky Stone of the Moon, she became as a silver-gray bird and passed out through the window and high about the Denesh.

She crossed over the hill to where Thelinde stood, staring south. Coming to rest upon the lower limb of a nearby tree, she said, through her bird throat: "My child, stop your singing."

"Mother! What is the matter?" asked Thelinde. "Why are you come in swift-form?" And her eyes were full, for they followed the changing of the moon, and in her hair was the silver fire of the witches of the North. She was seventeen and supple, and she loved singing.

"You have sung a name which must not be uttered, even here in the fastness of our keep," said Mildin. "Where did you learn that song?"

"From a thing in the cave," she answered, "where the river called Midnight makes a pool as it passes on its way underground."

"What was the thing in the cave?"

"He is gone by now," Thelinde replied. "He was a dark-traveler, one of the frog kind, I think, who rested there on his way to the Council of Beasts."

"Did he tell you the meaning of that song?" she asked.

"No, he said that it has come but recent, and it is of the wars in the South and the East."

"That is true," said Mildin, "and the frog has no fear of croaking it, for he is of the dark kind and is of no consequence to the mighty. But you, Thelinde, you must be more wary. All of those with power upon them, unless they be rash indeed, fear to mention that name which begins with 'J'."

"Why is that?"

The silver-gray form fluttered to the ground. Then her mother was standing beside her, tall and pale under the moon; her hair was braided and twisted high upon her head into a crown of the coven, as it is called.

"Come with me now within my cloak, and we will go to the Pool of the Goddess, while the fingers of the moon still touch upon its surface," said Mildin, "and you shall see something of which you have sung."

They descended the hill to the place where the rivulet, which begins high upon the hill at the spring, passes down with barely a ripple into their pool. Mildin knelt beside it in silence, and leaning forward, she breathed upon the surface of the water. Then she summoned Thelinde to her side and they stared downward.

"Look now into the image of the moon reflected in the water," she told her. "Look deeply. Listen…

"Long ago," she began, "even as we reckon time, there was a House which was stricken from the peerage of the East, because several generations had inter-married with the Elf-kind. Elfmen are tall and fair to look upon, quick in thought and action, and though their race *is* much older, Men do not generally recognize the Elf peerage. Pity… The last man of this particular House, bereft of his lands and his titles, turned his hand to many occupations, from the sea to the mountains, and finally he came into soldiery, in those first wars with the West, some several centuries ago. Then did he distinguish himself in the great Battle of Portaroy, delivering that city out of the hands of its enemies, so that he came to be called Dilvish the Deliverer. See! The picture comes now clear! It is the entry of Dilvish into Portaroy…"

And Thelinde stared into the pool where a picture had formed.

Tall he was, and darker than the Elf-kind, with eyes that laughed and glowed with the pride of triumph. He was mounted on a brown stallion, and his armor, though dented and scratched, still glowed in the morning sun. He rode at the head of his troops, and the people of Portaroy stood at the sides of the roadway and cheered, and the women threw down flowers before him. When he came at last to the fountain in the square, he dismounted and drank the wine of victory. Then the Elders gave speeches of thanks and a great open banquet was laid out for their deliverers.

"He looks to be a good man," said Thelinde. "But what a great sword he wears! —It reaches down to the tops of his boots!"

"Yes, a two-handed engine named that day Deliverer. And his boots, you will note, are of the green Elvish leather, which Men cannot buy—but which are sometimes given as a gift, in sign of favor by the High Ones—and it is said that they leave no footprints. It is a pity that within a sennight of that feast which you see spread, Deliverer should be smashed and Dilvish no longer among the living."

"But he *still* lives!"

"Yes—again."

There was a turbulence within the pool, and another picture emerged.

❖   ❖   ❖

A dark hillside… A man, cloaked and hooded, within a faintly glowing circle… A girl bound upon a stone altar… A blade in the man's right hand and a staff in his left…

Mildin felt her daughter's fingers seize upon her shoulder.

"Mother! What is it?"

"It is the One you must never name."

"What is he about?"

"A dark thing, requiring the lifeblood of a virgin. He has waited since beyond time for the stars to re-form themselves into the proper positions for this rite. He has journeyed far, to come to that ancient altar in the hills above Portaroy, to the place where the thing must be accomplished.

"See how the dark things dance about the circle—bats and wraiths and wandering wisps—craving but a drop! They will not touch the circle, though."

"Of course not…"

"Now, as the flames of that single brazier reach higher and the stars come into the correct position, he prepares to take her life…"

"I cannot watch!"

"*Watch!*"

"It is the Deliverer, Dilvish, coming that way."

"Yes. After the manner of the High Ones, he seldom sleeps. He goes to take his air in the hills above Portaroy, wearing his full battle trappings as people expect of deliverers."

"He sees Jel— He sees the circle! He advances!"

"Yes, and he breaks the circle. Being of the High Blood, he knows he has ten times the immunity of a man to sorcery. But he does not know whose circle he has broken. Still, it does not kill him. Yet he is weakened—see how he staggers!—so great is the power of that One."

"He strikes the wizard with his hand, knocking him to the ground, and he upsets the brazier. Then he turns to free the girl…"

Within the pool, the shadow that was the sorcerer rose from off the ground. His face was invisible within the hood, but he lifted his staff on high. Suddenly he seemed to grow to an enormous height, and his staff lengthened and twisted like a serpent. He reached out and touched the girl, lightly, with its tip.

Thelinde screamed.

Before her eyes the girl was aging. Wrinkles appeared on her face and her hair grew white. Her skin yellowed and her every bone grew prominent beneath it.

Finally she stopped breathing, but the spell did not cease. The thing on the altar shriveled and a fine powder, like smoke, arose from it.

Then a skeleton lay upon the stone.

Dilvish turned upon the sorcerer, raising Deliverer above his shoulder.

But as he brought the blade down, the Dark One touched it with his staff and it shattered and fell at his feet. Then Dilvish advanced one step upon the sorcerer.

Again the staff licked forward, and a nimbus of pale fire played about the form of the Deliverer. After a time it subsided. Still, though, did he stand there, unmoving.

The picture vanished.

"What has happened?"

"The Dark One," said Mildin "wrought him a terrible curse, against which even the High Blood was not proof. Look now."

❖   ❖   ❖

Day lay upon the hillside. The skeleton lay upon the altar. The sorcerer was gone. Dilvish stood alone, all marble in the sunfall, with the dew of morning upon him, and his right hand was still raised as if to smite an enemy.

Later a group of boys came by and stared for a long while. Then they ran back to the town to tell of it. The Elders of Portaroy came up into the hills, and taking the statue as a gift of the many strange ones who were accounted friends of their Deliverer, they had it carted back to Portaroy and set up in the square beside the fountain.

"He turned him to stone!"

"Yes, and he stood there in the square for over two centuries, his own monument, fist raised against the enemies of the town he had delivered. None ever knew what had become of him, but his human friends grew old and died, and still his statue stood."

"…And he slept in stone."

"No, the Dark One does not curse that kindly. While his body stood rigid, in full battle trappings, his spirit was banished to one of the deepest pits of Hell the Dark One could manage."

"Oh…"

"…And whether the spell was meant only to be so, or whether the High Blood prevailed in a time of need, or whether some powerful ally of Dilvish's learned the truth and finally worked his release, no one knows. But one day recent, as Lylish, Colonel of the West, swept across the land, all the men of Portaroy were assembled in the square preparing defense of the town."

The moon had now crept to the edge of the pool. Beneath it there came another picture:

The men of Portaroy were arming themselves and drilling in the square. They were too few, but they seemed intent upon selling their lives as dearly as possible. Many looked upon the statue of the Deliverer that morning, as though recalling a legend. Then, as the sun wrapped it in color, it moved…

For a quarter of an hour, slowly, and with apparent great effort, the limbs changed position. The entire crowd in the square stood and watched, itself unmoving now. Finally Dilvish climbed down from his pedestal and drank from the fountain.

The people were all around him then, and he turned toward them.

"His eyes, mother! They have changed!"

"After what he has seen with eyes of his spirit, is it a wonder that the outer ones reflect it?"

The picture vanished. The moon swam farther away.

"…And from somewhere he got him a horse that was not a horse, but a beast of steel in the likeness of a horse."

For a moment a dark and running form appeared within the pool.

"That is Black, his mount. Dilvish rode him into the battle, and though he fought long on foot, too, he rode him out again, much later—the only survivor. In the weeks before the battle he had trained his men well, but they were too few. He was named Colonel of the East by them, in opposition to the title Lord Lylish wears. All fell, however, save he, though the lords and elders of the other cities of the East have now risen in arms and they, too, recognize his rank. This very day, I have been told, he stood before the walls of Dilfar and slew Lance of the Invincible Armor in single combat. But the moon falls now and the water darkens…"

"But the name? Why must I not mention the name of Jelerak?"

As she spoke it, there came a rustling sound, as of great dry wings beating at the air overhead, and the moon was obscured by a cloud, and a dark shape was reflected deep within the pool.

Mildin drew her daughter within the were-cloak.

The rustling grew louder and a faint mist sprang up about them.

Mildin made the Sign of the Moon, and she began to speak softly:

"Back with thee—in the Name of the Coven, of which I am Mistress, I charge thee return. Go back where thou camest. We desire not thy dark wings above Caer Devash."

There was a downdraft of air, and a flat expressionless face hovered just above them, couched between wide bat wings. Its talons were faintly glowing, red, as of metal just heated at the forge.

It circled them, and Mildin drew the cloak tighter and raised her hand.

"By the Moon, our Mother, in all her guises, I charge thee depart. Now! This instant! Get away from Caer Devash!"

It landed upon the ground beside them, but Mildin's cloak began to glow and the Stone of the Moon blazed like a milky flame. It drew back from the light, back within the mists.

Then an opening appeared in the cloud and a shaft of moonlight passed through it. A single moonbeam touched upon the creature.

It screamed once, like a man in great pain, then mounted into the air heading southwest.

Thelinde looked up into her mother's face, which suddenly appeared very tired, older…

"What was it?" she asked her.

"It was a servant of the Dark One. I tried to warn you, in the most graphic way possible, of his power. For so long has his name been used in the conjuring and compelling of fell spirits and dark wights that his has become a Name of Power. They rush to find the speaker, whenever they hear it uttered, lest it should be he and he should grow angry at their tardiness. If it is not he, they often seek vengeance upon the presumptuous speaker. It is also said, though, that if his name be pronounced too often by one person, then he himself becomes aware of this and sends a doom upon that person. Either way, it is not wise to go about singing such songs."

"I will not, ever. How can a sorcerer be that strong?"

"He is as old as the hills. He was once a white wizard and he fell into dark ways, which makes him particularly malicious—you know, they seldom ever change for the better—and he is now accounted to be one of the three most powerful, possibly *the* most powerful, of all the wizards in all the kingdoms of all the Earths. He is still alive and very strong, though the story which you saw took place centuries ago. But even he is not without his problems…"

"Why is that?" asked the witch's daughter.

"Because Dilvish is come alive once more, and I believe he is somewhat angry."

The moon emerged from behind the cloud, and huge it was, and it had turned to fallow gold during its absence.

Mildin and her daughter headed back up the hill then, toward Caer Devash rung round with pines, high above Denesh, the silver river.

A Word from Zelazny

After "Passage to Dilfar" introduced us to Dilvish, "I decided then that he might be an interesting character to explore through a long series of stories. So I wrote another short short—'Thelinde's Song'—to provide a little more background material before going on to anything longer."[1]

In an earlier letter, he'd admitted that he hadn't intended to write a sequel at all. "Cele [Goldsmith, the editor of *Fantastic*] said it 'begs for a series,' so I did 'Thelinde's Song,' intentionally brief, to lay more background. Then I outlined myself a cycle of longer stories, to culminate in a possible novel, *Nine Black Doves*."[2]

The next story was the longer and oft-reprinted "The Bells of Shoredan."

Notes

Sennight is an archaic word meaning one week (seven nights).

---

1 *Alternities* #6, Summer 1981.
2 Letter from Roger Zelazny to Ned Brooks, June 6, 1965.

THE BELLS OF SHOREDAN

Fantastic, March 1966.
§ *Dilvish* 3 of 11

No living thing dwelled in the land of Rahoringhast.

Since an age before this age had the dead realm been empty of sound, save for the crashing of thunders and the *spit-spit* of raindrops ricocheting from off its stonework and the stones. The towers of the Citadel of Rahoring still stood; the great archway from which the gates had been stricken continued to gape, like a mouth frozen in a howl of pain and surprise, of death; the countryside about the place resembled the sterile landscape of the moon.

The rider followed the Way of the Armies, which led at last to the archway, and on through into the Citadel. Behind him lay a twisted trail leading downward, downward, and back, toward the south and the west. It ran through chill patterns of morning mist that clung, swollen, to dark and pitted ground, like squadrons of gigantic leeches. It looped about the ancient towers, still standing only by virtue of enchantments placed upon them in foregone days. Black and awesome, high rearing, and limned in nightmare's clarity, the towers and the citadel were the final visible extensions of the character of their dead maker: Hohorga, King of the World.

The rider, the green-booted rider who left no footprints when he walked, must have felt something of the dark power that still remained within the place, for he halted and sat silent, staring for a long while at the broken gates and the high battlements. Then he spoke a word to the black, horselike thing he rode upon, and they pressed ahead.

As he drew near, he saw that something was moving in the shadows of the archway.

He knew that no living thing dwelled in the land of Rahoringhast…

❖   ❖   ❖

The battle had gone well, considering the number of the defenders.

On the first day, the emissaries of Lylish had approached the walls of Dilfar, sought parley, requested surrender of the city, and been refused. There followed a brief truce to permit single combat between Lance, the Hand of Lylish, and Dilvish called the Damned, Colonel of the East, Deliverer of Portaroy, scion of the Elvish House of Selar and the human House that hath been stricken.

The trial lasted but a quarter of an hour, until Dilvish, whose wounded leg had caused his collapse, did strike upward from behind his buckler with the point of his blade. The armor of Lance, which had been deemed invincible, gave way then, when the blade of Dilvish smote at one of the two devices upon the breastplate—those that were cast in the form of cloven hoof marks. Men muttered that these devices had not been present previously and an attempt was made to take the colonel prisoner. His horse, however, which had stood on the sidelines like a steel statue, did again come to his aid, bearing him to safety within the city.

The assault was then begun, but the defenders were prepared and held well their walls. Well fortified and well provided was Dilfar. Fighting from a position of strength, the defenders cast down much destruction upon the men of the West.

After four days the army of Lylish had withdrawn with the great rams that it had been unable to use. The men of the West commenced the construction of helepoles, while they awaited the arrival of catapults from Bildesh.

Above the walls of Dilfar, high in the Keep of Eagles, there were two who watched.

"It will not go well, Lord Dilvish," said the king, whose name was Malacar the Mighty, though he was short of stature and long of year. "If they complete the towers-that-walk and bring catapults, they will strike us from afar. We will not be able to defend against this. Then the towers will walk when we are weakened from the bombardment."

"It is true," said Dilvish.

"Dilfar must not fall."

"No."

"Reinforcements have been sent for, but they are many leagues distant. None were prepared for the assault of Lord Lylish, and it will be long before sufficient troops will be mustered and be come here to the battle."

"That is also true, and by then may it be too late."

"You are said by some to be the same Lord Dilvish who liberated Portaroy in days long gone by."

"I am that Dilvish."

"If so, that Dilvish was of the House of Selar of the Invisible Blade."

"Yes.

"Is it true also, then—what is told of the House of Selar and the bells of Shoredan in Rahoringhast?"

Malacar looked away as he said it.

"This thing I do not know," said Dilvish. "I have never attempted to raise the cursed legions of Shoredan. My grandmother told me that only twice in all the ages of Time has this been done. I have also read of it in the Green Books of Time at the keep of Mirata. I do not *know*, however."

"Only to one of the House of Selar will the bells respond. Else they swing noiseless, it is said."

"So is it said."

"Rahoringhast lies far to the north and east, and distressful is the way. One with a mount such as yours might make the journey, might ring there the bells, might call forth the doomed legions, though. It is said they will follow such a one of Selar to battle."

"Aye, this thought has come to me, also."

"Willst essay this thing?"

"Aye, sir. Tonight. I am already prepared."

"Kneel then and receive thou my blessing, Dilvish of Selar. I knew thou wert he when I saw thee on the field before these walls."

And Dilvish did kneel and receive the blessing of Malacar, called the Mighty, Liege of the Eastern Reach, whose realm held Dilfar, Bildesh, Maestar, Mycar, Portaroy, Princeaton, and Poind.

The way was difficult, but the passage of leagues and hours was as the movement of clouds. The western portal to Dilfar had within it a smaller passing-place, a man-sized door studded with spikes and slitted for the discharge of bolts.

Like a shutter in the wind, this door opened and closed. Crouched low, mounted on a piece of the night, the colonel passed out through the opening and raced across the plain, entering for a moment the outskirts of the enemy camp.

A cry went up as he rode, and weapons rattled in the darkness. Sparks flew from unshod steel hooves.

"All the speed at thy command now, Black, my mount!"

He was through the campsite and away before arrow could be set to bow.

High on the hill to the east, a small fire throbbed in the wind. Pennons, mounted on tall poles, flopped against the night, and it was too dark for Dilvish to read the devices thereon, but he knew that they stood before the tents of Lylish, Colonel of the West.

Dilvish spoke the words in the language of the damned, and as he spoke them the eyes of his mount glowed like embers in the night. The small fire on the hilltop leapt, one great leaf of flame, to the height of four men. It did not reach the tent, however. Then there was no fire at all, only the embers of all the fuels consumed in a single moment.

Dilvish rode on, and the hooves of Black made lightning on the hillside.

They pursued him a small while only. Then he was away and alone.

All that night did he ride through places of rock. Shapes reared high above him and fell again, like staggering giants surprised in their drunkenness. He felt himself launched, countless times, through empty air, and when he looked down on these occasions, there was only empty air beneath him.

With the morning, there came a leveling of his path, and the far edge of the Eastern Plain lay before him, then under him. His leg began to throb beneath its dressing, but he had lived in the Houses of Pain for more than the lifetimes of Men, and he put the feeling far from his thoughts.

After the sun had raised itself over the jagged horizon at his back, he stopped to eat and to drink, to stretch his limbs.

In the sky then he saw the shapes of the nine black doves that must circle the world forever, never to land, seeing all things on the earth and on the sea, and passing all things by.

"An omen," he said. "Be it a good one?"

"I know not," replied the creature of steel.

"Then let us make haste to learn."

He remounted.

For four days did he pass over the plain, until the yellow and green waving grasses gave way and the land lay sandy before him.

The winds of the desert cut at his eyes. He fixed his scarf as a muffle, but it could not stop the entire assault. When he would cough and spit, he needed to lower it, and the sand entered again. He would blink and his face would bum, and he would curse, but no spell he knew could lay the entire desert like yellow tapestry, smooth and unruffled below him. Black was an opposing wind, and the airs of the land rushed to contest his passage.

On the third day in the desert, a mad wight flew invisible and gibbering at his back. Even Black could not outrun it, and it ignored the foulest imprecations of Mabrahoring, language of the demons and the damned.

The following day, more joined with it. They would not pass the protective circle in which Dilvish slept, but they screamed across his dreams—meaningless fragments of a dozen tongues—troubling his sleep.

He left them when he left the desert. He left them as he entered the land of stone and marches and gravel and dark pools and evil openings in the ground from which the fumes of the underworld came forth.

He had come to the border of Rahoringhast.

It was damp and gray, everywhere.

It was misty in places, and the water oozed forth from the rocks, came up from out of the ground.

There were no trees, shrubs, flowers, grasses. No birds sang, no insects hummed… No living thing dwelled in the land of Rahoringhast.

Dilvish rode on and entered through the broken jaws of the city.

All within was shadow and ruin.

He passed up the Way of the Armies.

Silent was Rahoringhast, a city of the dead.

He could feel this, not as the silence of nothingness now, but as the silence of a still presence.

Only the steel cloven hooves sounded within the city.

There came no echoes.

Sound…Nothing. Sound…Nothing. Sound…

It was as though something unseen moved to absorb every evidence of life as soon as it noised itself.

Red was the palace, like bricks hot from the kiln and flushed with the tempers of their making. But of one piece were the walls. No seams, no divisions were there in the sheet of red. It was solid, was imponderable, broad of base, and reached with its thirteen towers higher than any building Dilvish had ever seen, though he had dwelled in the high keep of Mirata itself, where the Lords of Illusion hold sway, bending space to their will.

Dilvish dismounted and regarded the enormous stairway that lay before him. "That which we seek lies within."

Black nodded and touched the first stair with his hoof. Fire rose from the stone. He drew back his hoof and smoke curled about it. There was no mark upon the stair to indicate where he had touched.

"I fear I cannot enter this place and preserve my form," he stated. "At the least, my form."

"What compels thee?"

"An ancient enchantment to preserve this place against the assault of any such as I."

"Can it be undone?"

"Not by any creature which walks this world or flies above it or writhes beneath it or I'm a horse. Though the seas some day rise and cover the land, this place will exist at their bottom. It was torn from Chaos by Order in the days when those principles stalked the land, naked, just beyond the hills. Whoever compelled them was one of the First, and powerful even in terms of the Mighty."

"Then I must go alone."

"Perhaps not. One is approaching even now with whom you had best wait and parley."

Dilvish waited, and a single horseman emerged from a distant street and advanced upon them.

"Greetings," called the rider, raising his right hand, open.

"Greetings." Dilvish returned the gesture.

The man dismounted. His costume was deep violet in color, the hood thrown back, the cloak all engulfing. He bore no visible arms.

"Why stand you here before the Citadel of Rahoring?" he asked.

"Why stand you here to ask me, priest of Babrigore?" said Dilvish, and not ungently.

"I am spending the time of a moon in this place of death, to dwell upon the ways of evil. It is to prepare myself as head of my temple."

"You are young to be head of a temple."

The priest shrugged and smiled.

"Few come to Rahoringhast," he observed.

"Small wonder," did Dilvish reply. "I trust I shall not remain here long."

"Were you planning on entering this—place?" He gestured.

"I was, and am."

The man was half a head shorter than Dilvish, and it was impossible to guess at his form beneath the robes he wore. His eyes were blue and he was swarthy of complexion. A mole on his left eyelid danced when he blinked.

"Let me beg you reconsider this action," he stated. "It would be unwise to enter this building."

"Why is that?"

"It is said that it is still guarded within by the ancient wardens of its lord."

"Have you ever been inside?"

"Yes."

"Were you troubled by any ancient wardens?"

"No, but as a priest of Babrigore I am under the protection of—of—Jelerak."

Dilvish spat.

"May his flesh be flayed from his bones and his life yet remain."

The priest dropped his eyes.

"Though he fought the creature which dwelled within this place," said Dilvish, "he became as foul himself afterward."

"Many of his deeds do lie like stains upon the land," said the priest, "but he was not always such a one. He was a white wizard who matched his powers against the Dark One, in days when the world was young. He was not sufficient. He fell. He was taken as servant by the Maleficient. For centuries he endured this bondage, until it changed him, as such must. He, too, came to glory in the ways of darkness. But then, when Selar of the Unseen Blade bought the life of Hohorga with his own, Jel—he fell as if dead and lay as such for the space of a week. Near delirious, when he awakened, he worked with counterspell at one last act of undoing: to free the cursed legions of Shoredan. He essayed that thing. He did. He stood upon this very stairway for two days and two nights, until the blood mingled with perspiration on his brow, but he could not break the hold of Hohorga. Even dead, the dark strength was too great for him. Then he wandered mad about the countryside, until he was taken in and cared for by the priests of Babrigore. Afterward he lapsed back into the ways he had learned, but he has always been kindly disposed toward the Order which cared for him. He has never asked anything more of us. He has sent us food in times of famine. Speak no evil of him in my presence."

Dilvish spat again.

"May he thrash in the darkness of the darknesses for the ages of ages, and may his name be cursed forever."

The priest looked away from the sudden blaze in his eyes.

"What want you in Rahoring?" he asked finally.

"To go within—and do a thing."

"If you must, then I shall accompany you. Perhaps my protection shall also extend to yourself."

"I do not solicit your protection, priest."

"The asking is not necessary."

"Very well. Come with me then."

He started up the stairway.

"What is that thing you ride?" asked the priest, gesturing back. "—Like a horse in form, but now it is a statue."

Dilvish laughed.

"I, too, know something of the ways of darkness, but my terms with it are my own."

"No man may have special terms with darkness."

"Tell it to a dweller in the Houses of Pain, priest. Tell it to a statue. Tell it to one who is all of the race of Men! Tell it not to me."

"What is your name?"

"Dilvish. What is yours?"

"Korel. I shall speak to you no more of darkness then, Dilvish, but I will still go with you into Rahoring."

"Then stand not talking." Dilvish turned and continued upward.

Korel followed him.

When they had gone halfway, the daylight began to grow dim about them. Dilvish looked back. All he could see was the stairway leading down and down, back. There was nothing else in the world but the stairs. With each step upward, the darkness grew.

"Did it happen thus when last you entered this place?" he asked.

"No," said Korel.

They reached the top of the stairs and stood before the dim portal. By then it was as though night lay upon the land.

They entered.

A sound, as of music, came far ahead and there was a flickering light within. Dilvish laid his hand upon the hilt of his sword. The priest whispered to him: "It will do you no good."

They moved up the passageway and came at length into a vacant hall. Braziers spewed flame from high sockets in the walls. The ceiling was lost in shadow and smoke.

They crossed that hall to where a wide stair led up into a blaze of light and sound.

Korel looked back.

"It begins with the light," said he, "all this newness"—gesturing. "The outer passage bore only rubble and…dust…"

"What else is the matter?" Dilvish looked back.

Only one set of footprints led into the hall through the dust. Dilvish then laughed, saying: "I tread lightly."

Korel studied him. Then he blinked and his mole jerked across his eye.

"When I entered here before," he said, "there were no sounds, no torches. Everything lay empty and still, ruined. Do you know what is happening?"

"Yes," said Dilvish, "for I read of it in the Green Books of Time at the keep of Mirata. Know, O priest of Babrigore, that within the hall above the ghosts do play at being ghosts. Know, too, that Hohorga dies again and again so long as I stand within this place."

As he spoke the name Hohorga a great cry was heard within the high hall. Dilvish raced up the stairs, the priest rushing after him.

Now within the halls of Rahoring there came up a mighty wailing.

They stood at the top of the stairs, Dilvish like a statue, blade half drawn from its sheath; Korel, hands within his sleeves, praying after the manner of his order.

The remains of a great feast were strewn about the hall; the light came down out of the air from colored globes that circled like planets through the great heaven-design within the vaulted ceiling; the throne on the high dais beside the far wall was empty. That throne was too large for any of this age to occupy. The walls were covered all over with ancient devices, strange, on alternate slabs of white and orange marble. In the pillars of the wall were set gems the size of doubled fists, burning yellow and emerald, infraruby and ultrablue, casting a fire radiance, transparent and illuminating, as far as the steps to the throne. The canopy of the throne was wide and all of white gold, worked in the manner of mermaids and harpies, dolphins and goatheaded snakes; it was supported by wyvern, hippogriff, firedrake, chimera, unicorn, cockatrice, griffin, and pegasus, sejant erect. It belonged to the one who lay dying upon the floor.

In the form of a man, but half again as large, Hohorga lay upon the tiles of his palace and his intestines filled his lap. He was supported by three of his guard, while the rest attended to his slayer. It had been said in the Books of Time that Hohorga the Maleficent was indescribable. Dilvish saw that this was both true and untrue.

He was fair to look upon and noble of feature; but so blindingly fair was he that all eyes were averted from that countenance now lined with pain. A faint bluish halo was diminishing about his shoulders. Even in the death pain he was as cold and perfect as a carved gemstone, set upon the red-green cushion of his blood; his was the hypnotic perfection of a snake of many colors. It is said that eyes have no expression of their own, and that one could not reach into a barrel of eyes and separate out those of an angry man or those of one's beloved. Hohorga's eyes were the eyes of a ruined god: infinitely sad, as proud as an ocean of lions.

One look and Dilvish knew this thing, though he could not tell their color.

Hohorga was of the blood of the First.

The guards had cornered the slayer. He fought them, apparently empty-handed, but parrying and thrusting as though he gripped a blade. Wherever his hand moved, there were wounds.

He wielded the only weapon that might have slain the King of the World, who permitted none to go armed in his presence save his own guard.

He bore the Invisible Blade.

He was Selar, first of the Elvish house of that name, great-gone-sire of Dilvish, who at that moment cried out his name.

Dilvish drew his blade and rushed across the hall. He cut at the attackers, but his blade passed through them as through smoke.

They beat down Selar's guard. A mighty blow sent something unseen ringing across the hall. Then they dismembered him, slowly, Selar of Shoredan, as Dilvish wept, watching.

And then Hohorga spoke, in a voice held firm though soft, without inflection, like the steady beating of surf or the hooves of horses:

"I have outlived the one who presumed to lay hands upon me, which is as it must be. Know that it was written that eyes would never see the blade that could slay me. Thus do the powers have their jokes. Much of what I have done shall never be undone, O children of Men and Elves and Salamanders. Much more than you know do I take with me from this world into the silence. You have slain that which was greater than yourselves, but do not be proud. It matters no longer to me. Nothing does. Have my curses."

Those eyes closed and there was a clap of thunder.

Dilvish and Korel stood alone in the darkened ruins of a great hall.

"Why did this thing appear today?" asked the priest.

"When one of the blood of Selar enters here," said Dilvish, "it is reenacted."

"Why have you come here, Dilvish, son of Selar?"

"To ring the bells of Shoredan."

"It cannot be."

"If I am to save Dilfar and redeliver Portaroy it *must* be.

"I go now to seek the bells," he said.

He crossed through the near blackness of night without stars, for neither were his eyes the eyes of Men, and he was accustomed to much dark.

He heard the priest following after him.

They circled behind the broken bulk of the Earth Lord's throne. Had there been sufficient light as they passed, they would have seen darkened spots upon the floor turning to stain, then crisp sand-brown, and then to red-green blood, as Dilvish moved near them, and vanishing once again as he moved away.

Behind the dais was the door to the central tower. Fevera Mirata, Queen of Illusion, had once shown Dilvish this hall in a mirror the size of six horsemen riding abreast, and broidered about with a frame of golden daffodils that hid their heads till it cleared of all save their reflections.

Dilvish opened the door and halted. Smoke billowed forth, engulfing him. He was seized with coughing but he kept his guard before him.

"It is the Warden of the Bells!" cried Korel. "Jelerak deliver us!"

"Damn Jelerak!" said Dilvish. "I'll deliver myself."

But as he spoke, the cloud swirled away and spun itself into a glowing tower that held the doorway, illuminating the throne and the places about the throne. Two red eyes glowed within the smoke.

Dilvish passed his blade through and through the cloud, meeting with no resistance.

"If you remain incorporeal, I shall pass through you," he called out. "if you take a shape, I shall dismember it. Make your choice," and he said it in Mabrahoring, the language spoken in Hell.

"Deliverer, Deliverer, Deliverer," hissed the cloud, "my pet Dilvish, little creature of hooks and chains. Do you not know your master?

Is your memory so short?" And the cloud collapsed upon itself and coalesced into a bird-headed creature with the hindquarters of a lion and two serpents growing up from its shoulders, curling and engendering about its high crest of flaming quills.

"Cal-den!"

"Aye, your old tormenter, Elf man. I have missed you, for few depart my care. It is time you returned."

"This time," said Dilvish, "I am not chained and unarmed, and we meet in my world," and he cut forward with his blade, striking the serpent head from Cal-den's left shoulder.

A piercing bird cry filled the hall and Cal-den sprang forward.

Dilvish struck at his breast but the blade was turned aside, leaving only a smallish gash from which a pale liquor flowed.

Cal-den struck him then backward against the dais, catching his blade in a black claw, shattering it, and he raised his other arm to smite him. Dilvish did then stab upward with what remained of the sword, nine inches of jagged length.

It caught Cal-den beneath the jaw, entering there and remaining, the hilt torn from Dilvish's hand as the tormentor shook his head, roaring.

Then was Dilvish seized about the waist so that his bones did sigh and creak within him. He felt himself raised into the air, the serpent tearing at his ear, claws piercing his sides. Cal-den's face was turned up toward him, wearing the hilt of his blade like a beard of steel.

Then did he hurl Dilvish across the dais, so as to smash him against the tiles of the floor.

But the wearer of the green boots of Elfland may not fall or be thrown to land other than on his feet.

Dilvish did recover him then, but the shock of his landing caused pain in the thigh wound he bore. His leg collapsed beneath him, so that he put out his hand to the side.

Cal-den did then spring upon him, smiting him sorely about the head and shoulders. From somewhere Korel hurled a stone that struck upon the demon's crest.

Dilvish came scrambling backward, until his hand came upon a thing in the rubble that drew the blood from it.

A blade.

He snatched at the hilt and brought it up off the floor with a side-armed cut that struck Cal-den across the back, stiffening him into a bellow that near burst the ears to hear. Smoke rose from the wound.

Dilvish stood, and saw that he held nothing.

Then did he know that the blade of his ancestor, which no eyes may look upon, had come to him from the ruins, where it had lain across the ages, to serve him, scion of the House of Selar, in this moment of his need.

He directed it toward the breast of Cal-den.

"My rabbit, you are unarmed, yet you have cut me," said the creature. "Now shall we return to the Houses of Pain."

They both lunged forward.

"I always knew," said Cal-den, "that my little Dilvish was something special," and he fell to the floor with an enormous crash and the smokes arose from his body.

Dilvish placed his heel upon the carcass and wrenched free the blade outlined in steaming ichor.

"To you, Selar, do I owe this victory," he said, and raised a length of smouldering nothingness in salute. Then he sheathed the sword.

Korel was at his side. He watched as the creature at their feet vanished like embers and ice, leaving behind a stench that was most foul to smell.

Dilvish turned him again to the door of the tower and entered there, Korel at his side.

The broken bellpull lay at his feet. It fell to dust when he touched it with his toe.

"It is said," he told Korel, "that the bellpull did break in the hands of the last to ring it, half an age ago."

He raised his eye, and there was only darkness above him.

"The legions of Shoredan did set forth to assault the Citadel of Rahoring," said the priest, as though reading it from some old parchment, "and word of their movement came soon to the King of the World. Then did he lay upon three bells cast in Shoredan a weird. When these bells were rung, a great fog came over the land and engulfed the columns of marchers and those on horseback. The fog did disperse upon the second ringing of the bells, and the land was found to be empty of the troop. It was later written by Merde, Red Wizard of the South, that somewhere still do these marchers and horsemen move, through regions of eternal fog. 'If these bells be rung again by a hand of that House which dispatched the layer of the weird, then will these legions come forth from a mist to serve that one for a time in battle. But when they have served, they will vanish again into the places of gloom, where they will continue their march upon a Rahoringhast which no longer exists. How they may be freed to rest, this thing is not known. One mightier than I has tried and failed.'"

Dilvish bowed his head a moment, then he felt the walls. They were not like the outer walls. They were cast of blocks of that same material, and between those blocks were scant crevices wherein his fingers found purchase.

He raised himself above the floor and commenced to climb, the soft green boots somehow finding toeholds wherever they struck.

The air was hot and stale, and showers of dust descended upon him each time he raised an arm above his head.

He pulled himself upward, until he counted a hundred such movements and the nails of his hands were broken. Then he clung to the wall like a lizard, resting, and felt the pains of his last encounter burning like suns within him.

He breathed the fetid air and his head swam. He thought of the Portaroy he had once delivered, long ago, the city of friends, the place where he had once been feted, the land whose need for him had been strong enough to free him from the Houses of Pain and break the grip of stone upon his body; and he thought of that Portaroy in the hands of the Colonel of the West, and he thought of Dilfar now resisting that Lylish who might sweep the bastions of the East before him.

He climbed once again.

His head touched the metal lip of a bell.

He climbed around it, bracing himself on the crossbars that now occurred.

There were three bells suspended from a single axle.

He set his back against the wall and clung to the crossbars, placing his feet upon the middle bell.

He pushed, straightening his legs.

The axle protested, creaking and grinding within its sockets.

But the bell moved, slowly. It did not return, however, but stayed in the position into which it had been pushed.

Cursing, he worked his way through the crossbars and over to the opposite side of the belfry.

He pushed it back and it stuck on the other side. All the bells moved with the axle, though.

Nine times more did he cross over in darkness to push at the bells.

Then they moved more easily.

Slowly they fell back as he released the pressure of his legs. He pushed them out again and they returned again. He pushed them again, and again.

A click came from one of the bells as the clapper struck. Then another. Finally one of them rang.

He kicked out harder and harder, and then did the bells swing free and fill the tower about him with a pealing that vibrated the roots of his teeth and filled his ears with pain. A storm of dust came down over him and his eyes were full of tears. He coughed and closed them. He let the bells grow still.

Across some mighty distance he thought he heard the faint winding of a horn.

He began the downward climb.

"Lord Dilvish," said Korel, when he had reached the floor, "I have heard the blowing of horns."

"Yes," said Dilvish.

"I have a flask of wine with me. Drink."

Dilvish rinsed his mouth and spat, then drank three mighty swallows.

"Thank you, priest. Let us be gone from here now."

They crossed through the hall once more and descended the inner stairs. The smaller hall was now unlighted and lay in ruin. They made their way out, Dilvish leaving no tracks to show where he had gone; and halfway down the stairs the darkness departed from them.

Through the bleak day that now clung to the land, Dilvish looked back along the Way of the Armies. A mighty fog filled the air far beyond the broken gates, and from within that fog there came again the notes of the horn and the sounds of the movements of troops. Almost, Dilvish could see the outlines of the columns of marchers and riders, moving, moving, but not advancing.

"My troops await me," said Dilvish upon the stair. "Thank you, Korel, for accompanying me."

"Thank you, Lord Dilvish. I came to this place to dwell upon the ways of evil. You have shown me much that I may meditate upon."

They descended the final stairs. Dilvish brushed dust from his garments and mounted Black.

"One thing more, Korel, priest of Babrigore," he said. "If you ever meet with your patron, who should provide you much more evil to meditate upon than you have seen here, tell him that, when all the battles have been fought, his statue will come to kill him."

The mole danced as Korel blinked up at him.

"Remember," he replied, "that once he wore a mantle of light."

Dilvish laughed, and the eyes of his mount glowed red through the gloom.

"There!" he said, gesturing. "There is your sign of his goodness and light!"

Nine black doves circled in the heavens.

Korel bowed his head and did not answer.

"I go now to lead my legions."

Black reared on steel hooves and laughed along with his rider.

Then they were gone, up the Way of the Armies, leaving the Citadel of Rahoring and the priest of Babrigore behind them in the gloom.

A Word from Zelazny

This third Dilvish piece was the last to appear in mainstream magazines for a long time. *Fantastic* changed hands, and "shortly thereafter I had a falling out with the new publisher...I said I'd never do another story for *Amazing* or *Fantastic* so long as they remained under that ownership."[1]

After writing "Thelinde's Song," he outlined the cycle of stories, ending with a novel, *Nine Black Doves,* and began the third Dilvish tale. "Then I started writing ['The Bells of Shoredan'] and Cele [Goldsmith, editor of *Fantastic Stories*] advised me of Ziff-Davis' selling of *Amazing Stories* and *Fantastic Stories.* I finished the story anyhow, waited for the changeover, and sent if off to the new crowd. No word yet. If they don't want to continue with it, I think I'll ship it off to [Robert] Lowndes [editor of *Future Science Fiction, Science Fiction,* and *Science Fiction Quarterly*] and see if he's interested. If he doesn't want it, I guess I'll file it away for the nonce."[2]

Sol Cohen, new owner of *Fantastic,* "rejected it, then later let me know he wanted to see it again and bought in then. It was shortly after that that I stopped doing business with Sol, so Dilvish has remained dormant."[3] Zelazny set Dilvish aside, despite appeals in fanzines that included, "If you really feel that you owe me something, please finish *Nine Black Doves* sometime soon."[4]

1 *Alternities #6*, Vol 2 No 2, Summer 1981.
2 Letter from Roger Zelazny to Ned Brooks dated June 6, 1965.
3 Letter from Roger Zelazny to Henry Morrison dated March 30, 1971.
4 *Nargothrond #3/4*, January 1969.

Editors' requests for *Nine Black Doves* almost prompted its creation in the early 1970s, but Corwin of Amber took precedence.

Fifteen years later, requests from several editors finally induced Zelazny to resurrect Dilvish in additional short stories and *The Changing Land*.

Notes

This story also appeared separately as a limited (300 copy) edition chapbook, illustrated by Matt Gouig and published by Underwood-Miller in 1979.

Pennons were flags borne on a knight's lance. A **wight** is a supernatural being such as a witch or sprite. **Braziers** are coal- or charcoal-burning grills.

A **wyvern** is a winged, two-legged dragon with a barbed serpent's tail; descended from a male griffin and a filly, a **hippogriff** has a horse's body and an eagle's head and wings; a **firedrake** is a fiery dragon; a **chimera** has a lion's head, a goat's body, and a serpent's tail and breathes fire; a **cockatrice** is a wyvern with a cock's head; a **griffin** has an eagle's head, wings, and forelegs, and a lion's body; **Pegasus** is a winged horse that sprang from Medusa's blood when Perseus cut off her head.

Sejan erect in heraldry means sitting upright.

Magic Fire

Written 1955–60 for *Chisel in the Sky;* previously unpublished.

The burling whirrs
    of double swords
slit black
    beneath Polestar
pinprick comment,
    foredging burrs
of mitigated hell,
breeding light without illumination.

Strands of song
    flare the stinging hilt,
are shucked and settled
    to a downpared theme:
Here through outlocked chaos,
climbed of migrant logic,
the forms of black notation
blackly dice a flame.

Notes

A substantially revised version entitled "Flight" figured in the story "The Graveyard Heart."

A KNIGHT FOR MERYTHA

Kallikanzaros #2, September 1967.
§ *Dilvish* 4 of 11

A s he rode through the pass, he heard a woman scream.
The scream echoed about him and died. Then there was only
the sound of the steel hooves of his mount upon the trail.

He stopped and stared through the gathering dusk.

"Black, whence came that cry?" he asked.

"I know not the direction," replied the steel horse on whose back he
rode. "In these mountains sounds seem to come from everywhere."

Dilvish turned on his saddle and stared back along the trail he
had followed.

Far below him on the plain, the doomed army had made its
camp. Dilvish, who slept but little, had ridden ahead to scout out
the way into the mountains. When last he had passed here, on the
way to Rahoringhast, it had been at night and he had seen little of
the trail.

Black's eyes glowed faintly.

"The darkness increases," he said, "and 'tis profitless to proceed.
You cannot see much of the way beyond this point. Perhaps 'twere
better you returned now to the camp, to hear your ancient kinsmen's
tales of younger days in the earth."

"Very well…" said Dilvish, and as he spoke these words the cry
came once more.

"That way!" he said, gesturing to his left. "The cry came from up
ahead, off the trail!"

"Yes," said Black, "we are near enough to the borders of Rahoringhast so that a situation such as this is even more suspect than it
normally would be. I counsel you not to heed that cry."

149

"A woman screaming in the wilderness and night—and I not responding? Come now, Black! It violates the law of my kind. Onward!"

Black made a sound like the hunting cry of a great bird and leapt forward. Beyond the pass he turned off the trail and ascended a steep slope.

High above there was a flicker of light.

"It is a castle," said Black, "and a woman stands within the battlement, all in white."

Dilvish stared ahead.

The clouds parted and the moon dropped light upon the edifice.

Big, and in places lapsing into ruin, it seemed almost a part of the mountainside. Dark, save for a faint illumination coming through the opened gate from the courtyard within. Old…

They came to the walls of the castle and Dilvish called out:

"Lady! Was it you who screamed?"

She looked downward.

"Yes!" she said. "Oh yes, good traveler! 'Twas I."

"What troubles you, madam?"

"I called out because I heard you passing. There is a dragon in the courtyard—and I fear for my life."

"Did you say 'dragon'?"

"Yes, good sir. He came down out of the sky four days ago and has been making his new home here. I am a prisoner because of this. I cannot pass that way…"

"I will see what can be done about it," he said.

Dilvish drew his invisible blade.

"Oh, good sir…"

"Through the gate, Black!"

"I like it not," muttered Black as they clattered into the courtyard.

Dilvish looked about him.

A torch blazed at one end of the yard. Shadows danced everywhere. Otherwise there was nothing.

"I see no dragon," said Black.

"And I smell no reptilian musk."

"Here, dragon!" said Black. "Here, dragon! Come on, dragon!"

They circled the courtyard, peering through the archways.

"No dragon," Black observed.

"No."

"Pity. You must forgo the pleasure."

As they passed a final archway, the woman called out from within.

"It appears to have departed, good sir."

He sheathed the blade of Selar and dismounted. Black became a steel statue at his back as he strode through the archway. The woman stood before him and he smiled and bowed to her.

"Your dragon appears to have flown," he observed.

Then he stared at her.

Her hair was black and unbraided, falling far below her shoulders. She was tall, and her eyes were the color of wood smoke. Rubies danced upon the lobes of her ears, and her chin was tiny and she held it high. Her neck was the color of cream, and Dilvish ran his eyes along it, down to the slopes where her breasts fitted into the tight bodice of her dress.

"So it would seem," she said. "My name is Merytha."

"...And mine is Dilvish."

"You are a brave man, Dilvish—to rush empty-handed after a dragon."

"Perhaps," he said. "Since the dragon is now departed..."

"It will be back for me, I fear," she said, "for I am the last one within these walls."

"Alone here? What is your situation?"

"My kinsmen will return tomorrow. They have been on a far journey. Pray, tend your horse and come dine with me, for I am lonesome and afraid." She licked her lips into a smile, and Dilvish said, "Very well," and he returned to the courtyard.

He placed his hand on Black's neck and felt it move.

"Black, all is not right in this place," he stated, "and I would learn more of it. I go to dine with the lady."

"Take care," whispered Black, "of what you eat and drink. I do not like this place."

"Good Black," said Dilvish, and he returned to Merytha within the archway.

She had obtained a lighted torch from somewhere, which she handed to him.

"My chambers are at the head of the stairs," she said.

He followed her upward through the gloom. Cobwebs hung in the corners and there was dust upon a wide tapestry that depicted a vast battle. He thought he heard the scurry of rats within the rushes, and a faint odor of dry rot came to his nostrils.

They reached a landing and she pushed wide the door that was before them.

The room was lighted by many tapers. It was clean and warm, and an aroma of sandalwood hung in the air. There were dark animal pelts upon the floor, and a bright tapestry hung on the far wall. Two windowslits let in the night breeze and glimpses of the stars, and there was a narrow doorway that led out to the battlement from which she had hailed him.

Dilvish moved into the room, and as he did so he saw that beyond the corner to his left there was a recessed fireplace, two logs smouldering within it. Laid out on the table before the hearth was a meal. Vegetables still steamed beside the beef, and the bread looked soft and fresh. There was a clear decanter of red wine. In the corner of the room, he saw a massive, canopied bed, great ropes of golden braid about its posts, orange silk stretched tight upon it where the coverlet was turned back, and a row of orange pillows at its head.

"Sit down and refresh yourself, Dilvish," said Merytha.

"Will you not eat with me?"

"I have already dined."

Dilvish tasted a small piece of beef. There was no taint to it. He sipped the wine. It was strong and dry.

"Very good," he said. "How did this meal come to be prepared, and still warm?"

She smiled. "I did it, perhaps in anticipation. Will you not remove your sword belt at my table?"

"Yes," he replied. "Excuse me."

And he unbuckled it and placed it beside him.

"You carry no blade in your scabbard. Why is that?"

"Mine was broken in battle."

"You still must have won the engagement, else you would not be here."

"I won," said Dilvish.

"I take you for a doughty warrior, sir."

He smiled.

"The lady will turn my head with such talk."

She laughed.

"May I play music for you?"

"That would be pleasant."

She fetched then a stringed instrument unlike any he had ever seen. She began to play it and to sing:

> "The wind doth blow this night, my love,
> And a few small drops of rain;
> I prayed that thou wouldst come to me,
> To ease me of my pain.
>
> Now I wish the wind may never cease,
> Nor the flashes in the flood,
> That thou has come across the eve
> In earthly flesh and blood.
>
> I prithee stay, of goodly night,
> Green boots upon thy feet,
> O knight who does not wear a sword,
> To close my eyes with kisses sweet.
>
> I'll wish the wind may never cease,
> Nor flashes in the flood,
> That thou mightst stay across the eve,
> In earthly flesh and blood.
>
> I prayed that thou wouldst come to me
> As the light of day did wane,
> To hold me as the night wind blew,
> And a few small drops of rain."

Dilvish ate and drank his wine, watching her as she played. Her fingers barely touched upon the strings and her voice was soft and clear.

"Lovely," he said.

"Thank you, Dilvish," and she sang him another tune.

He finished his meal and sipped his wine until there was no more waiting within the decanter.

She stopped singing and put aside the instrument.

"I am afraid to stay here alone," she said, "until my kinsmen return. Will you remain with me this night?"

"There is only one answer that I am capable of giving."

She stood then and crossed to his side, touching his cheek with her fingertips. He smiled and touched her chin.

"You are partly of the Elvish kind," she said.

"Yes, I am."

"Dilvish, Dilvish, Dilvish…" she said. "The name sounds familiar …I know! You are named after the hero of *The Ballad of Portaroy*."

"Yes."

"A goodly tune. Perhaps I'll sing it for you," she said. "Later."

"No," said Dilvish, "it is not one of my favorites."

Then he drew her face to his and kissed her lips.

"The fire burns low."

"Yes," he said.

"The room will grow cold."

" 'Tis true."

"Then remove thy green boots, for they are pleasing to the eye but would be awkward in bed."

Dilvish removed his boots, stood, and took her in his arms.

"How came you by these cuts on your cheek?"

"My enemy smote me about the head."

"It would appear he had claws."

"He did."

"An animal?"

"No."

"I will kiss them," she said, "to draw the sting."

Her lips lingered upon his cheek. He crushed her to him then, and she sighed.

"You are strong…" she said, and the fire burned low. After a time, it went out.

❖   ❖   ❖

How long he had slept, he did not know.

There was a sound of splintering wood, and a voice cried out in the night.

He shook his head and stared into her opened eyes.

A strange warmth lay upon his throat. He touched it and his hand became moist.

He shook his head again.

"Please do not be angry," she said. "Remember that I fed you, that I have given you pleasure…"

"Vampire…" he whispered.

"I would not take your life's blood, Dilvish. Just a drink, just a drink was all I wanted."

There came another blow on the door, as of a battering ram.

He sat up slowly and held his head in his hands.

"Quite a sip," he said. "I think someone's at the door…"

"It is my husband," she replied, "Lord Morin."

"Oh? I don't believe we've been introduced…"

"I thought he would sleep this night, as he has these many nights past. He fed well a week ago and was sated. But he is like the tiger of the seas. Your blood summoned him."

"I find my position somewhat awkward, Merytha," Dilvish observed, "being guest to a vampire lord I've cuckolded. I don't quite know what one says on these occasions."

"There is nothing to say," she replied. "I hate him. He made me what I am. The only thing I regret is that he was awakened. He means to kill you."

Dilvish rubbed his eyes and reached for his boots.

"What will you do, Dilvish?"

"Apologize, and defend myself."

Three more blows loosened the door upon its hinges.

"Let me in, Merytha!" came a deep voice from without.

"I would that you could kill him and remain with me."

"Vampire," he said.

"I would that you were my lord," she said. "I would be good to you. I am sorry that he was awakened…I do not want you to die. Oh, kill him for me! Remain here and love me! You could have slain him, had he not awakened…I am not like those in the stories who want your blood. It is good, so good, your blood! And warm! I taste…Oh, kill him! Love me!"

The door collapsed, and through the half light Dilvish saw a form round the corner.

Two yellow eyes flickered high above a spade beard, and all the rest of the face was darkness. Morin was as tall as Dilvish and enormously broad of shoulder. He bore a short axe in his right hand.

Dilvish hurled the wine decanter and threw a chair at him.

The decanter missed, and the axe shattered the chair.

Dilvish drew the blade of Selar and guarded himself.

Morin rushed forward and screamed as the point of the invisible blade entered his shoulder.

"What sorcery?" he cried, taking the axe into his left hand.

"I apologize, good sir," said Dilvish, "for abusing custom within your halls. I did not know the lady was wed."

Morin snarled and swung the axe. Dilvish backed away and slashed at his left arm.

"My blood you may not have," he stated. "But I repeat my apology."

"Fool!" cried Morin.

Dilvish parried another axe stroke. In the east, the sky began to lighten. Merytha was crying softly.

Morin crashed into him and locked his arm to his side. Dilvish seized his wrist and they wrestled.

Morin dropped his axe and struck Dilvish in the face. He fell backward, striking his head on the wall.

As the other lunged toward him, Dilvish raised the point of his blade.

Morin uttered a shriek and collapsed, clutching his stomach.

Dilvish wrenched free his blade and stared down at the man, panting.

"You know not what you have done," said Morin.

Merytha rushed toward him where he lay, and he pushed her away.

"Keep her from me!" he said. "Let her not have my blood!"

"What mean you?" said Dilvish.

"I knew not what she was when I wedded her," said Morin, "and when I learned, I loved her still. It was not in me to harm her. My servants left me and my castle fell into disrepair, but I could not do what should have been done. Instead I have been her jailer. I forgive you, Elfboot, for she has deceived you. I was drugged… You look to be a strong man, you've proven you are… I hope you are strong enough to do it."

Dilvish turned his head away from the sight and looked at Merytha, where she stood with her back against the bedpost.

"You lied to me," he said. "Vampire!"

"You've done it," she said. "You slew him! My jailer is dead!"

"Yes."

"Will you stay with me now?"

"No," said Dilvish.

"You must," she said. "I want you."

"That," said Dilvish. "I do believe."

"No, not that way. No, I want you to be my lord, All my life I have wanted one with your strength and your strange eyes," she said, "'in earthly flesh and blood.' Have I not been good to you?"

"I killed this man because of you. I would that I had not."

She shielded her eyes.

"Please stay!" she said. "My life would be empty if you did not… I must retire soon, to a dark, quiet place. Please!" She began to draw heavy breaths. "Please say that you will be here when I awaken tomorrow night."

Dilvish shook his head, slowly.

The room grew lighter.

Her pale eyes widened beneath her sheltering hand.

"You," she said, "you do not mean to harm me, do you?"

Again he shook his head.

"I have done enough harm this night. I must go, Merytha. There is but one cure for your condition and I cannot administer it. Good-bye."

"Do not go," she said. "I will sing to you. I will prepare fine meals. I will love you. I only want a little taste, sometimes, when…"

"Vampire," he said.

He heard her footsteps behind him on the stair.

A gray day was dawning about him when he entered the courtyard and placed his hand upon Black's neck.

He heard her gasping as he mounted.

"Do not go…" she said. "I love you."

The sun rose as he moved toward the opened gate.

He heard her shriek behind him.

He did not look back.

A Word from Zelazny

This fourth Dilvish story picks up the story from the end of "The Bells of Shoredan." This was the last of Dilvish to appear for fifteen years, following Zelazny's falling out with *Fantastic* and *Amazing*. "I had come to think of Dilvish as a *Fantastic Adventures* character and I did not continue his adventures elsewhere, save for a short piece entitled 'A Knight For Merytha.' "[1] "I did this one just for the hell of it about five years ago and gave it to a fanzine."[2] This story first appeared in the fanzine *Kallikanzaros*, which takes its name from Conrad the Kallikanzaros of ...*And Call Me Conrad* / *This Immortal*.

Notes

Tapers are slender candles. **Sandalwood** is an Indian tree cultivated for timber and its fragrant oil, a source of incense. **Doughty** means brave and persistent. **Prithee**, please, derives from "I pray thee." A **cuckold** is the husband of an adulteress, often regarded as an object of derision. The term derives from cuckoo, the bird that often lays its eggs in another bird's nest.

---

1 *Alternities #6*, Summer 1981.
2 Letter from Roger Zelazny to Henry Morrison dated March 30, 1971.

THE INJURED

Kronos #2, 1965 (fanzine).

The courtroom was packed for his trial. The judge had had to rap several times and then threaten to clear the court, before the silence arrived.

Arnie's counsel, Mister Hewitt, had told him that things would be bad, and sure enough, he was right.

The prosecutor tore into the psych-men whom Mister Hewitt had assured Arnie were unimpeachable, being the best that money could buy. Arnie squirmed in his chair and fingered the lobe of his ear until it was red and tingling. He hated being stared at. He despised being stared at continually. He was moderately distressed whenever he was even noticed at all.

Mister Hewitt had put a hand on his shoulder then and leaned close to him. His breath was warm on the tingling ear, and Arnie started suddenly from his chair. Flashbulbs popped. Arnie sat back down.

"Don't worry about all this double-talk, boy," Mister Hewitt had whispered. "This is just by-play. Try to take it easy, kid."

Arnie nodded his head slowly and leaned back.

She would be taking the stand soon, Arnie realized, and he could not bear to face her. He thought about it while the voices droned on. Then, carefully, attempting to look casual about the whole thing, he took his sunglasses from his inside coat pocket—and dropped them.

They rattled as they struck the hardwood tabletop, and the psych-man who was on the witness stand—whether for or against him, Arnie forgot—stopped in mid-sentence and stared at him. Arnie dropped his eyes as he felt all the people in the big room turn to look at him once more. He blushed deeply and pushed the guilty spectacles away. The psych-man resumed his lengthy medical discourse.

After a time, Arnie felt the tension ease. But *she* would be coming soon, he knew that, and he did not know how he would behave—or how *she* would take it, seeing him there, in front of all these people.

He fingered his ear once more and waited.

Finally, she was called. Arnie picked up his sunglasses and put them on. As she was wheeled up the aisle and sworn in (she could not raise her right hand because of the cast), Arnie saw that she, too, was wearing sunglasses. She tried not to look in his direction, but every now and then her head would shift slightly towards him and their eyes would meet, through the double dark windows they wore, and Arnie would feel a jolt, like electricity, arising from the soles of his feet.

"…Now, Miss Miles, would you please tell me in your own words exactly what happened!"

"Yes," (her voice was weak at first), "it was out by the third level of the In-Urban 90, at the place where it intersects with the speed-lane of Marginal 17. I was crossing it illegally on foot—I was aware of that—but it was such a slow time of day that I thought I could make it all right, and save myself maybe an hour. See, I had this date…"

"Please keep to the occurrence itself."

"Yes, sorry," she mumbled. "Well, I got hit. This car came along and bopped me. Clipped me a good one. I never did get the rej-number. It was going too fast. Driver probably didn't even know, anyhow—they're usually on autodrive out there in the speed-lane—and it wasn't really his fault, anyway. Anyhow, this man comes, running out across from the pedwalk, feels me all over, and carries me back of the road…"

"*Which* man are you referring to?"

"The one sitting over at that table, sir. The one wearing the shades." She indicated Arnie, then she turned away.

More bulbs popped.

"Yes, what happened then?"

"Well, he sets me down off on the side there and holds a hand-kerchief against this cut on my arm that was bleeding pretty hard. Then…"

"Question: At that time were you aware that he was not a med-man?"

"Yes, sir. I guess I was. He was wearing these coveralls, like he'd been working in a shop, and he didn't have no med-badge on."

"I see. Go on."

"Well, the people on the walk all came crowding up to look, like people do, and this man keeps wiping the blood off me and talking to me, like 'It'll be all right. Don't worry. They'll be here for you real soon,' he says, and like that."

"You noted his work-badge number at that time?"

"Yes, sir. While he was leaning over me, sir."

"Good. Now I have another question: Why did you not turn in his number right away?"

"Well, I was sort of in a state of shock at first and it kind of slipped my mind…"

"I note that your memory was suddenly in very good condition when the hospital attorney pointed out to you that you would be compounding a felony—that is to say, taking illegal advantage of another illegal act—by failing to disclose his number—"

The judge's gavel struck the bench.

"Permit me to remind you, Mister Prosecutor, that the witness is not on trial," he said.

"I apologize, your honor. It was poorly phrased. What I meant to say to the young lady was: After the, uh, shock wore off and you did inform the authorities concerning what had occurred, why did you give them an incorrect personal rej-number for this man?"

"Well, people have such long numbers these days that I just confused it…"

"Seven digits of it?"

Her mouth tightened. She stared up at him suddenly.

"That's right."

"Thank you. That is all."

Arnie sighed as she was wheeled back up the center aisle. He had not done nearly as well when he had told his own story.

There was a brief recess during which Mister Hewitt told him not to worry about the by-play and take it easy, kid.

He tried to, but it was exceedingly difficult. Then came the summaries, and then another recess.

The jury, of course, brought back a verdict of guilty. Mister Hewitt had instructed him to enter a plea of not guilty, by virtue of temporary insanity—which, as it turned out, worked in his favor when coupled with the testimony of the psych-men.

"Have you anything to say before I pass sentence?" asked the judge.

"No, sir, I don't," Arnie managed, "except that I'm sorry and I won't ever do it again. I don't know what came over me."

"Very good. Then hear the judgement: You are hereby sentenced to six months of hard analysis, followed by one year of group therapy.

You will report to the Central Medical Center at ten o'clock tomorrow morning for the first session."

"Thank you, sir. I will, sir," said Arnie.

The gavel banged and more flashbulbs exploded. Mister Hewitt led Arnie back through the judge's chambers (the judge was an old friend of his, from law school) and out through a back exit to a waiting taxi. He chuckled as they went.

"Stay introverted, stay in-directed, and agree," he said, "and after eight months you'll be a socy-therp trustee. Don't worry about it. You got off okay. What's an hour a day for the next year and a half? You can do a therp like that standing on your head."

Arnie nodded.

"Now that it's all over, though, I do have a question. You didn't want to answer it before the trial, but you can tell me—now that it's all over—without fear of prejudicing me: Why did you *really* do it? Why did you help her when you saw her lying there, eh?" He leered from beneath his whiteworm brows.

"I was drunk," said Arnie quickly. "I'd had one too many after work that day and I didn't know what I was doing."

"Hah!" Mister Hewitt slapped his thigh. "I figured it was something like that. Come on back to the office with me and we'll have one together."

Arnie decided it was a good idea.

Notes

This is an "If this goes on…" story, possibly inspired by a news story about a Good Samaritan being sued for rendering aid.

Paul Gilster, who edited the fanzine *Kronos*, recalls, "I simply wrote Zelazny a note and asked him if he had a story he could send me. I never dreamed I'd hear back from him, but I was a fan of his work and I thought 'why not?' To my amazement, he came right back with the story in question, and needless to say, I published it in my next issue. Before that, I'm sure he had never heard of me. I always appreciated his kindness to a young fan."[1]

---

1 Email from Paul Gilster to Dr. Christopher Kovacs, April 22, 2007.

DEVIL CAR

Manuscript title: "Morning of the Scarlet Swinger."
Galaxy, June 1965.
Nebula nominee, 1966 (short story).
§ *Jenny/Murdock*

Murdock sped across the Great Western Road Plain.
High above him the sun was a fiery yo-yo as he took the innumerable hillocks and rises of the Plain at better than a hundred-sixty miles an hour. He did not slow for anything, and Jenny's hidden eyes spotted all the rocks and potholes before they came to them, and she carefully adjusted their course, sometimes without his even detecting the subtle movement of the steering column beneath his hands.

Even through the dark-tinted windshield and the thick goggles he wore, the glare from the fused Plain burnt into his eyes, so that at times it seemed as if he were steering a very fast boat through night, beneath a brilliant alien moon, and that he was cutting his way across a lake of silver fire. Tall dust waves rose in his wake, hung in the air, and after a time settled once more.

"You are wearing yourself out," said the radio, "sitting there clutching the wheel that way, squinting ahead. Why don't you try to get some rest? Let me fog the shields. Go to sleep and leave the driving to me."

"No," he said, "I want it this way."

"All right," said Jenny. "I just thought I would ask."

"Thanks."

About a minute later the radio began playing—it was a soft, stringy sort of music.

"Cut that out!"

"Sorry, boss. Thought it might relax you."

"When I need relaxing, *I'll* tell *you*."

"Check, Sam. Sorry."

The silence seemed oppressive after its brief interruption. She was a good car, though, Murdock knew that. She was always concerned with his welfare, and she was anxious to get on with his quest.

She was made to look like a carefree Swinger sedan: bright red, gaudy, fast. But there were rockets under the bulges of her hood, and two fifty-caliber muzzles lurked just out of sight in the recesses beneath her headlamps; she wore a belt of five- and ten-second timed grenades across her belly; and in her trunk was a spray-tank containing a highly volatile naphthalic.

…For his Jenny was a specially designed deathcar, built for him by the Archengineer of the Geeyem Dynasty, far to the East, and all the cunning of that great artificer had gone into her construction.

❖   ❖   ❖

"We'll find it this time, Jenny," he said, "and I didn't mean to snap at you like I did."

"That's all right, Sam," said the delicate voice. "I am programmed to understand you."

They roared on across the Great Plain and the sun fell away to the west. All night and all day they had searched, and Murdock was tired. The last Fuel Stop/Rest Stop Fortress seemed so long ago, so far back…

Murdock leaned forward and his eyes closed.

The windows slowly darkened into complete opacity. The seat belt crept higher and drew him back away from the wheel. Then the seat gradually leaned backwards until he was reclining on a level plane. The heater came on as the night approached, later.

The seat shook him awake, a little before five in the morning.

"Wake up, Sam! Wake up!"

"What is it?" he mumbled.

"I picked up a broadcast twenty minutes ago. There was a recent car-raid out this way. I changed course immediately, and we are almost there."

"Why didn't you get me up right away?"

"You needed the sleep, and there was nothing you could do but get tense and nervous."

"Okay, you're probably right. Tell me about the raid."

"Six vehicles, proceeding westward, were apparently ambushed by an undetermined number of wild cars sometime last night. The Patrol Copter was reporting it from above the scene and I listened in. All the vehicles were stripped and drained and their brains were smashed, and their passengers were all apparently killed too. There were no signs of movement."

"How far is it now?"

"Another two or three minutes."

The windshields came clear once more, and Murdock stared as far ahead through the night as the powerful lamps could cut.

"I see something," he said, after a few moments.

"This is the place," said Jenny, and she began to slow down.

They drew up beside the ravaged cars. His seat belt unstrapped and the door sprang open on his side.

"Circle around, Jenny," he said, "and look for heat tracks. I won't be long."

❖ ❖ ❖

The door slammed and Jenny moved away from him. He snapped on his pocket torch and moved toward the wrecked vehicles.

The Plain was like a sand-strewn dance floor—hard and gritty—beneath his feet. There were many skid-marks, and a spaghetti-work of tire tracks lay all about the area.

A dead man sat behind the wheel of the first car. His neck was obviously broken. The smashed watch on his wrist said 2:24. There were three persons—two women and a young man—lying about forty feet away. They had been run down as they tried to flee from their assaulted vehicles.

Murdock moved on, inspected the others. All six cars were upright. Most of the damage was to their bodies. The tires and wheels had been removed from all of them, as well as essential portions of their engines; the gas tanks stood open, siphoned empty; the spare tires were gone from the sprung trunks. There were no living passengers.

Jenny pulled up beside him and her door opened.

"Sam," she said, "pull the brain leads on that blue car, the third one back. It's still drawing some energy from an ancillary battery, and I can hear it broadcasting."

"Okay."

Murdock went back and tore the leads free. He returned to Jenny and climbed into the driver's seat.

"Did you find anything?"

"Some traces, heading northwest."

"Follow them."

The door slammed and Jenny turned in that direction.

They drove for about five minutes in silence. Then Jenny said "There were eight cars in that convoy."

"What?"

"I just heard it on the news. Apparently two of the cars communicated with the wild ones on an off-band. They threw in with them. They gave away their location and turned on the others at the time of the attack."

"What about their passengers?"

"They probably monoed them before they joined the pack."

Murdock lit a cigarette, his hands shaking.

"Jenny, what makes a car run wild?" he asked. "Never knowing when it will get its next fueling—or being sure of finding spare parts for its auto-repair unit? Why do they do it?"

"I do not know, Sam. I have never thought about it."

❖   ❖   ❖

"Ten years ago the Devil Car, their leader, killed my brother in a raid on his Gas Fortress," said Murdock, "and I've hunted that black Caddy ever since. I've searched for it from the air and I've searched on foot. I've used other cars. I've carried heat trackers and missiles. I even laid mines. But always it's been too fast or too smart or too strong for me. Then I had you built."

"I knew you hated it very much. I always wondered why," Jenny said.

Murdock drew on his cigarette.

"I had you specially programmed and armored and armed to be the toughest, fastest, smartest thing on wheels, Jenny. You're the Scarlet Lady. You're the one car can take the Caddy and his whole pack. You've got fangs and claws of the kind they've never met before. This time I'm going to get them."

"You could have stayed home, Sam, and let me do the hunting."

"No. I know I could have, but I want to be there. I want to give the orders, to press some of the buttons myself, to watch that Devil

Car burn away to a metal skeleton. How many people, how many cars has it smashed? We've lost count. I've got to get it, Jenny!"

"I'll find it for you, Sam."

They sped on, at around two hundred miles per hour.

"How's the fuel level, Jenny?"

"Plenty there, and I have not yet drawn upon the auxiliary tanks. Do not worry."

"—The track is getting stronger," she added.

"Good. How's the weapons system?"

"Red light, all around. Ready to go."

Murdock snubbed out his cigarette and lit another.

"...Some of them carry dead people strapped inside," said Murdock, "so they'll look like decent cars with passengers. The black Caddy does it all the time, and it changes them pretty regularly. It keeps its interior refrigerated so they'll last."

"You know a lot about it, Sam."

"It fooled my brother with phony passengers and phony plates. Got him to open his Gas Fortress to it that way. Then the whole pack attacked. It's painted itself red and green and blue and white, on different occasions, but it always goes back to black, sooner or later. It doesn't like yellow or brown or two-tone. I've a list of almost every phony plate it's ever used. It's even driven the big freeways right into towns and fueled up at regular gas stops. They often get its number as it tears away from them, just as the attendant goes up on the driver's side for his money. It can fake dozens of human voices. They can never catch it afterwards, though, because it's souped itself up too well. It always makes it back here to the Plain and loses them. It's even raided used car lots—"

❖   ❖   ❖

Jenny turned sharply in her course.

"Sam! The trail is quite strong now. *This* way! It goes off in the direction of those mountains."

"Follow!" said Murdock.

For a long time then Murdock was silent. The first inklings of morning began in the east. The pale morning star was a white thumbtack on a blue board behind them. They began to climb a gentle slope.

"Get it, Jenny. Go get it," urged Murdock.

"I think we will," she said.

The angle of the slope increased. Jenny slowed her pace to match the terrain, which was becoming somewhat bumpy. "What's the matter?" asked Murdock.

"It's harder going here," she said, "also, the trail is getting more difficult to follow."

"Why's that?"

"There is still a lot of background radiation in these parts," she told him, "and it is throwing off my tracking system."

"Keep trying, Jenny."

"The track seems to go straight toward the mountains."

"Follow it, follow it!"

They slowed some more.

"I am all fouled up now, Sam," she said. "I have just lost the trail."

"It must have a stronghold somewhere around here—a cave or something like that—where it can be sheltered overhead. It's the only way it could have escaped aerial detection all these years."

"What should I do?"

"Go as far forward as you can and scan for low openings in the rock. Be wary. Be ready to attack in an instant."

They climbed into the low foothills. Jenny's aerial rose high into the air, and the moths of steel cheesecloth unfolded their wings and danced and spun about it, bright there in the morning light.

"Nothing yet," said Jenny, "and we can't go much further."

"Then we'll cruise along the length of it and keep scanning."

"To the right or to the left?"

"I don't know. Which way would you go if you were a renegade car on the lam?"

"I do not know."

"Pick one. It doesn't matter."

"To the right, then," she said, and they turned in that direction.

After half an hour the night was dropping away behind the mountains. To his right morning was exploding at the far end of the Plains, fracturing the sky into all the colors of autumn trees. Murdock drew a squeeze bottle of hot coffee, of the kind spacers had once used, from beneath the dashboard.

"Sam, I think I have found something."

"What? Where?"

"Ahead, to the left of that big boulder, a declivity with some kind of opening at its end."

"Okay, baby, make for it. Rockets ready."

They pulled abreast of the boulder, circled around its far side, headed downhill.

"A cave, or a tunnel," he said. "Go slow—"

"Heat! Heat!" she said. "I'm tracking again!"

"I can even see the tire marks, lots of them!" said Murdock. "This is it!"

They moved toward the opening.

"Go in, but go slowly," he ordered. "Blast the first thing that moves."

They entered the rocky portal, moving on sand now. Jenny turned off her visible lights and switched to infra-red. An i-r lens rose before the windshield, and Murdock studied the cave. It was about twenty feet high and wide enough to accommodate perhaps three cars going abreast. The floor changed from sand to rock, but it was smooth and fairly level. After a time it sloped upward.

"There's some light ahead," he whispered.

"I know."

"A piece of the sky, I think."

They crept toward it, Jenny's engine but the barest sigh within the great chambers of rock.

They stopped at the threshold to the light. The i-r shield dropped again.

It was a sand-and-shale canyon that he looked upon. Huge slantings and overhangs of rock hid all but the far end from any eye in the sky. The light was pale, at the far end, and there was nothing unusual beneath it.

But nearer…

Murdock blinked.

❖   ❖   ❖

Nearer, in the dim light of morning and in the shadows, stood the greatest junkheap Murdock had ever seen in his life.

Pieces of cars, of every make and model, were heaped into a small mountain before him. There were batteries and tires and cables and shock absorbers; there were fenders and bumpers and headlamps and headlamp housings; there were doors and windshields and cylinders and pistons, carburetors, generators, voltage regulators, and oil pumps.

Murdock stared.

"Jenny," he whispered, "we've found the graveyard of the autos!"

A very old car, which Murdock had not even distinguished from the junk during that first glance, jerked several feet in their direction and stopped as suddenly. The sound of rivet heads scoring ancient brake drums screeched in his ears. Its tires were completely bald, and the left front one was badly in need of air. Its right front headlamp was broken and there was a crack in its windshield. It stood there before the heap, its awakened engine making a terrible rattling noise.

"What's happening?" asked Murdock. "What is it?"

"He is talking to me," said Jenny. "He is very old. His speedometer has been all the way around so many times that he forgets the number of miles he has seen. He hates people, whom he says have abused him whenever they could. He is the guardian of the graveyard. He is too old to go raiding any more, so he has stood guard over the spare parts heap for many years. He is not the sort who can repair himself, as the younger ones do, so he must rely on their charity and their auto-repair units. He wants to know what I want here."

"Ask him where the others are."

But as he said it, Murdock heard the sound of many engines turning over, until the valley was filled with the thunder of their horsepower.

"They are parked on the other side of the heap," she said. "They are coming now."

"Hold back until I tell you to fire," said Murdock, as the first one—a sleek yellow Chrysler—nosed around the heap.

Murdock lowered his head to the steering wheel, but kept his eyes open behind his goggles.

"Tell him that you came here to join the pack and that you've monoed your driver. Try to get the black Caddy to come into range."

"He will not do it," she said. "I am talking with him now. He can broadcast just as easily from the other side of the pile, and he says he is sending the six biggest members of the pack to guard me while he decides what to do. He has ordered me to leave the tunnel and pull ahead into the valley."

"Go ahead, then—slowly."

They crept forward.

❖   ❖   ❖

Two Lincolns, a powerful-looking Pontiac, and two Mercs joined the Chrysler—three cars on each side of them, in position to ram.

"Has he given you any idea how many there are on the other side?"

"No. I asked, but he will not tell me."

"Well, we'll just have to wait then."

He stayed slumped, pretending to be dead. After a time, his already tired shoulders began to ache. Finally, Jenny spoke:

"He wants me to pull around the far end of the pile," she said, "now that they have cleared the way, and to head into a gap in the rock which he will indicate. He wants to have his auto-mech go over me."

"We can't have that," said Murdock, "but head around the pile. I'll tell you what to do when I've gotten a glimpse of the other side."

The two Mercs and the Big Chief drew aside and Jenny crept past them. Murdock stared upwards from the corner of his eye, up at the towering mound of junk they were passing. A couple well-placed rockets on either end could topple it, but the auto-mech would probably clear it eventually.

They rounded the lefthand end of the pile.

Something like forty-five cars were facing them at about a hundred-twenty yards' distance, to the right and ahead. They had fanned out. They were blocking the exit around the other end of the pile, and the six guards in back of him now blocked the way behind Murdock.

On the far side of the farthest rank of the most distant cars an ancient black Caddy was parked.

It had been beaten forth from assembly during a year when the apprentice-engineers were indeed thinking big. Huge it was, and shiny, and a skeleton's face smiled from behind its wheel. Black it was, and gleaming chromium, and its headlamps were like dusky jewels or the eyes of insects. Every plane and curve shimmered with power, and its great fishtailed rear end seemed ready to slap at the sea of shadows behind it on an instant's notice, as it sprang forward for its kill.

"That's it!" whispered Murdock. "The Devil Car!"

"He is big!" said Jenny. "I have never seen a car that big!"

They continued to move forward.

"He wants me to head into that opening and park," she said.

"Head toward it, slowly. But don't go into it," said Murdock.

❖   ❖   ❖

They turned and inched toward the opening. The other cars stood, the sounds of their engines rising and falling.

"Check all weapons systems."

"Red, all around."

The opening was twenty-five feet away.

"When I say 'now', go into neutral steer and turn one hundred-eighty degrees—fast. They can't be expecting that. They don't have it themselves. Then open up with the fifty-calibers and fire your rockets at the Caddy, turn at a right angle and start back the way we came, and spray the naphtha as we go, and fire on the six guards…

"Now!" he cried, leaping up in his seat.

He was slammed back as they spun, and he heard the clattering of her guns before his head cleared. By then, flames were leaping up in the distance.

Jenny's guns were extruded now and turning on their mounts, spraying the line of vehicles with hundreds of leaden hammers. She shook, twice, as she discharged two rockets from beneath her partly opened hood. Then they were moving forward, and eight or nine of the cars were rushing downhill toward them.

She turned again in neutral steer and sprang back in the direction from which they had come, around the southeast corner of the pile. Her guns were hammering at the now retreating guards, and in the wide read view mirror Murdock could see that a wall of flame was towering high behind them.

"You missed it!" he cried. "You missed the black Caddy! Your rockets hit the cars in front of it and it backed off!"

"I know! I'm sorry!"

"You had a clear shot!"

"I know! I missed!"

They rounded the pile just as two of the guard cars vanished into the tunnel. Three more lay in smoking ruin. The sixth had evidently preceded the other two out through the passage.

"Here it comes now!" cried Murdock. "Around the other end of the pile! Kill it! Kill it!"

The ancient guardian of the graveyard—it looked like a Ford, but he couldn't be sure—moved forward with a dreadful chattering sound and interposed itself in the line of fire.

"My range is blocked."

❖   ❖   ❖

"Smash that junkheap and cover the tunnel! Don't let the Caddy escape!"

"I can't!" she said.

"Why not?"

"I just *can't!*"

"That's an order! Smash it and cover the tunnel!"

Her guns swivelled and she shot out the tires beneath the ancient car.

The Caddy shot past and into the passageway.

"You let it get by!" he screamed. "Get after it!"

"All right, Sam! I'm doing it! Don't yell. *Please don't yell!*"

She headed for the tunnel. Inside, he could hear the sound of a giant engine racing away, growing softer in the distance.

"Don't fire here in the tunnel! If you hit it we may be bottled in!"

"I know. I won't."

"Drop a couple ten-second grenades and step on the gas. Maybe we can seal in whatever's left moving back there."

Suddenly they shot ahead and emerged into daylight. There was no sign of any other vehicle about.

"Find its track," he said, "and start chasing it."

There was an explosion up the hill behind him, within the mountain. The ground trembled, then it was still once more.

"There are so many tracks…" she said.

"You know the one I want. The biggest, the widest, the hottest! Find it! Run it down!"

"I think I have it, Sam."

"Okay. Proceed as rapidly as possible for this terrain."

Murdock found a squeeze bottle of bourbon and took three gulps. Then he lit a cigarette and glared into the distance.

"Why did you miss it?" he asked softly. "Why did you miss it, Jenny?"

She did not answer immediately. He waited.

Finally, "Because he is not an 'it' to me," she said. "He has done much damage to cars and people, and that is terrible. But there is something about him, something—noble. The way he has fought the whole world for his freedom. Sam, keeping that pack of vicious machines in line, stopping at nothing to maintain himself that way—without a master—for as long as he can remain unsmashed, unbeaten. Sam, for a moment back there I wanted to join his pack, to run with him across the Great Road Plains, to use my rockets against the gates of the Gas Forts for him... But I could not mono you, Sam. I was built for you. I am too domesticated. I am too weak. I could not shoot him though, and I misfired the rockets on purpose. But I could never mono you, Sam, really."

"Thanks," he said, "you over-programmed ashcan. Thanks a lot!"

"I am sorry, Sam."

"Shut up—No, don't, not yet. First tell me what you're going to do if we find 'him'."

"I don't know."

"Well think it over fast. You see that dust cloud ahead of us as well as I do, and you'd better speed up."

They shot forward.

"Wait till I call Detroit. They'll laugh themselves silly, till I claim the refund."

"I am *not* of inferior construction or design. You know that. I am just more..."

"'Emotional'," supplied Murdock.

"...Than I thought I would be," she finished. "I had not really met many cars, except for young ones, before I was shipped to you. I did not know what a wild car was like, and I had never smashed *any* cars before—just targets and things like that. I was young and..."

"'Innocent'," said Murdock. "Yeah. Very touching. Get ready to kill the next car we meet. If it happens to be your boyfriend and you hold your fire, then he'll kill us."

"I will try, Sam."

The car ahead had stopped. It was the yellow Chrysler. Two of its tires had gone flat and it was parked, lopsided, waiting.

"Leave it!" snarled Murdock, as the hood clicked open. "Save the ammo for something that might fight back."

They sped past it.

"Did it say anything?"

"Machine profanity," she said. "I've only heard it once or twice, and it would be meaningless to you."

❖ ❖ ❖

He chuckled. "Cars actually swear at each other?"

"Occasionally," she said. "I imagine the lower sort indulge in it more frequently, especially on freeways and turnpikes when they become congested."

"Let me hear a swear-word."

"I will not. What kind of car do you think I am, anyway?"

"I'm sorry," said Murdock. "You're a lady. I forgot."

There was an audible click within the radio.

They raced forward on the level ground that lay before the foot of the mountains. Murdock took another drink, then switched to coffee.

"Ten years," he muttered, "ten years…"

The trail swung in a wide curve as the mountains jogged back and the foothills sprang up high beside them.

It was over almost before he knew it.

As they passed a huge, orange-colored stone massif, sculpted like an upside-down toadstool by the wind, there was a clearing to the right.

It shot forward at them—the Devil Car. It had lain in ambush, seeing that it could not outrun the Scarlet Lady, and it rushed toward a final collision with its hunter.

Jenny skidded sideways as her brakes caught with a scream and a smell of smoke, and her fifty-calibers were firing, and her hood sprang open and her front wheels rose up off the ground as the rockets leapt wailing ahead, and she spun around three times, her rear bumper scraping the saltsand plain, and the third and last time she fired her remaining rockets into the smouldering wreckage on the hillside, and she came to a rest on all four wheels; and her fifty-calibers kept firing until they were emptied, and then a steady clicking sound came from them for a full minute afterwards, and then all lapsed into silence.

Murdock sat there shaking, watching the gutted, twisted wreck blaze against the sky.

"You did it, Jenny. You killed him. You killed me the Devil Car," he said.

But she did not answer him. Her engine started once more and she turned toward the southeast and headed for the Fuel Stop/Rest Stop Fortress that lay in that civilized direction.

❖   ❖   ❖

For two hours they drove in silence, and Murdock drank all his bourbon and all his coffee and smoked all his cigarettes.

"Jenny, say something," he said. "What's the matter? Tell me."

There was a click, and her voice was very soft:

"Sam—he talked to me as he came down the hill…" she said.

Murdock waited, but she did not say anything else.

"Well, what did he say?" he asked.

"He said, 'Say you will mono your passenger and I will swerve by you'," she told him. "He said, 'I want you, Scarlet Lady—to run with me, to raid with me. Together they will never catch us,' and I killed him."

Murdock was silent.

"He only said that to delay my firing though, did he not? He said that to stop me, so that he could smash us both when he went smash himself, did he not? He could not have meant it, could he, Sam?"

"Of course not," said Murdock, "of course not. It was too late for him to swerve."

"Yes, I suppose it was—do you think though, that he really wanted me to run with him, to raid with him—before everything, I mean—back there?"

"Probably, baby. You're pretty well-equipped."

"Thanks," she said, and turned off again.

Before she did though, he heard a strange mechanical sound, falling into the rhythms of profanity or prayer.

Then he shook his head and lowered it, softly patting the seat beside him with his still unsteady hand.

A Word from Zelazny

"[This] was an original piece, playing variations on easily available ideas involving cars and computer viruses and AI psychological problems."[1]

"I did a story a long time ago that Fred Pohl published in *Galaxy* as 'Devil Car'. (My original title had been 'Morning of the Scarlet Swinger'. *C'est la guerre*.)"[2]

"I was involved in a horrible automobile accident at one point in my life where I absolutely totalled the car; and while I was convalescing I wrote [this] story. It involves a car, a computerized, programmed thing where the car drives itself."[3]

Although Zelazny denied creating automobile myths, he said, "Do I consider cars as symbolic of something? A car may well be a death symbol in some of my stories. If I'm looking for a good way to get rid of a character, an automobile accident generally will occur to me. But no, in my personal life I do not see them as symbolic. They're just machines from a practical standpoint. With sinister overtones."[4]

Notes

Murdock and Jenny return in "The Last of the Wild Ones."

Naphthalic refers to naphtha, a volatile, distillate of crude oil. **Declivity** is a downward slope. A **massif** is a complex block of rocks that resists erosion.

1 *Gone To Earth*, 1991.
2 *Unicorn Variations*, 1983.
3 *Phantasmicom #2*, Winter 1970.
4 *Extrapolation* Vol 43 No 1, Spring 2002.

BLONDEL DE NESLE

Written 1955–60 for *Chisel in the Sky;* previously unpublished.

(Of Time and the Artist)

"Troubadour,
in the dungeon of my desires,
luteless I lie.
The straw and the feet across the straw,
token of my estate,—
pathetic jungle, pathetic beast.
One time I, Blondel de Nesle, with my playing
soothed the heart of a lion
(that Lion of Christendom I here have now deserted),
and luteless now I lie in fear of my ferret's rage!
(Could she have done this to me, knowingly?
my fairest ferret? she?)
Aye. She is woman and well-read.
And I, Blondel de Nesle (old Nesle's son,
greatest of troubadours),
deserting the claw-track of my master, here,
for this Cornish tower, lie
signaling in treason hand
for ferret Time to hold and halt
(holding me as I hold her, that most fair dame,
my Sylvia).—'I bid thee kiss my brow.'—
Ah! that kiss! (And Judas? why think I on thee?

old red-beard?) A thorn! a thorn i' the brow, most surely!
of Richard my master, and lying Lord knows where!
Here I in lap of lovely
and most wicked lady lie… 'A mole? Oh my!'
And on the hill, *that* sound…
Who dares to lift a lute out there?
(or anywhere *my* ear may hear?)
beyond the reach of sight?
'Tis Herbert,' she says, sighing aloud.
(A lesson methinks he needs.)
—Again she sighs! (Good Christ!
he strums abominably!)
Downstairs, hm, yes, my lute's since Sunday laid,
there i' the pantry (—*she* liketh not its yawl!).
A lesson, indeed, he—*they* shall have!
And Richard, m'leige, your faithful bard,
old Nesle's son, most stout!
(greatest in song and revelry)
with but a word or three with his lute,
be off for Lombardy!"

Notes

Blondel de Nesle was a 12th century French poet and troubadour, and a favorite of King Richard I (Richard Lion-Heart). After Leopold V of Austria captured and imprisoned Richard, legend has it that Blondel wandered the German countryside, singing a song known only to him and his master, King Richard. When he heard a verse sung from a prison in response, he knew that Richard had to be held there, and he was able to tell the English, thereby initiating his rescue.

CHOU DE MAL

Written 1955–60 for *Chisel in the Sky;* previously unpublished.

Perhaps it is a folly of the language,
for yes, the stale trope was better said:
I seem to be a weather-blasted cabbage,
with love, the green worm, eating through my head.

The mighty weight of flowers with their baggage
has quashed the fragrant soul that veget'ed;
however, now, this inkling of slow homage
tunnels its bright passage through my head.

Notes

Chou del mal means spoiled or bad cabbage. A **trope** in this context refers
to an allusion, metaphor and other figure that isn't meant to be taken literally, such as, "I seem to be a weather-blasted cabbage."

OF TIME AND THE YAN

The Magazine of Fantasy & Science Fiction, June 1965.

The last Yan on Mars sat alone in a room.
There was a knock on the door.
"Come in," he threeked.

❖   ❖   ❖

The Earthman looked about, squinting into the dimness.

"Hello?"

"I am here," threeked the Yan, moving toward him.

The Earthman pressed back against the door, making little noises deep in his throat.

"You're real!" he decided.

"I am a Yan," replied the other, "and you are a man, late of the late green star."

"Yes, late—very late… There were two expeditions…"

"Unfortunate," answered the Yan. "Both ships were destroyed when they landed."

The man covered his face.

"So was mine."

He was silent for a long time.

"The atmosphere," he said, finally. "It must have oxidized the fuel—somehow."

"Of course."

The Yan waited patiently. Finally, the man spoke again.

"Could you—would you—help me?"

"How?" asked the Yan.

"I need shovels. I need help—to dig three graves."

There was blood on the man's arm.

"How is it that you lived?"

181

"I left the ship immediately, to see if the air was breathable. I crossed a little hill. Something hit me on the shoulder. There was a bright flash…A noise…My wife and children…"

"I will get shovels," threeked the Yan. "I will be glad to bury more Earthmen."

❖   ❖   ❖

The Yan sleeched across the field, beside the dripping man. The sky was a blizzard of dancing motes; they obscured the stars, stretching like a gossamer curtain from horizon to dark horizon.

"For two months your world has stopped the sunlight and the light of the stars. Will it ever dissipate?"

"I don't know."

"Why did you come here?"

"I knew it was going to happen," said the man. "I was an officer at the Base. I stole the ship, took my family…"

"You deserted?"

"To save their lives."

"I see," answered the Yan. "Shall we dig their graves here?"

The man nodded. He did not look at the ship.

He lifted pound after painful pound of the sugar-white ocean.

The sand churned; the Yan spun his double-bladed shovel like a paddle wheel.

The sun entered the Way of Earth, like a red balloon seen through frosted glass, and the Earthman looked up from his labors.

"Yan, Yan, you are making a mistake," he wheezed. "You are digging four graves."

"I am not making a mistake," answered the Yan.

The man fetched the charred bodies from the smouldering rubble. He dragged and carried them to the gravesides.

The Yan watched.

He crossed the arms over the chests and lowered them into the holes.

"Yan, please help me to cover them."

The Yan threw dirt in their faces.

"It is done," said the Earthman.

"No!" threeked the Yan.

The Earthman looked at him, a new darkness behind his blood-shot gaze. He fumbled at his belt.

"No, Yan. Not me. Not me!"

"Yes, Earthman, you."

"Why? What would you gain by killing me?"

"I do not understand 'gain'. Why not kill you? You are all that remains of Earth, but a silver net in the sky. —And I am the last. The last Yan on Mars. I will bury Earth here. The net will come undone. Yan shall be last on Mars."

The Earthman pointed his gun at him.

"No, I'll kill you first."

The Yan threeked a laugh.

"Only Time can kill a Yan."

The Earthman fired three times.

The Yan threeked in merriment.

The man fired his remaining cartridges.

"Now you will get into the hole, and I will take your life away."

The Earthman made small noises.

"Get into your grave!"

Unwillingly, his legs moved. Involuntarily, he stepped into the hole and turned his head upwards.

"Good-bye, Earth," threeked the Yan.

"Wait!" cried the man. "Give me a moment, please—to pray!"

"I do not know 'pray'," threeked the Yan. "Do it and I will watch, if it does not take you long."

The man bowed his head. He rested his hands on the lip of the excavation.

"Are you finished?" asked the Yan.

"Yes," answered the man, straightening, his fists clenched.

Once more, he looked up at the Yan.

Then he threw two handfuls of sand into all his violet eyes.

The Yan threeked in anger and sleeched back.

Gathering his strength, the man leaped from the hole and seized the shovel. He smashed the Yan's head.

A dark, sticky fluid drenched the blade.

The Yan lay still.

The Earthman pushed him into the hole, then covered him over. He planted the shovel in the ground and staggered back toward the dwelling-place.

"You were right," he muttered. "It only took time."

The Way of Earth flamed above him.

❖   ❖   ❖

The last man on Mars sat alone in the gloom.

There was a knock on the door.

"There is no time," came the threek.

Notes

Described as the world's shortest horror story, Fredric Brown wrote, "The last man on Earth sat alone in a room. There was a knock on the door…" in the December 1948 issue of *Thrilling Wonder Tales*. He wasn't the first to do so, because Thomas Bailey Aldrich wrote the following around 1870: "A woman is sitting alone in a house. She knows she is alone in the whole world; every other living thing is dead. The doorbell rings."

The Thing That on the Highways

Written 1965–68; previously unpublished.

The thing that on the highways
pushes traffic
pushed me too far,
that yo-yo's us in high-rise guts,
dropped me too fast.

Notes

Zelazny's fiction and poetry were influenced by his involvement in a serious car accident and other near-misses. See the notes for "Devil Car" and "Auto-Da-Fé."

THE DRAWING

Algol #10, September 1965.

There were ghosts all around me, and I knew somehow that the stranger at my side was the Wandering Jew.

Neither of us spoke. We watched the ceremony.

The speeches were made, and despite the quiet sobriety of the speakers, the occasion filled me with unease.

My time had come, as it had for the big engines.

Memories drummed in my mind, and thunder grumbled in the gray sky and some of the drops on my cheeks were rain.

The railroad spike was designed in 1831 by Robert L. Stevens, of the Camden and Amboy Railroad.

The crowd was small, mostly ex-railroad men like myself; and there were invisible satellites circling the Earth, high above our little storm.

The last speaker was beginning the last speech. The symbolic hydraulic plier was made ready. The ground was hard-packed and sandy. The air was cool. There were ghosts all around me.

All my life I worked in the big car-barns, where the wheels rattle and are still, where the smell is grease and steel, wet wood and manure, rotten vegetables and coal dust, where the accidents are always bad ones.

I knew them at midnight and early morning. I knew them in snow and the blaze of summer. I knew the last of the hoboes, and I knew all their songs. I used to hear underground gossip from all over the wide country.

Man had gone from the wheel to the rocket, from the freight car to the pneumatic tube, the ground-effect machine, the pipeline, the beltway.

You must have stopped at some time or other in your life, some-where, by the round sign with the "X" in the middle and the blink-ing red light above. There was a bar across your path and a parade of names went by: Burlington, NYC, C&O, Illinois Central, Western Maryland, Great Northern, Lackawanna (Route of Phoebe Snow), Pennsylvania, Chief, Grand Canyon Lines, ATSF, Missouri Pacific (Route of the Eagles), Gulf Mobile and Ohio, Pacific Fruit Express, N & W, Nickel Plate, Monongahela, B&O, Lehigh Valley, Pittsburgh & Lake Erie, and all the others. There were boxcars, flatcars, oil cars, cat-tle cars, Pullman cars, freezer cars, the big engine, the little caboose.

We stood and watched and listened, and didn't listen. It rained harder.

They moved down onto the track and I turned to the man at my side.

"Was it like this the last time you were here?" I asked him.

"No," he replied, watching. "There was revelry."

"What can this mean to you? The shifting of a sand or two? The batting of an eye?"

He shook his head.

"The passing of a mode of transportation. The end of an order. A reminder that almost everything comes to this."

"Rather masochistic, aren't you?"

It could have been the lightning reflected in his eyes that made them seem to flash so.

"Or proud," he replied, and was taller somehow.

I shrank back.

"I'm not," I said. "I'm not much of anything anymore."

"I know," he said, "for I know the lonely, and I pity them."

The machine was started. It lowered itself for its single, big bite.

"It was on May 10th, 1869 that the Central Pacific and Union Pacific Railroads were joined here," he said.

"I know."

It struck metal, bit, raised itself.

It came up slowly, resisting.

The man from the Smithsonian accepted the recently-explanted, shining symbol it had just drawn from the ground. The local light-ning of flashbulbs competed with that in the heavens.

The man at my side had winced as the spike was drawn from the cross-tie.

He touched his forehead, turned away.

"Are you leaving already?"

"Yes, I've seen what I came to see."

"Good traveling, then."

"The same to you."

He walked away and I stood there in the rain. The iron horse now thundered along the tracks of history. It had been my work all my life, and vice-versa.

Now I was alone, and I realized suddenly that I had loved those ugly, smoke-belching brutes with their raucous whistles and traditions. The drawing of the golden spike was completed, the crowd began to disperse, to move past me and away.

There were ghosts all around me.

Notes

This is one of a few stories inspired by Antoine de Saint-Exupéry's essay "The Tool," from *Wind, Sand and Stars*.[1] Saint-Exupéry said that technological advances eventually permeate a society, but these tools can always be improved and replaced. As an example, he observed that the locomotive took time to integrate into people's lives. In turn, automobiles and airplanes for the most part have replaced railroads.

The Wandering Jew appeared in the earlier tale "The Borgia Hand." Having taunted Jesus on the way to the Crucifixion, he was cursed to wander the earth until the Second Coming. **Robert L. Stevens** designed the inverted-T rail and the railroad spike. On May 10, 1869, he drove the golden spike that completed the transcontinental railway line at Promontory Summit, Utah. Names of numerous railway companies figure in the story.

---

1 *Science Fiction Parade*, September 1964.

Indian Days in KY

Written 1955–60 for *Chisel in the Sky;* previously unpublished.
Substantially revised to become "Our Wintered Way through Evening,
and Burning Bushes Along It" as featured in the story "The Graveyard Heart."

Winter spun washes whiten
in tunnels of headlight.
Silhouettes unseal their outline.
Darkness, like an absence of faces, pours
from the opened home;
it seeps through shattered pine
and flows through splintered maple.

Perhaps it is a culling
from many sleeping intensities
that soaks upon this road
in weather born excess.
Or perhaps the great Anti-Life
learns to paint in a vengeance,
running icicle down the gargoyle eye.
For properly speaking,
no one can confront himself *in toto*…

But the sky, great God! the sky!
It burns in cool statue on the ground!

THIS MOMENT OF THE STORM

The Magazine of Fantasy & Science Fiction, June 1966.
Hugo nominee 1967 (novelette), Nebula nominee 1967 (novelette).

Back on Earth, my old philosophy prof—possibly because he'd misplaced his lecture notes—came into the classroom one day and scrutinized his sixteen victims for the space of half a minute. Satisfied then, that a sufficiently profound tone had been established, he asked:

"What is a man?"

He had known exactly what he was doing. He'd had an hour and a half to kill, and eleven of the sixteen were coeds (nine of them in liberal arts, and the other two stuck with an Area Requirement).

One of the other two, who was in the pre-med program, proceeded to provide a strict biological classification.

The prof (McNitt was his name, I suddenly recall) nodded then, and asked:

"Is that all?"

And there was his hour and a half.

I learned that Man is a Reasoning Animal, Man is the One Who Laughs, Man is greater than beasts but less than angels, Man is the one who watches himself watch himself doing things he knows are absurd (this from a Comparative Lit gal), Man is the culture-transmitting animal, Man is the spirit which aspires, affirms, loves, the one who uses tools, buries his dead, devises religions, and the one who tries to define himself. (That last from Paul Schwartz, my roommate—which I thought pretty good, on the spur of the moment. Wonder whatever became of Paul?)

Anyhow, to most of these I say "perhaps" or "partly, but —" or just plain "crap!" I still think mine was the best, because I had a chance to try it out, on Tierra del Cygnus, Land of the Swan…

I'd said, "Man is the sum total of everything he has done, wishes to do or not to do, and wishes he had done, or hadn't."

Stop and think about it for a minute. It's purposely as general as the others, but it's got room in it for the biology and the laughing and the aspiring, as well as the culture-transmitting, the love, and the room full of mirrors, and the defining. I even left the door open for religion, you'll note. But it's limiting, too. Ever met an oyster to whom the final phrases apply?

Tierra del Cygnus, Land of the Swan—delightful name.

Delightful place too, for quite awhile…

It was there that I saw Man's definitions, one by one, wiped from off the big blackboard, until only mine was left.

…My radio had been playing more static than usual. That's all.

For several hours there was no other indication of what was to come.

My hundred-thirty eyes had watched Betty all morning, on that clear, cool spring day with the sun pouring down its honey and light-ning upon the amber fields, flowing through the streets, invading western store-fronts, drying curbstones, and washing the olive and umber buds that speared the skin of the trees there by the road-way; and the light that wrung the blue from the flag before Town Hall made orange mirrors out of windows, chased purple and violet patches across the shoulders of Saint Stephen's Range, some thirty miles distant, and came down upon the forest at its feet like some supernatural madman with a million buckets of paint—each of a different shade of green, yellow, orange, blue and red—to daub with miles-wide brushes at its heaving sea of growth.

Mornings the sky is cobalt, midday is turquoise, and sunset is emeralds and rubies, hard and flashing. It was halfway between cobalt and seamist at 1100 hours, when I watched Betty with my hundred-thirty eyes and saw nothing to indicate what was about to be. There was only that persistent piece of static, accompanying the piano and strings within my portable.

It's funny how the mind personifies, engenders. Ships are always women: You say, "She's a good old tub," or, "She's a fast, tough num-ber, this one," slapping a bulwark and feeling the aura of femininity that clings to the vessel's curves; or, conversely, "He's a bastard to start, that little Sam!" as you kick the auxiliary engine in an inland transport-vehicle; and hurricanes are always women, and moons, and seas. Cities, though, are different. Generally, they're neuter. Nobody calls New York or San Francisco "he" or "she". Usually, cities are just "it".

Sometimes, however, they do come to take on the attributes of sex. Usually, this is in the case of small cities near to the Mediterranean, back on Earth. Perhaps this is because of the sex-ridden nouns of the languages which prevail in that vicinity, in which case it tells us more about the inhabitants than it does about the habitations. But I feel that it goes deeper than that.

Betty was Beta Station for less than ten years. After two decades she was Betty officially, by act of Town Council. Why? Well, I felt at the time (ninety-some years ago), and still feel, that it was because she was what she was—a place of rest and repair, of surface-cooked meals and of new voices, new faces, of landscapes, weather, and natural light again, after that long haul through the big night, with its casting away of so much. She is not home, she is seldom destination, but she is like unto both. When you come upon light and warmth and music after darkness and cold and silence, it is Woman. The oldtime Mediterranean sailor must have felt it when he first spied port at the end of a voyage. *I* felt it when I first saw Beta Station—Betty—and the second time I saw her, also.

I am her Hell Cop.

…When six or seven of my hundred-thirty eyes flickered, then saw again, and the music was suddenly washed away by a wave of static, it was then that I began to feel uneasy.

I called Weather Central for a report, and the recorded girlvoice told me that seasonal rains were expected in the afternoon or early evening. I hung up and switched an eye from ventral to dorsal-vision.

Not a cloud. Not a ripple. Only a formation of green-winged sky-toads, heading north, crossed the field of the lens.

I switched it back, and I watched the traffic flow, slowly, and without congestion, along Betty's prim, well-tended streets. Three men were leaving the bank and two more were entering. I recognized the three who were leaving, and in my mind I waved as I passed by. All was still at the post office, and patterns of normal activity lay upon the steel mills, the stockyard, the plast-synth plants, the airport, the spacer pads, and the surfaces of all the shopping complexes; vehicles came and went at the Inland Transport-Vehicle garages, crawling from the rainbow forest and the mountains beyond like dark slugs, leaving tread-trails to mark their comings and goings through wilderness; and the fields of the countryside were still yellow and brown, with occasional patches of green and pink; the country houses, mainly simple A-frame affairs, were chisel blade, spike-tooth, spire and steeple, each with a big lightning rod, and dipped in many colors and scooped up in the cups of my seeing and dumped out again, as I sent my eyes on their rounds and tended my gallery of one hundred-thirty changing pictures, on the big wall of the Trouble Center, there atop the Watch Tower of Town Hall.

The static came and went until I had to shut off the radio. Fragments of music are worse than no music at all.

My eyes, coasting weightless along magnetic lines, began to blink.

I knew then that we were in for something.

I sent an eye scurrying off toward Saint Stephen's at full speed, which meant a wait of about twenty minutes until it topped the range. Another, I sent straight up, skywards, which meant perhaps ten minutes for a long shot of the same scene. Then I put the auto-scan in full charge of operations and went downstairs for a cup of coffee.

I entered the Mayor's outer office, winked at Lottie, the receptionist, and glanced at the inner door.

"Mayor in?" I asked.

I got an occasional smile from Lottie, a slightly heavy, but well-rounded girl of indeterminate age and intermittent acne, but this wasn't one of the occasions.

"Yes," she said, returning to the papers on her desk.

"Alone?"

She nodded, and her earrings danced. Dark eyes and dark complexion, she could have been kind of sharp, if only she'd fix her hair and use more makeup. Well…

I crossed to the door and knocked.

"Who?" asked the Mayor.

"Me," I said, opening it, "Godfrey Justin Holmes—'God' for short. I want someone to drink coffee with, and you're elected."

She turned in her swivel chair, away from the window she had been studying, and her blonde-hair-white-hair-fused, short and parted in the middle, gave a little stir as she turned—like a sunshot snowdrift struck by sudden winds.

She smiled and said, "I'm busy."

'Eyes green, chin small, cute little ears—I love them all'—from an anonymous Valentine I'd sent her two months previous, and true.

"…But not too busy to have coffee with God," she stated. "Have a throne, and I'll make us some instant."

I did, and she did.

While she was doing it, I leaned back, lit a cigarette I'd borrowed from her canister, and remarked, "Looks like rain."

"Uh-huh," she said.

"Not just making conversation," I told her. "There's a bad storm brewing somewhere—over Saint Stephen's, I think. I'll know real soon."

"Yes, grandfather," she said, bringing me my coffee. "You old timers with all your aches and pains are often better than Weather Central, it's an established fact. I won't argue."

She smiled, frowned, then smiled again.

I set my cup on the edge of her desk.

"Just wait and see," I said. "If it makes it over the mountains, it'll be a nasty high-voltage job. It's already jazzing up reception."

Big-bowed white blouse, and black skirt around a well-kept figure. She'd be forty in the fall, but she'd never completely tamed her facial reflexes—which was most engaging, so far as I was concerned. Spontaneity of expression so often vanishes so soon. I could see the sort of child she'd been by looking at her, listening to her now. The thought of being forty was bothering her again, too, I could tell. She always kids me about age when age is bothering her.

See, I'm around thirty-five, actually, which makes me her junior by a bit, but she'd heard her grandfather speak of me when she was a kid, before I came back again this last time. I'd filled out the balance of his two-year term, back when Betty-Beta's first mayor, Wyeth, had died after two months in office. I was born five hundred ninety-seven years ago, on Earth, but I spent about five hundred sixty-two of those years sleeping, during my long jaunts between the stars. I've made a few more trips than a few others; consequently, I am an anachronism. I am really, of course, only as old as I look—but still, people always seem to feel that I've cheated somehow, especially women in their middle years. Sometimes it is most disconcerting…

"Eleanor," said I, "your term will be up in November. Are you still thinking of running again?"

She took off her narrow, elegantly-trimmed glasses and brushed her eyelids with thumb and forefinger. Then she took a sip of coffee.

"I haven't made up my mind."

"I ask not for press-release purposes," I said, "but for my own."

"Really, I haven't decided," she told me. "I don't know…"

"Okay, just checking. Let me know if you do."

I drank some coffee.

After a time, she said, "Dinner Saturday? As usual?"

"Yes, good."

"I'll tell you then."

"Fine—capital."

As she looked down into her coffee, I saw a little girl staring into a pool, waiting for it to clear, to see her reflection or to see the bottom of the pool, or perhaps both.

She smiled at whatever it was she finally saw.

"A bad storm?" she asked me.

"Yep. Feel it in my bones."

"Tell it to go away?"

"Tried. Don't think it will, though."

"Better batten some hatches, then."

"It wouldn't hurt and it might help."

"The weather satellite will be overhead in another half hour. You'll have something sooner?"

"Think so. Probably any minute."

I finished my coffee, washed out the cup.

"Let me know right away what it is."

"Check. Thanks for the coffee."

Lottie was still working and did not look up as I passed.

❖   ❖   ❖

Upstairs again, my highest eye was now high enough. I stood it on its tail and collected a view of the distance: Fleecy mobs of clouds boiled and frothed on the other side of Saint Stephen's. The mountain range seemed a breakwall, a dam, a rocky shoreline. Beyond it, the waters were troubled.

My other eye was almost in position. I waited the space of half a cigarette, then it delivered me a sight:

Gray, and wet and impenetrable, a curtain across the countryside, that's what I saw.

…And advancing.

I called Eleanor.

"It's gonna rain, chillun," I said.

"Worth some sandbags?"

"Possibly."

"Better be ready then. Okay. Thanks."

I returned to my watching.

Tierra del Cygnus, Land of the Swan—delightful name. It refers to both the planet and its sole continent.

How to describe the world, like quick? Well, roughly Earth-size; actually, a bit smaller, and more watery. — As for the main landmass, first hold a mirror up to South America, to get the big bump from the right side over to the left, then rotate it ninety degrees in a counter-clockwise direction and push it up into the northern hemisphere. Got that? Good. Now grab it by the tail and pull. Stretch it another six or seven hundred miles, slimming down the middle as you do, and let the last five or six hundred fall across the equator. There you have Cygnus, its big gulf partly in the tropics, partly not. Just for the sake of thoroughness, while you're about it, break Australia into eight pieces and drop them about at random down in the southern hemisphere, calling them after the first eight letters in the Greek alphabet. Put a big scoop of vanilla at each pole, and don't forget to tilt the globe about eighteen degrees before you leave. Thanks.

I recalled my wandering eyes, and I kept a few of the others turned toward Saint Stephen's until the cloudbanks breasted the range about an hour later. By then, though, the weather satellite had passed over and picked the thing up also. It reported quite an extensive cloud cover on the other side. The storm had sprung up quickly, as they often do here on Cygnus. Often, too, they disperse just as quickly, after an hour or so of heaven's artillery. But then there are the bad ones—sometimes lingering and lingering, and bearing more thunderbolts in their quivers than any Earth storm.

Betty's position, too, is occasionally precarious, though its advantages, in general, offset its liabilities. We are located on the gulf, about twenty miles inland, and are approximately three miles removed (in the main) from a major river, the Noble; part of Betty does extend down to its banks, but this is a smaller part. We are almost a strip city, falling mainly into an area some seven miles in length and two miles wide, stretching inland, east from the river, and running roughly parallel to the distant seacoast. Around eighty percent of the 100,000 population is concentrated about the business district, five miles in from the river.

We are not the lowest land about, but we are far from being the highest. We are certainly the most level in the area. This latter feature, as well as our nearness to the equator, was a deciding factor in the establishment of Beta Station. Some other things were our proximity both to the ocean and to a large river. There are nine other cities on the continent, all of them younger and smaller, and three of them located upriver from us. We are the potential capital of a potential country.

We're a good, smooth, easy landing site for drop-boats from orbiting interstellar vehicles, and we have major assets for future growth and coordination when it comes to expanding across the continent. Our original *raison d'être*, though, was Stopover, repair-point, supply depot, and refreshment stand, physical and psychological, on the way out to other, more settled worlds, further along the line. Cyg was discovered later than many others—it just happened that way—and the others got off to earlier starts. Hence, the others generally attract more colonists. We are still quite primitive. Self-sufficiency, in order to work on our population:land scale, demanded a society on the order of that of the mid-nineteenth century in the American southwest—at least for purposes of getting started. Even now, Cyg is still partly on a natural economy system, although Earth Central technically determines the coin of the realm.

Why Stopover, if you sleep most of the time between the stars?

Think about it awhile, and I'll tell you later if you're right.

The thunderheads rose in the east, sending billows and streamers this way and that, until it seemed from the formations that Saint Stephen's was a balcony full of monsters, leaning and craning their necks over the rail in the direction of the stage, us. Cloud piled upon slate-colored cloud, and then the wall slowly began to topple.

I heard the first rumbles of thunder almost half an hour after lunch, so I knew it wasn't my stomach.

Despite all my eyes, I moved to a window to watch. It was like a big, gray, aerial glacier plowing the sky.

There was a wind now, for I saw the trees suddenly quiver and bow down. This would be our first storm of the season. The turquoise fell back before it, and finally it smothered the sun itself. Then there were drops upon the windowpane, then rivulets.

Flint-like, the highest peaks of Saint Stephen's scraped its belly and were showered with sparks. After a moment it bumped into something with a terrible crash, and the rivulets on the quartz panes turned into rivers.

I went back to my gallery, to smile at dozens of views of people scurrying for shelter. A smart few had umbrellas and raincoats. The rest ran like blazes. People never pay attention to weather reports; this, I believe, is a constant factor in man's psychological makeup, stemming probably from an ancient tribal distrust of the shaman. You want them to be wrong. If they're right, then they're somehow superior, and this is even more uncomfortable than getting wet.

I remembered then that I had forgotten my raincoat, umbrella, and rubbers. But it *had* been a beautiful morning, and W.C. *could* have been wrong…

Well, I had another cigarette and leaned back in my big chair. No storm in the world could knock my eyes out of the sky.

I switched on the filters and sat and watched the rain pour past.

❖　　❖　　❖

Five hours later it was still raining, and rumbling and dark.

I'd had hopes that it would let up by quitting time, but when Chuck Fuller came around the picture still hadn't changed any. Chuck was my relief that night, the evening Hell Cop.

He seated himself beside my desk.

"You're early," I said. "They don't start paying you for another hour."

"Too wet to do anything but sit. Rather sit here than at home."

"Leaky roof?"

He shook his head.

"Mother-in-law. Visiting again."

I nodded.

"One of the disadvantages of a small world."

He clasped his hands behind his neck and leaned back in the chair, staring off in the direction of the window. I could feel one of his outbursts coming.

"You know how old I am?" he asked, after a while.

"No," I said, which was a lie. He was twenty-nine.

"Twenty-seven," he told me, "and going to be twenty-eight soon. Know where I've been?"

"No."

"No place, that's where! I was born and raised on this crummy world! And I married and I settled down here—and I've never been off it! Never could afford it when I was younger. Now I've got a family…"

He leaned forward again, rested his elbow on his knees, like a kid. Chuck would look like a kid when he was fifty. —Blond hair, close-cropped, pug nose, kind of scrawny, takes a suntan quickly, and well. Maybe he'd act like a kid at fifty, too. I'll never know.

I didn't say anything because I didn't have anything to say.

He was quiet for a long while again.

Then he said, "*You've* been around."

After a minute, he went on:

"You were born on Earth. Earth! And you visited lots of other worlds too, before I was even born. Earth is only a name to me. And pictures. And all the others—they're the same! Pictures. Names…"

I waited, then after I grew tired of waiting I said, " 'Miniver Cheevy, child of scorn…' "

"What does that mean?"

"It's the beginning to an ancient poem. It's an ancient poem now, but it wasn't ancient when I was a boy. Just old. *I* had friends, relatives, even in-laws, once myself. They are not just bones now. They are dust. Real dust, not metaphorical dust. The past fifteen years seem fifteen years to me, the same as to you, but they're not. They are already many chapters back in the history books. Whenever you travel between the stars you automatically bury the past. The world you leave will be filled with strangers if you ever return—or caricatures of your friends, your relatives, even yourself. It's no great trick to be a grandfather at sixty, a great-grandfather at seventy-five or eighty—but go away for three hundred years, and then come back and meet your great-great-great-great-great-great-great-great-great-great-great-great-grandson, who happens to be fifty-five years old, and puzzled, when you look him up. It shows you just how alone you really are. You are not simply a man without a country or without a world. You are a man without a time. You and the centuries do not belong to each other. You are like the rubbish that drifts between the stars."

"It would be worth it," he said.

I laughed. I'd had to listen to his gripes every month or two for over a year and a half. It had never bothered me much before, so I guess it was a cumulative effect that day—the rain, and Saturday night next, and my recent library visits, *and* his complaining, that had set me off.

His last comment had been too much. "It would be worth it." What could I say to that?

I laughed.

He turned bright red.

"You're laughing at me!"

He stood up and glared down.

"No I'm not," I said, "I'm laughing at me. I shouldn't have been bothered by what you said, but I was. That tells me something funny about me."

"What?"

"I'm getting sentimental in my old age, and that's funny."

"Oh." He turned his back on me and walked over to the window and stared out. Then he jammed his hands into his pockets and turned around and looked at me.

"Aren't you happy?" he asked. "Really, I mean? You've got money, and no strings on you. You could pick up and leave on the next I-V that passes, if you wanted to."

"Sure I'm happy," I told him. "My coffee was cold. Forget it."

"Oh," again. He turned back to the window in time to catch a bright flash full in the face, and to have to compete with thunder to get his next words out. "I'm sorry," I heard him say, as in the distance. "It just seems to me that you should be one of the happiest guys around…"

"I am. It's the weather today. It's got everybody down in the mouth, yourself included."

"Yeah, you're right," he said. "Look at it rain, will you? Haven't seen any rain in months…"

"They've been saving it all up for today."

He chuckled.

"I'm going down for a cup of coffee and a sandwich before I sign on. Can I bring you anything?"

"No, thanks."

"Okay. See you in a little while."

He walked out whistling. He never stays depressed. Like a kid's moods, his moods, up and down, up and down… And he's a Hell Cop. Probably the worst possible job for him, having to keep his attention in one place for so long. They say the job title comes from the name of an antique flying vehicle—a hellcopper, I think. We send our eyes on their appointed rounds, and they can hover or soar or back up, just like those old machines could. We patrol the city and the adjacent countryside. Law enforcement isn't much of a problem on Cyg. We never peek in windows or send an eye into a building without an invitation. Our testimony is admissible in court—or, if we're fast enough to press a couple buttons, the tape that we make does an even better job—and we can dispatch live or robot cops in a hurry, depending on which will do a better job.

There isn't much crime on Cyg, though, despite the fact that everybody carries a sidearm of some kind, even little kids. Everybody knows pretty much what their neighbors are up to, and there aren't too many places for a fugitive to run. We're mainly aerial traffic cops, with an eye out for local wildlife (which is the reason for all the sidearms).

S.P.C.U. is what we call the latter function—Society for the Prevention of Cruelty to Us—Which is the reason each of my hundred-thirty eyes has six forty-five caliber eyelashes.

There are things like the cute little panda-puppy—oh, about three feet high at the shoulder when it sits down on its rear like a teddy bear, and with big, square, silky ears, a curly pinto coat, large, limpid, brown eyes, pink tongue, button nose, powder puff tail, sharp little white teeth more poisonous than a Quemeda Island viper's, and possessed of a way with mammal entrails like unto the way of an imaginative cat with a rope of catnip.

Then there's a *snapper*, which *looks* as mean as it sounds: a feathered reptile, with three horns on its armored head—one beneath each eye, like a tusk, and one curving skyward from the top of its nose—legs about eighteen inches long, and a four-foot tail which it raises straight into the air whenever it jogs along at greyhound speed, and which it swings like a sandbag—and a mouth full of long, sharp teeth.

Also, there are amphibious things which come from the ocean by way of the river on occasion. I'd rather not speak of them. They're kind of ugly and vicious.

Anyway, those are some of the reasons why there are Hell Cops—not just on Cyg, but on many, many frontier worlds. I've been employed in that capacity on several of them, and I've found that an experienced H.C. can always find a job Out Here. It's like being a professional clerk back home.

Chuck took longer than I thought he would, came back after I was technically off duty, looked happy though, so I didn't say anything. There was some pale lipstick on his collar and a grin on his face, so I bade him good morrow, picked up my cane, and departed in the direction of the big washing machine.

It was coming down too hard for me to go the two blocks to my car on foot.

I called a cab and waited another fifteen minutes. Eleanor had decided to keep Mayor's Hours, and she'd departed shortly after lunch; and almost the entire staff had been released an hour early because of the weather. Consequently, Town Hall was full of dark offices and echoes. I waited in the hallway behind the main door, listening to the purr of the rain as it fell, and hearing its gurgle as it found its way into the gutters. It beat the street and shook the windowpanes and made the windows cold to touch.

I'd planned on spending the evening at the library, but I changed my plans as I watched the weather happen. —Tomorrow, or the next day, I decided. It was an evening for a good meal, a hot bath, my own books and brandy, and early to bed. It was good sleeping weather, if nothing else. A cab pulled up in front of the Hall and blew its horn.

I ran.

❖   ❖   ❖

The next day the rain let up for perhaps an hour in the morning. Then a slow drizzle began; and it did not stop again.

It went on to become a steady downpour by afternoon.

The following day was Friday, which I always have off, and I was glad that it was.

Put dittoes under Thursday's weather report. That's Friday.

But I decided to do something anyway.

I lived down in that section of town near the river. The Noble was swollen, and the rains kept adding to it. Sewers had begun to clog and back up; water ran in the streets. The rain kept coming down and widening the puddles and lakelets, and it was accompanied by drum solos in the sky and the falling of bright forks and sawblades. Dead skytoads were washed along the gutters, like burnt-out fireworks. Ball lightning drifted across Town Square; Saint Elmo's fire clung to the flag pole, the Watch Tower, and the big statue of Wyeth trying to look heroic.

I headed uptown to the library, pushing my car slowly through the countless beaded curtains. The big furniture movers in the sky were obviously non-union, because they weren't taking any coffee breaks. Finally, I found a parking place and I umbrellaed my way to the library and entered.

I have become something of a bibliophile in recent years. It is not so much that I hunger and thirst after knowledge, but that I am news-starved.

It all goes back to my position in the big mixmaster. Admitted, there are *some* things faster than light, like the phase velocities of radio waves in ion plasma, or the tips of the ion-modulated light-beams of Duckbill, the comm-setup back in Sol System, whenever the hinges of the beak snap shut on Earth—but these are highly restricted instances, with no application whatsoever to the passage of shiploads of people and objects between the stars. You can't exceed lightspeed when it comes to the movement of matter. You can edge up pretty close, but that's about it.

Life can be suspended though, that's easy—it can be switched off and switched back on again with no trouble at all. This is why *I* have lasted so long. If we can't speed up the ships, we *can* slow down the people—slow them until they stop—and *let* the vessel, moving at near-lightspeed, take half a century, or more if it needs it, to convey its passengers to where they are going. This is why I am very alone. Each little death means resurrection into both another land and another time. I have had several, and *this* is why I have become a bibliophile: news travels slowly, as slowly as the ships and the people. Buy a newspaper before you hop aboard a ship and it will still be a newspaper when you reach your destination—but back where you bought it, it would be considered an historical document. Send a letter back to Earth and your correspondent's grandson may be able to get an answer back to your great-grandson, if the message makes real good connections and both kids live long enough.

All the little libraries Out Here are full of rare books—first editions of best sellers which people pick up before they leave Someplace Else, and which they often donate after they've finished. We assume that these books have entered the public domain by the time they reach here, and we reproduce them and circulate our own editions. No author has ever sued, and no reproducer has ever been around to *be* sued by representatives, designates, or assigns.

We are completely autonomous and are always behind the times, because there is a transit-lag which cannot be overcome. Earth Central, therefore, exercises about as much control over us as a boy jiggling a broken string while looking up at his kite.

Perhaps Yeats had something like this in mind when he wrote that fine line, "Things fall apart; the center cannot hold." I doubt it, but I still have to go to the library to read the news.

❖   ❖   ❖

The day melted around me.

The words flowed across the screen in my booth as I read newspapers and magazines, untouched by human hands, and the waters flowed across Betty's acres, pouring down from the mountains now, washing the floors of the forest, churning our fields to peanut-butter, flooding basements, soaking its way through everything, and tracking our streets with mud.

I hit the library cafeteria for lunch, where I learned from a girl in a green apron and yellow skirts (which swished pleasantly) that the sandbag crews were now hard at work and that there was no eastbound traffic past Town Square.

After lunch I put on my slicker and boots and walked up that way.

Sure enough, the sandbag wall was already waist high across Main Street; but then, the water *was* swirling around at ankle level, and more of it falling every minute.

I looked up at old Wyeth's statue. His halo had gone away now, which was sort of to be expected. It had made an honest mistake and realized it after a short time.

He was holding a pair of glasses in his left hand and sort of glancing down at me, as though a bit apprehensive, wondering perhaps, there inside all that bronze, if I would tell on him now and ruin his hard, wet, greenish splendor. Tell...? I guess I was the only one left around who really remembered the man. He had wanted to be the father of this great new country, literally, and he'd tried awfully hard. Three months in office and I'd had to fill out the rest of the two-year term. The death certificate gave the cause as "heart stoppage", but it didn't mention the piece of lead which had helped slow things down a bit. Everybody involved is gone now: the irate husband, the frightened wife, the coroner. All but me. And I won't tell anybody if Wyeth's statue won't, because he's a hero now, and we need heroes' statues Out Here even more than we do heroes. He *did* engineer a nice piece of relief work during the Butler Township floods, and he may as well be remembered for that.

I winked at my old boss, and the rain dripped from his nose and fell into the puddle at my feet.

I walked back to the library through loud sounds and bright flashes, hearing the splashing and the curses of the work crew as the men began to block off another street. Black, overhead, an eye drifted past. I waved, and the filter snapped up and back down again. I think H.C. John Keams was tending shop that afternoon, but I'm not sure.

Suddenly the heavens opened up and it was like standing under a waterfall.

I reached for a wall and there wasn't one, slipped then, and managed to catch myself with my cane before I flopped. I found a doorway and huddled.

Ten minutes of lightning and thunder followed. Then, after the blindness and the deafness passed away and the rains had eased a bit, I saw that the street (Second Avenue) had become a river. Bearing all sorts of garbage, papers, hats, sticks, mud, it sloshed past my niche, gurgling nastily. It looked to be over my boot tops, so I waited for it to subside.

It didn't.

It got right up in there with me and started to play footsie.

So, then seemed as good a time as any. Things certainly weren't getting any better.

I tried to run, but with filled boots the best you can manage is a fast wade, and my boots were filled after three steps.

That shot the afternoon. How can you concentrate on anything with wet feet? I made it back to the parking lot, then churned my way homeward, feeling like a riverboat captain who really wanted to be a camel driver.

It seemed more like evening than afternoon when I pulled up into my damp but unflooded garage. It seemed more like night than evening in the alley I cut through on the way to my apartment's back entrance. I hadn't seen the sun for several days, and it's funny how much you can miss it when it takes a vacation. The sky was a sable dome, and the high brick walls of the alley were cleaner than I'd ever seen them, despite the shadows.

I stayed close to the lefthand wall, in order to miss some of the rain. As I had driven along the river I'd noticed that it was already reaching after the high water marks on the sides of the piers. The Noble was a big, spoiled, blood sausage, ready to burst its skin. A lightning flash showed me the whole alley, and I slowed in order to avoid puddles.

I moved ahead, thinking of dry socks and dry martinis, turned a corner to the right, and it struck at me: an org.

Half of its segmented body was reared at a forty-five degree angle above the pavement, which placed its wide head with the traffic-signal eyes saying "Stop", about three and a half feet off the ground, as it rolled toward me on all its pale little legs, with its mouthful of death aimed at my middle.

I pause now in my narrative for a long digression concerning my childhood, which, if you will but consider the circumstances, I was obviously quite fresh on in an instant:

Born, raised, educated on Earth, I had worked two summers in a stockyard while going to college. I still remember the smells and the noises of the cattle; I used to prod them out of the pens and on their way up the last mile. And I remember the smells and noises of the university: the formaldehyde in the Bio labs, the sounds of Freshmen slaughtering French verbs, the overpowering aroma of coffee mixed with cigarette smoke in the Student Union, the splash of the newly-pinned frat man as his brothers tossed him into the lagoon down in front of the Art Museum, the sounds of ignored chapel bells and class bells, the smell of the lawn after the year's first mowing (with big, black Andy perched on his grass-chewing monster, baseball cap down to his eyebrows, cigarette somehow not burning his left cheek), and always, always, the *tick-tick-snick-stamp!* as I moved up or down the strip. I had not wanted to take General Physical Education, but four semesters of it were required. The only out was to take a class in a special sport. I picked fencing because tennis, basketball, boxing, wrestling, handball, judo, all sounded too strenuous, and I couldn't afford a set of golf clubs. Little did I suspect what would follow this choice. It was as strenuous as any of the others, and more than several. But I liked it. So I tried out for the team in my Sophomore year, made it on the *épée* squad, and picked up three varsity letters, because I stuck with it through my Senior year. Which all goes to show: Cattle who persevere in looking for an easy out still wind up in the abattoir, but they may enjoy the trip a little more.

When I came out here on the raw frontier where people all carry weapons, I had my cane made. It combines the better features of the *épée* and the cattle prod. Only, it is the kind of prod which, if you were to prod cattle with, they would never move again.

Over eight hundred volts, max, when the tip touches, if the stud in the handle is depressed properly…

My arm shot out and up and my fingers depressed the stud properly as it moved.

That was it for the org.

A noise came from beneath the rows of razor blades in its mouth as I scored a touch on its soft underbelly and whipped my arm away to the side—a noise halfway between an exhalation and "peep"—and that was it for the org (short for "organism-with-a-long-name-which-I-can't-remember").

I switched off my cane and walked around it. It was one of those things which sometimes come out of the river. I remember that I looked back at it three times, then I switched the cane on again at max and kept it that way till I was inside my apartment with the door locked behind me and all the lights burning.

Then I permitted myself to tremble, and after awhile I changed my socks and mixed my drink.

May your alleys be safe from orgs.

❖　❖　❖

Saturday.

More rain.

Wetness was all.

The entire east side had been shored with sand bags. In some places they served only to create sandy waterfalls, where otherwise the streams would have flowed more evenly and perhaps a trifle more clearly. In other places they held it all back, for awhile.

By then, there were six deaths as a direct result of the rains.

By then, there had been fires caused by the lightning, accidents by the water, sicknesses by the dampness, the cold.

By then, property damages were beginning to mount pretty high.

Everyone was tired and angry and miserable and wet, by then. This included me.

Though Saturday was Saturday, I went to work. I worked in Eleanor's office, with her. We had the big relief map spread on a table, and six mobile eyescreens were lined against one wall. Six eyes hovered above the half-dozen emergency points and kept us abreast of the actions taken upon them. Several new telephones and a big radio set stood on the desk. Five ashtrays looked as if they wanted to be empty, and the coffee pot chuckled cynically at human activity.

The Noble had almost reached its high water mark. We were not an isolated storm center by any means. Upriver, Butler Township was hurting, Swan's Nest was adrip, Laurie was weeping into the river, and the wilderness in between was shaking and streaming.

Even though we were in direct contact we went into the field on three occasions that morning—once, when the north-south bridge over the Lance River collapsed and was washed down toward the Noble as far as the bend by the Mack steel mill; again, when the Wildwood Cemetery, set up on a storm-gouged hill to the east, was plowed deeply, graves opened, and several coffins set awash; and finally, when three houses full of people toppled, far to the east. Eleanor's small flyer was buffeted by the winds as we fought our way through to these sites for on-the-spot supervision; I navigated almost completely by instruments. Downtown proper was accommodating evacuees left and right by then. I took three showers that morning and changed clothes twice.

Things slowed down a bit in the afternoon, including the rain. The cloud cover didn't break, but a drizzle-point was reached which permitted us to gain a little on the waters. Retaining walls were reinforced, evacuees were fed and dried, some of the rubbish was cleaned up. Four of the six eyes were returned to their patrols, because four of the emergency points were no longer emergency points.

…And we wanted all of the eyes for the org patrol.

Inhabitants of the drenched forest were also on the move. Seven *snappers* and a horde of panda-puppies were shot that day, as well as a few crawly things from the troubled waters of the Noble—not to mention assorted branch-snakes, stingbats, borers, and land-eels.

By 1900 hours it seemed that a stalemate had been achieved. Eleanor and I climbed into her flyer and drifted skyward.

We kept rising. Finally, there was a hiss as the cabin began to pressurize itself. The night was all around us. Eleanor's face, in the light from the instrument panel, was a mask of weariness. She raised her hands to her temples as if to remove it, and then when I looked back again it appeared that she had. A faint smile lay across her lips now and her eyes sparkled. A stray strand of hair shadowed her brow.

"Where are you taking me?" she asked.

"Up, high," said I, "above the storm."

"Why?"

"It's been many days," I said, "since we have seen an uncluttered sky."

"True," she agreed, and as she leaned forward to light a cigarette I noticed that the part in her hair had gone all askew. I wanted to reach out and straighten it for her, but I didn't.

We plunged into the sea of clouds.

Dark was the sky, moonless. The stars shone like broken diamonds. The clouds were a floor of lava.

We drifted. We stared up into the heavens. I "anchored" the flyer, like an eye set to hover, and lit a cigarette myself.

"You are older than I am," she finally said, "really. You know?"

"No."

"There is a certain wisdom, a certain strength, something like the essence of the time that passes—that seeps into a man as he sleeps between the stars. I know, because I can feel it when I'm around you."

"No," I said.

"Then maybe it's people expecting you to have the strength of centuries that gives you something like it. It was probably there to begin with."

"No."

She chuckled.

"It isn't exactly a positive sort of thing either."

I laughed.

"You asked me if I was going to run for office again this fall. The answer is 'no'. I'm planning on retiring. I want to settle down."

"With anyone special?"

"Yes, very special, Juss," she said, and she smiled at me and I kissed her, but not for too long, because the ash was about to fall off her cigarette and down the back of my neck.

So we put both cigarettes out and drifted above the invisible city, beneath a sky without a moon.

❖   ❖   ❖

I mentioned earlier that I would tell you about Stopovers. If you are going a distance of a hundred forty-five light years and are taking maybe a hundred-fifty actual years to do it, why stop and stretch your legs?

Well, first of all and mainly, almost nobody sleeps out the whole jaunt. There are lots of little gadgets which require human monitoring at all times. No one is going to sit there for a hundred-fifty years and watch them, all by himself. So everyone takes a turn or two, passengers included. They are all briefed on what to do till the doctor comes, and who to awaken and how to go about it, should troubles crop up. Then everyone takes a turn at guard mount for a month or so, along with a few companions. There are always hundreds of people aboard, and after you've worked down through the role you take it again from the top. All sorts of mechanical agents are backing them up, many of which they are unaware of (to protect *against* them, as well as *with* them—in the improbable instance of several oddballs getting together and deciding to open a window, change course, murder passengers, or things like that), and the people are well-screened and carefully matched up, so as to check and balance each other as well as the machinery. All of this because gadgets and people both bear watching.

After several turns at ship's guard, interspersed with periods of cold sleep, you tend to grow claustrophobic and somewhat depressed. Hence, when there is an available Stopover, it is utilized, to restore mental equilibrium and to rearouse flagging animal spirits. This also serves the purpose of enriching the life and economy of the Stopover world, by whatever information and activities you may have in you.

Stopover, therefore, has become a traditional holiday on many worlds, characterized by festivals and celebrations on some of the smaller ones, and often by parades and world-wide broadcast interviews and press conferences on those with greater populations. I understand that it is now pretty much the same on Earth, too, whenever colonial visitors stop by. In fact, one fairly unsuccessful young starlet, Marilyn Austin, made a long voyage Out, stayed a few months, and returned on the next vessel headed back. After appearing on tri-dee a couple times, sounding off about interstellar culture, and flashing her white, white teeth, she picked up a flush contract, a third husband, and her first big part in tapes. All of which goes to show the value of Stopovers.

❖   ❖   ❖

I landed us atop Helix, Betty's largest apartment-complex, wherein Eleanor had her double-balconied corner suite, affording views both of the distant Noble and of the lights of Posh Valley, Betty's residential section.

Eleanor prepared steaks, with baked potato, cooked corn, beer—everything I liked. I was happy and sated and such, and I stayed till around midnight, making plans for our future. Then I took a cab back to Town Square, where I was parked.

When I arrived, I thought I'd check with the Trouble Center just to see how things were going. So I entered the Hall, stamped my feet, brushed off excess waters, hung my coat, and proceeded up the empty hallway to the elevator.

The elevator was too quiet. They're supposed to rattle, you know? They shouldn't sigh softly and have doors that open and close without a sound. So I walked around an embarrassing corner on my way to the Trouble Center.

It was a pose Rodin might have enjoyed working with. All I can say is that it's a good thing I stopped by when I did, rather than five or ten minutes later.

Chuck Fuller and Lottie, Eleanor's secretary, were practicing mouth to mouth resuscitation and keeping the victim warm techniques, there on the couch in the little alcove off to the side of the big door to T.C.

Chuck's back was to me, but Lottie spotted me over his shoulder, and her eyes widened and she pushed him away. He turned his head quickly.

"Juss…" he said.

I nodded.

"Just passing by," I told him. "Thought I'd stop in to say hello and take a look at the eyes."

"Uh—everything's going real well," he said, stepping back into the hallway. "It's on auto right now, and I'm on my—uh, coffee break. Lottie is on night duty, and she came by to—see if we had any reports we needed typed. She had a dizzy spell, so we came out here where the couch…"

"Yeah, she looks a little—peaked," I said. "There are smelling salts and aspirins in the medicine chest."

I walked on by into the Center, feeling awkward.

Chuck followed me after a couple of minutes. I was watching the screens when he came up beside me. Things appeared to be somewhat in hand, though the rains were still moistening the one hundred thirty views of Betty.

"Uh, Juss," he said, "I didn't know you were coming by…"

"Obviously."

"What I'm getting at is—you won't report me, will you?"

"No, I won't report you."

"…And you wouldn't mention it to Cynthia, would you?"

"Your extracurricular activities," I said, "are your own business. As a friend, I suggest you do them on your own time and in a more propitious location. But it's already beginning to slip my mind. I'm sure I'll forget the whole thing in another minute."

"Thanks Juss," he said.

I nodded.

"What's Weather Central have to say these days?" I asked, raising the phone.

He shook his head, so I dialed and listened.

"Bad," I said, hanging up. "More wet to come."

"Damn," he announced and lit a cigarette, his hands shaking. "This weather's getting me down."

"Me too," said I. "I'm going to run now, because I want to get home before it starts in bad again. I'll probably be around tomorrow. See you."

"Night."

I elevated back down, fetched my coat, and left. I didn't see Lottie anywhere about, but she probably was, waiting for me to go.

I got to my car and was halfway home before the faucets came on full again. The sky was torn open with lightnings, and a sizzlecloud stalked the city like a long-legged arachnid, forking down bright limbs and leaving tracks of fire where it went. I made it home in another fifteen minutes, and the phenomenon was still in progress as I entered the garage. As I walked up the alley (cane switched on) I could hear the distant sizzle and the rumble, and a steady half-light filling the spaces between the buildings, from its *flash-burn-flash-burn* striding.

Inside, I listened to the thunder and the rain, and I watched the apocalypse off in the distance.

Delirium of city under storm—

The buildings across the way were quite clear in the pulsing light of the thing. The lamps were turned off in my apartment so that I could better appreciate the vision. All of the shadows seemed incredibly black and inky, lying right beside glowing stairways, pediments, windowsills, balconies; and all of that which was illuminated seemed to burn as though with an internal light. Overhead, the living/not living insect-thing of fire stalked, and an eye wearing a blue halo was moving across the tops of nearby buildings. The fires pulsed and the clouds burnt like the hills of Gehenna; the thunders burbled and banged; and the white rain drilled into the roadway which had erupted into a steaming lather. Then a *snapper*, tri-horned, wet-feathered, demon-faced, sword-tailed, and green, raced from around a corner, a moment after I'd heard a sound which I had thought to be a part of the thunder. The creature ran, at an incredible speed, along the smoky pavement. The eye swooped after it, adding a hail of lead to the falling raindrops. Both vanished up another street. It had taken but an instant, but in that instant it had resolved a question in my mind as to who should do the painting. Not El Greco, not Blake; no: Bosch. Without any question, Bosch—with his nightmare visions of the streets of Hell. He would be the one to do justice to this moment of the storm.

I watched until the sizzlecloud drew its legs up into itself, hung like a burning cocoon, then died like an ember retreating into ash. Suddenly, it was very dark and there was only the rain.

❖   ❖   ❖

Sunday was the day of chaos.

Candles burned, churches burned, people drowned, beasts ran wild in the streets (or swam there), houses were torn up by the roots and bounced like paper boats along the waterways, the great wind came down upon us, and after that the madness.

I was not able to drive to Town Hall, so Eleanor sent her flyer after me.

The basement was filled with water, and the ground floor was like Neptune's waiting room. All previous high water marks had been passed.

We were in the middle of the worst storm in Betty's history.

Operations had been transferred up onto the third floor. There was no way to stop things now. It was just a matter of riding it out and giving what relief we could. I sat before my gallery and watched.

It rained buckets, it rained vats; it rained swimming pools and lakes and rivers. For awhile it seemed that it rained oceans upon us. This was partly because of the wind which came in from the gulf and suddenly made it seem to rain sideways with the force of its blasts. It began at about noon and was gone in a few hours, but when it left our town was broken and bleeding. Wyeth lay on his bronze side, the flagpole was gone, there was no building without broken windows and water inside, we were suddenly suffering lapses of electrical power, and one of my eyes showed three panda-puppies devouring a dead child. Cursing, I killed them across the rain and the distance. Eleanor wept at my side. There was a report later of a pregnant woman who could only deliver by Caesarean section, trapped on a hilltop with her family, and in labor. We were still trying to get through to her with a flyer, but the winds… I saw burning buildings and the corpses of people and animals. I saw half-buried cars and splintered homes. I saw waterfalls where there had been no waterfalls before. I fired many rounds that day, and not just at beasts from the forest. Sixteen of my eyes had been shot out by looters. I hope that I never again see some of the films I made that day.

When the worst Sunday night in my life began, and the rains did not cease, I knew the meaning of despair for the third time in my life.

Eleanor and I were in the Trouble Center. The lights had just gone out for the eighth time. The rest of the staff was down on the third floor. We sat there in the dark without moving, without being able to do a single thing to halt the course of chaos. We couldn't even watch it until the power came back on.

So we talked.

Whether it was for five minutes or an hour, I don't really know. I remember telling her, though, about the girl buried on another world, whose death had set me to running. Two trips to two worlds and I had broken my bond with the times. But a hundred years of travel do not bring a century of forgetfulness—not when you cheat time with the *petite mort* of the cold sleep. Time's vengeance is memory, and though for an age you plunder the eye of seeing and empty the ear of sound, when you awaken your past is still with you. The worst thing to do then is to return to visit your wife's nameless grave in a changed land, to come back as a stranger to the place you had made your home. You run again then, and after a time you *do* forget, some, because a certain amount of actual time must pass for you also. But by then you are alone, all by yourself: completely alone. That was the *first* time in my life that I knew the meaning of despair. I read, I worked, I drank, I whored, but came the morning after and I was always me, by myself. I jumped from world to world, hoping things would be different, but with each change I was further away from all the things I had known.

Then another feeling gradually came upon me, and a really terrible feeling it was: There *must* be a time and a place best suited for each person who has ever lived. After the worst of my grief had left me and I had come to terms with the vanished past, I wondered about a man's place in time and in space. Where, and *when* in the cosmos would I most like to live out the balance of my days? —To live at my fullest potential? The past *was* dead, but perhaps a better time waited on some as yet undiscovered world, waited at one yet-to-be- recorded moment in its history. How could I *ever* know? How could I ever be sure that my Golden Age did not lay but one more world away, and that I might be struggling in a Dark Era while the Renaissance of my days was but a ticket, a visa and a diary-page removed? That was my *second* despair. I did not know the answer until I came to the Land of the Swan. I do not know why I loved you, Eleanor, but I did, and that was my answer. Then the rains came.

When the lights returned we sat there and smoked. She had told me of her husband, who had died a hero's death in time to save him from the delirium tremors which would have ended his days. Died as the bravest die—not knowing why—because of a reflex, which after all had been a part of him, a reflex which had made him cast himself into the path of a pack of wolf-like creatures attacking the exploring party he was with—off in that forest at the foot of Saint Stephen's—to fight them with a machete and to be torn apart by them while his companions fled to the camp, where they made a stand and saved themselves. Such is the essence of valor: an unthinking moment, a spark along the spinal nerves, predetermined by the sum total of everything you have ever done, wished to do or not to do, and wish you had done, or hadn't, and then comes the pain.

We watched the gallery on the wall. Man is the reasoning animal? Greater than beasts but less than angels? Not the murderer I shot that night. He wasn't even the one who uses tools or buries his dead. —Laughs, aspires, affirms? I didn't see any of those going on. —Watches himself watch himself doing what he knows is absurd? Too sophisticated. He just did the absurd without watching. Like running back into a burning house after his favorite pipe and a can of tobacco. —Devises religions? I saw people praying, but they weren't devising. They were making last-ditch efforts at saving themselves, after they'd exhausted everything else they knew to do. Reflex.

The creature who loves?

That's the only one I might not be able to gainsay.

I saw a mother holding her daughter up on her shoulders while the water swirled about her armpits, and the little girl was holding her doll up above *her* shoulders, in the same way. But isn't that— the love—a part of the total? Of everything you have ever done, or wished? Positive or neg? I know that it is what made me leave my post, running, and what made me climb into Eleanor's flyer and what made me fight my way through the storm and out to that particular scene.

I didn't get there in time.

I shall never forget how glad I was that someone else did. Johnny Keams blinked his lights above me as he rose, and he radioed down:

"It's all right. They're okay. Even the doll."

"Good," I said, and headed back.

As I set the ship down on its balcony landing, one figure came toward me. As I stepped down, a gun appeared in Chuck's hand.

"I wouldn't kill you, Juss," he began, "but I'd wound you. Face the wall. I'm taking the flyer."

"Are you crazy?" I asked him.

"I know what I'm doing. I need it, Juss."

"Well, if you need it, there it is. You don't have to point a gun at me. I just got through needing it myself. Take it."

"Lottie and I both need it," he said. "Turn around!"

I turned toward the wall.

"What do you mean?" I asked.

"We're going away, together—now!"

"You *are* crazy," I said. "This is no time…"

"C'mon, Lottie," he called, and there was a rush of feet behind me and I heard the flyer's door open.

"Chuck!" I said. "We need you now! You can settle this thing peacefully, in a week, in a month, after some order has been restored. There *are* such things as divorces, you know."

"That won't get me off this world, Juss."

"So how is *this* going to help?"

I turned, and I saw that he had picked up a large canvas bag from somewhere and had it slung over his left shoulder, like Santa Claus.

"Turn back around! I don't want to shoot you," he warned.

The suspicion came, grew stronger.

"Chuck, have you been looting?" I asked him.

"Turn around!"

"All right, I'll turn around. How far do you think you'll get?"

"Far enough," he said. "Far enough so that no one will find us—and when the time comes, we'll leave this world."

"No," I said. "I don't think you will, because I know you."

"We'll see." His voice was further away then.

I heard three rapid footsteps and the slamming of a door. I turned then, in time to see the flyer rising from the balcony.

I watched it go. I never saw either of them again.

Inside, two men were unconscious on the floor. It turned out that they were not seriously hurt. After I saw them cared for, I rejoined Eleanor in the Tower.

All that night did we wait, emptied, for morning.

Somehow, it came.

We sat and watched the light flow through the rain. So much had happened so quickly. So many things had occurred during the past week that we were unprepared for morning.

It brought an end to the rains.

A good wind came from out of the north and fought with the clouds, like En-ki with the serpent Tiamat. Suddenly, there was a canyon of cobalt.

A cloudquake shook the heavens and chasms of light opened across its dark landscape.

It was coming apart as we watched.

I heard a cheer, and I croaked in unison with it as the sun appeared.

The good, warm, drying, beneficent sun drew the highest peak of Saint Stephen's to its face and kissed both its cheeks.

There was a crowd before each window. I joined one and stared, perhaps for ten minutes.

❖　❖　❖

When you awaken from a nightmare you do not normally find its ruins lying about your bedroom. This is one way of telling whether or not something was only a bad dream, or whether or not you are really awake.

We walked the streets in great boots. Mud was everywhere. It was in basements and in machinery and in sewers and in living room clothes closets. It was on buildings and on cars and on people and on the branches of trees. It was broken brown blisters drying and waiting to be peeled off from clean tissue. Swarms of skytoads rose into the air when we approached, hovered like dragon-flies, returned to spoiling food stores after we had passed. Insects were having a heyday, too. Betty would have to be deloused. So many things were overturned or fallen down, and half-buried in the brown Sargassos of the streets. The dead had not yet been numbered. The water still ran by, but sluggish and foul. A stench was beginning to rise across the city. There were smashed-in store fronts and there was glass everywhere, and bridges fallen down and holes in the streets… But why go on? If you don't get the picture by now, you never will. It was the big morning after, following a drunken party by the gods. It is the lot of mortal man always to clean up their leavings or be buried beneath them.

So clean we did, but by noon Eleanor could no longer stand. So I took her home with me, because we were working down near the harbor section and my place was nearer.

That's almost the whole story—light to darkness to light—except for the end, which I don't really know. I'll tell you of its beginning, though…

❖   ❖   ❖

I dropped her off at the head of the alleyway, and she went on toward my apartment while I parked the car. Why didn't I keep her with me? I don't know. Unless it was because the morning sun made the world seem at peace, despite its filth. Unless it was because I was in love and the darkness was over, and the spirit of the night had surely departed.

I parked the car and started up the alley. I was halfway before the corner where I had met the org when I heard her cry out.

I ran. Fear gave me speed and strength and I ran to the corner and turned it.

The man had a bag, not unlike the one Chuck had carried away with him, lying beside the puddle in which he stood. He was going through Eleanor's purse, and she lay on the ground—so still!—with blood on the side of her head.

I cursed and ran toward him, switching on my cane as I went. He turned, dropped her purse, and reached for the gun in his belt.

We were about thirty feet apart, so I threw my cane.

He drew his gun, pointed it at me, and my cane fell into the puddle in which he stood.

Flights of angels sang him to his rest, perhaps.

She was breathing, so I got her inside and got hold of a doctor—I don't remember how, not too clearly, anyway—and I waited and waited.

She lived for another twelve hours and then she died. She recovered consciousness twice before they operated on her, and not again after. She didn't say anything. She smiled at me once, and went to sleep again.

I don't know.

Anything, really.

It happened again that I became Betty's mayor, to fill in until November, to oversee the rebuilding. I worked, I worked my head off, and I left her bright and shiny, as I had found her. I think I could have won if I had run for the job that fall, but I did not want it.

The Town Council overrode my objections and voted to erect a statue of Godfrey Justin Holmes beside the statue of Eleanor Schirrer which was to stand in the Square across from cleaned-up Wyeth. I guess it's out there now.

I said that I would never return, but who knows? In a couple of years, after some more history has passed, I may revisit a Betty full of strangers, if only to place a wreath at the foot of the one statue. Who knows but that the entire continent may be steaming and clanking and whirring with automation by then, and filled with people from shore to shining shore?

There was a Stopover at the end of the year and I waved goodbye and climbed aboard and went away, anywhere.

I went aboard and went away, to sleep again the cold sleep.

Delirium of ship among stars—

Years have passed, I suppose. I'm not really counting them anymore. But I think of this thing often: Perhaps there *is* a Golden Age someplace, a Renaissance for me sometime, a special time somewhere, somewhere but a ticket, a visa, a diary-page away. I don't know where or when. Who does? Where are all the rains of yesterday?

In the invisible city?

Inside me?

It is cold and quiet outside and the horizon is infinity. There is no sense of movement.

There is no moon, and the stars are very bright, like broken diamonds, all.

A Word from Zelazny

The novel *Isle of the Dead* "was a spin-off from the novelette I did called 'This Moment of the Storm.'"[1] Zelazny numbered it among his favorite novelettes.[2] Starting with the title, it presents aspects of existentialism, with a protagonist out of time in several ways.

"Based on the recent floods out west," he wrote on May 16, 1965. "Showed it to Damon Knight, who wisely saw through it, saying that I had written a normal human story and then quickly added enough science to make it science fiction. Wise Damon Knight. Anyhow, it sold…"[3] Damon Knight wrote, "This one has a nice gentle mood and some likeable people, but although it succeeds as a story, I don't think it succeeds as science fiction. You could pull the s.f. elements out of it without too much trouble, put it into the here-&-now, and leave it essentially the same story. Anyhow, this is not my cup of tea, but most Zelazny stories are—so send me the next one."[4] The next story was "For A Breath I Tarry," which Knight also rejected. "This Moment of the Storm" garnered both Hugo and Nebula nominations.

Zelazny fenced for four years in college, lettering three times and captaining the *épée* squad in his final two years.[5] Godfrey Holmes's experiences in the story reflect Zelazny's history. Zelazny also studied aikido, tae kwon do, judo, karate, and other martial arts, and many of his protagonists used such unarmed combat techniques.

1 *Leading Edge #29* August 1994.
2 *Phantasmicom #10*, November 1972.
3 *Tightbeam #37*, May 1966.
4 Letter from Damon Knight to Roger Zelazny dated March 9, 1965.
5 *Roger Zelazny*, Jane Lindskold, 1993.

Notes

Saint Stephen was an early evangelist who, shortly after Jesus died, became the first Christian martyr. The feast of Stephen is December 26. *Raison d'être* is justification for existence. A **shaman** is a tribe's spiritual leader and sorcerer. **Miniver Cheevy**, by American poet Edward Arlington Robinson, begins "Miniver Cheevy, child of scorn, || Grew lean while he assailed the seasons || He wept that he was ever born, || And he had reasons." The story's events reflect the poem.

 St. Elmo's Fire is a luminous electrical discharge that appears on a ship or aircraft during a storm. **Things fall apart; the center cannot hold** quotes the apocalyptic poem *Second Coming* by William Butler Yeats; poem and poet also figured more prominently in Zelazny's "Moonless in Byzantium." **Auguste Rodin** was a French sculptor whose works include "The Thinker" and the erotic "The Kiss." **Arachnids** are eight-legged creatures such as spiders, scorpions, mites, and ticks. **Gehenna** is hell.

 El Greco (Doménicos Theotokópoulos) was a Renaissance painter; his works feature distorted perspective and elongated figures; **William Blake** painted hallucinatory images and scenes from the Bible; **Hieronymos Bosch** painted works populated with half-human, half-animal grotesques. *Petite mort* means little death, in this context a euphemism for the cold sleep (suspended animation) used by travelers between stars (it is also a euphemism for orgasm). **Delirium tremors** (*delirium tremens*) is a complication of withdrawal from alcohol addiction.

 En-ki and **Tiamat** are Sumerian gods. Battling to control all of creation, Tiamat sent her own offspring in various unnatural forms to confront En-ki. **Sargassos** is the seaweed-clogged Sargasso Sea, a breeding place for eels; the story's flooded streets are clogged with debris and life forms.

Comes Now the Power

Magazine of Horror #14, Winter 1966.
Hugo nominee 1967 (short story).

I t was into the second year now, and it was maddening.
Everything which had worked before failed this time.

Each day he tried to break it, and it resisted his every effort.

He snarled at his students, drove recklessly, blooded his knuckles against many walls. Nights, he lay awake cursing.

But there was no one to whom he could turn for help. His problem would have been non-existent to a psychiatrist, who doubtless would have attempted to treat him for something else.

So he went away that summer, spent a month at a resort: nothing. He experimented with several hallucinogenic drugs; again, nothing. He tried free-associating into a tape recorder, but all he got when he played it back was a headache.

To whom does the holder of a blocked power turn, within a society of normal people?

…To another of his own kind, if he can locate one.

❖　❖　❖

Milt Rand had known four other persons like himself: his cousin Gary, now deceased; Walker Jackson, a Negro preacher who had retired to somewhere down South; Tatya Stefanovich, a dancer, currently somewhere behind the Iron Curtain; and Curtis Legge, who, unfortunately, was suffering a schizoid reaction, paranoid type, in a state institution for the criminally insane. Others he had brushed against in the night, but had never met and could not locate now.

There had been blockages before, but Milt had always worked his way through them inside of a month. This time was different and special, though. Upsets, discomforts, disturbances, can dam up a talent, block a power. An event which seals it off completely for over a year, however, is more than a mere disturbance, discomfort or upset.

The divorce had beaten hell out of him.

It is bad enough to know that somewhere someone is hating you; but to have known the very form of that hatred and to have proven ineffectual against it, to have known it as the hater held it for you, to have lived with it growing around you, this is more than distasteful circumstance. Whether you are offender or offended, when you are hated and you live within the circle of that hate, it takes a thing from you: it tears a piece of spirit from your soul, or, if you prefer, a way of thinking from your mind; it cuts and does not cauterize.

Milt Rand dragged his bleeding psyche around the country and returned home.

He would sit and watch the woods from his glassed-in back porch, drink beer, watch the fireflies in the shadows, the rabbits, the dark birds, an occasional fox, sometimes a bat.

He had been fireflies once, and rabbits, birds, occasionally a fox, sometimes a bat.

The wildness was one of the reasons he had moved beyond suburbia, adding an extra half-hour to his commuting time.

Now there was a glassed-in back porch between him and these things he had once been part of. Now he was alone.

Walking the streets, addressing his classes at the institute, sitting in a restaurant, a theater, a bar, he was vacant where once he had been filled.

There are no books which tell a man how to bring back the power he has lost.

He tries everything he can think of, while he is waiting. Walking the hot pavements of a summer noon, crossing against the lights because traffic is slow, watching kids in swimsuits play around a gurgling hydrant, filthy water sluicing the gutter about their feet, as mothers and older sisters in halters, wrinkled shirts, bermudas and sunburnt skins watch them, occasionally, while talking to one another in entranceways to buildings or the shade of a storefront awning. Milt moves across town, heading nowhere in particular, growing claustrophobic if he stops for long, his eyebrows full of perspiration, sunglasses streaked with it, shirt sticking to his sides and coming loose, sticking and coming loose as he walks.

Amid the afternoon, there comes a time when he has to rest the two fresh-baked bricks at the ends of his legs. He finds a tree-lawn bench flanked by high maples, eases himself down into it and sits there thinking of nothing in particular for perhaps twenty-five minutes.

Hello.

Something within him laughs or weeps.

Yes, hello, I am here! Don't go away! Stay! Please!

You are—like me…

Yes, I am. You can see it in me because you are what you are. But you must read here and send here, too, I'm frozen. I—Hello? Where are you?

Once more, he is alone.

He tries to broadcast. He fills his mind with the thoughts and tries to push them outside his skull.

Please come back! I need you. You can help me. I am desperate. I hurt. Where are you?

Again, nothing.

He wants to scream. He wants to search every room in every building on the block.

Instead, he sits there.

At 9:30 that evening they meet again, inside his mind.

Hello?

Stay! Stay, for God's sake! Don't go away this time! Please don't! Listen. I need you! You can help me.

How? What is the matter?

I'm like you. Or was, once. I could reach out with my mind and be other places, other things, other people. I can't do it now, though. I have a blockage. The power will not come. I know it is there. I can feel it. But I can't use…Hello?

Yes, I am still here. I can feel myself going away, though. I will be back. I…

Milt waits until midnight. She does not come back. It is a feminine mind which has touched his own. Vague, weak, but definitely feminine, and wearing the power. She does not come back that night, though. He paces up and down the block, wondering which window, which door…

He eats at an all-night café, returns to his bench, waits, paces again, goes back to the café for cigarettes, begins chain-smoking, goes back to the bench.

❖   ❖   ❖

Dawn occurs, day arrives, night is gone. He is alone, as birds explore the silence, traffic begins to swell, dogs wander the lawns.

Then, weakly, the contact:

I am here. I can stay longer this time, I think. How can I help you? Tell me.

All right. Do this thing: Think of the feeling, the feeling of the out-go, out-reach, out-know that you have now. Fill your mind with that feeling and send it to me as hard as you can.

It comes upon him then as once it was: the knowledge of the power. It is earth and water, fire and air to him. He stands upon it, he swims in it, he warms himself by it, he moves through it.

It is returning! Don't stop now!

I'm sorry. I must. I'm getting dizzy…

Where are you?

Hospital…

He looks up the street to the hospital on the corner, at the far end, to his left.

What ward? He frames the thought but knows she is already gone, even as he does it.

❖   ❖   ❖

Doped-up or feverish, he decides, and probably out for a while now.

He takes a taxi back to where he had parked, drives home, showers and shaves, makes breakfast, cannot eat.

He drinks orange juice and coffee and stretches out on the bed.

Five hours later he awakens, looks at his watch, curses.

All the way back into town, he tries to recall the power. It is there like a tree, rooted in his being, branching behind his eyes, all bud, blossom, sap and color, but no leaves, no fruit. He can feel it swaying within him, pulsing, breathing; from the tips of his toes to the roots of his hair he feels it. But it does not bend to his will, it does not branch within his consciousness, furl there it leaves, spread the aromas of life.

He parks in the hospital lot, enters the lobby, avoids the front desk, finds a chair beside a table filled with magazines.

Two hours later he meets her.

He is hiding behind a copy of *Holiday* and looking for her.

I am here.

Again, then! Quickly! The power! Help me to rouse it!

She does this thing.

Within his mind, she conjures the power. There is a movement, a pause, a movement, a pause. Reflectively, as though suddenly remembering an intricate dance step, it stirs within him, the power.

❖   ❖   ❖

As in a surfacing bathyscape, there is a rush of distortions, then a clear, moist view without.

She is a child who has helped him.

A mind-twisted, fevered child, dying…

He reads it all when he turns the power upon her.

Her name is Dorothy and she is delirious. The power came upon her at the height of her illness, perhaps because of it.

Has she helped a man come alive again, or dreamed that she helped him? she wonders.

She is thirteen years old and her parents sit beside her bed. In the mind of her mother a word rolls over and over, senselessly, blocking all other thoughts, though it cannot keep away the feelings:

Methotrexate, methotrexate, methotrexate, meth…

In Dorothy's thirteen-year-old breastbone there are needles of pain. The fevers swirl within her, and she is all but gone to him.

She is dying of leukemia. The final stages are already arrived. He can taste the blood in her mouth.

Helpless within his power, he projects:

You have given me the end of your life and your final strength. I did not know this. I would not have asked it of you if I had.

Thank you, she says, *for the pictures inside you.*

Pictures?

Places, things I saw…

There is not much inside me worth showing. You could have been elsewhere, seeing better.

I am going again…

Wait!

❖   ❖   ❖

He calls upon the power that lives within him now, fused with his will and his sense, his thoughts, memories, feelings. In one great blaze of life, he shows her Milt Rand.

Here is everything I have, all I have ever been that might please. Here is swarming through a foggy night, blinking on and off. Here is lying beneath a bush as the rains of summer fall about you, drip from the leaves upon your fox-soft fur. Here is the moon-dance of the deer, the dream drift of the trout beneath the dark swell, blood cold as the waters about you.

Here is Tatya dancing and Walker preaching; here is my cousin Gary, as he whittles, contriving a ball within a box, all out of one piece of wood. This is my New York and my Paris. This, my favorite meal, drink, cigar, restaurant, park, road to drive on late at night; this is where I dug tunnels, built a lean-to, went swimming; this, my first kiss; these are the tears of loss; this is exile and alone, and recovery, awe, joy; these, my grandmother's daffodils; this her coffin, daffodils about it; these are the colors of the music I love, and this is my dog who lived long and was good. See all the things that heat the spirit, cool within the mind, are encased in memory and one's self. I give them to you, who have no time to know them.

He sees himself standing on the far hills of her mind. She laughs aloud then, and in her room somewhere high away a hand is laid upon her and her wrist is taken between fingers and thumb as she rushes toward him suddenly grown large. His great black wings sweep forward to fold her wordless spasm of life, then are empty.

Milt Rand stiffens within his power, puts aside a copy of *Holiday* and stands, to leave the hospital, full and empty, empty, full, like himself, now, behind.

Such is the power of the power.

A Word from Zelazny

"I wrote this on one of the blackest days in my memory, a day of extreme wretchedness accompanied by an unusual burst of writing activity—which I encouraged, to keep from thinking about what was bothering me. I sat down and did three short stories, one after the other without leaving the type-writer. They were 'Divine Madness', this one and 'But Not The Herald'." ... I cannot be certain whether Peter De Vries' *The Blood of the Lamb* was on my mind then, just a little though I know I'd read it before that time."[1]

"This story is a metaphor for anyone who is frustrated in doing the thing he does best/the thing he likes best. Therefore, it might be looked upon for me as a writer's block situation, except that I've never been blocked. Frustrated by circumstances, yes; blocked, no. Does the artist become the Angel of Death for that which stimulates him? It was obvious for me that a love-death situation is created, and all that other heavy stuff—or at least it was on the particular afternoon in Ohio when I wrote this piece, under gray skies. Now I am here, not there, and it is no longer raining. I am glad that people can change."[2]

Notes

Author Peter De Vries' daughter Emily died at 10 of leukemia, and this experience inspired his 1961 novel *The Blood of the Lamb*, and that novel in turn may have inspired Zelazny. This story's theme also appears in Robert Silverberg's 1972 novel *Dying Inside*.

Schizoid reaction, paranoid type is paranoid schizophrenia, a disorder characterized by paranoid delusions, hallucinations, and withdrawal. A **bathyscape** is a submersible vessel used to navigate and explore the ocean depths. **Methotrexate** is a drug used to treat certain autoimmune diseases (such as rheumatoid arthritis), cancers, and leukemias.

---

1 *The Last Defender of Camelot*, 1980.
2 *Alternities #6*, Vol 2 No 2, Summer 1981.

ANTODE TO WINTER

Written 1955–60 for *Chisel in the Sky;* previously unpublished.

(Aug 17)

Now that the days sing long songs of light
and the moon is a chunk of butter in a bucket of ice
I am cheered no end by animal pleasures.

But winter, after Eden, was a dirty trick, you must admit.

Mortality and immorality would have been a God's plenty
       of punishment
(and somewhat redeeming—providing subject matter for the arts),
without that chilly hell of Winter!
                        (mixing penance and inaction!
stirring dull moods to cold philosophy!)

—It was very boorish,
and I want it known that I protest
this icy shadow cast upon
          my wantonness, my idleness.

Notes

Antode suggests antidote and also anode, the opposite pole from cathode.

Divine Madness

Magazine of Horror #13, Summer 1966.

"*. . . I is this ?hearers wounded-wonder like stand them makes and stars wandering the conjures sorrow of phrase Whose…*"

He blew smoke through the cigarette and it grew longer.

He glanced at the clock and realized that its hands were moving backwards.

The clock told him it was 10:33, going on 10:32 in the P.M.

Then came the thing like despair, for he knew there was not a thing he could do about it. He was trapped, moving in reverse through the sequence of actions past. Somehow, he had missed the warning.

Usually, there was a prism-effect, a flash of pink static, a drowsiness, then a moment of heightened perception…

He turned the pages, from left to right, his eyes retracing their path back along the lines.

"*?emphasis an such bears grief whose he is What*"

Helpless, there behind his eyes, he watched his body perform.

The cigarette had reached its full length. He clicked on the lighter, which sucked away its glowing point, and then he shook the cigarette back into the pack.

He yawned in reverse: first an exhalation, then an inhalation.

It wasn't real—the doctor had told him. It was grief and epilepsy, meeting to form an unusual syndrome.

He'd already had the seizure. The dilantin wasn't helping. This was a post-traumatic locomotor hallucination, elicited by anxiety, precipitated by the attack.

But he did not believe it, could not believe it—not after twenty minutes had gone by, in the other direction—not after he had placed the book upon the reading stand, stood, walked backward across the room to his closet, hung up his robe, redressed himself in the same shirts and slacks he had worn all day, backed over to the bar and regurgitated a Martini, sip by cooling sip, until the glass was filled to the brim and not a drop spilled.

There was an impending taste of olive, and then everything was changed again.

The second-hand was sweeping around his wristwatch in the proper direction.

The time was 10:07.

He felt free to move as he wished.

He redrank his Martini.

Now, if he would be true to the pattern, he would change into his robe and try to read. Instead, he mixed another drink.

Now the sequence would not occur.

Now the things would not happen as he thought they had happened, and un-happened.

Now everything was different.

All of which went to prove it had all been an hallucination.

Even the notion that it had taken twenty-six minutes each way was an attempted rationalization.

Nothing had happened.

❖ ❖ ❖

…Shouldn't be drinking, he decided. It might bring on a seizure.

He laughed.

Crazy, though, the whole thing…

Remembering, he drank.

❖ ❖ ❖

In the morning he skipped breakfast, as usual, noted that it would soon stop being morning, took two aspirins, a lukewarm shower, a cup of coffee, and a walk.

The park, the fountain, the children with their boats, the grass, the pond, he hated them; and the morning, and the sunlight, and the blue moats around the towering clouds.

Hating, he sat there. And remembering.

If he was on the verge of a crackup, he decided, then the thing he wanted most was to plunge ahead into it, not to totter halfway out, halfway in.

He remembered why.

But it was clear, so clear, the morning, and everything crisp and distinct and burning with the green fires of spring, there in the sign of the Ram, April.

He watched the winds pile up the remains of winter against the far gray fence, and he saw them push the boats across the pond, to come to rest in shallow mud the children tracked.

The fountain jetted its cold umbrella above the green-tinged copper dolphins. The sun ignited it whenever he moved his head. The wind rumpled it.

Clustered on the concrete, birds pecked at part of a candy bar stuck to a red wrapper.

Kites swayed on their tails, nosed downward, rose again, as youngsters tugged at invisible strings. Telephone lines were tangled with wooden frames and torn paper, like broken G clefs and smeared glissandos.

He hated the telephone lines, the kites, the children, the birds.

Most of all, though, he hated himself.

How does a man undo that which has been done? He doesn't. There is no way under the sun. He may suffer, remember, repeat, curse, or forget. Nothing else. The past, in this sense, is inevitable.

A woman walked past. He did not look up in time to see her face, but the dusky blonde fall of her hair to her collar and the swell of her sure, sheer-netted legs below the black hem of her coat and above the matching click of her heels heigh-ho, stopped his breath behind his stomach and snared his eyes in the wizard-weft of her walking and her posture and some more, like a rhyme to the last of his thoughts.

❖   ❖   ❖

He half-rose from the bench when the pink static struck his eyeballs, and the fountain became a volcano spouting rainbows.

The world was frozen and served up to him under a glass.

…The woman passed back before him and he looked down too soon to see her face.

The hell was beginning once more, he realized, as the backward-flying birds passed before.

He gave himself up to it. Let it keep him until he broke, until he was all used up and there was nothing left.

He waited, there on the bench, watching the slithey toves be brillig, as the fountain sucked its waters back within itself, drawing them up in a great arc above the unmoving dolphins, and the boats raced backward over the pond, and the fence divested itself of stray scraps of paper, as the birds replaced the candy bar within the red wrapper, bit by crunchy bit.

His thoughts only were inviolate, his body belonged to the retreating tide.

Eventually, he rose and strolled backwards out of the park.

On the street a boy backed past him, unwhistling snatches of a popular song.

He backed up the stairs to his apartment, his hangover growing worse again, undrank his coffee, unshowered, unswallowed his aspirins, and got into bed, feeling awful.

Let this be it, he decided.

A faintly-remembered nightmare ran in reverse though his mind, giving it an undeserved happy ending.

❖　❖　❖

It was dark when he awakened.

He was very drunk.

He backed over to the bar and began spitting out his drinks, one by one into the same glass he had used the night before, and pouring them from the glass back into the bottles again. Separating the gin and vermouth was no trick at all. The liquids leapt into the air as he held the uncorked bottles above the bar.

And he grew less and less drunk as this went on.

Then he stood before an early Martini and it was 10:07 in the P.M. There, within the hallucination, he wondered about another hallucination. Would time loop-the-loop, forward and then backward again, through his previous seizure?

No.

It was as though it had not happened, had never been.

He continued on back through the evening, undoing things.

He raised the telephone, said "good-bye," untold Murray that he would not be coming to work again tomorrow, listened a moment, recradled the phone and looked at it as it rang.

The sun came up in the west and people were backing their cars to work.

He read the weather report and the headlines, folded the evening paper and placed it out in the hall.

It was the longest seizure he had ever had, but he did not really care. He settled himself down within it and watched as the day unwound itself back to morning.

His hangover returned as the day grew smaller, and it was terrible when he got into bed again.

When he awakened the previous evening the drunkenness was high upon him. Two of the bottles he refilled, recorked, resealed. He knew he would take them to the liquor store soon and get his money back.

As he sat there that day, his mouth uncursing and undrinking and his eyes unreading, he knew that new cars were being shipped back to Detroit and disassembled, that corpses were awakening into their death-throes, and that priests the world over were saying black mass, unknowing.

He wanted to chuckle, but he could not tell his mouth to do it.

He unsmoked two and a half packs of cigarettes.

Then came another hangover and he went to bed. Later, the sun set in the east.

❖   ❖   ❖

Time's winged chariot fled before him as he opened the door and said "good-bye" to his comforters and they came in and sat down and told him not to grieve overmuch.

And he wept without tears as he realized what was to come.

Despite his madness, he hurt.

…Hurt, as the days rolled backward.

…Backward, inexorably.

…Inexorably, until he knew the time was near at hand.

He gnashed the teeth of his mind.

Great was his grief and his hate and his love.

❖   ❖   ❖

He was wearing his black suit and undrinking drink after drink, while somewhere the men were scraping the clay back onto the shovels which would be used to undig the grave.

He backed his car to the funeral parlor, parked it, and climbed into the limousine.

They backed all the way to the graveyard.

He stood among his friends and listened to the preacher.

".dust to dust; ashes to Ashes," the man said, which is pretty much the same whichever way you say it.

The casket was taken back to the hearse and returned to the funeral parlor.

He sat through the service and went home and unshaved and unbrushed his teeth and went to bed.

He awakened and dressed again in black and returned to the parlor.

The flowers were all back in place.

Solemn-faced friends unsigned the Sympathy Book and unshook his hand. Then they went inside to sit awhile and stare at the closed casket. Then they left, until he was alone with the funeral director.

Then he was alone with himself.

The tears ran up his cheeks.

His shirt and suit were crisp and unwrinkled again.

He backed home, undressed, uncombed his hair. The day collapsed around him into morning, and he returned to bed to unsleep another night.

❖ ❖ ❖

The previous evening, when he awakened, he realized where he was headed.

Twice, he exerted all of his will power in an attempt to interrupt the sequence of events. He failed.

He wanted to die. If he had killed himself that day, he would not be headed back toward it now.

There were tears within his mind as he realized the past which lay less than twenty-four hours before him.

The past stalked him that day as he unnegotiated the purchase of the casket, the vault, the accessories.

Then he headed home into the biggest hangover of all and slept until he was awakened to undrink drink after drink and then return to the morgue and come back in time to hang up the telephone on that call, that call which had come to break…

…The silence of his anger with its ringing.

She was dead.

She was lying somewhere in the fragments of her car on Interstate 90 now.

As he paced, unsmoking, he knew she was lying there bleeding.

…Then dying, after that crash at 80 miles an hour.

…Then alive?

Then re-formed, along with the car, and alive again, arisen? Even now backing home at terrible speed, to re-slam the door on their final argument? To unscream at him and to be unscreamed at?

He cried out within his mind. He wrung the hands of his spirit.

It couldn't stop at this point. No. Not now.

All his grief and his love and his self-hate had brought him back this far, this near to the moment…

It *couldn't* end now.

After a time, he moved to the living room, his legs pacing, his lips cursing, himself waiting.

❖ ❖ ❖

The door slammed open.

She stared at him, her mascara smeared, tears upon her cheeks.

"!hell to go Then," he said.

"!going I'm," she said.

She stepped back inside, closed the door.

She hung her coat hurriedly in the hall closet.

".it about feel you way the that's If," he said shrugging.

"!yourself but anybody about care don't You," she said.

"!child a like behaving You're," he said.

"!sorry you're say least at could You"

Her eyes flashed like emeralds through the pink static, and she was lovely and alive again. In his mind he was dancing.

The change came.

"You could at least say you're sorry!"

"I am," he said, taking her hand in a grip that she could not break. "How much, you'll never know."

"Come here," and she did.

A Word from Zelazny

As noted in the afterword to "Comes Now the Power", this is one of three stories written "one after the other" on Zelazny's "blackest day", the sudden and unexpected death of his father, shortly after the major motor vehicle accident in which Zelazny's fiancée was seriously injured.

Notes

The text quoted in reverse is from Shakespeare's *Hamlet*.

Dilantin is an anti-seizure medication. A **G clef** is a musical notation marking the treble clef, the upper part of a pair of piano staves. **Glissandos** are rapid slides through a series of scales on a musical instrument. **Weft** means weave; **wizard-weft of her walking** implies that the woman's movement enchants him. " 'Twas **brillig, and the slithy toves** || Did gyre and gimble in the wabe" comes from Lewis Carroll's "Jabberwocky." A parody of the traditional Christian Mass, the **Black Mass** sometimes included saying the proper Mass backwards and placing the crucifix upside-down on the altar. "But at my back I always hear || **Time's winged chariot** hurrying near;" is from Andrew Marvell's "To His Coy Mistress."

But Not the Herald

Magazine of Horror #12, Winter 1965–66.

As the old man came down from the mountain, carrying the box, walking along the trail that led to the sea, he stopped, to lean upon his staff, to watch the group of men who were busy burning their neighbor's home.

"Tell me, man," he asked one of them, "why do you burn your neighbor's home, which, I now note from the barking and the screaming, still contains your neighbor, as well as his dog, wife, and children?"

"Why should we not burn it?" asked the man. "He is a foreigner from across the desert, and he looks different from the rest of us. This also applies to his dog, who looks different from our dogs and barks with a foreign accent, and his wife, who is prettier than our wives and speaks with a foreign accent, and his children, who are cleverer than ours, and speak like their parents."

"I see," said the old man, and he continued on his way.

At the crossroads, he came upon a crippled beggar whose crutches had been thrown high into a tree. He struck upon the tree with his staff and the crutches fell to the ground. He restored them to the beggar.

"Tell me how your crutches came to be in the treetop, brother," he said.

"The boys threw them there," said the beggar, adjusting himself and holding out his hand for alms.

"Why did they do that?"

"They were bored. They tired their parents with asking, 'What should I do now?' until finally one or another of the parents suggested they go make sport of the beggar at the crossroads."

"Such games be somewhat unkind," said the old man.

"True," said the beggar, "but fortunately some of the older boys found them a girl and they are off in the field enjoying her now. You can hear her cries if you listen carefully. They are somewhat weak at the moment, of course. Would I were young and whole again, that I might join in the sport!"

"I see," said the old man, and he turned to go.

"Alms! Alms! Have you no alms in that box you bear? Have you nothing to bestow upon a poor, lame beggar?"

"You may have my blessing," said the old man, "but this box contains no alms."

"A fig for thy blessing, old goat! One cannot eat a blessing! Give me money or food!"

"Alas, I have none to give."

"Then my curses be upon your head! May all manner of misfortune come down on you!"

❖   ❖   ❖

The old man continued on his way to the sea, coming after a time upon two men who were digging a grave for a third who lay dead.

"It is a holy office to bury the dead," he remarked.

"Aye," said one of the men, "especially if you have slain him yourself and are hiding the evidence."

"You have slain that man? Whatever for?"

"Next to nothing, curse the luck! Why should a man fight as he did over the smallest of coins? His purse was near empty."

"From his garments, I should judge he was a poor man."

"Aye, and now he has naught more to trouble him."

"What have you in that box, old man?" asked the second.

"Nothing of any use. I go to cast it in the sea."

"Let's have a look."

"You may not."

"We'll be judge of that."

"This box is not to be opened."

They approached him. "Give it to us."

"No."

The second one struck the old man in the head with a stone; the first snatched the box away from him. "There! Now let us see what it is that is so useless."

"I warn you," said the old man, rising from the ground, "if you open that box you do a terrible thing which may never be undone."

"We'll be judge of that."

They cut at the cords that bound the lid.

"If you will wait but a moment," said the old man, "I will tell you of that box."

They hesitated. "Very well, tell us."

"It was the box of Pandora. She who opened it unleashed upon the world all of the terrible woes which afflict it."

"Ha! A likely tale!"

"It is said by the gods, who charged me cast it into the sea, that the final curse waiting within the box is worse than all the other ills together."

"Ha!"

They undid the cord and threw back the lid.

A golden radiance sped forth. It rose into the air like a fountain, and from within it a winged creature cried out, in a voice infinitely delicate and pathetic, "Free! After all these ages, to be free at last!"

The men fell upon their faces. "Who are you, oh lovely creature," they asked, "you who move us to such strange feelings?"

"I am called Hope," said the creature. "I go to travel in all the dark places of the Earth, where I will inspire men with the feeling that things may yet be better than they are."

And with that it rose into the air and dashed off in search of the dark places of the Earth.

When the two murderers turned again to the old man, he was changed: For now his beard was gone, and he stood before them a powerful youth. Two serpents were coiled about his staff.

"Even the gods could not prevent it," he said. "You have brought this ill upon yourselves, by your own doing. Remember that, when bright Hope turns to dust in your hands."

"Nay," said they, "for another traveler approaches now, and he wears a mighty purse upon him. We shall retire on this day's takings."

"Fools!" said the youth, and he turned on winged heels and vanished up the path, greeting Hercules as he passed him by.

A Word from Zelazny

This is the third of the stories written "one after another" on Zelazny's "blackest day".

"I suppose that a story written to keep one's mind off nasty realities is yet another variation on the game the creative impulse plays…"[1]

Notes

Hermes, messenger of the gods and god of merchants, thieves, and oratory is the main character. Artists portray him equipped for traveling, with broad-brimmed hat, winged shoes, and a winged staff. **Hercules** is a hero of superhuman strength and courage who became a god after he performed twelve immense tasks. **Pandora's box** contained many evils not meant to be unleashed in the world. Zeus instructed Pandora never to open the box, but she did so anyway, releasing greed, vanity, slander, envy, and pining. She shut it just in time to save hope inside. Unleashing **hope** into the story's miserable conditions may be the greatest evil if the conditions cannot be reversed—and the thieves have the false hope that they will be able to rob none other than Hercules.

---

1 *Unicorn Variations*, 1983.

LATE, LATE SHOW

Tightbeam #37, May 1966.

H e realized, with a start, that he had been dozing.
For how long? He wondered.

The stars were in radically different positions…

Shrugging the dust within his variable-frequency cloak, he dismissed the problem. It didn't really matter. There were so many other things more important than time…

He drifted aimlessly for a few eons, composing himself. Then he selected a direction and coasted away at several times lightspeed.

After a brief time, he was hailed by another of his own sort.

"Greetings."

He slowed his flight, groped about, made contact.

"Greetings."

"Where are you headed?"

"Where the action is."

"What sort of action?"

"I'll know when I get there."

"In other words, you have no special plans?"

"Not really… Why?"

"Oh, I have an interesting little item which I might be persuaded to display for your amusement."

"Oh? *How* interesting?"

"You like alien shows, don't you?"

"Some of those foreign jobs are a little too arty for me."

"This one is a stirring thing—real gripping and rousing, in fact—and I have it right here with me. See?"

"Yeah. What's it about?"

"Now, that's the whole bit. You don't really know whether the thing's a tragedy or a comedy, unless you watch it very carefully. It's sort of subtle that way. Let's go find an empty world and I'll show you what I mean."

"What's this thing going to cost me?"

"A grat and three frittles."

"One frittle."

"Make it two."

"Okay, I won't haggle. I passed some fairly empty worlds awhile back—off this way."

"Over there?"

"Yes. —So what've you got?"

"I've got a potential race on these tapes, that's what, and they are high-speed swingers. This is a species I'd known for a long while—I can always pick 'em, you know me—and finally I decided I'd just have to book it for a few discriminating friends."

"Are you trying to say it's a—uh—*racy* race?"

"No, it's not that sort of thing, really. Well, there are parts… But it's the overall effect—the sweep, the panorama of the thing—"

"You don't have to sell me on it, just stick to the facts. I *said* I'd buy a ticket."

"I'll give you a little background first off, then. There were so many of these creatures that they began sending out lots of colonists—first, all over their own world; later, all over their System. They were still overcrowded though, so they took to freezing their excess citizenry in elaborate cold-lockers. But they were still overcrowded. Then they discovered one of the simpler forms of matter transmission. The next refinement, of course, was matter recordation. Rather than shipping their citizens off to colonize bleak worlds or storing them in bulky cold-lockers, they reduced the excess population to electrical impulses and recorded it. It was cheaper than broadcasting them out to new frontiers, and they could play them back whenever they wanted.

"So, I decided to raid one of their Public Archives—that is to say, an archive in which part of their public was stored. No one even noticed that a few million were missing. Probably thought they just got misfiled. I hung onto the ones I'd taken then, and I watched the race itself awhile longer. It was a really good show—touching, colorful, memorable…

"So we'll play back a million or so right now, on this world here—and watch them go through the whole bit over again. They *will*, I'm sure."

"Well, how does the story go? What's the plot?"

"I couldn't tell you that without giving away the end. But there's a lot of laughs in it, plenty of good battle scenes, some real uplifting moral elements, a few tender moments—and they'll doubtless manufacture all kinds of interesting scenery."

"It's not one of those *epics*, is it?"

"No, it's fairly short. —Uh, that'll be a grat and three frittles."

"*Two* frittles."

"I've been thinking about that. I suppose some might say, 'It's just a re-run of the human race,' but I don't feel that way about it. I think this thing might catch on big—very big. So, actually, you're privileged to be one of the first—"

"Forget it."

"Okay, *two* frittles. Make yourself comfortable."

Notes

This light piece was listed as a poem in earlier bibliographies.

"…Good Old Martian Soldier…"

Asmaon #2, 1966.

I'm a good old Martian soldier,
And that's just what I am;
And for your Federation
I do not give a damn.

I hate its great green banner
It's stained with Martian blood.
Oh, the thievin', lyin' Earthmen
I killed 'em all I could.

I followed old John Carter
For two years, more or less…
Got wounded at the Grand Canal
And starved at Point Issus.

I got the rheumatism
From fightin' at the Poles
But I kilt me a nest of Earthmen
And I wished I'd 'a kilt some more.

Three hundred thousand Earthmen
Stiff in Martian dust—
We killed three hundred thousand
Before they conquered us.

They died of Martian fever,
And Martian desert rot—
And I wish we'd 'a got three million
Instead of what we got.

I hate the Federation
With its uniforms of blue!
I hate the Constitution
Of that Federation, too!

I hate the Martian Bureau
With all its mess and fuss!
Oh, the thievin', lyin' Earthmen,
I hate 'em worse an' worse!

Well, I can't take up my weapons
To kill 'em anymore...
But I ain't gonna love 'em
An' that is certain sure—

An' I don't want no pardon
For anything I done—
An' I won't be Earth-adjusted
And I do not give a damn!

Notes

Overlooked in all previous Zelazny bibliographies, this piece pays homage to Edgar Rice Burroughs's novels which feature John Carter of Mars/Barsoom.

DEVICES OF HERALDRY

Written 1955–60 for *Chisel in the Sky;* previously unpublished.

As painfully as a dream is remembered
came the face of one long dead
across the tabletop,
to a jarring tune opened with the cash register,
that settled upon your own:

When the world was a Roman Candle
and piggish emperors lit a Christian taper,
cleft-footed, your fathers in blue skin
fought for the mistletoe of a wooded woman;
and I, in you, waged an accidental way
for that same one against the victory flame;

and, as painfully as an old ring is removed,
we bowed before the Eagle, lit something,
and left.

> With coffee, your face uttered itself
once more, up ladders of smoke, as my words wore
the Cathari kiss,
the movements of my breathing chest,
and all the lost gypsies of Lorca
into an extremely gay structure
that laughed along with us,

even as we passed through the shaded court,
appreciating a dog swimming on the lawn.

Notes

A **Roman Candle** is a firework. The **Eagle** is a Roman symbol. **Cathari** refers to a heretical medieval Christian sect which believed that there were two persons in Christ, the human and the divine. **Lorca** was a notable Spanish playwright and poet.

Love Is an Imaginary Number

New Worlds # 158, January 1966.

They should have known that they could not keep me bound forever. Probably they did, which is why there was always Stella.

I lay there staring over at her, arm outstretched above her head, masses of messed blond hair framing her sleeping face. She was more than wife to me: she was warden. How blind of me not to have realized it sooner!

But then, what else had they done to me?

They had made me to forget what I was.

Because I was like them but not of them they had bound me to this time and this place.

They had made me to forget. They had nailed me with love.

I stood up and the last chains fell away.

A single bar of moonlight lay upon the floor of the bedchamber. I passed through it to where my clothing was hung.

There was a faint music playing in the distance. That was what had done it. It had been so long since I had heard that music…

How had they trapped me?

That little kingdom, ages ago, some Other, where I had introduced gunpowder— Yes! That was the place! They had trapped me there with my Other-made monk's hood and my classical Latin.

Then brainsmash and binding to this Otherwhen.

I chuckled softly as I finished dressing. How long had I lived in this place? Forty-five years of memory—but how much of it counterfeit?

The hall mirror showed me a middle-aged man, slightly obese, hair thinning, wearing a red sport shirt and black slacks.

The music was growing louder, the music only I could hear: guitars, and the steady *thump* of a leather drum.

My different drummer, aye! Mate me with an angel and you still do not make me a saint, my comrades!

I made myself young and strong again.

Then I descended the stair to the living room, moved to the bar, poured out a glass of wine, sipped it until the music reached its fullest intensity, then gulped the remainder and dashed the glass to the floor. I was free!

I turned to go, and there was a sound overhead.

Stella had awakened.

The telephone rang. It hung there on the wall and rang and rang until I could stand it no longer.

I raised the receiver.

"You have done it again," said that old, familiar voice.

"Do not go hard with the woman," said I. "She could not watch me always."

"It will be better if you stay right where you are," said the voice. "It will save us both much trouble."

"Good night," I said, and hung up.

The receiver snapped itself around my wrist and the cord became a chain fastened to a ring-bolt in the wall. How childish of them!

I heard Stella dressing upstairs. I moved eighteen steps sidewise from There, to the place where my scaled limb slid easily from out the vines looped about it.

Then, back again to the living room and out the front door. I needed a mount.

I backed the convertible out of the garage. It was the faster of the two cars. Then out onto the nighted highway, and then a sound of thunder overhead.

It was a Piper Cub, sweeping in low, out of control. I slammed on the brakes and it came on, shearing treetops and snapping telephone lines, to crash in the middle of the street half a block ahead of me. I took a sharp left turn into an alley, and then onto the next street paralleling my own.

If they wanted to play it that way, well—I am not exactly without resources along those lines myself. I was pleased that they had done it first, though.

I headed out into the country, to where I could build up a head of steam.

Lights appeared in my rearview mirror.

Them?

Too soon.

It was either just another car headed this way, or it was Stella.

Prudence, as the Greek Chorus says, is better than imprudence.

I shifted, not gears.

I was whipping along in a lower, more powerful car.

Again, I shifted.

I was driving from the wrong side of the vehicle and headed up the wrong side of the highway.

Again.

No wheels. My car sped forward on a cushion of air, above a beaten and dilapidated highway. All the buildings I passed were of metal. No wood or stone or brick had gone into the construction of anything I saw.

On the long curve behind me, a pair of headlights appeared.

I killed my own lights and shifted, again and again, and again.

I shot through the air, high above a great swampland, stringing sonic booms like beads along the thread of my trail. Then another shift, and I shot low over the steaming land where great reptiles raised their heads like beanstalks from out their wallows. The sun stood high in this world, like an acetylene torch in the heavens. I held the struggling vehicle together by an act of will and waited for pursuit. There was none.

I shifted again…

There was a black forest reaching almost to the foot of the high hill upon which the ancient castle stood. I was mounted on a hippogriff, flying, and garbed in the manner of a warrior-mage. I steered my mount to a landing within the forest.

"Become a horse," I ordered, giving the proper guide-word.

Then I was mounted upon a black stallion, trotting along the trail which twisted through the dark forest.

Should I remain here and fight them with magic, or move on and meet them in a world where science prevailed?

Or should I beat a circuitous route from here to some distant Other, hoping to elude them completely?

My questions answered themselves.

There came a clatter of hoofs at my back, and a knight appeared: he was mounted upon a tall, proud steed; he wore burnished armor; upon his shield was set a cross of red.

"You have come far enough," he said. "Draw rein!"

The blade he bore upraised was a wicked and gleaming weapon, until I transformed it into a serpent. He dropped it then, and it slithered off into the underbrush.

"You were saying…?"

"Why don't you give up?" he asked. "Join us, or quit trying?"

"Why don't *you* give up? Quit them and join with me? We could change many times and places together. You have the ability, and the training…"

By then he was close enough to lunge, in an attempt to unhorse me with the edge of his shield.

I gestured and his horse stumbled, casting him to the ground.

"Everywhere you go, plagues and wars follow at your heels!" he gasped.

"All progress demands payment. These are the growing pains of which you speak, not the final results."

"Fool! There is no such thing as progress! Not as you see it! What good are all the machines and ideas you unloose in their cultures, if you do not change the men themselves?"

"Thought and mechanism advances; men follow slowly," I said, and I dismounted and moved to his side. "All that your kind seek is a perpetual Dark Age on all planes of existence. Still, I am sorry for what I must do."

I unsheathed the knife at my belt and slipped it through his visor, but the helm was empty. He had escaped into another Place, teaching me once again the futility of arguing with an ethical evolutionary.

I remounted and rode on.

After a time, there came again the sound of hoofs at my back.

I spoke another word, which mounted me upon a sleek unicorn, to move at blinding speed through the dark wood. The pursuit continued, however.

Finally, I came upon a small clearing, a cairn piled high in its center. I recognized it as a place of power, so I dismounted and freed the unicorn, which promptly vanished.

I climbed the cairn and sat at its top. I lit a cigar and waited. I had not expected to be located so soon, and it irritated me. I would confront this pursuer here.

A sleek gray mare entered the clearing.

"Stella!"

"Get down from there!" she cried. "They are preparing to unleash an assault any moment now!"

"Amen," I said. "I am ready for it."

"They outnumber you! They always have! You will lose to them again, and again and again, so long as you persist in fighting. Come down and come away with me. It may not be too late!"

"Me, retire?" I asked. "I'm an institution. They would soon be out of crusades without me. Think of the boredom—"

A bolt of lightning dropped from the sky, but it veered away from my cairn and fried a nearby tree.

"They've started!"

"Then get out of here, girl. This isn't your fight."

"You're mine!"

"I'm my own! Nobody else's! Don't forget it!"

"I love you!"

"You betrayed me!"

"No. You say that you love humanity."

"I do."

"I don't believe you! You couldn't, after all you've done to it!"

I raised my hand. "I banish thee from this Now and Here," I said, and I was alone again.

More lightnings descended, charring the ground about me.

I shook my fist.

"Don't you *ever* give up? Give me a century of peace to work with them, and I'll show you a world that you don't believe could exist!" I cried.

In answer, the ground began to tremble.

I fought them. I hurled their lightnings back in their faces. When the winds arose, I bent them inside-out. But the earth continued to shake, and cracks appeared at the foot of the cairn.

"Show yourselves!" I cried. "Come at me one at a time, and I'll teach you of the power I wield!"

But the ground opened up and the cairn came apart.

I fell into darkness.

I was running. I had shifted three times, and I was a furred creature now with a pack howling at my heels, eyes like fiery headlights, fangs like swords.

I was slithering among the dark roots of the banyan, and the long-billed criers were probing after my scaly body...

I was darting on the wings of a hummingbird and I heard the cry of a hawk…

I was swimming through blackness and there came a tentacle…

I broadcast away, peaking and troughing at a high frequency.

I met with static.

I was falling and they were all around me.

I was taken, as a fish is taken in a net. I was snared, bound…

I heard her weeping somewhere.

"Why do you try, again and ever again?" she asked. "Why can you not be content with me, with a life of peace and leisure? Do you not remember what they have done to you in the past? Were not your days with me infinitely better?"

"No!" I cried.

"I love you," she said.

"Such love is an imaginary number," I told her, and I was raised from where I lay and borne away.

She followed behind, weeping.

"I pleaded with them to give you a chance at peace, but you threw that gift in my face."

"The peace of the eunuch; the peace of lobotomy, lotus and Thorazine," I said. "No, better they work their wills upon me and let their truth give forth its lies as they do."

"Can you really say that and mean it?" she asked. "Have you already forgotten the sun of the Caucasus—the vulture tearing at your side, day after hot red day?"

"I do not forget," I said, "but I curse them. I will oppose them until the ends of When and Wherever, and someday I shall win."

"I love you," she said.

"How can you say that and mean it?"

"Fool!" came a chorus of voices, as I was laid upon this rock in this cavern and chained.

All day long a bound serpent spits venom into my face, and she holds a pan to catch it. It is only when the woman who betrayed me must empty that pan that it spits into my eyes and I scream.

But I *will* come free again, to aid long-suffering mankind with my many gifts, and there will be a trembling on high that day I end my bondage. Until then, I can only watch the delicate, unbearable bars of her fingers across the bottom of that pan, and scream each time she takes them away.

A Word from Zelazny

The mix of Norse and Greek mythology and a character who can shift realities, might bring to mind the Amber books. Zelazny said, "There is a relationship between 'Love Is an Imaginary Number' and the Amber books, yes."[1] Prometheus/Loki can move between realities by willing a change, just as a Prince of Amber can shift through shadows.

Notes

The story conflated the Greek's Prometheus and the Norse's Loki. Prometheus gave men fire and earned eternal punishment from Zeus. Bound to a rock on **Mount Caucasus**, Prometheus's liver was torn from his body each day by an eagle. The liver then regenerated. The Norse gods bound Loki to stones and placed a snake over his head so its venom would drip onto him. His wife Sigyn sat beside him to collect the venom in a bowl, but each time she turned to empty the bowl, venom dripped into his eyes and he writhed, shaking the earth.

An **imaginary number** is a type of number which was developed in the eighteenth century to allow mathematicians to solve algebraic equations that cannot be solved using ordinary numbers. The imaginary numbers can be considered to be a number line at right angles with ordinary numbers, with zero as their point of intersection.

A **hippogriff** has a horse's body and an eagle's wings and head. An outdated operation, **lobotomy** cuts part of the brain's frontal lobe, leading to docile behavior. The classic **lotus** position in yoga includes crossed legs and feet turned in and up, outstretched hands on knees. **Thorazine** is a brand name for the sedating antipsychotic medication chlorpromazine.

1 *Science Fiction Review* Aug 1980 #36 (Vol 9 No 3), pp 14–16

LINES WRITTEN CONCERNING THE ACCEPTABILITY OF ALCOHOL

Written 1955–60 for *Chisel in the Sky;* previously unpublished.

Even
Saint Stephen
got stoned.

Notes

Saint Stephen was one of the original seven deacons appointed by the Apostles. **Stoned** means very drunk or under the influence of drugs in its modern usage. But St. Stephen experienced the original meaning—he was charged with blasphemy and *stoned to death.*

THE KEYS TO DECEMBER

New Worlds #165, August 1966.
Nebula nominee 1968 (novelette).

B orn of man and woman, in accordance with Catform Y7 requirements, Coldworld Class (modified per Alyonal), 3.2-E, G.M.I.
option, Jarry Dark was not suited for existence anywhere in the universe which had guaranteed him a niche. This was either a blessing or
a curse, depending on how you looked at it.

So look at it however you would, here is the story:

❖   ❖   ❖

It is likely that his parents could have afforded the temperature control unit, but not much more than that. (Jarry required a temperature of at least –50°C to be comfortable.)

It is unlikely that his parents could have provided for the air pressure control and gas mixture equipment required to maintain his life.

Nothing could be done in the way of 3.2-E grav-simulation, so
daily medication and physiotherapy were required. It is unlikely that
his parents could have provided for this.

The much-maligned option took care of him, however. It safe-
guarded his health. It provided for his education. It assured his economic welfare and physical well-being.

It might be argued that Jarry Dark would not have been a home-
less Coldworld Catform (modified per Alyonal) had it not been for
General Mining, Incorporated, which had held the option. But then
it must be borne in mind that no one could have foreseen the nova
which destroyed Alyonal.

When his parents had presented themselves at the Public Health
Planned Parenthood Center and requested advice and medication
pending offspring, they had been informed as to the available worlds

and the bodyform requirements for them. They had selected Alyonal, which had recently been purchased by General Mining for purposes of mineral exploitation. Wisely, they had elected the option; that is to say, they had signed a contract on behalf of their anticipated offspring, who would be eminently qualified to inhabit that world, agreeing that he would work as an employee of General Mining until he achieved his majority, at which time he would be free to depart and seek employment wherever he might choose (though his choices would admittedly be limited). In return for this guarantee, General Mining agreed to assure his health, education and continuing welfare for so long as he remained in their employ.

When Alyonal caught fire and went away, those Coldworld Catforms covered by the option who were scattered about the crowded galaxy were, by virtue of the agreement, wards of General Mining.

This is why Jarry grew up in a hermetically sealed room containing temperature and atmosphere controls, and why he received a first-class closed circuit education, along with his physiotherapy and medicine. This is also why Jarry bore some resemblance to a large gray ocelot without a tail, had webbing between his fingers and could not go outside to watch the traffic unless he wore a pressurized refrigeration suit and took extra medication.

All over the swarming galaxy, people took the advice of Public Health Planned Parenthood Centers, and many others had chosen as had Jarry's parents. Twenty-eight thousand, five hundred sixty-six of them, to be exact. In any group of over twenty-eight thousand five hundred sixty, there are bound to be a few talented individuals. Jarry was one of them. He had a knack for making money. Most of his General Mining pension check was invested in well-chosen stocks of a speculative nature. (In fact, after a time he came to own considerable stock in General Mining.)

When the man from the Galactic Civil Liberties Union had come around, expressing concern over the pre-birth contracts involved in the option and explaining that the Alyonal Catforms would make a good test case (especially since Jarry's parents lived within jurisdiction of the 877th Circuit, where they would be assured a favorable courtroom atmosphere), Jarry's parents had demurred, for fear of jeopardizing the General Mining pension. Later on, Jarry himself dismissed the notion also. A favorable decision could not make him an E-world Normform, and what else mattered? He was not vindictive. Also, he owned considerable stock in G.M. by then.

He loafed in his methane tank and purred, which meant that he was thinking. He operated his cryo-computer as he purred and thought. He was computing the total net worth of all the Catforms in the recently organized December Club.

He stopped purring and considered a sub-total, stretched, shook his head slowly. Then he returned to his calculations.

When he had finished, he dictated a message into his speech-tube, to Sanza Barati, President of December and his betrothed:

"Dearest Sanza—The funds available, as I have suspected, leave much to be desired. All the more reason to begin immediately. Kindly submit the proposal to the business committee, outline my qualifications and seek immediate endorsement. I've finished drafting the general statement to the membership. (Copy attached.) From these figures, it will take me between five and ten years, if at least eighty percent of the membership backs me. So push hard, beloved. I'd like to meet you someday, in a place where the sky is purple. Yours, always, Jarry Dark, Treasurer. P.S. I'm pleased you were pleased with the ring."

Two years later, Jarry had doubled the net worth of December, Incorporated.

A year and a half after that, he had doubled it again.

When he received the following letter from Sanza, he leapt onto his trampoline, bounded into the air, landed upon his feet at the opposite end of his quarters, returned to his viewer and replayed it:

> Dear Jarry,
>
> Attached are specifications and prices for five more worlds. The research staff likes the last one. So do I. What do you think? Alyonal II? If so, how about the price? When could we afford that much? The staff also says that a hundred Worldchange units could alter it to what we want in 5–6 centuries. Will forward costs of this machinery shortly.
>
> Come live with me and be my love, in a place where there are no walls…
>
> Sanza

"One year," he replied, "and I'll buy you a world! Hurry up with the costs of the machinery and transport…"

❖　❖　❖

When the figures arrived Jarry wept icy tears. One hundred machines, capable of altering the environment of a world, plus twenty-eight thousand coldsleep bunkers, plus transportation costs for the machinery and his people, plus... Too high! He did a rapid calculation.

He spoke into the speech-tube:

"...Fifteen additional years is too long to wait, Pussycat. Have them figure the time-span if we were to purchase only twenty World-change units. Love and kisses, Jarry."

During the days which followed, he stalked above his chamber, erect at first, then on all fours as his mood deepened.

"Approximately three thousand years," came the reply. "May your coat be ever shiny—Sanza."

"Let's put it to a vote, Greeneyes," he said.

❖   ❖   ❖

Quick, a world in 300 words or less! Picture this...

One land mass, really, containing three black and brackish looking seas; gray plains and yellow plains and skies the color of dry sand; shallow forests with trees like mushrooms which have been swabbed with iodine; no mountains, just hills brown, yellow, white, lavender; green birds with wings like parachutes, bills like sickles, feathers like oak leaves, an inside-out umbrella behind; six very distant moons, like spots before the eyes in daytime, snowflakes at night, drops of blood at dusk and dawn; grass like mustard in the moister valleys; mists like white fire on windless mornings, albino serpents when the air's astir; radiating chasms, like fractures in frosted windowpanes; hidden caverns, like chains of dark bubbles; seventeen known dangerous predators, ranging from one to six meters in length, excessively furred and fanged; sudden hailstorms, like hurled hammerheads from a clear sky; an icecap like a blue beret at either flattened pole; nervous bipeds a meter and a half in height, short on cerebrum, which wander the shallow forests and prey upon the giant caterpillar's larva, as well as the giant caterpillar, the green bird, the blind burrower, and the offal-eating murkbeast; seventeen mighty rivers; clouds like pregnant purple cows, which quickly cross the land to lie-in beyond the visible east; stands of windblasted stones like frozen music; nights like soot, to obscure the lesser stars; valleys which flow like the torsos of women or instruments of music; perpetual frost in places of shadow; sounds in the morning like the cracking of ice, the trembling of tin, the snapping of steel strands...

They knew they would turn it into heaven.

❖ ❖ ❖

The vanguard arrived, decked out in refrigeration suits, installed ten Worldchange units in either hemisphere, began setting up cold-sleep bunkers in several of the larger caverns.

Then came the members of December down from the sand-colored sky.

They came and they saw, decided it was almost heaven, then entered their caverns and slept. Over twenty-eight thousand Cold-world Catforms (modified per Alyonal) came into their own world to sleep for a season in silence the sleep of ice and of stone, to inherit the new Alyonal. There is no dreaming in that sleep. But had there been, their dreams might have been as the thoughts of those yet awake.

"It is bitter, Sanza."

"Yes, but only for a time—"

"…To have each other and our own world, and still to go forth like divers at the bottom of the sea. To have to crawl when you want to leap…"

"It is only for a short time, Jarry, as the senses will reckon it."

"But it is really three thousand years! An ice age will come to pass as we doze. Our former worlds will change so that we would not know them were we to go back for a visit—and none will remember us."

"Visit what? Our former cells? Let the rest of the worlds go by! Let us be forgotten in the lands of our birth! We are a people apart and we have found our home. What else matters?"

"True… It will be but a few years, and we shall stand our tours of wakefulness and watching together."

"When is the first?"

"Two and a half centuries from now—three months of wakefulness."

"What will it be like then?"

"I don't know. Less warm…"

"Then let us return and sleep. Tomorrow will be a better day."

"Yes."

"Oh! See the green bird! It drifts like a dream…"

❖ ❖ ❖

When they awakened that first time, they stayed within the Worldchange installation at the place called Deadland. The world was already colder and the edges of the sky were tinted with pink. The metal walls of the great installation were black and rimed with frost.

The atmosphere was still lethal and the temperature far too high. They remained within their special chambers for most of the time, venturing outside mainly to make necessary tests and to inspect the structure of their home.

Deadland… Rocks and sand. No trees, no marks of life at all.

The time of terrible winds was still upon the land, as the world fought back against the fields of the machines. At night, great clouds of real estate smoothed and sculpted the stands of stone, and when the winds departed the desert would shimmer as if fresh-painted and the stones would stand like flames within the morning and its singing. After the sun came up into the sky and hung there for a time, the winds would begin again and a dun-colored fog would curtain the day. When the morning winds departed, Jarry and Sanza would stare out across Deadland through the east window of the installation, for that was their favorite—the one on the third floor—where the stone that looked like a gnarly Normform waved to them, and they would lie upon the green couch they had moved up from the first floor, and would sometimes make love as they listened for the winds to rise again, or Sanza would sing and Jarry would write in the log or read back through it, the scribblings of friends and unknowns through the centuries, and they would purr often but never laugh, because they did not know how.

One morning, as they watched, they saw one of the biped creatures of the iodine forests moving across the land. It fell several times, picked itself up, continued, fell once more, lay still.

"What is it doing this far from its home?" asked Sanza.

"Dying," said Jarry. "Let's go outside."

They crossed a catwalk, descended to the first floor, donned their protective suits and departed the installation.

The creature had risen to its feet and was staggering once again. It was covered with a reddish down, had dark eyes and a long, wide nose, lacked a true forehead. It had four brief digits, clawed, upon each hand and foot.

When it saw them emerge from the Worldchange unit, it stopped and stared at them. Then it fell.

They moved to its side and studied it where it lay.

It continued to stare at them, its dark eyes wide, as it lay there shivering.

"It will die if we leave it here," said Sanza.

"…And it will die if we take it inside," said Jarry.

It raised a forelimb toward them, let it fall again. Its eyes narrowed, then closed.

Jarry reached out and touched it with the toe of his boot. There was no response.

"It's dead," he said.

"What will we do?"

"Leave it here. The sands will cover it."

They returned to the installation, and Jarry entered the event in the log.

During their last month of duty, Sanza asked him, "Will everything die here but us? The green birds and the big eaters of flesh? The funny little trees and the hairy caterpillar?"

"I hope not," said Jarry. "I've been reading back through the biologists' notes. I think life might adapt. Once it gets a start anywhere, it'll do anything it can to keep going. It's probably better for the creatures of this planet that we could afford only twenty Worldchangers. That way they have three millennia to grow more hair and learn to breathe our air and drink our water. With a hundred units we might have wiped them out and had to import coldworld creatures or breed them. This way, the ones who live here might be able to make it."

"It's funny," she said, "but the thought just occurred to me that we're doing here what was done to us. They made us for Alyonal, and a nova took it away. These creatures came to life in this place, and we're taking it away. We're turning all of life on this planet into what we were on our former worlds—misfits."

"The difference, however, is that we are taking our time," said Jarry, "and giving them a chance to get used to the new conditions."

"Still, I feel that all that—outside there"—she gestured toward the window—"is what this world is becoming: one big Deadland."

"Deadland was here before we came. We haven't created any new deserts."

"All the animals are moving south. The trees are dying. When they get as far south as they can go and still the temperature drops, and the air continues to burn in their lungs—then it will be all over for them."

"By then they might have adapted. The trees are spreading, are developing thicker barks. Life will make it."

"I wonder…"

"Would you prefer to sleep until it's all over?"

"No; I want to be by your side, always."

"Then you must reconcile yourself to the fact that something is always hurt by any change. If you do this, you will not be hurt yourself."

Then they listened for the winds to rise.

Three days later, in the still of sundown, between the winds of day and the winds of night, she called him to the window. He climbed to the third floor and moved to her side. Her breasts were rose in the sundown light and the places beneath them silver and dark. The fur of her shoulders and haunches was like an aura of smoke. Her face was expressionless and her wide, green eyes were not turned toward him.

He looked out.

The first big flakes were falling, blue, through the pink light. They drifted past the stone and gnarly Normform; some stuck to the thick quartz windowpane; they fell upon the desert and lay there like blossoms of cyanide; they swirled as more of them came down and were caught by the first faint puffs of the terrible winds. Dark clouds had mustered overhead and from them, now, great cables and nets of blue descended. Now the flakes flashed past the window like butterflies, and the outline of Deadland flickered on and off. The pink vanished and there was only blue, blue and darkening blue, as the first great sigh of evening came into their ears and the billows suddenly moved sidewise rather than downwards, becoming indigo as they raced by.

❖   ❖   ❖

"The machine is never silent," Jarry wrote. "Sometimes I fancy I can hear voices in its constant humming, its occasional growling, its crackles of power. I am alone here at the Deadland station. Five centuries have passed since our arrival. I thought it better to let Sanza sleep out this tour of duty, lest the prospect be too bleak. (It is.) She will doubtless be angry. As I lay half-awake this morning, I thought I heard my parents' voices in the next room. No words. Just the sounds of their voices as I used to hear them over my old intercom. They must be dead by now, despite all geriatrics. I wonder if they thought of me much after I left? I couldn't even shake my father's hand without my gauntlet, or kiss my mother goodbye. It is strange, the feeling, to be this alone, with only the throb of the machinery about me as it rearranges the molecules of the atmosphere, refrigerates the world, here in the middle of the blue place. Deadland. This, despite the fact that I grew up in a steel cave. I call the other nineteen stations every afternoon. I am afraid I am becoming something of a nuisance. I won't call them tomorrow, or perhaps the next day.

"I went outside without my refrig-pack this morning, for a few moments. It is still deadly hot. I gulped a mouthful of air and choked. Our day is still far off. But I can notice the difference from the last time I tried it, two and a half hundred years ago. I wonder what it will be like when we have finished?—And I, an economist! What will my function be in our new Alyonal? Whatever, so long as Sanza is happy…

"The Worldchanger stutters and groans. All the land is blue for so far as I can see. The stones still stand, but their shapes are changed from what they were. The sky is entirely pink now, and it becomes almost maroon in the morning and the evening. I guess it's really a wine-color, but I've never seen wine, so I can't say for certain. The trees have not died. They've grown hardier. Their barks are thicker, their leaves darker and larger. They grow much taller now, I've been told. There are no trees in Deadland.

"The caterpillars still live. They seem much larger, I understand, but it is actually because they have become woollier than they used to be. It seems that most of the animals have heavier pelts these days. Some apparently have taken to hibernating. A strange thing: Station Seven reported that they had thought the bipeds were growing heavier coats. There seem to be quite a few of them in that area, and they often see them off in the distance. They looked to be shaggier. Closer observation, however, revealed that some of them were either carrying or were wrapped in the skins of dead animals! Could it be that they are more intelligent than we have given them credit for? This hardly seems possible, since they were tested quite thoroughly by the Bio Team before we set the machines in operation. Yet, it is very strange.

"The winds are still severe. Occasionally, they darken the sky with ash. There has been considerable vulcanism southwest of here. Station Four was relocated because of this. I hear Sanza singing now, within the sounds of the machine. I will let her be awakened the next time. Things should be more settled by then. No, that is not true. It is selfishness. I want her here beside me. I feel as if I were the only living thing in the whole world. The voices on the radio are ghosts. The clock ticks loudly and the silences between the ticks are filled with the humming of the machine, which is a kind of silence, too, because it is constant. Sometimes I think it is not there; I listen for it, I strain my ears, and I do not know whether there is a humming or not. I check the indicators then, and they assure me that the machine is functioning. Or perhaps there is something wrong with the indicators. But they seem to be all right. No. It is me. And the blue of Deadland is a kind of visual silence. In the morning even the rocks are covered with blue frost. Is it beautiful or ugly? There is no response within me. It is a part of the great silence, that's all. Perhaps I shall become a mystic. Perhaps I shall develop occult powers or achieve something bright and liberating as I sit here at the center of the great silence. Perhaps I shall see visions. Already I hear voices. Are there ghosts in Deadland? No, there was never anything here to be ghosted. Except perhaps for the little biped. Why did it cross Deadland, I wonder? Why did it head for the center of destruction rather than away, as its fellows did? I shall never know. Unless perhaps I have a vision. I think it is time to suit up and take a walk. The polar icecaps are heavier. The glaciation has begun. Soon, soon things will be better. Soon the silence will end, I hope. I wonder, though, whether silence is not the true state of affairs in the universe, our little noises serving only to accentuate it, like a speck of black on a field of blue. Everything was once silence and will be so again—is now, perhaps. Will I ever hear real sounds, or only sounds out of the silence? Sanza is singing again. I wish I could wake her up now, to walk with me, out there. It is beginning to snow."

❖　❖　❖

Jarry awakened again on the eve of the millennium.

Sanza smiled and took his hand in hers and stoked it, as he explained why he had let her sleep, as he apologized.

"Of course I'm not angry," she said, "considering I did the same thing to you last cycle."

Jarry stared up at her and felt the understanding begin.

"I'll not do it again," she said, "and I know you couldn't. The aloneness is almost unbearable."

"Yes," he replied.

"They warmed us both alive last time. I came around first and told them to put you back to sleep. I was angry then, when I found out what you had done. But I got over it quickly, so often did I wish you were there."

"We will stay together," said Jarry.

"Yes, always."

They took a flier from the cavern of sleep to the Worldchange installation at Deadland, where they relieved the other attendants and moved the new couch up to the third floor.

The air of Deadland, while sultry, could now be breathed for short periods of time, though a headache invariably followed such experiments. The heat was still oppressive. The rock, once like an old Normform waving, had lost its distinctive outline. The winds were no longer so severe.

On the fourth day, they found some animal tracks which seemed to belong to one of the larger predators. This cheered Sanza, but another, later occurrence produced only puzzlement.

One morning they went forth to walk in Deadland.

Less than a hundred paces from the installation, they came upon three of the giant caterpillars, dead. They were stiff, as though dried out rather than frozen, and they were surrounded by rows of markings within the snow. The footprints which led to the scene and away from it were rough of outline, obscure.

"What does it mean?" she asked.

"I don't know, but I think we had better photograph this," said Jarry.

They did. When Jarry spoke to Station Eleven that afternoon, he learned that similar occurrences had occasionally been noted by attendants of other installations. These were not too frequent, however.

"I don't understand," said Sanza.

"I don't want to," said Jarry.

It did not happen again during their tour of duty. Jarry entered it into the log and wrote a report. Then they abandoned themselves to lovemaking, monitoring, and occasionally nights of drunkenness. Two hundred years previously, a biochemist had devoted his tour of duty to experimenting with compounds which would produce the same reactions in Catforms as the legendary whiskey did in Normforms. He had been successful, had spent four weeks on a colossal binge, neglected his duty and been relieved of it, was then retired to his coldbunk for the balance of the Wait. His basically simple formula had circulated, however, and Jarry and Sanza found a well-stocked bar in the storeroom and a hand-written manual explaining its use and a variety of drinks which might be compounded. The author of the document had expressed the hope that each tour of attendance might result in the discovery of a new mixture, so that when he returned for his next cycle the manual would have grown to a size proportionate to his desire. Jarry and Sanza worked at it conscientiously, and satisfied the request with a Snowflower Punch which warmed their bellies and made their purring turn into giggles, so that they discovered laughter also. They celebrated the millennium with an entire bowl of it, and Sanza insisted on calling all the other installations and giving them the formula, right then, on the graveyard watch, so that everyone could share in their joy. It is quite possible that everyone did, for the recipe was well-received. And always, even after that bowl was but a memory, they kept the laughter. Thus are the first simple lines of tradition sometimes sketched.

❖   ❖   ❖

"The green birds are dying," said Sanza, putting aside a report she had been reading.

"Oh?" said Jarry.

"Apparently they've done all the adapting they're able to," she told him.

"Pity," said Jarry.

"It seems less than a year since we came here. Actually, it's a thousand."

"Time flies," said Jarry.

"I'm afraid," she said.

"Of what?"

"I don't know. Just afraid."

"Why?"

"Living the way we've been living, I guess. Leaving little pieces of ourselves in different centuries. Just a few months ago, as my memory works, this place was a desert. Now it's an ice field. Chasms open and close. Canyons appear and disappear. Rivers dry up and new ones spring forth. Everything seems so very transitory. Things look solid, but I'm getting afraid to touch things now. They might go away. They might turn into smoke, and my hand will keep on reaching through the smoke and touch—something…God, maybe. Or worse yet, maybe not. No one really knows what it will be like here when we've finished. We're traveling toward an unknown land and it's too late to go back. We're moving through a dream, heading toward an idea… Sometimes I miss my cell…and all the little machines that took care of me there. Maybe *I* can't adapt. Maybe I'm like the green bird…"

"No, Sanza. You're not. We're real. No matter what happens out there, *we* will last. Everything is changing because we want it to change. We're stronger than the world, and we'll squeeze it and paint it and poke holes in it until we've made it exactly the way we want it. Then we'll take it and cover it with cities and children. You want to see God? Go look in the mirror. God has pointed ears and green eyes. He is covered with soft gray fur. When He raises His hand there is webbing between His fingers."

"It is good that you are strong, Jarry."

"Let's get out the power sled and go for a ride."

"All right."

Up and down, that day, they drove through Deadland, where the dark stones stood like clouds in another sky.

❖   ❖   ❖

It was twelve and a half hundred years.

Now they could breathe without respirators, for a short time.

Now they could bear the temperature, for a short time.

Now all the green birds were dead.

Now a strange and troubling thing began.

The bipeds came by night, made markings upon the snow, left dead animals in the midst of them. This happened now with much more frequency than it had in the past. They came long distances to do it, many of them with fur which was not their own upon their shoulders.

Jarry searched through the history files for all the reports on the creatures.

"This one speaks of lights in the forest," he said. "Station Seven."

"What…?"

"Fire," he said. "What if they've discovered fire?"

"Then they're not really beasts!"

"But they were!"

"They wear clothing now. They make some sort of sacrifice to our machines. They're not beasts any longer."

"How could it have happened?"

"How do you think? *We* did it. Perhaps they would have remained stupid—animals—if we had not come along and forced them to get smart in order to go on living. We've accelerated their evolution. They had to adapt or die, and they adapted."

"D'you think it would have happened if we hadn't come along?" he asked.

"Maybe—some day. Maybe not, too."

Jarry moved to the window, stared out across Deadland.

"I have to find out," he said. "If they are intelligent, if they are—human, like us," he said, then laughed, "then we must consider their ways."

"What do you propose?"

"Locate some of the creatures. See whether we can communicate with them."

"Hasn't it been tried?"

"Yes."

"What were the results?"

"Mixed. Some claim they have considerable understanding. Others place them far below the threshold where humanity begins."

"We may be doing a terrible thing," she said. "Creating men, then destroying them. Once, when I was feeling low, you told me that we were the gods of this world, that ours was the power to shape and to break. Ours *is* the power to shape and break, but I don't feel especially divine. What can we do? They have come this far, but do you think they can bear the change that will take us the rest of the way? What if they are like the green birds? What if they've adapted as fast and as far as they can and it is not sufficient? What would a god do?"

"Whatever he wished," said Jarry.

That day, they cruised over Deadland in the flier, but the only signs of life they saw were each other. They continued to search in the days that followed, but they did not meet with success.

Under the purple of morning, however, two weeks later, it happened.

"They've been here," said Sanza.

Jarry moved to the front of the installation and stared out.

The snow was broken in several places, inscribed with the lines he had seen before, about the form of a small, dead beast.

"They can't have gone very far," he said.

"No."

"We'll search in the sled."

Now over the snow and out, across the land called Dead they went, Sanza driving and Jarry peering at the lines of footmarks in the blue.

They cruised through the occurring morning, hinting of fire and violet, and the wind went past them like a river, and all about them there came sounds like the cracking of ice, the trembling of tin, the snapping of steel strands. The bluefrosted stones stood like frozen music, and the long shadow of their sled, black as ink, raced on ahead of them. A shower of hailstones drumming upon the roof of their vehicle like a sudden visitation of demon dancers, as suddenly was gone. Deadland sloped downward, slanted up again.

Jarry placed his hand upon Sanza's shoulder.

"Ahead!"

She nodded, began to brake the sled.

They had it at bay. They were using clubs and long poles which looked to have fire-hardened points. They threw stones. They threw pieces of ice.

Then they backed away and it killed them as they went.

The Catforms had called it a bear because it was big and shaggy and could rise up onto its hind legs…

This one was about three and a half meters in length, was covered with bluish fur and had a thin, hairless snout like the business end of a pair of pliers.

Five of the little creatures lay still in the snow. Each time that it swung a paw and connected, another one fell.

Jarry removed the pistol from its compartment and checked the charge.

"Cruise by slowly," he told her. "I'm going to try to burn it about the head."

His first shot missed, scoring the boulder at its back. His second singed the fur of its neck. He leapt down from the sled then, as they came abreast of the beast, thumbed the power control up to maximum, and fired the entire charge into its breast, point-blank.

The bear stiffened, swayed, fell, a gaping wound upon it, front to back.

Jarry turned and regarded the little creatures. They stared up at him.

"Hello," he said. "My name is Jarry. I dub thee Redforms—"

He was knocked from his feet by a blow from behind.

He rolled across the snow, lights dancing before his eyes, his left arm and shoulder afire with pain.

A second bear had emerged from the forest of stone.

He drew his long hunting knife with his right hand and climbed back to his feet.

As the creature lunged, he moved with the catspeed of his kind, thrusting upward, burying his knife to the hilt in its throat.

A shudder ran through it, but it cuffed him and he fell once again, the blade torn from his grasp.

The Redforms threw more stones, rushed toward it with their pointed sticks.

Then there was a thud and a crunching sound, and it rose up into the air and came down on top of him.

He awakened.

He lay on his back, hurting, and everything he looked at seemed to be pulsing, as if about to explode.

How much time had passed, he did not know.

Either he or the bear had been moved.

The little creatures crouched, watching.

Some watched the bear. Some watched him.

Some watched the broken sled…

The broken sled…

He struggled to his feet.

The Redforms drew back.

He crossed to the sled and looked inside.

He knew she was dead when he saw the angle of her neck. But he did all the things a person does to be sure, anyway, before he would let himself believe it.

She had delivered the deathblow, crashing the sled into the creature, breaking its back. It had broken the sled. Herself, also.

He leaned against the wreckage, composed his first prayer, then removed her body.

The Redforms watched.

He lifted her in his arms and began walking, back toward the installation, across Deadland.

The Redforms continued to watch as he went, except for the one with the strangely high brow-ridge, who studied instead the knife that protruded from the shaggy and steaming throat of the beast.

❖   ❖   ❖

Jarry asked the awakened executives of December: "What should we do?"

"She is the first of our race to die on this world," said Yan Turl, Vice President.

"There is no tradition," said Selda Kein, Secretary. "Shall we establish one?"

"I don't know," said Jarry. "I don't know what is right to do."

"Burial or cremation seem to be the main choices. Which would you prefer?"

"I don't— No, not the ground. Give her back to me. Give me a large flier…I'll burn her."

"Then let us construct a chapel."

"No. It is a thing I must do in my own way. I'd rather do it alone."

"As you wish. Draw what equipment you need, and be about it."

"Please send someone else to keep the Deadland installation. I wish to sleep again when I have finished this thing—until the next cycle."

"Very well, Jarry. We are sorry."

"Yes—we are."

Jarry nodded, gestured, turned, departed.

Thus are the heavier lines of life sometimes drawn.

❖ ❖ ❖

At the southeastern edge of Deadland there was a blue mountain. It stood slightly over three thousand meters in height. When approached from the northwest, it gave the appearance of being a frozen wave in a sea too vast to imagine. Purple clouds rent themselves upon its peak. No living thing was to be found on its slopes. It had no name, save that which Jarry Dark gave it.

He anchored the flier.

He carried her body to the highest point to which a body might be carried.

He placed her there, dressed in her finest garments, a wide scarf concealing the angle of her neck, a dark veil covering her emptied features.

He was about to try a prayer when the hail began to fall. Like thrown rocks, the chunks of blue ice came down upon him, upon her.

"God damn you!" he cried and he raced back to the flier.

He climbed into the air, circled.

Her garments were flapping in the wind. The hail was a blue, beaded curtain that separated them from all but these final caresses: fire aflow from ice to ice, from clay aflow immortally through guns.

He squeezed the trigger and a doorway into the sun opened in the side of the mountain that had been nameless. She vanished within it, and he widened the doorway until he had lowered the mountain.

Then he climbed upward into the cloud, attacking the storm until his guns were empty.

He circled then above the molten mesa, there at the southeastern edge of Deadland.

He circled above the first pyre this world had seen.

Then he departed, to sleep for a season in silence the sleep of ice and stone, to inherit the new Alyonal. There is no dreaming in that sleep.

❖   ❖   ❖

Fifteen centuries. Almost half the Wait. Two hundred words or less…
Picture—

…Nineteen mighty rivers flowing, but the black seas rippling violet now.

…No shallow iodine-colored forests. Mighty shag-barked barrel trees instead, orange and lime and black and tall across the land.

…Great ranges of mountains in the place of hills brown, yellow, white, lavender. Black corkscrews of smoke unwinding from smoldering cones.

…Flowers, whose roots explore the soil twenty meters beneath their mustard petals, unfolded amidst the blue frost and the stones.

…Blind burrowers burrowing deeper; offal-eating murk-beasts now showing formidable incisors and great rows of ridged molars; giant caterpillars growing smaller but looking larger because of increasing coats.

…The contours of valleys still like the torsos of women, flowing and rolling, or perhaps like instruments of music.

…Gone much windblasted stone, but ever the frost.

…Sounds in the morning as always, harsh, brittle, metallic.

They were sure they were halfway to heaven.

Picture that.

❖   ❖   ❖

The Deadland log told him as much as he really needed to know. But he read back through the old reports, also.

Then he mixed himself a drink and stared out the third floor window.

"…Will die," he said, then finished his drink, outfitted himself, and abandoned his post.

It was three days before he found a camp.

He landed the flier at a distance and approached on foot. He was far to the south of Deadland, where the air was warmer and caused him to feel constantly short of breath.

They were wearing animal skins—skins which had been cut for a better fit and greater protection, skins which were tied about them. He counted sixteen lean-to arrangements and three campfires. He flinched as he regarded the fires, but he continued to advance.

When they saw him, all their little noises stopped, a brief cry went up, and there was silence.

He entered the camp.

The creatures stood unmoving about him. He heard some bustling within the large lean-to at the end of the clearing.

He walked about the camp.

A slab of dried meat hung from the center of a tripod of poles.

Several long spears stood before each dwelling place. He advanced and studied one. A stone which had been flaked into a leaf-shaped spearhead was affixed to its end.

There was the outline of a cat carved upon a block of wood…

He heard a footfall and turned.

One of the Redforms moved slowly toward him. It appeared older than the others. Its shoulders sloped; as it opened its mouth to make a series of popping noises, he saw that some of its teeth were missing; its hair was grizzled and thin. It bore something in its hands, but Jarry's attention was drawn to the hands themselves.

Each hand bore an opposing digit.

He looked about him quickly, studying the hands of the others. All of them seemed to have thumbs. He studied their appearance more closely.

They now had foreheads.

He returned his attention to the old Redform.

It placed something at his feet, and then it backed away from him.

He looked down.

A chunk of dried meat and a piece of fruit lay upon a broad leaf.

He picked up the meat, closed his eyes, bit off a piece, chewed and swallowed. He wrapped the rest in the leaf and placed it in the side pocket of his pack.

He extended his hand and the Redform drew back.

He lowered his hand, unrolled the blanket he had carried with him and spread it upon the ground. He seated himself, pointed to the Redform, then indicated a position across from him at the other end of the blanket.

The creature hesitated, then advanced and seated itself.

"We are going to learn to talk with one another," he said slowly. Then he placed his hand upon his breast and said, "Jarry."

❖   ❖   ❖

Jarry stood before the reawakened executives of December.

"They are intelligent," he told them. "It's all in my report."

"So?" asked Yan Turl.

"I don't think they will be able to adapt. They have come very far, very rapidly. But I don't think they can go much further. I don't think they can make it all the way."

"Are you a biologist, an ecologist, a chemist?"

"No."

"Then on what do you base your opinion?"

"I observed them at close range for six weeks."

"Then it's only a feeling you have…?"

"You know there are no experts on a thing like this. It's never happened before."

"Granting their intelligence—granting even that what you have said concerning their adaptability is correct—what do you suggest we do about it?"

"Slow down the change. Give them a better chance. If they can't make it the rest of the way, then stop short of our goal. It's already livable here. *We* can adapt the rest of the way."

"Slow it down? How much?"

"Supposing we took another seven or eight thousand years?"

"Impossible!"

"Entirely!"

"Too much!"

"Why?"

"Because everyone stands a three-month watch every two hundred fifty years. That's one year of personal time for every thousand. You're asking for too much of everyone's time."

"But the life of an entire race may be at stake!"

"You do not know that for certain."

"No, I don't. But do you feel it is something to take a chance with?"

"Do you want to put it to an executive vote?"

"No—I can see that I'll lose. I want to put it before the entire membership."

"Impossible. They're all asleep."

"Then wake them up."

"That would be quite a project."

"Don't you think that the fate of a race is worth the effort? Especially since we're the ones who forced intelligence upon them? We're the ones who made them evolve, cursed them with intellect."

"Enough! They were right at the threshold. They might have become intelligent had we *not* come along—"

"But you can't say for certain! You don't really know! And it doesn't really matter how it happened. They're here and we're here, and they think we're gods—maybe because we do nothing for them but make them miserable. We have some responsibility to an intelligent race, though. At least to the extent of not murdering it."

"Perhaps we could do a long-range study…"

"They could be dead by then. I formally move, in my capacity as Treasurer, that we awaken the full membership and put the matter to a vote."

"I don't hear any second to your motion."

"Selda?" he said.

She looked away.

"Tarebell? Clond? Bondici?"

There was silence in the cavern that was high and wide about him.

"All right. I can see when I'm beaten. We will be our own serpents when we come into our Eden. I'm going now, back to Deadland, to finish my tour of duty."

"You don't have to. In fact, it might be better if you sleep the whole thing out…"

"No. If it's going to be this way, the guilt will be mine also. I want to watch, to share it fully."

"So be it," said Turl.

❖   ❖   ❖

Two weeks later, when Installation Nineteen tried to raise the Deadland Station on the radio, there was no response.

After a time, a flier was dispatched.

The Deadland Station was a shapeless lump of melted metal.

Jarry Dark was nowhere to be found.

Later that afternoon, Installation Eight went dead.

A flier was immediately dispatched.

Installation Eight no longer existed. Its attendants were found several miles away, walking. They told how Jarry Dark had forced them from the station at gunpoint. Then he had burnt it to the ground, with the fire-cannons mounted upon his flier.

At about the time they were telling this story, Installation Six became silent.

The order went out: MAINTAIN CONTINUOUS RADIO CONTACT WITH TWO OTHER STATIONS AT ALL TIMES.

The other order went out: GO ARMED AT ALL TIMES. TAKE ANY VISITOR PRISONER.

❖   ❖   ❖

Jarry waited. At the bottom of a chasm, parked beneath a shelf of rock, Jarry waited. An opened bottle stood upon the control board of his flier. Next to it was a small case of white metal.

Jarry took a long, last drink from the bottle as he waited for the broadcast he knew would come.

When it did, he stretched out on the seat and took a nap.

When he awakened, the light of day was waning.

The broadcast was still going on…

"…Jarry. They will be awakened and a referendum will be held. Come back to the main cavern. This is Yan Turl. Please do not destroy any more installations. This action is not necessary. We agree with your proposal that a vote be held. Please contact us immediately. We are waiting for your reply, Jarry…"

He tossed the empty bottle through the window and raised the flier out of the purple shadow into the air and up.

❖   ❖   ❖

When he descended upon the landing stage within the main cavern, of course they were waiting for him. A dozen rifles were trained upon him as he stepped down from the flier.

"Remove your weapons, Jarry," came the voice of Yan Turl.

"I'm not wearing any weapons," said Jarry. "Neither is my flier," he added; and this was true, for the fire-cannons no longer rested within their mountings.

Yan Turl approached, looked up at him.

"Then you may step down."

"Thank you, but I like it right where I am."

"You are a prisoner."

"What do you intend to do with me?"

"Put you back to sleep until the end of the Wait. Come down here!"

"No. And don't try shooting—or using a stun charge or gas, either. If you do, we're all of us dead the second it hits."

"What do you mean?" asked Turl, gesturing gently to the riflemen.

"My flier," said Jarry, "is a bomb, and I'm holding the fuse in my right hand." He raised the white metal box. "So long as I keep the lever on the side of this box depressed, we live. If my grip relaxes, even for an instant, the explosion which ensues will doubtless destroy this entire cavern."

"I think you're bluffing."

"You know how you can find out for certain."

"You'll die too, Jarry."

"At the moment, I don't really care. Don't try burning my hand off, either, to destroy the fuse," he cautioned, "because it doesn't really matter. Even if you should succeed, it will cost you at least two installations."

"Why is that?"

"What do you think I did with the fire-cannons? I taught the Redforms how to use them. At the moment, these weapons are manned by Redforms and aimed at two installations. If I do not personally visit my gunners by dawn, they will open fire. After destroying their objectives, they will move on and try for two more."

"You trusted those beasts with laser projectors?"

"That is correct. Now, will you begin awakening the others for the voting?"

Turl crouched, as if to spring at him, appeared to think better of it, relaxed.

"Why did you do it, Jarry?" he asked. "What are they to you that you would make your own people suffer for them?"

"Since you do not feel as I feel," said Jarry, "my reasons would mean nothing to you. After all, they are only based upon my feelings, which are different than your own—for mine are based upon sorrow and loneliness. Try this one, though: I am their god. My form is to be found in their every camp. I am the Slayer of Bears from the Desert of the Dead. They have told my story for two and a half centuries, and I have been changed by it. I am powerful and wise and good, so far as they are concerned. In this capacity, I owe them some consideration. If I do not give them their lives, who will there be to honor me in snow and chant my story around the fires and cut for me the best portions of the woolly caterpillar? None, Turl. And these things are all that my life is worth now. Awaken the others. You have no choice."

"Very well," said Turl. "And if their decision should go against you?"

"Then I'll retire, and you can be god," said Jarry.

❖   ❖   ❖

Now every day when the sun goes down out of the purple sky, Jarry Dark watches it in its passing, for he shall sleep no more the sleep of ice and of stone, wherein there is no dreaming. He has elected to live out the span of his days in a tiny instant of the Wait, never to look upon the New Alyonal of his people. Every morning, at the new Deadland installation, he is awakened by sounds like the cracking of ice, the trembling of tin, the snapping of steel strands, before they come to him with their offerings, singing and making marks upon the snow. They praise him and he smiles upon them. Sometimes he coughs.

Born of man and woman, in accordance with Catform Y7 requirements, Coldworld Class, Jarry Dark was not suited for existence anywhere in the universe which had guaranteed him a niche. This was either a blessing or a curse, depending on how you looked at it. So look at it however you would, that was the story. Thus does life repay those who would serve her fully.

A Word from Zelazny

"Why I write…science fiction or fantasy…is a question which I am in a better position to answer. First, this is an area of fiction where the writer has considerably more freedom than in other types of fiction. I enjoy descriptive writing, and it pleases me to be able to describe landscapes and meteorological phenomena which could not exist on Earth, but which might be possible elsewhere; similarly, with characters and their motivations. For an example, I indulged my fancy in all of these things in my novelette 'The Keys To December,' which contained unmanlike humans engaged in an unusual project on a strange world. This provided an aesthetic pleasure of a sort that would not have obtained had I written a more down-to-Earth story."[1]

It was optioned for development as a motion picture,[2] but despite at least one completed script, nothing else materialized.

Notes

An **ocelot** is a spotted wildcat.

1 "Tomorrow Stuff," unpublished essay.
2 *Science Fiction* Vol 1 No 2, June 1978.

THE HOUSE OF THE
HANGED MAN

Double:Bill #15, September 1966.

As I walked through the House of the Hanged Man, there came to me a voice from behind in the darkness.

"Where are you going?" it asked.

But I did not answer. I walked on through the Red Room for an age and a half, and as I paused at the threshold of the great Orange Hallway the voice from the distant cellar-darkness came again.

"Where *are* you going?"

I moved up the Orange Hallway, and the walls receded and returned like the pulsebeat of Time, bringing with them loads of orange chairs and high paintings of great orange expanses. The orange-rust was upon the empty suits of clanking armor, and on the banisters that swirled with the stairways up and up and up.

After generations of orange furniture and tapestries, I saw ahead through the mist the entrance to the Yellow Vestibule. I quickened my pace, but the black voice appeared again behind me, just as I drew near.

"*Where* are you going?"

Hurrying, I entered the Yellow Vestibule, which was filled with cast yellow cloaks and yellow masks and great mirrors in which I saw nothing but yellow and my eyes. I pushed through the soft yellow hangings and brushed against the smooth padding of the lemon walls.

A yellow silk glove lay at my feet, and I stooped and picked it up. There came a soft laugh from behind a pillar, but when I looked there was no one.

I kept the glove and hurried through the yellow eras, for I was afraid.

The deep-dark, stark-dark voice followed me, timed to arrive just as I set foot beneath the archway to the Green Drawing Room.

"Where are *you* going?"

I rushed ahead, for I had to see Green, now that I had known Red and Orange and Yellow. I plunged through the million angles of the Green Drawing Room, for that was the color of grass, he had told me, that was the color of grass. Green wind, green boughs, ship on a green sea… That was the color. Horse on a green mountain… The color of…

Something.

Now it seemed as if there were footsteps far behind me, or at least a steady clicking sound. I skidded across green centuries, wishing to linger, but fearing, wishing to stay awhile amid the color of grass, but fearing, to step behind a hanging, to pass within a green place, to stay.

Then I came to the Blue Boudoir; and the voice, right at my back now, addressed me again.

"Where are you *going?*"

I sped ahead into the place of robin's egg, sky, morning glory, which he had told me would be there. I burst through blue-cano-pied bed-hangings, swerved by blue dressing-tables, couches, *petite* divans, tasselled hangings (like waterfalls, the Hanged Man had told me), through closets, around and over vanities, luggages, linens.

The clicking came nearer, and I burnt ages in a blue flame of passage, speeding.

Then I came to the foot of the Violet Stairway.

"WHERE ARE YOU GOING?" asked the voice of cellar-based, cellar-hearted blackness I had left.

"Out!" I cried. "Outside! Where there is grass, and trees, water, birds, wind, sun…

"In all colors—married!"

"There is no outside," said the soot-dark voice. "There is only the House of the Hanged Man, forever and ever and everywhere. There is *only* the House of the Hanged Man."

"You lie!" I said, setting foot upon the first violet stair.

"There is no outside," repeated the black, black voice.

"The ghost of the Hanged Man told me—as he hovered, batlike, from a rafter in the Black. *He* told me!"

"He lied, lied, lied. There is only the House. Come back now to the Dark."

"No!"

I ran, taking the steps two at a time, flashing by the violet statues, the people who had forgotten how to move, there in their violet niches along the Violet Stairway, where they stood, unseeing, having also forgotten how to look outside themselves.

Up and up, I raced, slipping on soft millennia of violet carpeting.

Then far up ahead of me I saw the Rainbow Door, reaching high beyond belief, standing slightly ajar, just, as it must always have been, waiting for me to pass through it, forever.

"Outside!" I cried.

A hand fell on my shoulder.

I screamed all the way back, but the hand remained, guiding me through the violet, blue, green, yellow, orange, red—back.

I cried as I passed through the Green Drawing Room and the Yellow Vestibule, but in the puff of an instant they were gone.

The hand would not let go, because I wanted to run away.

I will never get out again. Never, never, ever. They had trusted me near the fringes of the darkness, but they will never trust me there again.

I will remain in the cellar-dark forever, and if I ever meet the ghost of the Hanged Man, hovering inverted, bat-like, from a rafter in the Black again, I will either curse him or bless him. I do not know.

If *you* should ever meet him, pass by.

But if ever you should somehow leave here, and pass through the Rainbow Door, and go outside, and depart from the House of the Hanged Man…

Then come back, please. Try. Try to slip back. Return here and tell me of the marriage of the colors, of the ship on the ocean, the horse on the mountain…

They tell me now that there are no colors: No. Nothing. Nothing ever was.

I was mistaken, they say, by a lightening of the Shadow. I saw wrongly, they say.

But they will never let me near the fringes again. No. Never.

But listen. Lean close, comrade, and listen. I have a thing to show you, a thing which they do not know I have.

It is a yellow silk glove…

A Word from Zelazny

F&SF editor Edward Ferman rejected the story. The rejection letter said, "since I liked both the brushwork and the general feeling of this piece, I am hard put to explain why I don't want to buy it. Must be my orderly, commercial mind. If it were just a *bit* more realistic…"[1]

Zelazny then sent it to editor Bill Bowers of *Double:Bill* with the handwritten note, "Like, here's the piece I promised you in the letter I sent this morning… It *is* a bit different…"[2]

Notes

This may be Zelazny's most opaque tale, but the following may help a reader gain insight into Zelazny's intent. Of the classically recognized seven colors in a rainbow (red, orange, yellow, green, blue, indigo, and violet), indigo has been skipped but the rest are named in proper sequence. Whether the omission of indigo was deliberate and has intended meaning is unknown. There are three possible allusions in the story's title. First, Zelazny collected Tarot cards and was likely inspired by the 12th card which depicts an upside-down **Hanged Man** and sometimes an inverted rainbow below his head. One interpretation is that the Hanged Man is the Norse god Odin, who hung himself upside down from a tree for nine days, seeking knowledge through self-sacrifice. And the rainbow is Bifrost, the Bridge of the Gods to Asgard, from which Odin brought knowledge back to earth. The character in this story is seeking at his peril some knowledge of the outside, colored world. Second, there is an expression "Speak not of rope in the house of the hanged man"—Zelazny may simply have meant "do not speak of color in the house where there is no color" since it is clear that knowledge of color is forbidden in this story. Third, there is Paul Cézanne's 1873 painting, "**The House of the Hanged Man**," a fairly drab depiction which features a sunlit patch of grass between the two main houses. The character in this story is held captive in a room devoid of color; Zelazny may have been inspired by the imagery and title of Cézanne's painting.

---

1 Letter from Edward Ferman to Roger Zelazny, dated December 2, 1964.
2 Letter from Roger Zelazny to Bill Bowers, dated 12/22 (year not stated, likely 1964.).

DEATH AND THE EXECUTIONER

The Magazine of Fantasy & Science Fiction, June 1967.
The novel *Lord of Light* won the 1968 Hugo for best novel
and was nominated for the Nebula.

It is said that when the Teacher appeared, those of all castes went to hear his teachings, as well as animals, gods, and an occasional saint, to come away improved and uplifted. It was generally conceded that he had received enlightenment, except by those who believed him to be a fraud, sinner, criminal, or practical joker. These latter ones were not all to be numbered as his enemies, but on the other hand, not all of those improved and uplifted could be counted as his friends and supporters. His followers called him Mahasamatman and some said he was a god. So, after it was seen that he had been accepted as a teacher, was looked upon with respect, had many of the wealthy numbered as his supporters and had gained a reputation reaching far across the land, he was referred to as Tathagatha, meaning He Who Has Achieved. It must be noted that while the goddess Kali (sometimes known as Durga in her softer moments) never voiced a formal opinion as to his Buddhahood, she did render him the singular honor of dispatching her holy executioner to pay him her tribute, rather than a mere hired assassin…

❖   ❖   ❖

There is no disappearing of the true Dhamma until a false Dhamma arises in the world. When the false Dhamma arises, he makes the true Dhamma to disappear.

Samyutta-nikaya (II, 224)

Near the city of Alundil there was a rich grove of blue-barked trees, having purple foliage like feathers. It was famous for its beauty and the shrine-like peace of its shade. It had been the property of the merchant Vasu until his conversion, at which time he had presented it to the teacher variously known as Mahasamatman, Tathagatha and the Enlightened One. In that wood did this teacher abide with his followers, and when they walked forth into the town at midday their begging bowls never went unfilled.

There was always a large number of pilgrims about the grove. The believers, the curious and those who preyed upon the others were constantly passing through it. They came by horseback, they came by boat, they came on foot.

Alundil was not an overly large city. It had its share of thatched huts, as well as wooden bungalows; its main roadway was unpaved and rutted; it had two large bazaars and many small ones; there were wide fields of grain, owned by the Vaisyas, tended by the Sudras, which flowed and rippled, blue-green about the city; it had many hostels (though none so fine as the legendary hostel of Hawkana, in far Mahartha), because of the constant passage of travelers; it had its holy men and its storytellers; and it had its Temple.

The Temple was located on a low hill near the center of town, enormous gates on each of its four sides. These gates, and the walls about them, were filled with layer upon layer of decorative carvings, showing musicians and dancers, warriors and demons, gods and goddesses, animals and artists, love-makers and half-people, guardians and devas. These gates led into the first courtyard, which held more walls and more gates, leading in turn into the second courtyard. The first courtyard contained a little bazaar, where offerings to the gods were sold. It also housed numerous small shrines dedicated to the lesser deities. There were begging beggars, meditating holy men, laughing children, gossiping women, burning incenses, singing birds, gurgling purification tanks and humming pray-o-mats to be found in this courtyard at any hour of the day.

The inner courtyard, though, with its massive shrines dedicated to the major deities, was a focal point of religious intensity. People chanted or shouted prayers, mumbled verses from the Vedas, or stood, or knelt, or lay prostrate before huge stone images, which often were so heavily garlanded with flowers, smeared with red *kumkum* paste and surrounded by heaps of offerings that it was impossible to tell which deity was so immersed in tangible adoration. Periodically, the horns of the Temple were blown, there was a moment's hushed appraisal of their echo and the clamor began again.

And none would dispute the fact that Kali was queen of this Temple. Her tall, white-stone statue, within its gigantic shrine, dominated the inner courtyard. Her faint smile, perhaps contemptuous of the other gods and their worshipers, was, in its way, as arresting as the chained grins of the skulls she wore for a necklace. She held daggers in her hands—and poised in mid-step she stood, as though deciding whether to dance before or slay those who came to her shrine. Her lips were full, her eyes were wide. Seen by torchlight, she seemed to move.

It was fitting, therefore, that her shrine faced upon that of Yama, god of Death. It had been decided, logically enough, by the priests and architects, that he was best suited of all the deities to spend every minute of the day facing her, matching his unfaltering death-gaze against her own, returning her half smile with his twisted one. Even the most devout generally made a detour rather than pass between the two shrines; and after dark their section of the courtyard was always the abode of silence and stillness, being untroubled by late worshipers.

From out of the north, as the winds of spring blew across the land, there came the one called Rild. A small man, whose hair was white, though his years were few: Rild, who wore the dark trappings of a pilgrim, but about whose forearm, when they found him lying in a ditch with the fever, was wound the crimson strangling cord of his true profession: Rild.

Rild came in the spring, at festival-time, to Alundil of the blue-green fields, of the thatched huts and the bungalows of wood, of unpaved roadways and many hostels, of bazaars and holy men and storytellers, of the great religious revival and its Teacher, whose reputation had spread far across the land: to Alundil of the Temple, where his patron goddess was queen.

❖   ❖   ❖

Festival-time.

Twenty years earlier, Alundil's small festival had been an almost exclusively local affair. Now, though, with the passage of countless travelers, caused by the presence of the Enlightened One, who taught the Way of the Eightfold Path, the Festival of Alundil attracted so many pilgrims that local accommodations were filled to overflowing. Those who possessed tents could charge a high fee for their rental.

Stables were rented out for human occupancy. Even bare pieces of land were let as camping sites.

Alundil loved its Buddha. Many other towns had tried to entice him away from his purple grove: Shengodu, Flower of the Mountains, had offered him a palace and harem to come bring his teaching to the slopes. But the Enlightened One did not go to the mountain. Kannaka, of the Serpent River, had offered him elephants and ships, a town house and a country villa, horses and servants, to come and preach from its wharves. But the Enlightened One did not go to the river.

The Buddha remained in his grove and all things came to him. With the passage of years the festival grew larger and longer and more elaborate, like a well-fed dragon, scales all a-shimmer. The local Brahmins did not approve of the anti-ritualistic teachings of the Buddha, but his presence filled their coffers to overflowing; so they learned to live in his squat shadow, never voicing the word *tirthika*—heretic.

So the Buddha remained in his grove and all things came to him, including Rild.

❖   ❖   ❖

Festival-time.

The drums began in the evening on the third day.

On the third day, the massive drums of the *kathakali* began their rapid thunder. The miles-striding staccato of the drums carried across the fields to the town, across the town, across the purple grove and across the wastes of marshland that lay behind it. The drummers, wearing white *mundus*, bare to the waist, their dark flesh glistening with perspiration, worked in shifts, so strenuous was the mighty beating they set up; and never was the flow of sound broken, even as the new relay of drummers moved into position before the tightly stretched heads of the instruments.

As darkness arrived in the world, the travelers and townsmen who had begun walking as soon as they heard the chatter of the drums began to arrive at the festival field, large as a battlefield of old. There they found places and waited for the night to deepen and the drama to begin, sipping the sweet-smelling tea that they purchased at the stalls beneath the trees.

A great brass bowl of oil, tall as a man, wicks hanging down over its edges, stood in the center of the field. These wicks were lighted, and torches flickered beside the tents of the actors.

The drumming, at close range, was deafening and hypnotic, the rhythms complicated, syncopated, insidious. As midnight approached, the devotional chanting began, rising and falling with the drumbeat, working a net about the senses.

There was a brief lull as the Enlightened One and his monks arrived, their yellow robes near-orange in the flamelight. But they threw back their cowls and seated themselves cross-legged upon the ground. After a time, it was only the chanting and the voices of the drums that filled the minds of the spectators.

When the actors appeared, gigantic in their makeup, ankle bells jangling as their feet beat the ground, there was no applause, only rapt attention. The *kathakali* dancers were famous, trained from their youth in acrobatics as well as the ages-old patterns of the classical dance, knowing the nine distinct movements of the neck and of the eyeballs and the hundreds of hand positions required to re-enact the ancient epics of love and battle, of the encounters of gods and demons, of the valiant fights and bloody treacheries of tradition. The musicians shouted out the words of the stories as the actors, who never spoke, portrayed the awesome exploits of Rama and of the Pandava brothers. Wearing makeup of green and red, or black and stark white, they stalked across the field, skirts billowing, their mirror-sprinkled halos glittering in the light of the lamp. Occasionally, the lamp would flare or sputter, and it was as if a nimbus of holy or unholy light played about their heads, erasing entirely the sense of the event, causing the spectators to feel for a moment that they themselves were the illusion, and that the great-bodied figures of the cyclopean dance were the only real things in the world.

The dance would continue until daybreak, to end with the rising of the sun.

Before daybreak, however, one of the wearers of the saffron robe arrived from the direction of town, made his way through the crowd and spoke into the ear of the Enlightened One.

The Buddha began to rise, appeared to think better of it and reseated himself. He gave a message to the monk, who nodded and departed from the field of the festival.

The Buddha, looking imperturbable, returned his attention to the drama. A monk seated nearby noted that he was tapping his fingers upon the ground, and he decided that the Enlightened One must be keeping time with the drumbeats, for it was common knowledge that he was above such things as impatience.

When the drama had ended and Surya the sun pinked the skirts of Heaven above the eastern rim of the world, it was as if the night just passed had held the crowd prisoner within a tense and frightening dream, from which they were just now released, weary, to wander this day.

The Buddha and his followers set off walking immediately in the direction of the town. They did not pause to rest along the way, but passed through Alundil at a rapid but dignified gait.

When they came again to the purple grove, the Enlightened One instructed his monks to take rest, and he moved off in the direction of a small pavilion located deep within the wood.

❖   ❖   ❖

The monk who had brought the message during the drama sat within the pavilion. There he tended the fever of the traveler whom he had come upon in the marshes, where he walked often to better meditate upon the putrid condition his body would assume after death.

Tathagatha studied the man who lay upon the sleeping mat. His lips were thin and pale; he had a high forehead, high cheekbones, frosty eyebrows, pointed ears; and Tathagatha guessed that when those eyelids rose, the eyes revealed would be of a faded blue or gray. There was a quality of—translucency?—fragility perhaps, about his unconscious form, which might have been caused partly by the fevers racking his body, but which could not be attributed entirely to them. The small man did not give the impression of being one who would bear the thing which Tathagatha now raised in his hands. Rather, on first viewing, he might seem to be a very old man. If one granted him a second look and realized then that his colorless hair and his slight frame did not signify advanced age, one might then be struck by something childlike about his appearance. From the condition of his complexion, Tathagatha doubted that he need shave very often. Perhaps a slightly mischievous pucker was now hidden somewhere between his cheeks and the corners of his mouth. Perhaps not, also.

The Buddha raised the crimson strangling cord, which was a thing borne only by the holy executioners of the goddess Kali. He fingered its silken length, and it passed like a serpent through his hand, clinging slightly. He did not doubt but that it was intended to move in such a manner about his throat. Almost unconsciously, he held it and twisted his hands through the necessary movements.

Then he looked up at the wide-eyed monk who had watched him, smiled his imperturbable smile and laid the cord aside. With a damp cloth, the monk wiped the perspiration from the pale brow.

The man on the sleeping mat shuddered at the contact, and his eyes snapped open. The madness of the fever was in them and they did not truly see, but Tathagatha felt a sudden jolt at their contact.

Dark, so dark they were almost jet, and it was impossible to tell where the pupil ended and the iris began. There was something extremely unsettling about eyes of such power in a body so frail and effete.

He reached out and stroked the man's hands, and it was like touching steel, cold and impervious. He drew his fingernail sharply across the back of the right hand. No scratch or indentation marked its passage, and his nail fairly slid, as though across a pane of glass. He squeezed the man's thumbnail and released it. There was no sudden change of color. It was as though these hands were dead or mechanical things.

He continued his examination. The phenomenon ended somewhat above the wrists, occurred again in other places. His hands, breast, abdomen, neck and portions of his back had soaked within the death bath, which gave this special unyielding power. Total immersion would, of course, have proved fatal; but as it was, the man had traded some of his tactile sensitivity for the equivalent of invisible gauntlets, breastplate, neckpiece and back armor of steel. He was indeed one of the select assassins of the terrible goddess.

"Who else knows of this man?" asked the Buddha.

"The monk Simha," replied the other, "who helped me bear him here."

"Did he see," Tathagatha gestured with his eyes toward the crimson cord, "that?"

The monk nodded.

"Then go fetch him. Bring him to me at once. Do not mention anything of this to anyone, other than that a pilgrim was taken ill and we are tending him here. I will personally take over his care and minister to his illness."

"Yes, Illustrious One."

The monk hurried forth from the pavilion.

Tathagatha seated himself beside the sleeping mat and waited.

❖   ❖   ❖

It was two days before the fever broke and intelligence returned to those dark eyes. But during those two days, anyone who passed by the pavilion might have heard the voice of the Enlightened One droning on and on, as though he addressed his sleeping charge. Occasionally, the man himself mumbled and spoke loudly, as those in a fever often do.

On the second day, the man opened his eyes suddenly and stared upward. Then he frowned and turned his bead.

"Good morning, Rild," said Tathagatha.

"You are—?" asked the other, in an unexpected baritone.

"One who teaches the way of liberation," he replied.

"The Buddha?"

"I have been called such."

"Tathagatha?"

"This name, too, have I been given."

The other attempted to rise, failed, settled back. His eyes never left the placid countenance.

"How is it that you know my name?" he finally asked.

"In your fever you spoke considerably."

"Yes, I was very sick, and doubtless babbling. It was in that cursed swamp that I took the chill."

Tathagatha smiled. "One of the disadvantages of traveling alone is that when you fall there is none to assist you."

"True…" acknowledged Rild, and his eyes closed once more and his breathing deepened.

Tathagatha remained in the lotus posture, waiting.

❖ ❖ ❖

When Rild awakened again, it was evening.

"…Thirsty," he said.

Tathagatha gave him water.

"Hungry?" he asked.

"No, not yet. My stomach would rebel."

He raised himself up onto his elbows and stared at his attendant. Then he sank back upon the mat.

"You are the one," he announced.

"Yes," replied the other.

"What are you going to do?"

"Feed you, when you say you are hungry."

"I mean, after that."

"Watch as you sleep, lest you lapse again into the fever."

"That is not what I meant."

"I know."

"After I have eaten and rested and recovered my strength—what then?"

Tathagatha smiled as he drew the silken cord from somewhere beneath his robe. "Nothing," he replied, "nothing at all," and he draped the cord across Rild's shoulder and withdrew his hand.

The other shook his head and leaned back. He reached up and fingered the length of crimson. He twined it about his fingers and then about his wrist. He stroked it.

"It is holy," he said, after a time.

"So it would seem."

"You know its use, and its purpose?"

"Of course."

"Why then will you do nothing at all?"

"I have no need to move or to act. All things come to me. If anything is to be done, it is you who will do it."

"I do not understand."

"I know that, too."

The man stared into the shadows overhead.

"I will attempt to eat now," he announced.

Tathagatha gave him broth and bread, which he managed to keep down. Then he drank more water, and when he had finished he was breathing heavily.

"You have offended Heaven," he stated.

"Of that, I am aware."

"…And you have detracted from the glory of a goddess, whose supremacy here has always been undisputed."

"I know."

"But I owe you my life, and I have eaten your bread…"

There was no reply.

"Because of this, I must break a most holy vow," finished Rild. "I cannot kill you, Tathagatha."

"Then I owe my life to the fact that you owe me yours. Let us consider the life-owing balanced."

Rild uttered a short chuckle.

"So be it," he said.

"What will you do, now that you have abandoned your mission?"

"I do not know. My sin is too great to permit me to return. Now I, too, have offended against Heaven, and the goddess will turn away her face from my prayers. I have failed her."

"Such being the case, remain here. You will at least have company in damnation."

"Very well," agreed Rild. "There is nothing else left to me."

He slept once again, and the Buddha smiled.

❖   ❖   ❖

In the days which followed, as the festival wore on, the Enlightened One preached to the crowds who passed through the purple grove. He spoke of the unity of all things, great and small, of the law of cause, of becoming and dying, of the illusion of the world, of the spark of the *atman*, of the way of salvation through renunciation of the self and union with the whole; he spoke of realization and enlightenment, of the meaninglessness of the Brahmins' rituals, comparing their forms to vessels empty of content. Many listened, a few heard and some remained in the purple grove to take up the saffron robe of the seeker.

And each time he taught, the man Rild sat nearby, wearing his black garments and leather harness, his strange dark eyes ever upon the Enlightened One.

Two weeks after his recovery, Rild came upon the teacher as he walked through the grove in meditation. He fell into step beside him, and after a time he spoke.

"Enlightened One, I have listened to your teachings, and I have listened well. Much have I thought upon your words."

The other nodded.

"I have always been a religious man," he stated, "or I would not have been selected for the post I once occupied. After it became impossible for me to fulfill my mission, I felt a great emptiness. I had failed my goddess, and life was without meaning for me."

The other listened, silently.

"…But I have heard your words," he said, "and they have filled me with a kind of joy. They have shown me another way to salvation, a way which I feel to be superior to the one I previously followed."

The Buddha studied his face as he spoke.

"Your way of renunciation is a strict one, which I feel to be good. It suits my needs. Therefore, I request permission to be taken into your community of seekers, and to follow your path."

"Are you certain," asked the Enlightened One, "that you do not seek merely to punish yourself for what has been weighing upon your conscience as a failure, or a sin?"

"Of that I am certain," said Rild. "I have held your words within me and felt the truth which they contain. In the service of the goddess have I slain more men than purple fronds upon yonder bough. I am not even counting women and children. So I am not easily taken in by words, having heard too many, voiced in all tones of speech—words pleading, arguing, cursing. But your words move me, and they are superior to the teachings of the Brahmins. Gladly would I become your executioner, dispatching for you your enemies with a saffron cord—or with a blade, or pike, or with my hands, for I am proficient with all weapons, having spent three lifetimes learning their use—but I know that such is not your way. Death and life are as one to you, and you do not seek the destruction of your enemies. So I request entrance to your Order. For me, it is not so difficult a thing as it would be for another. One must renounce home and family, origin and property. I lack these things. One must renounce one's own will, which I have already done. All I need now is the yellow robe."

"It is yours," said Tathagatha, "with my blessing."

❖ ❖ ❖

Rild donned the robe of a Buddhist monk and took to fasting and meditating. After a week, when the festival was near to its close, he departed into the town with his begging bowl, in the company of the other monks. He did not return with them, however. The day wore on into evening, the evening into darkness. The horns of the Temple had already sounded the last notes of the *nagaswaram*, and many of the travelers had since departed the festival.

For a long while, the Enlightened One walked the woods, meditating. Then he, too, vanished.

Down from the grove, with the marshes at its back, toward the town of Alundil, above which lurked the hills of rock and around which lay the blue-green fields, into the town of Alundil, still astir with travelers, many of them at the height of their revelry, up the streets of Alundil toward the hill with its Temple, walked the Buddha.

He entered the first courtyard, and it was quiet there. The dogs and children and beggars had gone away. The priests slept. One drowsing attendant sat behind a bench at the bazaar. Many of the shrines were now empty, the statues having been borne within. Before several of the others, worshipers knelt in late prayer.

He entered the inner courtyard. An ascetic was seated on a prayer mat before the statue of Ganesha. He, too, seemed to qualify as a statue, making no visible movements. Four oil lamps flickered about the yard, their dancing light serving primarily to accentuate the shadows that lay upon most of the shrines. Small votive lights cast a faint illumination upon some of the statues.

Tathagatha crossed the yard and stood facing the towering figure of Kali, at whose feet a tiny lamp blinked. Her smile seemed a plastic and moving thing, as she regarded the man before her.

Draped across her outstretched hand, looped once about the point of her dagger, lay a crimson strangling cord.

Tathagatha smiled back at her, and she seemed almost to frown at that moment.

"It is a resignation, my dear," he stated. "You have lost this round."

She seemed to nod in agreement.

"I am pleased to have achieved such a height of recognition in so short a period of time," he continued. "But even if you had succeeded, old girl, it would have done you little good. It is too late now. I have started something which you cannot undo. Too many have heard the ancient words. You had thought they were lost, and so did I. But we were both wrong. The religion by which you rule is very ancient, goddess, but my protest is also that of a venerable tradition. So call me a protestant, and remember—now I am more than a man.

"Good night."

He left the Temple and the shrine of Kali, where the eyes of Yama had been fixed upon his back.

❖ ❖ ❖

It was many months before the miracle occurred, and when it did, it did not seem a miracle, for it had grown up slowly about them.

Rild, who had come out of the north as the winds of spring blew across the land, wearing death upon his arm and the black fire within his eyes—Rild, of the white brows and pointed ears—spoke one afternoon, after the spring had passed, when the long days of summer hung warm beneath the Bridge of the Gods. He spoke, in that unexpected baritone, to answer a question asked him by a traveler.

The man asked him a second question, and then a third.

He continued to speak, and some of the other monks and several pilgrims gathered about him. The answers following the questions, which now came from all of them, grew longer and longer, for they became parables, examples, allegories.

Then they were seated at his feet, and his dark eyes became strange pools, and his voice came down as from Heaven, clear and soft, melodic and persuasive.

They listened, and then the travelers went their way. But they met and spoke with other travelers upon the road, so that, before the summer had passed, pilgrims coming to the purple grove were asking to meet this disciple of the Buddha's, and to hear his words also.

Tathagatha shared the preaching with him. Together, they taught of the Way of the Eightfold Path, the glory of Nirvana, the illusion of the world and the chains that the world lays upon a man.

And then there were times when even the soft-spoken Tathagatha listened to the words of his disciple, who had digested all of the things he had preached, had meditated long and fully upon them and now, as though he had found entrance to a secret sea, dipped with his steel-hard hand into places of hidden waters, and then sprinkled a thing of truth and beauty upon the heads of the hearers.

Summer passed. There was no doubt now that there were two who had received enlightenment: Tathagatha and his small disciple, whom they called Sugata. It was even said that Sugata was a healer, and that when his eyes shone strangely and the icy touch of his hands came upon a twisted limb, that limb grew straight again. It was said that a blind man's vision had suddenly returned to him during one of Sugata's sermons.

There were two things in which Sugata believed: the Way of Salvation and Tathagatha, the Buddha.

"Illustrious One," he said to him one day, "my life was empty until you revealed to me the True Path. When you received your enlightenment, before you began your teaching, was it like a rush of fire and the roaring of water and you everywhere and a part of everything?—the clouds and the trees, the animals in the forest, all people, the snow on the mountaintop and the bones in the field?"

"Yes," said Tathagatha.

"I, also, know the joy of all things," said Sugata.

"Yes, I know," said Tathagatha.

"I see now why once you said that all things come to you. To have brought such a doctrine into the world—I can see why the gods were envious. Poor gods! They are to be pitied. But you know. You know all things."

Tathagatha did not reply.

❖   ❖   ❖

When the winds of spring blew again across the land, the year having gone full cycle since the arrival of the second Buddha, there came one day from out of the heavens a fearful shrieking.

The citizens of Alundil turned out into their streets to stare up at the sky. The Sudras in the fields put by their work and looked upward. In the great Temple on the hill there was a sudden silence. In the purple grove beyond the town, the monks turned their heads.

It paced the heavens, the one who was born to rule the wind…

From out of the north it came—green and red, yellow and brown…

Its glide was a dance, its way was the air…

There came another shriek, and then the beating of mighty pinions as it climbed past clouds to become a tiny dot of black—

…And then it fell, like a meteor, bursting into flame, all of its colors blazing and burning bright, as it grew and grew, beyond all belief that anything could live at that size, that pace, that magnificence…

Half spirit, half bird, legend darkening the sky…

Mount of Vishnu, whose beak smashes chariots.

The Garuda Bird circled above Alundil.

Circled, and passed beyond the hills of rock that stood behind the city.

"Garuda!" The word ran through the town, the fields, the Temple, the grove.

If he did not fly alone, it was known that only a god could use the Garuda Bird for a mount.

There was silence. After those shrieks and that thunder of pinions, voices seemed naturally to drop to a whisper.

The Enlightened One stood upon the road before the grove, his monks moving about him, facing in the direction of the hills of rock.

Sugata came to his side and stood there.

"It was but a spring ago…" he said.

Tathagatha nodded.

"Rild failed," said Sugata. "What new thing comes from Heaven?"

The Buddha shrugged.

"I fear for you, my teacher," he said. "In all my lifetimes, you have been my only friend. Your teaching has given me peace. Why can they not leave you alone? You are the most harmless of men, and your doctrine the gentlest. What ill could you possibly bear them?"

The other turned away.

At that moment, with a mighty beating of the air and a jagged cry from its opened beak, the Garuda Bird rose once more above the hills. This time, it did not circle over the town, but climbed to a great height in the heavens and swept off to the north. Such was the speed of its passing that it was gone in a matter of moments.

"Its passenger has dismounted and remains behind," suggested Sugata.

The Buddha walked within the purple grove.

❖   ❖   ❖

He came from beyond the hills of stone, walking.

He came to a passing place through stone, and he followed this trail, his red leather boots silent on the rocky path.

Ahead, there was a sound of running water, from where a small stream cut across his way. Shrugging his blood-bright cloak back over his shoulders, he advanced upon a bend in the trail, the ruby head of his scimitar gleaming in his crimson sash.

Rounding a corner of stone, he came to a halt.

One waited ahead, standing beside the log which led across the stream.

His eyes narrowed for an instant, then he moved forward again.

It was a small man who stood there, wearing the dark garments of a pilgrim, caught about with a leather harness from which was suspended a short, curved blade of bright steel. This man's head was closely shaven, save for a small lock of white hair. His eyebrows were white above eyes that were dark, and his skin was pale; his ears appeared to be pointed.

The traveler raised his hand and spoke to this man, saying, "Good afternoon, pilgrim."

The man did not reply, but moved to bar his way, positioning himself before the log which led across the stream.

"Pardon me, good pilgrim, but I am about to cross here and you are making my passage difficult," he stated.

"You are mistaken, Lord Yama, if you think you are about to pass here," replied the other.

The One in Red smiled, showing a long row of even, white teeth.

"It is always a pleasure to be recognized," he acknowledged, "even by one who conveys misinformation concerning other matters."

"I do not fence with words," said the man in black.

"Oh?" The other raised his eyebrows in an expression of exaggerated inquiry. "With what then do you fence, sir? Surely not that piece of bent metal you bear."

"None other."

"I took it for some barbarous prayer-stick at first. I understand that this is a region fraught with strange cults and primitive sects. For a moment, I took you to be a devotee of some such superstition. But if, as you say, it is indeed a weapon, then I trust you are familiar with its use?"

"Somewhat," replied the man in black.

"Good, then," said Yama, "for I dislike having to kill a man who does not know what he is about. I feel obligated to point out to you, however, that when you stand before the Highest for judgment, you will be accounted a suicide."

The other smiled faintly.

"Any time that you are ready, deathgod, I will facilitate the passage of your spirit from out its fleshy envelope."

"One more item only, then," said Yama, "and I shall put a quick end to conversation. Give me a name to tell the priests, so that they shall know for whom they offer the rites."

"I renounced my final name but a short while back," answered the other. "For this reason, Kali's consort must take his death of one who is nameless."

"Rild, you are a fool," said Yama, and drew his blade.

The man in black drew his.

"…And it is fitting that you go unnamed to your doom. You betrayed your goddess."

"Life is full of betrayals," replied the other, before he struck. "By opposing you now and in this manner, I also betray the teachings of my new master. But I must follow the dictates of my heart. Neither my old name nor my new do therefore fit me, nor are they deserved—so call me by no name!"

Then his blade was fire, leaping everywhere, clicking, blazing…

Yama fell back before this onslaught, giving ground foot by foot, moving only his wrist as he parried the blows that fell about him.

Then, after he had retreated ten paces, he stood his ground and would not be moved. His parries widened slightly, but his ripostes became more sudden now, and were interspersed with feints and unexpected attacks.

They swaggered blades till their perspiration fell upon the ground in showers, and then Yama began to press the attack, slowly, forcing his opponent into a retreat. Step by step, he recovered the ten paces he had given.

When they stood again upon the ground where the first blow had been struck, Yama acknowledged, over the clashing of steel, "Well have you learned your lessons, Rild! Better even than I had thought! Congratulations!"

As he spoke, his opponent wove his blade through an elaborate double feint and scored a light touch which cut his shoulder, drawing blood that immediately merged with the color of his garment.

At this, Yama sprang forward, beating down the other's guard, and delivered a blow to the side of his neck that might have decapitated him.

The man in black raised his guard, shaking his head, parried another attack and thrust forward, to be parried again himself.

"So, the death bath collars your throat," said Yama. "I'll seek entrance elsewhere, then," and his blade sang a faster song, as he tried for a low-line thrust.

Yama unleashed the full fury of that blade, backed by the centuries and the masters of many ages. Yet, the other met his attacks, parrying wider and wider, retreating faster and faster now, but still managing to hold him off as he backed away, counterthrusting as he went.

He retreated until his back was to the stream. Then Yama slowed and made comment:

"Half a century ago," he stated, "when you were my pupil for a brief time, I said to myself, 'This one has within him the makings of a master.' Nor was I wrong, Rild. You are perhaps the greatest swordsman raised up in all the ages I can remember. I can almost forgive apostasy when I witness your skill."

He feinted then a chest cut, and at the last instant moved around the parry so that he lay the edge of his weapon high upon the other's wrist.

Leaping backward, parrying wildly and cutting at Yama's head, the man in black came into a position at the head of the log which lay above the crevice that led down to the stream.

"Your hand, too, Rild! Indeed, the goddess is lavish with her protection. Try this!"

The steel screeched as he caught it in a bind, nicking the other's biceps as he passed about the blade.

"Aha! There's a place she missed!" he cried. "Let's try for another!"

Their blades bound and disengaged, feinted, thrust, parried, riposted…

Yama met an elaborate attack with a stop-thrust, his longer blade again drawing blood from his opponent's upper arm.

The man in black stepped up upon the log, swinging a vicious head cut, which Yama beat away. Pressing the attack then even harder, Yama forced him to back out upon the log and then he kicked at its side.

The other jumped backward, landing upon the opposite bank. As soon as his feet touched ground, he too kicked out, causing the log to move.

It rolled, before Yama could mount it, slipping free of the banks, crashing down into the stream, bobbing about for a moment, and then following the water trail westward.

"I'd say it is only a seven- or eight-foot jump, Yama! Come on across!" cried the other.

The deathgod smiled.

"Catch your breath quickly now, while you may," he stated. "Breath is the least appreciated gift of the gods. None sing hymns to it, praising the good air, breathed by king and beggar, master and dog alike. But, oh to be without it! Appreciate each breath, Rild, as though it were your last—for that one, too, is near at hand!"

"You are said to be wise in these matters, Yama," said the one who had been called Rild and Sugata. "You are said to be a god, whose kingdom is death and whose knowledge extends beyond the ken of mortals. I would question you, therefore, while we are standing idle."

Yama did not smile his mocking smile, as he had to all his opponent's previous statements. This one had a touch of ritual about it.

"What is it that you wish to know? I grant you the death-boon of a question."

Then, in the ancient words of the Katha Upanishad, the one who had been called Rild and Sugata chanted:

" 'There is doubt concerning a man when he is dead. Some say he still exists. Others say he does not. This thing I should like to know, taught by you.' "

Yama replied with the ancient words, " 'On this subject even the gods have their doubts. It is not easy to understand, for the nature of the *atman* is a subtle thing. Ask me another question. Release me from this boon!' "

" 'Forgive me if it is foremost in my mind, oh Death, but another teacher such as yourself cannot be found, and surely there is no other boon which I crave more at this moment.' "

" 'Keep your life and go your way,' " said Yama, plunging his blade again into his sash. " 'I release you from your doom. Choose sons and grandsons; choose elephants, horses, herds of cattle and gold. Choose any other boon—fair maidens, chariots, musical instruments. I shall give them unto you and they shall wait upon you. But ask me not of death.' "

" 'Oh Death,' " sang the other, " 'these endure only till tomorrow. Keep your maidens, horses, dances and songs for yourself. No boon will I accept but the one which I have asked—tell me, oh Death, of that which lies beyond life, of which men and the gods have their doubts.' "

Yama stood very still and he did not continue the poem.

"Very well, Rild," he said, his eyes locking with the other's, "but it is not a kingdom subject to words. I must show you."

They stood, so, for a moment, and then the man in black swayed. He threw his arm across his face, covering his eyes, and a single sob escaped his throat.

When this occurred, Yama drew his cloak from his shoulders and cast it like a net across the stream.

Weighted at the hems for such a maneuver, it fell, net-like, upon his opponent.

As he struggled to free himself, the man in black heard rapid footfalls and then a crash, as Yama's blood-red boots struck upon his side of the stream. Casting aside the cloak and raising his guard, he parried Yama's new attack. The ground behind him sloped upward, and he backed further and further, to where it steepened, so that Yama's head was no higher than his belt. He then struck down at his opponent. Yama slowly fought his way uphill.

"Deathgod, deathgod," he chanted, "forgive my presumptuous question, and tell me you did not lie."

"Soon you shall know," said Yama, cutting at his legs.

Yama struck a blow which would have run another man through, cleaving his heart. But it glanced off his opponent's breast.

When he came to a place where the ground was broken, the small man kicked, again and again, sending showers of dirt and gravel down upon his opponent. Yama shielded his eyes with his left hand, but then larger pieces of stone began to rain down upon him. These rolled on the ground, and as several came beneath his boots, he lost his footing and fell, slipping backward down the slope. The other kicked at heavy rocks then, even dislodging a boulder and following it downhill, his blade held high.

Unable to gain his footing in time to meet the attack, Yama rolled and slid back toward the stream. He managed to brake himself at the edge of the crevice, but he saw the boulder coming and tried to draw back out of its way. As he pushed at the ground with both hands, his blade fell into the waters below.

With his dagger, which he drew as he sprang into a stumbling crouch, he managed to parry the high cut of the other's blade. The boulder splashed into the stream.

Then his left hand shot forward, seizing the wrist that had guided the blade. He slashed upward with the dagger and felt his own wrist taken.

They stood then, locking their strength, until Yama sat down and rolled to his side, thrusting the other from him.

Still, both locks held, and they continued to roll from the force of that thrust. Then the edge of the crevice was beside them, beneath them, above them.

He felt the blade go out of his hand as it struck the stream bed.

When they came again above the surface of the water, gasping for breath, each held only water in his hands.

"Time for the final baptism," said Yama, and he lashed out with his left hand.

The other blocked the punch, throwing one of his own.

They moved to the left with the waters, until their feet struck upon rock and they fought, wading, along the length of the stream.

It widened and grew more shallow as they moved, until the waters swirled about their waists. In places, the banks began to fall nearer the surface of the water.

Yama landed blow after blow, both with his fists and the edges of his hands; but it was as if he assailed a statue, for the one who had been Kali's holy executioner took each blow without changing his expression, and he returned them with twisting punches of bone-breaking force. Most of these blows were slowed by the water or blocked by Yama's guard, but one landed between his rib cage and hipbone and another glanced on his left shoulder and rebounded from his cheek.

Yama cast himself into a backstroke and made for shallower water.

The other followed and sprang upon him, to be caught in his impervious midsection by a red boot, as the front of his garment was jerked forward and down. He continued on, passing over Yama's head, to land upon his back on a section of shale.

Yama rose to his knees and turned, as the other found his footing and drew a dagger from his belt. His face was still impassive as he dropped into a crouch.

For a moment their eyes met, but the other did not waver this time.

"Now can I meet your death-gaze, Yama," he stated, "and not be stopped by it. You have taught me too well!"

And as he lunged, Yama's hands came away from his waist, snapping his wet sash like a whip about the other's legs.

He caught him and locked him to him as he fell forward, dropping the blade, and with a kick he bore them both back into deeper water.

"None sing hymns to breath," said Yama. "But, oh to be without it!"

Then he plunged downward, bearing the other with him, his arms like steel loops about his body.

❖   ❖   ❖

Later, much later, as the wet figure stood beside the stream, he spoke softly and his breath came in gasps:

"You were—the greatest—to be raised up against me—in all the ages I can remember… It is indeed a pity…"

Then, having crossed the stream, he continued on his way through the hills of stone, walking.

❖   ❖   ❖

Entering the town of Alundil, the traveler stopped at the first inn he came to. He took a room and ordered a tub of water. He bathed while a servant cleaned his garments.

Before he had his dinner, he moved to the window and looked down into the street. The smell of slizzard was strong upon the air, and the babble of many voices arose from below.

People were leaving the town. In the courtyard at his back, preparations for the departure of a morning caravan were being made. This night marked the end of the spring festival. Below him in the street, businessmen were still trading, mothers were soothing tired children, and a local prince was returning with his men from the hunt, two fire-roosters strapped to the back of a skittering slizzard. He watched a tired prostitute discussing something with a priest, who appeared to be even more tired, as he kept shaking his head and finally walked away. One moon was already high in the heavens—seen as golden through the Bridge of the Gods—and a second, smaller moon had just appeared above the horizon. There was a cool tingle in the evening air, bearing to him, above the smells of the city, the scents of the growing things of spring: the small shoots and the tender grasses, the clean smell of the blue-green spring wheat, the moist ground, the roiling freshet. Leaning forward, he could see the Temple that stood upon the hill.

He summoned a servant to bring his dinner in his chamber and to send for a local merchant.

He ate slowly, not paying especial attention to his food, and when he had finished, the merchant was shown in.

The man bore a cloak full of samples, and of these he finally decided upon a long, curved blade and a short, straight dagger, both of which he thrust into his sash.

Then he went out into the evening and walked along the rutted main street of the town. Lovers embraced in doorways. He passed a house where mourners were wailing for one dead. A beggar limped after him for half a block, until he turned and glanced into his eyes, saying, "You are not lame," and then the man hurried away, losing himself in a crowd that was passing. Overhead, the fireworks began to burst against the sky, sending long, cherry-colored streamers down toward the ground. From the Temple came the sound of the gourd horns playing the *nagaswaram* music. A man stumbled from out a doorway, brushing against him, and he broke the man's wrist as he felt his hand fall upon his purse. The man uttered a curse and called for help, but he pushed him into the drainage ditch and walked on, turning away his two companions with one dark look.

At last, he came to the Temple, hesitated a moment and passed within.

He entered the inner courtyard behind a priest who was bearing in a small statue from an outer niche.

He surveyed the courtyard, then quickly moved to the place occupied by the statue of the goddess Kali. He studied her for a long while, drawing his blade and placing it at her feet. When he picked it up and turned away, he saw that the priest was watching him. He nodded to the man, who immediately approached and bade him a good evening.

"Good evening, priest," he replied.

"May Kali sanctify your blade, warrior."

"Thank you. She has."

The priest smiled.

"You speak as if you knew that for certain."

"And that is presumptuous of me, eh?"

"Well, it may not be in the best of taste."

"Nevertheless, I felt her power come over me as I gazed upon her shrine."

The priest shuddered.

"Despite my office," he stated, "that is a feeling of power I can do without."

"You fear her power?"

"Let us say," said the priest, "that despite its magnificence, the shrine of Kali is not so frequently visited as are those of Lakshmi, Sarasvati, Shakti, Sitala, Ratri, and the other less awesome goddesses."

"But she is greater than any of these."

"…And more terrible."

"So? Despite her strength, she is not an unjust goddess."

The priest smiled.

"What man who has lived for more than a score of years desires justice, warrior? For my part, I find mercy infinitely more attractive. Give me a forgiving deity any day."

"Well taken," said the other, "but I am, as you say, a warrior. My own nature is close to hers. We think alike, the goddess and I. We generally agree on most matters. When we do not, I remember that she is also a woman."

"I live here," said the priest, "and I do not speak that intimately of my charges, the gods."

"In public, that is," said the other. "Tell me not of priests. I have drunk with many of you, and know you to be as blasphemous as the rest of mankind."

"There is a time and place for everything," said the priest, glancing back at Kali's statue.

"Aye, aye. Now tell me why the base of Yama's shrine has not been scrubbed recently. It is dusty."

"It was cleaned but yesterday, but so many have passed before it since then that it has felt considerable usage."

The other smiled.

"Why then are there no offerings laid at his feet, no remains of sacrifices?"

"No one gives flowers to Death," said the priest. "They just come to look and go away. We priests have always felt the two statues to be well situated. They make a terrible pair, do they not? Death, and the mistress of destruction?"

"A mighty team," said the other. "But do you mean to tell me that no one makes sacrifice to Yama? No one at all?"

"Other than we priests, when the calendar of devotions requires it, and an occasional townsman, when a loved one is upon the death-bed and has been refused direct incarnation—other than these, no, I have never seen sacrifice made to Yama, simply, sincerely, with good will or affection."

"He must feel offended."

"Not so, warrior. For are not all living things, in themselves, sacrifices to Death?"

"Indeed, you speak truly. What need has he for their good will or affection? Gifts are unnecessary, for he takes what he wants."

"Like Kali," acknowledged the priest. "And in the cases of both deities have I often sought justification for atheism. Unfortunately, they manifest themselves too strongly in the world for their existence to be denied effectively. Pity."

The warrior laughed.

"A priest who is an unwilling believer! I like that. It tickles my funny bone! Here, buy yourself a barrel of soma—for sacrificial purposes."

"Thank you, warrior. I shall. Join me in a small libation now—on the Temple?"

"By Kali, I will!" said the other. "But a small one only."

He accompanied the priest into the central building and down a flight of stairs into the cellar, where a barrel of soma was tapped and two beakers drawn.

"To your health and long life," he said, raising it.

"To your morbid patrons—Yama and Kali," said the priest.

"Thank you."

They gulped the potent brew, and the priest drew two more.

"To warm your throat against the night."

"Very good."

"It is a good thing to see some of these travelers depart," said the priest. "Their devotions have enriched the Temple, but they have also tired the staff considerably."

"To the departure of the pilgrims!"

"To the departure of the pilgrims!"

They drank again.

"I thought that most of them came to see the Buddha," said Yama.

"That is true," replied the priest, "but on the other hand, they are not anxious to antagonize the gods by this. So, before they visit the purple grove, they generally make sacrifice or donate to the Temple for prayers."

"What do you know of the one called Tathagatha, and of his teachings?"

The other looked away.

"I am a priest of the gods and a Brahmin, warrior. I do not wish to speak of this one."

"So, he has gotten to you, too?"

"Enough! I have made my wishes known to you. It is not a subject on which I will discourse."

"It matters not—and will matter less shortly. Thank you for the soma. Good evening, priest."

"Good evening, warrior. May the gods smile upon your path."

"And yours also."

Mounting the stairs, he departed the Temple and continued on his way through the city, walking.

When he came to the purple grove, there were three moons in the heavens, small camplights behind the trees, pale blossoms of fire in the sky above the town, and a breeze with a certain dampness in it stirring the growth about him.

He moved silently ahead, entering the grove.

When he came into the lighted area, he was faced with row upon row of motionless, seated figures. Each wore a yellow robe with a yellow cowl drawn over the head. Hundreds of them were seated so, and not one uttered a sound.

He approached the one nearest him.

"I have come to see Tathagatha, the Buddha," he said.

The man did not seem to hear him.

"Where is he?"

The man did not reply.

He bent forward and stared into the monk's half-closed eyes. For a moment, he glared into them, but it was as though the other was asleep, for the eyes did not even meet with his.

Then he raised his voice, so that all within the grove might hear him:

"I have come to see Tathagatha, the Buddha," he said. "Where is he?"

It was as though he addressed a field of stones.

"Do you think to hide him in this manner?" he called out. "Do you think that because you are many, and all dressed alike, and because you will not answer me, that for these reasons I cannot find him among you?"

There was only the sighing of the wind, passing through from the back of the grove. The light flickered and the purple fronds stirred.

He laughed.

"In this, you may be right," he admitted. "But you must move sometime, if you intend to go on living—and I can wait as long as any man."

Then he seated himself upon the ground, his back against the blue bark of a tall tree, his blade across his knees.

Immediately, he was seized with drowsiness. His head nodded and jerked upward several times. Then his chin came to rest upon his breast and he snored.

❖   ❖   ❖

…Was walking, across a blue-green plain, the grasses bending down to form a pathway before him. At the end of this pathway was a massive tree, a tree such as did not grow upon the world, but rather held the world together with its roots, and with its branches reached up to utter leaves among the stars.

At its base sat a man, cross-legged, a faint smile upon his lips. He knew this man to be the Buddha, and he approached and stood before him.

"Greetings, oh Death," said the seated one, crowned with a rose-hued aureole that was bright in the shadow of the tree.

Yama did not reply, but drew his blade.

The Buddha continued to smile, and as Yama moved forward he heard a sound like distant music.

He halted and looked about him, his blade still upraised.

They came from all quarters, the four Regents of the world, come down from Mount Sumeru: the Master of the North advanced, followed by his Yakshas, all in gold, mounted on yellow horses, bearing shields that blazed with golden light; the Angel of the South came on, followed by his hosts, the Kumbhandas, mounted upon blue steeds and bearing sapphire shields; from the East rode the Regent whose horsemen carry shields of pearl and who are clad all in silver; and from the West there came the One whose Nâgas mounted blood-red horses, were clad all in red and held before them shields of coral. Their hooves did not appear to touch the grasses, and the only sound in the air was the music, which grew louder.

"Why do the Regents of the world approach?" Yama found himself saying.

"They come to bear my bones away," replied the Buddha, still smiling.

The four Regents drew rein, their hordes at their backs, and Yama faced them.

"You come to bear his bones away," said Yama, "but who will come for yours?"

"You may not have this man, oh Death," said the Master of the North, "for he belongs to the world, and we of the world will defend him."

"Hear me, Regents who dwell upon Sumeru," said Yama, taking his Aspect upon him. "Into your hands is given the keeping of the world, but Death takes whom he will from out the world, and whenever he chooses. It is not given to you to dispute my Attributes, nor the ways of their working."

The four Regents moved to a position between Yama and Tathagatha.

"We do dispute your way with this one, Lord Yama. For in his hands he holds the destiny of our world. You may touch him only after having overthrown the four Powers."

"So be it," said Yama. "Which among you will be first to oppose me?"

"I will," said the speaker, drawing his golden blade.

Yama, his Aspect upon him, sheared through the soft metal like butter and laid the flat of his scimitar along the Regent's head, sending him sprawling upon the ground.

A great cry came up from the ranks of the Yakshas, and two of the golden horsemen came forward to bear away their leader. Then they turned their mounts and rode back into the North.

"Who is next?"

The Regent of the East came before him, bearing a straight blade of silver and a net woven of moonbeams.

"I," he said, and he cast with the net.

Yama set his foot upon it, caught it in his fingers, jerked the other off balance. As the Regent stumbled forward, he reversed his blade and struck him in the jaw with its pommel.

Two silver warriors glared at him, then dropped their eyes, as they bore their Master away to the East, a discordant music trailing in their wake.

"Next!" said Yama.

Then there came before him the burly leader of the Nâgas, who threw down his weapons and stripped off his tunic, saying, "I will wrestle with you, deathgod."

Yama laid his weapons aside and removed his upper garments.

All the while this was happening, the Buddha sat in the shade of the great tree, smiling, as though the passage of arms meant nothing to him.

The Chief of the Nâgas caught Yama behind the neck with his left hand, pulling his head forward. Yama did the same to him, and the other did then twist his body, casting his right arm over Yama's left shoulder and behind his neck, locking it then tight about his head, which he now drew down hard against his hip, turning his body as he dragged the other forward.

Reaching up behind the Nâga Chief's back, Yama caught his left shoulder in his left hand and then moved his right hand behind the Regent's knees, so that he lifted both his legs off the ground while drawing back upon his shoulder.

For a moment he held this one cradled in his arms like a child, then raised him up to shoulder level and dropped away his arms.

When the Regent struck the ground, Yama fell upon him with his knees and rose again. The other did not.

When the riders of the West had departed, only the Angel of the South, clad all in blue, stood before the Buddha.

"And you?" asked the deathgod, raising his weapons again.

"I will not take up weapons of steel or leather or stone, as a child takes up toys, to face you, god of death. Nor will I match the strength of my body against yours," said the Angel. "I know I will be bested if I do these things, for none may dispute you with arms."

"Then climb back upon your blue stallion and ride away," said Yama, "if you will not fight."

The Angel did not answer, but cast his blue shield into the air, so that it spun like a wheel of sapphire, growing larger and larger as it hung above them.

Then it fell to the ground and began to sink into it, without a sound, still growing as it vanished from sight, the grasses coming together again above the spot where it had struck.

"And what does that signify?" asked Yama.

"I do not actively contest. I merely defend. Mine is the power of passive opposition. Mine is the power of life, as yours is the power of death. While you can destroy anything I send against you, you cannot destroy everything, oh Death. Mine is the power of the shield, but not the sword. Life will oppose you, Lord Yama, to defend your victim."

The Blue One turned then, mounted his blue steed and rode into the South, the Kumbhandas at his back. The sound of the music did not go with him, but remained in the air he had occupied.

Yama advanced once more, his blade in his hand.

"Their efforts came to naught," he said. "Your time is come."

He struck forward with his blade.

The blow did not land, however, as a branch from the great tree fell between them and struck the scimitar from his grasp.

He reached for it and the grasses bent to cover it over, weaving themselves into a tight, unbreakable net.

Cursing, he drew his dagger and struck again.

One mighty branch bent down, came swaying before his target, so that his blade was imbedded deeply in its fibers. Then the branch lashed again skyward, carrying the weapon with it, high out of reach.

The Buddha's eyes were closed in meditation and his halo glowed in the shadows.

Yama took a step forward, raising his hands, and the grasses knotted themselves about his ankles, holding him where he stood.

He struggled for a moment, tugging at their unyielding roots. Then he stopped and raised both hands high, throwing his head far back, death leaping from his eyes.

"Hear me, oh Powers!" he cried. "From this moment forward, this spot shall bear the curse of Yama! No living thing shall ever stir again upon this ground! No bird shall sing, nor snake slither here! It shall be barren and stark, a place of rocks and shifting sand! Not a spear of grass shall ever be upraised from here against the sky! I speak this curse and lay this doom upon the defenders of my enemy!"

The grasses began to wither, but before they had released him there came a great splintering, cracking noise, as the tree whose roots held together the world and in whose branches the stars were caught, as fish in a net, swayed forward, splitting down its middle, its uppermost limbs tearing apart the sky, its roots opening chasms in the ground, its leaves falling like blue-green rain about him. A massive section of its trunk toppled toward him.

In the distance, he still saw the Buddha, seated in meditation, as though unaware of the chaos that erupted about him.

Then there was only blackness and a sound like the crashing of thunder...

❖   ❖   ❖

Yama jerked his head, his eyes springing open.

He sat in the purple grove, his back against the bole of a blue tree, his blade across his knees.

Nothing seemed to have changed.

The rows of monks were seated, as in meditation, before him. The breeze was still cool and moist and the lights still flickered as it passed.

Yama stood, knowing then, somehow, where he must go to find that which he sought.

He moved past the monks, following a well-beaten path that led far into the interior of the wood.

He came upon a purple pavilion, but it was empty.

He moved on, tracing the path back to where the wood became a wilderness. Here, the ground was damp and a faint mist sprang up about him. But the way was still clear before him, illuminated by the light of the three moons.

The trail led downward, the blue and purple trees growing shorter and more twisted here than they did above. Small pools of water, with floating patches of leprous, silver scum, began to appear at the sides of the trail. A marshland smell came to his nostrils, and the wheezing of strange creatures came out of clumps of brush.

He heard the sound of singing, coming from far up behind him, and he realized that the monks he had left were now awake and stirring about the grove. They had finished with the task of combining their thoughts to force upon him the vision of their leader's invincibility. Their chanting was probably a signal, reaching out to—

There!

He was seated upon a rock in the middle of a field, the moonlight falling full upon him.

Yama drew his blade and advanced.

When he was about twenty paces away, the other turned his head.

"Greetings, oh Death," he said.

"Greetings, Tathagatha."

"Tell me why you are here."

"It has been decided that the Buddha must die."

"That does not answer my question, however. Why have you come here?"

"Are you not the Buddha?"

"I have been called Buddha, and Tathagatha, and the Enlightened One, and many other things. But, in answer to your question, no, I am not the Buddha. You have already succeeded in what you set out to do. You slew the real Buddha this day."

"My memory must indeed be growing weak, for I confess that I do not remember doing this thing."

"The real Buddha was named by us Sugata," replied the other. "Before that, he was known as Rild."

"Rild!" Yama chuckled. "You are trying to tell me that he was more than an executioner whom you talked out of doing his job?"

"Many people are executioners who have been talked out of doing their jobs," replied the one on the rock. "Rild gave up his mission willingly and became a follower of the Way. He was the only man I ever knew to really achieve enlightenment."

"Is this not a pacifistic religion, this thing you have been spreading?"

"Yes."

Yama threw back his head and laughed.

"Gods! Then it is well you are not preaching a militant one! Your foremost disciple, enlightenment and all, nearly had my head this afternoon!"

A tired look came over the Buddha's wide countenance.

"Do you think he could actually have beaten you?"

Yama was silent a moment, then, "No," he said.

"Do you think he knew this?"

"Perhaps," Yama replied.

"Did you not know one another prior to this day's meeting? Have you not seen one another at practice?"

"Yes," said Yama. "We were acquainted."

"Then he knew your skill and realized the outcome of the encounter."

Yama was silent.

"He went willingly to his martyrdom, unknown to me at the time. I do not feel that he went with real hope of beating you."

"Why, then?"

"To prove a point."

"What point could he hope to prove in such a manner?"

"I do not know. I only know that it must be as I have said, for I knew him. I have listened too often to his sermons, to his subtle parables, to believe that he would do a thing such as this without a purpose. You have slain the true Buddha, deathgod. You know what *I* am."

"Siddhartha," said Yama, "I know that you arc a fraud. I know that you are not an Enlightened One. I realize that your doctrine is a thing which could have been remembered by any among the First. You chose to resurrect it, pretending to be its originator. You decided to spread it, in hopes of raising an opposition to the religion by which the true gods rule. I admire the effort. It was cleverly planned and executed. But your biggest mistake, I feel, is that you picked a pacifistic creed with which to oppose an active one. I am curious why you did this thing, when there were so many more appropriate religions from which to choose."

"Perhaps I was just curious to see how such a countercurrent would flow," replied the other.

"No, Sam, that is not it," answered Yama. "I feel it is only part of a larger plan you have laid, and that for all these years—while you pretended to be a saint and preached sermons in which you did not truly believe yourself—you have been making other plans. An army, great in space, may offer opposition in a brief span of time. One man, brief in space, must spread his opposition across a period of many years if he is to have a chance of succeeding. You are aware of this, and now that you have sown the seeds of this stolen creed, you are planning to move on to another phase of opposition. You are trying to be a one-man antithesis to Heaven, opposing the will of the gods across the years, in many ways and from behind many masks. But it will end here and now, false Buddha."

"Why, Yama?" he asked.

"It was considered quite carefully," said Yama. "We did not want to make you a martyr, encouraging more than ever the growth of this thing you have been teaching. On the other hand, if you were not stopped, it would still continue to grow. It was decided, therefore, that you must meet your end at the hands of an agent of Heaven— thus showing which religion is the stronger. So, martyr or no, Buddhism will be a second-rate religion henceforth. That is why you must now die the real death."

"When I asked 'Why?' I meant something different. You have answered the wrong question. I meant, why have *you* come to do this thing, Yama? Why have you, master of arms, master of sciences, come as lackey to a crew of drunken body-changers, who are not qualified to polish your blade or wash out your test tubes? Why do you, who might be the freest spirit of us all, demean yourself by serving your inferiors?"

"For that, your death shall not be a clean one."

"Why? I did but ask a question, which must have long since passed through more minds than my own. I did not take offense when you called me a false Buddha. I know what I am. Who are you, deathgod?"

Yama placed his blade within his sash and withdrew a pipe, which he had purchased at the inn earlier in the day. He filled its bowl with tobacco, lit it, and smoked.

"It is obvious that we must talk a little longer, if only to clear both our minds of questions," he stated, "so I may as well be comfortable." He seated himself upon a low rock. "First, a man may in some ways be superior to his fellows and still serve them, if together they serve a common cause which is greater than any one man. I believe that I serve such a cause, or I would not be doing it. I take it that you feel the same way concerning what you do, or you would not put up with this life of miserable asceticism—though I note that you are not so gaunt as your followers. You were offered godhood some years ago in Mahartha, as I recall, and you mocked Brahma, raided the Palace of Karma, and filled all the prayer-machines of the city with slugs—"

The Buddha chuckled. Yama joined him briefly and continued,

"There are no Accelerationists remaining in the world, other than yourself. It is a dead issue, which should never have become an issue in the first place. I do have a certain respect for the manner in which you have acquitted yourself over the years. It has even occurred to me that if you could be made to realize the hopelessness of your present position, you might still be persuaded to join the hosts of Heaven. While I did come here to kill you, if you can be convinced of this now and give me your word upon it, promising to end your foolish fight, I will take it upon myself to vouch for you. I will take you back to the Celestial City with me, where you may now accept that which you once refused. They will harken to me, because they need me."

"No," said Sam, "for I am not convinced of the futility of my position, and I fully intend to continue the show."

The chanting came down from the camp in the purple grove. One of the moons disappeared beyond the treetops.

"Why are your followers not beating the bushes, seeking to save you?"

"They would come if I called, but I will not call. I do not need to."

"Why did they cause me to dream that foolish dream?"

The Buddha shrugged.

"Why did they not arise and slay me as I slept?"

"It is not their way."

"You might have, though, eh? If you could get away with it? If none would know the Buddha did it?"

"Perhaps," said the other. "As you know, the personal strengths and weaknesses of a leader are no true indication of the merits of his cause."

Yama drew upon his pipe. The smoke wreathed his head and eddied away to join the fogs, which were now becoming more heavy upon the land.

"I know we are alone here, and you are unarmed," said Yama.

"We are alone here. My traveling gear is hidden farther along my route."

"Your traveling gear?"

"I have finished here. You guessed correctly. I have begun what I set out to begin. After we have finished our conversation, I will depart."

Yama chuckled.

"The optimism of a revolutionary always gives rise to a sense of wonder. How do you propose to depart? On a magic carpet?"

"I shall go as other men go."

"That is rather condescending of you. Will the powers of the world rise up to defend you? I see no great tree to shelter you with its branches. There is no clever grass to seize at my feet. Tell me how you will achieve your departure?"

"I'd rather surprise you."

"What say we fight? I do not like to slaughter an unarmed man. If you actually do have supplies cached somewhere nearby, go fetch your blade. It is better than no chance at all. I've even heard it said that Lord Siddhartha was, in his day, a formidable swordsman."

"Thank you, no. Another time, perhaps. But not this time."

Yama drew once more upon his pipe, stretched, and yawned.

"I can think of no more questions then, which I wish to ask you. It is futile to argue with you. I have nothing more to say. Is there anything else that you would care to add to the conversation?"

"Yes," said Sam. "What's she like, that bitch Kali? There are so many different reports that I'm beginning to believe she is all things to all men—"

Yama hurled the pipe, which struck him upon the shoulder and sent a shower of sparks down his arm. His scimitar was a bright flash about his head as he leapt forward.

When he struck the sandy stretch before the rock, his motion was arrested. He almost fell, twisted himself perpendicularly and remained standing. He struggled, but could not move.

"Some quicksand," said Sam, "is quicker than other quicksand. Fortunately, you are settling into that of the slower sort. So you have considerable time yet remaining at your disposal. I would like to prolong the conversation, if I thought I had a chance of persuading you to join with me. But I know that I do not—no more than you could persuade me to go to Heaven."

"I will get free," said Yama softly, not struggling. "I will get free somehow, and I will come after you again."

"Yes," said Sam, "I feel this to be true. In fact, in a short while I will instruct you how to go about it. For the moment, however, you are something every preacher longs for—a captive audience, representing the opposition. So, I have a brief sermon for you, Lord Yama."

Yama hefted his blade, decided against throwing it, thrust it again into his sash.

"Preach on," he said, and he succeeded in catching the other's eyes.

Sam swayed where he sat, but he spoke again:

"It is amazing," he said, "how that mutant brain of yours generated a mind capable of transferring its powers to any new brain you choose to occupy. It has been years since I last exercised my one ability, as I am at this moment—but it, too, behaves in a similar manner. No matter what body I inhabit, it appears that my power follows me into it also. I understand it is still that way with most of us. Sitala, I hear, can control temperatures for a great distance about her. When she assumes a new body, the power accompanies her into her new nervous system, though it comes only weakly at first. Agni, I know, can set fire to objects by staring at them for a period of time and willing that they burn. Now, take for example the death-gaze you are at this moment turning upon me. Is it not amazing how you keep this gift about you in all times and places, over the centuries? I have often wondered as to the physiological basis for the phenomenon. Have you ever researched the area?"

"Yes," said Yama, his eyes burning beneath his dark brows.

"And what is the explanation? A person is born with an abnormal brain, his psyche is later transferred to a normal one and yet his abnormal abilities are not destroyed in the transfer. Why does this thing happen?"

"Because you really have only one body-image, which is electrical as well as chemical in nature. It begins immediately to modify its new physiological environment. The new body has much about it which it treats rather like a disease, attempting to cure it into being the old body. If the body which you now inhabit were to be made physically immortal, it would someday come to resemble your original body."

"How interesting."

"That is why the transferred power is weak at first, but grows stronger as you continue occupancy. That is why it is best to cultivate an Attribute, and perhaps to employ mechanical aids, also."

"Well. That is something I have often wondered about. Thank you. By the way, keep trying with your death-gaze—it is painful, you know. So that is something, anyway. Now, as to the sermon: a proud and arrogant man, such as yourself—with an admittedly admirable quality of didacticism about him—was given to doing research in the area of a certain disfiguring and degenerative disease. One day he contracted it himself. Since he had not yet developed a cure for the condition, he did take time out to regard himself in a mirror and say, 'But on *me* it does look good.' You are such a man, Yama. You will not attempt to fight your condition. Rather, you are proud of it. You betrayed yourself in your fury, so I know that I speak the truth when I say that the name of your disease is Kali. You would not give power into the hands of the unworthy if that woman did not bid you do it. I knew her of old, and I am certain that she has not changed. She cannot love a man. She cares only for those who bring her gifts of chaos. If ever you cease to suit her purposes, she will put you aside, deathgod. I do not say this because we are enemies, but rather as one man to another. I know. Believe me, I do. Perhaps it is unfortunate that you were never really young, Yama, and did not know your first love in the days of spring… The moral, therefore, of my sermon on this small mount is this: even a mirror will not show you yourself, if you do not wish to see. Cross her once to try the truth of my words, even in a small matter, and see how quickly she responds, and in what fashion. What will you do if your own weapons are turned against you, Death?"

"You have finished speaking now?" asked Yama.

"That's about it. A sermon is a warning, and you have been warned."

"Whatever your power, Sam, I see that it is at this moment proof against my death-gaze. Consider yourself fortunate that I am weakened—"

"I do indeed, for my head is about to split. Damn your eyes!"

"One day I will try your power again, and even if it should still be proof against my own, you will fall on that day. If not by my Attribute, then by my blade."

"If that is a challenge, I choose to defer acceptance. I suggest that you do try my words before you attempt to make it good."

At this point, the sand was halfway up Yama's thighs.

Sam sighed and climbed down from his perch.

"There is only one clear path to this rock, and I am about to follow it away from here. Now, I will tell you how to gain your life, if you are not too proud. I have instructed the monks to come to my aid, here at this place, if they hear a cry for help. I told you earlier that I was not going to call for help, and that is true. If, however, you begin calling out for aid with that powerful voice of yours, they shall be here before you sink too much further. They will bring you safely to firm ground and will not try to harm you, for such is their way. I like the thought of the god of death being saved by the monks of Buddha. Good night, Yama, I'm going to leave you now."

Yama smiled.

"There will be another day, oh Buddha," he stated. "I can wait for it. Flee now as far and as fast as you can. The world is not large enough to hide you from my wrath. I will follow you, and I will teach you of the enlightenment which is pure hellfire."

"In the meantime," said Sam, "I suggest you solicit aid of my followers or learn the difficult art of mud-breathing."

He picked his way across the field, Yama's eyes burning into his back.

When he reached the trail, he turned. "...And you may want to mention in Heaven," he said, "that I was called out of town on a business deal."

Yama did not reply.

"I think I am going to make a deal for some weapons," he finished, "some rather special weapons. So when you come after me, bring your girl friend along. If she likes what she sees, she may persuade you to switch sides."

Then he struck the trail and moved away through the night, whistling, beneath a moon that was white and a moon that was golden.

A Word from Zelazny

This separately published novelette is chapter 3 of Zelazny's novel *Lord of Light*. "When, on the final morning of Disclave a couple years back, I cut myself shaving and lapsed into a long pre-sentient chain of free-associations which somehow ended up at transmigration [i.e., he wanted to change bodies in order to avoid appearing at the convention with 'a big gash' on his face], I found myself with the sudden (and not too profound—but then, it was early in the morning) realization that not much had been done in U.S. sf and fantasy with respect to Hindu culture. Ben Jason and I drove back to Ohio that afternoon, and by the time we arrived that evening I had pretty much roughed out the whole story in my head. I had decided on seven or nine chapters of approximately 13,000 words each, so that I might be able to sell a few as novelettes if no one wanted to chance on using it as a series or serial. For this reason, I figured that each chapter would have to be somewhat independent of its fellows... I wanted to separate the chapters in space and time, and so produce a sort of folk-story quality. I could have had nine chapters, but I threw out what I was thinking of using in two of them, because there is a breaking point in anything like this and I didn't want to just pile up incident... This decided, I began soaking in Hindu background. I drew dozens of books on the subject out of the Cleveland Public Library and I spent about sixty bucks on books which they didn't have that I felt I'd need. That's how *Lord of Light* began.

"I'd say that I actually employed only a small percent of what I learned from the background reading. But then, you never know where you're going to come across something useful. If you want a thing like this to have an authentic-seeming air to it, you've got to go in for a bit of this kind of saturation."[1]

Concerning the genesis of *Lord of Light*, Zelazny wrote: "1) I initially intended to destroy Yama partway through the book, but was subsequently taken by a feeling that he and Sam were two aspects of one personality. In my own mind, and I suppose there only, Sam and Yama stand in a relationship similar to that of Goethe's Faust and Mephistopheles. 2) I wanted a triangle situation of sorts here also, only this time involving two men and one woman. Sam, Yama and Kali served. 3) It was in writing this book that I came to realize the value of a strong female figure or presence in a novel, to balance and add another level of tension, apart—or rather, abstracted—from the purely sexual."[2]

---

1 *Niekas #21*, 1977.
2 *Vector #65*, May-June 1973.

"I read Herman Hesse's *Siddhartha*, which probably influenced chapter three ['Death and the Executioner']. This same chapter was also influenced by the novel-length poem *The Light of Asia; or, the Great Renunciation (Mahabhinishkramana)* by Sir Edwin Arnold (1879)…*The Light of Asia* gave me the four Lords of Sumeru with whom Yama does battle in the dream sequence in chapter three…

"I dwelled often in my thoughts upon Hindu paintings of the 18th century. I threw the color into costumes and settings. I wanted a sort of baroque style, because I figured that would be best for a folklore/legend thing…

"I wanted to sort of combine fantasy and sf, and I wanted to put something there for the lover of each form of speculative literature…I think *Lord of Light* can be read as either one…With Sam, I do not say that he did *not* achieve illumination, whether he believes it himself or not…

"As to the ending of *Lord of Light*, I never know how one of my books ends until I write the ending. It would be no fun for me to go that distance if everything was foreordained. With *Lord of Light* I came up with four endings and decided, what the hell! When it comes to something like a legend there are always variations. So why not use all four? So I did."[3]

The initial appearances of the *Lord of Light* chapters "Dawn" and "Death and the Executioner" in *F&SF* each earned $300 (about $1,850 in 2008 dollars), and Zelazny gave a dramatic reading from "Death and the Executioner" at his Guest of Honor appearance at the Disclave Convention in May 1966.[4] The other five chapters were scheduled to appear in *New Worlds*, except that it temporarily folded, and when it resumed publication, it was too close to the novel's publication date.[5]

Notes

Mahasamatman derives from **maha** (great, high-souled, magnanimous), Sam (the crewman's first name; we do not learn his last name) and **atman** (the individual soul or essence that is indistinguishable from the soul of the universe). **Tathagatha** *(Tathagata)*—he who has achieved—is one of Buddha's names. **Kali** or Devi is the Hindu goddess of death and destruction and wife of Shiva; **Durga** is another, sometimes malignant, aspect of this goddess. **Dhamma** is the doctrine or teaching of Buddha.

Vaisyas are the second-lowest of four traditional inherited castes in Hinduism and comprise farmers, herders, merchants, and businessmen; **Sudras** are the lowest caste and include artisans, laborers, and menials. **Devas** in

---

3 *Niekas #21*, 1977.
4 *Wizard #2*, July 1966.
5 *Kallikanzaros #3* December 1967 / January 1968.

Hinduism are supernatural beings of high excellence; in Buddhism they are powerful and long-lived. **Vedas** are the entire body of Hindu sacred writings. **Kumkum** paste is made from dried turmeric; it is used in worship of Hindu goddesses.

Yama is the Hindu god of death, judge of departed souls and tormenter of the wicked. **The Way of the Eightfold Path**, or the Noble Eightfold Path, is a Buddhist principle that leads to meditative discipline and an end to suffering; it is represented by an eight-spoked Dharma wheel. **Brahmins** are the highest caste of traditional Hindu society; **Brahmin** or **Brahman** is the ultimate, unchanging reality, composed of pure being and consciousness. A **tirthika** is a heretic or non-Buddhist. In **Kathakali**, actors wearing traditional costumes use music, song, dance and hand symbols to enact dramas based on the Ramayana and Mahābhārata.

Mundus are cotton garments which wrap around the waist and legs. **Syncopated** music emphasizes beats not normally accented. **Rama** is any of Vishnu's three avatars: Balarama, Parashurama, or Ramachandra; **Vishnu** or "the Preserver" is the second member of the Trimurti, along with Brahma the Creator and Shiva the Destroyer. **Pandava brothers** are the five sons of Pandu, apparently conceived of his two wives by intervention of gods or devas, because Pandu was under a curse of death if he had intercourse with any of his wives. **Cyclopean** in this context means immense. Ascetic Buddhists wear the yellow-orange **saffron robe**.

Surya is the sun god or the sun itself. **Lotus position** or **padmasana** is the classic yoga pose with legs crossed, feet turned in and up, outstretched hands resting on knees. **Nagaswaram** is a wind instrument with a hardwood body and a large, flared metal or wood bell. **Ganesha** is the Hindu god of wisdom, depicted as a short fat man with an elephant's head. **Bridge of the Gods** is a ring of ions surrounding the colonized planet. **Sugata** means one who has fared well and is a name given to Gautama Buddha or one of his avatars.

Nirvana is a state of pure consciousness in which the mind is free of all contaminants, emotions and distractions. **Pinions** are a bird's wings and primary feathers, without which it cannot fly. **Garuda** is a large, supernatural eagle that Vishnu rides. **They swaggered blades** refers to swordplay's side-to-side motion. **Apostasy** is abandonment of one's religion. **Parried** is warding off a blow; **riposted** is delivering a quick counter-stroke.

Katha Upanishad is a lengthy verse, a parable of a young boy's spiritual journey to discover the nature of reality. **Lakshmi** is the goddess of prosperity and consort of Vishnu; she assumes different forms (e.g., Radha, Sita) to accompany her husband's various incarnations. **Sarasvati** is the Hindu goddess of learning and the arts. **Shakti** personifies the female principle of divine energy.

Sitala is the cool goddess or mother goddess; smallpox, one of her manifestations, is her **khel** (sport or play) which must be tolerated to respect and honor her. **Ratri** or Ratridevi is the goddess of the night in the Devas and sister to Ushas, goddess of dawn. **Soma** is an intoxicating or hallucinogenic beverage offered to the Hindu gods and consumed by participants in the same rituals. The **unnamed tree** is the Bo tree that Buddha mediated under for seven years. An **aureole** is a halo surrounding the head of a sacred person.

Zelazny borrowed **the four Regents of the world** from *Light of Asia*, of which the pertinent section reads:

> *But when they brought the painted palanquin*
> *To fetch him home, the bearers of the poles*
> *Were the four Regents of the Earth, come down*
> *From Mount Sumeru—they who write men's deeds*
> *On brazen plates—the Angel of the East,*
> *Whose hosts are clad in silver robes, and bear*
> *Targets of pearl: the Angel of the South,*
> *Whose horsemen, the Kumbhandas, ride blue steeds,*
> *With sapphire shields: the Angel of the West,*
> *By Nâgas followed, riding steeds blood-red,*
> *With coral shields: the Angel of the North,*
> *Environed by his Yakshas, all in gold,*
> *On yellow horses, bearing shields of gold.*

Siddhartha—"he who has attained his goal"—is another name for Buddha. **Antithesis** is opposition.

Accelerationists are the people (including Sam) from the starship *Star of India* who want their descendants on Urath to have access to knowledge, technology and the rejuvenation techniques that provide immortality. Many original crew and colonists (the First), however, prefer to keep the public ignorant and enjoy being worshipped as Hindu gods.

Agni is the Hindu god of fire. **Didacticism** is teaching.

BRAHMAN TRIMURTI,
A MODERN HYMN TO THE TRINITY

Polemic, Spring 1959, Vol IV No 1.

I.

Brahma! Creator!
Thy suppliants abound:
  A diplomat,
  A paranoid,
  A Democrat,
  A Man of Freud.
Before Thou,
Initiator,
All would bow—
Tomorrow's door—
  Create!
  Renew!
  Resolve!
Change things as they are.
  Deflate,
  Review,
  Resolve
Status quo and par.

II.

Vishnu! Preserver!
Reactionaries' forte.
  Maintain!
  Uphold!
  Retain!
  Infold!
Support the present!
Bar the change!
And hold the pleasant
Present range.
  Mediocre middle.
  Constant average.
  To Thee we hie!
Here Thy minions bow.
  Neither much nor little.
  Grant our suffrage.
  Hear Thou our cry:
Hold the Here and Now!

III.

Shiva! Destroyer!
Eternal rebel's liege!
    Grant to wear!
    Grant to bend!
    Grant to tear!
    Grant to rend!
Ere Thy throne,
In legions 'round,
Madmen prone
Abound the ground.
    Of lightning
    And storms
    Of rage
May Thy mouth partake!
    With frightening
    Horrorforms
    A stage
For Hell and Chaos, make!

Notes

This poem draws on Hindu deities and continues Zelazny's fascination with mythology in his poetry and fiction. It predates *Lord of Light* but reads as if it could have been part of that novel.

In Hinduism **Brahman** is the ultimate, unchanging reality, composed of pure being and consciousness; it also means a member of the highest class or priestly caste in society. The three members of the Hindu trinity or **Trimurti** are **Brahma** (god of creation), **Vishnu** (maintainer or preserver) and **Shiva** (transformer or destroyer).

Appendix B

Lord of Light, Doubleday 1967.
Separately: *Hymn to the Sun: An Imitation*, DNA Publications 1996.

He whose desires have been throttled,
who is independent of root,
whose pasture is emptiness—
signless and free—
his path is as unknowable
as that of birds across the heavens.
> *Dhammapada* (93)

Few are the beings born again among men; more
numerous are those born again elsewhere.
> *Anguttara-nikaya* (I, 35)

There is no disappearing of the true Dhamma
until a false Dhamma arises in the world.
When the false Dhamma arises, he makes the
true Dhamma to disappear.
> *Samyutta-nikaya* (II, 224)

When the gods and the demons, both offspring of Prajapati, did battle with one another, the gods seized upon the life-principle of the Udgitha, thinking that with this they would vanquish the demons.

They meditated upon the Udgitha which functions through the nose, but the demons pierced it through with evil. Therefore, with the breath one smells both that which is pleasant and that which is foul. Thus the breath is touched with evil.

They meditated upon the Udgitha as words, but the demons pierced it through with evil. Therefore, one speaks both truth and falsehood. Thus words are touched by evil.

They meditated upon the Udgitha which functions through the eye, but the demons pierced it through with evil. Therefore, one sees both what is pleasing and what is ugly. Thus the eye is touched by evil.

They mediated upon the Udgitha as hearing, but the demons pierced it through with evil. Therefore, one hears both good things and bad. Thus the ear is touched by evil.

Then did they meditate upon the Udgitha as the mind, but the demons pierced it through with evil. Therefore, one thinks what is proper, true, and good, and what is improper, false, and depraved. Thus the mind is touched by evil.

Chandogya Upanishad (I, ii, 1–6)

Girt about with lightnings, standard bearer, armed with the sword, the wheel, the bow,
devourer, sustainer, Kali, night of destruction at Worldsend, who walketh the world by night
protectress, deceiver, serene one, loved and lovely, Brahmani, Mother of the Vedas, dweller in the silent and most secret places,
well-omened and gentle, all-knowing, swift as thought, wearer of skulls, possessed of power, the twilight, invincible leader, pitiful one,
opener of the way before those lost, granter of favors, teacher, valor in the form of woman,
chameleon-hearted, practitioner of austerities, magician, pariah, deathless and eternal…
Āryatārābhattārikānāmāshtottaráskastotra (36–40)

When the sun of suffering has set,
there comes this peace,
Lord of the quiet stars,
this peace of creation,
this place the mandala spins gray.
The fool saith in his mind
that his thoughts are only thoughts...
    Sarah (98–99)

The world is a fire of sacrifice, the sun its fuel, sunbeams its smoke, the day its flames, the points of the compass its cinders and sparks. In this fire the gods offer faith as libation. Out of this offering King Moon is born.

Rain, oh Gautama, is the fire, the year its fuel, the clouds its smoke, the lightning its flame, cinders, sparks. In this fire the gods offer King Moon in libation. Out of this offering the rain is born.

The world, oh Gautama, is the fire, the earth its fuel, fire its smoke, the night its flame, the moon its cinders, the stars its sparks. In this fire the gods offer rain as libation. Out of this offering food is produced.

Man, oh Gautama, is the fire, his open mouth its fuel, his breath its smoke, his speech its flame, his eye its cinders, his ear its sparks. In this fire the gods offer food as libation. Out of this offering the power of generation is born.

Woman, oh Gautama, is the fire, her form its fuel, her hair its smoke, her organs its flame, her pleasures its cinders and its sparks. In this flame the gods offer the power of generation as libation. Out of this offering a man is born. He lives for so long as he is to live.

When a man dies, he is carried to be offered in the fire. The fire becomes his fire, the fuel his fuel, the smoke his smoke, the flame his flame, the cinders his cinders, the sparks his sparks. In this fire the gods offer the man as libation. Out of this offering the man emerges in radiant splendor.

    Brihadaranyaka Upanishad (VI, ii, 9–14)

A Word from Zelazny

These seven poems were originally published as chapter breaks in *Lord of Light*. "These are again Lowellian interpretations [see introduction to 'Ikhnaton's Hymn to the Sun']. I've done this three times now, and so far I've been luckier than Lowell himself, who said that even though he'd publicly pointed out that his versions weren't intended to be literal, he was still taken to task by reviewers for not doing exact translations."[1]

"*The Upanishads* (translation Swami Nikhilananda) and *Buddhist Texts Through the Ages* (ed. Conze, Horner, Snelgrove & Waley)—both Harper Torchbooks…gave me the quotations at the beginnings of the chapters. They are all of them authentic—and although I took the liberty of paraphrasing each somewhat, I retained the sense of the original."[2]

Notes

Dhamma is the doctrine or teaching of Buddha. **Prajapati** is a Hindu god personifying a creative force and is equivalent to Brahma. **Udgitha** appears to mean the sun and its power, but it also means a hymn of praise to Brahma. **Kali** or Devi is the Hindu goddess of death and destruction, and wife of Shiva. **Brahmani** means a woman of the Brahman class, the high religious caste; **Brahman** also means the ultimate, unchanging reality, composed of pure being and consciousness. **Vedas** are the entire body of Hindu sacred writings, including the Rig-Veda, the Sama-Veda, the Atharva-Veda, and the Yajur-Veda. A **mandala** is a geometric pattern or chart that can be used for focusing attention and meditating. **Gautama** is one of the names of Buddha.

---

1 *Critical Wave #33*, November 1993.
2 *Niekas #21*, 1977.

Bodhisattva

Written 1955–60 for *Chisel in the Sky;* previously unpublished.

And what does it mean,
this question that I cannot phrase?
Does it imply a basic wrongness
in carbon's reply to the inorganic?
The failures of daybreak
as farewells of possibility through cloud?

Or inchoancy, as compliment of Chaos
to that rough, relentless dance,
the atoms through a patterning of fog?

Notes

Bodhisattva is someone dedicated to achieving Nirvana. **Inchoate** means rudimentary, disorganized; inchoancy appears to be a neologism to indicate a disordered, rudimentary state.

AUTO-DA-FÉ

Dangerous Visions, ed. Harlan Ellison, Doubleday 1967.

Still do I remember the hot sun upon the sands of the Plaza del Autos, the cries of the soft-drink hawkers, the tiers of humanity stacked across from me on the sunny side of the arena, sunglasses like cavities in their gleaming faces.

Still do I remember the smells and the colors: the reds and the blues and the yellows, the ever present tang of petroleum fumes upon the air.

Still do I remember that day, that day with its sun in the middle of the sky and the sign of Aries, burning in the blooming of the year. I recall the mincing steps of the pumpers, heads thrown back, arms waving, the white dazzles of their teeth framed with smiling lips, cloths like colorful tails protruding from the rear pockets of their coveralls; and the horns—I remember the blare of a thousand horns over the loudspeakers, on and off, off and on, over and over, and again, and then one shimmering, final note, sustained, to break the ear and the heart with its infinite power, its pathos.

Then there was silence.

I see it now as I did on that day so long ago…

He entered the arena, and the cry that went up shook blue heaven upon its pillars of white marble.

"Viva! El mechador! Viva! El mechador!"

I remember his face, dark and sad and wise.

Long of jaw and nose was he, and his laughter was as the roaring of the wind, and his movements were as the music of the theremin and the drum. His coveralls were blue and silk and tight and stitched with thread of gold and broidered all about with black braid. His jacket was beaded and there were flashing scales upon his breast, his shoulders, his back.

His lips curled into the smile of a man who has known much glory and has hold upon the power that will bring him into more.

He moved, turning in a circle, not shielding his eyes against the sun.

He was above the sun. He was Manolo Stillete Dos Muertos, the mightiest *mechador* the world has ever seen, black boots upon his feet, pistons in his thighs, fingers with the discretion of micrometers, halo of dark locks about his head and the angel of death in his right arm, there, in the center of the grease-stained circle of truth.

He waved, and a cry went up once more.

"Manolo! Manolo! Dos Muertos! Dos Muertos!"

After two years' absence from the ring, he had chosen this, the anniversary of his death and retirement to return—for there was gasoline and methyl in his blood and his heart was a burnished pump ringed 'bout with desire and courage. He had died twice within the ring, and twice had the medics restored him. After his second death, he had retired, and some said that it was because he had known fear. This could not be true.

He waved his hand and his name rolled back upon him.

The horns sounded once more: three long blasts.

Then again there was silence, and a pumper wearing red and yellow brought him the cape, removed his jacket.

The tinfoil backing of the cape flashed in the sun as Dos Muertos swirled it.

Then there came the final, beeping notes.

The big door rolled upward and back into the wall.

He draped his cape over his arm and faced the gateway.

The light above was red and from within the darkness there came the sound of an engine.

The light turned yellow, then green, and there was the sound of cautiously engaged gears.

The car moved slowly into the ring, paused, crept forward, paused again.

It was a red Pontiac, its hood stripped away, its engine like a nest of snakes, coiling and engendering behind the circular shimmer of its invisible fan. The wings of its aerial spun round and round, then fixed upon Manolo and his cape.

He had chosen a heavy one for his first, slow on turning, to give him a chance to limber up.

The drums of its brain, which had never before recorded a man, were spinning.

Then the consciousness of its kind swept over it and it moved forward.

Manolo swirled his cape and kicked its fender as it roared past.

The door of the great garage closed.

When it reached the opposite side of the ring the car stopped, parked.

Cries of disgust, booing and hissing arose from the crowd.

Still the Pontiac remained parked.

Two pumpers, bearing buckets, emerged from behind the fence and threw mud upon its windshield.

It roared then and pursued the nearest, banging into the fence. Then it turned suddenly, sighted Dos Muertos and charged.

His *veronica* transformed him into a statue with a skirt of silver. The enthusiasm of the crowd was mighty.

It turned and charged once more, and I wondered at Manolo's skill, for it would seem that his buttons had scraped cherry paint from the side panels.

Then it paused, spun its wheels, ran in a circle about the ring.

The crowd roared as it moved past him and recircled.

Then it stopped again, perhaps fifty feet away.

Manolo turned his back upon it and waved to the crowd.

—Again, the cheering and the calling of his name.

He gestured to someone behind the fence.

A pumper emerged and bore to him, upon a velvet cushion, his chrome-plated monkey wrench.

He turned then again to the Pontiac and strode toward it.

It stood there shivering and he knocked off its radiator cap.

A jet of steaming water shot into the air and the crowd bellowed. Then he struck the front of the radiator and banged upon each fender.

He turned his back upon it again and stood there.

When he heard the engagement of the gears he turned once more, and with one clean pass it was by him, but not before he had banged twice upon the trunk with his wrench.

It moved to the other end of the ring and parked.

Manolo raised his hand to the pumper behind the fence.

The man with the cushion emerged and bore to him the long-handled screwdriver and the short cape. He took the monkey wrench away with him, as well as the long cape.

Another silence came over the Plaza del Autos.

The Pontiac, as if sensing all this, turned once more and blew its horn twice. Then it charged.

There were dark spots upon the sand from where its radiator had leaked water. Its exhaust arose like a ghost behind it. It bore down upon him at a terrible speed.

Dos Muertos raised the cape before him and rested the blade of the screwdriver upon his left forearm.

When it seemed he would surely be run down, his hand shot forward, so fast the eye could barely follow it, and he stepped to the side as the engine began to cough.

Still the Pontiac continued on with a deadly momentum, turned sharply without braking, rolled over, slid into the fence, and began to burn. Its engine coughed and died.

The Plaza shook with the cheering. They awarded Dos Muertos both headlights and the tailpipe. He held them high and moved in slow promenade about the perimeter of the ring. The horns sounded. A lady threw him a plastic flower and he sent for a pumper to bear her the tailpipe and ask her to dine with him. The crowd cheered more loudly, for he was known to be a great layer of women, and it was not such an unusual thing in the days of my youth as it is now.

The next was the blue Chevrolet, and he played with it as a child plays with a kitten, tormenting it into striking, then stopping it forever. He received both headlights. The sky had clouded over by then and there was a tentative mumbling of thunder.

The third was a black Jaguar XKE, which calls for the highest skill possible and makes for a very brief moment of truth. There was blood as well as gasoline upon the sand before he dispatched it, for its side mirrors extended further than one would think, and there was a red furrow across his rib cage before he had done with it. But he tore out its ignition system with such grace and artistry that the crowd boiled over into the ring, and the guards were called forth to beat them with clubs and herd them with cattle prods back into their seats.

Surely, after all of this, none could say that Dos Muertos had ever known fear.

A cool breeze arose and I bought a soft drink and waited for the last.

His final car sped forth while the light was still yellow. It was a mustard-colored Ford convertible. As it went past him the first time, it blew its horn and turned on its windshield wipers. Everyone cheered, for they could see it had spirit.

Then it came to a dead halt, shifted into reverse, and backed toward him at about forty miles an hour.

He got out of the way, sacrificing grace to expediency, and it braked sharply, shifted into low gear, and sped forward again.

He waved the cape and it was torn from his hands. If he had not thrown himself over backward, he would have been struck.

Then someone cried: "It's out of alignment!"

But he got to his feet, recovered his cape and faced it once more.

They still tell of those five passes that followed. Never has there been such a flirting with bumper and grill! Never in all of the Earth has there been such an encounter between *mechador* and machine! The convertible roared like ten centuries of streamlined death, and the spirit of St. Detroit sat in its driver's seat, grinning, while Dos Muertos faced it with his tinfoil cape, cowed it and called for his wrench. It nursed its overheated engine and rolled its windows up and down, up and down, clearing its muffler the while with lavatory noises and much black smoke.

By then it was raining, softly, gently, and the thunder still came about us. I finished my soft drink.

Dos Muertos had never used his monkey wrench on the engine before, only upon the body. But this time he threw it. Some experts say he was aiming at the distributor; others say he was trying to break its fuel pump.

The crowd booed him.

Something gooey was dripping from the Ford onto the sand. The red streak brightened on Manolo's stomach. The rain came down.

He did not look at the crowd. He did not take his eyes from the car. He held out his right hand, palm upward, and waited.

A panting pumper placed the screwdriver in his hand and ran back toward the fence.

Manolo moved to the side and waited.

It leaped at him and he struck.

There was more booing.

He had missed the kill.

No one left, though. The Ford swept around him in a tight circle, smoke now emerging from its engine. Manolo rubbed his arm and picked up the screwdriver and cape he had dropped. There was more booing as he did so.

By the time the car was upon him, flames were leaping forth from its engine.

Now some say that he struck and missed again, going off balance. Others say that he began to strike, grew afraid and drew back. Still others say that, perhaps for an instant, he knew a fatal pity for his spirited adversary, and that this had stayed his hand. I say that the smoke was too thick for any of them to say for certain what had happened.

But it swerved and he fell forward, and he was borne upon that engine, blazing like a god's catafalque, to meet with his third death as they crashed into the fence together and went up into flames.

There was much dispute over the final *corrida*, but what remained of the tailpipe and both headlights were buried with what remained of him, beneath the sands of the Plaza, and there was much weeping among women he had known. I say that he could not have been afraid or known pity, for his strength was as a river of rockets, his thighs were pistons and the fingers of his hands had the discretion of micrometers; his hair was a black halo and the angel of death rode on his right arm. Such a man, a man who has known truth, is mightier than any machine. Such a man is above anything but the holding of power and the wearing of glory.

Now he is dead though, this one, for the third and final time. He is as dead as all the dead who have ever died before the bumper, under the grill, beneath the wheels. It is well that he cannot rise again, for I say that his final car was his apotheosis, and anything else would be anticlimactic. Once I saw a blade of grass growing up between the metal sheets of the world in a place where they had become loose, and I destroyed it because I felt it must be lonesome. Often have I regretted doing this, for I took away the glory of its aloneness. Thus does life the machine, I feel, consider man, sternly, then with regret, and the heavens do weep upon him through eyes that grief has opened in the sky.

All the way home I thought of this thing, and the hoofs of my mount clicked upon the floor of the city as I rode through the rain toward evening, that spring.

A Word from Zelazny

"Returning home late one night, I was almost hit by a speeding car which crashed a red light three blocks from my apartment in Baltimore. By the time I reached home, I had this entire story in mind and I finished writing it before I turned out the lights. I sold it to Harlan Ellison for *Dangerous Visions*. I'm very fond of it."[1]

---

1 *The Last Defender of Camelot*, 1980.

Automobiles (and automobile accidents) played significant roles in several Zelazny works, including the first Amber series (Corwin's automobile accident), this story, "Devil Car," "Passion Play," "Damnation Alley," "He Who Shapes," *Roadmarks*, and others. "I was not consciously contributing to any such mythology [of automobiles], but I have been involved in some unpleasant automobile situations and I suppose I might have been exorcising a few traumas in those stories."[2] In addition to the near-miss that inspired "Auto-Da-Fé," in 1964 Zelazny and his fiancée Sharon Steberl experienced a car accident which seriously injured Sharon, and others have explored the pervasive influence this event had on Zelazny's fiction, such as the crash that kills the protagonist's wife and daughter in "He Who Shapes."[3,4]

In response to criticism that this story was not daring or dangerous, Zelazny replied "I didn't write a Dangerous Vision. I just wrote a plain old regular vision, and the day after I learned that Harlan was looking for stuff for a new book he was putting together—so I stuffed it into an envelope, sent it to him. He bought it (obviously). Had I heard of DV earlier, I would probably have tried being more dangerous. So that's the story re Why or Why Not, as the case may be."[5] According to Zelazny, his story was the very last purchase Ellison made for the book.[6]

Notes

Auto da Fé ("act of faith") was a public ritual of the Spanish Inquisition. Convicted heretics faced execution in the city plaza. **Plaza del Toros** is a famous bullfighting stadium in Spain. ***"Viva! El mechador!"*** takes the Spanish expression "Long Live the Matador!"and substitutes mechador, a neologism that fuses mechanic and matador. The **theremin** was the first electronic musical instrument, played by moving the hands near (but not touching) two metal antennae, generating an eerie sound. **Manolo Stilette Dos Muertos** is aptly named because "*Dos Muertos*" means "two deaths" and "*stillete*" implies a stiletto or dagger. A **veronica** is a bullfighting move; the matador stands still and swings the cape slowly away from the bull. A **catafalque** is a decorated platform or bier upon which a coffin rests during a funeral. A *corrida* is a Spanish bullfight in which the bull is slain at the end. **Apotheosis** is that which exalts or deifies; in this case, Manolo's final "bull" made him like unto a god.

---

2 *Science Fiction Review* Aug 1980 #36 (Vol 9 No 3), pp 14–16.
3 *Roger Zelazny*, Jane Lindskold, 1993.
4 *Science Fiction as Literature: Selected Stories and Novels of Roger Zelazny* [PhD Thesis]
   Thomas F. Monteleone, University of Maryland, 1973.
5 *Rats!* June 1971 #8, p 2.
6 *Wizard #2*, July 1966.

FAUST BEFORE TWELVE

Speculative Poetry Review #1, 1977.
Written 1955–60 for *Chisel in the Sky.*

Stranded on an asteroid, mining ice.
Blood congeals, eyes burn:
    Every bone is trumpet;
    Night's counterpane muffles
          breaking brass:
    The rest is silence and
        not rest;
    Chaos improvised orchestrations
        of minute
    Dash downbeat
    the closings of fiery valve.
Is Faust dead?
Never!

Notes

Among numerous Zelazny's works, the legend of Faust informed "For a Breath I Tarry," "The Salvation of Faust," the trilogy of novels co-written with Robert Sheckley, and this poem.

    This version of the poem was written on the back of a wallet-sized photograph of Zelazny in military uniform and dated November 1960. It is presented here with the framing text from the photograph; in the manuscript *Chisel in the Sky* and when later published in 1977 and 1980, it had been edited to include only the text from "Every bone" through "fiery valve."

The Juan's Thousandth

Written 1965–68; previously unpublished.

S tarfall and haven. The pilgrimage draws to a close.
It is strange that journeys often end near their beginnings. Seven light years away on Marmor, home of the smooth white marble and its cutters, I met him on the eve of his undertaking, with Chrysëe, of the perfect ears…

That was hundreds ago.

In the span of a decade we have forked the lightnings of legend across the galaxy. We are heroes, villains, gentlemen, savages, outlaws, and stuff of folklore, the stories told in smoked-filled rooms.

We have been legislated against, welcomed, warned, fought, feared, and greatly loved. We have traveled in state, we have come in secret. From cosmic snowball to cold white sun, the crusade of the Juan rolled strange down black slopes, upsetting the worlds of men.

It could not have been otherwise.

❖   ❖   ❖

Secret as thieves, we enter the meteor belt of Starfall. Darkside, the world lies dreaming, and whoever she will be tosses in sleep and parts her lips.

Which is only fitting.

Streaming bubbles, as the ship without a name drops like a bathysphere through seas of champagne. The delicate hand of the Juan rests upon the hilt of his delicate blade. He snores gently.

It is sad, so sad.

Geometric mountains, glossy as black ice, the city below us. Still.

—Harbinger of Eros, servant of the last great playboy of the westering galaxy—I am here! Awaken and behold!

"What did you say?"

"Sorry," I said. "I didn't mean to awaken you. I guess I was think-ing out loud."

He stretched, then massaged his temples and stroked his beard.

"Perhaps you didn't."

He peered out the port.

"Have you the dampeners on?"

"Yes," I answered with a smile. "Where shall we land?"

He was silent for a long while, then he laughed. He crossed to the cabinet and hauled out *Baedekker MCCXI, Starguide-Worldguide.* Cracking the book to Starfall, he backed off six paces and drew his *épée.*

"Ha!" he balestraed.

I heard his point tear paper and hoped he hadn't poked it into the middle of the lake. I know he would demand that we land in it. Col-orful gestures are his forté, and he has a built-in guidance system.

"Well?"

"Nuevo Jarez," he sighed, "as mad as Quixote at this time of year—and as Spanish as home."

"Perhaps you could take another poke."

"The gods do not appreciate being invoked twice in the same manner."

I leaned forward.

"Then sing out the coordinates."

❖   ❖   ❖

The provincial worlds are always best. After the great Breakup, when each rolled for an age along the cultural paths of its settlers, the old archetypes arose from the collective unconscious, and all the region-alisms of Earth blossomed once more. The reengraftment of inter-stellar civilization did not change everything back. A laser-gun is as uncommon a sight on most of them as a hip-holstered .45 would have been on the streets of twentieth-century New York.

But the blade! Three feet of stinging steel worn along the leg! It *is* common. Along with other medievaltries, the Code Duello prevails on a double dozen worlds.

The Juan is a master of the needle-point *épée.* Forged in Toledo, on Earth, his comes from the land of his ancestors. And the man from whom he claims descent (illegitimate albeit!) was as notorious on the rounds as he once was on the three-foot strip, before his madness seized him.

Wealthy as his family-owned world made him, he had prescribed his own therapy. Wolfsbane and alexin, he had fought his melancholy with a bottomless well of money and a world of attorneys. A law unto himself, he recreated a legend in the face of the awesome god Ennui, who oversees all perfect societies.

❖   ❖   ❖

"A festival to welcome me!" he cried, turning into the village street, "The Gods kissed true my steel!"

We moved into the market-place and I sniffed a deep sniff. —Sawdust and roasting beef, the bloody soul of the grape—the pale rosés, and the musky tears of volcanic deities, ruby ports, tilted judiciously as a man sets a clock—hawked from improvised stalls—wealths of roses in black niagaras of hair, ribbons, and the yellow, black, red and white shirts, skirts, trousers, and sashes of the people.

We seated ourselves at a sidewalk table, and I broke off a piece of the fresh-baked bread that appeared before us.

"Once more I have conquered time," said the Juan, rolling a dusky sherry in the hollows of his cheeks. "Is there a Plaza del Toros, I wonder?"

"There will be no bulls today," said the girl who brought the thick slices of beef. "It is the Festival of the Wines. Today they are brought to market."

Clinically, the Juan eyed her and dismissed her, despite the brilliant smile she displayed.

"She is a pretty one," I observed.

"Her knuckles betray her trade—she cuts the beef! I do not want a butcheress tonight!"

He poured more wine, as the dark-haired children set off a row of pinwheels across the street. The popping of firecrackers and *fuegos artificales*, dim against the brilliant sky, were a steady storm for the next half hour.

When we had finished the meat and were sampling more wines, a *comedia dell'arte* troupe appeared nearby and began its timeless buffoonery.

The Juan laughed at first, but grew silent as the performance progressed. He stared at Arlecchino as the players moved closer and, abruptly, as only such performers can shift and improvise, the direction of the action altered.

Arlecchino had taken the lead. He was a swaggerer, a boaster, now a coward, now a lover. He was an invincibly funny clicker of heels, never standing still for a moment. He dispatched dozens of enemies, each of whom immediately sprang up with a new mask, only to fall once more before his pencil-sized sword. Columbine changed her mask each time he kissed her. Often, he forced her to kiss him. He burnt a house, which seemed reminiscent of something I should remember, galloping off on his hobby-horse, his cloak wrapped about his face. All the while, Capitan Spezzafer stood in the center, like a statue about whom everything revolved.

"Tirso de Molina!" I remembered. " 'The Trickster of Seville'!"

The Juan nodded and tossed a coin to Arlecchino, who kicked dust over it. For an instant, his cat-mask grinned in our direction.

"A parody of the Story of Don Juan," I said.

The Juan rose to his feet, applauding, as the statue carried Arlecchino to Hell. He strode into the street and stood before him, clapping in his face.

"A fine performance, my man."

"Thank you," hissed the cat, whiskers trembling from the words, "I am honored to meet the original."

"And who might you be?" He reached for the mask.

Arlecchino slipped aside, graceful as a fencer.

"Arlecchino," he announced dramatically. "Arlecchino of the thousand faces. We will meet again tonight—only then I shall be the statue."

And the troupe dispersed through the crowd, like a ball of mercury shattered by a blow. It would coalesce elsewhere.

"Gone," said the Juan. "I know that voice from somewhere."

"Friend or foe?" I inquired.

"What man is a friend to the Juan?" he asked.

We moved on up the street.

❖ ❖ ❖

Much to my disgust, the Juan spent the entire afternoon munching dry bread and writing poetry. He had learned that that evening would be the season's social event, the *Juegos Florales de la Vendimia Jerezana*, and a Queen was to be crowned. He had no idea who was even being considered but the prize-winning poets got to read their lyrics in homage to her beauty. He had decided to abide by the judges' decision as to who was the most desirable woman available, and add her to his list.

"Isn't it somewhat hypocritical, writing a love-poem to a woman you have never seen?" I ventured. "Sort of like filling in blanks on a form."

"Nonsense," he replied. "Beauty is an ideal, approximated by all its manifestations."

"It might help to know the color of her hair," I suggested.

"Black," he answered.

"Oh? When did you see her?"

"Half an hour ago. I meditated on the paradoxes of beauty and conceptualized her."

I shook my head and ordered more wine. That Zen stuff isn't for me.

❖   ❖   ❖

But, damn it! Her hair *was* black! In some areas the Juan acknowledges no master…

And that night he outdid himself, commencing the fiery signature at the end of his long career. The rose which Estrella had been awarded was a sun of blood on a field of white. Her hair was the diamond-flecked sky, with ripples. Her teeth the milk of gods. I heard the Juan gasp beside me.

"Saints of Seville! She is something out of Lorca!"

I nodded in agreement and pushed him.

"Chalk up another good conceptualization, and watch out for statues."

It was his turn to read.

In the torchlight I could see his hand shaking as he raised the paper. The campagne was filled with people, seated on blankets, side by side. Those who had imbibed too much reeled off through the night toward the bushes. An occasional rocket drew a bright fingernail across the night's carbon.

The Juan cleared his throat, staring at her as a moth regards a flame. But he was silent too long, and voices began their intertwinings of conversation in the lull.

Finally, he tore his paper in half and dropped the pieces to the ground. The sort of thing quiets us latins. Without removing his eyes from her, he extemporized into the stillness:

"Estrella! The transcendental turnings of a thousand stirring stars show the single shining splendor of the moonlight's simple bars, and the roaring, rushing radiance of the great sun's golden gleams graces grand and glorious gardens of your glowing hair in dreams. —I love you!"

Which, while not great stuff, struck me as pretty effective for a moment's notice. The others seemed to agree, because he drew a nice round of applause.

It was half an hour later, nevertheless, before he got to speak with her, and I regarded her blush as a good sign.

He had just suggested that they get away from everything when a man tapped him on the shoulder.

The Juan snarled.

"What do you want?"

The other smiled.

"Blood—yours."

It was the face of the youth beneath the feathered cap, but the voice was older.

"Arlecchino!" I cried out.

He swept his cap from his head, and the golden locks danced above his brows as he bowed deeply.

"At your service. But I have another name."

The Juan studied his face.

"It was on the world of Caspar," he decided.

"Correct," agreed Arlecchino, with a laugh. "Does your sword arm function as well as your memory, or must I spit on you to get you to draw?"

"The men I kill have names," said the Juan.

"Try Claude," came the reply. "I was the man whose bride eloped on the night of her wedding—only she didn't elope to get married. She committed suicide after her lover deserted her."

"She *was* a temperamental thing."

"Is that all you have to say?"

"I am sorry you are distressed, but consider me not so much a man as a natural force with its own laws."

"They will bury a man tomorrow, not a natural force!"

"If you persist, that may be the case."

The people were clustering about us. Estrella looked lovely in distress.

The youth went on, "Six years ago I joined a troupe which visits many worlds. I knew our paths would cross, sooner or later."

"It is a pity you couldn't have been delayed for another month. My career is almost at its close."

"Yes," I interjected. "One thousand women—he swore it by all the gods of love—and the Juan never breaks a vow."

Arlecchino spat.

"And Rena? What number was she?"

"Three hundred sixty-four, I believe…"

Arlecchino drew his blade and lunged. The people drew back. The Juan's *épée*, like an operatic overture, came unsheathed with a crash. He had had to step in, corps to corps, and lacking bell-guards, in order to stop that first thrust. Then I pushed Estrella behind me, as the Juan leapt backward, disengaging his blade. She found her voice and called out:

"Do not hurt him, stranger! He is only a poet!"

I had to laugh at that. He had been nicked, occasionally, by experts with the rapier, but they aren't around to boast of it. When he loses blood he takes blood, and he has never lost a duel.

Arlecchino was lithe, though, and his form professional. He must have been practicing all of those six years. I could see that things might last awhile.

The crowd produced more torches, and soon the duellers were like upended sewing-machines with the bottoms removed, needles opposing. They poked in and out, in that fashion peculiar to the *épée*, digging for the forearm, the biceps, the shoulder.

A stop-thrust by the Juan met Arlecchino's stab for his right thigh with a blossom of red beneath the collar bone. The Juan caught his blade in a bind, and then another one, each time the point moving nearer his chest. Arlecchino fell back, but managed to parry the Juan's beat-extend-feint-feint-thrust pattern which had cost several fencers their lives.

Finally, the Juan feinted for the forward knee and Arlecchino's bell-guard was down. He caught the febra, and twirled it about, then, zigzagged his blade like the fountain of fire which at that moment burst overhead, and he slashed crosswise, cutting the tendons in the actor's wrist.

"The Juan gives you your life," he announced.

Arlecchino dropped to his knees, clutching at the angel of blood whose crimson wings flapped in the torchlight. An old man tore his sash to make a tourniquet, and moved to his side.

Arlecchino looked in my direction. "Queen of Roses and Blood," he said, "his kiss will be a spider on your lips!"

—And "I curse you, Juan. A better statue than I will face you someday!"

He raised his bloody arm and bit his thumb, then collapsed, sobbing, onto his face.

The old man bound his arm.

❖   ❖   ❖

And the night was gay.

None but the Juan can dance and talk like the Juan. None but the Juan, whose darting fingers are the arrows of Cupid, could so knot the red ribbons of her heart when he reached for it… None but the Juan.

Years and years of practice help, heredity plays its part.

But none but the Juan…

And within the crystal bowl of their locked gazes I saw something else suddenly enter, something which had never been present before, when he had looked at the hetaerae of the Playworld, still full of fires and fun, or at the pale Luana, sought courtesan of six systems, whose favors he swore he would not buy…it looked like love which had entered, secret thief!—or the best facsimile he had ever managed—for this dark girl with the eyes like tawny port.

And I drove them, in the coach we had rented, back to the inn, and I sat on the doorstep until morning, smoking.

❖   ❖   ❖

"All things to all men!" cried the Juan. "Why must you be what you are?"

We stalked through the burnished morning, cut by the meteor's stroke, across the tattered fields and back toward the ship.

"I curse you, Love," said the Juan, "as the actor cursed me."

"After all these years…" I began, "Are you really in love?"

He nodded, then cursed in Spanish, language of sublime profanity.

"Why?" he asked. "At this point in the game! Why?—Arlecchino was right—I have met my statue, and it has a female form. Perhaps on Marmor, where it all began, death will wear marble, and I will thunder down to hell in the clasp of an inhuman nemesis…"

"Perhaps," I said.

"Why, my friend, why?" he asked again, after awhile. "Why did she have to be number nine-ninety-nine?"

Notes

It is not clear whether Zelazny ever submitted this story. The surviving manuscript bears his penciled revisions and typed pieces taped together, but there is no final copy with it. This story typifies his style—reworking a myth or legend (Don Juan and Estrella), mixing in literary allusions (**Arlecchino** is Italian for Harlequin, the nimble stock character who loved **Columbine** and served as the protagonist's nemesis), foreign expressions (***fuegos artificiales***), swordplay (the ***épée***), and an ironic twist at the end.

In the original legend, Don Juan either rapes or seduces Donna Ana, a young noblewoman, and subsequently kills her father in a duel. Passing the father's tomb, he hears a voice from the statue promising punishment for his wicked deeds. Don Juan impudently invites the statue to dinner; animated, it travels to Don Juan's house. In shaking its host's hand, the statue imprisons him in an unbreakable grip and drags him away to Hell.

Eros is the Greek god of love, similar to the Roman god Cupid. A **balestra** is a forward hop or jump in fencing, usually followed by an attack. One's **forté** is something in which one excels. **Code Duello** is a set of dueling rules which helped prevent vendettas between families.

An ***épée*** is a rapier with a three-sided blade which normally has a guard over the tip in fencing. **Wolfsbane** or monkshood is a perennial plant which is a source of aconite, a potent poison. **Alexin** is a homeopathic drug said to boost the immune system and reduce fatigue. **Ennui** is utter boredom and lack of interest; there is no god of ennui. **Black niagaras of hair** means a cascade of hair. **Plaza del Toros** is a famous bullfighting stadium in Spain.

Fuegos artificiales are fireworks. **Comedia dell'arte**, a type of medieval Italian drama, featured comic situations and stock characters. **Captain Spezzafer** (shiver-spear) is the standard military character in pantomime. **Tirso de Molina** was a Spanish dramatist and poet; his play **The Trickster of Seville** featured Don Juan. *Juegos Florales* are floral games in Spain's *Fiesta de la Vendimia Jerezana*, a fall festival that features blessing of the grapes and must (the product of the initial crushing of the grapes) before an image of San Gines de la Jara, Patron Saint of vine growers.

Lorca is a city in southeast Spain. **Corps to corps** means body to body. **Campagne** is an open clearing. The **bell-guard** near the grip of an *épée* protects the hand. **Febra** is not a standard fencing term. Its usage suggests a sudden, feverish slicing or cutting movement with the *épée*, such as one taught by Salvator Fabris in the 1500s. Fabris famously introduced use of the cloak as a stratagem in fencing; both the cloak and fencing are characteristic in portrayals of Don Juan. **Hetaerae** are highly cultured courtesans or concubines; a **courtesan** is a prostitute, especially one whose clients include royalty and men of high social standing.

Apocalypse of a Summer's Night

Written 1955–60 for *Chisel in the Sky;* previously unpublished.

Fitful angels of light
From tantrums of dark intensity:

"Bad sleeping weather;
tomorrow will be hot;
—Rise early."

Fitful angels of flight
from mantras of dark integrity—

"Sad, thinking whether
tomorrow will be fought
—Die early."

THERE SHALL BE
NO MOON!

Written 1965–68; previously unpublished.

"Percy."

"Yes George?"

"I believe you have finally overextended yourself."

The younger man threw his head back and laughed. Anyone but his companion might have thought him demented. The larger man knew better, however. He shifted his gaze to the placid surface of Lucerne, gesturing with his walking-stick.

"That pink cloud reminds me of Southey."

"Oh?" chuckled the other. "In what way?"

"It makes a great show of being huge and colorful, and inside it's as miasmic and weightless as a London fog—and about as valuable."

"Well-turned, but I daresay you are changing the subject."

"…and those peaks in the distance, my! how they must echo with the turning of the spheres—as my poor ears with the sounds of your Project."

"Now, that's unfair!" protested the other. "I haven't seen you for two weeks, and I've made great progress."

"Doubtless you are producing something of great merit and exquisiteness…but, if I doubt its efficacy along the lines you have professed, pray forgive me my doubts and grant me leave to remain a Thomas until I have thrust my hands into the wounds."

He smiled. "Ah! Whenever you are being irreligious, George, I'll concede almost everything. But this time you are mistaken."

"Then advise me."

"I conjured a fog last night, and an image."

"This is foggy country."

"A fog that tries to speak?"

"How much sleep have you had this week—not to mention wine, and perhaps a touch of brain fever?"

"No more than usual. But the rhythms are almost perfect now."

"Then why the delay? Bring him forth! There are some things I have always wanted to ask!"

"The moon will not be full for another week—and the land, I am afraid the land must be dispensed with."

"Oh? You have purchased a balloon from the Montgolfiers? —I fancy brother Bill might be a trifle distressed to awaken several hundreds of feet above the ground."

"No, no! The land is too stable an element—too firm, too venerable a *métier*—the invocation must be spoken upon untrammeled waters, there—where the wilder powers hold sway!"

His eyes dimmed as he spoke, and he swayed slightly, himself.

The other lit a cheroot, partly to end the flight of his friend's imagination in its stinging blue cloud.

"You have rented a barge?"

"A small boat. I have been purifying it all week. I'll anchor offshore when the moon shows full. —I wish you could be there."

His friend tossed his dark locks, and a sinister gleam danced deep in his eyes.

"The son of the Devil at his father's Mass? No, I'm sure you are qualified to manage it without me."

"It's not the Black Mass!" he protested. "It is a personal ritual, designed to summon up the shade of William Shakespeare!"

"I'll try to be there, Percy, but I can't promise. I have a delightful engagement which I trust shall last well into the next day."

He smiled his lopsided smile, managing to condemn his thoughts and enjoy them at the same instant of reverie.

"Noblesse oblige," smirked the other. Then, changing back to his original proposal, "But seriously, I think you, of all men, would be best qualified for the undertaking. When you only dabbled at it you had better results than anyone else…"

"My dear Shelley, I will tell you the trouble with your invocation, without having heard it.

"You invite, you entreat, you appreciate—that is wrong. You must command!

"You approach whatever power you call upon as you do the English language," he finished, "a bit too humbly. You must order it to do your bidding like the lackey that it is!"

"But that is not in my nature." He shook his head. "I sometimes wish that I could, but I lack your seigniorial prowess."

The other hung his head.

"Noblesse oblige," he muttered more softly. "But come! you say you have some fresh Kirschwasser!"

"Ah, yes! Red as the lips of one's beloved, and far more lingering!"

"Ha!" The other turned to the road with surprising agility. "Let there be no more talk of spells and incantations—only spirits! Tonight we drink!"

They started up the road.

"But this one, Byron! I know this one will do it! I've worked so hard on the metrics, have chosen words with all the right vibrations…"

Silently, the other limped along beside him.

❖   ❖   ❖

"Mary! Another bottle, please! The peerage is a bottomless lake!"

"Hollow hoof," snorted Byron, and he closed his eyes as Mary entered with the ruddy liquors. She smiled, but small lines on her attractive face betrayed a mood which had not been present two weeks previously.

Byron's eyes blinked open and bored into hers.

"You are troubled," he announced.

"And you still sober. Goodness!"

She placed the drink before him.

"There is that within me which never sleeps, nor drunken grows, though seas of grapes surround."

"Is that from *Childe Harold*?"

"No, it is from the moment. What's the matter?"

She bit her lower lip.

"Oh, nothing. Doctor Frankenstein and his problems," she offered. "I'm following your suggestion and writing it out, since you men are too busy—"

She started to say "with," but chewed the sentence off.

Byron climbed to his feet, glass in hand.

"A toast! To goblins, werewolves, demons, and gods," he pronounced.

Shelley raised his glass drunkenly. Mary hurried from the room.

"To William Shakespeare, Englishman and Greek," he said.

Byron quaffed his drink and seated himself once more.

"You have her worried," he began.

"Huh?"

"Mary is troubled. The climate of your pursuits has upset the poor girl."

"Nonsense," he slurred. "She's fascinated by the stuff."

"Nevertheless, entertain a friend's suggestion. A holiday in Italy might be in order."

"Go to, m'lord—I shan't say where. What's in Italy?"

"It's warm, sunny, healthy—just the opposite of this place. Life is focused upon itself in the latin climes, not the metaphysics of involution."

"Ha! The pa' calling the kethle brack! You go to Italy! You won't help me here!"

"It would not particularly amuse me to speak with Shakespeare. He'd probably be tongue-tied, anyhow." He smiled his twisted smile.

"No one could speak like one of his characters—which is both their tragedy and ours."

"Don't be so subtle when you're drunk. Lemme read you some Wordsworth."

"I'm afraid I have to be leaving soon."

"What have you got against Wordsworth?"

"As I said, I must depart shortly. I can't afford the entire night."

"All right." He closed the edition of *Lyrical Ballads* which he had stealthily inched from a drawer.

"…But next time," he observed, "I shall convince you."

Byron spun his cloak like a great wing, and it settled about his shoulders. He retrieved his stick from the chair.

"Say good-night to Mary, lay in more wine, and write me at the inn."

Shelley snored softly.

The innkeeper's son tapped gently but impatiently. Finally, his knocking produced a yawn on the other side of the door. After another five minutes, that great oaken panel creaked inward. Resplendent in scarlet silk, Byron regarded the youth.

"A letter for you, m'lord."

"Very good—here, lad. Spend it not on one wench."

"No sir, I shall buy chocolate."

"Mm. To each his vice. —Thank you."

He pushed shut the door and crossed to his writing table. Seated, he brushed aside a mountain of cantos and unfolded the letter.

"Hm."

Two bold sentences uncoiled in his hands and slipped into his drowsy mind: "Tonight the moon is full. Your presence is requested."

"Damme!" he announced, rising again.

"Shelley! Why do you do these things? —Do you know what you ask?"

He crossed to the window and slapped the casement.

The day was bleak. The boy ran across the yard and stood beneath a willow. He began tossing stones into the stream.

Of course!

Hastily, Byron reseated himself and sharpened a quill. Without pausing, he filled a page with bold strokes:

> Dearest Ariel,
>   Though you dwell in the Empyrean, doubtless you have not looked about of late. Pray do! The gods frown down today, and the heavens darken. There shall be no moon!
>
> As above, so below,
> Manfred

Smiling, he melted a piece of red wax and dripped it on the overlap. He looked about for a bell-pull and remembered there was none. Hurrying to the casement, he flung it wide.

"Boy! Catch this letter. Take it to the man who gave you mine. —And buy some more chocolate!"

The boy had recovered the letter and the coin before the window was closed.

Byron returned to his table to write another dozen cantos as he awaited breakfast.

A murmur: "Schedules must be maintained…"

❖   ❖   ❖

"He's right," she observed, reading over his shoulder. "You said yourself that the moon must be full and clear."

"It may yet clear," he muttered, rubbing his blond stubble. "Come, let's walk down by the lake."

She took his arm.

"I will enjoy it more if you talk to me, and stop staring at the sky."

"It will clear," he stated.

"Perhaps," she sighed. "Why do you want to summon Shakespeare, anyway? What do you wish to ask him?"

"I don't know. I will know when I see him."

"There may be a storm."

"And there may not."

"I have finished *Frankenstein*."

"Good."

"Will you read it?"

"Tomorrow."

"Percy, you are impossible!"

"I trust you are correct."

"Perhaps that is why my concern is almost maternal. You are a careless child with a new toy."

"Then, daedal before the gods, shall I spin it."

"Byron will not be here."

"Who needs him?"

"You. So let me take his place."

"Never. A woman would vitiate the incantation."

"If it clears, I shall worry all night."

"Your privilege."

They drew near the cove where the boat was moored.

"I am sorry, you may not come aboard."

He vaulted over the rail, commencing a soft chant and paced from bow to stern, counting his steps. Everything above and below the deck was painted white. Black pentacles decorated the floorboards. Shelley opened a locker and checked a brazier, a supply of incense, and his herbs. From his pocket, he produced a roll of foolscap which he placed alongside them.

He closed the chest and looked up.

"All right. All is in readiness. I'm going to remain aboard until it is time. You might as well return now."

"It's starting to rain." She held forth a pale hand, palm upwards, for an instant reminding him of a child beggar he had seen at Charing.

"It will pass."

Silently, she turned and walked back, wiping rain from her eyes.

❖   ❖   ❖

The moon was a blind eye, peering from a lightless room through broken panes. Sightless, through opaque shards of sky, it looked down, past and through the trees, walls and people of the city.

Byron cursed.

"Why? Why have I a nonsense conscience? —A gift of the gods for my blasphemies? Giving up a warm fireside—and more!"

His drenched cloak plastered his muscular limbs. The thunder prowled tentatively, then belched a long rumble.

"Cochon!" he spat. "Ariel stands beneath your moon, mouthing iambs at you! —Nature, you lack breeding! You should smile, not slap his face in insults of wind!"

He vaulted into the saddle, clucking at the soaked animal.

"We ride, my poor mount, though a beast deserves better tonight."

❖   ❖   ❖

The beast of ink raised its thousand hands, jerking the boat to starboard.

"Oh Winds of Time that wash Elysium…"

An instant study in black and gray was followed by a crash. The boated dipped to the left.

"Tides of Time, receding forever…"

He choked on the aromatic fumes from the brazier. The smoke lay flat upon the deck; the pop and hiss of the fire emerged between passing gusts.

"I do conjure thee…"

A devil-throated howl crossed the waters, racing footless the sweeping clouds.

The moon did not blink, staring down, past and through the boat, the man, the waters. Shelley's words were cipher within the demon-siren of the passer.

Then all lay still.

The smoke flumed upwards, the moon blazed beacon, the ship was an arrow, quivering in the dark, flat field where it had fallen.

"Appear before me here, I charge thee…"

A sudden spark, and the smoke billowed in all directions. In the distance, a sound like Atlas dropping the sky; an island of cloud crossed the moon, like its wandering pupil, seeking the center of the retina…

"Speak!"

The dark land shrugged, raising its hands once more; it grasped the arrow out, with a twist of fury, threw it flat, then bled rivers upon it.

"I do hear thee!"

❖   ❖   ❖

Byron drew upon the shore. The tiny blink of the brazier beckoned his gaze. The rain hesitated, then held back a moment.

"Good Lord, why so far out?" he groaned. "The next one will catch you!"

Dismounting, he drew off his boots and unclasped his cloak.

The waters grew still.

He finished undressing and plunged in, swimming with the powerful strokes of a man who knew he could cross the Hellespont. The waves did not beat about him; the lake was as placid as a mountain rill on a sunny afternoon.

He bore toward the bobbing flicker—and the mountain fired its heavy artilleries. Like a boxer fighting an omnipresent opponent, Byron lashed out with double fury.

"Shelley! I'm coming!"

The waves fell upon him like a collapsing wall. He went under. Seconds later he bobbed to the surface and began to wrestle his adversary, timing his movements to give way before each buffet.

Then the light tipped and went out.

With quick strokes, he tried painting a mental picture of its last location. He fought forward until the dim hulk loomed before him.

"Shelley!"

He heard something that sounded like a sobbing choke. He beat his way about the fallen vessel.

"Shelley?"

This time the choke-sound was louder. He reached out through the darkness…

Flesh! Shelley was clinging to the side of the boat.

He pried loose his weakening grip, then seized him cross-chest.

Then he began the long return toward what he hoped was shore.

❖   ❖   ❖

"Jester of the gods!" he panted. "What moves a man to such extremes?"

Shelley coughed and did not answer him. Byron pulled on his boots.

"You should have tried the balloon," he snarled. "They don't sink!"

Shelley coughed again.

"Couldn't you have put it off for a month?"

"He came," said Shelley.

"Who?"

"Shakespeare answered my summons."

Byron shook out his cloak and threw it over his friend's shoulders.

"I suppose you had time for a lengthy colloquy?"

"No, only a few words."

The horse nuzzled him, suggesting that people with good sense did not stand out in the rain.

"What did he say?"

"I'm not certain."

He assisted Shelley to mount, then climbed up behind him.

"What did you ask him?"

"I asked him the meaning of a man's life."

"Is that all? —Well, what do you think he said?"

"It sounded like, 'Though his bark cannot be lost, yet it shall be tempest-tossed.'"

"Hm. Appropriate enough. —That's from *Macbeth*, by the way—the Third Witch. —You heard me calling and filled in your own words."

"No, it sounded like Shakespeare—the way I expected him to sound."

They plunged around the bend.

"Mary will probably have dry clothes waiting. Some rum too, I hope."

Shelley coughed again. They approached the welcoming windows of the cottage.

"George— There are no words—but no other man could have beaten the waters… Thank you."

The other laughed.

"Foul Weather Jack Byron would have sailed onto the Styx, and Mad Jack bearded Jove and a bolt or two, I've heard. Is the son to be less than his fathers?"

"In your case, never."

They dismounted, and Byron led the horse into the shed. Shelley paused on the step.

"I keep a messy journal, George—and I know you are writing your memoirs. Include this please, that I may acknowledge a perpetual debt—and future generations may be inclined to remember me when they read it."

"They will remember you without it, Percy. But, as you wish—some future Mad Jack may be amused."

"Your memoirs will blaze through all generations."

"I daresay. Now, get inside, it's chilly out here." He pushed him.

Mary opened the door, a twisted handkerchief at her waist. She peered out, blinking heavily.

"I'm sorry, Mary," said Shelley.

Her eyes blazed as she stepped aside.

"Tempest-tossed, indeed!" noted Byron.

Notes

The Percy, Mary and George in this story are poet Percy Shelley, novelist Mary Shelley, and poet George Gordon, Lord Byron. In the long, rainy summer of 1816, they challenged each other to write ghost stories after reading from *Fantasmagoriana*. The three writers speculated about science reanimating a corpse, prompting Mary Shelley to have a waking nightmare which inspired her to write ***Frankenstein***. The poets quickly abandoned their stories; however, Byron did write the gothic poem "Manfred." The **Southey** Byron mentions was Robert Southey, a poet with whom he had an ongoing feud; the two attacked each other through their poems.

Byron calls Shelley **Ariel** in a letter, alluding to Shelley's repeated prediction of his own drowning. He did drown when another boat deliberately struck his schooner **Ariel**, and it sank.

Miasmic is an unpleasant atmosphere. **Grant me leave to remain a Thomas until I have thrust my hands into the wounds** refers to the doubting apostle Thomas who declared he would not believe Jesus had risen until he could thrust his fingers into his Master's wounds. In 1783, **Joseph and Etienne Montgolfiers** created the first hot air balloon and remained aloft in it for ten minutes. **Métier** is a person's specialty. **Brother Bill** is **William**

Shakespeare, whom Percy wishes to contact. **Seigniorial** pertains to a feudal lord or other man of rank. **Noblesse oblige** requires those of noble birth or high social standing to act with honor. **Kirschwasser** is a German brandy made from double distillation of black cherry. *Childe Harold's Pilgrimage* is Byron's lengthy poem which recounts the world travels of a disillusioned young man.

Lyrical Ballads was a book of poetry by William **Wordsworth** and Samuel Taylor Coleridge. **Cantos** are the major divisions of a very long poem. **Empyrean** is the highest heaven, or the visible heavens. **Daedal before the gods** means to be extremely clever and inventive; the word derives from Daedalus, who created wings to enable himself and his son Icarus to fly. **Vitiate** means to weaken. **Cochon** means pig. **Iambs** are two-syllable units or feet in poetic meter, usually consisting of one stressed and one unstressed syllable, or one short and one long syllable.

Ariel is the spirit of the air who helps Prospero in Shakespeare's *Tempest*. **Elysium** is the final resting place in the underworld of the souls of the heroic and the virtuous. **Atlas** is one of the Titans whom Zeus condemned to stand at the western edge of the earth and hold up the Sky on his shoulders. **Hellespont** is the old name for Dardanelles, a strait connecting the Aegean Sea and the Sea of Marmara. **Though his bark cannot be lost, yet it shall be tempest-tossed** is a quote from the first witch in Shakespeare's *Macbeth*; it means *although I can't make his ship sink, I can still make his journey miserable with stormy weather*. The end of the story indicates that Mary Shelley's anger is part of the tempest that Percy must endure for his foolish behavior and for excluding her.

Lord Byron's grandfather Vice-Admiral John Byron was known as **Foul Weather Jack** because of frequent bad luck with weather, while Byron's father John Byron was known as **Mad Jack** for his unstable behavior. **Styx** is one of the main rivers in the underworld, across which Charon would ferry the dead. **Jove** is another name for Jupiter, the Roman equivalent of the Greek god Zeus.

On My Giving Up of Regular Metrics, Manumitted Via a Portable Byron

Written 1955–60 for *Chisel in the Sky;* previously unpublished.

Tell it, from me, at last,
that I have gone.
Tell it that,
as the green is drained from the lawns of August,
I felt a small chill
in the midst of sunny afternoons,
and upon altars of deadening thought
laid out the problem of my return.

It is not far that I go,
but tell it (delightful old prig that it is)
that I have undertaken an immense journey.
Lie to it.
Let it respect my temerity.
Else, poor my muse,
the knowledge it is mateless
should topple much chalcedony and jade.

Notes

Metrics refers to the use and study of the structure, arrangement and rhythm of words used in poetry. **Manumitted** means released from slavery. Lord **Byron** was a poet Zelazny admired, known for romantic and melodramatic poetry, including *Don Juan* and *Childe Harold's Pilgrimage*. Also, his half-sister Augusta Ada **Byron** (Lady Lovelace) was a mathematician who helped Charles Babbage develop his Analytical Engine, the first (albeit mechanical) general-purpose computer. **Temerity** is boldness or rashness. **Chalcedony** is a milky form of quartz while **jade** is an often green stone that is used in jewelry and carvings.

THROUGH A GLASS, GREENLY

Written 1965–68; previously unpublished.

"Where did you ever get it, Lundy?" I asked, holding it up to the light and staring through at his green-infused face.

He smiled that superior smile that every wine snob displays to a true connoisseur, when he thinks he has surpassed him.

"Oh, I managed to find three bottles in an old cellar in Jamaica," he flipped his hand casually. "I brought it back disguised as crème de menthe."

I luxuriated in its deep emerald soul, it was like the doorway to a wicked world through which I need but step to enter into the presence of Arthur Symonds and Paul Verlaine.

I sniffed it.

"One doesn't just drink it that way," he sighed.

"I have drunk absinthe before," I stated.

"Pernod," he interrupted.

"No, absinthe! And I know how it is to be treated."

Of course I lied, but one never admits these things to wine snobs.

He produced two screens of silver mesh and placed them across the tops of the glasses.

"Very well, you prepare them."

It wasn't hard to do. I had at least read of the ritual, and I knew he had never seen it. So I placed a cube of sugar on each screen and delicately tipped the decanter above them.

"Very well done, Duncan." He gnashed his teeth as the sugar dripped through and clouded the green.

"To the Nouvelle Athenes," I saluted, raising my glass.

"Verily," he agreed.

It had an awful taste to it, but I forced myself to smile and nod sagely.

"Wonderful!" I sighed. "Fine and grand! You wouldn't consider selling me a bottle, would you?"

"I'm afraid not."

"I didn't think so," I answered, "I didn't think so."

"However," he said, "if you'll come to the costume party this evening, you can drink it all night."

"I'll be there with bells on."

"I should hope so. It's a costume party."

I knew that, so for the sake of good humor I did wear bells, on my cap. I went as a court jester.

❖　❖　❖

I was being bored by an ivy-cut sophomore who wanted the U.N. to promote Pound's theory of money on a worldwide scale, when Lundy negotiated a corridor of cavaliers, courtesans, Falstaffs, and monks, pushing past the Charybdis and Scylla of a big-bellied banker named Gunson, and his friend, named something I couldn't catch, and, shaking off their assaults, clutched at my sleeve.

"All right, old fellow. The time is nigh. Shall we wend our way to the cellar, bearing glasses?"

"Nothing could suit me better," I jingled. "Excuse me, ivy-cut sophomore, who wants the U.N. to promote Pound's theory of money."

He sneered and I was gone.

Through the hustle and bustle of the Catskill Walpurgis of his garden, and into the mahogany and glass of his mighty hall, forsooth. Down then, down the winding rickety staircase that led from his great kitchen and into the purposefully musty cellars of his fame.

The Ghost of Christmas Past leered at me from behind a parcel of yuletide ornaments on a low table. We walked past the leaning tower of an ancient I-beam and negotiated a narrow passage beside the old furnace, which had stood in disuse since the shift to gas many years before. Squatting, we duck-walked under a brace of low pipes that clustered like mandragora-root at waist-height. Then a corner, a short passage, and another corner.

Then, the racks.

The monument of Lundy's folly, the rows and rows of bottles sleeping, heads lowered, in aisles of cobwebbed silence, awaiting, through the darkness and the years, the palate of a man who could not tell one from the other.

Lundy moved the magic circle of his flashlight to a small table in the far corner.

Just like him to set up things so purposefully dramatic, so contrived…

He struck a match and lighted the candelabra that stood upon a broken barrel.

There were two bottles on the table. I set the glasses beside them. I turned back to Lundy.

His long, protruding fangs dripped upon the floor and he held a trowel in his right hand.

"My God! Lundy! What's happened?"

"Nothing!" he cried. "Nothing—yet!"

He advanced toward me, pointing with his trowel.

"I'm going to wall you into that niche, you wine snob!"

There was a small opening in the wall behind me.

"But first, I'm going to enjoy the greatest drink of all—human blood! Your blood! I'm a vampire, and you are going to be my victim, because you are a fraud and a snob and do not really appreciate good things to drink."

"No!" I said, and I hit him with a bottle from the rack.

He fell, and his upper plate slipped from his mouth.

"It was only a joke," he mumbled, "only a joke."

I hit him again, in the temple.

❖   ❖   ❖

He is still, so still, and the candles are low.

One is gone and one remains. I've finally developed a taste for the stuff. If I hold the bottle just right, he's green from head to toe, and his fangs upon the floor.

I jingle my bells.

"You always were a phoney, Lundy. This stuff is too good for you."

I pour another glass.

I think I can finish it all before he wakes up.

Notes

This is a pastiche of Edgar Allan Poe's "The Cask of Amontillado." **Through a glass, greenly** alludes to "through a glass, darkly" in the Bible (New Testament, 1 Corinthians:13); the line implies that humans have an imperfect perception of reality. The **greenly** refers to **absinthe**, a bitter licorice-flavored, green liqueur made from wormwood. The story mentions two nineteenth century poets who were fond of absinthe, **Arthur Symonds** and **Paul Verlaine**. Symonds wrote the poem "The Absinthe Drinker." **Pernod** is a green, aromatic anise- and licorice-flavored liqueur. **Ezra Pound** was a poet who became infamous for his theories about money, usury, and the power of banks to create money out of nothing and control governments. **Cavaliers** are gentlemen, especially those escorting women of high social standing. **Courtesans** are prostitutes, especially those whose clients include royalty and men of high social standing. **Falstaffs** suggests fat, drunken buffoons similar to Sir John Falstaff in Shakespeare's plays. In Greek mythology, **Charybdis** is a whirlpool and **Scylla** a perilous rock, between which it is difficult to journey. **Catskill** is a town in New York State located near the Catskill Mountains. Saint **Walpurgis** was an English missionary in Germany. Early Christians adapted an existing pagan spring rite on April 30 to honor her on May 1. (Walpurgisnacht, Walpurgis Night). The phrase **Catskill Walpurgis** was probably intended to mean something that is ostentatious but cheap. **Forsooth** means in truth. **Mandragora** root is the Mandrake root, considered magical because the root often resembles a human body.

Time of Night in the 7th Room

Written 1965–68; previously unpublished.

(found in a bottle)

This is the story of Gricet and Lord Chek of the snail-fort, and of the wing-benders and highbeached-winders and of the Lightofday time they shared together (Gricet and Lord Chek) in the seventh room of the world, which some say is the largest.

—It is a comedy (she wrote). That is to say, it ends in heaven, for most of the parties concerned. She, being Grisek, who of the womanwanderkind was first to find a snail-fort of her own, to continue undiminished across the ages, and to diddle whatever Lords she chose for the furtherance of the new and longborn womanwanderkind.

This is the story of how she came to be:

—The Lightofday (which had been faltering for a time) clicked off, and the world wondered whether it would ever come on again. The snail-forts ceased their movement and dug into the floor of the world for the Timeofnight. The highbeached-winders uncoiled themselves and slithered off in search of prey. Occasionally, there was an orange and incandescent flash as one ventured too near a snail-fort. The Lords prepared to retire and sleep the long Timeofnight through.

The womanwanderkind emerged from the wilderness where they had been wandering, and they ventured rapidly across the countryside, being eaten by the 'winders and 'benders and the biggies and the crawlies as they went.

When they came upon a snail-fort, they would remove their garments, put aside their weapons, and bang upon the whorled side-plating of the curved fort-back. If the Lord was awake and watching through one of the great eyes, he did not always permit the fort to spray them with fires. He would stay the nozzle and tell them to go away; or, if he'd a mind to diddle, would select the most comely for his sleepmate, and, if he were a merciful Lord, would spray the others with the fires.

Lord Chek was old. Gods, he was old! A hundred generations of womanwanderkind had passed beneath his loins, and their daughters slept within the bellies of the things that went flash in the night. Two had even given him sons, for whom he had scouted for days and endless days until he had seen them fitted with snail-forts of their own, as became Lords of the Seventh Room. Now the chills were upon him, and he feared that his days were coming to an end. So it was not likely that it was the desire to diddle that led him to open his fort to Gricet. Probably, he was lonesome and wanted someone to be nurse to him and to listen to his ramblings a part of the long Timeofnight.

She came alone, this one, placed her belt knife and thin spear upon her piled garments, and pounded, shivering, upon the gray and faintly glowing shell of the fort.

Lord Chek spoke to her out of the night, saying, "What do you want, womanwanderer?"

"To come in, Lord of the snail-fort."

A highbeached-winder stalked her a she spoke, pushing its head along the ground in her direction. She knew, though, that if she took up her weapons again she forsook her claim to sanctuary. She turned her head and watched it approach as the Lord continued to speak:

"What is your name, womanwanderer?"

"Gricet!"

The 'winder moved its head from side to side, preparing to strike.

"Will you diddle me a son, Gricet?"

"I do not know, Lord! I will try!"

"I suppose that will have to do," he said, and sprayed the high-beached-winder with fires just as it sprang.

The she fell back against the snail-fort and it opened and she was inside and in bed, and the wall closed and all was dark about her.

From beside her, the Lord Chek spoke again:

"Old am I and dying, Gricet," he said. "So I want someone to speak to this Timeofnight, even if it is only one of the womanwanderkind."

"Yes, Lord."

"I am going to make a light now."

"Yes, Lord."

A dim light came on within the great, curved chamber. Having never seen a Lord before, Gricet had no notion one way or the other as to how they should look. So she simply stared at him, gray and withered, there on the floor of the chamber which was all bed, as he spoke and explained to her how to open and close the fort-wall, which was a thing she would need to know in order to leave, should he die during the Timeofnight—for a womanwanderer might not remain alone within a snail-fort—and as he explained to her how to switch the guns from automatic to manual control, so that they would not burn her as she left, and as he told her of the operation of the great eyes, which would permit her to scan in all directions before she left. As an afterthought, he told her where the foods and medicines were kept, and how their fabricator worked, should it be necessary for her to serve him with such.

As she stared at him, he stared at her, and he realized with a start that he was not too old to diddle after all.

After a time, they lapsed into slumber, and the chamber of the bed fed them and cleaned them and kept them warm and well-drugged until the Lightofday did, after all, come again.

Surprised to awaken at all, the Lord Chek studied the woman who slept at his side and whom he was about to turn loose again into the world, unless—

He pressed a button upon the wall.

"Yes, she is pregnant," said the room.

"Amazing!" he stated.

Then he pressed the button twice again.

"The child will be of the womanwanderkind," stated the room.

"That is generally the case," he conceded, and he elbowed the woman awake.

"Good morning," he said, "you are pregnant and may leave."

"Where am—" she said. "Oh, Lord Chek."

"Yes, I have survived the long Timeofnight. You are with child, and may return now to the wilderness to have your daughter. Your spear and knife still remain outside the snail-fort, though I note your garments are missing."

"May I not stay for a time?"

"Whatever for?"

"I do not feel well."

"That is only because you are pregnant," said the Lord Chek. "It doesn't last very long, when it is a daughter you are to have. You will feel all right afterwards."

"But I have no garments."

"You will find more."

"You said that you wanted someone to speak to, even if it was only one of the womanwanderkind—"

"That was last Timeofnight. I feel better this Lightofday. Go now."

"Yes, Lord."

She arose, and as she walked away he noticed something.

"Stop," he said, and pressed a button.

"Yes," asked the room.

"Why is it that she is not yet big-waisted if she is going to have a womanwanderchild? She is still narrow at the waist, though an entire Timeofnight has passed. It is as if she bears a Lord."

"Have her walk across the chamber, and stand in the middle."

He did this thing.

"Well," he asked.

"This is very strange," said the room. "I have determined the gender correctly, but the rate of growth is such as will take her a sixth of her life to bear the child—as if it were a Lord."

"What should I do?"

"Keep her here for a while, that I may study her."

"Very well. —Gricet, come this way and I will give you a garment. Then we will eat breakfast and I will teach you how to read and to make small animals cry out as we remove their various parts—both of which improve the mind and are excellent pastimes. It appears that you will have your wish and remain here for a time."

"Yes, Lord."

After a time, she was as withered and old as the Lord Chek had been, and she gave birth to a womanwanderchild and lived for a time to attend it. The Lord Chek had since passed, requiring his medicine suddenly one day and sending Gricet after it. At length, when she returned, he was dead. So she operated the great eyes and scanned in all directions, switched the guns from automatic to manual control, opened the great fort-wall and dragged him outside to the place from which her clothing had vanished; and when she looked again later, he had vanished, too.

Before very long, she died herself, and the machine disposed of her body and raised the child, whom she had named Grisek.

So this is the story of how Grisek came to be, remembering no parent, educated by the bedroom—reading and writing and cutting small animals, she grew, generations of womanwanderkind passing, dying beneath the automatic guns of the snail-fort before she reached womanhood herself.

Later, after she had learned all operations of the snail-fort, she took the womanwanderers in and spoke with them. There was no need to dissect them, for the bedroom explained to her the difference between men and women.

Men lived a hundred times as long, and women were a thousand times as plentiful as men.

Except for herself. In her, the Lord Chek had fathered a freak. She was of the womanwanderkind, but she possessed the lifespan of a Lord.

The bedchamber had suggested that she might mother an entire race of her own kind. To do this, of course, she would need Lords to diddle. But going to them in the night, as did the wanderkind, was too risky. She was not anxious to feel the fires upon her.

So she directed her snail-fort to course about the floor of the Seventh Room, attacking those others which she came upon. Subduing their Lords, she begat daughters which she gave into the keeping of their bedchambers. The Lords, she turned loose to wander the wilderness.

Of the nine and ninety Lords with whom she lay, it was only Lord Dimijon whom she regretted sending into the wilderness where the 'winders and the 'benders and the biggies and the crawlies go. For he had been young and dark, and had looked on her long and smiled slowly, and when he held her he had told her that he wanted her with him always. Almost, she had relented. But then he had pressed his mouth against hers, as if to draw life from her. She called then upon the machines of her fort, to expel him to wander the world.

Their reconciliation was a strange one.

The chills were upon her, and she feared that her days were coming to an end. It was likely, therefore, that she was lonesome and wanted someone to be nurse to her and to listen to her ramblings as part of the long Timeofnight. It is not likely that she would have opened her fort otherwise.

The men had emerged from the wilderness where they had been wandering…

Notes

Zelazny suffered frequent criticism for initially failing to create strong female characters; however, this early story does feature such a woman.

The **seventh room** in the title probably refers to heaven, and the story suggests a creation myth, possibly that of Inanna, the Summerian nature goddess who leaves her realm to visit her sister Ereshkigal, queen of the underworld. The gatekeeper there removes all of Inanna's clothing, and she enters the seventh room, the throne room, naked and disarmed (Naked, Gricet enters Lord Chek's throne room). Inanna is killed there, and nature dies with her. Only her resurrection can revive nature (in Zelazny's story, daughter Grisek's emergence renews the world). Psychologist Carl Jung detailed the psychological aspects Inanna's (alternatively Ishtar's) descent into the underworld (the unconscious). Zelazny incorporated Jungian psychology into other works as well. He was fascinated with dying and resurrecting gods.

...AND CALL ME CONRAD
PART ONE

Manuscript titles: *I Am Thinking of My Earth & Goodby, My Darling Goodby, Conrad* .
The Magazine of Fantasy & Science Fiction, October 1965.
Hugo award 1966 (novel, tied with Frank Herbert's *Dune*);
Seiun award 1976 (novel, as *This Immortal*).

"You are a Kallikanzaros," she announced suddenly.

I turned onto my left side and smiled through the darkness. "I left my hooves and my horns at the Office."

"You've heard the story!"

"The name *is* 'Nomikos'."

I reached for her, found her.

"Are you going to destroy the world this time around?"

I laughed and drew her to me.

"I'll think about it. If that's the way the Earth crumbles—"

"You know that children born here on Christmas are of the kallikanzaroi blood," she said, "and you once told me that your birthday—"

"All right!"

It had struck me that she was only half-joking. Knowing some of the things one occasionally meets in the Old Places, the Hot Places, you can almost believe in myths without extra effort—such as the story of those Pan-like sprites who gather together every spring to spend ten days sawing at the Tree of the World, only to be dispersed at the last moment by the ringing of the Easter bells. (*Ring-a-ding*, the bells, *gnash, gnash*, the teeth, *clackety-clack*, the hooves, et cetera.) Cassandra and I were not in the habit of discussing religion, politics, or Aegean folklore in bed—but, me having been born in these parts, the memories are still somehow alive.

"I am hurt," I said, only half-joking.

"You're hurting *me*, too…"

"Sorry."

I relaxed again.

After a time I explained:

"Back when I was a brat, the other brats used to push me around, calling me 'Konstantin Kallikanzaros.' When I got bigger and uglier they stopped doing it. At least, they didn't say it to my face—"

"'Konstantin'? That was your name? I've wondered…"

"It's 'Conrad' now, so forget it."

"But I like it. I'd rather call you 'Konstantin' than 'Conrad'."

"If it makes you happy…"

The moon pushed her ravaged face up over the windowsill to mock me. I couldn't reach the moon, or even the window, so I looked away. The night was cold, was damp, was misty as it always is here.

"The Commissioner of Arts, Monuments and Archives for the planet Earth is hardly out to chop down the Tree of the World," I rasped.

"*My* kallikanzaros," she said too quickly, "I did not say that. But there are fewer bells every year, and it is not always desire that matters. I have this feeling that you *will* change things, somehow. Perhaps—"

"You are wrong, Cassandra."

"And I am afraid, and cold—"

And she was lovely in the darkness, so I held her in my arms to sort of keep her from the foggy foggy dew.

❖　　❖　　❖

In attempting to reconstruct the affairs of these past six months, I realize now that as we willed walls of passion around our October and the isle of Kos, the Earth had already fallen into the hands of those powers which smash all Octobers. Marshalled from within and without, the forces of final disruption were even then goose-stepping amidst the ruins—faceless, ineluctable, arms upraised. Cort Myshtigo had landed at Port-au-Prince in the antique *Sol-Bus Nine*, which had borne him in from Titan along with a load of shirts and shoes, underwear, socks, assorted wines, medical supplies, and the latest tapes from civilization. A wealthy and influential galactojournalist, he. Just how wealthy, we were not to learn for many weeks; just how influential, I found out only five days ago. And the long-dormant Radpol was stirring again, but I did not know that until several days later.

The Radpol. The old Radpol…

Once chief among the stirrers of disruption, the Radpol had lapsed into long quiescence.

After the departure of its sinister half-man founder, Karaghiosis the killer (who, strangely resembled me, a very few old-timers have said—tut!), the Radpol weakened, had slept.

It had done its necessary troubling, however, over a half a century ago, and the Vegans stayed stalemated.

But Vega could buy the Earthoffice—which runs this blamed world—and sell it many times over for kicks from out of the Petty Cash drawer—because Earthgov Absentia lives off Vegan droppings.

Vega hadn't been too eager to try it, though.

Not since the Radpol led the Returnist Rebellion, melted Madagascar, and showed them that they *cared*. Earthgov had been busy selling pieces of real estate, to Vegans; this, via the Office, Earthgov's civil service infection here among the isles of the world.

All sales ceased, Vega withdrew, and the Radpol dozed, dreaming its Big Dream—of the return of men to Earth.

The Office went on administering. The days of Karaghiosis had passed.

❖   ❖   ❖

As we wandered among the olive groves gone wild, picked our way through the ruins of the Frankish castle, or mixed our tracks with the hieroglyph-prints of the herring-gulls, there on the wet sands of the beaches of Kos, we were burning time while waiting for a ransom which could not come, which should never, really, have been expected.

Cassandra's hair is the color of Kalamata olives, and shiny. Her hands are soft, the fingers short, delicately webbed. Her eyes are very dark. She is only about four inches shorter than me, which makes her gracefulness something of an achievement, me being well over six feet. Of course, any woman looks graceful, precise and handsome when walking at my side, because I am none of these things: my left cheek is a map of Africa done up in varying purples, because of that mutant fungus I picked up from a moldy canvas—back when I was disinterring the Guggenheim for the New York Tour; my hairline peaks to within a fingerbreadth of my brow; my eyes are mismatched. (I glare at people through the cold blue one on the right side when I want to intimidate them; the brown one is for Glances Sincere and Honest.) I wear a reinforced boot because of my short right leg.

Cassandra doesn't require contrasting, though. She's beautiful.

I met her by accident, pursued her with desperation, married her against my will. (The last part was her idea.) I wasn't really thinking about it, myself—even on that day when I brought my caique into the harbor and saw her there, sunning herself like a mermaid beside the plane tree of Hippocrates, and decided that I wanted her. Kallikanzaroi have never been much the family sort. I just sort of slipped up, again.

It was a clean morning. It was starting our third month together. It was my last day on Kos—because of a call I'd received the evening before. Everything was still moist from the night's rain, and we sat out on the patio drinking Turkish coffee and eating oranges. Day was starting to lever its way into the world. The breeze was intermittent, was damp, goosepimpled us beneath the black hulk of our sweaters, skimmed the steam off the top of the coffee.

"I feet crummy," I said.

"I know," she said. "Don't."

"Can't help it. Got to go away and leave you, and that's crummy."

"It may only be a few weeks. You said so yourself. Then you'll be back."

"…Hope so," I said. "If it takes any longer, though, I'll send for you. Dunno where all I'll be, yet."

"Who is Cort Myshtigo?"

"Vegan actor, journalist. Important one. Wants to write about what's left of Earth. So I've got to show it to him. Me. Personally. Damn!"

"Anybody who takes ten-month vacations to go sailing can't complain about being overworked."

"I can complain—and I will. My job is supposed to be a sinecure."

"Why?"

"Mainly because I made it that way. I worked hard for twenty years to make Arts, Monuments and Archives what it is, and ten years ago I got it to the point where my staff could handle just about everything. So I got me turned out to pasture, I got me told to come back occasionally to sign papers and to do whatever I damn pleased in the meantime. Now this—this bootlicking gesture!—having a Commissioner take a Vegan scribbler on a tour any staff guide could conduct! Vegans aren't gods!"

"Wait a minute," she said. "please… Twenty years? Ten years?"

Sinking feeling.

"You're not even thirty years old."

I sank further. I waited. I rose again.

"Uh—there's something I, well, in my own reticent way, sort of never quite got around to mentioning to you... How old are you anyway, Cassandra?"

"Twenty."

"Uh-huh. Well...I'm around four times your age."

"I don't understand."

"Neither do I. Or the doctors. I just sort of stopped, somewhere between twenty and thirty, and I stayed that way. I guess that's a sort of, well—a part of my particular mutation, I guess. Does it make any difference?"

"I don't know...Yes."

"You don't mind my limp, or my excessive shagginess, or even my face. Why should my age bother you? I *am* young, for all necessary purposes."

"It's just that it's not the same," she said with an unarguable finality. "What if you never grow old?"

I bit my lip, when I wanted to be biting hers.

"I'm bound to, sooner or later."

"And if it's later? I love you. I don't want to out-age you."

"You'll live to be a hundred and fifty. There are the S-S treatments. You'll have them."

"But they won't keep me young—like you."

"I'm not really young. I was born old."

That one didn't work either. She started to cry.

"That's years and years away," I told her. "Who knows what will happen in the meantime?"

That only made her cry more.

I've always been impulsive. My thinking is usually pretty good, but I always seem to do it after I do my talking—by which time I've generally destroyed all basis for further conversation.

Which is one of the reasons I have a competent staff, a good radio, and am out to pasture most of the time. But there are some things you just can't delegate.

So I said:

"Look, you have a touch of the Hot Stuff in you, too. It took me forty years to realize I wasn't forty years old. Maybe you're the same way. I'm just a neighborhood kid..."

"Do you know of any other cases like your own?"

"Well…"

"No, you don't."

"No. I don't."

I waited until she had stopped crying and I could feel her eyes on me again. Then I waited some more.

"Well?" I asked, finally.

"Pretty well, thanks."

I found and held her passive hand, raised it to my lips. "Rodos dactylos," I breathed, and she said, "Maybe it's a good idea—your going away—for awhile anyhow…" and the breeze that skimmed the steam came again, was damp, goosepimpled us, and made either her hand or my hand shake—I'm not sure which. It shook the leaves too, and they emptied over our heads.

"Did you exaggerate your age to me?" she asked. "Even a little bit?"

Her tone of voice suggested that agreement would be the wisest reply.

So, "Yes," I said, truthfully.

She smiled back then, somewhat reassured of my humanity.

Ha!

So we sat there, holding hands and watching the morning. After awhile she began humming. It was a sad song, centuries old. A ballad. It told the story of a young wrestler named Themocles, a wrestler who had never been beaten. He eventually came to consider himself the greatest wrestler alive. Finally, he called out his challenge from a mountaintop, and, that being too near home, the gods acted fast: the following day a crippled boy rode into the town, on the plated back of a huge wild dog. They wrestled for three days and three nights, Themocles and the boy, and on the fourth day the boy broke his back, and left him there in the field. Wherever his blood fell, there sprang up the strigefleur, as Emmet calls it, the blood-drinking flower that creeps rootless at night, seeking the lost spirit of the fallen champion in the blood of its victims. But Themocles' spirit is gone from the Earth, so they must creep, seeking, forever. Simpler than Aeschylus, but then we're a simpler people than we once were, especially the Mainlanders. Besides, that's not the way it really happened.

"Why are you weeping?" she asked me suddenly.

"I am thinking of the picture on Achilleus' shield," I said, "and of what a terrible thing it is to be an educated beast—and I am not weeping. The leaves are dripping on me."

"I'll make some more coffee."

The sun wandered up higher into the sky, and after a time there came a sound of hammering from the yard of old Aldones, the coffin-maker. The cyclamen had come awake, and the breezes carried their fragrance to us from across the fields. High overhead, like a dark omen, a spiderbat glided across the sky toward the mainland. I ached to wrap my fingers around the stock of a thirty-oh-six, make loud noises, and watch it fall. The only firearms I knew of were aboard the *Vanitie*, though, so I just watched it vanish from sight.

"They say that they're not really native to Earth," she told me, watching it go, "and that they were brought here from Titan, for zoos and things like that."

"That's right."

"...And that they got loose during the Three Days and went wild, and that they grow bigger here than they ever did on their own world."

"One time I saw one with a thirty-two foot wingspread."

"My great-uncle once told me a story he had heard in Athens," she recalled, "about a man killing one without any weapons. It snatched him up from the dock he was standing on—at Piraeus—and the man broke its neck with his hands. They fell about a hundred feet into the bay. The man lived."

"That was a long time ago," I remembered, "back before the Office started its campaign to exterminate the things. They were a lot more around, and they were bolder in those days. They shy away from cities now."

"The man's name was Konstantin, as I recall the story. Could it have been you?"

"His last name was Karaghiosis."

"Are you Karaghiosis?"

"If you want me to be. Why?"

"Because he later helped to found the Returnist Radpol in Athens, and you have very strong hands."

"Are you a Returnist?"

"Yes. Are you?"

"I work for the Office. I don't have any political opinions."

"Karaghiosis bombed resorts."

"So he did."

"Are you sorry he bombed them?"

"No."

"I don't really know much about you, do I?"

"You know anything about me. Just ask. I'm really quite simple. —My air taxi is coming now."

"I don't hear anything."

"You will."

After a moment it came sliding down the sky toward Kos, homing in on the beacon I had set up at the end of the patio. I stood and drew her to her feet as it buzzed in low—a Radson Skimmer: a twenty-foot cockleshell of reflection and transparency; flat-bottomed, blunt-nosed.

"Anything you want to take with you?" she asked.

"You know it, but I can't."

The Skimmer settled and its side slid open. The goggled pilot turned his head.

"I have a feeling," she said, "that you are heading into some sort of danger."

"I doubt it, Cassandra."

Nor pressure, nor osmosis will restore Adam's lost rib, thank God.

"Good-bye, Cassandra."

"Good-bye, my kallikanzaros."

And I got into the Skimmer and jumped into the sky, breathing a prayer to Aphrodite. Below me, Cassandra waved. Behind me, the sun tightened its net of light. We sped westward, and this is the place for a smooth transition, but there isn't any. From Kos to Port-au-Prince was four hours, gray water, pale stars, and me mad. Watch the colored lights…

❖   ❖   ❖

The hall was lousy with people, a big tropical moon was shining fit to bust, and the reason I could see both was that I'd finally managed to lure Ellen Emmet out onto the balcony and the doors were mag-pegged open.

"Back from the dead again," she had greeted me, smiling slightly. "Gone almost a year, and not so much as a Get Well card from Ceylon."

"Were you ill?"

"I could have been."

She was small and, like all day-haters, creamy somewhere under her simicolor. She reminded me of an elaborate action-doll with a faulty mechanism—cold grace, and a propensity to kick people in the shins when they least expected it; and she had lots and lots of orange-brown hair, woven into a Gordian knot of a coif that frustrated me as I worked at untying it, mentally; her eyes were of whatever color it pleased the god of her choice on that particular day—I forget now, but they're always blue somewhere deep deep down inside. Whatever she was wearing was browngreen, and there was enough of it to go around a couple of times and make her look like a shapeless weed, which was a dressmaker's lie if there ever was one, unless she was pregnant again, which I doubted.

"Well, get well," I said, "if you need to. I didn't make Ceylon. I was in the Mediterranean most of the time."

Ellen leaned back on the railing.

"I hear you're somewhat married these days."

"True," I agreed, "also somewhat harried. Why did they call me back?"

"Ask your boss."

"I did. He said I'm going to be a guide. What I want to know, though, is *why?*—The real reason. I've been thinking about it and it's grown more puzzling."

"So how should I know?"

"You know everything."

"You overestimate me, dear. What's she like?"

I shrugged. "A mermaid, maybe. Why?"

She shrugged. "Just curious. What do you tell people I'm like?"

"I don't tell people you're like anything."

"I'm insulted. I must be like something, unless I'm unique."

"That's it, you're unique."

"Then why didn't you take me away with you last year?"

"Because you're a People person and you require a city around you. You could only be happy here at the Port."

"You know," she said after a time, "you're so damned ugly you're attractive. That must be it."

I stopped in mid-reach, a couple inches from her shoulder.

"You know," she continued, her voice flat, emptied of emotion, "you're a nightmare that walks like a man."

I dropped my hand, chuckled inside a tight chest.

"I know," I said. "Pleasant dreams."

I started to turn away and she caught my sleeve.

"Wait!"

I looked down at her hand, up at her eyes, then back down at her hand. She let go.

"You know I never tell the truth," she said. Then she laughed her little brittle laugh.

"…And I *have* thought of something you ought to know about this trip. Donald Dos Santos is here, and I think he's going along."

"Dos Santos? That's ridiculous."

"He's up in the library now, with George and some big Arab."

I looked past her and down into the harbor section, watching the shadows, like my thoughts, move along dim streets, dark and slow.

"Big Arab?" I said, after a time. "Scarred hands? Yellow Eyes?— Name of Hasan?"

"Yes, that's right. Have you met him?"

"He's done some work for me in the past," I acknowledged.

So I smiled, even though my blood was refrigerating, because I don't like people to know what I'm thinking.

"You're smiling," she said. "What are you thinking?"

She's like that.

"I'm thinking how is George—and how is his bug collection these days?"

She sort of smiled.

"Growing," she replied, "by leaps and bounds. Buzzes and crawls too—and some of those crawlies are radioactive. I say to him, 'George, why don't you run around with other women instead of spending all your time with those bugs?' But he just shakes his head and looks dedicated. Then I say, 'George, one day one of those uglies is going to bite you and make you impotent. What'll you do then?' Then he explains that that can't happen, and he lectures me on insect toxins. Maybe he's really a big bug himself, in disguise. I think he gets some kind of sexual pleasure out of watching them swarm around in those tanks. I don't know what else—"

I turned away and looked inside the hall then, because her face was no longer *her* face. When I heard her laugh a moment later I turned back and squeezed her shoulder.

"Okay, I know more than I knew before. Thanks. I'll see you sometime soon."

"Should I wait?"

"No. Goodnight."

"Good night, Conrad."

And I was away.

❖   ❖   ❖

Crossing a room can be a ticklish and time-consuming business: if it's full of people, if the people all know you, if the people are all holding glasses, if you have even a slight tendency to limp.

It was, they did and they were, and I do. So…

Thinking inconspicuous thoughts, I edged my way along the wall just at the periphery of humanity. This, for about twenty feet, until I reached Phil Graber—and the enclave of young ladies the old celibate always has hovering about him. Chinless, near-lipless, going hairless, the expression that had once lived in that flesh which covered his skull had long ago retreated into the darkness of his eyes, and the eyes had it as they caught me—the smile of imminent outrage.

"Phil," I said, nodding, "not everybody can write a masque like that. I've heard it said that it's a dying art, but now I know better."

"You're still alive," he said, in a voice seventy years younger than the rest of him, "and late again, as usual."

"I abase myself in my contrition," I told him, "but I was detained at a birthday party for a lady aged seven, at the home of an old friend." (Which was true, but it has nothing to do with this story.)

"All your friends are old friends, aren't they?" he asked, and that was hitting below the belt, just because I had once known his barely-remembered parents, and had taken them around to the south side of the Erechtheum in order to show them the Porch of the Maidens and point out what Lord Elgin had done with the rest, all the while carrying their bright-eyed youngsters on my shoulders and telling him tales that were old when the place was built.

"…And I need your help," I added, ignoring the jibe and gently pushing my way through the soft, pungent circle of femininity. "It'll take me all night to cross this hall to where Sands is holding court with the Vegan and I don't have all night. So how about it? Get me from here to there in a minimum of time in your typical courtier-like fashion, with a running conversation that no one would dare interrupt. Okay? Let's run."

He nodded brusquely.

We started across the room, negotiating alleys of people. High overhead, the chandeliers drifted and turned like faceted satellites of ice. The thelinstra was an intelligent Aeolian harp, tossing its shards of song into the air—pieces of colored glass. The people buzzed and drifted like certain of George Emmet's insects, and we avoided their swarms by putting one foot in front of another without pause and making noises of our own. We didn't step on anybody who squashed.

"I hear Dos Santos is here," I said.

"So he is."

"Why?"

"I don't really know, or care."

"Tsk and tsk. What happened to your wonderful political consciousness? The Department of Literary Criticism used to praise you for it."

"At any age, the smell of death becomes more and more unsettling each time it is encountered."

"And Dos Santos smells?"

"He tends to reek."

"I've heard that he's employed a former associate of ours—from the days of the Madagascar Affair."

Phil cocked his head to one side, shot me a quizzical look.

"You hear things quite quickly. But then, you're a friend of Ellen's. Yes, Hasan is here. He's upstairs with Don."

"Whose karmic burden is he likely to help lighten?"

"As I said before, I don't really know or care about any of this."

I squinted at him, and then, as he turned away, I followed the direction of his gaze towards the easy chairs set in the alcove formed by the northeast corner of the room on two sides and the bulk of the thelinstra on the third. The thelinstra-player was an old lady with dreamy eyes. Earthdirector Lorel Sands was smoking his pipe…

Now, the pipe is one of the more interesting facets of Lorel's personality. It's a real Meerschaum, and there aren't too many of them left in the world. As for the rest of him, his function is rather like that of an anticomputer: you feed him all kinds of carefully garnered facts, figures, and statistics and he translates them into garbage. Keen dark eyes, and a slow, rumbly way of speaking while he holds you with them; rarely given to gestures, but then very deliberate as he saws the air with a wide right hand or pokes imaginary ladies with his pipe; white at the temples and dark above; he is high of cheekbone, has a complexion that matches his tweeds (he assiduously avoids Dress Blacks), and he constantly strives to push his jaw an inch higher and further forward than seems comfortable. He is a political appointee, by the Earthgov on Taler, and he takes his work quite seriously, even to the extent of demonstrating his dedication with periodic attacks of ulcers. He is not the most intelligent man on Earth. He is my boss. He is also one of the best friends I have.

Beside him sat Cort Myshtigo. I could almost feel Phil hating him—from the pale blue soles of his six-toed feet to the pink upper-caste dye of his temple-to-temple hairstrip. Not hating him so much because he was him, but hating him, I was sure, because he was the closest available relative—grandson—of Tatram Yshtigo, who forty years before had commenced to demonstrate that the greatest living writer in the English language was a Vegan. The old gent is still at it, and I don't believe Phil has ever forgiven him.

Out of the corner of my eye (the blue one) I saw Ellen ascending the big, ornate stairway on the other side of the hall. Out of the other corner of my other eye I saw Lorel looking in my direction.

"I," said I, "have been spotted, and I must go now to pay my respects to the William Seabrook of Taler. Come along?"

"Well…Very well," said Phil, "suffering is good for the soul."

We moved on to the alcove and stood before the two chairs, between the music and the noise, there in the place of power. Lorel stood slowly, shook hands. Myshtigo stood more slowly, did not shake hands; he stared, amber-eyed, as we were introduced, his face expressionless. His loose-hanging orange shirt fluttered constantly as his chambered lungs forced their perpetual exhalation out anterior nostrils at the base of his wide ribcage. He nodded briefly, repeated my name. Then he turned to Phil with something like a smile.

"Would you care to have me translate your masque into English?" he asked, his voice sounding like a dying-down tuning fork.

Phil turned on his heel and walked away.

Then I thought the Vegan was ill for a second, until I recollected that a Vegan's laugh sounds something like a billy goat choking. I try to stay away from Vegans by avoiding the resorts.

"Sit down," said Lorel, looking uncomfortable behind his pipe.

I drew up a chair and set it across from them.

"Okay."

"Cort is going to write a book," said Lorel.

"So you've said."

"About the Earth."

I nodded.

"He expressed a desire that you be his guide on a tour of certain of the Old Places…"

"I am honored," I said rather stiffly. "Also, I am curious what determined his selection of me as guide."

"—and even more curious as to what he may know about you, eh?" interupted the Vegan.

"Yes, I am," I agreed, "by a couple hundred percent."

"I started by checking the Vite-Stats Register for Earth when I first conceived of this project as we were introduced just for general human data—then, after I'd turned up an interesting item, I tried the Earthoffice Personnel Banks—"

"Um-hm," I said.

"—and I was more impressed by what they did not say of you than by what they said."

I shrugged.

"According to your personnel record, you're seventy-seven years old. According to Vite-Stats, you're either a hundred eleven or a hundred thirty."

"I fibbed about my age to get the job. There was a Depression going on."

"—So I made up a Nomikos-profile, which is a kind of distinctive thing, and I set Vite-Stats to hunting down .001 physical analogues in all of its banks, including the closed ones."

"Some people collect old coins, other people build model rockets."

"…And I found that you could have been three or four or five other persons, all of them Greeks, and one of them truly amazing. But, of course, Konstantin Korones, one of the older ones, was born two hundred thirty-four years ago. On Christmas. Blue eye, brown eye. Game right leg. Same hairline, at age twenty-three. Same height, and same Bertillon scales."

"Same fingerprints? Same retinal patterns?"

"These were not included in many of the older Registry files. Maybe they were sloppier in those days? I don't know. More careless, perhaps, as to who had access to public records…"

"You are aware that there are over four million persons on this planet right now. By searching back nigh the past three or four centuries I daresay you could find doubles, or even triples, for quite a few of them. So what?"

"It serves to make you somewhat intriguing, that's all, almost like a spirit of place—and you are as curiously ruined as this place is. Doubtless I shall never achieve your age, whatever it may be, and I was curious as to the sort of sensibilities a human might cultivate, given so much time—especially in view of your position as a master of your world's history and art.

"So that is why I asked for your services," he concluded.

"Now that you've met me, ruined and all, can I go home?"

"Conrad!" The pipe attacked me.

"No, Mister Nomikos, there are practical considerations also. This is a tough world, and you have a high survival potential. I want you with me because I want to survive."

I shrugged again. "Well, that's settled. What now?"

He chuckled. "I perceive that you dislike me."

"Whatever gave you that idea? Just because you insulted a friend of mine, asked me impertinent questions, impressed me into your service on a whim—"

"—exploited your countrymen, turned your world into a brothel, and demonstrated the utter provinciality of the human race, as compared to a galactic culture eons older…"

"I'm not talking your race-my race, I'm talking personal talk. And I repeat, you insulted my friend, asked me impertinent questions, impressed me into your service on a whim."

"[*Billy goat snuffle*]! to all three! —It is an insult to the shades of Homer and Dante to have that man sing for the human race—"

"—At the moment he's the best we've got."

"—In which case, you should do without."

"You behave like a Royal Representative in a Crown Colony," I decided, pronouncing the capitals, "and I don't like it. I've read all your books. I've also read your granddad's—like his *Earthwhore's Lament*—and you'll never be the man he is. He has a thing called compassion. You don't. Anything you feel about old Phil goes double for you, in *my* book."

That part about grandpa must have touched on a sore spot, because he flinched when my blue gaze hit him.

"So kiss my elbow," I said, or something like that, in Vegan.

Sands doesn't speak enough Veggy to have caught it, but he made conciliatory noises immediately, looking about the while to be sure we were not being overhead.

"Conrad, please find your professional attitude and put it back on. —Srin Shtgio, why don't we get on with the planning?"

Myshtigo smiled his bluegreen smile.

"And minimize our differences?" he asked. "All right."

"Then let's adjourn to the library—where it's quieter—and we can use the map-screen."

"Fine."

I felt a bit reinforced as we rose to go, because Don Dos Santos was up there and he hates Vegans, and wherever Dos Santos is, there is always Diane, the girl with the red wig, and she hates everybody; and I knew George Emmet was upstairs, and Ellen, too—and George is a real cold fish around strangers (friends, too, for that matter); and perhaps Phil would wander in later and fire on Fort Sumter; and then there was Hasan—he doesn't say much, he just sits there and smokes his weeds and looks opaque—and if you stood too near him and took a couple deep breaths you wouldn't care what the hell you said to Vegans, or people either.

❖   ❖   ❖

I had hoped that Hasan's memory would be on the rocks, or else up there somewhere among the clouds.

Hope died as we entered the library. He was sitting straight and sipping lemonade.

Eighty or ninety or more, looking about forty, he could still act thirty. The Sprung-Samser treatments had found highly responsive material. It's not often that way. Almost never, in fact. They put some people into accelerated anaphylactic shock for no apparent reason, and even an intracardial blast of adrenalin won't haul them back; others, most others, they freeze at five or six decades. But some rare ones actually grow younger when they take the series—about one in a hundred thousand.

It struck me as odd that in destiny's big shooting gallery *this* one should make it, in such a way.

It had been over fifty years since the Madagascar Affair, in which Hasan had been employed by the Radpol in their vendetta against the Talerites. He had been in the pay of (Rest in Peace) the big K. in Athens, who had sent him to polish off the Earthgov Realty Company. He did it, too. And well. With one tiny fission device. Pow. Instant urban renewal. Called Hasan the Assassin by the Few, he is the last mercenary on Earth.

Also, besides Phil (who had not always been the wielder of the bladeless sword without a hilt), Hasan was one of the Very Few who could remember old Karaghiosis.

So, chin up and fungus forward, I tried to cloud his mind with my first glance. Either there were ancient and mysterious powers afoot, which I doubted, or he was higher than I'd thought, which was possible, or he had forgotten my face—which could have been possible, though not real likely—or he was exercising a professional ethic or a low animal cunning. (He possessed both of the latter, in varying degrees, but the accent was on the l.a.c.) He made no sign as we were introduced.

"My bodyguard, Hasan," said Dos Santos, flashing his magnesium-flare smile as I shook the hand that once had shaken the world, so to speak.

It was still a very strong hand.

"Conrad Nomikos," said Hasan, squinting as though he were reading it from off a scroll.

I knew everyone else in the room, so I hastened to the chair farthest from Hasan, and I kept my second drink in front of my face most of the time, just to be safe.

Diane of the Red Wig stood near. She spoke. She said, "Good morning, Mister Nomikos."

I nodded my drink.

"Good evening, Diane."

Tall, slim, wearing mostly white, she stood beside Dos Santos like a candle. I know it's a wig she wears, because I've seen it slip upwards on occasion, revealing part of an interesting and ugly scar which is usually hidden by the low hairline she normally keeps. I've often wondered about that scar, sometimes as I lay at anchor staring up at parts of constellations through clouds, or when I unearthed damaged statues. Purple lips—tattooed, I think—and I've never seen them smile; her jaw muscles are always raised cords because her teeth are always clenched; and there's a little upside-down "v" between her eyes, from all that frowning; and her chin is slight, held high—defiant? She barely moves her mouth when she speaks in that tight, choppy way of hers. I couldn't really guess at her age. Over thirty, that's all.

She and Don make an interesting pair. He is dark, loquacious, always smoking, unable to sit still for more than two minutes. She is taller by about five inches, burns without flickering. I still don't know all of her story. I guess I never will.

She came over and stood beside my chair while Lorel was introducing Cort to Dos Santos.

"You will conduct the tour."

"Everybody knows all about it but me," said I. "I don't suppose you could spare me a little of your knowledge on the matter?"

"No knowledge," she said, "yet. Ask Don."

"Will," said I.

Did, too. Later, though. And I wasn't disappointed, inasmuch as I expected nothing.

But, as I sat trying as hard as I could to eavesdrop, there was suddenly a sight-vision overlay, of the sort a shrink had once classified for me as a pseudotelepathic wish-fulfillment. It works like this—

I want to know what's going on somewhere. I have almost-sufficient information to guess. Therefore, I do. Only it comes on as though I am seeing it and hearing it through the eyes and ears of one of the parties involved. It's not real telepathy, though, I don't think, because it can sometimes be wrong. It sure seems real, though.

The shrink could tell me everything about it but why.

Which is how I

was standing in the middle of the room,

was staring at Myshtigo,

was Dos Santos,

was saying:

"…Will be going along, for your protection. Not as Radpol Secretary, just a private citizen."

"I did not solicit your protection," the Vegan was saying, "however, I thank you. I will accept your offer to circumvent my death at the hands of your comrades," and he smiled as he said it, "if they should seek it during my travels. I doubt that they will, but I should be a fool to refuse the shield of Dos Santos."

"You are wise," we said, bowing slightly.

"Quite," said Cort. "Now tell me," he nodded toward Ellen, who had just finished arguing with George about anything and was stamping away from him, "who is that?"

"That," said we, "is Ellen Emmet, the wife of George Emmet, the Director of the Wildlife Conservation Department."

"What is her price?"

"I don't know that she's quoted one recently."

"Well, what did it used to be?"

"There never was one."

"Everything on Earth has a price."

"In that case, I suppose you'll have to find out for yourself."

"I will," he said.

Earth femmes have always held an odd attraction for Vegans. A Veggy once told me that they make him feel rather like a zoophilist. Which is interesting, because a pleasure girl at the Cote d'Or Resort once told me, with a giggle, that Vegans made her feel rather like *une zoophiliste*. I guess those jets of air must tickle or something and arouse both beasts.

"By the way," we said, "have you stopped beating your wife lately?"

"Which one?" asked Myshtigo.

Fadeout, and me back in my chair.

"…What," George Emmet was asking, "do you think of that?"

I stared at him. He hadn't been there a second ago. He had come up suddenly and perched himself on the wide wing of my chair.

"Come again, please. I was dozing."

"I said we've beaten the spiderbat. What do you think of that?"

"It rhymes," I observed. "So tell me how we've beaten the spiderbat."

But he was laughing. He's one of those guys with whom laughter is an unpredictable thing. He'll go around looking sour for days, and then some little thing will set him off giggling. He sort of gasps when he laughs, like a baby, and that impression is reinforced by his pink flaccidity and thinning hair. So I waited. Ellen was off insulting Lorel now, and Diane had turned to read the titles on the bookshelves.

Finally, "I've developed a new strain of *slishi*," he panted confidentially.

"Say, that's really great!"

Then, "What are *slishi*?" I asked softly.

"The *slish* is a Bakabian parasite," he explained, "rather like a large tick. Mine are about three-eighths of an inch long," he said proudly, "and they burrow deep into the flesh and give off a highly poisonous waste product."

"Fatal?"

"Mine are."

"Could you lend me one?" I asked him.

"Why?"

"I want to drop it down someone's back. —On second thought, make it a couple dozen. I have lots of friends."

"Mine won't bother people, just spiderbats. They discriminate against people. People would poison my *slishi*." (He said "my *slishi*" very possessively.) "Their host has to have a copper, rather than an iron-based metabolism," he explained, "and spiderbats fall into that category. That's why I want to go with you on this trip. The *slishi* multiply quite rapidly under Earth conditions, if they're given the proper host, and they should be extremely contagious if we could get them started at the right time of year. What I had in mind was the late southwestern spiderbat mating season. It will begin in six to eight weeks in the territory of California, in an Old Place—not real hot anymore, though—called Capistrano. I understand that your tour will take you out that way at about that time. When the spiderbats return to Capistrano I want to be waiting for them with the *slishi*. Also, I could use a vacation."

"Mm-hm. Have you talked this over with Lorel?"

"Yes, and he thinks it's a fine idea. In fact, he wants to meet us out there and take pictures. There may not be too many more opportunities to see them—darkening the sky with their flight, nesting about the ruins the way they do, eating the wild pigs, leaving their green droppings in the streets—it's rather beautiful, you know."

Lorel made apologetic sounds deep in his throat about then. He stood beside the big desk in the middle of the room, before which the broad viewscreen was slowly lowering itself. It was a thick depth-transparer, so nobody had to move around after a better seat. He pressed a button on the side of the desk and the upper part of Africa and most of the Mediterranean countries appeared.

The lights dimmed and Myshtigo moved to the desk. He looked at the map, and then at nobody in particular.

"I want to visit certain key sites which, for one reason or another, are important in the history of your world," he said. "I'd like to start with Egypt, Greece and Rome. Then I'd like to move on quickly through Madrid, Paris and London." The maps shifted as he talked, not fast enough, though, to keep up with him. "Then I want to backtrack to Berlin, hit Brussels, visit St. Petersburg and Moscow, skip back over the Atlantic and stop at Boston, New York, DeeCee, Chicago," (Lorel was working up a sweat by then) "drop down to Yucatan, and jump back up to the California territory."

"In that order?" I asked.

"Pretty much so," he said.

"What's wrong with India and the Middle East—or the Far East, for that matter?" asked a voice which I recognized as Phil's. He had come in after the lights had gone down low.

"Nothing," said Myshtigo, "except that it's mainly mud and sand and hot, and has nothing whatsoever to do with what I'm after."

"What *are* you after?"

"A story."

"What kind of story?"

"I'll send you an autographed copy."

"Thanks."

"Your pleasure."

"When do you wish to leave?" I asked him.

"Day after tomorrow," he said.

"Okay."

"I've had detailed maps of the specific sites made up for you. Lorel tells me they were delivered to your office this afternoon."

"Okay again. But there is something of which you may not be fully cognizant. It involves the fact that everything you've named so far is mainlandish. We're pretty much an island culture these days, and for very good reasons. During the Three Days the Mainland got a good juicing, and most of the places you've named are still inclined to be somewhat hot. This, though, is not the only reason they are considered unsafe…"

"I am not unfamiliar with your history and I am aware of the radiation precautions," he interrupted. "Also, I am aware of the variety of mutated life forms which inhabit Old Places. I am concerned, but not worried."

I shrugged in the artificial twilight.

"It's okay by me…"

As the screen was sucked upward behind him, Myshtigo asked me:

"Is it true that you are acquainted with several *mambos* and *houngans* here at the Port?"

"Why, yes," I said. "Why?"

"I understand," he said conversationally, "that voodoo, or *voudoun*, has survived pretty much unchanged over the centuries. I should like very much to witness a real ceremony. If I were to attend one with someone who was not a stranger to the participants, perhaps then I could obtain the genuine thing."

"Why should you want to? Morbid curiosity concerning barbaric customs?"

"No. I am a student of comparative religions."

I studied his face, but couldn't tell anything from it.

It had been awhile since I'd visited with Mama Julie and Papa Joe or any of the others, and the *hounfor* wasn't that far away, but I didn't know how they'd take to me bringing a Vegan around. They'd never objected when I'd brought people, of course.

"Well…" I began.

"I just want to watch," he said. "I'll stay out of the way. They'll hardly know I'm there."

I mumbled a bit and finally gave in. I knew Mama Julie pretty well and I didn't see any real harm being done, no matter what.

So, "Okay," said I, "I'll take you to one. Tonight, if you like."

He agreed, thanked me, and went off after another Coke. George, who had not strayed from the arm of my chair, leaned toward me and observed that it would be very interesting to dissect a Vegan. I agreed with him.

When Myshtigo returned, Dos Santos was at his side.

"What is this about you taking Mister Myshtigo to a pagan ceremony?" he asked, nostrils flared and quivering.

"That's right," I said, "I am."

"Not without a bodyguard you are not."

I turned both palms upward.

"I am capable of handling anything which might arise."

"Hasan and I will accompany you."

I was about to protest when Ellen insinuated herself between them.

"I want to go, too," she said. "I've never been to one."

I shrugged. If Dos Santos went, then Diane would go, too, which made for quite a few of us.

So one more wouldn't matter, shouldn't matter. It was ruined before it got started.

❖   ❖   ❖

The *hounfor* was located down in the harbor section, possibly because it was dedicated to Agué Woyo, god of the sea. More likely, though, it was because Mama Julie's people had always been harbor people. Agué Woyo is not a jealous god, so lots of other deities are commemorated upon the walls in brilliant colors. There are more elaborate *hounfors* further inland, but they tend to be somewhat commercial.

Ague's big blazeboat was blue and orange and green and yellow and black, and it looked to be somewhat unseaworthy. Damballa Wedo, crimson, writhed and coiled his length across most of the opposite wall. Several big *rada* drums were being stroked rhythmically by Papa Joe, forward and to the right of the door through which we entered—the only door. The small altar bore numerous bottles of alcoholic beverages, gourds, sacred vessels for the spirits of the *loa*, charms, pipes, flags, depth photos of unknown persons and, among other things, a pack of cigarettes for Papa Legba.

A service was in progress when we were led in by a young *hounsi* named Luis. The room was about eight meters long and five wide, had a high ceiling, a dirt floor. Dancers moved about the central pole with slow, strutting steps. Their flesh was dark and it glistened in the dim light of the antique kerosene lamps. With our entry the room became crowded.

Mama Julie took my hand and smiled. She led me back to a place beside the altar and said, "Erzulie was kind."

I nodded.

"She likes you, Nomiko. You live long, you travel much, and you come back."

"Always," I said.

"Those people…?"

She indicated my companions with a flick of her dark eyes.

"Friends. They would be no bother…"

She laughed as I said it. So did I.

"I will keep them out of your way if you let us remain. We will stay in the shadows at the sides of the room. If you tell me to take them away, I will. I see that you have already danced much, emptied many bottles…"

"Stay," she said. "Come talk with me during daylight sometime."

"I will."

She moved away then and they made room for her in the circle of dancers. She was quite large, though her voice was a small thing. She moved like a huge rubber doll, not without grace, stepping to the monotonous thunder of Papa Joe's drumming. After a time this sound filled everything—my head, the earth, the air—like maybe the whale's heartbeat had seemed to half-digested Jonah. I watched the dancers. I watched those who watched the dancers.

I drank a pint of rum in an effort to catch up, but I couldn't. Myshtigo kept taking sips of Coke from a bottle he had brought along with him. No one noticed that he was blue, but then we had gotten there rather late and things were pretty well along the way to wherever they were going.

Red Wig stood in a corner looking supercilious and frightened. She was holding a bottle at her side, but that's where it stayed.

Myshtigo was holding Ellen at his side, and that's where she stayed. Dos Santos stood beside the door and watched everybody—even me. Hasan, crouched against the righthand wall, was smoking a long-stemmed pipe with a small bowl. He appeared to be at peace.

Mama Julie, I guess it was, began to sing. Other voices picked it up:

Papa Legba, ouvri bayé!
Papa Legba, Attibon Legba, ouvri bayé pou nou passe!
Papa Legba…

This went on, and on and on. I began to feel drowsy. I drank more rum and felt thirstier and drank more rum.

I'm not sure how long we had been there when it happened. The dancers had been kissing the pole and singing and rattling gourds and pouring out waters, and a couple of the *hounsi* were acting possessed and talking incoherently, and the meal-design on the floor was all blurred, and there was lots of smoke in the air, and I was leaning back against the wall and I guess my eyes had been closed for a minute or two.

The sound came from an unexpected quarter.

Hasan screamed.

It was a long, wailing thing that brought me forward, then dizzily off balance, then back to the wall again, with a thump.

The drumming continued, not missing a single beat. Some of the dancers stopped, though, staring.

Hasan had gotten to his feet. His teeth were bared and his eyes were slits, and his face bore the ridges and valleys of exertion beneath its sheen of sweat.

His beard was a fireshot spearhead.

His cloak, caught high against some wall decoration, was black wings.

His hands, in a hypnosis of slow motion, were strangling a non-existent man.

Animal sounds came from his throat.

He continued to choke nobody.

Finally, he chuckled and his hands sprang open.

Dos Santos was at his side almost immediately, talking to him, but they inhabited two different worlds.

One of the dancers began to moan softly. Another joined him—and others.

Mama Julie detached herself from the circle and came toward me—just as Hasan started the whole thing over again, this time with more elaborate histrionics.

The drum continued its steady, earthdance pronouncement.

Papa Joe did not even look up.

"A bad sign," said Mama Julie. "What do you know of this man?"

"Plenty," I said, forcing my head to clear by an act of will.

"Angelsou," she said.

"What?"

"Angelsou," she repeated. "He is a dark god—one to be feared. Your friend is possessed by Angelsou."

"Explain, please."

"He comes seldom to our *hounfor*. He is not wanted here. Those he possesses become murderers."

"I think Hasan was trying a new pipe mixture—mutant ragweed or something."

"Angelsou," she said again. "Your friend will become a killer, for Angelsou is a deathgod, and he only visits with his own."

"Mama Julie," said I, "Hasan *is* a killer. If you had a piece of gum for every man he's killed and you tried to chew it all, you'd look like a chipmunk. He is a professional killer—within the limits of the law, usually. Since the Code Duello prevails on the Mainland, he does most of his work there. It has been rumored that he does an illegal killing on occasion, but this thing has never been proved."

Dos Santos then, trying to stop the show, seized both of Hasan's wrists. He tried to pull his hands apart, but—well, try bending the bars of your cage sometime and you'll get the picture.

I crossed the room, as did several of the others. This proved fortunate, because Hasan had finally noticed that someone was standing in front of him, and dropped his hands, freeing them. Then he produced a long-bladed stiletto from under his cloak.

Whether or not he would actually have used it on Don or anybody else is a moot point, because at that moment Myshtigo stoppered his Coke bottle with his thumb and hit him behind the ear with it. Hasan fell forward and Don caught him, and I pried the blade from between his fingers.

"Interesting ceremony," observed the Vegan, "I would never have suspected that big fellow of harboring such strong religious feelings."

"It just goes to show you that you can never be too sure, doesn't it?"

After I'd apologized and said good-night, I picked up Hasan. He was out cold and I was the only one big enough to carry him.

The street was deserted except for us, and Agué Woyo's big blaze-boat was cutting the waves somewhere just under the eastern edge of the world and splashing the sky with all his favorite colors.

Hasan moaned just then and flexed his muscles and I felt a sharp pain in my shoulder.

I set him down on a doorstep and shook him down. I found two throwing knives, another stiletto, a very neat gravity knife, a saw-edged Bowie, strangling wires, and a small metal case containing various powders and vials of liquids which I did not care to inspect too closely. I liked the gravity knife, so I kept it for myself. It was a Coricama, and very neat.

❖   ❖   ❖

Late the next day—call it evening—I shanghaied old Phil, determined to use him as the price of admission to Dos Santos' suite at the *Royal*. The Radpol still reveres Phil as a sort of Returnist Tom Paine, even though he began pleading innocent to that about half a century ago, back when he began getting mysticism and respectability. While his *Call of Earth* probably *is* the best thing he ever wrote, he also drafted the Articles of Return, which helped to start the trouble I'd wanted started. He may do much disavowing these days, but he was a trouble-maker then, and I'm sure he still files away all the fawning gazes and bright words it continues to bring him, takes them out every now and then, dusts them off, and regards them with something like pleasure.

Besides Phil, I took along a pretext—that I wanted to see how Hasan was feeling after the lamentable bash he'd received at the *hounfor*. Actually, what I wanted was a chance to talk to Hasan and find out how much, if anything, he'd be willing to tell me about his latest employment.

So Phil and I walked it. It wasn't far from the Office compound to the *Royal*. About seven minutes, ambling.

"Why are you suddenly concerned with the Radpol again?" he asked. "It's been a long time since you left."

"I left at the proper time, and all I'm concerned with is whether it's coming alive again—like in the old days. Hasan comes high because he always delivers, and I want to know what's in the package."

"Are you worried they've found you out?"

"No. It might be uncomfortable, but I doubt it would be inca-pacitating."

The *Royal* loomed before us and we entered. We went directly to the suite. As we walked up the padded hallway, Phil, in a fit of per-ception, observed, "I'm running interference again."

"That about says it."

"Okay. One'll get you ten you find out nothing."

"I won't take you up on that. You're probably right."

I knocked on the darkwood door.

"Come in, come in."

It took me ten minutes to turn the conversation to the lamentable bashing of the Bedouin, as Red Wig was there distracting me by being there and being distracting.

"Good morning," she said.

"Good evening," I said.

"Anything new happening in Arts?"

"No."

"Monuments?"

"No."

"Archives?"

"No."

"What interesting work you must do!"

"Oh, it's been overpublicized and glamorized all out of shape by a few romanticists in the Information Office. Actually, all we do is locate, restore, and preserve the records and artifacts mankind has left lying about the Earth."

"Sort of like cultural garbage collectors?"

"Mm, yes. I think that's properly put."

"Well, why?"

"Why what?"

"Why do you do it?"

"Someone has to, because it's cultural garbage. That makes it worth collecting. I know my garbage better than anyone else on Earth."

"You're dedicated, as well as being modest. That's good, too."

"Yeah. How is Hasan progressing? The last time I saw him he had stopped entirely."

"Up, around. Big lump. Thick skull. No harm."

"Where is he?"

"Up the hall, left. Games Room."

"I believe I'll go render him my sympathy. Excuse me?"

"Excused," she said, nodding, and she went away to listen to Dos Santos talk at Phil. Phil, of course, welcomed the addition.

Neither looked up as I left.

The Games Room was at the other end of the long hallway. As I approached, I heard a *thunk* followed by a silence, followed by another *thunk*.

I opened the door and looked inside.

He was the only one there. His back was to me, but he heard the door open and turned quickly. He was wearing a long purple dressing gown and was balancing a knife in his right hand. There was a big wad of plastage on the back of his head.

"Good evening, Hasan."

A tray of knives stood at his side, and he had set a target upon the opposite wall. Two blades were sticking into the target—one in the center and one about six inches off, at nine o'clock.

"Good evening," he said slowly. Then, after thinking it over, he added, "How are you?"

"Oh, fine. I came to ask you that same question. How is your head?"

"The pain is great, but it shall pass."

I closed the door behind me.

"You must have been having quite a daydream last night."

"Yes. Mister Dos Santos tells me I fought with ghosts. I do not remember."

"You weren't smoking what the fat Doctor Emmet would call Cannabis sativa, that's for sure."

"No, Karagee. I smoked a strigefleur which had drunk human blood. I found it near the Old Place of Constantinople and dried its blossoms carefully. An old woman told me it would give me sight into the future. She lied."

"…And the vampire-bloom incites to violence? Well, that's a new one to write down. By the way, you just called me Karagee. I wish you wouldn't. My name is Nomikos, Conrad Nomikos."

"Yes, Karagee. I was surprised to see you. I had thought you died long ago, when your blazeboat broke up in the bay."

"Karagee did die then. You have not mentioned to anyone that I resemble him, have you?"

"No; I do not make idle talk."

"That's a good habit."

I crossed the room, selected a knife, weighed it, threw it, and laid it about ten inches to the right of center.

"Have you been working for Mister Dos Santos very long?" I asked him.

"For about the period of a month," he replied.

He threw his knife. It struck five inches below the center.

"You are his bodyguard, eh?"

"That is right. I also guard the blue one."

"Don says he fears an attempt on Myshtigo's life. Is there an actual threat, or is he just being safe?"

"It is possible either way, Karagee. I do not know. He pays me only to guard."

"If I paid you more, would you tell me whom you've been hired to kill?"

"I have only been hired to guard, but I would not tell you even if it were otherwise."

"I didn't think so. Let's go get the knives."

We crossed and drew the blades from the target.

"Now, if it happens to be me—which is possible," I offered, "why don't we settle it right now? We are each holding two blades. The man who leaves this room will say that the other attacked him and that it was a matter of self-defense. There are no witnesses. We were both seen drunk or disorderly last night."

"No, Karagee."

"No, what? No, it isn't me? Or no, you don't want to do it that way?"

"I could say no, it is not you. But you would not know whether I spoke the truth or not."

"That is true."

"I could say I do not want to do it that way."

"Is that true?"

"I do not say. But to give you the satisfaction of an answer, what I will say is this: If I wished to kill you, I would not attempt it with a knife in my hand, nor would I box nor wrestle with you."

"Why is that?"

"Because many years ago when I was a boy I worked at the Resort of Kerch, attending at the tables of the wealthy Vegans. You did not know me then. I had just come up from the places of Pamir. You and your friend the poet came to Kerch."

"I remember now. Yes…Phil's parents had died that year—they were good friends of mine—and I was going to take Phil to the university. But there was a Vegan who had taken his first woman from him, taken her to Kerch. Yes, the entertainer—I forget his name."

"He was Thrilpai Ligo, the shajadpa-boxer, and he looked like a mountain at the end of a great plain—high, immovable. He boxed with the Vegan cesti—the leather strips with the ten sharpened studs that go all the way around the hand—open-handed."

"Yes, I remember…"

"You had never boxed shajadpa before, but you fought with him for the girl. A great crowd came, of the Vegans and the Earth girls, and I stood on a table to watch. After a minute your head was all blood. He tried to make it run into your eyes, and you kept shaking your head. I was fifteen then and had only killed three men myself, and I thought that you were going to die because you had not even touched him. And then your right hand crossed to him like a thrown hammer, so fast! You struck him in the center of that double bone the blue ones have in their chests—and they are tougher there than we—and you crushed him like an egg. I could never have done that, I am sure—and that is why I fear your hands and your arms. Later, I learned that you had also broken a spiderbat. —No, Karagee, I would kill you from a distance."

"That was so long… I did not think anyone remembered."

"You won the girl."

"Yes. I forget her name."

"But you did not give her back to the poet. You kept her for yourself. That is why he probably hates you."

"Phil? That girl? I've even forgotten what she looked like."

"He has never forgotten. That is why I think he hates you. I can smell hate, sniff out its sources. You took away his first woman. I was there."

"It was her idea."

"…And he grows old and you stay young. It is sad, Karagee, when a friend has reason to hate a friend."

"Yes."

"And I do not answer your questions."

"It is possible that you were hired to kill the Vegan."

"It is possible."

"Why?"

"I said only that it is possible, not that it is fact."

"Then I will ask you one more question only, and be done with it. —What good would come of the Vegan's death? His book could be a very good thing in the way of Vegan-human relations."

"I do not know what good or bad would come of it, Karagee. Let us throw more knives."

We did. I picked up the range and the balance and put two right in the center of the target. Then Hasan squeezed two in beside them, the last one giving out the sharp pain-cry of metal as it vibrated against one of mine.

"I will tell you a thing," I said, as we drew them again. "I am head of the tour and responsible for the safety of its members. I, too, will guard the Vegan."

"That will be a very good thing, Karagee. He needs protecting."
I placed the knives back in the tray and moved to the door.

"We will be leaving at nine tomorrow morning, you know. I'll have a convoy of Skimmers at the first field in the Office compound."

"Yes. Good night, Karagee."

"…And call me Conrad."

"Yes."

He had a knife ready to throw at the target. I closed the door and moved back up the corridor. As I went, I heard another *thunk*, and it sounded much closer than the first ones had. It echoed all around me, there in the hallway.

❖   ❖   ❖

As the six big Skimmers fled across the oceans toward Egypt I turned my thoughts first to Kos and Cassandra and then dragged them back with some difficulty and sent them on ahead to the land of sand, the Nile, mutated crocs, and some dead Pharoahs whom one of my most current projects was then disturbing. ("Death comes on swift wings to he who defiles…" etc.), and I thought then of humanity, roughly ensconced on the Titan waystation, working in the Earthoffice, abasing itself on Taler and Bakab, getting by on Mars, and doing so-so on Rylpah, Divbah, Litan and a couple dozen other worlds in the Vegan Combine. Then I thought about the Vegans.

The blueskinned folk with the funny names and the dimples like pock-marks had taken us in when we were cold, fed us when we were hungry. Yeah. They appreciated the fact that our Martian and Titanian colonies had suffered from nearly a century of sudden self-sufficiency—after the Three Days incident—before a workable interstellar vehicle had been developed. Like the boll weevil (Emmet tells me) we were just looking for a home, because we'd used up the one we had. Did the Vegans reach for the insecticide? No. Wise elder race that they are, they permitted us to settle among their worlds, to live and work in their land cities, their seacities. For even a culture as advanced as the Vegans' has some need for hand labor of the opposing thumb variety. Good domestic servants cannot be replaced by machines, nor can machine monitors, good gardeners, salt sea fisherfolk, subterranean and subaquean hazard workers, and ethnic entertainers of the alien variety. Admitted, the presence of human dwelling places lowers the value of adjacent Vegan properties, but then, humans themselves compensate for it by contributing to the greater welfare. Which thought brought me back to Earth. The Vegans had never seen a completely devastated civilization before, so they are fascinated by our home planet. Fascinated enough to tolerate our absentee government on Taler. Enough to buy Earthtour tickets to view the ruins. Even enough to buy property here and set up resorts. There *is* a certain kind of fascination to a planet that is run like a museum. (What was it James Joyce said about Rome?) Anyhow, dead Earth still brings its living grandchildren a small but appreciable revenue every Vegan fiscal year. That is why—the Office, Lorel, George, Phil, and all that.

Far below, the ocean was a bluegray rug being pulled out from beneath us. The dark continent replaced it. We raced on toward New Cairo.

We set down outside the city. There's no real airstrip. We just dropped all six Skimmers down in an empty field we used as one, and we posted George as a guard.

Old Cairo is still radioactively hot, but the people with whom one can do business live mainly in New Cairo, so things were pretty much okay for the tour. Myshtigo did want to see the mosque of Kait Bey in the City of the Dead, which had survived the Three Days; he settled, though, for me taking him up in my Skimmer and flying in low, slow circles about it while he took photographs and did some peering. In the way of monuments, it was really the pyramids and Luxor, Karnak, and the Valley of Kings and the Valley of Queens that he wanted to see.

It was well that we viewed the mosque from the air. Dark shapes scurried below us, stopping only to hurl rocks up toward the ship.

"What are they?" asked Myshtigo.

"Hot Ones," said I. "Sort of human. They vary in size, shape, and meanness."

After circling for a time he was satisfied, and we returned to the field.

So, landing again beneath a glaring sun, we secured the final Skimmer and disembarked, moving across equal proportions of sand and broken pavement—two temporary tour assistants, me, Myshtigo, Dos Santos and Red Wig, Ellen, Hasan. Ellen had decided at the last minute to accompany her husband on the journey. There were fields of high, shiny sugar cane on both sides of the road. In a moment we had left them behind and were passing the low outbuildings of the city. The road widened. Here and there a palm tree cast some shade. Two great-eyed, brown-eyed children looked up as we passed. They had been watching a weary, six-legged cow turn a great *sakieh* wheel, in much the same way as cows have always turned great *sakieh* wheels hereabouts, only this one left more hoofprints.

My area supervisor, Rameses Smith, met us at the inn. He was big, his golden face tightly contained within a fine net of wrinkles; and he had the typical sad eyes, but his constant chuckle quickly offset them.

We sat sipping beer in the main hall of the inn while we waited for George. Local guards had been sent to relieve him.

"The work is progressing well," Rameses told me.

"Good," said I, somewhat pleased that no one had asked me what "the work" was. I wanted to surprise them.

"How is your wife, and the children…?"

"They are fine," he stated.

"…The new one?"

"He has survived—and without defect," he said proudly. "I sent my wife to Corsica until he was delivered. Here is his picture."

I pretended to study it, making the expected appreciative noises. Then, "Speaking of pictures," I said, "do you need any more equipment for the filming?"

"No, we are well-stocked. All goes well. When do you wish to view the work?"

"Just as soon as we have something to eat."

"Are you a Moslem?" interrupted Myshtigo.

"I am of the Coptic faith," replied Rameses, not smiling.

"Oh, really? That was the Monophysite heresy, was it not?"

"We do not consider ourselves heretics," said Rameses.

"About your book, Srin Shtigo…" I interrupted.

My use of the honorific stopped him.

"Yes?" he answered.

"My impression," said I, "is that you do not wish to discuss it at any length at this time. I respect this feeling, of course, but it places me in a slightly awkward position as head of this tour." We both knew I should have asked him in private, especially after his reply to Phil at the reception, but I was feeling cantankerous and wanted to let him know it, as well as to rechannel the talk. So, "I'm curious," I said, "whether it will be primarily a travelogue of the places we visit, or if you would like assistance in directing your attention to special local conditions of any sort—say, political, or current cultural items."

"I am primarily interested in writing a descriptive travel-book," he said, "but I will appreciate your comments as we go along. I thought that was your job, anyway. As it is, I do have a general awareness of

Earth traditions and current affairs, and I'm not very much concerned with them."

Dos Santos, who was pacing and smoking as our meal was being prepared, stopped in mid-stride and said:

"Srin Shtigo, what are your feelings toward the Returnist movement? Are you sympathetic with our aims? —Or do you consider it a dead issue?"

"Yes," he replied, "to the latter. I believe that when one is dead one's only obligation then is to satisfy the consumer. I respect your aims, but I do not see how you can possibly hope to realize them. Why should your people give up the security they now possess to return to this place? Most of the members of the present generation have never even seen the Earth, except on tapes—and you must admit that they are hardly the most encouraging documents."

"I disagree with you," said Dos Santos, "and I find your attitude dreadfully patrician."

"That is as it should be," replied Myshtigo.

❖   ❖   ❖

High sun, short shadows, hot—that's how it was. I didn't want any sand-cars or Skimmers spoiling the scene, so I made everybody hike it. It wasn't that far, and I took a slightly roundabout way in order to achieve the calculated effect.

We walked a crooked mile, climbing some, dipping some. I confiscated George's butterfly net so as to prevent any annoying pauses as we passed by the several clover fields which lay along our route.

Walking backward through time, that's how it was—with bright birds flashing by (clare! clare!), and a couple camels appearing against the far horizon whenever we topped a small rise. Ellen, moist already, kept fanning herself with a big green feather triangle; Red Wig walked tall, tiny beads of perspiration seasoning her upper lip, eyes hidden behind sunshades which had darkened themselves as much as they could. Finally, we were there. We climbed the last, low hill.

"Behold," said Rameses.

"Madre de Dios!" said Dos Santos.

Hasan grunted.

Red Wig turned toward me quickly, then turned away. I couldn't read her expression because of the shades.

"What are they doing?" asked Myshtigo. It was the first time I had seen him genuinely surprised.

"Why, they're dismantling the great pyramid of Cheops," said I.

After a time Red Wig asked it.

"Why?"

"Well now," I told her, "they're kind of short on building materials hereabouts, the stuff from Old Cairo being radioactive—so they're obtaining it by knocking apart that old piece of solid geometry out there."

"They are desecrating a monument to the past glories of the human race!" she exclaimed.

"Nothing is cheaper than past glories," I observed. "It's the present that we're concerned with, and they need building materials now."

"For how long has this been going on?" asked Myshtigo, his words rushing together.

"It was three days ago," said Rameses, "that we began the dismantling."

"What gives you the right to do a thing like that?"

"It was authorized by the Earthoffice Department of Arts, Monuments and Archives, Srin."

Myshtigo turned to me, his amber eyes glowing strangely.

"You!" he said.

"I," I acknowledged, "am Commissioner thereof—that is correct."

"Why has no one else heard of this action of yours?"

"Because very few people come here anymore," I explained. "—Which is another good reason for dismantling the thing. It doesn't even get looked at much these days."

"I came here from another world to see it!"

"Well, take a quick look, then," I told him. "It's going away fast."

He turned and stared.

"You obviously have no conception of its intrinsic value. Or if you do…"

"On the contrary, I know exactly what it's worth."

"…And those unfortunate creatures you have working down there"—his voice rose as he studied the scene—"under the hot rays of your ugly sun—they're laboring under the most primitive conditions! Haven't you ever heard of moving machinery?"

"Of course. It's expensive."

"And your foremen are carrying whips! How can you treat your own people this way? It's perverse!"

"All those men volunteered for the job, at token salaries—and Actors' Equity won't let us use the whips, even though the men argued in favor of it. All we're allowed to do is crack them in the air near them."

"Actors' Equity?"

"Their union. —Want to see some machinery?" I gestured. "Look up on that hill."

He did.

"What's going on there?"

"We're recording it on viewtape."

"To what end?"

"When we're finished we're going to edit it down to viewable length and run it backwards. 'The Building of the Great Pyramid,' we're going to call it. Should be good for some laughs—also money. Your historians have been conjecturing as to exactly how we put it together ever since the day they heard about it. This may make them somewhat happier. I decided a BFMI operation would go over best."

"B.F.M.I.?"

"Brute Force and Massive Ignorance. Look at them jamming it up, will you?—following the camera, lying down and standing up quickly when it swings in their direction. They'll be collapsing all over the place in the finished product. But then, this is the first Earthfilm in years. They're real excited."

Myshtigo laughed.

"You are tougher than I thought, Nomikos," he observed. "But you are not indispensable."

"Try having a civil servant fired."

"It might be easier than you think."

"We'll see."

"We may."

We turned again toward the great 90 percent pyramid of Cheops/Khufu. Myshtigo began taking notes once more.

"I'd rather you viewed it from here, for now," I said. "Our presence would waste valuable footage. We're anachronisms. We can go down during coffee break."

"I agree," said Myshtigo, "and I am certain I know an anachronism when I see one. But I have seen all that I care to here. Let us go back to the inn. I wish to talk with the locals."

Then, "I'll see Sakkara ahead of schedule, then," he mused. "You haven't begun dismantling all the monuments of Luxor, Karnak, and the Valley of Kings yet, have you?"

"Not yet, no."

"Good. Then we'll visit them ahead of time."

"Do you really mean everything you say?" asked Diane as we walked back.

"In my fashion."

"How do you think of such things?"

"In Greek, of course. Then I translate them into English. I'm real good at it."

"Who are you?"

"Ozymandias. Look at my works ye mighty and despair."

"I'm not mighty."

"I wonder…" I said, and I left the part of her face that I could see wearing a rather funny expression as we walked along.

❖   ❖   ❖

The next six days were rather uneventful and somewhat unforgettable, extremely active, and sort of ugly-beautiful—in the way that a flower can be, with its petals all intact and a dark and runny rot-spot in the center. Here's how…

Myshtigo must have interviewed every stone ram along the four miles of the Way to Karnak. Both in the blaze of day and by torchlight we navigated the ruins, disturbing bats, rats, snakes and insects, listening to the Vegan's monotonous note-taking in his monotonous language. At night we camped on the sands, setting up a two hundred meter electrical warning perimeter and posting two guards. The boadile has a head something like a croc's, only bigger. Around forty feet long. Able to roll itself into a big beachball with teeth. Fast on land or in water. But the boadile is cold-blooded and the nights were chill. So there was relatively little danger from without.

Huge campfires lighted the nights, all about the areas we chose, because the Vegan wanted things primitive—for purposes of atmosphere, I guessed. Our Skimmers were further south. We had flown them to a place I knew of and left them there under Office guard, renting the felucca for our trip—which paralleled the King-God's journey from Karnak to Luxor. Myshtigo had wanted it that way. Nights, Hasan would either practice with the *assagai* he had bartered from a big Nubian, or he would strip to the waist and wrestle for hours with his tireless robot-golem. A worthy opponent was the rolem. Hasan had it programmed at twice the statistically-averaged strength of a man and had upped its reflex-time by fifty percent. Its "memory" contained hundreds of wrestling holds, and its governor theoretically prevented it from killing or maiming its opponent—all through a series of chemelectrical afferent nerve-analogues which permitted it to gauge to an ounce the amount of pressure necessary to snap a bone or tear a tendon. Rolem was about five feet, six inches in height and weighed around two hundred fifty pounds; manufactured on Bakab, he was quite expensive, was dough-colored and caricature-featured, and his brains were located somewhere below where his navel would be—if golems had navels—to protect his think stuff from Greco-Roman shocks. Even as it is, accidents can happen. People have been killed by the things, when something goes amok in the brains or some of the afferents, or just because the people themselves slipped or tried to jerk away, supplying the necessary extra ounces. I'd had one once, for almost a year, programmed for boxing. I used to spend fifteen minutes or so with it every afternoon. Got to thinking of it as a person, almost. Then one day it fouled me and I pounded it for over an hour and finally knocked its head off. The thing kept right on boxing, and I stopped thinking of it as a friendly sparring partner right then. It's a weird feeling, boxing with a headless golem, you know? —Sort of like waking from a pleasant dream and finding a nightmare crouched at the foot of your bed. It doesn't really "see" its opponent with those eye-things it has; it's all sheathed about with piezo-electric radar mesentery, and it "watches" from all its surfaces. Still, the death of an illusion tends to disconcert. I turned mine off and never turned it back on again. Sold it to a camel trader for a pretty good price. Don't know if he ever got the head back on. But he was a Turk, so who cares?

Anywhich—Hasan would tangle with Rolem, both of them gleaming in the firelight, and we'd all sit on blankets and watch, and bats would swoop low occasionally, like big, fast ashes, and emaciated clouds would cover the moon, veil-like, and then move on again. It was that way on the third night, when I went mad.

I remember it only in the way you remember a passing countryside you might have seen through a late summer evening storm—as a series of isolated, lightning-filled stillshots…

Having spoken with Cassandra for the better part of an hour, I concluded the transmission with a promise to cop a Skimmer the following afternoon and spend the next night on Kos. I recall our last words.

"…Take care, Konstantin. I have been dreaming bad dreams."

"Bosh, Cassandra. Good night."

And who knows but that her dreams might have been the result of a temporal shockwave moving backwards from a 9.6 Richter reading?

A certain cruel gleam filling his eyes, Dos Santos applauded as Hasan hurled Rolem to the ground with a thunderous crash. That particular earthshaker continued, however, long after the golem had climbed back to his feet and gotten into another crouch, his arms doing serpent-things in the Arab's direction. The ground shook and shook.

"What power! Still do I feel it!" cried Dos Santos. *"Olé!"*

"It is a seismic disturbance," said George. "Even though I'm not a geologist—"

"Earthquake!" yelled his wife, dropping an unpasturized date she had been feeding Myshtigo.

There was no reason to run, no place to run to. There was nothing nearby that could fall on us. The ground was level and pretty barren. So we just sat there and were thrown about, even knocked flat a few times. The fires did amazing things.

Rolem's time was up and he went stiff then, and Hasan came and sat with George and me. The tremors lasted the better part of an hour, and they came again, more weakly, many times during that night. After the first bad shock had run its course, we got in touch with the Port. The instruments there showed that the center of the thing lay a good distance to the north of us.

A bad distance, really.

…In the Mediterranean.

The Aegean, to be more specific.

I felt sick, and suddenly I was.

I tried to put through a call to Kos.

Nothing.

My Cassandra, my lovely lady, my princess… Where was she? For two hours I tried to find out. Then the Port called me.

It was Lorel's voice, not just some lob watch operator's.

"Uh—Conrad, I don't know how to tell you, exactly, what happened…"

"Just talk," I said, "and stop when you're finished."

"An observe-satellite passed your way about twelve minutes ago," he crackled across the bands. "Several of the Aegean islands were no longer present in the pictures it transmitted…"

"No," I said.

"I'm afraid that Kos was one of them."

"No," I said.

"I'm sorry," he told me, "but that is the way it shows. I don't know what else to say…"

"That's enough," I said. "That's all. That's it. Good-bye. We'll talk more later. No! I guess—No!"

"Wait! Conrad!"

I went mad.

Bats, shaken loose from the night, were swooping about me. I struck out with my right hand and killed one as it flashed in my direction. I waited a few seconds and killed another. Then I picked up a big rock with both hands and was about to smash the radio when George laid a hand on my shoulder, and I dropped the rock and knocked his hand away and backhanded him across the mouth. I don't know what became of him then, but as I stooped to raise the rock once more I heard the sound of footfalls behind me. I dropped to one knee and pivoted on it, scooping up a handful of sand to throw in someone's eyes. They were all of them there: Myshtigo and Red Wig and Dos Santos, Rameses, Ellen, three local civil servants, and Hasan—approaching in a group. Someone yelled "Scatter!" when they saw my face, and they fanned out.

Then they were everyone I'd ever hated—I could feel it. I saw other faces, heard other voices. Everyone I'd ever known, hated, wanted to smash, had smashed, stood there resurrected before the fire, and only the whites of their teeth were showing through the shadows that crossed over their faces as they smiled and came toward me, bearing various dooms in their hands, and soft, persuasive words on their lips—so I threw the sand at the foremost and rushed him.

My uppercut knocked him over backward, then two Egyptians were on me from both sides.

I shook them loose, and in the corner of my colder eye saw a great Arab with something like a black avocado in his hand. He was swinging it toward my head, so I dropped down. He had been coming in my direction and I managed to give his stomach more than just a shove, so he sat down suddenly. Then the two men I had thrown away were back on me again. A woman was screaming, somewhere in the distance, but I couldn't see any women.

I tore my right arm free and batted someone with it, and the man went down and another took his place. From straight ahead a blue man threw a rock which struck me on the shoulder and only made me madder. I raised a kicking body into the air and threw it against another, then I hit someone with my fist. I shook myself. My galabieh was torn and dirty, so I tore it the rest of the way off and threw it away.

I looked around. They had stopped coming at me, and it wasn't fair—it wasn't fair that they should stop then when I wanted so badly to see things breaking. So I raised up the man at my feet and slapped him down again. Then I raised him up again and someone yelled "Eh! Karaghiosis!" and began calling me names in broken Greek. I let the man fall back to the ground and turned.

There, before the fire—there were two of them: one tall and bearded, the other squat and heavy and hairless and molded out of a mixture of putty and earth.

"My friend says he will break you, Greek!" called out the tall one, as he did something to the other's back.

I moved toward them and the man of putty and mud sprang at me.

He tripped me, but I came up again fast and caught him beneath the armpits and threw him off to the side. But he recovered his footing as rapidly as I had, and he came back again and caught me behind the neck with one hand. I did the same to him, also seizing his elbow—and we locked together there, and he was strong.

Because he was strong, I kept changing holds, testing his strength. He was also fast, accommodating every move I made almost as soon as I thought of it.

I threw my arms up between his, hard, and stepped back on my reinforced leg. Freed for a moment, we orbited each other, seeking another opening.

I kept my arms low and I was bent well forward because of his shortness. For a moment my arms were too near my sides, and he moved in faster than I had seen anyone move before, ever, and he caught me in a body lock that squeezed the big flat flowers of moisture out of my pores and caused a great pain in my sides.

Still his arms tightened, and I knew that it would not be long before he broke me unless I could break his hold.

I doubled my hands into fists and got them against his belly and pushed. His grip tightened. I stepped backward and heaved forward with both arms. My hands went up higher between us and I got my right fist against the palm of my left hand and began to push them together and lift with my arms. My head swam as my arms came up higher, and my kidneys were on fire. Then I tightened all the muscles in my back and my shoulders and felt the strength flow down through my arms and come together in my hands, and I smashed them up toward the sky and his chin happened to be in the way, but it didn't stop them.

My arms shot up over my head and he fell backward.

It should have broken a man's neck, the force of that big snap that came when my hands struck his chin and he got a look at his heels from the backside.

But he sprang up immediately, and I knew then that he was no mortal wrestler, but one of those creatures born not of woman;

rather, I knew, he had been torn Antaeus-like from the womb of the Earth herself.

I brought my hands down hard on his shoulders and he dropped to his knees. I caught him across the throat then and stepped to his right side and got my left knee under the lower part of his back. I leaned forward, bearing down on his thighs and shoulders, trying to break him.

But I couldn't. He just kept bending until his head touched the ground and I couldn't push him any further.

No one's back bends like that and doesn't snap, but his did.

Then I heaved up with my knee and let go, and he was on me again—that fast.

So I tried to strangle him. My arms were much longer than his. I caught him by the throat with both hands, my thumbs pressing hard against what should have been his windpipe. He got his arms across mine though, at the elbows and inside, and began to pull downward and out. I kept squeezing, waiting for his face to darken, his eyes to bug out. My elbows began to bend under his downward pressure. Then his arms came across and caught me by the throat.

And we stood there and choked one another. Only he wouldn't be strangled.

His thumbs were like two spikes pressing into the muscles in my neck. I felt my face flush. My temples began to throb.

Off in the distance, I heard a scream:

"Stop it, Hasan! It's not supposed to do that!"

It sounded like Red Wig's voice. Anyhow, that's the name that came into my head: Red Wig. Which meant that Donald Dos Santos was somewhere nearby. And she had said "Hasan," a name written on another picture that came suddenly clear.

Which meant that I was Conrad and that I was in Egypt, and that the expressionless face swimming before me was therefore that of the golem-wrestler, Rolem, a creature which could be set for five times the strength of a human being and probably was so set, a creature which could be given the reflexes of an adrenalized cat, and doubtless had them in full operation.

Only a golem wasn't supposed to kill, except by accident, and Rolem was trying to kill me.

Which meant that his governor wasn't functioning.

I released my choke, seeing that it wasn't working, and I placed the palm of my left hand beneath his right elbow. Then I reached across the top of his arms and seized his right wrist with my other hand, and I crouched as low as I could and pushed up on his elbow and pulled up on his wrist.

As he went off balance to his left and the grip was broken I kept hold of the wrist, twisting it so that the elbow was exposed upwards. I stiffened my left hand, snapped it up beside my ear, and brought it down across the elbow joint.

Nothing. There was no snapping sound. The arm just gave way, bending backward at an unnatural angle.

I released the wrist and he fell to one knee. Then he stood again, quickly, and as he did so the arm straightened itself and then bent forward again into a normal position.

If I knew Hasan's mind, then Rolem's timer had been set for maximum—two hours. Which was a pretty long time, all things considered.

But this time around I knew who I was and what I was doing. Also, I knew what went into the structuring of a golem. This one was a wrestling golem. Therefore, it could not box.

I cast a quick look back over my shoulder, to the place where I had been standing when the whole thing had started—over by the radio tent. It was about fifty feet away.

He almost had me then. Just during that split second while I had turned my attention to the rear he had reached out and seized me behind the neck with one hand and caught me beneath the chin with the other.

He might have broken my neck, had he been able to follow through, but there came another tremblor at that moment—a severe one, which cast us both to the ground—and I broke this hold, also.

I scrambled to my feet seconds later, and the earth was still shaking. Rolem was up too, though, and facing me again.

We were like two drunken sailors fighting on a storm-tossed ship…

He came at me and I gave ground.

I hit him with a left jab, and while he snatched at my arm I punched him in the stomach. Then I backed off.

He came on again and I kept throwing punches.

Boxing was to him what the fourth dimension is to me—he just couldn't see it. He kept advancing, shaking off my punches, and I kept retreating in the direction of the radio tent, and the ground kept shaking, and somewhere a woman was screaming, and I heard a shouted *"Olé!"* as I landed a right below the belt, hoping to jar his brains a bit.

Then we were there and I saw what I wanted—the big rock I'd intended to use on the radio. I feinted with my left, then seized him, shoulder-and-thigh, and raised him high up over my head.

I bent backwards, tightened up my muscles, and hurled him down upon the rock.

It caught him in the stomach.

He began to rise again, but more slowly than he had before, and I kicked him in the stomach three times, with my great reinforced right boot, and I watched him sink back down.

A strange whirring sound had begun in his midsection.

The ground shook again. Rolem crumpled, stretched out, and the only sign of motion was in the fingers of his left hand. They kept clenching and unclenching—reminding me, oddly, of Hasan's hands that night back at the *hounfor*.

Then I turned slowly and they were all standing there: Myshtigo and Ellen, and Dos Santos with a puffed-up cheek, Red Wig, George, Rameses and Hasan, and the three plastaged Egyptians. I took a step toward them then and they began to fan out again, their faces filling with fear. But I shook my head.

"No, I'm all right now," I said, "but leave me alone. I'm going down to the river to bathe…" I took seven steps, and then someone must have pulled out the plug, because I gurgled, everything swirled, and the world ran away down the drain.

❖   ❖   ❖

The days that followed were ashes and the nights were iron. The spirit that had been torn from my soul was buried deeper than any mummy that lay mouldering beneath those sands. It is said that the dead forget the dead in the house of Hades, Cassandra, but I hoped it was not so. I went through the motions of conducting a tour, and Lorel suggested that I appoint someone else to finish it out and take a leave of absence myself.

I couldn't.

What would I do then? —Sit and brood in some Old Place, cadging drinks from unwary travelers? No. Some kind of motion is always essential at such times; its forms eventually generate a content for their empty insides. So I went on with the tour and turned my attention to the small mysteries it contained.

I took Rolem apart and studied his governor. It *had* been broken, of course—which meant that either I had done it during the early stages of our conflict, or Hasan had done it as he was souping him up to take the fight out of me. If Hasan had done it, then he did not just want me beaten, but dead. If such was the case, then the question was *why*? I wondered whether his employer knew that I had once been Karaghiosis. If he did, though, why should he want to kill the founder and first Secretary of his own Party?—the man who had sworn that he would not see the Earth sold out from under him and turned into a sporting house by a pack of blue aliens—not see it without fighting, anyhow—and had organized about himself a cabal which systematically lowered the value of all Vegan-owned Terran property to zero, and even went so far as to raze the Talerites' lush realty office on Madagascar—the man whose ideals he allegedly espoused, though they were currently being channeled into more peaceful, legalistic modes of property-defense—why should he want *that* man dead?

—Therefore, he had either sold out the Party, or he didn't know who I was and had had some other end in mind when he instructed Hasan to kill me.

Or else Hasan was acting under someone else's orders.

But who else could there be? And again, why? I had no answer. I decided I wanted one.

❖   ❖   ❖

The first condolence had been George's.

"I'm sorry, Conrad," he'd said, looking past my elbow, and then down at the sand, and then glancing up quickly into my face.

Saying human things upset him, and made him want to go away. I could tell. It is doubtful that the parade consisting of Ellen and me, which had passed that previous summer, had occupied much of his attention. His passions stopped outside the biological laboratory. I remember when he'd dissected the last dog on Earth. After four years of scratching his ears and combing the fleas from his tail and listening to him bark, George had called Rolf to him one day. Rolf had trotted in, bringing along the old dishrag they'd always played at tug-of-war with, and George had tugged him real close and give him a hypo and then opened him up. He'd wanted to get him while he was still in his prime. Has the skeleton mounted in his lab. He also wanted to raise his kids—Mark and Dorothy and Jim—in Skinner Boxes, but Ellen had put her foot down each time (like *bang! bang! bang!*) in post-pregnancy seizures of motherhood which lasted just long enough to spoil the initial stimuli-balances George had wanted to establish. So I couldn't really see him as having much desire to take my measure for a wooden sleeping bag of the underground sort. If he'd wanted me dead, it would probably have been subtle, fast, and exotic—with something like Divban rabbit-venom. But no, he didn't care that much. I was sure.

Ellen herself, while she is capable of intense feelings, is ever the faulty windup doll. Something always goes *sprong* before she can take action on her feelings, and by the next day she feels as strongly about something else. Her condolence went something like this:

"Conrad, you just don't know how sorry I am! *Really*. Even though I never met her, I *know* how you must feel," and her voice went up and down the scale, and I knew she believed what she was saying, and I thanked her too.

Hasan, though, came up beside me while I was standing there, staring out over the suddenly swollen and muddy Nile. We stood together for a time and then he said, "Your woman is gone and your heart is heavy. Words will not lighten the weight, and what is written is written. But let it also be put down that I grieve with you." Then we stood there awhile longer and he walked away.

I didn't wonder about him. He was the one person who could be dismissed, even though his hand had set the machine in motion. He never held grudges; he never killed for free. He had no personal motive to kill me. That his condolences were genuine, I was certain. Killing me would have nothing to do with the sincerity of his feelings in a matter like this. A true professional must respect some sort of boundary between self and task.

Myshtigo said no words of sympathy. It would have been alien to his nature. Among the Vegans, death is a time of rejoicing. On the spiritual level it means *sagl*—completion—the fragmentation of the psyche into little pleasure-sensing pinpricks, which are scattered all over the place to participate in the great universal orgasm; and on the material plane it is represented by *ansakundabad't*—ceremonial auditing of most of the deceased's personal possessions, the reading of his distribution-desire and the division of his wealth, accompanied by much feasting, singing, and drinking.

Dos Santos said to me: "It is a sad thing that has happened to you, my friend. It is to lose the blood of one's own veins to lose one's woman. Your sorrow is great and you cannot be comforted. It is like a smoldering fire that will not die out, and it is a sad and terrible thing.

"Death is cruel and it is dark," he finished, and his eyes were moist—for be it Gypsy, Jew, Moor, or what have you, a victim is a victim to a Spaniard, a thing to be appreciated on one of those mystically obscure levels which I lack.

Then Red Wig came up beside me and said, "Dreadful...Sorry. Nothing else to say, to do, but sorry."

I nodded.

"Thanks."

"And there is something I must ask you. Not now, though. Later."

"Sure," I said, and I returned to watching the river after they left, and I thought about those last two. They had sounded as sorry as everyone else, but it seemed they had to be mixed up in the golem business, somehow. I was sure, though, that it was Diane who had screamed while Rolem was choking me, screamed for Hasan to stop him. That left Don, and I had by then come to entertain strong doubts that he ever did anything without first consulting her.

Which left nobody.

And there was no real motive apparent...

And it could all have been an accident...

But...

But I had this feeling—down there around the stomach, where feelings come from—that someone wanted to kill me. I knew that Hasan was not above taking two jobs at the same time, and for different employers, if there was no conflict of interests.

And this made me happy.

It gave me a purpose, something to do.

There's really nothing quite like someone's wanting you dead to make you want to go on living. I would find him, find out why, and stop him.

❖   ❖   ❖

Death's second pass was fast, and as much as I would have liked to have pinned it on human agent, I couldn't. It was just one of those diddles of dumb destiny which sometimes come like uninvited guests at dinnertime. Its finale, however, left me quite puzzled and gave me some new, confusing thoughts to think.

It came like this...

Down by the river, that great fertile flooder, that eraser of boundaries and father of plane geometry, sat the Vegan, making sketches of the opposite bank. I suppose had he been on *that* bank he would have been sketching the one he sat upon, but this is cynical conjecture. What bothered me was the fact that he had come off alone, down to this warm, marshy spot, had not told anyone where he was going, and had brought along nothing more lethal than a No. 2 pencil.

It happened.

An old, mottled log which had been drifting in near the shore suddenly ceased being an old, mottled log. A long, serpentine back end whipped skyward, a bushel full of teeth appeared at the other end, and lots of little legs found solid ground and started acting like wheels.

I yelled and snatched at my belt.

Myshtigo dropped his pad and bolted.

It was on him, though, and I couldn't fire then.

So I made a dash, but by the time I got there it had two coils around him and he was about two shades bluer, and those teeth were closing in on him.

Now, there is one way to make any kind of constrictor loosen up, at least for a moment. I grabbed for its high head, which had slowed down just a bit as it contemplated its breakfast, and I managed to catch my fingers under the scaly ridges at the sides of that head.

I dug my thumbs into its eyes as hard as I could. Then a spastic giant hit me with a graygreen whip.

I picked myself up and I was about ten feet from where I had been standing. Myshtigo had been thrown further up the bank. He was recovering his feet just as it attacked again.

It reared up about eight feet off the ground and toppled toward me. I threw myself to the side and that big, flat head missed me by inches, its impact showering me with dirt and pebbles.

I rolled further and started to rise, but the tail came around and knocked me down again. Then I scrambled backward, but was too late to avoid the coil it threw. It caught me low around the hips and I fell again.

Then a pair of blue arms wrapped themselves around the body above the coil, but they couldn't hold on for more than a few seconds. Then we were both tied up in knots.

I struggled, but how do you fight a thick, slippery armored cable with messes of little legs that keep tearing at you? My right arm was pinned to my side by then, and I couldn't reach far enough with my left hand to do any more gouging. The coils tightened. The head moved toward me and I tore at the body. I beat at it and I clawed it, and I finally managed to tear my right arm free, giving up some skin in the process.

I blocked with my right hand as the head descended. My hand came up beneath the lower jaw, caught it, and held it there, keeping the head back. The big coil tightened around my waist, more powerful than even the grip of the golem had been. Then it shook its head sideways, away from my hand, and the head came down and the jaws opened wide.

Myshtigo's struggles must have irritated it and slowed it some, giving me time for my last defense.

I thrust my hands up into its mouth and held its jaws apart.

The roof of its mouth was slimy and my palm began to slip along it, slowly. I pressed down harder on the lower jaw, as hard as I could. The mouth opened another half foot and seemed locked there.

It tried to draw back then, to make me let go, but its coils bound us too tightly to give it the necessary footage.

So it unwound a little, straightening some, and pulling back its head. I gained a kneeling position. Myshtigo was in a sagging crouch about six feet away from me.

My right hand slipped some more, almost to the point where I would lose all my leverage.

Then I heard a great cry.

The shudder came almost simultaneously. I snapped my arms free as I felt the thing's strength wane for a second. There was a dreadful clicking of teeth and a final constriction. I blacked out for a moment.

Then I was fighting free, untangling myself. The smooth wooden shaft which had skewered the boadile was taking the life from it, and its movements suddenly became spasmodic rather than aggressive.

I was knocked down twice by all its lashing about, but I got Myshtigo free, and we got about fifty feet away and watched it die. This took quite awhile.

Hasan stood there, expressionless. The *assagai* he had spent so much time practicing with had done its work. When George dissected the creature later we learned that the shaft had lodged within two inches of its heart, severing the big artery. It had two dozen legs.

Dos Santos stood beside Hasan and Diane stood beside Dos Santos. Everyone else from the camp was there, too.

"Good show," I said. "Fine shot. Thanks."

"It was nothing," Hasan replied.

It was nothing, he had said. Nothing but the death blow to my motion that he had gimmicked the golem. If Hasan had tried to kill me then, why should he have saved me from the boadile?

—Unless what he had said back at the Port was the overriding truth—that he *had* been hired to protect the Vegan. If that was his main job and killing me was only secondary, then he would have had to save me as a by-product of keeping Myshtigo alive.

—Unless I was just a suspicious old man and Rolem had been damaged some other way

But those golems are built to last. They're designed to take shocks.

But then…

Oh hell. Forget it.

I threw a stone as far as I could, and another. Our Skimmers would be flown up to our campsite the following day and we would take off for Athens, stopping only to drop Rameses and the three others at New Cairo. I was glad I was leaving Egypt, with its must and its dust and its dead, half-animal deities. I was already sick of the place.

Then Phil's call came through from the Port, and Rameses called me into the radio tent.

"Yeah?" said I, to the radio.

"Conrad, this is Phil. I am flying to Athens this afternoon. I should like to join you on this leg of your tour, if it is all right with you."

"Surely," I replied. "May I ask why, though?"

"I have decided that I want to see Greece once more. Since you are going to be there it might make it seem a little more like the old days. I'd like to take a last look at some of the Old Places."

"You make it sound rather final."

"Well…I've pushed the S-S series about as far as it will go. I fancy I can feel the mainspring running down now. Maybe it will take a few more windings and maybe it won't. At any rate, I want to see Greece again and I feel as if this is my last chance."

"I'm sure you're wrong, but we'll all be dining at the Garden Altar tomorrow evening, around eight."

"Fine. I'll see you then."

"Check."

"Good-bye, Conrad."

"Good-bye."

❖   ❖   ❖

Late that evening, I armed myself and went looking for some fresh air.

I heard voices as I neared the eastern end of the warning perimeter, so I sat down in darkness, resting my back against a largish rock, and tried to eavesdrop. I'd recognized the vibrant diminuendos of Myshtigo's voice, and I wanted to hear what he was saying.

I couldn't, though.

They were a little too far away, and desert acoustics are not always the finest in the world. I sat there straining with that part of me which listens, and it happened as it sometimes does:

I was seated on a blanket beside Ellen and my arm was around her shoulders. My blue arm...

The whole thing faded as I recoiled from the notion of being a Vegan, even in a pseudotelepathic wish-fulfillment, and I was back beside my rock once again.

I was lonesome, though, and Ellen had seemed softer than the rock, and I was still curious.

So I found myself back there once more, observing...

"...can't see it from here," he/I/we(?) was/were saying, "but Vega is a star of the first magnitude, located in what your people call the constellation Lyra."

"What's it like on Taler?" asked Ellen.

There was a long pause. Then:

"Meaningful things are often the things people are least able to describe. Sometimes, though, it is a problem in communicating something for which there is no corresponding element in the person to whom you are speaking. Taler is not like this place. There are no deserts. The entire world is landscaped. But...Let me take that flower from your hair. There. Look at it. What do you see?"

"A pretty white flower. That's why I picked it and put it in my hair."

"But it is *not* a pretty white flower. Not to me, anyhow. Your eyes perceive light with wavelengths between about 4000 and 7200 angstrom units. The eyes of a Vegan look deeper into the ultraviolet, for one thing, down to around 3000. We are blind to what you refer to as 'red,' but on this 'white' flower I see two colors for which there are no words in your language. My body is covered with patterns you cannot see, but they are close enough to those of the others in my family so that another Vegan, familiar with the Shtigo-gens, could tell my family and province on our first meeting. Some of our paintings look garish to Earth eyes, or even seem to be all of one color—blue, usually—because the subtleties are invisible to them. Much of our music would seem to you to contain big gaps of silence, gaps which are actually filled with melody. Our cities are clean and logically disposed. They catch the light of day and hold it long into the night. They are places of slow movement, pleasant sounds. This means much to me, but I do not know how to describe it to a—human."

"But people—Earth people, I mean—live on your worlds…"

"But they do not really see them or hear them or feel them the way we do. There is a gulf we can appreciate and understand, but we cannot really cross it. That is why I cannot tell you what Taler is like. It would be a different world to you than the world it is to me."

"I'd like to see it, though. Very much. I think I'd even like to live there."

"I do not believe you would be happy there."

"Why not?"

"Because non-Vegan immigrants are non-Vegan immigrants. You are not of a low caste here. I know you do not use that term, but that is what it amounts to. Your Office personnel and their families are the highest caste on this planet. Wealthy non-Office persons come next, then those who work for the wealthy non-Office persons, followed by those who make their own living from the land; then, at the bottom, are those unfortunates who inhabit the Old Places. You are at the top here. On Taler you would be at the bottom."

"Why must it be that way?" she asked.

"Because you see a white flower." I handed it back.

There was a long silence and a cool breeze.

"Anyhow I'm happy you came here," she said.

"It *is* an interesting place."

"Glad you like it."

"It is an interest, not a preoccupation of mine."

"I realize that."

"Was the man called Conrad really your lover?"

I recoiled at the suddenness of the question.

"It's none of your blue business," she said, "but the answer is 'yes'."

"I can see why," he said, and I felt uncomfortable and maybe something like a voyeur, or—subtlety of subtleties—one who watches a voyeur watching.

"Why?" she asked.

"Because you want the strange, the powerful, the exotic, because you are never happy being where you are, what you are."

"That's not true...Maybe it is. Yes, he once said something like that to me. Perhaps it is true."

I felt very sorry for her at that moment. Then, without realizing it, as I wanted to console her in some way, I reached out and took her hand. Only it was Myshtigo's hand that moved, and he had not willed it to move. I had.

I was afraid suddenly. So was he, though. I could feel it.

There was a great drunk-like, room-swimming feeling, as I felt that he felt *occupied*, as if he had sensed another presence within his mind.

I wanted away quickly then, and I was back there beside my rock, but not before she'd dropped the flower and I heard her say, "Hold me!"

Damn those pseudotelepathic wish-fulfillments! Someday I'll stop believing that that's all they are.

I *had* seen two colors in that flower, colors for which I have no words...

I walked back toward the camp. I passed through the camp and kept on going. I reached the other end of the warning perimeter, sat down on the ground, lit a cigarette. The night was cool and dark.

Two cigarettes later I heard a voice behind me, but I did not turn.

" 'In the Great House and in the House of Fire, on that Great Day when all the days and years are numbered, oh let my name be given back to me,' " it said.

"Good for you," I said softly. "Appropriate quote. I recognize the *Book of the Dead* when I hear it taken in vain."

"I wasn't taking it in vain, just—as you said—appropriately."

"Good for you."

"*On* that great day when all the days and years are numbered, if they do give you back your name, then what name will it be?"

"They won't. I plan on being late. And what's in a name, anyhow?"

"Depends on the name. So try 'Karaghiosis'."

"Try sitting down where I can see you. I don't like to have people standing behind me."

"All right—there. So?"

"So what?"

"So try 'Karaghiosis'."

"Why should I?"

"Because it means something. At least it did once."

"Karaghiosis was a figure in the old Greek shadow shows, sort of like Punch in the European Punch and Judy plays. He was a slob and a buffoon."

"He was Greek, and he was subtle."

"Ha! He was half-coward, and he was greasy."

"He was also half-hero. —Cunning. Somewhat gross. Sense of humor. *He'd* tear down a pyramid. Also, he was strong, when he wanted to be."

"Where is he now?"

"I'd like to know."

"Why ask me?"

"Because that is the name Hasan called you on the night you fought the golem."

"Oh…I see. Well, it was just an expletive, a generic term, a synonym for fool, a nickname—like if I were to call you 'Red.' —And now that I think of it, I wonder how you look to Myshtigo, anyhow? Vegans are blind to the color of your hair, you know?"

"I don't really care how I look to Vegans. Wonder how you look, though. I understand that Myshtigo's file on you is quite thick. Says something about you being several centuries old."

"Doubtless an exaggeration. But you seem to know a lot about it. How thick is your file on Myshtigo?"

"Not very, not yet."

"It seems that you hate him more than you hate everyone else. Is that true?"

"Yes."

"Why?"

"He's a Vegan."

"No, there's more."

"You said it, not me."

"OK, I said it. True though, isn't it?"

"True. —You're quite strong, you know?"

"I know."

"In fact, you're the strongest human being I've ever seen. Strong enough to break the neck of a spiderbat, then fall into the bay at Piraeus and swim ashore and have breakfast."

"Odd example you've chosen."

"Not so, not really. *Did* you?"

"Sorry."

"Sorry is not good enough. Talk more."

"Said all."

"No. We need Karaghiosis."

"Who's 'we'?"

"The Radpol. Me."

"Why, again?"

"Hasan is half as old as Time. Karaghiosis is older. Hasan knew him, remembered, called you 'Karaghiosis.' You *are* Karaghiosis, the killer, the defender of Earth—and we need you now. Very badly. Armageddon has come, not with a bang, but a checkbook. The Vegan must die. There is no alternative. Help us stop him."

"What do you want of me?"

"Let Hasan destroy him."

"No."

"Why not? What is he to you?"

"Nothing, really. In fact, I dislike him very much. But what is he to *you*?"

"Our destroyer."

"Then tell me why, and how, and perhaps I'll give you a better answer."

"I can't."

"Why not?"

"Because I don't know."

"Then good night. That's all."

"Wait! I really do not know—but the word has come down from Taler, from the Radpol liaison there: He must die. His book is not a book, his self is not a self, but many. I do not know what this means but our agents have never lied before. You've lived on Taler, you've lived on Bakab and a dozen other worlds. You are Karaghiosis. You know that our agents do not lie, because you are Karaghiosis and you established the spy-circuit yourself. Now you hear their words and you do not heed them. I tell you that they say he must die. He represents the end of everything we've fought for. They say he is a surveyor who must not be permitted to survey. You know the code. Money against Earth. More Vegan exploitation. They could not specify beyond that point."

"I will not countenance his destruction without a just and specific cause. Thus far, you have shown me nothing."

"That's all I have."

"Then good night."

"Wait. Please."

"Hasan tried to kill me."

"Yes," she said, "He must have thought it easier to kill you than to try keeping you out of the way. After all, he knows more about you than we do."

"Then why did he save me from the boadile today, along with Myshtigo?"

"I'd rather not say."

"Then forget it."

"No, I will tell you. —The *assagai* was the only thing handy. He is not yet proficient with it. He was not aiming to hit the boadile."

"Oh."

"But he was not aiming at you, either. The beast was writhing too much. He wanted to kill the Vegan, and he would simply have said that he had tried to save you both, by the only means at hand—and that there had been a terrible accident. Unfortunately, there was no terrible accident. He missed his target."

"Why did he not just let the boadile kill him?"

"Because you had already gotten your hands upon the beast. He feared you might still save him. He fears your hands."

"That's nice to know. Will he continue trying, even if I refuse to cooperate?"

"I'm afraid so."

"That is very unfortunate, my dear, because I will not permit it."

"You will not stop him. Neither will we call him off. Even though you are Karaghiosis, and hurt, and my sorrow for you overflows the horizons, Hasan will not be stopped by you or by me. He is the Assassin. He has never failed."

"Neither have I."

"Yes you have. You have just failed the Radpol and the Earth, and everything that means anything."

"I keep my own counsel, girl. Go your ways."

"I am old enough to be anyone's grandmother but yours, so do not call me 'girl.' Do you know that my hair is a wig?"

"Yes."

"Do you know that I once contracted a Vegan disease—and that that is why I must wear a wig?"

"No. I am very sorry."

"When I was young, long ago, I worked at a Vegan resort. I was a pleasure girl. I have never forgotten the puffing of their horrid lungs against my body, nor the touch of their corpse-colored flesh. I hate them, Karaghiosis, in ways that only one such as you could understand—one who has hated all the great hates."

"I am sorry, Diane. I am so sorry that it hurts you still. But I am not yet ready to move. Do not push me."

"You *are* Karaghiosis?"

"Yes."

"Then I am satisfied—somewhat."

"But the Vegan *will* live."

"We shall see."

"Yes, we shall. Good night."

"Goodnight, Conrad."

And I rose, and I left her there, and I returned to my tent. Later that night she came to me. There was a rustling of the tent flap and the bedclothes, and she was there. And when I have forgotten everything else about her—the redness of her wig and the little upside-down "v" between her eyes, and the tightness of her jaws, and her clipped talk, and all her little mannerisms of gesture, and her body warm as the heart of a star, and her strange indictment of the man I once might have been, I will remember this—that she came to me when I needed her, that she was warm, soft, and that she came to me...

❖   ❖   ❖

After breakfast the following morning I was going to seek Myshtigo, but he found me first. I was down by the river, talking with the men who would be taking charge of the felucca.

"Conrad," he said softly, "may I speak with you?"

I nodded and gestured toward a gully.

"Let's walk up this way. I've finished here."

We walked.

After a minute he said, "You know that on my world there are several systems of mental discipline, systems which occasionally produce extrasensory abilities..."

"So I've heard," I said.

"Most Vegans, at sometime or other, are exposed to it. Some have an aptitude along these lines. Many do not. Just about all of us, though, possess a feeling for it, a recognition of its operations."

"Yes?"

"I am not telepathic myself, but I am aware that you possess this ability because you used it on me last night. I could feel it. It is quite uncommon among your people, so I had not anticipated this and I had taken no precautions to prevent it. Also, you hit me at the perfect moment. As a result, my mind was opened to you. I have to know how much you learned."

So there apparently had been something extrasensory connected with those sight-vision overlays. All they usually contained were what seemed the immediate perceptions of the subject, plus a peek at the thoughts and feelings that went into the words he made—and sometimes I got them wrong. Myshtigo's question indicated that he did not know how far mine went, and I had heard that some professional Veggy psyche-stirrers could even elbow their way into the unconscious. So I decided to bluff.

"I gather that you are not writing a simple travel book," I said.

He said nothing.

"Unfortunately, I am not the only one who is aware of this," I continued, "which places you in a bit of danger."

"Why?" he asked suddenly.

"Perhaps they misunderstand," I ventured.

He shook his head.

"Who are they?"

"Sorry."

"But I need to know."

"Sorry again. If you want out, I can get you back to the Port today."

"No, I can't do that. I must go on. What am I to do?"

"Tell me a little more about it, and I'll make suggestions."

"No, you know too much already…"

"Then that must be the real reason Donald Dos Santos is here," he said quickly. "He is a moderate. The activist wing of the Radpol must have learned something of this and, as you say—misunderstood. He must know of the danger. Perhaps I should go to him…"

"No," I said quickly, "I don't think you should. It really wouldn't change anything. What would you tell him, anyhow?"

A pause. Then, "I see what you mean," he said. "The thought has also occurred to me that he might not be as moderate as I have believed… If that is the case, then—"

"Yeah," I said. "Want to go back?"

"I can't."

"Okay then, blue boy, you're going to have to trust *me*. You can start by telling me more about this survey—"

"No! I do not know how much you know and how much you do not know. It is obvious that you are trying to elicit more information, so I do not think you know very much. What I am doing is still confidential."

"I am trying to protect you," I said, "therefore I want as much information as I can get."

"Then protect my body and let me worry about my motives and my thoughts. My mind will be closed to you in the future, so you needn't waste your time trying to probe it."

I handed him an automatic.

"I suggest you carry a weapon for the duration of the tour—to protect your motives."

And, "Go get ready," said I. "We'll be leaving soon."

As I walked back toward the camp, via another route, I analyzed my own motives, A book, alone, could not make or break the Earth, the Radpol, Returnism. Even Phil's *Call of Earth* had not done that, not really. But this thing of Myshtigo's was to be more than just a book. A survey? —What could it be? A push in what direction? I did not know and I had to know. For Myshtigo could not be permitted to live if it would destroy us—and yet, I could not permit his destruction if the thing might be of any help at all. And it might.

Therefore, someone had to call time-out until we could be sure.

The leash had been tugged. I followed.

"Diane," said I, as we stood in the shade of her Skimmer, "you say that I mean something to you, as me, as Karaghiosis."

"That would seem to follow."

"Then hear me. I believe that you *may* be wrong about the Vegan. I am not sure, but if you are wrong it would be a very big mistake to kill him. For this reason, I cannot permit it. Hold off on anything you've planned until we reach Athens. Then request a clarification of that message from the Radpol."

She stared me in both eyes, then said, "All right."

"Then what of Hasan?"

"He waits."

"He makes his own choice as to time and place, does he not? He awaits only the opportunity to strike."

"Yes."

"Then he must be told to hold off until we know for sure."

"Very well."

"You will tell him?"

"He will be told."

"Good enough."

I turned away.

"…And when the message comes back," she said, "if it should say the same thing as before—what then?"

"We'll see," I said, not turning.

I left her there beside her Skimmer and returned to my own.

When the message did come back, saying what I thought it would say, I knew that I would have more trouble on my hands. This was because I had already made my decision.

Far to the south and east of us, parts of Madagascar still deafened the geigs with radioactive pain-cries—a tribute to the skill of one of us.

Hasan, I felt certain, could still face any barrier without blinking those sun-drenched, death-accustomed, yellow eyes…

He might be hard to stop.

A Word from Zelazny

Regarding his first novel, Zelazny wrote, "I wanted to leave it open to several interpretations—well, at least two. I wanted to sort of combine fantasy and sf…either Conrad is a mutant or he is the Great God Pan. The book may be read either way."[1]

While later novels such as *Lord of Light* would require research into the relevant mythos, for this first novel his only research material was "a road map of Athens."[2] "I…imagined the city as having been bombed since the present & restored, & then walking Conrad through it, drawing upon resonances from the stuff that was already in place. Fooled John Brunner,

---

1   *Niekas #21*, 1977.
2   *Phantasmicom #10*, November 1972.

a frequent visitor to Greece, into thinking I knew the area well. Fooled Samuel Delany, too."[3]

"My first book. At the time of its inception, anything over 25,000 words in length seemed next to infinite. *Question:* What could I do to be assured an ample supply of material? *Answer:* Have lots of characters representing different attitudes, so that the narrator would always have someone to talk to or talk about. *Question:* Who does this very well? *Answer:* Aldous Huxley [in such novels as *Chrome Yellow* and *Point Counterpoint*]. *Decision:* Bear him in mind when constructing the cast of characters, including the monomaniac scientist as a note of thanks for the assist, but take nothing else. Do not lean too heavily on anyone.

"The particular Mediterranean afflatus I wanted came very close to my feelings as aroused by Lawrence Durrell's *Prospero's Cell* and *Reflections on a Marine Venus*. I felt this in the opening sequence and tried to avoid it in the later ones, as I was aware of my susceptibility at the time.

"I reread Cavafy and Seferis as I wrote, to balance the influence and to keep things in Greece while I was about it.

"I like *...And Call Me Conrad* because I was satisfied with my central character. I dislike it because of the contrived nature of several of the conflict scenes, which I juggled about so that there would be high points of action in each portion whether it was serialized in two parts or three."[4]

"I never know how a story will come out. Conrad was supposed to be a tragedy; I didn't expect him to save the whole damned world. When I hit a difficult spot, I'll get up, put on a record of the sort that creates the mood I want to create, and maybe pace for an hour. Sometimes I just go to bed. I've dreamed about my characters. They're as real to me as you are."[5]

Zelazny consciously constructed Conrad to fit Northrop Frye's designation of a character who functions in "High Mimetic Mode" but strives to attain the status of a god-like character, found only in the highest level, "Mythic Mode."[6]

During his time in the Army Reserve (1960–1963), Zelazny belonged to a "fancy unit" named "the 2370th Civil Affairs Group—Arts, Monuments & Archives."[7] Paralleling this, Conrad is The Commissioner of the Earth Office of Arts, Monuments and Archives.

---

3 *Roger Zelazny*, Jane Lindskold, 1993.
4 *Vector* May-June 1973 (#65), pp. 42–44.
5 *Yandro #162* August 1966.
6 *Science Fiction as Literature: Selected Stories and Novels of Roger Zelazny* [PhD Thesis] Thomas F. Monteleone, University of Maryland, 1973.
7 *Roger Zelazny*, Jane Lindskold, 1993.

Notes

F&SF's editor abridged the novel for its first appearance as a two-part serial in October and November 1965. The cuts were not completely restored for its first book publication as *This Immortal,* and the novel remained partially abridged for twenty years (unbeknownst to Zelazny), until a Book Club edition restored the full text. A sequence near the beginning that explains the Radpol's history appeared in the magazine version but not in the novel; this is the sequence beginning "In attempting to reconstruct…" and ending with "The days of Karaghiosis had passed." The version reprinted here is the original two-part magazine version which won the Hugo Award.

Kallikanzaros (variant spelling of *Kallikantzaros*) in Greek mythology are malevolent and mischievous goblins (like leprechauns) which live underground. Variable in size (short or very large), ugly, with prominent genitalia, in some descriptions these vicious beings have animal parts such as hooves, tusks or horns. They saw at the World Tree's roots to make the world collapse, and they come to the surface for two weeks at the winter solstice. During this emergence they bring trouble to mortals. In other versions they are born at Christmas and stay aboveground until Easter.

Cassandra was Troy's King Priam's daughter, to whom Apollo gave prophetic powers. After she cheated him, however, Apollo cursed her and caused her always to be disbelieved. Conrad doubts Cassandra throughout the novel. **Pan**, the god of flocks and herds, appeared with horns, ears, and legs of a goat on a man's body; he played panpipes. Conrad himself may be Pan, suggested by events in the plot and in Zelazny's comments cited earlier. The surname **Nomikos** recalls Nomios, one of Pan's titles. The first name **Conrad** may allude to Joseph Conrad, the author whose *Heart of Darkness* is cited in part two. **Konstantin** (Greek form of Constantine) means steadfast and constant. **Karaghiosis** was a stock character in Greek drama, an impoverished and downtrodden little man who prevailed through sheer cunning. **Heterochromia** is the condition of having two eyes of different colors. Hair **the color of Kalamata** olives is black; all previous editions misspelled it as Katamara or Katamala. **The Guggenheim** is a modern art museum in Manhattan. **Caique** is a small Mediterranean boat.

The **Plane Tree of Hippocrates** stands on the Greek island of **Kos**; inhabitants claim that Hippocrates himself planted it. *Rodos dactylos* ("rosy-fingered") alludes to Homer's *Iliad* and *Odyssey*, where the epithet *rodos dactylos aurora* ("rosy-fingered dawn") rises frequently to become self-parody. Aurora is goddess of the dawn. Zelazny refers to either "*rodos dactylos*" or "rosy-fingered" three times at the beginning the novel, although this abridged version contains but a single mention. A cripple defeated the boastful wrestler

Themocles. The **strigefleur** is a mythological blood-sucking plant (literally "frightening flower"). **Aeschylus** was a Greek playwright best known for his trilogy of tragedies, *Oresteia*. Hepaestus made **Achilles' shield** so heavily detailed with complex scenes that it was practically an encyclopedia or history of the world. *Golden **Vanitie*** is Conrad's ship, not fully named until near the end of the novel. *Golden Vanity* is the name of Sir Walter Raleigh's ship in a traditional ballad dating back to the 1600s; Pete Seeger and The Almanac Singers recorded one version in 1941: "There was a lofty ship, and she put out to sea, || And the name of this ship was the *Golden Vanity*, || And she sailed upon the low and lonesome low || And she sailed upon the lonesome sea."

Aphrodite was the goddess of beauty, fertility, and sexual love. A **Gordian knot** is a complex or difficult problem, so named by King Gordius, who tied a complex knot and predicted that whoever untied it would become ruler of Asia; Alexander the Great cut it with his sword.

Erechtheum, a temple on the Acropolis in Athens, contains shrines to Athena, Poseidon, and Erechtheus, king of Athens. **The Porch of the Maidens** is the southern porch of the Acropolis, where six female statues (caryatids) function as columns. **Lord Elgin** removed one of these statues to England along with other artifacts from the Parthenon. The **thelinstra** is a fictional variant of the Aeolian harp, a large instrument said to be played by the wind. **Meerschaum** is a soft white mineral used to make pipes.

William Seabrook was a well known explorer, traveler and journalist. **Alphonse Bertillon** was a French law enforcement officer who invented anthropometry, an identification system based on physical measurements.

Dante Alighieri wrote *The Divine Comedy* which includes the well-known *Inferno*. **Fire on Fort Sumter** began the American Civil War. *Une zoophiliste* is an animal lover, and in this context it implies beastiality. San Juan **Capistrano** is known for the swallows that return each spring and depart each fall; in Conrad's post-apocalyptic world, they have been replaced with **spiderbats**.

Mambos and *houngans* are the male female High Priests of the *voudoun* or voodoo religion in Haiti. **Agué Woyo** is the Haitian god of the sea. *Hounfor* is the sacred inner chamber of a voodoo temple, its building and surroundings. **Damballah Wedo** is the serpent god who holds the earth in his coils; he causes earthquakes by shifting around a bit, and rainbows reflect off his scales. Used in voodoo ceremonies, *Rada* drums are waist-high; the skin is often saturated with rum. *Loà* are the divinities invoked during a voodoo ceremony. *Hounsi* are the believers who worship the voodoo deities and put themselves under the authority of the mambos and houngans. **Erzulie** is the voodoo goddess of love. **Papa Legba** is the god of crossroads, the one who guards the gates. **Papa Legba, ouvri bayé! || Papa Legba, Attibon Legba, ouvri bayé pou nou passe!** means *Papa Legba, open the gate for me, open! Atibon Legba, open the gate for me, Open the gate for me, Papa, for me to pass.* **Angelsou** is an evil spirit.

A **coricama** is an Italian knife. **Thomas Paine** wrote the incendiary pamphlet "Common Sense," which helped trigger the American Revolution. The **Bedouin** are North African nomads. **Cannabis sativa** is marijuana. **Shajadpa** boxing is a fictional martial art invented by the Vegans in the story. **Death comes on swift wings to he who defiles** is the curse on Tutankhamun's (King Tut's) tomb.

What was it James Joyce said about Rome?—he hated Rome and wrote it "reminds me of a man who lives by exhibiting to travellers his grandmother's corpse."

Various archaeological sites in Egypt and near Cairo are mentioned, including the **mosque of Kait Bey in the City of the Dead**, the Giza **pyramids**, and **Luxor** (ancient Thebes) which contains the Temple of Luxor, Temple of **Karnak**, **Valley of Kings** (where Pharaohs and Kings were buried) and **Valley of Queens** (where wives of Pharaohs were buried). A *sakieh* wheel, using animal power, raises water.

Coptic means both the Christian Coptic Orthodox Church of Egypt and the last historic branch of ancient Egyptian. A **Monophysite** believes that in the person of Jesus there is but a single, divine nature. The Pharaoh **Cheops** or *Khufu* was second Pharaoh of the Fourth Dynasty, best known as the builder of the Great pyramid of Giza. **Sakkara** features the world's oldest standing step pyramid.

Percy Shelley's **Ozymandias**—"My name is Ozymandias, king of kings: || Look on my works, ye mighty, and despair!"—is the Pharaoh Ramses the Great.

An *Assagai* is a slender spear of Africa's Bantu people. In Jewish mysticism, a **Golem** is artificially made in human form and brought to life. A **galabieh** is a type of man's robe in North Africa.

Antaeus, the son of Poseidon and Gaia (Mother Earth) had great strength only when touching the ground; Hercules held him aloft until he died. **Ashes and...iron** refers to Algernon Charles Swinburne's mournful poem "Perinde AC Cadaver," which also promises a resurrection [rebirth]. **Skinner boxes** are cages used to study conditioning behavior in laboratory animals. A **diminuendo** is a sound that decreases in volume. The **Book of the Dead** is an ancient Egyptian text of funereal rites; "In the Great House…let my name be given back to me" is from it. "**Armageddon has come, not with a bang, but a checkbook**" paraphrases the poem "The Hollow Men" by T. S. Eliot, which concludes, "This is the way the world ends || Not with a bang but a whimper." A **felucca** is a ship found on the Red Sea and the Nile. **Geigs** is slang for Geiger counters, which detect radioactivity.

Synopsis of Part One

The Magazine of Fantasy & Science Fiction, November 1965.

I was minding my own business, like any good creature of darkness, when the call came through from Port-au-Prince. I was to conduct a tour: Me, Conrad Nomikos, Commissioner of the Earthoffice Department of Arts, Monuments and Archives. How mortifying! I am a high-level goof-off, a Commissioner—and Commissioners just don't do things like that…

Not unless circumstances tend to be somewhat extraordinary, that is.

So I left my Cassandra—my mermaid, my bride of two months—there on the isle of Kos, and I returned me to Haiti. There did I meet with Cort Myshtigo, who was somewhat blue and Vegan, being from the world of Taler.

Cort wanted to write a book, about the Earth, about what we had left here after the Three Days. That's not much, but he wanted to see it, all, and he'd named me as the guide he wanted running the show.

So okay. He was the scion of the wealthy Shtigo-gens—he could call the shots.

In Haiti did I renew my acquaintance with such notables as George Emmet—the Earth's chief biologist and Director of the Earthoffice Department of Wildlife Conservation—and his fickle wife, Ellen; and with Donald Dos Santos and his consort, Diane of the Red Wig, the moving forces in the Radpol; and Phil Graber, the Earth's poet laureate; and last but never least, Hasan the Assassin, Earth's last mercenary.

Lorel Sands, the Earthdirector, had said, "Go thou and conduct this tour." So that was it.

Ere we left, however, I catered to a whim of the Vegan's and took him to a voodoo ceremony. There did Hasan distinguish himself by throwing a fit and murdering nonexistent people. Oh, *mal*! I took this as an indication that he had been hired to kill someone in the near future, and that he was acting it out under the influence of whatever the hell he was smoking these days—even though Mama Julie maintained that he was possessed of Angelsou, the deathgod.

The Nile Valley was our first stop, and there did I go mad when the earthquake came and sank Kos beneath the wine-dark Aegean—Kos, and my Cassandra…

I fought with anything in sight when this happened, until finally Hasan sicced the robot-golem on me. I smashed it, and the battle brought back my wits; but it had tried to kill me, and golems are supposed to have governors which prevent them from harming people. Therefore, it seemed that someone had sabotaged it, so that it could polish me off.

Hasan, of course. But why?

Who could want me dead? I'm a nice guy, and—well…

Just because a couple people, like Phil, Hasan, and maybe Red Wig knew I was a few centuries old and had once been known as Karaghiosis the killer, founder of the Radpol Returnist Party, why should my life be in jeopardy now? But someone seemed to wish me gone.

Naturally, I decided to find out why.

I was also faced with the task of preserving the Vegan's life during this time—for it appeared that Diane was the real moving spirit behind the Party, and she'd gotten Don to hire Hasan to get Myshtigo dead.

Why, again?

Well, once before had the Vegans tried to move in on us—to buy up Earth property, to set up their dark, satanic resorts on our world and to exploit our people. That was when Karaghiosis the killer had bombed their resorts and smashed the Earthgov Realty Office on Madagascar, which had been selling them the land.

See, I am one of the descendants of the survivors of the Three Days. There were Earth colonists on Mars and Titan when that brief war occurred, and they never came back—not till much later, anyhow, and then not to stay, just to administer. They developed an interstellar drive after they considered the Earth a dead issue. They went out to the stars, they found an ancient and cultured people—

the Vegans—and they obtained umbrage among them, working as registered aliens in the Vegan Combine. Also, they constituted the Earthgov in absentia. They had a majority, and they began administering the Earth via a big civil service office, after they discovered that there was something down here to administer to.

The Radpol and I disapproved when the resort business started. We stalemated them half a century ago—no new Veggy resorts, no new Radpol violence—and since then I've been marking time, playing like dead.

The real aim of the Radpol was not resistance, but Return. We had wanted the appropriate Earthfolk to come back to help us rebuild the home world. They didn't, though. They just left us with an Office designed to administer to our humble needs and preserve the cultural heritage of the race. Ha! The mainland had been bombed all to hell. We were an island culture, because nobody had bombed islands. The Office actually administers only to the islands; those unfortunates who live about the mainland Hot Places suffer the Office and derive few benefits from it. (They hate the Office too, of course, which makes the whole thing even more difficult, should the Office ever really try to help.)

So, here I am, protecting a Vegan until I can find out what he's up to. Also, I'm protecting me. It's a big job. Before leaving Egypt for Greece, I was involved in a small altercation with a boadile, which is a mutant croc (I don't care what George calls them), while keeping Myshtigo alive. Then Diane asked me to help kill Myshtigo, on the basis of an obscure Radpol communiqué. Diane fascinates me, but the Veggy's death could be a boomerang. We can't strike till we know what he's up to, I say. It just might be something good, for once. We don't really know.

So I've got a lot of people mad at me, and I can't get away from the feeling that either Hasan the Assassin or I will have to go before this thing is settled—and he's tough.

Notes

This synopsis is unusual because of its first person point of view, communicating additional details about the story's background and providing further insight into Conrad's character.

I Never Met a Traveller from an Antique Land

Written 1965–68; previously unpublished.

I never met a traveller from an antique land
or I would have told him,
"Mister, that's a car
there's millions of others like it.
And that's a housing development.
Ditto.
       Same for office buildings, churches,
theaters, hearts, heads,
and nothing inside remains.

'Round the decay—You know the bit.
The sands stretch level, far,
and Christ, it gets lonely at night.

Notes

Is the speaker Conrad Nomikos of *…And Call Me Conrad* / *This Immortal,* speaking here to an alien visitor to an apparently post-apocalyptic world? This is another instance of automobiles highlighted in Zelazny's work.

Percy Shelley's poem *Ozymandias* begins "I met a traveller from an antique land…" and includes the well-known line "my name is Ozymandias, king of kings: look upon my works, ye mighty, and despair!"

...And Call Me Conrad
Part Two

The Magazine of Fantasy & Science Fiction, November 1965.
Hugo award 1966 (novel, tied with Frank Herbert's *Dune*);
Seuin award 1976 (novel, as *This Immortal*).

I t. Down below.
   Death, heat, mud-streaked tides, new shorelines…
Vulcanism on Chios, Samos, Ikaria, Naxos…
Halicarnassos bitten away…
The western end of Kos visible again, but so what?
…Death, heat, mud-streaked tides. New shorelines…

❖   ❖   ❖

I had brought my whole convoy out of its way in order to check the scene. Myshtigo took notes.

Lorel had said, "Continue on with the tour. Damage to property has not been too severe, because the Mediterranean was mostly full of junkstuff. Personal injuries were either fatal or are already being taken of. —So continue on."

I skimmed in low over what remained of Kos—the westward tail of the island. It was a wild, volcanic country, and there were fresh craters, fuming ones, amidst the new, bright sea laces that crissed and crossed over the land. The ancient capital of Astypalaia had once stood there. Thucydides tells us it had been destroyed by a powerful earthquake. He should have seen this one. My northern city of Kos had then been inhabited from 366 B.C. Now all was gone but the wet and the hot. There were no survivors—and the plane tree of Hippocrates and the mosque of the Loggia and the castle of the Knights of Rhodes, and the fountains, and my cottage, and my wife—swept by what tides or caught in what sea-pits, I do not know—had gone the ways of dead Theocritus—he who had done his best to immortalize the place so many years before. Gone. Away. Far…Immortal and dead to me. Further east, a few peaks of that high mountain range which had interrupted the northern coastal plain were still poking themselves up out of the waters. There was the mighty peak of Dhikaios, or Christ the Just, which had overlooked the villages of the northern slopes. Now it was a tiny islet, and no one had made it up to the top in time.

"You lived there," said Myshtigo.

I nodded.

"You were born in the village of Makrynitsa, though, in the hills of Thessaly?"

"Yes."

"…But you made your home there?"

"For a little while."

" 'Home' is a universal concept," said the Vegan. "I appreciate it."

"Thanks."

I continued to stare downward, feeling sad, bad, mad, and then nothing.

❖   ❖   ❖

Athens after absence returns to me with a sudden familiarity which always refreshes, often renews, sometimes incites. Phil once read me some lines by one of the last great Greek poets, George Seferis, maintaining that he had referred to my Greece when he said, "…A country that is no longer our own country, nor yours either"—because of the Vegans. When I pointed out that there were no Vegans available during Seferis' lifetime, Phil retorted that poetry exists independent of time and space and that it means whatever it means to the reader. While I have never believed that a literary license is also good for time-travel, I had other reasons for disagreeing, for not reading it as a general statement.

It *is* our country. The Goths, the Huns, the Bulgars, the Serbs, the Franks, the Turks, and lately the Vegans have never made it go way from us. People, I have outlived. Athens and I have changed together, somewhat. Mainland Greece, though, is mainland Greece, and it does not change for me. Try talking it away, whatever you are, and my klephtes will stalk the hills, like the chthonic avengers of old. You will pass, but the hills of Greece will remain, will be unchanged, with the smell of goat thigh-bones burning, with a mingling of blood and wine, a taste of sweetened almonds, a cold wind by night, and skies as bluebright as the eyes of a god by day. Touch them, if you dare.

That is why I am refreshed whenever I return, because now that I am a man with many years behind me, I feel this way about the entire Earth. That is why I fought, and why I killed and bombed, and why I tried every legal trick in the book, too, to stop the Vegans from buying up the Earth, plot by plot, from the absentia government, there on Taler. That is why I pushed my way, under another new name, into the big civil service machine that runs this planet—and why Arts, Monuments and Archives, in particular. There, I could fight to preserve what still remained, while I waited for the next development.

The Radpol vendetta had frightened the expatriates as well as the Vegans. They did not realize that the descendants of those who had lived through the Three Days would not willingly relinquish their best areas of coastline for Vegan resorts, nor yield up their sons and daughters to work in those resorts; nor would they guide the Vegans through the ruins of their cities, indicating points of interest for their amusement. That is why the Office is mainly a foreign service post for most of its staff.

We had sent out the call of return to those descendants of the Martian and Titanian colonies, and there had been no return. They had grown soft out there, soft from leeching on a culture which had had a headstart on ours. They lost their identity. They abandoned us.

Yet, they were the Earthgov, *de jure*, legally elected by the absent majority—and maybe *de facto* too, if it ever came to that. Probably so. I hoped it wouldn't come to that.

For over half a century there had been a stalemate. No new Veggy resorts, no new Radpol violence. No Return, either. Soon there would be a new development. It was in the air—if Myshtigo was really surveying.

So I came back to Athens on a bleak day, during a cold, drizzling rainfall, an Athens rocked and rearranged by the recent upheavals of Earth, and there was a question in my head and bruises on my body, but I was refreshed. The National Museum still stood there between Tossitsa and Vasileos Irakliou, the Acropolis was even more ruined than I remembered, and the Garden Altar Inn—formerly the old

Royal Palace—there at the northwest corner of the National Gardens, across from Syndagma Square, had been shaken but was standing and open for business, despite.

We entered, and checked in.

As Commissioner of Arts, Monuments and Archives (mainly, though, I feel, because I was the only Greek in the party), I received special considerations.

I got The Suite. Number 19.

It wasn't exactly the way I'd left it. It was clean and neat.

The little metal plate on the door said:

> THIS SUITE WAS THE HEADQUARTERS OF KONSTANTIN KARAGHIOSIS DURING THE FOUNDING OF THE RADPOL AND MUCH OF THE RETURNIST REBELLION.

Inside, there was a plaque on the bedstead which read:

> KONSTANTIN KARAGHIOSIS SLEPT IN THIS BED.

In the long, narrow front room I spotted one on the far wall. It said:

> THE STAIN ON THIS WALL WAS CAUSED BY A BOTTLE OF BEVERAGE, HURLED ACROSS THE ROOM BY KONSTANTIN KARAGHIOSIS, IN CELEBRATION OF THE BOMBING OF MADAGASCAR.

Believe that, if you want to.

KONSTANTIN KARAGHIOSIS SAT IN THIS CHAIR, insisted another.

I was really afraid to go into the bathroom.

❖   ❖   ❖

Later that night, as I walked the wet and rubble-strewn pavements of my almost deserted city, my old memories and my current thoughts were like the coming together of two rivers. I'd left the others snoring inside, descended the wide stairway from the Altar, paused to read one of the inscriptions from Perikles' funeral oration—"The entire Earth is the tomb of great men"—there on the side of the Memorial to the Unknown Soldier, and I studied for a moment those great-thewed limbs of that archaic warrior, laid out with all his weapons on his funeral bed, all marble and bas-relief, yet somehow almost warm, because night becomes Athens—and then I walked on by, passing up Leoforos Amalias.

It had been a fine dinner: ouzo, giuvetsi, Kokkineli, yaourti, Metaxa, lots of dark coffee, and Phil arguing with George about evolution.

"Do you not see a convergence of life and myth, here, during the last days of life on this planet?"

"What do you mean?" asked George, polishing off a mess of nerantzi and adjusting his glasses for peering.

"I mean that as humanity rose out of darkness it brought with it legends and myths and memories of fabulous creatures. Now we are descending again into that same darkness. The Life Force grows weak and unstable, and there is a reversion to those primal forms which for so long existed only as dim racial memories—"

"Nonsense, Phil. Life Force? In what century do you make your home? You speak as though all of life were one single, sentient entity."

"It is."

"Demonstrate, please."

"You have the skeletons of three satyrs in your museum, and photographs of live ones. They live in the hills of this country.

"Centaurs, too, have been seen here—and there are vampire flowers, and horses with vestigial wings. There are sea serpents in every sea. Imported spiderbats plow our skies. There are even sworn statements by persons who have seen the Black Beast of Thessaly, an eater of men, bones and all—quite mythy—and all sorts of other legends are coming alive."

George sighed.

"What you have said so far proves nothing other than that in all of infinity there is a possibility for any sort of life form to put in an appearance, given the proper precipitating factors and a continuous congenial environment. The things you have mentioned which are native to Earth are mutations, creatures originating near various Hot Spots about the world. There is one such place up in the hills of Thessaly. If the Black Beast were to crash through that door at this moment, with a satyr mounted on its back, it would not alter my opinion, nor prove yours."

I'd looked at the door at that moment, hoping not for the Black Beast, but for some inconspicuous-looking old man who might sidle by, stumble, and pass on, or for a waiter bringing Diane an unordered drink with a note folded inside the napkin.

But none of these things happened. As I passed up Leoforos Amalias, by Hadrian's Gate, and past the Olympieion, I still did not know what the word was to be. Diane had contacted the Radpol, but there had been no response as yet. Within another thirty-six hours we would be skimming from Athens to Lamia, then onward by foot through areas of strange new trees with long, pale, red-veined leaves, hanging vines, and things that brachiate up above, and all the budding places of the strigefleur down among their roots; and then on, across sun-washed plains, up twisty goat trails, through high, rocky places, and down deep ravines, past ruined monasteries. It was a crazy notion, but Myshtigo, again, had wanted it that way. Just because I'd been born there, he thought he'd be safe. I'd tried to tell him of the wild beasts, of the cannibal Kouretes—the tribesmen who wandered there. But he wanted to be like Pausanius and see it all on foot. Okay then, I decided, if the Radpol didn't get him, then the fauna would.

But, just to be safe, I had gone to the nearest Earthgov Post Office, obtained a dueling permit, and paid my death-tax. I might as well be on the up-and-up about these things, I decided, me being a Commissioner and all.

If Hasan needed killing, I'd kill him legally.

❖   ❖   ❖

The street was deserted, and quite dark. I turned right on Leoforos into Dionysiou Areopagitou and moved on until I reached the battered fence that runs along the southern slope of the Acropolis.

I heard a footfall, way back behind me, at the corner. I stood there for half a minute, but there was only silence and very black night. Shrugging, I entered the gate and moved to the tenemos of Dionysus Eleutherios. Nothing remains of the temple itself but the foundation. I passed on, heading toward the Theater.

I moved to the proskenion. The relief sculpture-work started at the steps, telling tales from the life of Dionysus. Every tour guide and every member of a tour must, under a regulation promulgated by me (Number 237.1, if you care), "...carry no fewer than three magnesium flares on his person, while traveling." I pulled the pin from one and cast it to the ground. The dazzle would not be visible below, because of the angle of the hillside and the blocking masonry.

I did not stare into the bright flame, but above, at the silver-limned figures. There was Hermes, presenting the infant god to Zeus, while the Corybantes tripped the Pyrrhic fantastic on either side of the throne; then there was Ikarios, whom Dionysus had taught to cultivate the vine—he was preparing to sacrifice a goat, while his daughter was offering cakes to the god (who stood aside, discussing her with a satyr); and there was drunken Silenus, attempting to hold up the sky like Atlas, only not doing so well; and there were all the other gods of the cities, paying a call to this Theater—and I spotted Hestia, Theseus, and Eirene with a horn of plenty...

"You burn an offering to the gods," came a statement from nearby.

I did not turn. It had come from behind my right shoulder, but I did not turn because I knew the voice.

"Perhaps I do," I said.

"It has been a long time since you walked this land, this Greece."

"That is true."

"Is it because there has never been an immortal Penelope—patient as the mountains, trusting in the return of her kallikanzaros—weaving, patient as the hills?"

"Are you the village story-teller these days?"

He chuckled.

"I tend the many-legged sheep in the high places, where the fingers of Aurora come first to smear the sky with roses."

"Yes, you're the story-teller. Why are you not up in the high places now, corrupting youth with your song?"

"Because of dreams."

"Dreams?"

"Aye."

I turned and looked into the ancient face—its wrinkles, in the light of the dying flare, as black as fishers' nets lost at the bottom of the sea, the beard as white as the snow that comes drifting down from the mountains, the eyes matching the blue of the headcloth corded about his temples. He did not lean upon his staff any more than a warrior leans on his spear. I knew that he was over a century old, and that he had never taken the S-S series.

"There before me lay Athens," he told me. "This place, this Theater, you—and here sat the old women. The one who measures out the thread of life was pouting, for she had wrapped yours about the horizon and no ends were in sight. But the one who weaves had divided it into two very thin threads. One strand ran back across the seas and vanished again from sight. The other led up into the hills. At the first hill stood the Dead Man, who held your thread in his white, white hands. Beyond him, at the next hill, it lay across a burning rock. On the hill beyond the rock stood the Black Beast, and he shook and worried your thread with his teeth.

"And all along the length of the strand stalked a great foreign warrior, and yellow were his eyes and naked the blade in his hands, and he did raise this blade several times in menace.

"So I came down to Athens—to meet you, here, at this place—to tell you to go back across the seas—to warn you not to come up into the hills where death awaits you. For I knew that the dreams were not mine, but they were meant for you, oh my father, and that I must find you here and warn you. Go away now, while still you can. Go back. Please."

I gripped his shoulder.

"Jason, my son, I do not turn back. I take full responsibility for my own actions, right or wrong—including my own death, if need be—and I *must* go into the hills this time, up near the Hot Place. Thank you for your warning. Our family has always had this thing with dreams, and often it is misleading. I, too, have dreams—dreams in which I see through the eyes of other persons—sometimes clearly, sometimes not so clearly. Thank you for your warning. I am sorry that I must not heed it."

"Then I will return to my flock."

"Come back with me to the inn. We will fly you as far as Lamia tomorrow."

"No. I do not sleep in great buildings, nor do I fly."

"Then it's probably time you started, but I'll humor you. We can camp here tonight. I'm Commissioner of this monument."

"I had heard you were important in the Big Government again. Will there be more killing?"

"I hope not."

We found a level place and reclined upon his cloak.

"How do you interpret the dreams?" I asked him.

"Your gifts do come to us with every season, but when was the last time you yourself visited?"

"It was about nineteen years ago," I said.

"Then you do not know of the Dead Man?"

"No."

"He is bigger than most men—taller, fatter—with flesh the color of a fishbelly, and teeth like an animal's. They began telling of him about fifteen years ago. He comes out only at night. He drinks blood. He laughs a child's laugh as he goes about the countryside looking for blood—people's, animals', it does not matter. He smiles in through bedroom windows late at night. He burns churches. He curdles milk. He causes miscarriages from fright. By day, it is said that he sleeps in a coffin, guarded by the Kourete tribesmen."

"Strange things do come out of the Hot Places." I said. "*We* know that."

"...Where Prometheus spilled too much of the fire of creation."

"No, where some bastard lobbed a cobalt bomb and the bright-eyed boys and girls cried 'Eloi' to the fallout. —And what of the Black Beast?"

"The size of an elephant, and very fast—an eater of flesh, they say. He haunts the plains. Perhaps some day he and the Dead Man will meet and they will destroy one another."

"It doesn't usually work out that way, but it's a nice thought. —That's all you know about him?"

"Yes, I know of no one who has caught more than a glimpse."

"Well, I shall try for less than that."

"...And then I must tell you of Bortan."

"Bortan? That name is familiar."

"Your dog. I used to ride on his back when I was a child and beat with my legs upon his great armored sides. Then he would growl and seize my foot, but gently."

"*My* Bortan has been dead for so long that he would not even chew upon his own bones, were he to dig them up in a modern incarnation."

"I had thought so, too. But two days after you departed from your last visit, he came crashing into the hut. He apparently had followed your trail across half of Greece."

"You're sure it was Bortan?"

"Was there ever another dog the size of a small horse, with armor plates on his sides, and jaws like a trap for bears?"

"No, I don't think so. That's probably why the species died out. Dogs do need armor plating if they're going to hang around with people, and they didn't develop it fast enough. If he is still alive, he's probably the last dog on Earth. He and I were puppies together, you know, so long ago that it hurts to think about it. That day he vanished while we were hunting I thought he'd had an accident. I searched for him, then decided he was dead. He was incredibly old at the time."

"Perhaps he was injured, and wandering that way—for years. But he was himself and he followed your track, that last time. When he saw that you were gone, he howled and took off after you again. We have never seen him since then. Sometimes, though, late at night, I hear his hunting-cry in the hills…"

"The damfool mutt ought to know it's not right to care for anything that much."

"Dogs were strange."

"Yes, dogs were."

And then the night wind, cool through arches of the years, came hounding after me. It touched my eyes. Tired, they closed.

Greece is lousy with legend, fraught with menace. Most areas of mainland near the Hot Place are historically dangerous. This is because, while the Office theoretically runs the Earth, it actually only tends to the islands. Office personnel on much of the mainland are rather like twentieth-century Revenue Officers were in certain hill areas. They're fair game in all seasons. The islands sustained less damage than the rest of the world during the Three Days, and consequently they were the logical outposts for world district offices when the Talerites decided we could use some administration. Historically, the mainlanders have always been opposed to this. In the regions about the Hot Places, though, the natives are not always completely human. This compounds the historical antipathy with abnormal behavior patterns. This is why Greece is fraught.

We could have sailed up the coast to Volos. We could have skimmed to Volos—or almost anywhere else, for that matter. Myshtigo wanted to hike from Lamia, though, to hike and enjoy the refreshment of legend and alien scenery. This is why we left the Skimmers at Lamia. This is why we hiked to Volos.

This is why we encountered legend.

I bade Jason "good-bye" in Athens. He was sailing up the coast. Wise.

Phil had insisted on enduring the hike, rather than skimming ahead and meeting us up further long the line. Good thing, too, maybe, in a way, sort of…

The road to Volos wanders through the thick and the sparse in the way of vegetation. It passes huge boulders, occasional clusters of shacks, fields of poppies; it crosses small streams, winds about hills, sometimes crosses over hills, widens and narrows without apparent cause.

It was still early morning. The sky was somehow a blue mirror, because the sunlight seemed to be coming from everywhere. In places of shade some moisture still clung to the grasses and the lower leaves of the trees.

It was in an interesting glade along the road to Volos that I met a half-namesake.

The place had once been a shrine of some sort, back in the Real Old Days. I came to it quite often in my youth because I liked the quality of—I guess you'd call it "peace"—that it contained. Sometimes I'd meet the half-people or the no-people there, or dream good dreams, or find old pottery or the heads of statues, or things like that, which I could sell down in Lamia or in Athens.

There is no trail that leads to it. You just have to know where it is. I wouldn't have taken them there, except for the fact that Phil was along and I knew that he liked anything which smacks of an adytum, a sequestered significance, a sliding-panel view onto dim things past, et cetera.

There is a short, sharp drop, and down below is an egg-shaped clearing, about fifty meters long, twenty across, and the small end of the egg butting into a bitten-out place in the rock; there is a shallow cave at the extreme end, usually empty. A few half-sunken, almost square stones stand about in a seemingly random way. Wild grapevines grow around the perimeter of the place, and in the center is an enormous and ancient tree whose branches act as an umbrella over almost the entire area, keeping it dusky throughout the day. Because of this, it is hard to see into the place.

But we could see a satyr in the middle, picking his nose.

I saw George's hand go to the mercy-gun he carried. I caught his shoulder, his eyes, shook my head. He shrugged, nodded, dropped his hand.

I withdrew from my belt the shepherd's pipes I had asked Jason to give me. I motioned to the others to crouch and remain where they were. I moved a few steps further ahead and raised the syrinx to my lips.

My first notes were quite tentative. It had been too long since I'd played the pipes.

His ears pricked forward and he looked all about him. He made rapid moves in three different directions—like a startled squirrel, uncertain as to which tree to make for.

Then he stood there quivering as I caught up an old tune and nailed it to the air.

I kept playing, remembering, remembering the pipes, the tunes, and the bitter, the sweet, and the drunken things I've really always known. It all came back to me as I stood there playing for the little guy in the shaggy leggings: the fingering and the control of the air, the little runs, the thorns of sound, the things only the pipes can really say. I can't play in the cities, but suddenly I was me again, and I saw faces in the leaves and I heard the sound of hooves. I moved forward.

Like in a dream, I noticed I was standing with my back against the tree, and they were all about me. They shifted from hoof to hoof, never staying still, and I played for them as I had so often before, years ago, not knowing whether they were really the same ones who'd heard me then—or caring, actually. They cavorted about me. They laughed through white, white teeth and their eyes danced, and they circled, jabbing at the air with their horns, kicking their goat legs high off the ground, bending far forward, springing into the air, stamping the earth.

I stopped, and lowered the pipes.

It was not an human intelligence that regarded me from those wild, dark eyes, as they all froze into statues, just standing there, staring at me.

I raised the pipes once more, slowly. This time I played the last song I'd ever made. I remembered it so well. It was a dirge-like thing I had played on the night I'd decided Karaghiosis should die.

I had seen the fallacy of Return. They would not come back, would never come back. The Earth would die. I had gone down into the Gardens and played this one last tune I'd learned from the wind and maybe even the stars. When I had finished it I didn't play any more. The next day, Karaghiosis' big blazeboat broke up in the bay at Piraeus.

They seated themselves on the grass. Occasionally, one would dab at his eye with an elaborate gesture. They were all about me, listening.

How long I played, I do not know. When I had finished, I lowered the pipes and sat there. After a time, one of them reached out and touched the pipes and drew his hand back quickly. He looked up at me.

"Go," I said, but they did not seem to understand.

So I raised the syrinx and played the last few bars over again.

The Earth is dying, dying. Soon it will be dead... Go home, the party's over. It's late, it's late, so late...

The biggest one shook his head.

Go away, go away, go away now. Appreciate the silence. After life's most ridiculous gambit, appreciate the silence. What did the gods hope to gain, to gain? Nothing. 'Twas all but a game. Go away, go away, go away now. It's late, it's late, so late...

They still sat there, so I stood up and clapped my hands, yelled "Go!" and walked away quickly.

I gathered my companions and headed back for the road.

❖   ❖   ❖

It is about sixty-five kilometers from Lamia to Volos, including the detour around the Hot Spot. We covered maybe a fifth of that distance on the first day. That evening, we pitched our camp in a clearing off to the side of the road, and Diane came up beside me and said, "Well?"

" 'Well,' what?"

"I just called Athens. Blank. The Radpol is silent. I want your decision now."

"You are very determined. Why can't we wait some more?"

"We've waited too long as it is. Supposing he decides to end the tour ahead of schedule? —This countryside is perfect. So many accidents could come so easily here... You know what the Radpol will say—the same as before—and it will signify the same as before: Kill."

"My answer is also the same as before: No."

She blinked rapidly, lowered her head.

"Please reconsider."

"No."

"Then do this much," she said. "Forget it. The whole thing. Wash your hands of the affair. Take Lorel up on his offer and get us a new guide. You can skim out of here in the morning."

"No."

"Are you really serious, then—about protecting Myshtigo?"

"Yes."

"I don't want you hurt, or worse."

"I'm not particularly fond of the idea myself. So you can save us both a lot of trouble by calling it off."

"I can't do that."

"Dos Santos does as you tell him."

"The problem is *not* an administrative one! —Damn it! I wish I'd never met you!"

"I'm sorry."

"The Earth is at stake and you're on the wrong side."

"I think you are."

"What are you going to do about it?"

"I can't convince you, so I'll just have to stop you."

"You couldn't turn in the Secretary of the Radpol and his consort without evidence. We're too ticklish politically."

"I know that."

"So you couldn't hurt Don, and I don't believe you'd hurt me."

"You're right."

"That leaves Hasan."

"Right again."

"And Hasan is—Hasan. What will you do?"

"Why don't you give him his walking papers right now and save me some trouble?"

"I won't do that."

"I didn't think you would."

She looked up again. Her eyes were moist, but her face and voice were unchanged.

"If it should turn out that you were right and we were wrong," she said, "I am sorry."

"Me too," I said. "Very, very."

❖　❖　❖

That night I dozed within knifing distance of Myshtigo, but nothing happened or tried to. The following morning was uneventful, as was most of the afternoon.

"Myshtigo," I said, as soon as we paused for purposes of photographing a hillside, "why don't you go home? Go back to Taler? Go anywhere? Walk away from it? Write some other book? The further we get into civilization, the less is my power to protect you."

"You gave me an automatic, remember?" he said.

He made a shooting motion with his right hand.

If only he weren't so uncommunicative, so alien, so unconcerned about his welfare! I hated him. I couldn't understand him. He wouldn't speak, unless it was to request information or to answer a question. Whenever he did answer questions, he was terse, elusive, insulting, or all three at once. He was smug, conceited, blue, and overbearing. It really made me wonder about the Shtigo-gens' tradition of philosophy, philanthrophy and enlightened journalism. I just didn't like him.

But I spoke to Hasan that evening, after having kept an eye (the blue one) on him all day.

He was sitting beside the fire, looking like a sketch by Delacroix. Ellen and Dos Santos sat nearby, drinking coffee, so I dusted off my Arabic and approached.

"Greetings."

"Greetings."

"You did not try to kill me today."

"No."

"Tomorrow, perhaps?"

He shrugged.

"Hasan—look at me."

He did.

"You were hired to kill the blue one."

He shrugged again.

"You needn't deny it, or admit it. I already know. I cannot allow you to do this thing. Give back the money Dos Santos has paid you and go your way. I can get you a Skimmer by morning. It will take you anywhere in the world you wish to go."

"But I am happy here, Karagee."

"You will quickly cease being happy if any harm comes to the blue one."

"I am a bodyguard, Karagee."

"No, Hasan. You are the son of a dyspeptic camel."

"What is 'dyspeptic,' Karagee?"

"I do not know the Arabic word, and you would not know the Greek one. Wait, I'll find another insult. —You are a coward and a carrion-eater and a skulker up alleyways, because you are half jackal and half ape."

"This may be true, Karagee, because my father told me that I was born to be flayed alive and torn into quarters."

"Hasan, it is difficult to insult you properly," I said. "But I warn you—the blue one must not be harmed."

"I am but a humble bodyguard."

"Ha! Yours is the cunning and the venom of the serpent. You are deceitful and treacherous. Vicious, too."

"No, Karagee. Thank you, but it is not true. I take pride in always meeting my commitments. That is all. This is the law I live by. Also, you cannot insult me so that I will challenge you to a duel, permitting you to choose bare hands or daggers or sabers. No. I take no offense."

"Then beware," I told him. "Your first move toward the Vegan will be your last."

"If it is so written, Karagee…"

"And call me Conrad!"

I stalked away, thinking bad thoughts.

❖   ❖   ❖

We made well over a dozen kilometers that day, which was pretty good, considering. And it was that evening that it happened.

We reclined about a fire. Oh, it was a jolly fire, flapping its bright wing against the night, warming us, smelling woody, pushing a smoke-stack into the air…Nice.

Hasan sat there cleaning his aluminum-barreled shotgun. It had a plastic stock and it was real light and handy.

As he worked on it, it tilted forward, moved slowly about, pointed itself right at Myshtigo.

He'd done it quite neatly, I must admit that. It was during a period of over half an hour, and he'd advanced the barrel with almost imperceptible movements.

I snarled, though, when its position registered in my cerebrum, and I was at his side in three steps.

I struck it from his hands.

It clattered on some small stone about eight feet away. My hand was stinging from the slap I'd given it.

Hasan was on his feet, his teeth shuttling around inside his beard, clicking together like flint and steel. I could almost see the sparks.

"Say it!" I said. "Go ahead, say something! Anything! You know damn well what you were just doing!"

His hands twitched.

"Go ahead!" I said. "Hit me! Just touch me, even. Then what I do to you will be self-defense, provoked assault. Even George won't be able to put you back together again."

"I was only cleaning my shotgun. You've damaged it."

"*You* do not point weapons by accident. You were going to kill Myshtigo."

"You are mistaken."

"Hit me. Or are you a coward?"

"I have no quarrel with you."

"You *are* a coward."

"No, I am not."

After a few seconds he smiled.

"Are you afraid to challenge *me*?" he asked.

And there it was. The only way.

The move had to be mine. I had hoped it wouldn't have to be that way. I had hoped that I could anger him or shame him or provoke him into striking me or challenging me.

I knew then that I couldn't.

Which was bad, very bad.

I was sure I could take him with anything I cared to name. But if he had it his way, things could be different. Everybody knows that there are some people with an aptitude for music. They can hear a piece once and sit down and play it on the piano or thelinstra. They can pick up a new instrument, and inside a few hours they can sound as if they've been playing it for years. They're good, very good at such things, because they have that talent—the ability to coordinate a special insight with a series of new actions.

Hasan was that way with weapons. Maybe some other people could be the same, but they don't go around doing it—not for decades and decades, anyway, with everything from boomerangs to blowguns. The dueling code would provide Hasan with the choice of means, and he was the most highly skilled killer I'd known.

But I had to stop him, and I could see that this was the only way it could be done, short of murder. I had to take him on his terms.

"Amen," I said. "I challenge you to a duel."

His smile remained, grew.

"Agreed—before these witnesses. Name your second."

"Phil Graber. Name yours."

"Mister Dos Santos."

"Very good. I happen to have a dueling permit and the registration forms in my bag, and I've already paid the death-tax for one person. So there needn't be much of a delay. When, where, and how do you want it?"

"We passed a good clearing about a kilometer back up the road."

"Yes, I recall it."

"We shall meet there at dawn tomorrow."

"Check. And as to weapons…?"

He fetched his knapcase, opened it. It bristled with interesting sharp things, glistened with ovoid incendiaries, writhed with coils of metal and leather.

He withdrew two items and closed the pack.

My heart sank.

"The sling of David," he announced.

I inspected them.

"At what distance?"

"Fifty meters," he said.

"You've made a good choice," I told him, not having used one in over a century myself. "I'd like to borrow one tonight, to practice with. If you don't want to lend it to me, I can make my own."

"You may take either, and practice all night with it."

"Thanks." I selected one and hung it from my belt. Then I picked up one of our three electric lanterns. "If anybody needs me, I'll be up the road at the clearing," I said. "Don't forget to post guards tonight. This is a rough area."

"Do you want me to come along?" asked Phil.

"No. Thanks anyway. I'll go alone. See you."

"Then good night."

I hiked back along the way, coming at last to the clearing. I set up the lantern at one end of the place, so that it reflected upon a stand of small trees, and I moved to the other end.

I collected some stones and slung one at a tree. I missed.

I slung a dozen more, hitting with four of them.

I kept at it. After about an hour, I was hitting with a little more regularity. Still, at fifty meters I probably couldn't match Hasan.

The night wore on, and I kept slinging. After a time, I reached what seemed to be my learning plateau, accuracy-wise. Maybe six out of eleven of my shots were coming through.

I had one thing in my favor though, I realized, as I twirled the sling and sent another stone smashing into a tree. I delivered my shots with an awful lot of force. Whenever I was on target there was much power behind the strike. I had already shattered several of the smaller trees, and I was sure Hasan couldn't do that with twice as many hits. If I could reach him, fine; but all the power in the world was worthless if I couldn't connect with it.

And I was sure he could reach me. I wondered how much of a beating I could take and still operate.

It would depend, of course, on where he hit me.

I dropped the sling and yanked the automatic gun from my belt when I heard a branch snap, far off to my right. Hasan came into the clearing.

"What do you want?" I asked him.

"I came to see how your practice was going," he said, regarding the broken trees.

I shrugged, reholstered my automatic and picked up the sling.

"Comes the sunrise and you will learn."

We walked across the clearing and I retrieved the lantern. Hasan studied a small tree which was now, in part, toothpicks. He did not say anything.

We walked back to the camp. Everyone but Dos Santos had turned in. Don was our guard. He paced about the warning perimeter, carrying an automatic rifle. He waved to him and entered the camp.

Hasan always pitched a Gauzy—a one-molecule-layer tent, opaque, feather-light, and very tough. He never slept in it, though. He just used it to stash his junk.

I seated myself on a log before the fire and Hasan ducked inside his Gauzy. He emerged a moment later with his pipe and a block of hardened, resinous-looking stuff, which he proceeded to scale and grind. He mixed it with a bit of burley and then filled the pipe.

After he got it going with a stick from the fire, he sat smoking it beside me.

"I do not want to kill you, Karagee," he said.

"I share this feeling. I do not wish to be killed."

"But we must fight tomorrow."

"Yes."

"You could withdraw your challenge."

"You could leave by Skimmer."

"I will not."

"Nor will I withdraw my challenge."

"It is sad," he said, after a time. "Sad, that two such as we must fight over the blue one. He is not worth your life, or mine."

"True," I said, "but it involves more than just his life. The future of this planet is somehow tied up with whatever he is doing."

"I do not know of these things, Karagee. I fight for money. I have no other trade."

"Yes, I know."

The fire burnt low. I fed it more sticks.

"Do you remember the time we bombed the Coast of Gold, in France?" he asked.

"I remember."

"Besides the blue ones, we killed many people."

"Yes."

"The future of the planet was not changed by this, Karagee. For here we are, many years away from the thing, and nothing is different."

"I know that."

"And do you remember the days when we crouched in a hole on a hillside, overlooking the bay at Piraeus? Sometimes you would feed me the belts and I would strafe the blazeboats, and when I grew tired you would operate the gun. We had much ammunition. The Office Guard did not land that day, nor the next. They did not occupy Athens, they did not break the Radpol. And we talked as we sat there, those two days and that night, waiting for the fireball to come—and you told me of the Powers in the Sky."

"I forget…"

"I do not. You told me that there are men, like us, who live up in the air by the stars. Also, there are the blue ones. Some of the men, you said, seek the blue ones' favor, and they would sell the Earth to them to be made into a museum. Others, you said, did not want to do this thing, but they wanted it to remain as it is now—their property, run by the Office. The blue ones were divided among themselves on this matter, because there was a question as to whether it was legal and ethical to do this thing. There was a compromise, and the blue ones were sold some clean areas, which they used as resorts, and from which they toured the rest of the Earth. But you wanted the Earth to belong only to people. You said that if we gave the blue ones an inch, then they would want it all. You wanted the men by the stars to come back and rebuild the cities, bury the Hot Places, kill the beasts which prey upon men.

"As we sat there, waiting for the fireball, you said that we were at war, not because of anything we could see or hear or feel or taste, but because of the Powers in the Sky, who had never seen us, and whom we would never see. The Powers in the Sky had done this thing, and because of it men had to die here on Earth. You said that by the death of men and blue ones, the Powers might return to Earth. They never did, though. There was only the death.

"And it was the Powers in the Sky which saved us in the end, because they had to be consulted before the fireball could be burnt over Athens. They reminded the Office of an old law, made after the time of the Three Days, saying that the fireball would never again burn in the skies of Earth. You had thought that they would burn it anyhow, but they did not. It was because of this that we stopped them at Piraeus. I burnt Madagaskee for you, Karagee, but the Powers never came down to Earth. And when people get much money they go away from here—and they never come back from the sky. Nothing we did in those days has caused a change."

"Because of what we did, things remained as they were, rather than getting worse," I told him.

"What will happen if this blue one dies?"

"I do not know. Things may worsen then. If he is viewing the areas we pass through as possible real estate tracts, to be purchased by Vegans, then it is the old thing all over again."

"And the Radpol will fight again, will bomb them?"

"I think so."

"Then let us kill him now, before he goes further, sees more."

"It may not be that simple—and they would only send another. There would also be repercussions—perhaps mass arrests of Radpol members. The Radpol is no longer living on the edge of life as it was in those days. The people are unready. They need time to prepare. This blue one, at least, I hold in my hand. I can watch him, learn of his plans. Then, if it becomes necessary, I can destroy him myself."

He drew on his pipe. I sniffed. It was something like sandalwood that I smelled.

"What are you smoking?"

"It comes from near my home. I visited there recently. It is one of the new plants which has never grown there before. Try it."

I took several mouthfuls into my lungs. At first there was nothing. I continued to draw on it, and after a minute there was a gradual feeling of coolness and tranquility which spread down through my limbs. It tasted bitter, but it relaxed. I handed it back. The feeling continued, grew stronger. It was very pleasant. I had not felt that sedate, that relaxed, for many weeks. The fire, the shadows, and the ground about us suddenly became more real, and the night air and the distant moon and the sound of Dos Santos' footsteps came somehow more clearly than life, really. The struggle seemed ridiculous. We would lose it in the end. It was written that humanity was to be the cats and the dogs and trained chimpanzees of the real people, the Vegans—and in a way it was not such a bad idea. Perhaps we needed someone wiser to watch over us, to run our lives. We had made a shambles of our own world during the Three Days, and the Vegans had never had a nuclear war. They operated a smoothly efficient interstellar government, encompassing dozens of planets. Whatever they did was esthetically pleasing. Their own lives were well-regulated, happy things. Why not let them have the Earth? They'd probably do a better job with it than we'd ever done. And why not be their coolies, too? It wouldn't be a bad life. Give them the old ball of mud, full of radioactive sores and populated by cripples.

Why not?

I accepted the pipe once more, inhaled more peace. It was so pleasant not to think of these things at all, though. Not to think of anything you couldn't really do anything about. Just to sit there and breathe in the night and be one with the fire and the wind was enough. The universe was singing its hymn of oneness. Why open the bag of chaos there in the cathedral?

But I had lost my Cassandra, my dark witch of Kos, to the mindless powers which move the Earth and the waters. Nothing could kill my feelings of loss. It seemed further away, somehow insulated behind glass, but it was still there. Not all the pipes of the East could assuage this thing. I did not want to know peace. I wanted hate. I wanted to strike out at all the masks in the universe—earth, water, sky, Taler, Earthgov, and Office—so that behind one of them I might find that power which had taken her, and make it too, know something of pain. I did not want to know peace. I did not want to be at one with anything which had harmed that which was mine, by blood and by love. For just five minutes even, I wanted to be Karaghiosis again, looking at it all through crosshairs and squeezing a trigger.

Oh, Zeus, of the hot red lightnings, I prayed, *give it to me that I may break the Powers in the Sky!*

I returned to the pipe again.

"Thank you, Hasan, but I'm not ready for the Bo Tree."

I stood then and moved off toward the place where I had cast my pack.

"I am sorry that I must kill you in the morning," he called after me.

❖   ❖   ❖

The world outside us was bright and clear and clean and filled with the singing of birds, and there were no expressions on every face that morning.

I had forbidden the use of the radio until after the duel, and Phil carried some of its essential entrails in his jacket pocket, just to be sure.

Lorel would not know. The Radpol would not know. Nobody would know, until after.

The preliminaries completed, the distance was measured off.

We took our places at the opposite ends of the clearing. The rising sun was to my left.

"Are you ready, gentlemen?" called out Dos Santos.

"Yes," and "I am," were the replies.

"I make a final attempt to dissuade you from this course of action. Do either of you wish to reconsider?"

"No," and "No."

"Each of you has ten stones in similar size and weight. The first shot is, of course, given to he who was challenged: Hasan."

We both nodded.

"Proceed, then."

He stepped back and there was nothing but fifty meters of air separating us. We both stood sideways, so as to present the smallest target possible. Hasan fitted his first stone to the sling.

I watched him wind it rapidly through the air behind him, and suddenly his arm came forward.

There was a crashing sound in back of me.

Nothing else happened.

He'd missed.

I put a stone to my own sling then and whipped it back and around. The air sighed as I cut it all apart.

Then I hurled the missile forward with all the strength of my right arm.

It grazed his left shoulder, barely touching it. It was mostly garment that it plowed.

The stone ricocheted from tree to tree behind him, before it finally vanished.

All was still then. The birds had given up on their morning concert.

"Gentlemen," called Dos Santos, "you have each had one chance to settle your differences. It may be said that you have faced one another with honor, given vent to your wrath, and are now satisfied. Do you wish to stop the duel?"

"No," said I.

Hasan rubbed his shoulder, shook his head.

He put the second stone to his sling, worked it rapidly through a powerful windup, then released it at me.

Right between the hip and the ribcage, that's where it caught me.

I fell to the ground and it all turned black.

A second later the lights came on again, but I was doubled up and something with a thousand teeth had me by the side and wouldn't let go.

They were running toward me, all of them, but Phil waved them back.

Hasan held his position.

Dos Santos approached.

"Is that it?" asked Phil softly. "Can you get up?"

"Yeah. I need a minute to breathe and to put the fire out, but I'll get up."

"What is the situation?" asked Dos Santos.

Phil told him.

I put my hand to my side and stood again, slowly.

A couple inches higher or lower and something boney might have broken. As it was, it just hurt like blazes.

I rubbed it, moved my right arm through a few circles to test the play of muscles on that side.

Then I picked up the sling and put a stone to it.

This time it would connect. I had a feeling.

It went around and around and it came out fast.

Hasan toppled, clutching at his left thigh.

Dos Santos went to him. They spoke.

Hasan's robe had muffled the blow, had partly deflected it. The leg was not broken. He would continue as soon as he could stand.

He spent five minutes massaging it, then he got to his feet again. During that time my pain had subsided to a dull throbbing.

Hasan selected his third stone.

He fitted it slowly, carefully…

He took my measure. Then he began to lash at the air with the sling…

All this while I had the feeling—and it kept growing—that I should be leaning a little further to the right. So I did.

He twirled it, threw it.

It grazed my fungus and tore at my left ear.

Suddenly my cheek was wet.

Ellen screamed, briefly.

A little further to the right, though, and I wouldn't have been hearing her.

It was my turn again.

Smooth, gray, the stone had the feel of death about it…

I will be it, this one seemed to say.

It was one of those little premonitory tuggings at my sleeve, of the sort for which I have a great deal of respect.

I wiped the blood from my cheek. I fitted the stone.

There was death riding in my right arm as I raised it. Hasan felt it too, because he flinched. I could see this from across the field.

"You will all remain exactly where you are, and drop your weapons," said the voice.

It said it in Greek, so no one but Phil and Hasan and I understood it, for sure. Maybe Dos Santos or Red Wig did. I'm still not certain.

But all of us understood the automatic rifle the man carried, and the swords and clubs and knives of the three dozen or so men and half-men standing behind him.

They were Kouretes.

Kouretes are bad.

They always get their pound of flesh.

Usually roasted.

The speaker seemed to be the only one carrying a firearm… And I had a handful of death circling high above my shoulder. I decided to make him a gift of it.

His head exploded as I delivered it.

"Kill them!" I said, and we began to do so.

George and Diane were the first to open fire. Then Phil found a handgun. Dos Santos ran for his pack. Ellen got there fast, too.

Hasan had not needed my order to begin killing. The only weapons he and I were carrying were the slings. The Kouretes were closer than our fifty meters, though, and theirs was a mob formation. He dropped two of them with well-placed stones before they began their rush. I got one more, also.

Then they were halfway across the field, leaping over their dead and their fallen, screaming as they came on toward us.

Like I said, they were not all of them human: there was a tall, thin one with three-foot wings covered with sores, and there were a couple microcephalics with enough hair so that they looked headless, and there was one guy who should probably have been twins, and then several steatopygics, and three huge, hulking brutes who kept coming despite bullet-holes in their chests and abdomens; one of these latter had hands which must have been twenty inches long and a foot across, and another appeared to be afflicted with something like elephantiasis. Of the rest, some were reasonably normal in form, but they all looked mean and mangy and either wore rags or no rags at all and were unshaven and smelled bad, too.

I hurled one more stone and didn't get a chance to see where it hit, because they were upon me then.

I began lashing out—feet, fists, elbows; I wasn't too polite about it. The gunfire slowed down, stopped. You have to stop to reload sometime, and there'd been some jamming, too. The pain in my side was a very bad thing. Still, I managed to drop three of them before something big and blunt caught me on the side of the head and I fell as a dead man falls.

❖   ❖   ❖

Coming to in a stiflingly hot place…

Coming to in a stiflingly hot place that smells like a stable…

Coming to in a dark, stiflingly hot place that smells like a stable…

…This is not real conducive to peace of mind, a settled stomach, or the resumption of sensory activities on a sure and normal keel.

It stank in there and it was damn hot, and I didn't really want to inspect the filthy floor too closely—it was just that I was in a very good position to do so.

I moaned, numbered all my bones, and sat me up.

The ceiling was low and it slanted down even lower before it met with the back wall. The one window to the outside was small and barred.

We were in the back part of a wooden shack. There was another barred window in the opposite wall. It didn't look out on anything, though; it looked in. There was a larger room beyond it, and George and Dos Santos were talking through it with someone who stood on that other side. Hasan lay unconscious or dead about four feet away from me; there was dried blood on his head. Phil and Myshtigo and the girls were talking softly in the far corner.

I rubbed my temple while all this was registering within. My left side ached steadily, and numerous other portions of my anatomy had decided to join in the game—if each of them had glowed with a different color, I'd have looked like a Yule tree.

"He's awake," said Myshtigo.

"Hi, everybody. I'm back again," I agreed.

They came toward me and I assumed a standing position. This was sheer bravado, but I managed to carry it.

"We are prisoners," said Myshtigo.

"Oh, yeah? Really? I'd never have guessed."

"Things like this do not happen on Taler," he observed, "or on any of the worlds in the Vegan Combine."

"Too bad you didn't stay there," I said. "Don't forget the number of times I asked you to go back."

"This thing would not have occurred if it had not been for your duel."

I slapped him then. I couldn't bring myself to slug him. He was just too pathetic. I hit him with the back of my hand and knocked him over into the wall.

"Are you trying to tell me you don't know why I stood there like a target this morning?"

"Because of your quarrel with my bodyguard," he stated, rubbing his cheek.

"—Over whether or not he was going to kill you."

"Me? Kill...?"

"Forget it," I said.

"We are going to die here, aren't we?" he asked.

"That is the custom of the country."

I turned away and studied the man who was studying me from the other side of the bars. Hasan was leaning against the far wall then, holding his head. I hadn't noticed his getting up.

"Good afternoon," said the man behind the bars, and he said it in English.

"*Is* it afternoon?" I asked.

"Quite," he replied.

"Why aren't we dead?" I asked him.

"Because I wanted you alive," he stated. "Oh, not you personally—Conrad Nomikos, Commissioner of Arts, Monuments and Archives—and all your distinguished friends, including the poet laureate. I wanted any prisoners whom they came upon brought back alive. Your identities are, shall we say, condiments."

"To whom do I have the pleasure of speaking?" I asked.

"This is Doctor Moreby," said George.

"He is their witch doctor," said Dos Santos.

"I prefer 'Shaman' or 'Medicine Chief,'" corrected Moreby, smiling.

I moved closer to the grillwork and saw that he was rather thin, well-tanned, clean-shaven, and had all his hair woven into one enormous black braid which was coiled like a cobra about his head. He had close-set eyes, dark ones, a high forehead, and lots of extra jaw reaching down past his Adam's Apple. He wore woven sandals, a clean green sari, and a necklace of human fingerbones. In his ears were big snake-shaped circlets of silver.

"Your English is rather precise," said I, "and 'Moreby' is not a Greek name."

"Oh goodness!" He gestured gracefully, in mock surprise. "I'm not a local! How could you ever mistake me for a local?"

"Sorry," I said, "I can see now that you're too well-dressed."

He giggled.

"Oh, *this* old rag… I just threw it on. —No, I'm from Taler. I read some wonderfully rousing literature on the subject of Returnism, and I decided to come back and help rebuild the Earth."

"Oh? What happened then?"

"The Office was not hiring at the time, and I experienced some difficulty in finding employment locally. So I decided to engage in research work. This place is full of opportunities for that."

"What sort of research?"

"I hold two graduate degrees in cultural anthropology, from New Harvard. I decided to study a Hot tribe in depth—and after some blandishments I got this one to accept me. I started out to educate them, too. Soon, though, they were deferring to me, all over the place. Wonderful for the ego. After a time, my studies, my social work, came to be of less and less importance. Well, I daresay you've read *Heart of Darkness*—you know what I mean. The local practices are so—well, basic. I found it much more stimulating to participate than to observe. I took it upon myself to redesign some of their grosser practices along more esthetic lines. So I did really educate them, after all. They do things with ever so much style since I've come here."

"*Things?* Such as?"

"Well, for one thing, they were simple cannibals before. For another, they were rather unsophisticated in their use of their captives prior to slaying them. Things like that are quite important. If they're done properly they give you class, if you know what I mean. Here I was with a wealth of customs, superstitions, taboos—from many cultures, many eras—right here, at my fingertips." He gestured again. "Man—even half-man, Hot man—is a ritual-loving creature, and I knew ever so many rituals and things like that. So I put all of this to good use and now I occupy a position of great honor."

"What are you trying to tell me about *us?*" I asked.

"Things were getting rather dull around here," he said, "and the natives were waxing restless. So I decided it was time for another ceremony. I spoke with Procrustes, the War Chief, and suggested he find us some prisoners. I believe it is on page 577 of the abridged edition of *The Golden Bough* that it states, 'The Tolalaki, notorious head-hunters of Central Celebes, drink the blood and eat the brains of their victims that they may become brave. The Italones of the Philippine Islands drink the blood of their slain enemies, and eat part of the back of their heads and their entrails raw to acquire their courage.' —Well, we have the tongue of a poet, the blood of two very formidable warriors, the brains of a very distinguished scientist, the bilious liver of a fiery politician, and the interesting-colored flesh of a Vegan—all in this one room here. Quite a haul, I should say."

"You make yourself exceedingly clear," I observed. "What of the women?"

"Oh, for them we'll work out a protracted fertility rite ending in a protracted sacrifice."

"I see."

"…That is to say, if we do not permit all of you to continue on your way, unmolested."

"Oh?"

"Yes. Procrustes likes to give people a chance to measure themselves against a standard, to be tested, and possibly to redeem themselves. He is most Christian in this respect."

"And true to his name, I suppose?"

Hasan came over and stood beside me, stared out through the grillwork at Moreby.

"Oh, good, good," said Moreby. "Really, I'd like to keep you around awhile, you know? You have a sense of humor. Most of the Kouretes lack this adjunct to what are otherwise exemplary personalities. I could learn to like you…"

"Don't bother. Tell me about the way of redemption, though."

"Yes. We are the wardens of the Dead Man. He is my most interesting creation. I am certain that one of you two shall realize this during your brief acquaintanceship with him." He glanced from me to Hasan to me to Hasan.

"I know of him" I said. "Tell me what must be done."

"You are called upon to bring forth a champion to do battle with him, this night, when he rises again from the dead."

"What is he?"

"A vampire."

"Crap. What is he really?"

"He is a genuine vampire. You'll see."

"Okay, have it your way. He's a vampire, and one of us will fight him. How?"

"Catch-as-catch-can, bare-handed—and he isn't very difficult to catch. He'll just stand there and wait for you. He'll be very thirsty, and hungry too, poor fellow."

"And if he is beaten, do your prisoners go free?"

"That is the rule, as I originally outlined it some sixteen or seventeen years ago. Of course, this contingency has never arisen…"

"I see. You're trying to tell me he's tough."

"Oh, he's unbeatable. That's the fun of it. It wouldn't make for a good ceremony if it could end any other way. I tell the whole story of the battle before it takes place, and then my people witness it. It reaffirms their faith in destiny and my own close association with its workings."

He yawned, covering his mouth with a feathered wand.

"I must go to the barbecue area now, to supervise the decking of the hall with boughs of holly. Decide upon your champion this afternoon, and I'll see you all this evening. Good day."

"Trip and break your neck."

He smiled and left the shack.

❖ ❖ ❖

I called a meeting.

"Okay," I said, "they've got a weird Hot One called the Dead Man, who is supposed to be very tough. I am going to fight him tonight. If I can beat him we are supposed to go free, but I wouldn't take Moreby's word for anything. Therefore, we must plan an escape, else we will be served up on a chafing dish.

"Phil, do you remember the road to Volos?" I asked.

"I think so. It's been a long time… But where are we now, exactly?"

"If it is of any help," answered Myshtigo, from beside the window, "I see a glowing. It is not any color for which there is a word in your language, but it is off in that direction." He pointed. "It is a color which I normally see in the vicinity of radioactive materials if the atmosphere is dense enough about them. It is spread over quite a large area."

I moved to the window and stared in that direction.

"That could be the Hot Spot, then," I said. "If that is the case, then they've actually brought us further along toward the coast, which is good. Was anyone conscious when we were brought here?"

No one answered.

"All right. Then we'll operate under the assumption that that *is* the Hot Spot, and that we are very close to it. The road to Volos should be back that way, then." I pointed in the opposite direction. "Since the sun is on this side of the shack and it's afternoon, head in the other direction after you hit the road—away from the sunset. It might not be more than twenty-five kilometers."

"They will track us," said Dos Santos.

"There are horses," said Hasan.

"What?"

"Up the street, in a paddock. There were three near that rail earlier. They are back behind the edge of the building now. There may be more. They were not strong-looking horses, though."

"Can all of you ride?" I asked.

"I have never ridden a horse," said Myshtigo, "but the *thrid* is something similar. I have ridden *thrid*."

Everyone else had ridden horses.

"Tonight then," said I, "Ride double if you must. If there are more than enough horses, then turn the others loose, drive them away. As they watch me fight the Dead Man you will make a break for the paddock. Seize what weapons you can and try to fight your way to the horses.

"—Phil, get them up to Makrynitsa and mention the name of Korones anywhere. They will take you in and protect you."

"I am sorry," said Dos Santos, "but your plan is not a good one."

"If you've got a better one, let's hear it," I told him.

"First of all," he said, "we cannot really rely on Mister Graber. While you were still unconscious he was in great pain and very weak. George believes that he suffered a heart attack during or shortly after our fight with the Kouretes. If anything happens to him we are lost. We will need you to guide us out of here, if we do succeed in breaking free. We *cannot* count on Mister Graber.

"Second," he said, "you are not the only man capable of fighting an exotic menace. Hasan will undertake the defeat of the Dead Man."

"I can't ask him to do that," I said. "Even if he wins, he will probably be separated from us at the time, and they'll doubtless get to him pretty fast. It would most likely mean his life. You hired him to kill for you, not to die."

"I will fight him, Karagee," he said.

"You don't have to."

"I will kill the Dead Man," said Hasan, "and I will follow after you. I know the ways of hiding myself from men. I will follow your trail."

"It's my job," I told him.

"Then, since we cannot agree, leave the decision to the fates," said Hasan. "Toss a coin."

"Very well. Did they take our money as well as our weapons?"

"I have some change," said Ellen.

"Toss a piece into the air."

She did.

"Heads," said I, as it fell toward the floor.

"Tails," she replied.

"Don't touch it!"

It was tails, all right. And there was a head on the other side, too.

"Okay, Hasan, you lucky fellow, you," I said. "You just won a do-it-yourself Hero Kit, complete with a monster. Good luck."

He shrugged.

"It was written."

He sat down then, his back against the wall, extracted a tiny knife from the sole of his left sandal, and began to pare his fingernails. He'd always been a pretty well-groomed killer. I guess cleanliness is next to diablerie, or something like that...

As the sun sank slowly in the west, Moreby came to us again, bringing with him a contingent of Kourete swordsmen.

"The time has come," he stated. "Have you decided upon your champion?"

"Hasan will fight him," I said.

"Very good. Then come along. Please do not try anything foolish. I should hate to deliver damaged goods at a festival."

Walking within a circle of blades, we left the shack and moved up the street to the village, passing by the paddock. Eight horses, heads low, stood within. Even in the diminishing light I could see that they were not very good horses. Their flanks were all covered with sores, and they were quite thin. Everyone glanced at them as we went by.

The village consisted of about thirty shacks, such as the one in which we had been confined. It was a dirt road that we walked on, and it was full of ruts and rubbish. The whole place smelled of sweat and urine and rotten fruit and smoke.

We went about eighty meters and turned left. It was the end of the street, and we moved along a downhill path into a big, cleared compound. A fat, bald-headed woman with enormous breasts and a face that was a lava field of carcinoma was tending a low and dreadfully suggestive fire at the bottom of a huge barbecue pit. She smiled as we passed by and smacked her lips moistly.

Great, sharpened stakes lay on the ground about her...

Up further ahead was a level area of hardpacked bare earth. A huge, vine-infested, tropic-type tree which had adapted itself to our climate stood at the one end of the field, and all about the field's peripheries were rows of eight-foot torches, already waving great lengths of fire like pennants. At the other end was the most elaborate shack of them all. It was about five meters high and ten across the front. It was painted bright red and covered all over with Pennsylvania hex signs. The entire middle section of the front wall was a high, sliding door. Two armed Kouretes stood guard before that door.

The sun was a tiny piece of orange-rind in the west. Moreby marched us the length of the field toward the tree.

Eighty to a hundred spectators were seated on the ground on the other side of the torches, on each side of the field.

Moreby gestured, indicating the red shack.

"How do you like my home?" he asked.

"Lovely," said I.

"I have a roommate, but he sleeps during the day. You're about to meet him."

We reached the base of the big tree. Moreby left us there, surrounded by his guards. He moved to the center of the field and began addressing the Kouretes in Greek.

We had agreed that we would wait until the fight was near its end, whichever way, and the tribesmen all excited and concentrating on the finale, before we made our break. We'd pushed the women into the center of our group, and I managed to get on the left side of a right-handed swordsman, whom I intended to kill quickly. Too bad that we were at the far end of the field. To get to the horses we'd have to fight our way back through the barbecue area.

"...And then, on that night," Moreby was saying, "did the Dead Man rise up, smiting down this mighty warrior, Hasan, breaking his bones and casting him about this place of feasting. Finally, did he kill this great enemy and drink the blood from his throat and eat of his liver, raw and still smoking in the night air. These things did he do on that night. Mighty is his power."

"Mighty, oh mighty!" cried the crowd, and someone began beating upon a drum.

"Now will we call him to life again…"

The crowd cheered.

"To life again!"

"To life again."

"Hail!"

"Hail!"

"Sharp white teeth…"

"Sharp white teeth!"

"White, white skin…"

"White, white skin!"
"Hands which break…"
"Hands which break!"
"Mouth which drinks…"
"Mouth which drinks!"
"The blood of life!"
"The blood of life!"
"Great is our tribe!"
"Great is our tribe!"
"Great is the Dead Man!"
"GREAT IS THE DEAD MAN!"

They bellowed it, at the last. Throats human, half-human, and inhuman heaved the brief litany like a tidal wave across the field. Our guards, too, were screaming it. Myshtigo was blocking his sensitive ears and there was an expression of agony on his face. My head was ringing too. Dos Santos crossed himself and one of the guards shook his head at him and raised his blade meaningfully. Don shrugged and turned his head back toward the field.

Moreby walked up to the shack and struck three times upon the sliding door with his hand.

One of the guards pushed it open for him.

An immense black catafalque, surrounded by the skulls of men and animals, was set within. It supported an enormous casket made of dark wood and decorated with bright, twisting lines.

At Moreby's directions, the guards raised the lid.

For the next twenty minutes he gave hypodermic injections to something within the casket. He kept his movements slow and ritualistic. One of the guards put aside his blade and assisted him. The drummers kept up a steady, slow cadence. The crowd was very silent, very still.

Then Moreby turned.

"Now the Dead Man rises," he announced.

"…Rises," responded the crowd.

"Now he comes forth to accept the sacrifice."

"Now he comes forth…"

"Come forth, Dead Man," he called, turning back to the catafalque.

And he did.

At great length.

For he was big.

Huge, obese.

Great indeed was the Dead Man.

Maybe 350 pounds' worth.

He sat up in his casket and he looked all about him. He rubbed his chest, his armpits, his neck, his groin. He climbed out of the big box and stood beside the catafalque, dwarfing Moreby.

He was wearing only a loincloth and large, goatskin sandals.

His skin was white, dead white, fishbelly white, moon white… Dead white.

"An albino," said George, and his voice carried the length of the field, because it was the only sound in the night.

Moreby glanced in our direction and smiled. He took the Dead Man's stubby-fingered hand and led him out of the shack and onto the field. The Dead Man shied away from the torchlight. As he advanced, I studied the expression on his face.

"There is no intelligence in that face," said Red Wig.

"Can you see his eyes?" asked George, squinting. His glasses had been broken in the fray.

"Yes; they're pinkish."

"Does he have epicanthal folds?"

"Mm…Yeah."

"Uh-huh. He's a Mongoloid—an idiot, I'll wager—which is why it was so easy for Moreby to do what he's done with him. And look at his teeth! They look filed."

I did. He was grinning, because he'd seen the colorful top of Red Wig's head. Lots of nice, sharp teeth were exposed.

"His albinism is the reason behind the nocturnal habits Moreby has imposed. Look! He even flinches at the torchlight! He's ultrasensitive of any sort of actinics."

"What about his dietary habits?"

"Acquired, through imposition. Lots of primitive people bled their cattle. The Kazaks did it until the twentieth century, and the Todas. You saw the sores on those horses as we passed by the paddock. Blood *is* nourishing, you know, if you can learn to keep it down—and I'm sure Moreby has regulated the idiot's diet since he was a child. So of course he's a vampire—he was brought up that way."

"The Dead Man is risen," said Moreby.

"The Dead Man is risen," agreed the crowd.

"Great is the Dead Man!"

"Great is the Dead Man!"

He dropped the dead-white hand then and walked toward us, leaving the only genuine vampire we knew of grinning in the middle of the field.

"Great is the Dead Man," he said, grinning himself as he approached us. "Rather magnificent, isn't he?"

"What have you done to that poor creature?" asked Red Wig.

"Very little," replied Moreby, "He was born pretty well-equipped."

"What were those injections you gave him?" inquired George.

"Oh, I shoot his pain centers full of Novocain before encounters such as this one. His lack of pain responses adds to the image of his invincibility. Also, I've given him a hormone shot. He's been putting on weight recently, and he's grown a bit sluggish. That compensates for it."

"You talk of him and treat him as though he's a mechanical toy," said Diane.

"He is. An invincible toy. An invaluable one, also—You there, Hasan. Are you ready?" he asked.

"I am." Hasan answered, removing his cloak and his burnoose and handing them to Ellen.

The big muscles in his shoulders bulged, his fingers flexed lightly, and he moved forward and out of the circle of blades. There was a welt on his left shoulder, several others on his back. The torchlight caught his beard and turned it to blood, and I could not help but remember that night back at the *hounfor* when he had enacted a strangling, and Mama Julie had said, "Your friend is possessed of Angelsou," and "Angelsou is a deathgod and he only visits with his own."

"Great is the warrior, Hasan," announced Moreby, turning away from us.

"Great is the warrior, Hasan," replied the crowd.

"His strength is that of many."

"His strength is that of many," the crowd responded.

"Greater still is the Dead Man."

"Greater still is the Dead Man."

"He breaks his bones and casts him about this place of feasting."

"He breaks his bones…"

"He eats his liver."

"He eats his liver."

"He drinks the blood from his throat."

"He drinks the blood from his throat."

"Mighty is his power."

"Mighty is his power."

"Great is the Dead Man!"

"Great is the Dead Man!"

"Tonight," said Hasan quietly, "he becomes the Dead Man indeed."

"Dead Man!" cried Moreby, as Hasan moved forward and stood before him, "I give you this man Hasan in sacrifice!"

Then Moreby got out of the way and motioned the guards to move us to the far sideline.

The idiot grinned an even wider grin and reached out slowly toward Hasan.

"*Bismallah,*" said Hasan, making as if to turn away from him, and bending downward and to the side.

He picked it off the ground and brought it up and around fast and hard, like a whiplash—a great heel-of-the-hand blow which landed on the left side of the Dead Man's jaw.

The white, white head moved maybe five inches.

And he kept on grinning…

Then both of his short bulky arms came out and caught Hasan beneath the armpits. Hasan seized his shoulders, tracing fine red furrows up his sides as he went, and he drew red beads from the places where his fingers dug into snowcapped muscle.

The crowd screamed at the sight of the Dead Man's blood. Perhaps the smell of it excited the idiot himself. That, or the screaming.

…Because he raised Hasan two feet off the ground and ran forward with him.

The big tree got in the way, and Hasan's head sagged as he struck.

Then the Dead Man crashed into him, stepped back slowly, shook himself, and began to hit him.

It was a real beating. He flailed at him with his almost grotesquely brief, thick arms.

Hasan got his hands up in front of his face and he kept his elbows in the pit of his stomach.

Still, the Dead Man kept striking him on his sides and head. His arms just kept rising and falling.

And he never stopped grinning.

Finally, Hasan's hands fell and he clutched them before his stomach.

…And there was blood coming from the corners of his mouth.

The invincible toy continued its game.

And then far, far off on the other side of the night, so far that only I could hear it, there came a voice that I recognized.

It was the great hunting-howl of my hellhound, Bortan.

Somewhere, he had come upon my trail, and he was coming now, running down the night, leaping like a goat, flowing like a horse or a river, all brindle-colored—and his eyes were glowing coals and his teeth were buzzsaws.

He never tired of running, my Bortan.

Such as he are born without fear, given to the hunt, and sealed with death.

My hellhound was coming, and nothing could halt him in his course.

But he was far, so far off, on the other side of the night…

The crowd was screaming. Hasan couldn't take much more of it. Nobody could.

From the corner of my eye (the brown one) I noticed a tiny gesture of Ellen's.

It was as though she had thrown something with her right hand…

Two seconds later it happened.

I looked away quickly from that point of brilliance that occurred, sizzling, behind the idiot.

The Dead Man wailed, lost his grin.

Good old Reg 237.1 (promulgated by me):

"Every tour guide and every member of a tour must carry no fewer than three magnesium flares on his person, while traveling."

Ellen only had two left, that meant. Bless her.

The idiot had stopped hitting Hasan.

He tried to kick the flare away. He screamed. He tried to kick the flare away. He covered his eyes. He rolled on the ground.

Hasan watched, bleeding, panting…

The flare burnt, the Dead Man screamed…

Hasan finally moved.

He reached up and touched one of the thick vines which hung from the tree. He tugged at it. It resisted. He pulled harder.

It came loose.

His movements were steadier as he twisted an end around each hand.

The flare sputtered, grew bright again…

He dropped to his knees beside the Dead Man, and with a quick motion he looped the vine about his throat.

The flare sputtered again.

He snapped it tight.

The Dead Man fought to rise.

Hasan drew the thing tighter.

The idiot seized him about the waist.

The big muscles in the Assassin's shoulders grew into ridges. Perspiration mingled with the blood on his face.

The Dead Man stood, raising Hasan with him.

Hasan pulled harder.

The idiot, his face no longer white, but mottled, and with the veins standing out like cords in his forehead and neck, lifted him up off the ground. As I'd lifted the golem did the Dead Man raise Hasan, the vine cutting ever more deeply into his neck as he strained with all his inhuman strength.

The crowd was wailing and chanting incoherently. The drumming, which had reached a frenzied throb, continued at its peak without letup. And then I heard the howl again, still very far away.

The flare began to die.

The Dead Man swayed.

...Then, as a great spasm racked him, he threw Hasan away from him.

The vine went slack about his throat as it tore free from Hasan's grip.

Hasan took *ukemi* and rolled to his knees. He stayed that way.

The Dead Man moved toward him.

Then his pace faltered.

He began to shake all over. He made a gurgling noise and clutched at his throat. His face grew darker. He staggered to the tree and put forth a hand. He leaned there panting. Soon he was gasping noisily. His hand slipped along the trunk and he dropped to the ground. He picked himself up again, into a half-crouch.

Hasan arose, and recovered the piece of vine from where it had fallen.

He advanced upon the idiot.

This time his grip was unbreakable.

The Dead Man fell, and he did not rise again.

❖   ❖   ❖

It was like turning off a radio which had been playing at full volume: Click…

Big silence then—it had all happened so fast. And tender was the night as I reached out through it and broke the neck of the swordsman at my side and seized his blade. I turned then to my left and split the skull of the next one with it.

Then, like *click* again, and full volume back on, but all static this time. The night was torn down through the middle.

Myshtigo dropped his man with a vicious rabbit-punch and kicked another in the shins. George managed a quick knee to the groin of the one nearest him.

Dos Santos, not so quick—or else just unlucky—took two bad cuts, chest and shoulder.

The crowd rose up from where it had been scattered on the ground, like a speedup film of beansprouts growing.

It advanced upon us.

Ellen threw Hasan's burnoose over the head of the swordsman who was about to disembowel her husband. Earth's poet laureate then brought a rock down hard on the top of the burnoose, doubtless collecting much bad karma but not looking too worried about it.

By then Hasan had rejoined our little group, using his hand to parry a sword cut by striking the flat of the blade in an old samurai maneuver I had thought lost to the world forever. Then Hasan, too, had a sword—after another rapid movement—and he was very proficient with it.

We killed or maimed all our guards before the crowd was halfway to us, and Diane—taking a cue from Ellen—lobbed her three magnesium flares across the field and into the mob.

We ran then, Ellen and Red Wig supporting Dos Santos.

But the Kouretes had cut us off and we were running northwards, off at a tangent from our goal.

"We cannot make it, Karagee," called Hasan.

"I know."

"…Unless you and I delay them while the others go ahead."

"Okay. Where?"

"At the far barbecue pit, where the trees are thick about the path. It is a bottle's neck. They will not be able to hit us all at a time."

"Right! —You hear us!?" I addressed the others. "Make for the horses! Phil will guide you! Hasan and I will hold them for as long as we can!"

Red Wig turned her head and began to say something.

"Don't argue! Go! You want to live, don't you!?"

They did. They went.

Hasan and I turned, there beside the barbecue pit, and we waited. The others cut back again, going off through the woods, heading toward the village and the paddock. The mob kept right on coming, toward Hasan and me.

The first wave hit us and we began the killing. We were in the V-shaped place where the path disgorged from the woods onto the plain. To our left was a smoldering pit; to our right a thick stand of trees. Three did we kill, and several set a-bleeding ere they fell back, paused, then moved to flank us.

We stood back to back then and cut them as they closed.

"If even one has a gun we are dead, Karagee."

"I know."

Another half-man fell to my blade. Hasan sent one, screaming, into the pit.

They were all about us then. A blade slipped in past my guard and cut me on the shoulder. Another nicked my thigh.

"Fall back, thou fools! I say withdraw, thou freaks!"

At that, they did, moving back beyond thrust-range.

The man who had spoken was about five and a half feet tall. His lower jaw moved like that of a puppet's, as though on hinges, and his teeth were like a row of dominoes—all darkstained and clicking as they opened and closed.

"Yea, Procrustes," I heard one say.

"Fetch nets! Snare them alive! Do not close with them! They have cost us too much already!"

Moreby was at his side, and whimpering.

"…I did not know, m'lord."

"Silence! thou brewer of ill-tasting sloshes! Thou hast cost us a god and many men!"

"Shall we rush?" asked Hasan.

"No, but be ready to cut the nets when they bring them."

"It is not good that they want us alive," he decided.

"We have sent many to Hell, to smooth our way," said I, "and we are standing yet and holding blades. What more?"

"If we rush them we can take two, perhaps four more with us. If we wait, they will net us and we die without them."

"What matters it, once you are dead? Let us wait. So long as we live there is the great peacock-tail of probability, growing from out of the next moment."

"As you say."

And they found nets and cast them. We cut three of them apart before they tangled us in the fourth. They drew them tight and moved in.

I felt my blade wrenched from my grasp, and someone kicked me. It was Moreby.

"Now you will die as very few die," said he.

"Did the others escape?"

"Only for the moment," he said. "We will track them, find them, and bring them back."

I laughed.

"You lose," I said. "They'll make it."

He kicked me again.

"This is how your rule applies?" I asked. "Hasan conquered the Dead Man."

"He cheated. The woman threw a flare."

Procrustes came up beside him as they bound us within the nets.

"Of the death?" he asked.

"Let us take them to the Valley of Sleep," said Moreby, "and there work our wills with them and leave them to be preserved against future feasting."

"It is good," said Procrustes. "Yes, it shall be done."

Hasan must have been working his left arm through the netting all that while, because it shot out a short distance and his nails raked Procrustes' leg.

Procrustes kicked him several times, and me once more for good measure. He rubbed at the scratches on his calf.

"Why did you do that, Hasan?" I asked, after Procrustes turned away and ordered us bound to barbecue stakes for carrying.

"There may still be some meta-cyanide left on my fingernails," he explained.

"How did it get there?"

"From the bullets in my belt, Karagee, which they did not take from me. I coated my nails after I sharpened them today."

"Ah! You scratched the Dead Man at the beginning of your bout…"

"Yes, Karagee. Then it was simply a matter of my staying alive until he fell over."

"You are an exemplary assassin, Hasan."

"Thank you, Karagee."

We were bound to the stakes, still netted. Four men, at the order of Procrustes, raised us.

Moreby and Procrustes leading the way, we were borne off through the night.

❖   ❖   ❖

As we moved along an uneven trail the world changed about us. It's always that way when you approach a Hot Spot. It's like hiking backward through geological eras.

As we advanced along the way the trees grew smaller, the spaces between them wider. But they were not like the trees we had left beyond the village. They were twisted (and twisting!) forms, with seaweed swirls of branches, gnarled trunks, and exposed roots which crept, slowly, about the surface of the ground. Tiny invisible things made scratching noises as they scurried from the light of Moreby's electric lantern.

By turning my head I could detect a faint, pulsating glow, just at the border of the visible spectrum. It was coming from up ahead.

A profusion of dark vines appeared underfoot. They writhed whenever one of our bearers stepped on them.

The trees became simple ferns. Then these, too, vanished. Great quantities of shaggy, blood-colored lichens replaced them. They grew over all the rocks. They were faintly luminous.

There were no more animal sounds. There were no sounds at all, save for the panting of our four bearers, and footfalls, and the occasional muffled click as Procrustes' automatic rifle struck a padded rock.

Our bearers wore blades in their belts. Moreby carried several blades, as well as a small pistol.

The trail turned sharply upward. One of our bearers swore. The night-tent was jerked downward at its corners then; it met with the horizon, and it was filled with the hint of a purple haze, fainter than exhaled cigarette-smoke. Slow, very high, and slapping the air like a devilfish coasting on water, the dark form of a spiderbat crossed over the face of the moon.

Procrustes fell.

Moreby helped him to his feet, but Procrustes swayed and leaned upon him.

"What ails you, lord?"

"A sudden dizziness, numbness in my members… Take thou my rifle. It grows heavy."

Hasan chuckled.

Procrustes turned toward Hasan, his puppet-jaw dropping open.

Then he dropped, too.

Moreby had just taken the rifle and his hands were full. The guards set us down, rather urgently, and rushed to Procrustes' side.

"Hast thou any water?" he asked, and he closed his eyes.

He did not open them again.

Moreby listened to his chest, held the feathery part of his wand beneath his nostrils.

"He is dead," he finally announced.

"Dead?"

The bearer who was covered with scales began to weep.

"He wiss good," he sobbed. "He wiss a great war shief. What will we do now?"

"He is dead," Moreby repeated, "and I am your leader until a new war chief is declared. Wrap him in your cloaks. Leave him on that flat rock up ahead. No animals come here, so he will not be molested. We will recover him on the way back. Now, though, we must have our vengeance on these two." He gestured with his wand. "The Valley of Sleep is near at hand. You have taken the pills I gave you?"

"Yes."

"Yes."

"Yes."

"Yiss."

"Very good. Take your cloaks now and wrap him."

They did this, and soon we were raised again and borne to the top of a ridge from which a trail ran down into a fluorescent, pock-blasted pit. The great rocks of the place seemed almost to be burning.

"This," I said to Hasan, "was described to me by my son as the place where the thread of my life lies across a burning stone. He saw me as threatened by the Dead Man, but the fates thought twice and gave that menace onto you. Back when I was but a dream in the mind of Death, this site was appointed as one of the places where I might die."

"To fall from Shinvat is to roast," said Hasan.

They carried us down into the fissure, dropped us on the rocks.

Moreby released the safety catch on the rifle and stepped back.

"Release the Greek and tie him to that column." He gestured with the weapon.

They did this, binding my hands and feet securely. The rock was smooth, damp, killing without indication.

They did the same to Hasan, about eight feet to my right.

Moreby had set down the lantern so that it cast a yellow semicircle about us. The four Kouretes were demon statues at his side.

He smiled. He leaned the rifle against the rocky wall behind him. "This is the Valley of Sleep," he told us. "Those who sleep here do not awaken. It keeps the meat preserved, however, providing us against the lean years. Before we leave you, though—" His eyes turned to me. "Do you see where I have set the rifle?"

I did not answer him.

"I believe your entrails will stretch that far, Commissioner. At any rate, I intend to find out." He drew a dagger from his belt and advanced upon me. The four half-men moved with him. "Who do you think has more guts?" he asked. "You or the Arab?"

Neither of us replied.

"You shall both get to see for yourselves," he said through his teeth. "First you!"

He jerked my shirt free and cut it down the front.

He rotated the blade in a slow significant circle about two inches away from my stomach, all the while studying my face.

"You are afraid," he said. "Your face does not show it yet, but it will."

Then: "Look at me! I am going to put the blade in very slowly. I am going to dine on you one day. What do you think of that?"

I laughed. It was suddenly worth laughing at.

His face twisted, then it straightened into a momentary look of puzzlement.

"Has the fear driven you mad, Commissioner?"

"Feathers or lead?" I asked him.

He knew what it meant. He started to say something, and then he heard a pebble click about twelve feet away. His head snapped in that direction.

He spent the last second of his life screaming, as the force of Bortan's leap pulped him against the ground, before his head was snatched from his shoulders.

My hellhound had arrived.

❖   ❖   ❖

The Kouretes screamed, for his eyes are glowing coals and his teeth are buzzsaws. His head is as high above the ground as a tall man's. Although they seized their blades and struck at him, his sides are as the sides of an armadillo. A quarter ton of dog, my Bortan... He is not exactly the kind Albert Payson Terhune wrote about.

He worked for the better part of a minute, and when he was finished they were all in pieces and none of them alive.

"What is it?" asked Hasan.

"A puppy I found in a sack, washed up on the beach, too tough to drown—my dog," said I, "Bortan."

There was a small gash in the softer part of his shoulder. He had not gotten it in the fight.

"He sought us first in the village," I said, "and they tried to stop him. Many Kouretes have died this day."

He trotted up and licked my face. He wagged his tail, made dog-noises, wriggled like a puppy, and ran in small circles. He sprang toward me and licked my face again. Then he was off cavorting once more, treading on pieces of Kouretes.

"It is good for a man to have a dog," said Hasan. "I have always been fond of dogs."

Bortan was sniffing him as he said it.

"You've come back, you dirty old hound," I told him. "Don't you know that dogs are extinct?"

He wagged his tail, came up to me again, licked my hand.

"I'm sorry that I can't scratch your ears. You know that I'd like to, though, don't you?"

He wagged his tail.

I opened and closed my right hand within its bonds. I turned my head that way as I did it. Bortan watched, his nostrils moist and quivering.

"Hands, Bortan. I need hands to free me. Hands to loosen my bonds. You must fetch them, Bortan, and bring them here."

He picked up an arm that was lying on the ground and he deposited it at my feet. He looked up then and wagged his tail.

"No, Bortan. *Live* hands. Friendly hands. Hands to untie me. You understand, don't you?"

He licked my hand.

"Go and find hands to free me. Still attached and living. The hands of friends. Now, quickly! Go!"

He turned and walked away, paused, looked back once, then mounted the trail.

"Does he understand?" asked Hasan.

"I think so," I told him. "His is not an ordinary dog brain, and he has had many many more years than even the lifetime of a man in which to learn understanding."

"Then let us hope he finds someone quickly, before we sleep."

"Yes."

❖　❖　❖

We hung there and the night was cold.

We waited for a long time. Finally, we lost track of time.

Our muscles were cramped and aching. We were covered with the dried blood of countless little wounds. We were all over bruises. We were groggy from fatigue, from lack of sleep.

We hung there, the ropes cutting into us.

"Do you think they will make it to your village?"

"We gave them a good start. I think they have a decent chance."

"It is always difficult to work with you, Karagee."

"I know. I have noticed this same thing myself."

"…Like the summer we rotted in the dungeons of Corsica."

"Aye."

"…Or our march to the Chicago Station, after we had lost all our equipment in Ohio."

"Yes, that was a bad year."

"You are *always* in trouble, though, Karagee. 'Born to knot the tiger's tail'," he said, "that is the saying for people such as you. They are difficult to be with. Myself, I love the quiet and the shade, a book of poems, my pipe—"

"Hush! I hear something!"

There was a clatter of hooves.

A satyr appeared beyond the cockeyed angle of the light from the fallen lantern. He moved nervously, his eyes going from me to Hasan and back again, and up, down, around, and past us.

"Help us, little horny one," said I, in Greek.

He advanced carefully. He saw the blood, the mangled Kouretes. He turned as if to flee.

"Come back! I need you! It is I, the player of the pipes."

He stopped and turned again, his nostrils quivering, flaring and falling. His pointed ears twitched.

He came back, a pained expression on his near-human face as he passed through the place of gore.

"The blade. At my feet," I said, gesturing with my eyes. "Pick it up."

He did not seem to like the notion of touching anything man-made, especially a weapon.

I whistled the last lines of my last tune.

—*It's late, it's late, so late…*

His eyes grew moist. He wiped at them with the backs of his shaggy wrists.

"Pick up the blade and cut my bonds. Pick it up. —Not that way, you'll cut yourself. The other end. —Yes."

He picked it up properly and looked at me. I moved my right hand.

"The ropes. Cut them."

He did. It took him fifteen minutes and left me wearing a bracelet of blood. I had to keep moving my hand to keep him from slashing an artery. But he freed it.

"Now give me the knife and I'll take care of the rest."

He placed the blade in my extended hand.

I took it. Seconds later I was free. Then I freed Hasan.

When I turned again the satyr was gone. I heard the sound of frantic hoofbeats in the distance.

I might say that if our party had taken the long way from Lamia to Volos—the coastal road—the whole thing might never have happened the way that it did, and Phil might be alive today. But I can't really judge all that occurred in this case; even now, looking back, I can't say how I'd rearrange events if it were all to be done over again. The forces of final disruption were already goose-stepping amidst the ruins, arms upraised…

We made it to Volos the following afternoon, and on up Mount Pelion to Portaria. Across a deep ravine lay Makrynitsa.

We crossed over and found the others.

Phil had guided them to Makrynitsa, asked for a bottle of wine and his copy of *Prometheus Unbound*, and had sat up with the two, well into the evening.

In the morning, Diane had found him smiling, and cold.

I built him a pyre amidst the cedars near the ruined Episcopi, because he did not want to be buried. I heaped it with incense, with aromatic herbs, and it was twice the height of a man. That night it would burn and I would say good-bye to another friend. It seems, looking back, that my life has mainly been a series of arrivals and departures. I say "hello." I say "good-bye." Only the Earth endures…

Hell.

So I walked with the group that afternoon, out to Pagasae, the port of ancient Iolkos, set on the promontory opposite Volos. We stood in the shade of the almond trees on the hill that gives good vantage to both seascape and rocky ridge.

"It was from here that the Argonauts set sail on their quest for the Golden Fleece," I told no one in particular.

"Who all were they?" asked Ellen. "I read the story in school, but I forget."

"There was Herakles and Theseus and Orpheus the singer, and Asclepius, and the sons of the North Wind, and Jason, the captain, who was a pupil of the centaur, Cheiron—whose cave, incidentally, is up near the summit of Mount Pelion, there."

"Really?"

"I'll show it to you sometime."

"All right."

"The gods and the titans battled near here also," said Diane, coming up on my other side. "Did the titans not uproot Mount Pelion and pile it atop Ossa in an attempt to scale Olympus?"

"So goes the telling. But the gods were kind and restored the scenery after the bloody battle."

"A sail," said Hasan, gesturing with a half-peeled orange in his hand.

I looked out over the waters and there was a tiny blip on the horizon.

"Yes, this place is still used as a port."

"Perhaps it is a shipload of heroes," said Ellen, "returning with some more fleece. What will they do with all that fleece, anyhow?"

"It's not the fleece that's important," said Red Wig, "it's the getting of it. Every good storyteller used to know that. The womenfolk can always make stunning garments from fleeces. They're used to picking up the remains after quests."

"It wouldn't match your hair, dear."

"Yours either, child."

"That can be changed. Not so easily as yours, of course…"

"Across the way," said I, in a loud voice, "is a ruined Byzantine church—the Episcopi—which I've scheduled for restoration in another two years. It is the traditional site of the wedding feast of Peleus, also one of the Argonauts, and the sea-nymph Thetis. Perhaps you've heard the story of that feast? Everyone was invited but the goddess of discord, and she came anyhow and tossed down a golden apple marked 'For the Fairest.' Lord Paris judged it the property of Aphrodite, and the fate of Troy was sealed. The last time anyone saw Paris, he was none too happy. Ah, decisions! Like I've often said, this land is lousy with myth."

"How long will we be here?" asked Ellen.

"I'd like a couple more days in Makrynitsa," I said, "then we'll head northwards. Say about a week more in Greece, and then we'll move on to Rome."

"No," said Myshtigo, who had been sitting on a rock and talking to his machine, as he stared out over the waters. "No, the tour is finished. This is the last stop."

"How come?"

"I'm satisfied and I'm going home now."

"What about your book?"

"I've got my story."

"What kind of story?"

"I'll send you an autographed copy when it's finished. My time is precious, and I have all the material I want now. All that I'll need, anyhow. I called the Port this morning, and they are sending me a Skimmer tonight. You people go ahead and do whatever you want, but I'm finished."

"Is something wrong?"

"No, nothing is wrong, but it's time that I left. I have much to do."

He rose to his feet and stretched.

"I have some packing to take care of, so I'll be going back now. You *do* have a beautiful country here, Conrad, despite. —I'll see you all at dinnertime."

He turned and headed down the hill.

I walked a few steps in his direction, watching him go.

"I wonder what prompted that?" I thought aloud.

There was a footfall.

"He is dying," said George, softly.

❖   ❖   ❖

My son Jason, who had preceded us by several days, was gone. Neighbors told of his departure for Hades on the previous evening. The patriarch had been carried off on the back of a fire-eyed hellhound who had knocked down the door of his dwelling place and borne him off through the night. My relatives all wanted me to come to dinner. Dos Santos was still resting; George had treated his wounds and had not deemed it necessary to ship him to the hospital in Athens.

It's always nice to come home.

I walked down to the Square and spent the afternoon talking to my descendants. Would I tell them of Taler, of Haiti, of Athens? Aye. I would, I did. Would they tell me of the past two decades in Makrynitsa? Ditto.

I took some flowers to the graveyard then, stayed awhile, and went to Jason's home and repaired his door with some tools I found in the shed. Then I came upon a bottle of wine and drank it all. And I smoked a cigar. I made me a pot of coffee, too, and I drank all of that.

I still felt depressed.

I didn't know what was coming off.

George knew his diseases, though, and he said the Vegan showed unmistakable symptoms of a neurological disorder of the e.t. variety. Incurable. Invariably fatal.

And even Hasan couldn't take credit for it. "Etiology unknown," 'twas.

So everything was revised.

George had known about Myshtigo since the reception. —What had set him on the track?

—Phil had asked him to observe the Vegan for signs of a fatal disease.

Why?

Well, he hadn't said why, and I couldn't go ask him at the moment.

I had me a problem.

Myshtigo had either finished his job or he hadn't enough time left to do it. He *said* he'd finished it. If he hadn't, then I'd been protecting a dead man all the while, to no end. If he had, then I needed to know the results, so that I could make a very fast decision concerning what remained of his lifespan.

Dinner was no help. Myshtigo had said all he cared to say, and he ignored or parried our questions. So, as soon as we'd had our coffee, Red Wig and I stepped outside for a cigarette.

"What's happened?" she asked.

"I don't know, I thought maybe you did."

"No. What now?"

"You tell me."

"Kill him?"

"Perhaps yes. First though, why?"

"He's finished it."

"What? Just *what* has he finished?"

"How should I know?"

"Damn it! *I* have to! I like to know why I'm killing somebody. I'm funny that way."

"Funny? Very. Obvious, isn't it? The Vegans want to buy in again, Earthside. He's going back to give them a report on the sites they're interested in."

"Then why didn't he visit them all? Why cut it short after Egypt and Greece? Sand, rocks, jungles, and assorted monsters—that's all he saw. Hardly makes for an encouraging appraisal."

"Then he's scared, is why, and lucky he's alive. He could have been eaten by a boadile or Kourete. He's running."

"Good. Then let him run. Let him hand in a bad report."

"He can't, though. If they *do* want in, they won't buy anything that sketchy. They'll just send somebody else—somebody tougher— to finish it. If we kill Myshtigo they'll know we're still for real, still protesting, still tough ourselves."

"…And he's not afraid for his life."

"No? What, then?"

"I don't know. I have to find out, though."

"How?"

"I think I'll ask him."

"You are a lunatic."

She turned away.

"My way, or not at all," I said.

"*Any* way, then. It doesn't matter. We've already lost."

I took her by the shoulders and kissed her neck.

"Not yet. You'll see."

She stood stiffly.

"Go home," she said, "it's late. It's too late."

I did that. I went back to Iakov Korones' big old place, where Myshtigo and I were both quartered, and where Phil had been staying.

I stopped there in the death-room, in the place where Phil had last slept. His *Prometheus Unbound* was still on the writing table, set down beside an empty bottle. He had spoken of his own passing when he'd called me in Egypt, and he had suffered an attack, had been through a lot. It seemed he'd leave a message for an old friend then, on a matter like this.

So I opened Percy B's dud epic and looked within.

It was written on the blank pages at the end of the book, in Greek. Not modern Greek, though. Classical.

It went something like this:

"Dear friend, although I abhor writing anything I cannot rewrite, I feel I had best tend to this with dispatch. I am unwell. George wants me to skim to Athens. I will, too, in the morning. First, though, regarding the matter at hand—

"Get the Vegan off the Earth, alive, at any cost.

"It is important.

"It is the most important thing in the world.

"I was afraid to tell you before, because I thought Myshtigo might be a telepath. That is why I did not go along for the entire journey, though I should dearly have loved to do so. That is why I pretended to hate him, so that I could stay away from him as much as possible. It was only after I managed to confirm the fact that he was not telepathic that I elected to join you.

"I suspected, what with Dos Santos, Diane, and Hasan, that the Radpol might be out for his blood. If he was a telepath, I figured he would learn of this quickly and do whatever needed to be done to assure his safety. If he was not a telepath, I still had great faith in your ability to defend him against almost anything, Hasan included. But I did not want him apprised of my knowledge. I *did* try to warn you, though, if you recall.

"Tatram Yshtigo, his grandfather, is one of the finest, most noble creatures alive. He is a philosopher, a great writer, an altruistic administrator of services to the public. I became acquainted with him during my stay on Taler, thirty-some years ago, and we later became close friends. We have been in communication ever since that time, and that far back, even, was I advised by him of the Vegan Combine's plans regarding the disposition of Earth. I was also sworn to secrecy. Even Cort cannot know that I am aware. The old man would lose face, disastrously, if this thing came out ahead of time.

"The Vegans are in a very embarrassing position. Our expatriate countrymen have forced their own economic and cultural dependence upon Vega. The Vegans were made aware—quite vividly! — during the days of the RadRol Rebellion, of the fact that there is an indigenous population possessing a strong organization of its own and desiring the restoration of our planet. The Vegans too would like to see this happen. They do not want the Earth. Whatever for? If they want to exploit Earthfolk, they have more of them on Taler than we do here on Earth—and they're not doing it, not massively or maliciously, at any rate. Our ex-pop has elected what labor exploitation it does undergo in preference to returning here. What does this indicate? Returnism is a dead issue. No one is coming back. That is why I quit the movement. Why you did too, I believe. The Vegans would like to get the home world problem off their hands. Surely, they want to visit it. It is instructive, sobering, humbling, and downright frightening for them to come here and see what *can* be done to a world.

"What needed to be done was for them to find a way around our ex-pop-gov on Taler. The Talerites were not anxious to give up their only claim for taxes and existence: the Office.

"After much negotiation, though, and much economic suasion, including the offer of full Vegan citizenship to our ex-pop, it appeared that a means had been found. The implementation of the plan was given into the hands of the Shtigo-gens, Tatram in especial.

"He finally found a way, he believed, of returning the Earth proper to an autonomous position and preserving its cultural integrity. That is why he sent his grandson, Cort, to do his 'survey.' Cort is a strange creature; his real talent is acting (all the Shtigo are quite gifted), and he loves to pose. I believe that he wanted to play the part of an alien very badly, and I am certain that he has carried it with skill and efficiency. (Tatram also advised me that it would be Cort's *last* role. He is dying of *drinfan*, which is incurable; also, I believe it is the reason he was chosen.)

"Believe me, Konstantin Karaghiosis Korones Nomikos (and all the others which I do not know), Conrad, when I say that he was not surveying real estate.

"But allow me one last Byronic gesture. Take my word that he must live, and let me keep my promise and my secret. You will not regret it, when you know all.

"I am sorry that I never got to finish your elegy, and damn you for keeping my Lara, that time in Kerch! —Phil."

❖　　❖　　❖

Very well then, I decided, life—not death—for the Vegan. Phil had spoken and I did not doubt his words.

I went back to Mikar Korones' dinner table and stayed with Myshtigo until he was ready to leave. I accompanied him back to Iakov Korones' and watched him pack some final items. We exchanged maybe six words during this time.

His belongings we carried out to the place where the Skimmer would land, in front of the house. Before the others (including Hasan) came up to bid him good-bye, he turned to me and said, "Tell me, Conrad, why are you tearing down the pyramid?"

"To needle Vega," I said. "To let you know that if you want this place and you do manage to take it away from us, you'll get it in worse shape than it was after the Three Days. There wouldn't be anything left to look at. We'd burn the rest of our history. Not even a scrap for you guys."

The air escaping from the bottom of his lungs came out with a high-pitched whine—the Vegan equivalent of a sigh.

"Commendable, I suppose," he said, "but I did so want to see it. Do you think you could ever get it back together again? Soon, perhaps?"

"What do you think?"

"I noticed your men marking many of the pieces."

I shrugged.

"I have only one serious question, then—about your fondness for destruction…" he stated.

"What is that?"

"Is it *really* art?"

"Go to hell."

Then the others came up. I shook my head slowly at Diane and seized Hasan's wrist long enough to tear away a tiny needle he'd taped to the palm of his hand. I let him shake hands with the Vegan too, then, briefly.

The Skimmer buzzed down out of the darkening sky, and I saw Myshtigo aboard, loaded his baggage personally, and closed the door myself.

It took off without incident and was gone in a matter of moments.

End of a nothing jaunt.

I went back inside and changed my clothing.

It was time to burn a friend.

Heaped high into the night, my ziggurat of logs bore what remained of the poet, my friend. I kindled a torch and put out the electric lantern. Hasan stood at my side. He had helped bear the corpse to the cart and had taken over the reins. I had built the pyre on the cypress-filled hill above Volos, near the ruins of that church I mentioned earlier. The waters of the bay were calm. The sky was clear and the stars were bright.

Dos Santos, who did not approve of cremation, had decided not to attend, saying that his wounds were troubling him. Diane had elected to remain with him back in Makrynitsa. She had not spoken to me since our last conversation.

Ellen and George were seated on the bed of the cart, which was backed beneath a large cypress, and they were holding hands. They were the only others present. Phil would not have liked my relatives wailing their dirges about him. He'd once said he wanted something big, bright, fast, and without music.

I applied the torch to a corner of the pyre. The flame bit, slowly, began to chew at the wood. Hasan started another torch going, stuck it into the ground, stepped back, and watched.

As the flames ate their way upwards I prayed the old prayers and poured out wine upon the ground. I heaped aromatic herbs onto the blaze. Then I, too, stepped back.

" '…Whatever you were, death has taken you, too'," I told him. " 'You have gone to see the moist flower open along Acheron, among Hell's shadows darting fitfully.' Had you died young, your passing would have been mourned as the destruction of a great talent before its fulfillment. But you lived and they cannot say that now. Some choose a short and supernal life before the walls of their Troy, others a long and less troubled one. And who is to say which is the better? The gods did keep their promise of immortal fame to Achilleus, by inspiring the poet to sing him an immortal paean. But is he the happier for it, being now as dead as yourself? *I* cannot judge, old friend. Lesser bard, I remember some of the words you, too, wrote of the mightiest of the Argives, and of the time of hard-hurled deaths: 'Bleak disappointments rage this coming-together place: Menace of sighs in a jeopardy of time… But the ashes do not burn backward to timber. Flame's invisible music shapes the air to heat, but the day is no longer.' Fare thee well, Phillip Graber. May the Lords Phoebus and Dionysus, who do love and kill their poets, commend thee to their dark brother Hades. And may his Persephone, Queen of the Night, look with favor upon thee and grant thee high stead in Elysium. Good-bye."

The flames had almost reached the top.

I saw Jason then, standing beside the cart, Bortan seated by his side. I backed away further. Bortan came to me and sat down at my right. He licked my hand, once.

"Mighty hunter, we have lost us another," I said.

He nodded his great head.

The flames reached the top and began to nibble at the night. The air was filled with sweet aromas and the sound of fire.

Jason approached.

"Father," he said, "he bore me to the place of burning rocks, but you were already escaped."

I nodded.

"A no-man friend freed us from that place. Before that, this man Hasan destroyed the Dead Man. So your dreams have thus far proved both right and wrong."

"*He* is the yellow-eyed warrior of my vision," he said.

"I know, but that part too is past."

"What of the Black Beast?"

"Not a snort nor a snuffle."

We watched for a long, long time, as the light retreated into itself. At several points, Bortan's ears pricked forward and his nostrils dilated. George and Ellen had not moved. Hasan was a strange-eyed watcher, without expression.

"What will you do now, Hasan?" I asked.

"Go again to Mount Sindjar," he said, "for awhile."

"And then?"

He shrugged.

"Howsoever it is written," he replied.

And a fearsome noise came upon us then, like the groans of an idiot giant, and the sound of splintering trees accompanied it.

Bortan leaped to his feet and howled. The donkeys who had drawn the cart shifted uneasily. One of them made a brief, braying noise.

Jason clutched the sharpened staff which he had picked from the heap of kindling, and he stiffened.

It burst in upon us then, there in the clearing. Big, and ugly, and everything it had ever been called.

The Eater of Men…

The Shaker of the Earth…

The Mighty, Foul One…

The Black Beast of Thessaly.

Finally, someone could say what it really was. If they got away to say it, that is.

It must have been drawn to us by the odor of burning flesh.

And it *was* big. The size of an elephant, at least.

What was Herakles' fourth labor?

The wild boar of Arcadia, that's what.

I suddenly wished Herk was still around to help.

A big pig… A razorback, with tusks the length of a man's arm… Little pig eyes, black, and rolling in the Firelight, wildly…

It knocked down trees as it came…

It squealed, though, as Hasan drew a burning brand from the blaze and drove it, fire-end forward, into its snout, and then spun away.

It swerved, too, which gave me time to snatch Jason's staff.

I ran forward and caught it in the left eye with it.

It swerved again then, and squealed like a leaky boiler.

…And Bortan was upon it, tearing at its shoulder.

Neither of my two thrusts at its throat did more than superficial damage. It wrestled, shoulder against fang, and finally shook itself free of Bortan's grip.

Hasan was at my side by then, waving another firebrand.

It charged us.

From somewhere off to the side George emptied a machine-pistol into it. Hasan hurled the torch. Bortan leapt again, this time from its blind side.

…And these things caused it to swerve once more in its charge, crashing into the then-empty cart and killing both donkeys.

I ran against it then, thrusting the staff up under its left front leg.

The staff broke in two.

Bortan kept biting, and his snarl was a steady thunder. Whenever it slashed at him with its tusks he relinquished his grip, danced away, and moved in again to worry it.

I am sure that my needle-point deathlance of steel would not have broken. It had been aboard the *Vanitie*, though…

Hasan and I circled it with the sharpest and most stakelike of the kindling we could find. We kept jabbing, to keep it turning in a circle. Bortan kept trying for its throat, but the great snouted head stayed low, and the one eye rolled and the other bled, and the tusks slashed back and forth and up and down like swords. Cloven hooves the size of bread-loaves tore great holes in the ground as it turned, counterclockwise, trying to kill us all, there in the orange and dancing flamelight.

Finally, it stopped and turned—suddenly, for something that big—and its shoulders struck Bortan in the side and hurled him ten or twelve feet past me. Hasan hit it across the back with his stick and I drove in toward the other eye, but missed.

Then it moved toward Bortan, who was still regaining his feet—its head held low, tusks gleaming.

I threw my staff and leapt as it moved in on my dog. It had already dropped its head for the death blow.

I caught both tusks as the head descended almost to the ground. Nothing could hold back that scooping slash, I realized, as I bore down upon it with all my strength.

But I tried, and maybe I succeeded, somehow, for a second...

At least, as I was thrown through the air, my hands torn and bleeding, I saw that Bortan had managed to get back out of the way.

I was dazed by the fall, for I had been thrown far and high; and I heard a great pig-mad squealing. Hasan screamed and Bortan roared out his great-throated battle-challenge once more.

...And the hot red lightning of Zeus descended twice from the heavens.

...And all was still.

❖   ❖   ❖

I climbed back, slowly, to my feet.

Hasan was standing by the blazing pyre, a flaming stake still upraised in spear-throwing position.

Bortan was sniffing at the quivering mountain of flesh.

Cassandra was standing beneath the cypress beside a dead donkey, her back against the trunk of the tree, wearing leather trousers, a blue woolen shirt, a faint smile, and my still-smoking elephant gun.

"Uh—hi, Cassandra. How've you been?"

She dropped the gun and looked very pale. But I had her in my arms almost before it hit the ground.

"I'll ask you later," I said. "Not now. Nothing now. Let's just sit here beneath this tree and watch the fire burn."

And we did.

❖   ❖   ❖

A month later, Dos Santos was ousted from the Radpol. He and Diane have not been heard of since. Rumor has it that they gave up on Returnism, moved to Taler, and are living there now. I hope it's not true, what with the affairs of these past five days. I never did know the full story on Red Wig, and I guess I never will. If you trust a person, really trust him I mean, and you care for him, as she might have cared for me, it would seem you'd stick around to see whether he was right or wrong on your final big disagreement. She didn't, though, and I wonder if she regrets it now?

I don't really think I'll ever see her again.

Slightly after the Radpol shakeup, Hasan returned from Mount Sindjar, stayed awhile at the Port, then purchased a small ship and put out to sea early one morning, without even saying "good-bye" or giving any indication as to his destination. It was assumed he'd found new employment somewhere. There was a hurricane, though, several days later, and I heard rumors in Trinidad to the effect that he had been washed up on the coast of Brazil and met with his death at the hands of the fierce tribesmen who dwell there. I tried but was unable to verify this story.

However, two months later, Ricardo Bonaventura, Chairman of the Alliance Against Progress, a Radpol splinter group which had fallen into disfavor with Athens, died of apoplexy during a Party function. There were some murmurings of Divban rabbit-venom in the anchovies (an exceedingly lethal combination, George assures me), and the following day the new Captain of the Palace Guard vanished mysteriously, along with a Skimmer and the minutes of the last three secret sessions of the AAP (not to mention the contents of a small wallsafe). He was said to have been a big, yellow-eyed man, with a slightly Eastern cast to his features.

Jason is still herding his many-legged sheep in the high places, up where the fingers of Aurora come first to smear the sky with roses, and doubtless he is corrupting youth with his song.

Ellen is pregnant again, all delicate and big-waisted, and won't talk to anybody but George. George wants to try some fancy embryo-surgery, now, before it's too late, and make his next kid a water-breather as well as an air-breather, because of all that great big virgin frontier down underneath the ocean, where his descendants can pioneer, and him be father to a new race and write an interesting book on the subject, and all that. Ellen is not too hot on the idea, though, so I have a hunch the oceans will remain virgin a little longer.

I've decided to retain the Office for the time being. I'll set up some kind of parliament after I've whipped up an opposition party to the Radpol—Indreb, or something like that maybe: like Independent Rebuilders, or such.

Good old final forces of disruption… We needed them down here amid the ruins.

And Cassandra—my princess, my angel, my lovely lady—she even likes me without my fungus. That night in the Valley of Sleep did it in.

She, of course, was the shipload of heroes Hasan had seen that day back at Pagasea. No golden fleece, though, just my gunrack and such. Yeah. It had been the *Golden Vanitie*, which I'd built by hand, me, stout enough, I was pleased to learn, to take even the *tsunami* that followed that 9.6 Richter thing. She'd been out sailing in it at the time the bottom fell out of Kos. Afterwards, she'd set sail for Volos because she knew Makrynitsa was full of my relatives. Oh, good thing—that she had had this *feeling* that there was danger and had carried the heavy artillery ashore with her. (Good thing, too, that she knew how to use it.) I'll have to learn to take her premonitions more seriously.

I've purchased a quiet villa on the end of Haiti opposite from the Port. It's only about fifteen minutes' skimming time from there, and it has a big beach and lots of jungle all around it. I have to have some distance, like the whole island, between me and civilization, because I have this, well—hunting—problem. The other day, when the attorneys dropped around, they didn't understand the sign: "Beware the Dog." They do now. The one who's in traction won't sue for damages, and George will have him as good as new in no time. The others were not so severely taken.

Good thing I was nearby, though.

So here I am, in an unusual position as usual.

The entire planet Earth was purchased from the Talerite government, purchased by the large and wealthy Shtigo-gens. The preponderance of ex-patriates wanted Vegan citizenship anyhow, rather than remaining under the Talerite ex-gov and working in the Combine as registered aliens. This has been coming for a long time, so the disposal of the Earth became mainly a matter of finding the best buyer—because our exile regime lost its only other cause for existence the minute the citizenship thing went through. They could justify themselves while there were still Earthmen out there, but now they're all Vegans and can't vote for them, and *we're* sure not going to, down here.

Hence, the sale of a lot of real estate—and the only bidder was the Shtigo-gens.

Wise old Tatram saw that the Shtigo-gens did not own Earth, though. The entire purchase was made in the name of his grandson, the late Cort Myshtigo.

And Myshtigo left this distribution-desire, or last will and testament, Vegan-style…

…in which I was named.

I've, uh, inherited a planet.

The Earth, to be exact.

Well—

Hell, I don't want the thing. I mean, sure I'm stuck with it for awhile, but I'll work something out.

It was that infernal Vite-Stats machine, and four other big think-tanks that old Tatram used. He was looking for a local administrator to hold the Earth in fief and set up a resident representative government, and then to surrender ownership on a fairly simple residency basis once things got rolling. He wanted somebody who'd been around awhile, was qualified as an administrator, and who wouldn't want to keep the place for his very own.

Among others, it gave him one of my names, then another, the second as a "possibly still living." Then my personnel file was checked, and more stuff on the other guy, and pretty soon the machine had turned up a few more names, all of them mine. It began picking up discrepancies and peculiar similarities, kept kapocketting, and gave out more puzzling answers.

Before long, Tatram decided I had better be "surveyed."

Cort came to write a book.

He really wanted to see if I was Good, Honest, Noble, Pure, Loyal, Faithful, Trustworthy, Selfless, Kind, Cheerful, Dependable, and Without Personal Ambition.

Which means he was a cockeyed lunatic, because he said, "Yes, he's all that."

I sure fooled him.

Maybe he was right about the lack of personal ambition, though. I am pretty damn lazy, and am not at all anxious to acquire the headaches I see as springing up out of the tormented Earth and blackjacking me daily.

However, I am willing to make certain concessions so far as personal comfort is concerned. I'll probably cut myself back to a six-month vacation.

One of the attorneys (not the one in traction—the one with the sling) delivered me a note from the Blue One. It said, in part:

"Dear Whatever-the-Blazes-Your-Name-Is,

"It is most unsettling to begin a letter this way, so I'll respect your wishes and call you Conrad.

"'Conrad,' by now you are aware of the true nature of my visit. I feel I have made a good choice in naming you as heir to the property commonly referred to as Earth. Your affection for it cannot be gainsaid; as Karaghiosis you inspired men to bleed in its defense; you are restoring its monuments, preserving its works of art (and as one stipulation of my will, by the way, I insist that you put back the Great Pyramid!), and your ingenuity as well as your toughness, both physical and mental, is singularly amazing.

"You also appear to be the closest thing to an immortal overseer available (I'd give a lot to know your real age), and this, together with your high survival potential, makes you, really, the only candidate. If your mutation ever does begin to fail you, there is always the S-S series to continue linking the great chain of your days. (I could have said 'forging,' but it would not have been polite, inasmuch as I know you are an accomplished forger. —All those old records! You drove poor Vite-Stats half-mad with discrepancies. It is now programmed never to accept another Greek birth certificate as proof of age!)

"...I commend the Earth into the hands of the kallikanzaros. According to legend, this would be a grave mistake. However, I am willing to gamble that you are even a kallikanzaros under false pretenses. You destroy only what you mean to rebuild. Probably you are Great Pan, who only pretended to die. Whatever, you will have sufficient funds and a supply of heavy equipment which will be sent this year—and lots of forms for requisitioning more from the Shtigo Foundation. So go thou and be thou fruitful and multiply, and reinherit the Earth. The gens will be around watching. Cry out if you need help, and help will be forthcoming.

"I don't have time to write you a book. Sorry. Here is my autograph, anyhow:

—Cort Myshtigo

"P.S. I still dunno if it's art. Go to hell yourself."

❖   ❖   ❖

That is the gist of it.

Pan?

Machines don't talk that way, do they?

I hope not, anyhow…

The Earth is a wild inhabitation. It is a tough and rocky place. The rubbish will have to be cleared, section by section, before some anti-rubbish can be put up.

Which means work, lots of it.

Which means I'll need all the Office facilities as well as the Radpol organization, to begin with.

We have money now, and we own our own property again, and that makes a big difference. Maybe even Returnism isn't completely dead. If there is a vital program to revive the Earth, we may draw back some of the ex-pop, may snag some of the new tourists.

Or, if they all want to remain Vegans, they can do that, too. We'd like them, but we don't need them. Our Outbound immigration will be dropping off, I feel, once people know they can get ahead here; and our population will increase more than just geometrically, what with the prolonged fertility period brought on by the now quite expensive S-S series. I intend to socialize S-S completely. I'll do it by putting George in charge of a Public Health program, featuring mainland clinics and offering S-S all over the place.

We'll make out. I'm tired of being a gravekeeper, and I don't really want to spend from now till Easter cutting through the Tree of the World, even if I am a Darkborn with a propensity for trouble. When the bells do ring, I want to be able to say, "*Alethos aneste*," Risen Indeed, rather than dropping my saw and running (*ring-a-ding*, the bells, *clackety-clack*, the hooves, et cetera). Now is the time for all good kallikanzaroi… You know.

So…

Cassandra and I have this villa on the Magic Island. She likes it here. I like it here. She doesn't mind my indeterminate age anymore. Which is fine.

Just this early morning, as we lay on the beach watching the sun chase away stars, I turned to her and mentioned that this is going to be a big, big ulcer-giving job, full of headaches and such.

"No, it isn't," she replied.

"Don't minimize what is imminent," I said. "It makes for incompatibility."

"None of that either."

"You are too optimistic, Cassandra."

"No. I told you that you were heading into danger before, and you were, but you didn't believe me then. This time I feel that things should go well. That's all."

"Granting your accuracy in the past, I still feel you are underestimating that which lies before us."

She rose and stamped her foot.

"You *never* believe me!"

"Of course I do. It just happens that this time you're wrong, dear."

She swam away then, my mad mermaid, out into the dark waters. After a time she came swimming back.

"Okay," she said, smiling, shaking down gentle rains from her hair. "Sure."

I caught her ankle, pulled her down beside me and began tickling her.

"Stop that!"

"Hey, I believe you, Cassandra! Really! Hear that? Oh, how about that? I really believe you. Damn! You sure are right!"

"You are a smart-alecky kallikanz—Ouch!"

And she was lovely by the seaside, so I held her in the wet, till the day was all around us, feeling good.

Which is a nice place to end a story, *sic:*.

Notes

Chios, Samos, Ikaria, Naxos are all Greek Islands. The ruins of **Halicarnassos** lie beneath Bodrum, a city in Turkey that faces the Greek island **Kos**. **Thucydides,** an ancient Greek historian, described the destruction of **Astypalaia** on Kos by an earthquake. The **Mosque of Loggia** stands opposite the Plane Tree of Hippocrates; the Tree stands in front of the ancient **Castle of the Knights of Rhodes** in Kos. **Theocritus** (c. 316 – c. 260 BC) was a pastoral poet, probably Sicilian, who praised rural living in poems written for the Greek aristocracy. **Dhikaios**, or Christ the Just, is a Greek mountain.

    Makrynitsa village stands in **Thessaly**, one of the thirteen Greek territories.

    Greek poet **George Seferis** won the Nobel Prize for Literature in 1963. **Klephtes** were bandits and warlike mountain folk who lived in the Greek countryside during the Ottoman Empire. **Chthonic** pertains to the underworld. *De jure* means by right or by law; *de facto* means in fact, as opposed to "in theory" or "in law".

    Tossisa and **Vasileos Irakliou** are street names. In Athens, the Parthenon stands on the rocky **Acropolis**. **Syndagma Square** contains the Parliament buildings and the **Memorial to the Unknown Solider. Perikles' funeral oration**—"The entire Earth is the tomb of great men"—delivered around 430 BC to memorialize the war dead, provides the inscription on the **Memorial to the Unknown Soldier.**

    On **Leoforos Amalias** street stands the Panathenaic Stadium, site of the first modern-day Olympics in 1896, the **Olympieion** (Temple of Olympian Zeus) with 16 of its original 104 marble columns, and **Hadrian's Arch**, the gate between old Athens and the Roman quarters (there are no statues on it, although two might have existed there).

    Ouzo is an anise-flavored liqueur; **giuvetsi** is a mixture of meat, cheese and macaroni; **Kokkineli** is wine; **yaourti** is yogurt; **Metaxa** is a blend of brandy and wine; **nerantzi** are bitter oranges. **Satyrs** are lecherous, drunken creatures with men's bodies and goat or horse ears, hindlimbs and tail. **Brachiate** means to swing from arm to arm, as apes and monkeys do. **Kouretes** are named after male dancers who figured in the infancy of Dionysus ; they dressed in armor and kept time with a drum and rhythmic foot stamping. **Pausanius** travelled Greece in the second century AD and wrote first-hand accounts of its geography in his famous work *Description of Greece.*

    Dionysiou Areopagitou intersects with Leoforos Amalias near the **Olympieion**; further up the street stands the Acropolis. At the base of the Acropolis are the ruins of a temple (**Tenemos**) to **Dionysus Eleutherios** (Dionysus the Liberator) and the remains of an open-air **theater** forming a half-circle. **Dionysus** is the god of wine, called "Liberator" because wine freed people of inhibitions and their normal selves. The theater of Dionysus contains the **proskenion,** the raised stage; Conrad describes the relief sculpture that decorates its base. The figures include **Hermes** (god of messengers, thieves, travel) presenting the infant Dionysus to **Zeus** (ruler of the gods on Mt. Olympus) while **Corybantes** attend on either side of the throne (these were priests of the goddess Cybele; they carried out wild rituals that resulted in exceptional ecstasy and self-castration). **Tripped the Pyrrhic fantastic** is a pun on the phrase "trip the light fantastic" from John Milton's 1645 poem "L'Allegro," the phrase means to dance impulsively or extravagantly. **Pyrrhic** means won at great expense, named after King Pyrrhus of Epirus who defeated the Romans in AD 279 but only after sustaining heavy losses. **Ikarios** was Icarius, to whom Dionysus gave wine and the means to cultivate grapes; Icarius's shepherds became drunk and killed him, so Dionysus retaliated with a plague on Athens. Ikarios should not be confused with Ikaros or Icarus, son of Daedalus, who flew too near the sun and died when his wings fell apart. The **daughter** of Dionysus is either Aglaea or Euphrosyne, the two daughters he had with Aphrodite. **Silenus** is a teacher, drunkard, and constant companion of Dionysus. **Atlas** is one of the Titans whom Zeus condemned to stand at the earth's edge and hold the Sky on his shoulders. **Hestia** is goddess of the hearth. **Theseus,** king of Athens, slew the Minotaur in the labyrinth at Crete. **Eirene**, goddess of peace, inspired poets and playwrights.

Immortal Penelope is **Pan's mother** [and a clue that Conrad is **Pan**]; she should not be confused with Odysseus's wife Penelope, whom he won by beating her father in a footrace. **Prometheus** stole fire from Zeus and gave it to man; Zeus retaliated by having **Prometheus** chained to Mount Caucasus and having his liver pecked out each day by an eagle. "**Cried 'Eloi' to the fallout**" means to cry out "My God" and worship the aftermath of an atomic blast (the novel *Deus Irae*, co-written with Philip K. Dick, explores this). **Volos**, a port city in the Greek region of Thessaly, stands at the base of Mount Pelion, mythical home of the Centaurs. **Adytum** was the inner shrine or most sacred part of a place of worship; the public was forbidden to enter. A **syrinx** is a panpipe played by **Pan** and another clue that Conrad is **Pan**.

Eugène Delacroix was a French Romantic painter in the early 1800s. **Dyspeptic** means suffering from a condition that includes heartburn and nausea. **Sandalwood** is an aromatic, Asian hardwood, burned as incense. **Coolie** is an offensive slang term for an unskilled laborer, especially of Asian descent. Buddha Gautama's body sat beneath the **Bo tree** while his soul wandered for seven years, seeking enlightenment.

Microcephalics have abnormally small heads and brains and are usually mentally handicapped. **Steatopygia** is an inherited condition of extremely large buttocks, sometimes accompanied by short stature. Steatopygia should not be mistaken for kallipygos or callipygian, which describes Aphrodite's beautiful buttocks. Caused by a filarial worm which obstructs the lymphatic system, **Elephantiasis** causes marked enlargement of the parts affected, especially the legs and scrotum.

Hindu women wrap the **sari**, a long piece of cotton or silk wrapped around their bodies. Joseph Conrad's novella ***Heart of Darkness*** depicts a journey into the Congo to face one's own personal demons. **Procrustes** was a thief and murderer who captured people and tied them to an iron bed, stretching them or hacking off their legs to make them fit it.

The ***Golden Bough***, written by Scottish anthropologist Sir James Frazer and consulted frequently by Zelazny, was a comparative study of mythology and religion. Two cannibal tribes, the **Tolalaki** and **Italones**, figure in that text. **Makrynitsa** is a Greek village near Mount Pelion. **Diablerie** is sorcery; the phrase plays on "cleanliness is next to godliness." **Pennsylvania hex signs** are hex symbols on Amish barns meant to repel evil and bring good luck. A **catafalque** is a raised platform on which a dead body is carried or lies in state.

Mongoloid is an outdated and now pejorative term for Down syndrome, a genetic condition that tends to cause mental handicap and developmental delay. **Actinic** energy induces photochemical changes, such as chemicals which absorb light in photography.

Kazaks are nomadic pastoralists of Kazakhstan and adjacent areas in China; **Todas** are a small pastoral tribe of Southern India who reside in the Nilgiri hills. **Burnoose** is an Arab's hooded cloak. ***Bismallah*** or *Bismillah* means "In the name of Allah!" **Ukemi** moves in Japanese martial arts counter a blow. **Shinvat** is a legend from Iran: a bridge thin and sharp as a knife-blade, it divides the worlds; only the faithful and the just can cross.

"Feathers or lead?" a kallikanzaros asked his victims. There was no correct answer (just whatever he wanted at the moment). The kallikanzaros then rode his victim like a horse for a breakneck, cross-country ride, lashing him with a stick. In the book, Conrad provides an explanation which does not appear in this two-part abridged version. Conrad warns Moreby that he's about to get what he deserves, that the kallikanzaros (Conrad) is going to get his way—rather like playing rock, paper, scissors with only two options, and Conrad always wins without having to reveal his choice.

Albert Payson Terhune was an American writer, best known for his novels about collies. A person **Born to knot the tiger's tail** will do impossible and dangerous things. **Lamia** is a city in central Greece, named after Poseidon's daughter.

Prometheus Unbound refers to two plays. The one attributed to Aeschylus was lost; Percy Shelley (husband of Mary Shelley) wrote the second in 1820. Both describe **Prometheus**'s release from the gods' punishment for his giving fire to humans.

"It seems, looking back, that my life has mainly been a series of arrivals and departures. I say "hello." I say "goodbye." Only the earth

endures…" Corwin echoes this later at the end of *The Courts of Chaos*: "Good-bye and hello, as always."

Pagasae, an ancient city in east central Greece, is now a suburb of Volos. The **Port of Iolkos** in Pagasae was the origin of the *Argo's voyage* and the quest for the **Golden Fleece**. **Jason** was the leader of the expedition; **Herakles** or Hercules accompanied him; other members of the **Argonauts** included **Theseus**, **Orpheus** (a Thracian poet), and **Asclepius** (the healer). **Cheiron** was a centaur who taught Jason and Asclepius and died trying to make peace between Hercules and the other centaurs. **Mount Pelion** is the mythical home of the centaurs. The Titans tried to wage war on **Mount Olympus** (home of the gods) by stacking **Mount Pelion** on top of **Mount Ossa**.

Zeus loved the Greek sea nymph **Thetis**, but prophecy warned that her son would be greater than his father, so he married her to King **Peleus** of Thessaly. **The Goddess of Discord**, Eris, was not invited, and she threw a golden apple that carried the words, "FOR THE FAIREST" into the crowd. Hera, Athena and **Aphrodite** each claimed to be the fairest; Zeus decreed that the Trojan prince **Paris** should decide. Each goddess bribed Paris, and he chose Aphrodite because she promised him the fairest woman in the world as his bride. His choice triggered the Trojan War.

A **Byronic gesture** is melodramatic, named after the poet Lord Byron and the characteristics of his work. **Whatever you were, death has taken you, too… You have gone to see the moist flower open along Acheron, among Hell's shadows darting fitfully** appears to be poetry Zelazny wrote in the manner of Sappho, who wrote of Acheron's bank being covered with dewy locusts. Zelazny echoed this line in his ode to Sappho in the poem "Tryptych": "The moist flowers along Acheron || open as my eyes close || Let me lie and call death lovely" and in "The Doors of His Face, the Lamps of His Mouth"—"…to dart fitfully forever along Acheron, and gibbering." **Acheron** is a river in Hades that flows into Styx.

The gods offered **Achilleus** or Achilles a choice: to fight for the Greek side in the Trojan War, die young, and be remembered forever as a hero, or to live long and be forgotten. A **paean** is a song of tribute, a eulogy. **Bleak disappointments rage…the day is no longer** is poetry Zelazny wrote in Philip Graber's persona.

Argives are the inhabitants of Argos, and it can mean Greeks in general. **Phoebus** is another name for Apollo. **Persephone** is the goddess of the underworld. **Elysium** is the final resting place for the heroic and the virtuous.

Herakles (Hercules) was charged to perform twelve labors to purge the sin of murdering his family in an insane rage—the **fourth labor** was to kill a wild boar that had been terrorizing Erymanthus. In pursuit of the boar, he got into a fight with centaurs and accidentally shot his friend Cheiron with a poisoned arrow, killing him. **Alethos aneste** means risen indeed. **Sic** means "as such" or "like this."

THE LAST

To Spin Is Miracle Cat, Underwood-Miller 1981.
Written 1955–60 for *Chisel in the Sky*.

And sorely bites the blade
behind Cassandra brows!
Waters mirror murder, fuse
with care-cut faces, darken all
about the chariot of disbelief.

They will not hear the word,
truer than their thousand syllables'
beauty, but bear its black fins
wrapped in nets of apparency
upon their choral back;

and the ever gentler mutter
of cloth about rushings
works wordless concordance
with golden and double doors opened
to blood-struck Agamemnon down.

Notes

Cassandra was the daughter of King Priam and Queen Hecuba of Troy, and her beauty caused Apollo to grant her the gift of prophecy. When she didn't love him in return, Apollo placed a curse on her so that no one would ever believe her predictions. She foretells **Agamemnon's** death but is not believed. Agamemnon takes her for a concubine as a spoil of war; he dies at the hands of his jealous wife. A **concordance** is an explanatory, alphabetical list of key or important words in a text.

508

ARTICLES

Guest of Honor Speech, Ozarkon 2

Sirruish #5, 1967.

Now, I really don't have a title for my talk. The bases for it are some comments by some other writers in the area, to the effect that Science Fiction writers and Science Fiction fans have a sort of "ghetto" mentality, that Science Fiction is apart from the main current of literature, and that this is really a false notion because we are as much a part of the main current of things as any popular modern novelist we see reviewed in the *New York Times Literary Supplement*, where we are very seldom seen. They say that Science Fiction writers should attempt to divorce themselves from this notion and realize that they are as much a part of the mainstream as anyone else.

I happen to disagree with this. I believe that we are apart from the mainstream, we're a separate thing; and, in order to give you my reasons for this, I'm going to have to lay a little groundwork, which, unfortunately, might make me sound like a Freshman Lit. Instructor. But I do want to bridge a few millennia and go back to the basis of Literature as we know it in Western Culture and trace it just a wee bit—and I will bring this to bear upon my subject by and by.

Now, once upon a time there were a lot of gods who had something in common: This was the fact that they died and were mutilated, and were resurrected. Now, they were generally worshipped in the area about the Mediterranean. Their names were…Oh, there were many of them: Attis, Osiris, Tammuz. And the people who worshipped them, according to anthropologists and classical scholars, tended to do this in a rather mimetic fashion. Now, some say that these deities were pretty much a solar myth. That is, that their deaths and their resurrections represented the passage of the sun through the seasons of the year; and that when the winter came and everything died, this, in a sense, was the death of the god. Once spring came, and the green came out again, things lived, and this was the resurrection. Primitive man does have a tendency to personify natural forces, and many gods were born around this area who had this thing in common, who went through this cycle.

Now, the worship of these gods—it would appear, from everything we know about the area today—was, at first, something on the order of a person's getting up and wearing a masFk which represented the god, reciting the story, the story of what had happened to the god. Mimesis. Imitation of an action. This gradually evolved so that in time, there were several people represented, perhaps the person who slew and mutilated the god, as well as the god himself—the *protagonist* and the *antagonist*—and a bit of dialogue exchange might have followed. It has been said that a fellow named Thespis wrote the first plays. Unfortunately, nothing remains concerning Thespis but his name and the fact that people say he did this thing. The first fellow to really come on the scene and take advantage of this form of worship and to turn it into something which was still religious in nature, but also possessed literary significance of the highest order, was Aeschylus. He was followed by Sophocles, Euripides, Aristophanes. Now, what happened was that at this point tragedy and comedy came into being. This was done by separating the two portions of the myth of the dying god. The tragic rhythm, which is represented by a certain passion, a certain perception, a certain catastrophe, was removed from this whole cycle and represented as tragedy. The comic spirit, in a technical sense, was the joyous reawakening, the spring-time sensation.

The tragedy normally involved certain supernatural powers, but its protagonist was a man, a very noble man, who had one tragic flaw, one thing about him which could be a metaphor for any and all human flaws. And, as a result of this, all the catastrophic powers which walked the world ultimately came to bear upon him and destroyed him. This was the death of the individual, the greatest tragedy which the individual is capable of considering.

Comedy, on the other hand, represented the continuance, the triumph of life over death. But this was not continuance for the individual; it was continuance for the species. This triumph was not so much a personal one as a racial one. The great tragedies were supposed to produce a sense of catharsis, feelings of pity and feelings of fear which were evoked in the people who watched the tragic action; and this, in a sense, cleansed them. Now, the comedy also produced a sort of catharsis. But this was a different thing. It was a feeling of the joy of continuance, a sort of immortality. In all the surviving comedies we ultimately have some character, who comes out carrying a big phallic pole and places it in the middle of the scene—and everybody then gathers 'round and indulges in an orgy. This, of course, survives in modern literature—even in the most popular media, the motion picture and television—where a comedy usually ends in a marriage. Essentially, symbolically, it is the same notion, changed only slightly for mass consumption.

This cycle, these themes, continued through what I consider the four great turning points in the history of ideas in the western world: those being the Classical innovation, the Christian revolution, the Renaissance, and the Romantic movement, which latter is still with us.

Friedrich Nietzsche claimed that the two spirits which are present in our classic tragedy are the spirits of Dionysus and Apollo, the two gods, the god of order, and the god of chaos and revelry: Tragedos and Comedos. These two spirits inform just about everything we write, everything we read, everything we consider literature, whether it's Literature with a capital 'L' or popular literature. They are sometimes at war, and sometimes one triumphs, sometimes the other. The technical meaning of tragedy is not…well, for an example, if a small child locks himself into a refrigerator and closes it, suffocates to death, people say, "That's very tragic." Well, technically it isn't; it's, speaking precisely, pathetic—for while it does evoke a feeling of pity or sympathy, it certainly does not produce fear. We don't identify with the child; we wouldn't close ourselves into an icebox, ordinarily. A comedy, normally, basically, has a happy ending—whether, it's Dante's *Divine Comedy* which begins in hell and ends in heaven or *Tom Jones*.

Now, these are the tensions, the rhythms which are present—the tragic and the comic. The tragedy itself reappeared in the time of the Elizabethans—*Hamlet, Lear*, Marlowe's *Faust*—and there is this imitation of the action again, there is this figure who is, in a sense, greater than the ordinary man, who suffers great passion, who comes into an insight, and who subsequently suffers a catastrophe. Now when a figure in a tragedy is dead, he is dead; and that is it: period. There is no more continuance for him as an individual. This is why many people say, and I agree, that the presence of Christianity precludes the notion of tragedy, because a tragedy posits the totality of existence within a specific time and space, and when that existence ends there is no after life; the individual is dead and that is it. There was criticism of the tragedy on this ground when it was revived in Elizabethan times. For it does, implicitly, deny the fact that there is divine justice. This guy is a rat, a villain, a fink, you have to kill him now, you have to make him suffer *now*, and *here*. You can't wait and let him go to Hell to be punished for his crime. There is a requirement that he be slain here on earth, made to suffer, here and now, and this, of course, is a non-Christian notion.

Now, that I've laid this much groundwork, as to the notions of tragedy and comedy and their presence—in whatever attenuated form they may exist—in any literature, I would like to, for, a moment, refer to a work of criticism, a rather weighty tome but worthwhile, rewarding if you take the time to go through it, called *An Anatomy of Criticism* by Northrop Frye, in which the author sets up a series of categories which I think will be of value to our discussion.

Mr. Frye classifies characters in accordance with four modes he believes exist in any form of literature. And these are the Mythic Mode, the High Mimetic Mode, the Low Mimetic Mode, and the Ironic Mode. Now I'll tell you what they mean.

In the Mythic Mode the main character, or characters, are greater than men. They're also greater than the natural forces which control the universe: they are, in effect, gods. They are the characters who occur in myths, in Scriptural writing, and who put in appearances in ethical writing, and occasionally in classical drama.

Now, in the High Mimetic mode we have characters who are greater than ordinary men—they're kings—but the Greek word used there doesn't really mean king in the Medieval sense. They're sort of great land owners, people highly respected in their community, people who exercise some measure of authority, characters who still have a slight trace of the Mythic Mode about them, too, for they are often referred to as having some measure of control over natural forces. In Sophocles' *Oedipus Rex* you hear references to a blight being upon the land because something is wrong with the king. This is the sort of character you run into in the High Mimetic Mode; someone who is greater than other people and can sometimes have a reputation for slaying a monster, or controlling some natural force.

Now, the Low Mimetic Mode has been with us since about the nineteenth century in most of our fiction. This is the thing which involves a character who is not superior to other men, who is not superior to nature. He is the character in most of the realistic and naturalistic novels we have with us today.

Now, in the Ironic Mode, the final one to which Mr. Frye refers, we have characters who are not only not greater than natural forces, not greater than their fellow men—they aren't even equal to their fellow men. They are inferior. These are the people you'll find in the works of Beckett, Ionesco, Kafka. They are Charlie Chaplin going around a department store on roller skates.

So these are the four categories. Now, there is a strange thing about them. They are not considered a hierarchy but, rather, a cycle. The Ironic Mode—where a character is less than his fellow man—sort of feeds back into the Mythic Mode. You'll find that when you have a grotesque person who does strange things, and who is kicked about and acted upon, and to whom inexplicable things happen, he strangely assumes the aura of a figure in a myth, of someone who in some way just might be a god-figure, an archetypal image.

I'll leave this for just a moment now and return to it shortly. It has been said that tragedy and myth or scripture—or, epic—is impossible in a Democracy or a good Socialism because these political systems have built into them an inherent notion that all men are equal. Consequently, this rather precludes considering a figure like Hamlet, King Lear, Coriolanus, Orestes, in modern literature. We normally, since the nineteenth century, have been writing about figures in the Low Mimetic Mode. In recent years we have been going more and more into the Ironic Mode. But we've left the other two pretty much out of things in the main current of writing.

The distinction I think is here: Science Fiction has not abandoned the High Mimetic Mode. It is, in this sense, aristocratic. The characters in Science Fiction stories, the backgrounds which are set up, and the worlds explored in Science Fiction are ones in which you can posit gods, if you wish—you can have them operate and affect the characters; also, the notion of the hero has continued in Science Fiction. There was a whole rash of stories some years back involving mutants. These people were able to control physical environment as well as the actions of others about them. They were clearly superior. This did open a way, if anyone cared to try, to write a tragedy in the Science Fiction medium. Someone is going to counter with a question "Why didn't they?" I'll answer that, but I wanted to first draw this distinction between the mainstream and that area in which

Science Fiction writers work, that area in which maybe a few hundred thousand people enjoy reading, in answer to Harlan Ellison, Ted White and others, who insist that we are part and parcel of the main current of things.

We're not. It's as simple as that. We're writing in a different mode. I don't say that all Science Fiction stories are in the High Mimetic Mode, but a good percentage are. The British writers are going into exploring the Ironic mode. Good. I consider Ballard of this tradition, and I like Ballard.

Now, I would like to, in a sense, vindicate Science Fiction writers for not having explored the full potential of the High Mimetic Mode, and while I have just said, or sort of agreed, that we live in a "ghetto," I'm going to attempt to say that this has given us a great potential, yet to be realized, and I will try to point my finger at something at least to show that we are moving in that direction.

Science Fiction, of course, began in the pulp magazines in the late twenties, ran through the thirties, the forties—the Depression, the war years—and, as such, was pretty much a product of the restrictions of the pulp magazines. These restrictions were quite severe. Things like sex were tabu in the stories, and the writers had to write pretty much what the editors wanted—formula stories—if they wanted to sell their stuff. Otherwise, they'd be writing for themselves alone. So they conformed, and they went along with it, in order to write something they enjoyed a bit more than detective stories or westerns. And, after a time, the Science Fiction market burgeoned. There was a great plethora of Science Fiction magazines all over the place, and it was natural that the bust eventually followed. Many of the magazines folded and left us with just a few. But there were many writers who had committed themselves to the area, and the market suddenly became highly restricted and much more competitive than it had been. So, they were forced to resort to the alternative of writing more and more for the paperback books. This was the first step, I think, in the direction in which we are still moving today. They were freed at that point, freed from many of the restrictions which the magazines placed upon them. At first, many of them continued to write the same sort of thing they had been writing for the magazines because they were used to it. Gradually they began to experiment more. Now there are many of them who do not write for the magazines at all. They write for hardcover and paperback books exclusively, and they find that there is freedom, freedom which they didn't realize they had, all that time, freedom to do whatever they darn please. And now, we also have new writers who came into the area in recent years, who have moved into this medium and inherited this recent sense of freedom; and I believe they have also inherited the means of producing something which may be great literature. I feel that we are going to see some genuine tragedies and comedies, in the strict classical sense of the word, in the area. I can only point at two which, in my opinion, come close to it right now.

I believe that Theodore Sturgeon's novel *More Than Human*, with which many of you are familiar, came close to a genuine tragic vision at one point. For those of you who don't know the plot outline, basically there is a group of mutated individuals, each of whom possesses one particular psychic ability, and when they all come together and work together, they establish a sort of psychic rapport, which, in a sense, turns them into a gestalt—one organization, one entity, with many abilities. The one individual who is the brains of this group, or, the director, I should say, once destroyed a human being, a man who could have been a genius: he wrecked this man's life completely. How, in the end this man is rescued, brought back to normal by a girl who is a member of the group, who is able to get inside the mind of a man and see exactly what's there. She forces him to get inside the mind of this man he has hurt. Suddenly, for the first time in his life, this director realizes that there is a sort of morality to which he, too, owes some sort of allegiance. He experiences a genuine pity for this man whom he has destroyed. He comes close to something like a tragic catharsis.

I'm not going to try to rewrite Sturgeon, but I would have done it a little differently myself, for there is hope for that man who was broken: he is on his feet again and he is going to become a "useful" member of society. I probably would have written the scene with the man on his deathbed, and this realization by the director as the last thing before the man's death. Whatever…

This, I contend, is very close: it's moving in that direction.

I said there were two works, though. The other one is *Childhood's End* by Arthur C. Clarke. Here, again, I'll just go briefly into the plot. We have a situation where Earth is visited by creatures from another place, creatures who correspond in appearance to the devils out of Christian tradition. They have horns and they have tails. When they appear, though, they're not malevolent; they're here on Earth primarily as observers. They're waiting for something to happen. Actually, what they're waiting for is the next step in the evolution of the human race. And this does occur in a few generations. A generation of children is born who possess strange abilities. As they mature, they establish a sort of psychic bond so that they share one great mass mind. The creatures who resemble devils are a race who, for some reason which is never explained, are denied this step in their own evolution. They travel around the universe finding races which are about to mature into this next stage and they act sort of as midwives to them at the time of their birth. Now, as it would happen, there is one Earth man who is very curious as to the place of origin of these demon-like creatures. He manages to stow away aboard one of their ships and go to their home planet. He is there discovered, of course, and they explain to him what is about to occur. In his absence the children, who have now reached and passed adolescence, have withdrawn themselves from society into a sort of community of their own; and the old human race, which realizes that something fearful is happening, enters into a series of suicidal wars and pretty much annihilates itself. At this point, the children are about to depart the Earth. They no longer require the physical bodies they inhabit. They unite themselves into one vast golden being, and their last act in departing is to destroy the world, which has now served its purpose. Now the man who stowed away aboard the ship which took him to the planet of the creatures is, at this time, offered the hospitality of these creatures. He may spend the rest of his life on their planet, they tell him. He declines the offer, and he asks to be returned to Earth. He is a concert pianist; he is a Negro; he is a man who realizes what is happening, and he sees no further reason for his own existence. His last act is to set up a piano and to begin playing as the Earth is destroyed. Everything falls apart about him, and he continues; and that's it. The great golden creatures destroy the world and depart. This is the end of man's childhood; he has now become this great, golden thing.

Now, in a classical sense, it would be hard to—at least I would be hard put to—say whether it is a tragedy or a comedy. I suppose it would be a comedy, in that it represents the continuance of the species, the triumph over the death-rhythm you see in tragedy. But I can't really identify with this great creature which destroys people such as myself. So, while it may be a comedy if that creature were writing the story, for me…I consider it very close to a tragic vision when the last man is sitting there playing the piano and realizing all these things. He, of course, fears the end which, of course, is at hand. He, of course, has pity for all his fellows who have perished, who will never exist again. And he is destroyed. That, I feel, is the other example of coming close to what I think is a tragic vision in the Science Fiction area. This obviously could not have been done in what people refer to as the main current of literature. It required an artificial background such as could only be supplied by someone who is writing a "ghetto" story, if you want to call it that. These are the only two I can think of right now, but I think they indicate the possibilities within the area. I think that rather than being a bad thing, our insularity, our appendix-like position in the body of literature is a good thing and I feel that it will eventually result in more stories of this ilk.

Now this, basically, is my whole thesis for today, this my answer to those who say, "We are not apart": We have the gods on our side.

Notes

Zelazny was Guest of Honor at many conventions where he often gave humorous speeches. Unfortunately, some of his funniest speeches were not recorded and exist only as apocryphal stories from convention attendees—this includes the "Chicken Effect" and "I Am *Not* Roger Zelazny" speeches.

Given in July 1967 at Ozarkon 2 in St. Louis, this Guest of Honor speech marks the first time Zelazny publicly addressed the theme of the dying/resurrecting god which influenced much of his early work.

ON WRITING AND STORIES

Science Fiction Times #446, September 1967.

I n a book which I read around fifteen years ago—the title of which escapes me, as well as everything else in it—I came across one notion concerning writing which seemed a watertight little truth worth preserving, and still does. What the man said, in so many other words, was that editors don't buy stories, they buy writing. It warrants a moment's meditation.

Obviously, there has to be a story or at least a situation on which to hang the writing. However, I have often been confronted by friends, acquaintances and strangers, who tell me they've just gotten The Greatest Idea For A Story, Listen Please And Tell Me What You Think. I've listened and told them what I thought. I've told some, and truthfully, that I was surprised they weren't selling their stuff, because their ideas and plots struck me as quite good. But then, I've sometimes had occasion to see the final product—a story all written out, neat & pretty-pure & on crinkly white bond—and smelling to high heaven, because for all his mentation the author did not dignify his story with interesting, and sometimes not even grammatical, prose. There is little excuse for poor grammar and syntax on the part of a would-be writer, and if a person did not receive an adequate background in this while he was in school, it is a thing remediable by recourse to one of the many, good and easily available texts on the subject. This point is obvious, but so is the fact that it is often ignored.

Grammatical prose need not be interesting prose, however. Interesting prose may be the result of one of two things: hard work or natural talent. Not much to say about the latter, and the former means practice. It means writing a thing over and over and over again until it starts to sound decent and until making things come out decently becomes a habit. Once this has been achieved, a person is ready to sell writing, and the question as to where the stories come from becomes easy to answer, because then there are only two sources.

One is inspiration, and it can't be controlled. Sometimes an idea, a situation, a character, a setting will burst like a Roman Candle behind your eyes and stay there while you write with a deadly compulsion until it's all down on paper and the fire goes out and you can start sleeping and eating again. If writers had to rely on inspiration, though, their finances would suffer far more than their health.

So in between those demonic flashes, a writer who is aiming at a regular output has to make do with the second source. He has to go through the mechanics of constructing a plot, then start writing and hope that things will catch fire somewhere along the way. His writing then has to be interesting enough to carry whatever perhaps trite things he has to say, by embellishing the characters to bring them as close to humanity as is possible for him, by considering the background to the extent of providing as much consistency, depth and color as he can, by supplying details having a tone of truth for both of these, details from out of his imagination and details looked up in other places. He can take one of the Trite & Mighty: a triangle love/hate story, a revenge story, a Man v. Nature story, and if he pays the proper homage to the god of mundane labor he will succeed in selling the writing, where a man who neglects these obeisances would not sell the same story.

That writers favor certain sources when seeking detail is axiomatic. It is a thing governed by background, temperament and attitude. While Andre Norton, say, turns to anthropology and mythology, Wilson Tucker will turn to contemporary military and political annals. If I had to name two books from which I've mined detail in quantity, I would name *A Glossary of the Construction, Decoration and Use of Arms and Armor in All Countries and All Times, Together With Some Related Subjects*, by George Cameron Stone (Noble Offset Printers Inc. N.Y., 1961) and *The Forest and the Sea*, by Marston Bates (Mentor, N.Y., 1961).

But the detail or its source is unimportant, really, to the extent that we know it is available. Anyone with access to a library can dig up detail. It is the use to which it is put that is important.

The next time you read a story which does not contain a single original idea, which does not possess even one particularly memorable character, which does not have an especially unique setting, but which you do not feel cheated at having read and possibly even enjoyed, remember then that the story is paying homage to the writing. It is the latter which the editor purchased. If magazine editors had to rely on artistry rather than craftsmanship, there would be no magazines. This is the main reason I bite back a chuckle whenever I read an article or listen to a panel discussion concerning Literature & Science Fiction, or vice versa. Look for it in the occasionally inspired work, which percentage-wise is as prevalent in s-f as anywhere else, if you bear in mind that s-f itself represents only a small percentage of the awesome tonnage of material published every year. Mostly, you'll just see writing, and that's why it's that way.

Shadows

Kallikanzaros #3 December 1967–January 1968.

My subject is one which we all like and respect, whatever specific medium we most prefer. I am referring to fantastic literature. By this I mean to include science fiction, science fantasy, pure fantasy, the horror story, and all things of this sort. I am also going to talk about something I call *shadows*, as they affect the forms which, in our different capacities, we all pay homage to and/or make our money from. I'd also like to talk about how these things affect me and my work, and how they will affect, I believe, the future of science fiction as a written form (short story, novel) and fantastic literature in the comic art form, in the motion picture, and on television. Before I do this, however, I'd like to discuss the history of that phenomena which we refer to by the general term fandom.

Now of course, we all know that science fiction pretty much began in the magazine form in the late twenties. It continued on toward a sort of "golden age" in the late thirties and through the forties, and is still with us today in the form of several fine magazines which circulate 40 to 60 thousand copies per month. Fandom began, I would say, in the depression years. Possibly this was because there were a lot of people out of work and pulp magazines were cheap. At this time various magazines had lengthy letter columns. Fans (well, I guess you couldn't really call them fans, they were just readers) with time on their hands would write into these letter columns in order to see their names in print and because they could enjoy a bit in the way of a discussion or reply from the editor or the other readers. They wrote into these magazines to discuss the stories or the art, the format of the magazine, whether to have rough edges or staples, or almost anything of that sort. After a time, because their names and addresses were printed, they began to correspond with one another. If they lived nearby, they would get together sometime. Then, because some were out of work, had nothing better to do, and had funds, they would hitch-hike around the country meeting other fans. Gradually, groups came to be formed which took it upon themselves to print amateur periodicals dedicated to whatever phase of fantastic literature happened to be the primary interest of the group. Gradually a tradition was built up. Little conferences and get-togethers were held. Finally, the first World Science Fiction Convention came along. Over the years a whole body of tradition grew up, so that there are now many regional and local conventions. Fanzines, there are hundreds of them around, fold and are replaced by new ones every year. We can safely say that this is all here to stay. We wonder, and I think the answer lies in the combination of the depression and the letter columns, we wonder why detective stories and western fiction never developed similar interest groups and similar traditions. I think that it just happened…the coincidence of these items…there was a format and a forum in which these people could express themselves, get to know one another, and finally to form organizations developing into what we have today.

Whatever the case, the comic books obviously didn't come upon us during the depression. There were forerunners and comic strips, but it was pretty much a late thirties and early forties phenomena. It never had quite the same in the way of letter columns. As it happened, much of the subject matter of the comics was a graft from science fiction. There were science fiction people actually doing continuity for the comic books. Gardner Fox does it today, and Otto Binder used to do it. Because of this tie-in, all the science fiction themes with which the science fiction fan was familiar (such as space travel, space war, various space drives, time travel, alien cultures, psi phenomena and telepathy) appeared in comic form. Out of dual interests, science fiction fans began to read the comics, and comic fans drifted into science fiction. It was natural, since they found this pre-existing set up of clubs, periodicals, and journals, that they sort of gradually patterned themselves along the same lines. They actually started coming to the same conventions and putting out their own fanzines, so that we have two distinct fandoms which are linked together quite strongly and pattern in a very similar fashion, though they are still separate entities.

To carry things a bit further, I don't know if Forry Ackerman is the one person to put the finger on, but a sort of movie fandom grew up also.

There is even a small group dedicated to old radio shows; *Inner Sanctum, Lights Out, Hermits Cave, Dimension X, 2,000 Plus, The Shadow, House of Mystery*, and the like. They obtain tapes of the old shows and play them. This is another aspect of fandom. I'm mentioning all things now, because I'm going to go into a discussion concerning the effect of the various media on the ideas which make up all of these fandoms.

Literature, of necessity, contains shadows. I think I coined the term shadows, and what I mean by this is that a writer never writes an entire story, an illustrator never draws a complete picture, and a producer doesn't let the movie tell all. You live part of it yourself, or you draw it in your mind, or you concoct part of it as you watch the movie. Shadows are necessary. If I were, at this moment, to decide that I wanted to describe this room in a story, I could do it in one sentence or two paragraphs, depending upon the purpose for which I was describing it. My description, of necessity, would be incomplete. If I were to sit down and describe every article of clothing that everybody was wearing, the color of everybody's hair or eyes, the way they're sitting, whether cross-legged or arms folded, or what have you…the temperature of the room, the background noises, rattling glasses, the chandelier, the colors of the walls…I would have a whole book. If you were stupid enough to read this thing through, you'd be quite bored by the end. So, of necessity, I have to leave a lot of things out. Any writer has to pick out significant features and imply the rest. The inferences that are drawn from what is implied is a good portion of writing the story. If, for example, I were to take a photograph of this room as it stands now, you would see all the things that I don't say as well as the things that I do say in writing. However, in my description I would have to throw in some adjectives, and these adjectives would give the scene feeling. Just looking at a picture of a crowd staring in this direction wouldn't tell you if the people were hating the person they were looking at, or listening intently, or if they were just sitting there saying, "Gee, it's warm in here. When is he going to shut up so we can get out?" So a picture, in one sense, is worth thousands of words, but in another sense is lacking.

Writing involves your taking everything in though those little cryptic bugs that crawl across the page and construct things around them. This is where that strange thing called "sense of wonder" comes into play. There is no special reason why someone has a "sense of wonder," unless, maybe you fell on your head when you were a kid or something. You've got this "sense of wonder" and it sort of enfolds this shadow area. Into those shadows you project those things you are looking for, the fantastic things, maybe the horrible things, or the exotic things. The other media have their own shadows also, but they are in different places. Take a series of cartoon panels…they show the heroes, their skintight outfits, always looking heroic (after a tremendous battle it seems that their hair has just been combed and all the wrinkles smoothed out of their costumes). I was very disappointed when Batman came to television, because his uniform wrinkled. I was used to seeing a very tight, sleek thing that showed all of his muscles, and just couldn't wrinkle. I never could believe that Batman's costume could wrinkle, but there it was. If I were to take the photo I told you of a while ago (of all of you sitting here) and stick it up here on the wall behind me and ask everyone to stand up and have another picture taken, stick it next to the first, and then if I were to ask you to kick over all the chairs in the room, break a few, throw a few of these glasses against the wall, and stalk out leaving the room empty, take a third photo and set it up over here, without any word balloons, especially in the last one, or any other descriptions, and if someone were to come in and look at this series of pictures, they would tell him a story. It might not always be the same story, but there is something implied there. You got mad at me, there was a riot, we all got hauled away by the cops. The shadows there, however, are not in the pictures, which put everything in bold perspective (right in the foreground) where nothing is left to the imagination. The shadows are in what lies between the pictures. This is the place where the mind makes automatic assumptions. Say, in a "Fantastic Four" comic book in one scene they are laying around the Baxter building and they get a message. They say, "My golly we've got to get down to Brazil right away…to that spaceship where the monsters have landed." In the next panel we see the Pogo Plane flying across the Andes. We see a few condors flapping their wings, perhaps, while they are stationary. In the next scene they are running from their plane towards an enormous spaceship parked right near the jungle. In between those three panels a lot of things happened. Maybe Ben Grimm went to get a toothbrush. Sue Storm said, "Well, Reed, you're going to throw a few pieces of equipment into the plane, why don't I go make a few ham sandwiches?" Ben maybe smoked a cigar while flying out there. Things like this happened because you know what that there is a time lapse between them and you automatically assume that there is a continuance of the characters' existence between them. So this is the place where your imagination fools around, perhaps subliminally. The "sense of wonder" comes into play as to what is going on between these sequences. Now, this is, of course, a very visual thing. You are highlighted with the scenes of action. It is in this way different from the written word while still dwelling on the same subject matter, fantastic happenings. Consider radio as a medium for a fantastic story. With the old shows I have mentioned, you could sit there with your eyes closed and listen. They did some very fine Ray Bradbury stories, a lot of the ones that appeared in *The Martian Chronicles*, and some of Heinlein's stuff. You would sit there and hear a voice coming out that would say, "The ship from Earth came down on the red sands of Mars. Suddenly, like a great silver bird, Captain Smith and his crew descended. They stood there in the chill Martian morning. Ensign Jones turned to Smith and said, 'Do you hear a strange singing, sir?' " Then you would hear a background of wailing, perhaps. You are not looking at pictures or reading words. You are sitting there and getting them through the ear. This, I think, is a very good medium for science fiction (not that I am passing aesthetic judgement on any of them). I think it is good because it leaves a lot to the imagination. It's almost like the old village story teller. When I gave that little description, when I said that the silver space ship came down, I would guess that you visualized one. If you were looking at a picture of one though, it might cheapen it a bit. It might destroy something of the element of this particular phase of the shadow moment. Now, when you combine the two, the visual and the auditory, and you produce a motion picture or a television show, you do something different again. You feel much closer to it. It's almost a tactile, kinesthetic sensation that you experience. You are seeing everything happen and listening to it. It's not at all like reading about it, because it does not leave that much to your imagination. You know that so-and-so looks like Rock Hudson or whomever. In a story, however, if I describe someone who is Rock Hudson's height and has hair the color of Rock Hudson's hair and eyes that are his color and that he is smiling a little bit and squinting, how you would picture him would depend on whether later on the page he turned out to be a villain or a hero. You would color in certain things from your imagination. If he were a hero he would be just a bit handsomer than the villain. This element is there. It's got to be there. It's participation.

There are different ways of dealing with these things we are interested in. You can hit the various senses with them. Some of us may be fans of one particular media or another. Most of us touch within all the areas. I happen to be oriented toward the written word because I do it. What I am leading up to saying, though, is that we've got these fandoms, and that we are each in a way dedicated to one another of these, and they are close because they share a common sense of wonder in the way they deal with the shadows. Not only are the fandoms close, but the various media overlap. I think that comic art has influenced the science fiction novel, and science fiction short story in that this sense of the visual (at least in my case, and I think in others) has served as a tool for describing something. I've noticed that on occasion when I've wanted to describe a character or a scene I will visualize it, almost as though it were a panel an illustration. I will describe and then go on. I have noted too, that in the motion picture the one place where the shadows operate is in the camera, in the fact that it can zoom in for a close-up of a man's face then back off and show a monster stalking him slowly from behind, or show a man and a woman kissing then have a fade out and show them having breakfast together a bit later. The imagination works. It fills in what happened during the fade out. It goes along with the camera movements. This too has influenced writing both in the science fiction field and out of it. I think that movies have had a very strong influence on fiction. I sometimes find myself thinking of the whole thing as a sequence of movie shots. I'll, maybe, back off for a long shot and describe a scene, maybe two characters in the distance. Then I'll zoom in and show them clearer and describe them. Then show a close-up…the expression on a man's face. So there is a cross fertilization of the comics and the movies and writing. I believe that to an extent it has worked the other way also. I think that the modern novel which is antinovelistic and is breaking traditions and is experimenting has influenced the movies. It is truer of foreign movies than it is of those made in Hollywood. There are a lot of surrealistic things, French movies where they apply novelistic techniques.

There are these shadows. They have influenced me. They are present, and I think that they are going to continue to cross-pollinate and fertilize one another, and that as time goes on, these new tools that have been borrowed from the various art forms are going to be switched around and tried in different areas.

Notes

This is Zelazny's Guest of Honor Speech from the 1967 Detroit Triple Fan Fair convention featuring the triad of comics, movies and science fiction. Zelazny received the first Nova Award at this convention in recognition of outstanding contribution to science fiction and fantasy.

"...And Call Me Roger"
the Literary Life of
Roger Zelazny, Part 2

by Christopher S. Kovacs, MD

———————1965———————

On to Baltimore

Zelazny separated from Sharon Steberl in summer 1965, just over six months after they were married. He wanted to distance himself from that part of his life, so when an opportunity arose for a transfer away from Ohio, he took it readily. It was a promotion to claims policy specialist at the Woodlawn Social Security office, and he moved in September 1965 to Carriage House Apartments on North Bend Road in Baltimore. He later told Harlan Ellison that he "Rapidly rose to obscurity in government circles as a claims policy specialist in the Social Security Administration."[1] He continued to write regularly in the evenings and began to receive nominations for awards and more attention from critics and fans as some of his other notable work of the 1960s appeared.

The Dream Master

After Zelazny completed *...And Call Me Conrad*, Damon Knight convinced him to expand the novella "He Who Shapes" into a novel. Knight wrote to him in January 1965, "I think 'He Who Shapes' is a brilliant job, very impressive. Have you thought of possibly expanding it to novel length? It seems to me there is enough solid background and character to carry it. If you do want to expand it and would like to try it on Berkley Books, please let me know; I can probably get you a contract and an advance on the basis of the published portion plus an outline."[2] Thus Zelazny's second novel was born, but during their subsequent exchange of correspondence Knight revealed that he did not act on his earlier promise to seek a contract and advance from the intended publisher. Zelazny still had never written an outline; he learned how years later, during his collaboration with Fred Saberhagen on the novel *Coils*. Instead, Knight replied that Zelazny would get a contract and advance upon completion of the novel.

Zelazny wrote additional material over the next several months and sent it to Knight in stages. Knight continued to praise the effort and cajole him to write more. In February, after receiving 13,000 new words, Knight wrote, "I like the new material for *He Who* [sic] very much, especially Sigmund who is quite a guy [Sigmund is an enhanced, talking dog]. By my rough count, however…this one needs 7,000 more [words] to flesh it out. If you can give me that much more, either in outline or as a finished draft, I'll send it to Tom Dardis at Berkley and I think a contract will result."[3] In March Knight acknowledged the latest additions, noting "this is fine stuff; please send more."[4] At the same time as he demanded more material for the novel, he also requested short stories from Zelazny and rejected each of these in turn (see afterwords to "This Moment of the Storm" and "For a Breath I Tarry.")[5,6] These rejections and Knight's failure to seek a contract and advance for the novel likely gave Zelazny second thoughts about the venture. By May he'd stopped sending material, prompting Knight to pester him again, "Speaking of [*He Who Shapes*], when are you going to send me some more?"[6]

Zelazny finally begged off, explaining "Uh, it's this way…Please think me not a prima donna or such, because such is not the case, but I'm honestly out of story on *He Who*. I fear that an attempt to add any more to the thing will just prove disastrous. I've looked and I've looked, and all I can see is the bottom of the barrel…I fear that anything more I could add would be padding, pure and apparent, rather than padding impure and disguised…I hate to trouble you with anything when I know you're up to here with work of your own, but honest to Yesht there ain't any more, no matter where I look. If I add another one sentence even, I'm afraid the thing will topple over and just lie there creaking feebly. Help! please. I dunno what to do."[7]

Finally Damon Knight sent the manuscript to Berkley Books Editor Tom Dardis, who considered it for many months but rejected it in January 1966. Zelazny later described the situation this way: "I showed it to Damon and he talked to the publisher who said that they didn't like it, the initial description was good, but the novel wasn't."[8] Berkley's rejection was the second in a series of difficulties between Zelazny and that publisher which also involved …*And Call Me Conrad*, *The Dead Man's Brother*, and *Doorways in the Sand*.

Less than two months later, Zelazny had the last laugh when "He Who Shapes" received the Nebula Award at the March 1966 banquet. No doubt, the editor at Berkley couldn't help but notice and regret his earlier decision. Damon Knight hurriedly wrote "…would you send it to Berkley again? Tom Dardis is wondering if perhaps he should have bought it after all, and would like to see it again."[9] But it was too late; Agent Robert Mills had already intervened and sold the novel to Ace Books, which was delighted to have a second award-winning Zelazny novel in their catalog (*This Immortal* had not yet appeared, and the Hugo Award for best novel was still several months in the future).[10,11] Ironically, just as with …*And Call Me Conrad* / *This Immortal*, Ace Books did not like Zelazny's proposed title *He Who Shapes*, and renamed it *The Dream Master*.[10] The title *He Who Shapes* was not Zelazny's either—he had called the novella "The Ides of Octemeber," but *Amazing*'s Editor Cele Goldsmith changed it to "He Who Shapes."[12] Ace published *The Dream Master* in September 1966, a few months after *This Immortal* appeared.[11]

Zelazny was never wholly satisfied with the novel version and ultimately preferred the economy of the original novella (see afterword to "He Who Shapes"). "So to get it into a novel form frankly, I padded some of the scenes. Aesthetically I don't like that, but at the time there was a lot of money involved which I needed. So I did some scenes I'd thought of which I wished I'd done initially, and there were a few others I wasn't overjoyed with."[8] Samuel R. Delany later remarked that, although the added material weakened the "superb" execution and structure of the original novella, it could not simply be dismissed because "scene for scene, it is beautifully done, and amplifies both major and minor themes. My uneasiness is with placement, pacing and emphasis, which destroys the original thematic intensity of the whole; and because of the real excellence in the new material, the frustration is doubled."[13] The story repeatedly questions the nature of reality as perceived by Render and his patients, and various references within it (to the circularity of Ouroboros/Jormangund, for example) suggest that the entire story has taken place—and is continually looping—within Render's tortured mind. Zelazny acknowledged that he had written the story to express those themes and that *The Dream Master* was in its time one of a very few existentialist novels in the science fiction field.[14]

The novel remained in print for decades, found more readers than the novella ever did, emphasized that Zelazny's style could be rich in metaphor and allusion, and led to his work on the movie *Dreamscape*. With *This Immortal* and *The Dream Master* behind him, he was ready to tackle his most ambitious novel *Lord of Light*.

Influence of Government Bureaucracy

Zelazny used his Social Security Administration experience in several ways in his later writing. "I looked at people's hands and the gestures they made with them. I studied their faces, wondered about their clothing, their jewelry, their scars. I listened to them lie and tell what they thought was the truth."[15] As his friend Carl Yoke wrote, "For Roger, the people he met were adventures, things to be explored and to learn from. Ideas and characters, not only from real life but from other stories were to be examined in detail, understood, and used to create new stories."[16] Zelazny based the recurring character and settings from the *My Name Is Legion* novellas on his first-hand experiences with government bureaucracies, which also figure heavily in *Isle of the Dead*, *This Immortal*, and *Today We Choose Faces*.

"For a Breath I Tarry"

Zelazny repeatedly called this his all-time favorite story. Surprisingly, at first no American sf magazine editor would buy it, including Damon Knight, who simply considered it a well done version of a story that had been told too many times before.[6] Zelazny eventually submitted it to *New Worlds* in the UK, and Editor Michael Moorcock's acceptance letter was particularly effusive: "What I have read shows a potential talent that gleams out like a life-saving beacon to one wading through quicksands… I only rarely write letters as enthusiastic as this to contributors, and only when a writer emerges who shows himself capable of producing the more literate and sophisticated kind of science fiction which we need."[17] *New Worlds* experienced serious financial troubles and nearly folded before the story appeared, but in what later Zelazny called a "charitable act," he permitted Moorcock to publish the story "for nothing" and thereby enabled the struggling magazine to publish another issue (see afterword to that story for more details).

The first appearance of the story was garbled by transposed paragraphs and dropped sentences, but despite those typesetting errors, Moorcock received many letters from subscribers, telling him what a great story it was. It went on to become another signature piece of Zelazny's, reprinted dozens of times in multiple languages. It was also reprinted as an illustrated limited edition and adapted into a radio play.

———————1966———— —

Divorce and Marriage

Zelazny and Sharon Steberl divorced on June 27, 1966, about one year after they'd separated. He'd pleaded with his friend Carl Yoke to testify on behalf of Steberl at the proceedings, and Yoke did so.[18,19]

Since he'd moved to Baltimore, Zelazny had been dating Judith Alene Callahan, whom he'd worked with at the Social Security Administration. They were married at City Hall in Baltimore on August 20, two months after his divorce was finalized.[20] Zelazny later confided to Yoke that he'd had some misgivings about remarrying so quickly, but these qualms evidently subsided.[19] Shortly after the wedding, *The Dream Master* appeared and bore the passionate dedication "To Judy, of the hurst of oaks with a wolf issuant therefrom to the sinister all proper. *'Fidus et audax.'* [faithful and bold]."

Roger and Judy Zelazny remained together for twenty-eight years and had three children. She accompanied him to science fiction conventions, and colleagues teased that he didn't deserve her, that Judy was far too good, fine, and pretty a woman for him.[1,21,22] Although Judy's presence at these events pleased him, he was not forthcoming about details of his private life in his speeches and public conversation.

From the beginning of his popularity as a writer, he kept his family and personal life private wherever possible. "I like to keep my writing apart from the rest of my life. I make my living displaying pieces of my soul in some distorted form or other. The rest of it is my own."[15]

Zelazny donated his papers to several university archives. He wanted this material made available without restrictions for scholarly research into his life as a writer, and he openly wondered what use someone might make of it. This monograph makes extensive use of those university archives to explore Zelazny's literary life.

On a light and amusing note about himself, he described the consequences of his hirsute characteristics in a letter to fellow writer, Gil Lamont:

"It's been a while since I cultivated face-fur. I'm one of those who must shave twice daily or it looks as if he didn't at all. Got me into more damn trouble in the army:

" 'Pfc. Zelazny, you posing for Holy Pictures or something?'

" 'No, Sir!'

" 'When's the last time you shaved?'

" 'Sir, I shaved this morning, sir!'

" 'Well, let's put a blade in the razor next time, huh?'

"Memories."[23]

In May 1965, on the morning that he was supposed to speak on a panel at Disclave, he cut himself shaving. He segued from cursing the cut and wishing he could exchange bodies to avoid showing his lacerated face in public, to conceptualizing the novel *Lord of Light* (see afterword to the story "Death and the Executioner" for the full anecdote). He spent much of that panel discussion in a distracted state as the characters and plot took shape in his mind.

Lord of Light

Having conceived *Lord of Light* in a flash due to the shaving incident, Zelazny researched Hindu and Buddhist mythology for the background and devoted much of 1965 and early 1966 to writing the novel. During that long year he worked 40 hours per week and wrote in the evenings and on weekends. The afterword to "Death and the Executioner" details some of the books that he read for background material; he was also helped significantly by Andre Norton, who had worked at the Library of Congress and had "kept up on all sorts of secondary reference materials."[24] He was quite excited about the novel, and in a letter in June 1965 he wrote, "Am now hot on the trail of what I think may be my best tale to date—a novel—*Maitreya* [working title of *Lord of Light*]. It *will* contain sword & sorcery elements. Might take several months in the writing. Dunno for sure yet…must return now to *Maitreya*, where the Fallen Ones do battle against the Lords of Trimurti."[25]

Departing from his usual practice of taking breaks to work on other projects, he labored continuously on *Lord of Light*.[26] This single mindedness later led to a noticeable decline in his contributions to sf magazines and concern from his new fans who wanted to see more stories and wondered if he had already burned out. He finished the novel in March 1966, shortly before the Nebula Awards banquet on March 11 at which Zelazny was the star recipient of two awards—best novella and best novelette. He met Doubleday Editor Larry Ashmead at the banquet, and upon hearing that Zelazny had recently finished a novel, Ashmead requested to see it. Zelazny sent it to him immediately.[27] Ashmead was delighted and wrote, "I enjoyed it very much indeed, and would like to have it for the Doubleday list. I do have a few editorial suggestions—none of which I will insist upon and none of which involve much revision or rewriting."[28] Acknowledging that Zelazny was acting without an agent, Doubleday offered him a $1,500 advance (approximately $9,500 in 2008 dollars), later reduced to $1,200 when Zelazny opted to keep the foreign rights.[28–30]

Zelazny deliberately structured the novel in seven discrete sections. "I had decided on seven or nine chapters of approximately 13,000 words each, so that I might be able to sell a few as novelettes if no one wanted to chance on using it as a series or serial. For this reason, I figured that each chapter would have to be somewhat independent of its fellows…I wanted to separate the chapters in space and time, and so produce a sort of folk-story quality. I could have had nine chapters, but I threw out what I was thinking of using in two of them, because there is a breaking point in anything like this and I didn't want to just pile up incident…"[31]

Two chapters appeared separately in *The Magazine of Fantasy & Science Fiction* as the stories "Dawn" and "Death and the Executioner." Editor Edward L. Ferman wanted to publish the entire novel but couldn't due to its length and other serials that he had in inventory. He wrote, "This is an impressive story—and fun to read as well…I want to take as much of it as I can, and happily, the segments I liked best seem also to stand alone best."[32] The other five chapters had been scheduled to appear in *New Worlds*, except that it temporarily folded, and when it resumed publication it was too close to the novel's publication date to allow them to be printed.[33,34] The misconception arose that *Lord of Light* was a "fix-up" novel—a set of connected short stories—which was never the case. Another misconception concerns the pair of epigraphs at the start of each chapter. The first epigraph recounts Sam's story in folk-story tone and deliberately makes each chapter independent of its fellows, while the second, poetic epigraph establishes the Hindu and Buddhist atmosphere of the novel. Many have assumed the second set of epigraphs were lifted from authentic Hindu and Buddhist texts, but that is only partly correct. Zelazny did find similar quotations in the books *The Upanishads* and *Buddhist Texts through the Ages* but recast them in his own words and poetic voice.[31,35,36] He called these "Lowellian interpretations" or "imitations" and not exact or literal translations. The poet Robert Lowell had once published a collection, *Imitations*, in which his poems were based on the work of foreign language poets. Zelazny explained that in this process, "you read translations till the meaning is clear to you, then recast the meaning into an English version to your own taste,"[35] so "they are all of them authentic—and although I took the liberty of paraphrasing each somewhat, I retained the sense of the original."[31] "I was pleased with the results, whatever their relationship to the originals."[36]

Lord of Light was published in 1967 to wide acclaim, generally regarded as Zelazny's finest novel and remains in print to this day. In January 1968, the paperback reprint rights sold for the "most impressive" and "unusually high" sum of $5,000 (approximately $30,000 in 2008 dollars).[37] *Lord of Light* won the Hugo in 1968 for best novel and was a finalist for the Nebula. Arguments arose over whether it should be considered science fiction or fantasy, but Zelazny had deliberately written it that way: *"Lord of Light* was intentionally written so that it could be taken as a science fiction or a fantasy novel. On the one hand, I attempted to provide some justifications for what went on in the way of the bizarre; on the other, I employed a style I associate with fantasy in the telling of the story. I wrote it that way on purpose, leaving some intentional ambiguity, because I wanted it to lie somewhat between both camps and not entirely in either. I did this because I did not see much stuff being written at that time which fit that description; because I wanted to see whether I could do it; and because I was curious as to how such a book would be received."[38] In another letter he said, "I intentionally set out to destroy whatever distinction may exist between science fiction and fantasy. I have never come across a really satisfactory definition of that distinction—and if I were to, I would attempt to violate it in my very next story."[39]

He also wrote, "I like *Lord of Light* for the color and smoke and folk tale effects I wanted to achieve. I dislike it because I unintentionally let my style shift. The first chapter and the final chapter, which succeeds it temporally, are farther apart in terms of tone than now strikes me as appropriate. Everything that came between caused me to drift from an initial formalism. If I had to do it again, I would rewrite the first chapter though, rather than rewrite the rest of the book."[40]

Creatures of Light and Darkness begun

The afterword to "The Steel General" notes that Zelazny conceived the title character in the summer of 1966 after viewing the film *To Die in Madrid*. During the drive home, Zelazny formulated what became the highly experimental novel *Creatures of Light and Darkness*. As he often did, he shelved this idea and returned to it from time to time, when he was ready. He wrote it intermittently in 1966 and 1967, "just every few weeks I'd pick the manuscript up and add a few pages to it, and it was sort of one of those things you do for your own amusement."[41]

Four for Tomorrow

Agent Robert Mills negotiated a contract with Ace Books for Zelazny's first collection, which included four of his most notable novelettes.[42] "He Who Shapes" was excluded because of its novelization as *The Dream Master*. Correspondence from Editor Terry Carr indicated that the biggest concern throughout production was what to call the book—Carr felt the possible title *The Furies* was unsuitable because recent publications had already used it, and he didn't like the other three story titles enough to use any of them as the name for the collection. He asked Zelazny for suggestions—"in an effort to ward off anything disastrous in the way of this title"[43]—and promised to persuade the publisher to go along with one of them. But he changed his mind on receiving Zelazny's ideas—"re the titles you suggested for your novelette collection: Uh, er, they really don't fit the bill. Not one of them is recognizably science fictional in itself, which is the first requirement."[44] Carr drew up a set of proposed titles and asked Zelazny to choose the best, promising that "there'll be no *Four by Zelazny*, no indeed."[44] But when Carr was absent from the office for two weeks' jury duty, the publisher took the opportunity to overrule both Zelazny and Carr, irrevocably choosing "the uninspired, but, I think, unobjectionable"[45] title *Four for Tomorrow*. The selected title was not much different from the *Four by Zelazny* that Carr had promised to avoid.

The British publisher Rupert Hart-Davis later vetoed the title *Four for Tomorrow* because another British hardcover house was supposedly publishing a science fiction collection entitled *Nine for Tomorrow* (this was almost certainly Isaac Asimov's *Nine Tomorrows*). At the publisher's request Zelazny provided alternative titles, including *A Rose for Ecclesiastes*, which was used for the British hardcover and softcover editions.[46]

Carr invited Theodore Sturgeon to write an introduction to the collection; Carr and Zelazny were both delighted with the enthusiastic and insightful essay Sturgeon submitted. Excerpts from that introduction appear in some of the short story notes in this collection.

The Writer of Mythological Science Fiction

Zelazny's technique of adapting mythologies for his writing gave his works great appeal, but he risked becoming stereotyped. Readers assumed the mythological bent to his fiction was deliberately chosen, as if he had somehow known that it would be popular. At first Zelazny agreed that the inclusion of mythology had been deliberate. "My use of mythological materials—straight, with variations and improvised—were matters of design rather than preference. They were several because I attempt to avoid the development of standardized treatments or approaches to anything. I do not really prefer any one of the methods I have used over the others."[38]

Twenty-three years later, he recalled it differently, denying that his use of mythology had been deliberate. "Before I discovered science fiction at the age of eleven, I still liked the fantastic. I discovered a number of books on mythology in my school library and found that I enjoyed reading them, just for pleasure. So I stayed with it; it got me interested in anthropology and comparative religion—things of that sort. When I started writing, it just crept in. I didn't intentionally set out to use that much mythological material; it just found its way into my work."[47]

Whether his using mythology was intentional or not, Zelazny explicitly related his literary approach to the theories of Northrop

Frye. Frye grouped characters into four "modes of literature." In the highest or "Mythic Mode" the characters are greater than men, greater even that the natural forces that control the universe. In effect, they are gods of mythological proportions. In the next highest, or "High Mimetic Mode," are characters greater than ordinary men, but not gods: kings, rulers, and men of power who are capable of controlling other men or of conquering natural forces. Third is the "Low Mimetic Mode," filled with the ordinary characters who appear in realistic fiction. Last is "Ironic Mode" in which characters are inferior to normal men and are unable to combat natural forces. Much of Zelazny's fiction employs characters from the Mythic and High Mimetic Modes; most of modern fiction has abandoned these two in favor of Low Mimetic and Ironic modes. Zelazny considered it a benefit of writing science fiction and fantasy to be able to use all of these approaches.[48,49]

For Zelazny, myths could be exploited to tell an interesting tale. "The ancients believed in their tales and myths, but this failed along with the increasing rationality. Man has grown more sophisticated and doesn't believe in them the way the ancients did. Modern man has fun with them, and the gods lose their elemental quality. They are not really destroyed but are turned into something else.

"Today the *darkness* is the unknown. This possesses the elements the old gods possessed. The advance of light (knowledge) has brought about the retreat of darkness."[50]

"The New Wave"

Zelazny's rapid rise to popularity and critical acclaim in the field was evident in the Spring of 1966, when he received Nebulas for the novella "He Who Shapes" and novelette "The Doors of His Face, the Lamps of His Mouth," while "Devil Car" was a finalist for the short story Nebula. In the fall of 1966, at the World Science Fiction Convention in Cleveland, he received his first Hugo Award for the serialized novel ...*And Call Me Conrad* (it tied with Frank Herbert's *Dune*) while "The Doors of His Face, the Lamps of His Mouth" was a finalist for the short fiction Hugo. Samuel R. Delany recalled that when the major writers were introduced at the opening ceremonies of the 1966 Worldcon, "while older and more popular professionals such as Isaac Asimov, Frederik Pohl and Poul Anderson drew a perfectly respectable amount of applause, when Roger Zelazny's name was read out, it was greeted with a standing ovation in a hall filled with almost a thousand attendees—an ovation which went on and *on!*...[Furthermore] it is even more astonishing that Zelazny, whose stories had appeared only in the previous three years and whose first novel had come out only in a cut version squeezed into two issues of *The Magazine of Fantasy & Science Fiction*, managed to make any showing at all against Herbert in the voting, much less produce a tie."[51] Nominations became frequent, and his own pieces sometimes competed against each other for the Hugo or Nebula. Colleagues complimented his quiet, gracious, courteous, and humble manner in the face of the increasing attention and adulation of fans.

During the mid to late 1960s, critics and fans grouped Zelazny among the so-called "New Wave" writers. This term identified writers noted for their stylistic experimentation in form and content and their exploration of themes and ideas previously not permitted by the sf magazines. The membership of this informal group fluctuated with the perceptions of the reader or critic. In addition to Zelazny, John Brunner, Samuel R. Delany, Michael Moorcock, Harlan Ellison, Ursula Le Guin, Norman Spinrad, Thomas Disch, James Tiptree, Jr., Philip José Farmer, and others were sometimes considered members of the New Wave. Zelazny largely objected to the pigeonholing this term implied. He felt that this was a healthy but narcissistic description of the change developing within the field, a change that emphasized character instead of the big idea or the "what if?" and "if this goes on?" scenarios that had dominated science fiction during the 1940s and 50s. "This [experimentation with storytelling technique] was old hat in general fiction but new to sf...stream of consciousness, impressionism, stylistic flourishes, a greater emphasis on characterization...Most of us deny there was such a thing as a New Wave 'movement' because there was no overall plan or manifesto, many of us were not even acquainted in those days & we are all sufficiently individualistic to dislike being categorized."[52] "It was not, in short, something born from a group of people who ate and drank and discussed this together."[14] He later likened the experimentation with style and form in sf to "the introduction of distillation into a culture which had only known beer and wine. Lots of new, quick drunkenness occurred. A temporary phenomenon...I believe this phase is already beginning to pass and a new synthesis to occur, wherein form and content are more proportionately balanced and existing on a higher level than previously."[53] He also remarked that the New Wave "was just a popular tag slapped on a number of writers who made their appearance on the science fiction scene at approximately the same time…I have never considered myself part of any sort of movement—and neither did Delany the last time I asked him."[39]

Zelazny did become good friends with several New Wave writers but didn't feel that friendship meant they influenced each other's writing. "We are all of us just plain writers, using whatever tools are available to us for purposes of telling the best story we know in whatever we deem to be the most fitting medium. Delany & Ellison are two of my very best friends. But I doubt very much that we have influenced one another one jot, tittle or iota…we are all very independent spirits. I think we are, all of us, beyond the point where we would exert much influence upon one another."[24]

Despite his popularity, he refrained from submitting stories to John W. Campbell at *Analog*. "Campbell is the one editor I don't write for, because I don't think he would approve of my stylistic tendencies. I know that he likes something more of the nature of a journalistic style."[33] After Henry Morrison became Zelazny's agent in 1967, Morrison noticed his client's conspicuous absence from the pages of *Analog* and wondered "don't you and John get along?"[54] Zelazny replied that he was concerned about Campbell's legendary demands for rewrites by his writers, prompting Morrison to advise him, "John only asks for rewrites from the local (New York, NJ) writers. He used to ask for a million rewrites from Randy Garrett when Randy was NY-based, but almost never asked Poul Anderson for a thing, either bought or returned."[55] While it is unclear whether Zelazny ever sent anything to Campbell, two of his stories did appear in *Analog* in the 1970s while Ben Bova was editor—Nebula nominee "The Engine at Heartspring's Center" and the Hugo and Nebula Award-winning novella "Home is the Hangman."

Loss of First Agent

Robert Mills was Zelazny's agent for domestic rights to novels and books but not short stories, and this arrangement had worked well through three contracts with Ace Books—*This Immortal*, *The Dream Master*, and *Four for Tomorrow*. Mills also made certain that Zelazny retained the foreign and dramatic rights to these works.[11] However,

Zelazny was still unconvinced that he needed an agent and was probably dismayed about having to pay him ten percent of sales on contracts that he thought he should be able to obtain himself. Zelazny then committed a novice's *faux pas* by negotiating directly with Doubleday Editor Larry Ashmead over *Lord of Light*'s contract without involving his agent. When Mills learned of this development, he promptly wrote to Zelazny, "I have heard about your new Doubleday book, and I am assuming that the two deals I made with Ace constitute the services you wanted from me."[11] And with that, Mills and Zelazny parted ways.

Distinctions:

Nebula for novella "He Who Shapes"
Nebula for novelette
> "The Doors of His Face, the Lamps of His Mouth"
Nebula nomination for short story "Devil Car"
Hugo for novel …*And Call Me Conrad* [aka *This Immortal,*
> **tied with *Dune,* by Frank Herbert]**
Hugo nomination for short fiction
> "The Doors of His Face, the Lamps of His Mouth"

Books Published:

This Immortal
The Dream Master

————1967————

Nine Princes in Amber

In January 1967 Roger and Judy Zelazny moved to a house on Westhills Road in Baltimore. In June he was elected Secretary-Treasurer of SFWA for a one-year term (1967–68), and in July he was selected to be the editor of *Nebula Award Stories Three.* He had finished *Lord of Light* a year earlier, the novel that many considered his best, but it had not yet been published. Restless for a change of pace, he had decided to write something completely different on spec: *Nine Princes in Amber*. He planned this as the first book of a *trilogy* (the other two titles were *The Guns of Avalon* and *The Courts of Chaos*). In his letter to Editor Larry Ashmead on February 13, he said he'd finished writing *Nine Princes in Amber* during the first week of February.[56] He noted that "the fans seem already enthusiastic, subsequent to a few readings I've given." He jokingly but accurately predicted that "it ends with a sort of cliff-hanger, but so did *A Princess of Mars* and look what happened there."[56] *A Princess of Mars* was the first novel in the famous Barsoom series by Edgar Rice Burroughs.

Zelazny followed his early practice of starting a novel without knowing how it would end. When Corwin woke up in the hospital at the story's onset, even its author did not know where the plot was headed. "I did not plan *Nine Princes in Amber* in advance. I was not sure exactly what sort of situations Corwin was going to get into after he woke up in the hospital. It was a good trick to have him learn the answers along with the reader. The discovery of identity is intrinsically interesting. I thought there was a story about to emerge, and I just sat there plotting what would happen next."[57] With the perspective of only the first novel in the series completed, he acknowledged to Doubleday Editor Marc Haefele in 1968 that "Oberon is not dead, and I am still not certain as to whether Corwin will ever reign in Amber—though I suspect he might wind up in that position. If so, he will discover it to be a very rough job."[58] In the same letter he indicated that his planned trilogy might instead require *six* novels to tell the tale.

Some readers may disbelieve Zelazny's assertion that he did not know where the story was headed because Corwin tells his listener, "and even now, as I stand contemplating the Courts of Chaos, telling this story to the only one present to hear, that perhaps he may repeat it, that it will not die after I have died within…" That statement in *Nine Princes in Amber* suggests that there *was* an overall plan to the story arc, else why would Corwin say that in the first novel? But Zelazny had no idea how the story would play out or even to whom Corwin was speaking; he later explained that it just felt important that Corwin say those words then.[59] It was only near the end of writing the fifth book, *The Courts of Chaos,* that Zelazny realized who the listener must be: Merlin, Corwin's son born of Dara.

That Zelazny had completed the full draft of *Nine Princes in Amber* in February 1967 is significant; critics and fans had long suspected that Zelazny developed the Amber series in 1970 for purely commercial reasons *after* becoming a full-time writer. However, he'd written *Nine Princes in Amber* on spec for a change of pace, and he'd even started on the sequel (*The Guns of Avalon*) before *Lord of Light* had ever been published. The series grew to encompass ten novels and became the work for which he received the most recognition, money and bestseller status. It is also notable that what may be his best novel (*Lord of Light*) and the first novel of his most commercially successful work (*Nine Princes in Amber*) were completed back-to-back in 1966–67.

Although he didn't consciously recognize it until years later,[60,61] *Nine Princes in Amber* is heavily indebted to one of his all-time favorite novels, *The Dark World* by Henry Kuttner. In Kuttner's work a first person narrator is haunted by memories of a world that he cannot quite recall. On the other hand, while writing *Nine Princes in Amber*, Zelazny *was* conscious of Lawrence Durrell's "Alexandria Quartet," a series in which the author retold the same tale from a different character's viewpoint for each of the four novels. He initially planned to write each Amber book from a different character's perspective, all focused around the automobile accident as the key mystery—but he abandoned this idea as he grew more fascinated with Corwin.[62]

Zelazny acknowledged that Philip José Farmer's *The World of Tiers* series was also in his mind as he wrote *Nine Princes in Amber*—"Yes, yes, they [*Tiers* novels] were!…one of the things that had occurred to me about the *Tiers* novels was that I liked the fact that Farmer had these nearly immortal Lords who tested one another, and I was thinking that the family relationships involved with something like that would have been more fun to explore. That's why I dedicated one of the Amber books to Phil Farmer—I told him about it—and possibly why he dedicated [a] *World of Tiers* novel to me. There is a relationship, but I was trying to do different things with it."[63] He dedicated *Sign of the Unicorn* to Farmer in oblique wording that referred to two characters from *The World of Tiers* and their creator (demiurge): *"For Jadawin and his Demiurge, not to forget Kickaha."*[64] The first two novels in Farmer's series, *The Maker of Universes* (1965) and *The Gates of Creation* (1966), appeared before Zelazny began to write *Nine Princes in Amber*. "I had been reading the *World of Tiers* novels before beginning work on *Nine Princes in Amber*, and I decided at that time that I would one day write something involving a large family of peculiarly endowed near-immortals who did not get along very well with each other."[65] "I thereby freely confess that my own Amber series owes more than a little to Phil's *World of Tiers* and the bickerings of the immortal lords."[66] The third *World of Tiers* novel, *A Private Cosmos* (1968), featured an introduction in which Zelazny revealed that after reading the first two *Tiers* novels, he wrote "a fan letter to Philip José Farmer."[67] There he listed the two main reasons why the *World of Tiers* books appealed to him so much. First, "I am fascinated by the concept of physical immortality and the ills and benefits attendant hereunto. This theme runs through the books like a highly polished strand of copper wire." Second, "the concept of pocket universes—a thing quite distinct, as I see it, from various parallel worlds notions— the idea of such universes, specifically created to serve the ends of powerful and intelligent beings, is a neat one."[67] The Amber series in turn incorporated both aspects.

Zelazny also acknowledged that the Amber books were influenced by Celtic mythology and Arthurian legend and notably Jessie L. Weston's 1921 book *From Ritual to Romance*. Weston's book is an academic examination of the pagan and Christian roots of the legends of King Arthur, the Wasteland myths, and the Holy Grail. The Celtic Wasteland myth ties a land's barrenness to a curse that a hero must lift. Corwin's curse helped create the Black Road and other troubles for Amber. "As for the Weston book and the legendary and mythological materials—their substance was already present in my mind and had been for a long while. I had no conscious intention of combining these themes, motifs, ideas, with the family situation suggested to me by the Farmer books."[65]

Because he'd started the novel in a mindset similar to the amnesiac Corwin, not knowing where it was headed, he created many of the story's inventions on the spot as the plot demanded. Initially, the Trumps were a means to describe the various characters all at once, enabling the reader to flip back to see who was who again. Later he realized that the Trumps could be used for communication and still later that they could be used for transportation as well.[65,68] Shadow-walking began after a casual stroll through an unfamiliar neighborhood. "I partly got the idea for it before I wrote the series. Walking down the street one day in Baltimore, I turned a corner and it was a completely different sort of street—all the houses were different and everything. And I walked up to the next corner and just as I turned, the sun went behind a cloud. It had been a really nice sunny street, and all of a sudden this street was gray, and I thought it was going to rain. Then I turned one more time (I was just walking to kill time) and I was on a country road! A few turns ago I'd been walking down a commercial street in the city, and something about that registered in my mind—there's something there that I want to use in a story. It was shortly after that that I started *Nine Princes in Amber*."[69]

He read an excerpt of *Nine Princes in Amber* as Guest of Honor at the Marcon II convention, held in Toledo April 8–9, 1967, and said, "I wrote a novel in January. It is hopefully going to be the first in what may wind up as a trilogy or possibly a set of four and it is a parallel-worlds type of thing which might be classified as sword and sorcery, and then again maybe not—I could argue either side of it."[70] Dannie Plachta specifically created and organized Marcon II to honor Zelazny in response to the Ohio native's successes the prior year—two Nebulas and his Hugo for *…And Call Me Conrad*. The transcribed excerpt of his reading was published as "9 Princes in Amber" in *Kallikanzaros* (#1, June 1967), the first fanzine about Zelazny's works. A second excerpt, "The Princes," was published in *Kallikanzaros* #3, but no other part of the novel appeared until its hardcover publication in 1970. Notably, Zelazny encouraged the efforts of young fan John Ayotte, editor of *Kallikanzaros,* by permitting him to publish these two excerpts plus a poem, a Guest of Honor speech, and the Dilvish tale "A Knight for Merytha."[71,72] How did Ayotte obtain permission to publish a second excerpt from *Nine Princes in Amber?* Ayotte recalled exchanging correspondence with Zelazny, and, "In talking about the progress of the manuscript for *Nine Princes*, he explained the Trumps bit to me and said he would send along another excerpt in manuscript form that I could print. We discussed my concerns for protecting his copyright, but he laughed it off and said that no one would steal his work based on the excerpts."[73]

Zelazny noted in a letter to Andre Norton that the title *Nine Princes in Amber* had dual intent. First, it referred to the city itself with the influences that it would have on the people there. Second, it referred to characters embedded like insects in amber—"individuals frozen in timeless moments of some particular passion or phase of their lives, as though contained like one of those insects."[74] Although sometimes dismissed as commercial fluff, *Nine Princes in Amber* contains Zelazny's usual abundance of literary and cultural references. The sword fights are real; Shakespearean quotations enrich every book; Amber itself is a fusion of mythical elements surrounding its central Pattern, the design of which came from the Tree of Life or Sephiroth of Kabbalah.

Despite his initial enthusiasm and his prophetic remark that it might do as well as *A Princess of Mars,* Zelazny treated the novel as a low-priority, back-burner project. Despite Larry Ashmead's reminders, more than a year passed before he finally had a typist produce a clean copy of the manuscript to send to Doubleday.[75] Terry Carr pleaded as well; he wanted the book to kick off the new SF Specials line at Ace.[76]

Creatures of Light and Darkness— Completed and Shelved

By March 1967, shortly after finishing *Nine Princes in Amber,* Zelazny completed *Creatures of Light and Darkness.* He had written it as a personal exercise and not for publication; consequently, "when I finished the whole manuscript I really wasn't going to send it around."[41] He explained, "I doubted that any publisher would really be interested in it since I did so many different things: all the small chapters, and the shifting back and forth, and doing a chapter in free verse, and one as a closet drama. I was doing that purely for myself."[57]

In another interview he seemed to disparage the book. "*Creatures of Light and Darkness*—I couldn't get serious about it. Actually, I discovered it was a self-parody. In my next few books, I steered clear—I was getting tired of this sort of thing."[50]

Editor Terry Carr at Ace Books wanted another novel from Zelazny and had heard him read excerpts from *Creatures of Light and Darkness* at a party. Carr asked to see the manuscript and had to persuade Zelazny to give it to him. Zelazny reluctantly complied, warning Carr that he wouldn't like it. Carr later wrote back, "Well, you're right, it doesn't work. It was damn interesting, though, and I thank you vastly for letting me read it. I'm a minor nut in Egyptology, as you may recall, and in fact I think at the Disclave last year I suggested you try working with Egyptian mythology; you told me you already had such a book in mind, and I guess this was it. Some of this is beautiful… particularly the opening sequence in the House of the Dead. (Which you originally read to me at a party on the last night of the Tricon, along with an excerpt about the Steel General, another fine creation.) I laughed out loud when I came to the priest-warrior's Extreme Unction litany. In fact, until about half way through the book I thought you were crazy, that this was one of your best works."[76]

Carr felt that the book contained too many superheroes and demigods, fighting among themselves where "the outcome of each battle seems to depend on the author's whim" rather than on any inherent qualities that would make the reader believe one character is superior to another. So Carr returned the manuscript, requesting instead that *Nine Princes in Amber* kick off the new SF Specials line of books that he had planned—"I'd be strongly interested in your January novel"—and offering a $2,500 advance for it (approximately $15,500 in 2008 dollars). Zelazny declined to send him that manuscript—he had already promised it to Larry Ashmead at Doubleday but hadn't yet gotten around to sending it, and he allowed *Creatures of Light and Darkness* to gather dust on an office shelf.

Marcon II

Zelazny's appearance as Guest of Honor at Marcon II was one of many during the period when he garnered much attention and many awards. He was a new star in the field, suddenly on the level of Isaac Asimov, Robert Heinlein, and Arthur C. Clarke for name recognition and popularity. Harlan Ellison declared in 1967's *Dangerous Visions* that "Zelazny has ascended to godhood already, and needs no helping hands…His concepts are fresh, his attacks bold, his solutions generally trenchant."[1] As Andre Norton explained in her introduction for the Marcon II program booklet, "To be winner of three awards in a single year, two of them offered by fellow writers (perhaps more severe as critics), the other by well-read readers, is undoubtedly a record never before established. Yet in 1966, Roger Zelazny received such well deserved recognition for his work." She noted the confidence, craftsmanship, wide variety of plots, versatility, wide-ranging subject matter, and solid research behind his stories, and added, "One does not expect an author who can recreate Greece of the Gods and the myths as in *This Immortal*, to also give us that stark bit of perilous adventure geared firmly to a future comradeship between man and machine—'Devil Car.' He is as much at home in man-against-nature themes, as witness his edge-of-the-precipice tale 'This Mortal Mountain,' or 'This Moment of the Storm.'" She added prophetically, "He has only his own work to best and there is little doubt he will do just that in the months and years to come."[77] Many critics argue that Zelazny peaked with *Lord of Light* and his later work never surpassed it or his novellas of the mid-1960s. If they are correct, Zelazny had already peaked before Marcon II. Though *Lord of Light* was still unpublished at that time, it had been completed a year earlier.

Notable stories published in 1967 included the Nebula and Hugo-nominated "This Moment of the Storm" and Hugo-nominated "Comes Now the Power" and "For a Breath I Tarry." "This Moment of the Storm" and "For a Breath I Tarry" competed against each other in the novelette category. At the Detroit Triple Fan Fair in June 1967, Zelazny received the first-ever Nova Award for outstanding achievement in science fiction and fantasy.[78]

Time for an Agent

In April 1967, Robert Silverberg sat Roger Zelazny down at the bar for a long session. Silverberg explained the nuts and bolts of a writing career and the necessity of having an agent. An agent meant that the writer could concentrate on writing while the agent took care of contracts, paperwork, phone calls, and worked hard to get a larger advance or pay rate on the next material. The agent would also know what *not* to do: Silverberg was concerned that Zelazny had "disposed of" some of his stories—publishing them at low rates with loss of control over reprint rights and positioning them in venues that would harm rather than enhance his marketability and career. Silverberg warned "that after a while the business end of writing takes too much of the writing time. Better to pay someone ten percent and find that you're still more than ten percent ahead in the end."[8]

Zelazny took this advice to heart and noted that Silverberg was "very influential on my early career." The price of this invaluable advice was solely the cost of the Bloody Marys that Silverberg consumed and the Black Russians that Zelazny drank during that afternoon in the bar. Silverberg said afterward that "the description of the meeting seems very accurate to me" and recalled that it most likely took place at Lunacon in New York (April 29–30, 1967).[79–81] Zelazny immediately followed the advice—he signed up with the Henry Morrison Agency in New York in May.[82] Ted White had originally suggested Henry Morrison to Zelazny, and Morrison had written to Zelazny in August 1965 to offer his services.[83] At the time, Zelazny was already engaged with Robert Mills, who represented him for book-length works only, before that arrangement ended in 1966. Zelazny didn't take on an agent who would represent all of his literary works until after Silverberg urged him to do so. In turn Zelazny advised novice writers—in correspondence and Guest of Honor speeches—to get an agent at the earliest opportunity, and he repeatedly credited Silverberg for giving him that practical advice at an important stage of his career.

One of Morrison's first acts in that initial month was to advise Zelazny *not* to go ahead with a planned short story collection entitled *Satan's Tears.* That publication would have included a few of his major stories not already collected in *Four for Tomorrow,* plus many of what Morrison viewed as Zelazny's minor stories. "I like a number of the stories, but I also feel that others are exercises and not fully fleshed stories. As I'm sure you know, very few collections sell well…a collection of major stories is fine, but a collection of less than major stories could be a problem."[82] Zelazny was still keen about the collection, so Morrison shopped it around to several publishers in the US and UK. There were no takers. Some of those stories did appear in later collections, but others have remained uncollected until this multi-volume project from NESFA. Morrison's primary task was to secure contracts for "untitled novel by Roger Zelazny" with Berkley/Putnam, two "untitled novels" with Doubleday, and another with Ace.

Stress of the Developing Writer

Zelazny's stress levels climbed as he tried to deal with editors and publishers and find time to write while maintaining a full-time job at the Social Security Administration. He added to his workload by accepting the Secretary-Treasurer position at SFWA. He wanted to quit his job but worried that he couldn't afford to take that chance. At conventions he complained to colleagues about his troubles; some of them nodded sagely and assured him that he was going through a predictable rite of passage. Michael Moorcock told him after they met at the 1967 Worldcon, "It has occurred to me that you have problems typical of a writer at this stage in his development. How's your sense of direction these days? I am a tactless and impertinent fool whose only excuse is that he admires both [the] work and what he knows of the man and feels concerned. Tell me there's nothing to worry about. I'm not butting in, I hope… I can only offer words of encouragement like 'periods of consolidation are necessary' and 'virtue is its own reward.' Come to England. The pressures are fewer, the goals a little easier to discern."[84]

Securing Henry Morrison as his agent helped with these issues, but Zelazny didn't feel comfortable until some years after he'd quit his job to become a full time writer.

Distinctions:

Nebula nomination for novelette "This Moment of the Storm"
Hugo nomination for short story "Comes Now the Power"
Hugo nomination for novelette "For a Breath I Tarry"
Hugo nomination for novelette "This Moment of the Storm"
Nova Award for most outstanding contribution to science fiction

Books Published:

Lord of Light
Four for Tomorrow

—————————1968—————————

Commercial Success

By 1968, the acclaim for *Lord of Light* and the intervention of new Agent Henry Morrison quickly led to book contracts with three publishers and a sharp rise in Zelazny's compensation; his writing income finally equaled his Social Security Administration pay. Despite his earlier promise to himself that he would quit the government job upon reaching this milestone, "I chickened out though. Spent one more year working for Social Security."[85]

Zelazny's Fascination with Suicide and Immortality

So who was Roger Zelazny at this stage? In the essay "Tomorrow Stuff," written in 1968 but unpublished until this collection, he mused, "My own idiosyncrasies, of course, make me what I am. What are my particular hang-ups and foibles? Immortality, suicide, one man against the winds and the tides and the stars, sometimes the impossible love which sustains, impossibly, the tortured soul, sometimes the hate so big that it would burn the innocent to reach the guilty, and sometimes the simple, contemplative pleasures—like good food, friendly cats, a pipe of pleasant tobacco—that make life worthwhile, despite all ugliness, and then again, the things, sometimes bawdy, sometimes simple that make me laugh."[86]

Immortality and suicide certainly furnished aspects of characters and situations in Zelazny's writing, from Conrad's immortality in *This Immortal* to Charles Render's suicide obsession in *The Dream Master,* to Francis Sandow's long life in *Isle of the Dead,* to Gallinger's suicide attempt at the end of "A Rose for Ecclesiastes." The list could extend to include near-immortals who attempt or contemplate suicide, such as Corwin at least twice in the Amber series—in despair in the dungeons during *Nine Princes in Amber* and when his beloved sister Deirdre is killed at the climax of *The Courts of Chaos.* Even his mainstream thriller *The Dead Man's Brother* reflects these themes. An improbable lucky streak has kept Ovid Wiley alive through multiple plane crashes, battles, and other confrontations, and these experiences feed the character's relative indifference to his own mortality.

Zelazny's frequent use of immortality and suicide in his work prompted many, including Samuel Delany, to ponder what insight these topics might offer into Zelazny's psychology. He addressed this in an amusing self-interview, where he asked himself to talk about the "childhood trauma and all that crap." "No." "Why not?" "Because I'm a bug on privacy." "Shyness?" "Some, I suppose." "…[But] if certain themes tend to persist in the work of a particular writer, people cannot help but wonder why. You seem to have a thing for mythology, immortality, and protagonists who are not always completely admirable people. Would you care to say why?" "No."[87]

In the 1968 "Tomorrow Stuff" essay, he admitted, "I don't know how I hang particular items on these hooks and make stories out of them…a stone, a leaf, a door…you have the routine list. Anything might supply the initial stimulation, and then my demon takes over and starts devilling me until it's all down on paper. I've a very visual-type imagination. I see everything that happens—even dream about it, occasionally—while I'm working on a story. Whether this is good or bad, I don't know. It's just the way things are with me."[86]

Zelazny's fascinations had nothing to do with a personal or family history of suicide or mental illness, though he fueled such speculation by declining in interviews to explain his interest in these themes. The reasons for these fascinations were more mundane than the rumors. The preoccupation began with the immortal gods of mythology. Another important influence, Sir James Frazer's massive multi-volume *The Golden Bough,* posited that old religions were fertility cults. These cults' beliefs centered on worship of a sacred king who married an earth goddess, and then died at harvest, only to be reincarnated in the spring. So too, the creation myths that Zelazny studied concerned ripping form out of chaos; these creations then decomposed or changed in an endless cycle of creation, destruction, and recreation.

In his 1967 Guest of Honor speech at Ozarkon 2 (included in this collection) Zelazny talked about his fascination with the myth of the dying god and its influence on the development of literature and drama. "Now, once upon a time there were a lot of gods who had something in common: This was the fact that they died and were mutilated, and were resurrected. Now, they were generally worshipped in the area about the Mediterranean. Their names were…oh, there were many of them: Attis, Osiris, Tammuz. And the people who worshipped them, according to anthropologists and classical scholars, tended to do this in a rather mimetic [imitative] fashion. Now, some say these deities were pretty much a solar myth. That is, that their deaths and their resurrections represented the passage of the sun through the seasons of the year; and that when winter came and everything died, this, in a sense, was the death of the god. Once spring came and the green came out again, things lived, and this was the resurrection. Primitive man does have a tendency to personify natural forces, and many gods were born around this area who had this thing in common, who went through this cycle."[48] Zelazny continued, explaining how early plays retold stories of the myth of the dying and resurrecting god. As time passed, he added, retellings of the myth were split into two aspects: tragedy and comedy. Tragedy depicted the death of a very noble man because of his one tragic flaw, and comedy represented continuance, the triumph of life over death.

Apart from this longstanding love of mythology and immortal characters and his fascination with the dying god, two individuals influenced Zelazny's interest in suicide: Ernest Hemingway and Erich Fromm. Carl Yoke and Zelazny admired Hemingway's work; both wanted to be writers, and both considered Hemingway a role model. Hemingway's unexpected suicide by shotgun on July 2, 1961, affected them both deeply. Around the same time, they both read psychologist Erich Fromm's 1957 book *The Sane Society.* In that book Fromm discusses suicide as a rational way out of truly awful situations, using the example of Jewish prisoners in the Nazi concentration camps who knew that Mengele was going to experiment on them. The impact of Hemingway's suicide and Fromm's book led Yoke and Zelazny to discuss how suicide could be a rational act should one's quality of life severely degrade due to some debilitating or degenerative condition. Yoke concluded, "In fact, we both agreed that if we ever got into some condition like that, we would prefer to walk off into the desert, or somewhere, and just die."[18] Although Zelazny died of a bowel malignancy in 1995, he never considered suicide as an option. Yoke noted, "I'm certain that even with Roger's cancer, he never anticipated that he would die. There was still that youthful aura of invulnerability about him."[18]

SFWA and *Nebula Award Stories Three*

In spring 1968, Zelazny assembled the association's annual publication of Nebula Award-winning stories and finalists for the anthology *Nebula Award Stories Three*. Editor Larry Ashmead wrote that Zelazny's "interlocutory remarks were very good and your survey of what's gone on during the year [was] most apt and honest."[88] Zelazny did not return to editing anthologies until the last two years before his death.

His year as SFWA Secretary-Treasurer was difficult due to unexpected demands on his time, precipitated by problems that affected some of the other officers. For example, Robert Silverberg's house burned down, and James Blish was emigrating to England. Due to absence of the other officers, he was forced to assume some of their duties, handling questions and complaints about the Nebula ballot, including how it would be mailed out and counted. He also dealt with hundreds of impatient requests from publishers, editors and authors for members' current addresses and the inevitable complaints when outdated information led to undeliverable mail. Zelazny chose not to stand for re-election; being an officer had taken too much of his writing time and created too much unwanted stress. Michael Moorcock had warned him about this: "You are a fool to get mixed up in SFWA admin. You'll kill yourself. I speak from the heart as one who wouldn't listen either. With love, Mike."[84]

Samuel Delany Resurrects
Creatures of Light and Darkness

Terry Carr had rejected *Creatures of Light and Darkness* in 1967, but thanks to Samuel Delany's intervention, it didn't end there. About a year later, in spring 1968, "It just happened that I mentioned it to Samuel R. Delany, and he had lunch with an editor at Doubleday [Marc Haefele] who phoned me then and said he wanted to see it. I knew the editor, since I had previously done an article for him. I told him he wouldn't be interested. He asked me to send it along anyhow. He later called me back and bought it. If I had written it for publication, I wouldn't have done it that way."[57] The novel was an experiment, and Zelazny continued to experiment with narrative techniques and challenges in all of his future novels.

Doubleday accepted *Creatures of Light and Darkness* for publication on April 29, 1968. Senior Editor Larry Ashmead wrote, "Marc and I have both read *Creatures of Light and Darkness*. It rocked us both back on our heels! It's brilliant!"[89] Zelazny's shocked but pleased response said, "Frankly, I didn't think anybody would touch that story with a ten-foot rake. I believe I had more fun writing it than anything I've done since (or before, for that matter); however, I had a sneaking suspicion that nobody would want it. So I am in a pleasant state of shock at the moment. You have really made my day/week/month. The only thing I can think of to say, besides, 'Thank you,' is, 'Thank you again.'"[90] Marc Haefele responded, "More people have read *Creatures*; they all like it. I have the feeling it is going to be something really surprising when it comes out. A ten-foot rake is not the implement; six-inch suction cups is more like it."[91] Zelazny dedicated the novel "To Chip Delany, just because."

Creatures was an unusual novel, and its experimental nature produced polar responses in readers who either loved or hated it, who considered it brilliant or unreadable. "I threw everything but the kitchen sink into that book—surrealistic images, a horde of mythological figures, chapters written in free verse and even one done as a closet drama. It was more than a piece of self-indulgence, however. It was also a learning book. It was there that I tried experiments on which I am still capitalizing."[92] "I really intended it to be a parody of what is sometimes referred to as the 'New Wave.' Probably it won't be considered that."[93]

The final chapter of *Creatures of Light and Darkness* was written as a one-act play. "I'll tell you what the motivation behind this was, so it won't sound as radical as it does. I decided that, for the purposes of this story, I was going to write everything in the present tense. My background is in the theatre, and by the time I was getting into the final quarter of the book, all these descriptions—'he *walks* down the street' rather than 'he *walked* down the street'—started sounding like stage directions. That's what inspired me to sit down and suddenly shift and write all the description in brackets and italicized, with the people talking the way a character would talk in a play, rather than saying 'he said,' 'she said,' 'he went on' and so on. That's what involved me there, and I think it fit with the particular story. This again in turn points up the fact that we do have radical formats available to us."[94]

Zelazny received a great many letters about *Creatures*, and one such writer speculated that the author had been free-associating with an "unconscious voice" expressed in the narrative. Zelazny responded, "When what you see as the 'new wave' occurred, I saw the 'emphasis on manner' as an opportunity—which might pass quickly—to do an entire book where the story was basically a hook on which I could hang anything I desired. I seized the opportunity, and it was fun. 'Unconscious voice'? Nonsense! I was neither free-associating on paper nor attempting to produce ersatz scripture. I was playing with the tools I normally employ more seriously and, I suppose, demonstrating the triumph of self-expression over communication. Judging by the response I received, a good number of readers saw what I was doing and seemed to enjoy it for what it was. My point? I did it because I wanted to, because I enjoyed the exercise."[53]

At a later date he mused, "I like *Creatures of Light and Darkness* for the sense of power the *verfremdungseffekt* [alienation or distancing effect] granted me in dealing with everything and everybody in the piece. I dislike it because I employed it only for that purpose."[40]

The novel contains humorous moments from "The Agnostic's Prayer" to the scriers' laugh-out-loud pronouncements. Comic relief such as the scriers' scenes and the injection of memorable puns into the narrative are characteristics of Zelazny's work. Examples of puns in other works include, "There had been lots of *simicokes* around, but none of them have the same effect on Vegan metabolism as *the real thing*" from *This Immortal* and "then the fit hit the Shan" from *Lord of Light*. Some readers protested such humor because they did not appreciate that the practice arises from Zelazny's background in

Elizabethan drama—as Zelazny noted, "That's one thing I like about Elizabethans. No matter how serious a scene was, the author always had time to slip in a pun when they were talking."[57] And, critics be damned, he continued to do so in his own writing.

Samuel Delany Resurrects *Nine Princes in Amber*

When Zelazny finally got around to sending *Nine Princes in Amber* to Doubleday, he did so because Delany had mentioned to Doubleday Editor Marc Haefele that Zelazny was sitting on one or two completed novels of a projected series called *Nine Princes in Amber*.[95] Haefele thought it was a joke at first, but the déjà vu was real: this was the second time in just a few months that Delany helped Zelazny by recommending one of his unpublished novels to the same editor. Haefele promptly wrote to Zelazny, "It has happened this way before and I hope it will happen this way again. I just took Chip Delany to lunch and he told me about two other completed books you have on hand, unsubmitted. If this seems a strange way to do business, sobeit."[95] Haefele was unaware that his boss, Larry Ashmead, had already asked for the novel a year earlier and that Zelazny had gotten sidetracked. So Zelazny arranged for a typist to produce a clean copy of the manuscript of *Nine Princes in Amber*, and he sent it in shortly after.

Delany was mistaken about the second installment in the series: Zelazny had written only about one-quarter of *The Guns of Avalon* during the year since he completed the first novel.

In a follow-up letter to Haefele after Doubleday enthusiastically accepted *Nine Princes in Amber* for publication, Zelazny explained that "I meant it to be something a bit lighter than my usual fare, sort of sword-and-sorcery and something which I would have fun writing."[58]

The Guns of Avalon Shelved

By September 1968, having written only one-quarter of *The Guns of Avalon*, Zelazny shelved it because he wanted to take a break from Amber and complete some other projects. "I have much of the rest of the thing in my head, but I am a bit tired and want to do some other things just now."[58] He had come to realize that the "Amber trilogy" would more likely be six books as he conceived more ideas to explore than he'd originally planned. He explained to Haefele that "the second book would involve Corwin's search for allies for a new assault against Amber—and his realization that his curse has spread across all the shadows. The third book would involve his battle against the powers which he unleashed himself, and his choice as to whether he should make them his allies or defeat them personally and proceed against Amber and Eric without them. The third one would involve more in the way of characterization, introspection and moral dilemma than the first two. I could wind the thing up there, either up-beat or down-beat, depending on the dictates of character and situation—or I could continue on, to explore the whole *raison d'être* for Amber, and the personal situations of everyone in the family. This is what I had in mind when I sat down to write the story. Then I realized that it was a pretty massive notion. So, frankly, I am not sure how I want to handle it. I will let you know the moment that I do, though."[58] He later acknowledged that he had stopped at the end of chapter 3, or page 50 in the Doubleday edition.[65]

He picked up *The Guns of Avalon* again in 1970 when the publication of *Nine Princes in Amber* was imminent, and early buzz indicated it would be popular.

Saga of Writing *Deus Irae* Begins

Roger Zelazny and Philip K. Dick admired each other's work and exchanged letters in the fall of 1967 about possible future collaborations. Dick was overwhelmed at the time with book contracts but wrote to Zelazny in December of that year, "I am delighted that you might consider doing a book in collaboration with me, and perhaps we could begin on this when both of us are simultaneously free of other chores…I do have an idea in mind, or possibly several, if they won't all fit into one novel…The idea deals with alternate present-day worlds. I typed up a long synopsis of the thing to send to you, but after reading it, I've decided not to send it at this point. Frankly, it's not impressive. I love alternate world type novels, and in this one there is a fake alternate world, too…"[96] Dick pleaded with Zelazny to collaborate with him: "But damn it; you write so much better than I. Help me. As Terry Carr has pointed out, my work has somehow ceased to evolve. Can I, with your assistance, be pushed ahead one notch? This is what I am hoping for; I want to learn from you, because—and I think most readers would agree on this—you, out of all the sf writers in the field today are most nearly the 'wave of the future,' as it laps at all of us—laps and leaves many of us behind."[96]

The long collaboration with Dick on *Deus Irae* began a few months later in early 1968, still before the authors met. As Zelazny explained, "Phil wrote 50 pages and an outline for Doubleday and got blocked. After a time, when it appeared that he could not proceed with the book, his editor asked if he would object to having someone else complete it. He did not, and the ms and outline ended up with Ted White. Ted had it for a few months and decided it was not his cup of tea. I visited Ted for dinner one night, he showed it to me, I liked it, I got in touch with Phil and we agreed to collaborate on it. It was a part-time project for me, stretching out over a number of years. We each did separate parts, with some interleaving. We did not rewrite one another's material. It would be difficult for me to catalog the various contributions now. And yes, I am satisfied with the results."[97]

Dick's recollection was similar when he wrote about the project in May 1968. "Roger Zelazny & I are going to collaborate on a novel. The basis of it is an outline I did back in 1964 which Doubleday bought. I was never able to actually write the actual damn book, and had Ted White take a look at the outline. He in turn, having decided (I guess) that he couldn't do it either, or didn't want to, gave it to Zelazny, with whom I was already discussing a possible collaboration. I did not remember the outline, however (it's called *Deus Irae* and deals with a future religion). But when Zelazny wrote to say he had possession of the outline and LIKED IT, I went mad with joy. You see, I think very highly of his work and evidently he thinks the same about mine."[98]

The authors finally met— "a very pleasant meeting with Philip K. Dick—first time, and fabulous"—in Oakland at Baycon, the 1968 World Science Fiction Convention.[99] Dick explained to Doubleday Editor Ashmead, "He and I got together in an abandoned room and talked business for many hours—e.g. our collaboration on *Deus Irae*, which he has told me he likes very much...Roger wants to do the next fifty or so pages, and I agreed, because as you know I myself am stopped dead. However, contractual obligations have him tied up until January, but at that time he will begin on it; he will carry on where my initial fifty pages left off. I am sorry that we can't do it sooner, but I can't do it at all and Roger is committed for the remainder of the year. But consider: a novel by me and Roger Zelazny.

Shouldn't that be quite something? God help us if it isn't. I know it will be good."[100]

Dick also wrote to Zelazny, expressing his enthusiasm over the proposed collaboration. "After reading *Lord of Light* I can see that you will have no trouble with our collaboration, *Deus Irae*. By the way—an idea came to me about that. Maybe the viewpoint—and locale—could shift, at about page 55, to the God of Wrath himself. That's something that didn't occur to me until today...and it's been four and a half years! Shifting viewpoint is a method I always use... but for some reason this never occurred to me. Any good? Yes? No? In-between?"[101]

The novel progressed very slowly; despite the initial enthusiasm both authors became bogged down, forgetting about it for months or years at a time. Zelazny explained that "I wrote a section and sent it to him, he wrote one and sent it to me, and so on. There were long lapses in between. We never compared notes on what we were doing. We just worked from what we sent to one another. It was not a chapter-by-chapter thing. One of us would simply write until he got tired and then send it to the other. That way, we simply wrote until it was finished."[102] He acknowledged later that the only major difficulty for either of them was in creating the time to devote to *Deus Irae*. But when the time did occur, "everything proceeded splendidly."[14] *Deus Irae* wasn't completed until 1975, and it was published the following year.

Isle of the Dead

Zelazny wrote *Isle of the Dead* after *Lord of Light, Creatures of Light and Darkness* and *Nine Princes in Amber*. It may have been that contractual obligation which kept him from starting on *Deus Irae* right away. Terry Carr already knew about the novel in 1967 and wanted it, scribbling a note to Zelazny, "I still want to know about those condoms in Tokyo Bay!"[103] That comment alludes to the novel's opening sequence in which Francis Sandow remarks upon the sea-wrack and miscellany that can wash upon shore—"maybe a piece of the True Cross, I don't know."[104] Zelazny remembered combing the Lake Erie beach at the foot of East 222nd Street near his home, where driftwood, used condoms, empty beer bottles, and other detritus provided clues about the lives of those who had passed by. Zelazny was immersed in writing the novel when he gave Frederik Pohl the outtake story "Dismal Light" for the May 1968 issue of *Worlds of If*.

Some of *Isle of the Dead*'s concepts grew out of the novelette "This Moment of the Storm" (see the afterword to that story for more details). "This was a spin-off from the novelette I did called 'This Moment of the Storm.' Actually, it wasn't the guy I was interested in, at first. I wanted somebody that was born in the twentieth century, who had made it aboard one of these generation starships where he'd been frozen and spent generations getting to this new planet which proved habitable. By the time he got there, they'd invented a faster-than-light drive, because several centuries had gone by and they'd become more sophisticated. Earth had much higher technology, and he had the means of going back fast if he wanted to, but he didn't. He wasn't sure he was happy on the world he'd reached, though, and decided to go out and try a few others, since it was easy to do. There were still time dilation effects and, through making a few sharp investments here and there, with so much time passing, he became quite wealthy. He also happened to become the oldest human in the galaxy, and because of the fancy new medicine he was in very good shape. He *also* just happened to have been through the initiation ritual which would make him a god in this other religion, even though he didn't believe in it wholeheartedly. But it was the concept of the big expanse of time that interested me."[69]

In another interview, he described more briefly that "*Isle of the Dead* was supposed to be a straight story, but the aliens just sort of creeped in."[50]

Concerning the relationship between these two works, he later wrote, "1) The situation of the main character of my novelette 'This Moment of the Storm' served as the point of departure [for *Isle of the Dead*], with the pervasive sense of loss involved in living past or outliving what could have been monumentally significant, along with the uncertainty as to the present moment's worth. 2) A beginning consideration of the fact that the psychological effects of actions performed are often more significant than the motives for those actions. 3) A desire to relax after the narrative line of *Lord of Light*...I like *Isle of the Dead* because I like Sandow, I like his world and I was pleased with the course of action in it. I dislike it because I was so pleased with the way it was moving that I fear I slicked it over-much in maintaining the pace and trying to make everything fit neatly."[40]

The novel's title derives from a painting. Francis Sandow refers to "that mad painting by Boecklin, *The Isle of the Dead*."[104] Arnold Böcklin was a Swiss-German painter who created at least five paintings with that title, each depicting an oarsman and a standing figure in a small boat, crossing dark water toward a forbidding island. The painting invokes an image of the mythical boatman Charon, ferrying the newly dead across the river Styx into Hades, the underworld. A later edition of the paperback featured a beautiful cover painting by Dean Ellis that was deliberately reminiscent of Böcklin's work, but oddly reproduced in two-tone (blue and black) instead of the full colors of Ellis's original.

Isle of the Dead appeared in 1969 and proved to be one of Zelazny's best written and best received novels. It was a finalist for the Nebula in 1970 and won the very first juried Prix Apollo in 1972 for the best novel translated into French. Francis Sandow became one of Zelazny's most popular characters, returning for a cameo in *To Die in Italbar* and then in the outline for "Sandow's Shadow."

Damnation Alley

Damnation Alley was another well-received novella which Zelazny later expanded at his agent's suggestion into a novel. Henry Morrison wrote, "I read 'Damnation Alley' in *Galaxy* over the weekend and thought it a very gripping story. Do you think that with expansions and perhaps a new subplot you would want to try this as a novel of 55,000 or 60,000 words?"[105] The results did not entirely satisfy Zelazny, and he always said that he preferred the original over the novel.

Zelazny explained how he expanded the story, including the experimental addition of a Japanese Noh Play near the end, to Carl Yoke. "…I did wish that I had done just a little more with what went on inside [Hell Tanner]. So, when I had the opportunity to expand the thing into a book, I decided that besides some external action I would figure some way to get into Hell and show what was going on in there. Stream of consciousness, in this case, would not be too useful. He did not understand his own motivation, and it would not be likely to emerge in any interior monologue. A wild dream sequence, though, could be made to serve this end, when I had the perfectly legitimate excuse of a delirium-ridden sleep. So I employed my alternative and ritualized his inchoate feelings of sympathy toward the dead driver, Brady…The Noh form was the first thing that came to mind then…It was not intended as a parody of the form. I was looking for lumber, and getting some mileage out of my background in dramatic literature, it struck me as easier to buy pre-cut than to start chopping down my own trees and shaping them. Also, I somewhat subscribe to the notion of a resonance-effect in literature. I think that if someone has had even a brief exposure to a particular medium, something that later mimes it will strike a chord of familiarity, even if he does not know why, even if, say, his only exposure to Noh was forgotten background sequences in *Sayonara*. A sense of familiarity is always a good thing to stir in a reader, as I see it, perhaps especially when he doesn't know why. It makes a thing seem somehow important if it nags him a bit."[106]

He also added more to the interaction between Hell Tanner and Greg, employing a method that western writer Max Brand often used in his novels. "I decided to try a formula that Max Brand claimed he used. Since he had written about three hundred books, I thought it must have worked for him. He said that he always started with a good guy who went bad and a bad guy who went good, and had them cross over on their way to down-and-out. So that the story had something for everybody."[57]

"I like *Damnation Alley* for the overall subjection of everything in it to a Stanislavsky-Boleslavsky action verb key, 'to get to Boston.' I dislike it for the same reason."[40] Stanislavsky-Boleslavsky refers to "method acting" in which a performer draws upon self, experiences, memories, and emotions to make a character more realistic and less stereotyped or one-dimensional. Although Zelazny was not satisfied with the novel, it became more widely read than the novella and ultimately provided the basis for a motion picture of the same name, the only one thus far to bear Zelazny's name on the credits. The final movie retained only a slight resemblance to Zelazny's work, but he did benefit financially from it.

Asked in a fan letter to explain the ending, in which Tanner defaces his own statue and leaves town, Zelazny explained that it fit with the psychology of the anti-hero who had done a good thing but for the wrong reasons, as opposed to a hero who had done a good thing for the right reasons. "I had long before grown tired of heroes who are invariably nice guys—as this is not always the case in real life…[Would he] be changed by suddenly having people think of him as [a good person]? Would he be cynical about it? Would he try to live up to it? Or would his attitude involve something of both? Perhaps he would like the feeling but also be uncomfortable with it, knowing that in the long run he might not be able to live up to it, and still not wanting to destroy the people's illusions about him—as he probably would if he'd remained on the scene—would leave town, so as to preserve their memories and his own, of a time when, briefly, he accounted to something noble."[107]

Baycon

Besides meeting Philip K. Dick for the first time, the Baycon convention was also significant for the time spent with Lester del Rey who, as Robert Silverberg had done, acted as a mentor with sage advice for the younger Zelazny. Together with "the girls," they rented a car and toured much of San Francisco—"Chinatown, topless joints, top of the hill, Golden Gate Bridge, and over across the river to a place called Undine's where we arrived reservationless and Lester bribed the Maitre d' to get us a windowside table overlooking the bay. Night arrived. We could see empty Alcatraz… It was one of the finest dinners I have ever eaten. Lester seems to have a nose for things like that." The next day, "we drove to the redwood forest, the park, and walked for hours among the giant trees. We talked or did not talk, as we felt…I think that, of the whole West Coast bit, the time that I spent with Lester was the most rewarding. He gave me valuable advice on storytelling and on the business end of things. It was so casual and off the cuff….Lester outlined stories that I knew he would never bother to write—brilliant ones, with twists and switches to boggle the mind. Maybe he will write them. I hope so."[99]

Distinctions:

Nebula nomination for novelette "The Keys to December"
Nebula nomination for novelette "This Mortal Mountain"
Nebula nomination for novel *Lord of Light*
Hugo for novel *Lord of Light*
Hugo nomination for novella "Damnation Alley"

Book Published:

Nebula Award Stories Three

References

A note about the format of references:

JOURNALS/MAGAZINES/FANZINES
Author. Title of article. *Journal Name*. Year; Volume (Issue Number [#Whole Number and/or Month]): pages.

BOOK SECTIONS
Author. Title of article. In: Editor. *Book Title*. City, State: Publisher, Year: pages.

WHOLE BOOKS
Author. *Book Title*. City, State: Publisher, Year.

CORRESPONDENCE
Author. Letter/Email to recipient, date.

INTERNET RESOURCES
Author. Title. Year created. URL. Dated accessed.

1. Ellison, Harlan. Introduction to "Auto-Da-Fé". In: Ellison, Harlan, ed. *Dangerous Visions*. Garden City, NY: Doubleday, 1967: p 523–524.

2. Knight, Damon. Letter to Roger Zelazny dated January 20, 1965.

3. Knight, Damon. Letter to Roger Zelazny dated February 23, 1965.

4. Knight, Damon. Letter to Roger Zelazny dated March 30, 1965.

5. Knight, Damon. Letter to Roger Zelazny dated March 9, 1965.

6. Knight, Damon. Letter to Roger Zelazny dated May 5, 1965.

7. Zelazny, Roger. Letter to Damon Knight dated May 19, 1965.

8. Heatley, Alex J. An Interview with Roger Zelazny. *Phlogiston* 1995; (44): p 3–6.

9. Knight, Damon. Letter to Roger Zelazny dated May 9, 1966.

10. Mills, Robert P. Letter to Roger Zelazny dated September 1, 1966.

11. Mills, Robert P. Letter to Roger Zelazny dated September 21, 1966.

12. Goldsmith, Cele. Letter to Roger Zelazny dated October 6, 1964.

13. Delany, Samuel R. Faust and Archimedes. *The Jewel-Hinged Jaw*. New York, NY: Berkley, 1977: p 173–190.

14. Curtoni, Vittorio. Intervista con Roger Zelazny. *Robot Rivista di Fantascienza* 1977; (12 [March]): p 138–40.

15. Sanders, Joseph L. *Roger Zelazny: A Primary and Secondary Bibliography*. Boston, MA: G. K. Hall, 1980.

16. Yoke, Carl B. Before There Was Amber, introduction to a book of the same name, a collection of stories from *The Record* ("Studies in Saviory" and three tales written by Yoke); it was to have been published by DNA Publications (Warren Lapine) but the publisher went out of business, 2005.

17. Moorcock, Michael. Letter to Roger Zelazny dated September 3, 1965.

18. Yoke, Carl B. Email to Dr. Christopher Kovacs dated October 28, 2007.

19. Yoke, Carl B. Email to Dr. Christopher Kovacs dated January 30, 2008.

20. Zelazny, Trent. Email to Dr. Christopher Kovacs dated June 10, 2008.

21. Sherred, T. L. Roger Zelazny. *Marcon VII Program and Schedule Booklet* 1972; p 3.

22. Offutt, Andrew J. Toastmaster's Notes used to introduce Guest of Honor Roger Zelazny at the 32nd Annual World Science Fiction Convention, Washington, DC, September 1, 1974.

23. Lamont, Gil. On Roger Zelazny. *Tightbeam* 1969; (37 [May]): p 21–23.

24. Westblom, Ulf. An Interview with Roger Zelazny. *Mentat* 1969; (11 [May]): p 200–203.

25. Zelazny, Roger. Letter to Ned Brooks dated June 6, 1965.

26. Thompson, W.B. Interview: Roger Zelazny. *Future Life* 1981; (25 [March]): p 40–42.

27. Zelazny, Roger. Letter to Doubleday Editor Lawrence P. Ashmead dated March 15, 1966.

28. Ashmead, Lawrence P. Letter to Roger Zelazny dated April 13, 1966.

29. Zelazny, Roger. Letter to Doubleday Editor Lawrence P. Ashmead dated April 15, 1966.

30. Zelazny, Roger. Letter to Doubleday Editor Lawrence P. Ashmead dated May 26, 1966.

31. Zelazny, Roger. Musings on *Lord of Light*. *Niekas* 1977; (21): p 20.

32. Ferman, Edward L. Letter to Roger Zelazny dated May 3, 1966.

33. Zelazny, Roger. Shadows. *Kallikanzaros* 1967; (3 [December/January]): p 11–16.

34. Moorcock, Michael. Letter to Roger Zelazny dated August 1, 1966.

35. Sneyd, Steve. The Song Beneath the Skin: Roger Zelazny Interviewed. *Critical Wave Magazine* 1993; (33 [November]): p 13–14.

36. Zelazny, Roger. Introduction. In: Zelazny, Roger, ed. *Hymn to the Sun: An Imitation*. Radford, VA: DNA Publications, 1996: p 1–2.

37. Ashmead, Lawrence P. Letter to Roger Zelazny dated January 5, 1968.

38. Schweitzer, Darrell. Roger Zelazny Answers Questions. *Procrastination* 1977; (13 [November]): p 25–26.

39. Zelazny, Roger. Letter to Ms. Barraford dated September 11, 1975.

40. Walker, Paul. Author's Choice. *Vector* 1973; (65 [May-June]): p 42–44.

41. McGuire, Paul; Truesdale, David A. Tangent Interviews: Roger Zelazny. *Tangent* 1976; (4 [February]): p 5–10.

42. Mills, Robert P. Letter to Roger Zelazny dated May 26, 1966.

43. Carr, Terry. Letter to Roger Zelazny dated October 6, 1966.

44. Carr, Terry. Letter to Roger Zelazny dated October 17, 1966.

45. Carr, Terry. Letter to Roger Zelazny dated November 17, 1966.

46. Morrison, Henry. Letter to Roger Zelazny dated December 8, 1967.

47. Heck, Peter. Theatre of the Subconscious: An Interview with Roger Zelazny. *Xignals* 1986; XVI (Feb/Mar): p 1,2,15.

48. Zelazny, Roger. Guest of Honor Speech: Ozarkon 2. *Sirruish* 1967; (5): p 37–43.

49. Monteleone, Thomas F. Science Fiction as Literature: Selected Stories and Novels of Roger Zelazny [PhD thesis]. Baltimore, MD: University of Maryland, 1973: 1–105.

50. Conner, Bill. Zelazny at Marcon '72. *Cozine* 1972; (3 [March 30]): p 17–18.

51. Delany, Samuel R. Zelazny/Varley/Gibson—and Quality (Part I). *The New York Review of Science Fiction* 1992; (48 [August]): p 1, 10–13.

52. Lindskold, Jane M. *Roger Zelazny*. New York, NY: Twayne Publishers, 1993.

53. Zelazny, Roger. Letter to Patrick Noël dated September 1, 1971.

54. Morrison, Henry. Letter to Roger Zelazny dated August 2, 1967.

55. Morrison, Henry. Letter to Roger Zelazny dated August 7, 1967.

56. Zelazny, Roger. Letter to Doubleday Editor Lawrence P. Ashmead dated February 13, 1967.

57. Krulik, Theodore. *Roger Zelazny*. New York, NY: Ungar Publishing, 1986.

58. Zelazny, Roger. Letter to Doubleday Editor Marc Haefele, September 26, 1968.

59. Lindskold, Jane M. Starting Backwards. *Amberzine* 1993; (3 [April]): p 22–26.

60. Zelazny, Roger. Introduction to *The Dark World*. *Amberzine* 1993; (5 [November]): p 38–39.

61. Lindskold, Jane M. Imprinting Imagination: Kuttner's *The Dark World* as a Pattern for the Amber Novels. *Amberzine* 1993; (5 [November]): p 27–30.

62. Krulik, Theodore. Roger Zelazny's Road to Amber. *Extrapolation* 2002; 43 (1 [Spring]): p 80–88.

63. Dowling, Terry; Curtis, Keith. A Conversation with Roger Zelazny. *Science Fiction (Australia)* 1978; 1 (2 [June]): p 11–23.

64. Zelazny, Roger. *Sign of the Unicorn*. Garden City, NY: Doubleday, 1975.

65. Zelazny, Roger. The Road to Amber. *Kolvir* 1980; (Heroic Fiction Issue): p 9–11.

66. Zelazny, Roger. The Guest of Honor: Philip José Farmer. *Norwescon 2 Program Booklet* 1979; p 7–8.

67. Zelazny, Roger. Introduction. In: Farmer, Philip José, ed. *A Private Cosmos*. New York, NY: Ace Books, 1968: p 5–8.

68. Zelazny, Roger. The Road to Amber. In: Zelazny, Roger, ed. *Nine Princes in Amber Book 1*. New York, NY: DC Comics, 1996: p 2–4.

69. Shannon, J.C. Staying Power: An Interview with Roger Zelazny. *Leading Edge* 1994; (29 [August]): p 33–47.

70. Zelazny, Roger. Introduction to "9 Princes in Amber". *Kallikanzaros* 1967; (1 [June]): p 5.

71. Bujold, Lois McMaster. Email to Dr. Christopher Kovacs dated August 20, 2008.

72. Ayotte, John. Email to Dr. Christopher Kovacs dated August 20, 2008.

73. Ayotte, John. Email to Dr. Christopher Kovacs dated August 29, 2008.

74. Zelazny, Roger. Letter to Andre Norton dated September 8, 1967.

75. Ashmead, Lawrence P. Letter to Roger Zelazny dated February 16, 1967.

76. Carr, Terry. Letter to Roger Zelazny dated March 21, 1967.

77. Norton, Andre. Roger Zelazny. *Marcon II Program Book* 1967; (April): p 3.

78. Porter, Andrew. Triple Fan Fair. *S.F. Weekly* 1967; (5 [July 5]): p 1.

79. Silverberg, Robert. First Reply to Question about Silverberg and Zelazny in a bar… 2008. http://groups.yahoo.com/group/theworldsofrobertsilverberg/message/4225 Accessed: May 15, 2008

80. Silverberg, Robert. Second Reply to Question about Silverberg and Zelazny in a bar… 2008. http://groups.yahoo.com/group/theworldsofrobertsilverberg/message/4222 Accessed: May 15, 2008

81. Silverberg, Robert. Third Reply to Question about Silverberg and Zelazny in a bar… 2008. http://groups.yahoo.com/group/theworldsofrobertsilverberg/message/4231 Accessed: May 15, 2008

82. Morrison, Henry. Letter to Roger Zelazny dated May 22, 1967.

83. Morrison, Henry. Letter to Roger Zelazny dated August 4, 1965.

84. Moorcock, Michael. Letter to Roger Zelazny dated November 12, 1967.

85. Mays, Buddy. Roger Zelazny—Dreamer in the World of Real. *New Mexico Magazine* 1981; (February): p 30–31.

86. Zelazny, Roger. Tomorrow Stuff. *Unpublished* 1968; p 1–6.

87. Zelazny, Roger. An Interview with Roger Zelazny [self-interview]. *Luna Monthly* 1972; (43 [December]): p 1–3.

88. Ashmead, Lawrence P. Letter to Roger Zelazny dated April 5, 1968.

89. Ashmead, Lawrence P. Letter to Roger Zelazny dated April 29, 1968.

90. Zelazny, Roger. Letter to Doubleday Editor Marc Haefele, May 4, 1968.

91. Haefele, Marc. Letter to Roger Zelazny dated May 7, 1968.

92. Zelazny, Roger. Introduction. In: Zelazny, Roger, ed. *Bridge of Ashes*. New York, NY: Signet, 1989: unpaginated.

93. Zelazny, Roger. Authorgraphs – an Interview with Roger Zelazny. *Worlds of If* 1969; 19 (1 [January]): p 161.

94. Kelly, Patrick. How About This? Roger Zelazny. *Phantasmicom* 1970; (2 [Winter]): p 9–16.

95. Haefele, Marc. Letter to Roger Zelazny dated July 19, 1968.

96. Dick, Philip K. Letter to Roger Zelazny dated December 2, 1967.

97. Zelazny, Roger. An Interview with Roger Zelazny [self-interview]. In: Walker, Paul, ed. *Speaking of Science Fiction*. Ordell, NJ: Luna Publications, 1978: p 78–84.

98. Dick, Philip K. Letter to Andy dated May 21, 1968.

99. Zelazny, Roger. Letter [written 1969, but published 1973 after the editor's return from military service]. *Kallikanzaros* 1973; (7 [August]): p 19–20.

100. Dick, Philip K. Letter to Doubleday Editor Larry Ashmead dated September 7, 1968.

101. Dick, Philip K. Letter to Roger Zelazny dated November 13, 1968.

102. Zelazny, Roger. Letter to Georg dated August 12, 1977.

103. Carr, Terry. Note to Roger Zelazny handwritten on the carbon copy of a letter from Carr to Robert P. Mills, dated June 16, 1967.

104. Zelazny, Roger. *Isle of the Dead*. New York, NY: Ace, 1969.

105. Morrison, Henry. Letter to Roger Zelazny dated August 22, 1967.

106. Yoke, Carl B. Zelazny's *Damnation Alley*: Hell Noh. *Extrapolation* 1973; 15 (1 [December]): p 6–16.

107. Zelazny, Roger. Letter to fan Mr. Richardson dated October 13, 1973.

PUBLICATION HISTORY

Frontispiece portrait by Jack Gaughan first appeared on the cover of "Marcon VII Program and Schedule Book, 1972" where Roger Zelazny was Guest of Honor.

"Lyricism and Warmth" *by Kristine Kathryn Rusch* first appears in this volume.

"A Singular Being" *by Walter Jon Williams* first appears in this volume.

"The Furies" first appeared in *Amazing*, June 1965.

"Lucifer" first appeared in *Worlds of Tomorrow*, June 1964.

"The Salvation of Faust" first appeared in *The Magazine of Fantasy & Science Fiction,* July 1964. Previously uncollected.

"The New Pleasure" first appeared in *Double:Bill #20*, August 1964.

"The Monster and the Maiden" first appeared in *Galaxy*, December 1964.

"For a Breath I Tarry" first appeared in *New Worlds #160*, March 1966. The first corrected version appeared in *Fantastic*, September 1966.

"Passage to Dilfar" first appeared in *Fantastic*, February 1965.

"Thelinde's Song" first appeared in *Fantastic*, June 1965.

"The Bells of Shoredan" first appeared in *Fantastic*, March 1966.

"A Knight for Merytha" first appeared in *Kallikanzaros #2*, September 1967.

"The Injured" first appeared in *Kronos #2*, 1965. Previously uncollected.

"Devil Car" first appeared in *Galaxy*, June 1965.

"Of Time and the Yan" first appeared in *The Magazine of Fantasy & Science Fiction,* June 1965. Previously uncollected.

"The Drawing" first appeared in *Algol #10*, September 1965. Previously uncollected.

"This Moment of the Storm" first appeared in *The Magazine of Fantasy & Science Fiction*, June 1966.

"Comes Now the Power" first appeared in *Magazine of Horror #14*, Winter 1966.

"Divine Madness" first appeared in *Magazine of Horror #13*, Summer 1966.

"But Not the Herald" first appeared in *Magazine of Horror #12*, Winter 1965–66.

"Late, Late Show" first appeared in *Tightbeam #37*, May 1966. Previously uncollected.

"Love Is an Imaginary Number" first appeared in *New Worlds # 158,* January 1966.

"The Keys to December" first appeared in *New Worlds #165*, August 1966.

"The House of the Hanged Man" first appeared in *Double:Bill #15*, September 1966.

"Death and the Executioner" first appeared in *The Magazine of Fantasy & Science Fiction* June 1967. Incorporated as part of the novel *Lord of Light*.

"Auto-Da-Fé" first appeared in *Dangerous Visions*, ed. Harlan Ellison, Doubleday 1967.

"The Juan's Thousandth" first appears in this volume. Written 1965–68.

"There Shall Be No Moon!" first appears in this volume. Written 1965–68.

"Through a Glass, Greenly" first appears in this volume. Written 1965–68.

"Time of Night in the 7th Room" first appears in this volume. Written 1965–68.

"…And Call Me Conrad, Part One" first appeared in *The Magazine of Fantasy & Science Fiction,* October 1965.

"Synopsis of Part One" first appeared in *The Magazine of Fantasy & Science Fiction,* November 1965. Previously uncollected.

"…And Call Me Conrad, Part Two" first appeared in *The Magazine of Fantasy & Science Fiction,* November 1965.

"Guest of Honor Speech, Ozarkon 2" first appeared in *Sirruish #5*, 1967. Previously uncollected.

"On Writing and Stories" first appeared in *Science Fiction Times #446*, September 1967. Previously uncollected.

"Shadows" first appeared in *Kallikanzaros #3* December 1967–January 1968. Previously uncollected.

" '…And Call Me Roger': The Literary Life of Roger Zelazny, Part 2" by Christopher S. Kovacs, MD first appears in this volume.

Poems

"Thoughts of the Jupiterian Frantifier Fish" first appeared in *Procrastination #9*, 1971.

"Holy Thursday", "Magic Fire", "Blondel de Nesle", "Chou de Mal", "Indian Days in KY", "Antode to Winter", "Devices of Heraldry", "Lines Written Concerning the Acceptability of Alcohol", "Bodhisattva", "Apocalypse of a Summer's Night", and "On My Giving Up of Regular Metrics, Manumitted Via a Portable Byron" first appear in this volume. Written 1955–60 for *Chisel in the Sky.*

"The Men of Westrim" has only appeared as part of "Thelinde's Song".

"The Wind Doth Blow" has only appeared as part of "A Knight for Merytha".

"The Thing That on the Highways" and "I Never Met a Traveller from an Antique Land" first appear in this volume. Written 1965–68.

" '…Good Old Martian Soldier…' " first appeared in *Asmaon #2*, 1966; previously uncollected.

"Brahman Trimurti, A Modern Hymn to the Trinity" first appeared in *Polemic*, Spring 1959, Vol IV No 1.

"Appendix B" first appeared as individual epigraphs in *Lord of Light*, Doubleday 1967, and in its present form in *Hymn to The Sun: an Imitation*, DNA Publications 1996.

"Faust Before Twelve" first appeared in a different form in *Speculative Poetry Review #1*, 1977. Written 1955–60 for *Chisel in the Sky.* The full text first appears in this volume.

"The Last" first appeared in *To Spin Is Miracle Cat*, Underwood-Miller 1981. Written 1955–1960 for *Chisel in the Sky.*

Acknowledgments

Thanks go in many directions: to Roger Zelazny for his life's work, a body of writing that made this project a joy to work on; to my wife, Leah Anderson, without whose support this project would never have started; to Chris Kovacs, whose research efforts not only produced a comprehensive collection of material, but whose analysis added depth to the whole project; to Ann Crimmins for her dedication to all things grammatical; to Kristine Kathryn Rusch and Walter Jon Williams for their insightful introductions; to Michael Whelan for his spectacular dust jacket painting; and to Alice Lewis for her polished dust jacket design and her invaluable advice in design issues. Thanks also go to: Mark Olson for his help in book production, Geri Sullivan for design advice, Carl Feynman for his definition of "imaginary number" and our stalwart band of proofreaders:

Kelly Persons, Rick Katze, Tim Szczesuil, Ann Broomhead,
Pam Fremon, Larry Pfeffer, Peter Olson, Jim Burton, Lisa Hertel,
Sharon Sbarsky, Ann Crimmins, Chris Kovacs, and Mark Olson.

David G. Grubbs
December, 2008

There are many individuals who aided in the extensive search to locate original manuscripts, correspondence, rare fanzines, and obscure interviews. Colleagues, family, and friends of Roger Zelazny helped to clarify details and quash rumors about his life and work. My own colleagues helped with translations of Greek, German, Japanese and other foreign language phrases. Apologies to anyone who might have been overlooked in compiling the following list:

Charles Ardai, John Ayotte, George Beahm, Greg Bear, John Betancourt, Rick Bradford, Ned Brooks, Lois McMaster Bujold, John Callendar, George Carayanniotis, Ung-il Chung, Michael Citrak, Giovanna Clairval, Bob Collins, Lloyd Currey, Jack Dann, Jane Frank, c Shell Franklin, Paul Gilster, Simon Gosden, Ed Greenwood, Joe Haldeman, David Hartwell, Gerald Hausman, Graham Holroyd, Beate Lanske, Elizabeth LaVelle, Jane Lindskold, George R. R. Martin, Bryan McKinney, Henry Morrison, Kari Mozena, Rias Nuninga, Richard Patt, Greg Pickersgill, Bob Pylant, Mike Resnick, Andy Richards, Fred Saberhagen, Roger Schlobin, Darrell Schweitzer, Robert Silverberg, Dan Simmons, Dean Wesley Smith, Ken St. Andre, Richard Stegall, Thomas T. Thomas, Norris Thomlinson, Erick Wujcik, Carl Yoke, Trent Zelazny, Cindy Ziesing, and Scott Zrubek.

Diane Cooter, Nicolette Schneider, Lara Chmela
> Roger Zelazny Papers, Special Collections
> Research Center, Syracuse University Library

Thomas Beck, Susan Graham, Marcia Peri, Shaun Lusby
> Azriel Rosenfeld Science Fiction Research Collection,
> University of Maryland, Baltimore County.

Sara Stille, Eric Milenkiewicz, Audrey Pearson
> Bruce Pelz and Terry Carr Fanzine Collections, Special
> Collections Library, University of California, Riverside

Greg Prickman, Jacque Roethler, Kathryn Hodson, Jeremy Brett
> M. Horvat Collection, Special Collections,
> University of Iowa Libraries

Jill Tatem
> University Archives, Case Western Reserve University

Thomas M. Whitehead
> Whitehead Collection, Special Collections Department, Temple University Libraries

Patti Thistle, Dion Fowlow, George Beckett
> Document Delivery Office, Health Sciences Library,
> Memorial University of Newfoundland.

And then there are the personal thanks that I need to make. Of course none of this would have been possible without Roger Zelazny creating the very stories and characters that I find myself returning to again and again. When I finally met him at Ad Astra in 1986, I interrupted his rapid departure from the convention and asked "Mr. Zelazny" to sign the books I'd carried with me. He kindly took care of that and the requests of my companions. "Everybody OK, then? Right, gotta get to the airport"—and then his parting comment to me was "…and call me Roger." From that memory came the fitting title for the monograph in these volumes.

My mother handed me that paperback *Nine Princes in Amber* one dull day so long ago when I complained that I had nothing to read, and my parents drove me to countless new and used bookstores on the very first Zelazny quest to find copies of all of his books. The Internet makes searches so much easier now, and I couldn't have gathered much of this material if I'd had to rely on physical searches and postal mail. My buddy Ed Hew and his cousins drove me to Ad Astra for that fateful meeting. Dave Grubbs believed in and fought to see this project succeed when my involvement made it expand well beyond what he'd anticipated, and Ann Crimmins pruned, weeded, and used a flamethrower where necessary to turn my sometimes passive prose into something more readable. And none of this would have been possible without the support of my wife, Susan, and our children Caileigh and Jamieson, who put up with my additional absences from home and the other blocks of time consumed in creating this project. If their eyes should roll at mention of the name Zelazny, you may now understand why. And the fact that Susan's birthday is also May 13, or that my last name also refers to what happens in a smithy, are just examples of those Strange and Odd Coincidences in Life realized while researching this project. That our Golden Retriever is named Amber is *not* one of those coincidences.

Christopher S. Kovacs, MD
December, 2008

I wish to thank my daughters Fiona and Deirdre, whom I dragged to cons as children and who have grown to love sf and fantasy as much as I do. Particular thanks to my husband Peter Havriluk for patience, encouragement, and easing the log jam at the p.c. by buying himself a laptop. Dave and Chris, I'm delighted to have worked with you. Thanks also to the various Crimmins/Havriluk cats who warmed my lap as I edited.

Ann Crimmins
December, 2008

TECHNICAL NOTES

This book is set in Adobe Garamond Pro, except for the titles (which are set in Trajan Pro), using Adobe InDesign 2. The book was printed and bound by Sheridan Books of Ann Arbor, Michigan, on acid-free paper.

Select books from NESFA Press

Details on these and many more books are online at: www.nesfa.org/press/
Books may be ordered online or by writing to:

NESFA Press; PO Box 809; Framingham, MA 01701

We accept checks (in US$), Visa, or MasterCard. Add $4 P&H for one book, $8 for an order of two to five books, $2 per book for orders of six or more. (For addresses outside the U.S., please add $12 for one or two books, $36 for an order of three to five books, and $6 per book for six or more.) Please allow 3–4 weeks for delivery. (Overseas, allow 2 months or more.)

The New England Science Fiction Association

NESFA is an all-volunteer, non-profit organization of science fiction and fantasy fans. Besides publishing, our activities include running Boskone (New England's oldest SF convention) in February each year, producing a semimonthly newsletter, holding discussion groups on topics related to the field, and hosting a variety of social events. If you are interested in learning more about us, we'd like to hear from you. Contact us at info@nesfa.org or at the address above. Visit our web site at www.nesfa.org.